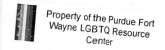

Seasons

Seasons

Anne Azel

P.D. Publishing, Inc.
Clayton, North Carolina

ISBN-13: 978-1-933720-23-4
ISBN-10: 1-933720-23-9

First edition (in two parts): 2000 (1-930928-00-9 and 1-930928-08-4)
Second edition: 2005 (0-9765664-0-0)

9 8 7 6 5 4 3

Cover art by B.L. Magill
Cover design by Barb Coles
Edited by Day Petersen

Published by:

P.D. Publishing, Inc.
P.O. Box 70
Clayton, NC 27528

http://www.pdpublishing.com

Acknowledgements:

My thanks to Tigger for all she does for me.

Dedication

To Donna.

Autumn Winds

Chapter 1

The news photographer waited, as instructed, huddled by an old brick wall on the cold autumn day until the funeral ended. The press was not allowed into the cathedral, but the list of attendees read like a *Who's Who* of the rich and famous and his editor was eager to get some good pictures as the mourners came out. Each public face would no doubt show the politically correct degree of grief.

The photographer shivered, pulling up the wool collar of his jacket against the bitter wind. They didn't come more famous than the "Remarkable Williams Family". Philip "Philly" Williams had been a Welsh immigrant to Canada. Through hard work and brilliant financial dealings, he had carved a place for himself among a surprised Canadian establishment.

Always a nonconformist, at fifty-three he had surprised the conservative Canadian establishment again by marrying Alexandria Thasos, the prima ballerina of the Royal Winnipeg Ballet Company. She was twenty-two. To everyone's greater surprise, the stormy marriage had endured until Williams' mysterious, fatal boating accident at the age of seventy-six.

Alexandria gave her "Philly" three equally remarkable offspring: Roberta, Elizabeth, and William. Roberta, the oldest, had won Oscars as an actor, screenwriter, and director. She was like her father: brilliant, ruthless, and driven. As one critic wrote, "Robbie Williams can make anyone a star and all it will cost them is their soul."

Number two was Elizabeth, a reclusive physicist who had knowledge of quantum mechanics to a degree so complex that few could understand. It was said within enlightened circles that only she and God completely understood the dynamics involved in the creation of the universe.

The baby, black sheep of the family, was "Billy-the-Kid". His wild ways had won him three world championships in Formula One racing and, finally, the brushed stainless steel coffin that was at this moment being carried from the cathedral.

The photographer moved away from the protection of the brick wall and out into the biting wind to lean against the dirty yellow barricades that had been put up by the police at the request of the concerned mayor.

The crowd buzzed in anticipation of the procession of celebrities. The coffin was carried by Billy-the-Kid's racing team. They wore their team colours: black with a slash of red down the pant leg.

The grey steel of the coffin was partly hidden by the black and white checkered flag that Alexandria had dramatically unrolled on her son's coffin only moments before. His two sisters had placed his red helmet at one end. It had done its job well; Billy's handsome head had remained undamaged, although separated from his neck by the crash.

Alexandria descended the long flight of stairs behind the coffin, dramatically wrapped in black mink, though not the same one she had worn at her husband's memorial service. A brilliant red clasp at her throat emphasized her long neck and repeated the racing motif. She appeared distraught at her son's death. Closer observation through the camera lens showed the photographer that her eyes were dry.

One step behind the dramatic Alexandria walked the surviving siblings: Roberta, tall, dark, and bristling with energy, defiantly sneering at the gawkers; and mousy Elizabeth, who seemed to be bowed, not in grief, but in the heady contemplation of the universe.

Following them with quiet dignity, apparently completely forgotten by the others, was Billy's wife, Janet. In her arms she held a baby. Billy's child. The photographer took a number of close-up shots. It was the first public appearance by the third generation. The infant would have a hell of a tradition to live up to.

The party paused on the last few stairs, watching as the coffin was slipped into the black hearse. It was then that the photographer took the picture that would appear on newsstands all over the world.

There stood Alexandria, dramatically posed, with Elizabeth one step behind, lost in thought and partially hidden by the black swirl of mommy's furs. Alone to the right towered Roberta. She was not looking at the coffin; instead her head was turned to the left, looking past her sister to where Billy's wife stood with quiet dignity, her arms wrapped protectively around her child. Janet Williams' strawberry blonde hair was the only spot of light in the dark scene.

The expression on Roberta's face was one of calculating curiosity, as if she had just become aware that her brother had left a family and was evaluating her responsibilities and options regarding them.

A black, stretch limousine pulled slowly forward and the racing team, now no longer burdened with Billy's body, turned and filed down each side. Those on the left opened the doors to receive the Williams family. Alexandria and Elizabeth stepped forward and disappeared into the luxurious interior. Roberta crossed the steps and took Janet Williams' elbow, guiding the surprised woman and her child down to the vehicle. All three disappeared into the car and the racing team closed the doors, waiting for the next limo, which would carry them to the graveside.

Inside the limo there was silence for a moment, then Alexandra shifted. "Thank you, Roberta. Beautifully choreographed, as always. Although I'm not sure if we shouldn't have stood longer on the steps for the press."

The two sisters exchanged a ghost of a smile. "Nonsense, Alexandria, the light today is far too harsh. It would not have done you justice," Robbie responded practically, noting the wide-eyed shock on Janet's face. *Billy had good taste*, she thought, her eyes slowly traveling up the small woman's body.

Alexandria sniffed. "Perhaps. That is your field so I shall bow to your judgment, Robbie. Beth, do straighten your shoulders, dear." Beth did so immediately, a red tide washing up her neck and over her face.

"I read your paper on your observations of the event horizon of Cygnus X-1. Can I assume that you feel the calculated Schwarzschild's radius is not upheld by the current data?" questioned Robbie, turning her neon blue eyes in the direction of her sister.

Janet relaxed, no longer under Roberta's scrutiny. She saw Elizabeth relax too, as her big sister came to her aid by leading the conversation to waters where she felt comfortable.

"Certainly the light wave front has failed to collapse and hovers around thirty kilometers from the star. That would be the expected Schwarzschild's radius if X-1 is a massive black hole. What is interesting," the recluse continued, warming to her only interest, "is that under the principles of quantum mechanics, particles appear to escape from a black hole. This, of course, would have been impossible using classic mechanics."

Robbie nodded. "The uncertainty principle?" she muttered as she followed her sister's train of thought.

Beth smiled. "Planck's constant comes into play where—"

Alexandria waved a hand in annoyance. "Girls, Billy's wife doesn't need to have her mind strained to the limit with Williams' thought play. Be polite."

"My name is Janet," said a soft, firm voice from the corner. All eyes turned to look at the petite blonde in surprise.

At the sound of the voice the small child on her lap awoke, beamed and reached up. "Mommy, mommy."

Janet's green eyes turned away from the family and focused on her daughter. Her face broke into a radiant smile. "Hi, Rebecca," Janet Williams cooed, letting the tot play with the leather glove she had removed.

Robbie stirred uncomfortably. Elizabeth withdrew into herself. Alexandria looked in amazement at the baby as if she had just realized that she was now a grandmother. "I am not to be called Grandmother!" she proclaimed.

With startled eyes that then quickly turned cool green, Janet looked up. "If my daughter and I should ever meet you again, Mrs. Williams, how would you like us to address you?"

Robbie's laugh exploded in the limo, causing the driver to look into his rear view mirror in surprise. In response, Beth cringed in her corner, and Alexandria gathered herself up for one of her more notable tirades, but was forestalled by a large, strong hand on her arm. "Alexandria is not maternal in nature. We call her Alexandria to her face, and anything we dare behind her back," explained Robbie, those extraordinary eyes focused on Janet.

Janet nodded, realizing that Roberta had once again come to the rescue.

"Really, Roberta," exclaimed Alexandria. "What will...Janice think?"

"What do we care what she thinks? And her name is Janet," drawled Robbie with the raise of an eyebrow.

"Why did you lead me over to this limo?" Janet met and held those remarkable eyes as they turned back to her.

"Show," Robbie explained bluntly, stretching out her long legs so that her calf touched Janet's ankle.

This time Alexandria laughed. "Robbie is always directing, aren't you, dear?"

"Always," murmured Robbie, still looking into Janet's eyes.

Janet didn't look away. Backing down was out of the question. She had heard rumours that Robbie was gay and very wild. *Is Roberta coming on to me? No, unlikely. I'm Billy's widow, after all, and I'm carrying our two-year-old in my arms. That alone should discourage any interest. No, this was just another little Williams' mind game. But why, I'm not sure.*

"Billy failed to inform the family that he had married. You came as quite a surprise when we read about his wedding in the papers. And of course the birth announcement that followed. I didn't think Billy—"

"Roberta! You go too far. She is a Williams by marriage, I realize, but we hardly know her," Alexandria interrupted.

The limo came to a stop, forestalling any further discussion. Alexandria, followed by Elizabeth, got out one side while Robbie got out the other. "Roberta, would you mind?" Janet, held up the baby. Robbie blinked in confusion, then rallied, stepped forward and took the baby, though awkwardly. Anticipating that the baby would be fussy with the stiff, cold woman, Janet got out of the limo quickly.

Much to both Robbie and Janet's surprise, the little child looked into those blue eyes and gave a delighted squeal, burying her head against Robbie's neck and her chubby little arms into her aunt's dark, thick hair. When Robbie tried to give her back, the two-year-old scrunched up her face and hung on tighter.

Janet's eyes twinkled at the look of bewilderment that came over Roberta's face. Her hand rose to cover a nervous grin then touched her forehead in thought. "Listen, maybe you'd better hold on to her just for a little while," she suggested. "This is not the place for a scene."

Robbie's eyes narrowed; Janet stared back innocently. "Stay right beside me," Robbie ordered, and Janet nodded, obligingly placing her hand around the tall woman's elbow.

4 ❖ *Anne Azel*

They looked at each other at the touch. The wind blew their hair gently about their coat collars. Leaves rustled overhead. Then they walked over to join Alexandria and Elizabeth by the grave.

The photographer captured the knot of Williamses on film. Roberta, now holding the third generation, played the role of head of the family. Alexandria and Elizabeth performed their roles as grieving mother and sister, and the little wife held onto Roberta's strong arm for support as she watched the coffin of her husband being placed on the grave supports. The picture appeared on page two.

At the end of the interment service, each family member stepped forward and dropped a red rose tied with a black ribbon onto the checkered flag that covered the coffin. Robbie gave her rose to the baby first, then retrieved it and dropped it by the red helmet. The child's serious blue eyes followed it with intense interest. The last to place her rose was Janet. She leaned down over the coffin. "Thanks," she whispered and then straightened, tears welling in her eyes as she made her way back to Roberta's side.

Robbie instinctively wrapped her long arm around the grieving woman and wondered what her self-centred brother had ever done in his life for which he should be thanked. The family moved off, Robbie with one arm supporting the beautiful child and the other wrapped around the distraught wife. Alexandria and Elizabeth followed.

At the limo, Robbie turned to meet her sister's eye. Elizabeth gave the smallest of nods, following her mother into the vehicle, this time sitting beside her. Janet got in next and waited to take her child. To her surprise, Roberta held on to the little girl and gracefully slipped in beside her.

The conversation on the way to the hotel consisted of Janet telling bedtime stories to Rebecca who sat comfortably in Robbie's lap and played sleepily with her aunt's gold chain. The little girl watched her mother's face intently as the woman wove simple but beautiful fairy tales. The three Williamses sat in wonder, watching Janet who emanated love for her child as she told her stories.

When the child finally fell asleep in Robbie's arms, she whispered to Janet, "Are you staying at the hotel with us?"

"No, no, I plan to drive back home tonight," the widow demurred.

Robbie shook her head impatiently. "Where is your car?"

"Back at the funeral home," Janet replied as the limo pulled up to the hotel. "I can get a taxi from here."

Alexandria made a noise that fell somewhere between a squeal and a snort. "My dear, there is the reception. We have eight hundred guests waiting to pay their respects; do behave. Roberta?"

Robbie trained her eyes on Janet, who looked as though she was about to rebel. "You will come with me and trust me to see that things are done right. Don't worry; I won't expose you to any of Alexandria's friends."

"Roberta!" protested her mother.

Janet dropped the scowl and almost smiled.

Ignoring Alexandria, Robbie turned to her sister. "Sorry, Sis, you'll have to run shotgun while I baby sit."

Elizabeth nodded, but said nothing. As far as Beth was concerned, Roberta's word was law.

They all trooped out, Roberta keeping the heir apparent in her arms. It was important that the press see a united Williams front. They walked a gauntlet of reporters in the lobby. Robbie wrapped a protective arm around Janet and covered the baby's face by folding up her collar as they bee-lined for the waiting elevator.

On the top floor, the manager ushered them into a private suite where they took off their coats and freshened their make-up. Janet used the time to wash and change the baby and settle her to continue her nap. Then they went to greet their guests in an adjoining hall.

The evening was a blur for Janet, who was emotionally drained. Robbie steered her around, and when she saw that her eyes were no longer focused, she ushered her back into the bedroom and left her to sleep with Rebecca.

Several hours later, Robbie returned to find mother and daughter still asleep; Rebecca safely under the covers with her mom's protective arm over her, and Janet on top of the covers wearing only her slip. Her strawberry blonde hair washed across the pillow.

For a minute, Robbie leaned against the doorjamb and enjoyed the view. *She is a beautiful woman — photogenic features; wonder if she can act.* Robbie looked at her watch. She needed Janet out of there and home safely before the press re-formed in greater numbers in the morning. They would not be expecting Billy's widow to disappear from the hotel in the middle of the night. It was important to keep Janet as isolated as possible until the Williams family knew more about her. She pushed herself away from the doorframe and walked to the bed. "Janet. Janet. Hey," Robbie called, giving the petite woman's bare shoulder a shake. The skin was warm and silky soft under Robbie's hand. She quickly pulled her hand away.

"Huh? Oh. What time is it?" the blonde asked, clearly not fully awake.

"Time to go before the press regroups. I'll get you a coffee while you get dressed." Robbie turned and left.

Janet got up and busied herself getting washed and dressed, and then seeing to Rebecca.

Robbie returned some time later with a coffee, a glass of milk, and some cookies on a tray. "Here, the limo is downstairs. It will take us over to where your car is parked, then I'll drive home with you."

"Really, I'm okay. I can manage from here."

"Feed the kid," was Robbie's response as she left the room.

When she returned, Robbie had changed to jeans and a suede jacket over a brushed cotton shirt, and was carrying an overnight bag and a laptop case. Janet was just getting Rebecca into her coat. "This isn't necessary," she protested.

"Yes, it is. You are tired and emotional, and you plan to drive some five hundred miles through the night with the only Williams heir," Robbie stated bluntly.

Her temper rising at this woman's clear intention to meddle in her life, Janet snapped, "Damn the Williamses!"

"Too late, we already are. I will drive and you can take care of..."

"Rebecca," Janet supplied sharply.

"Rebecca." Robbie looked at the child as she registered her name. She reached into her coat pocket and pulled out her cellular phone. "Rowe, we are leaving the hotel now. I'll be gone two days, maybe more." She clicked the phone off.

"I don't need your help," Janet said with determination, the edge in her voice obvious.

"Good, because you are not getting it; Rebecca is." Robbie picked up Rebecca and led Janet out and down to the elevator. They left by a side door and entered the limo that pulled up as they stepped outside. As soon as they were safely in the car, the driver accelerated away. The trip back to the funeral home was made in silence.

The limo pulled up beside the only vehicle remaining in the parking lot. It was an old, slightly battered Chevy truck with an extended cab. There was a moment's silence. Then Robbie snorted, "What...is...that?"

"My truck," Janet answered, getting out with some difficulty with Rebecca, her purse, and the diaper bag in her arms. She walked over to the dusty, red vehicle, shifted

Rebecca to one arm, and fumbled in her coat pocket for her keys. Her gloves fell out and Rebecca stirred restlessly.

Strong arms lifted the child from her. "Here, open the damn door before you drop the kid on its head," Robbie grumbled.

Janet stooped and picked up her gloves. Then, finding the right key, she walked around and unlocked the passenger door. Robbie followed, her face devoid of expression. Janet placed the diaper bag inside and turned to scoop the sleeping child from Robbie's arms, bringing the three of them together for an instant. Robbie's body felt very warm. That was probably why Rebecca liked being close to her. The faintest fragrance of spice drifted over to Janet as she looked up and met Robbie's eyes.

The taller woman spoke. "I'm driving. You can be pissed off as much as you want. It is still going to happen."

Frustrated, Janet sighed and pulled Rebecca away and into her arms. The sleepy little child reached a hand over Janet's shoulder. "Obbie, Obbie come," she whined.

Janet placed the child into her car seat in the back, carefully fastening her in. She looked at her little girl, wondering why she had bonded so quickly to this strange woman. Roberta Williams did look remarkably like her brother, Billy, but Rebecca had never met her father so it was unlikely that was the reason.

Janet wiggled back out of the back seat and flipped the passenger seat back into place, turning to face Roberta. "Thank you, Ms. Williams, for your concern. Rebecca and I will be fine," she said, taking out her keys again.

Robbie stepped forward, trapping Janet between her body and the doorframe. Her hand folded around Janet's and she squeezed.

"That hurts," Janet snapped, and the hand around her own relaxed a little.

"Let go of the car keys," Robbie ordered. "You can't care for a tired baby and drive." For a minute their eyes held in a battle of wills. "Please," growled the director and Janet acquiesced, opening her hand and letting the keys drop. Robbie scooped them up, went around to the driver's side and hopped in, turning to look at the annoyed woman.

"On the rare occasions when I feel compelled to be responsible for others, it is for a damn good reason. Don't question my authority," Robbie stated calmly, her blue eyes the colour of ice. Janet looked at her daughter. "Don't even think it," came the response to the plan that had barely taken root in Janet's mind to take her daughter and walk off. The petite woman looked back at the driver, then got in and slammed the door.

"This is kidnapping," she growled, staring out the front window in anger as she did up her seat belt.

Robbie leaned forward and turned the key. The engine started with protest. "Add it to my list of crimes," responded the director bitterly. "Shit! Is this the best vehicle that my brother owns?"

Anger spurred Janet to say more than she normally would have. "Billy and I never lived together."

"Yeah, well how did you end up with the kid then?" Robbie asked sarcastically.

"That's not your concern," muttered Janet, her hands folded in her lap to keep them from shaking.

The strong jaw of the driver tightened as she pulled out on the street. "Is she Billy's?"

Janet gave her a sneer and didn't answer. They drove on, Robbie expertly moving through the city traffic and then out on the highway taking them north.

Some hours later, Robbie pulled into a self-serve gas station and got out. Janet watched the famous director pumping gas and cleaning the windows. She looked as dynamic in blue jeans as she had in the black tailored coat of brushed silk she had worn at the funeral.

The coat was classic over a grey, wool suit, beautifully tailored and set off with a red silk blouse. Elizabeth had worn grey, too, with a red silk scarf as an accent. Show, Janet now realized. The whole funeral, right down to the costumes, had all been arranged by Roberta to perpetuate the Williams' mystique.

Billy had talked bitterly about the myth the first night they had met. How the famous Williams family consciously perpetuated their legend as talented, united, and caring. According to Billy, they consciously enhanced their image by carefully staging any public gathering, all the while protesting that they didn't enjoy the limelight. Billy had said that it was all a sham, a myth, and that the truth was very different. Looking back on the day, the funeral had been more a play than a time of grieving.

Robbie climbed back into the truck. "You hungry?" she asked. "It's eight o'clock, and the sandwiches they served at the reception were for show not substance."

Janet considered. She was actually starving but it meant disturbing Rebecca and having to spend more time with the objectionable Roberta. Hunger won out. "Yes, something to eat would be good. Rebecca might be a bit cranky, though. She doesn't like to be waked up."

"Well, if she starts to bawl, we'll stuff a hamburger or something in her mouth," Robbie suggested, looking back at the little bundle asleep in her car seat. She had a small fist balled up in her eye. *She's kinda cute for a baby.*

Janet gave Roberta a weary look. *This woman clearly has no idea about children.* She opened her heavy door and jumped down, then flipped back the seat, undid the straps, and pulled Rebecca out. Right on cue, Rebecca started to cry. Janet bounced her and talked softly to her as Roberta locked up the truck and came around.

The tall figure looked down at the fretting baby. "Make her stop," she commanded.

"I'm trying, Ms. Williams, but she is a baby and her schedule has been really upset today."

Robbie reached out her arms, saying, "Gimme." Janet handed over her heavy daughter. The director looked down at the startled baby face. "Shut up, okay," she said and, much to Janet's surprise, Rebecca laughed and grabbed for Robbie's chain. Robbie looked down at Janet and raised an eyebrow, a smug look on her face.

Shaking her head in disbelief, Janet laughed. "Just for that bit of showing off, Ms. Williams, you can feed her the strained peas."

"The name is Robbie, and no kid should have to start life on strained peas," she growled, heading for the diner with Rebecca over her shoulder.

Not sure just how to take the unusual woman, Janet followed. "All children start out on strained peas. Rebecca is starting to eat solids, but I thought it best to have her on the bottled foods while we were on the road."

"If we all started out eating that crap, no wonder the world is such a fucking mess," Robbie muttered, holding the door for Janet to go ahead.

"Robbie?"

"Hmm," the tall woman responded, liking the way Janet said her name.

Janet slid into a booth and Robbie, still holding Rebecca, slid in the other side. "If you are going to be part of Rebecca's life, you have to remember not to swear in front of her," Janet chided softly.

Surprised, Robbie glanced first at Janet, then Rebecca, and then back to Janet again. "Who said anything about being in the kid's life?" she exclaimed.

Janet smiled and looked down at her daughter, who once again had wrapped her little arms around Robbie's neck and was happily chewing on Robbie's collar. She looked back up at Robbie. A slow blush was creeping up her neck. "You're here, aren't you? And you have taken Rebecca every chance you had."

"Hey, wait." The red was now glowing on high, defined cheekbones.

"Excuse me, would you like a highchair for your little one?" asked the waitress, looking down at Robbie.

"Agh!" Robbie looked down at the floor.

"Yes, she would," translated Janet. "Don't they look alike?" she added as a tease.

The waitress smiled, reaching out to smooth Rebecca's dark, sleep rumpled hair, "She's got mom's hair. Are you going to look just like your mommy?" she cooed.

Janet hid a grin behind the hand that was propped up on the table. Robbie buried her face in Rebecca's neck. "Can we have menus too, please?" asked Janet.

"Sure thing." The waitress moved off.

In annoyance, Robbie looked up at Janet. "What'd you do that for?"

Grinning broadly, Janet put her head to one side to observe the hot and bothered director. "This was your idea," she reminded sweetly. Robbie scowled and was just about to respond when the highchair showed up.

"Here you are." The waitress placed the wooden highchair at the end of the table, and the menus on the blue tablecloth before she left.

Janet smiled at Robbie and waited. Robbie's scowl got deeper as she eased off the bench and lifted Rebecca up to put her in the highchair. Rebecca laughed gleefully and swung her legs up, making it impossible to slide her into the chair. Robbie tried again, another gleefully aborted attempt.

"This kid has your sick sense of humour," Robbie muttered, grabbing Rebecca's legs with one hand and stuffing them gently under the highchair's tray as she successfully lowered Rebecca into place on her the third attempt. Rebecca promptly grabbed hold of Robbie's gold chain, making it impossible for her to straighten up.

Prudently, Janet decided that this was the time to come to the rescue before there was one of the famous Williams' scenes. "Rebecca," she called softly and her daughter immediately forgot Robbie and let go of the chain, reaching her little arms out to her mom. Janet took the hands and kissed them. "That's a good girl."

Robbie sighed and slid back into the booth, looking at the mother and daughter with confused eyes. *Why the hell am I here anyway? Why should I be making Billy's family my responsibility?*

"So, are you going to try feeding her now that you've mastered highchair?" Janet asked, leading Robbie on as she read her menu.

"I can feed her," Robbie muttered with irritation, looking at her own menu.

"Ready to order?" asked the waitress, who had returned to their table.

"I'll have a cheese omelette," Robbie ordered from behind the menu, "and...my daughter will have scrambled eggs."

"I'll have bacon and eggs with extra toast, please," requested Janet with a smile. The waitress smiled back and went to put in the order. Janet looked over at Robbie. "Your daughter?"

"Hey, you started it. What am I going to say now — that I've never seen the kid before today?" Robbie leaned forward and propped her chin on her hand. "Do immature humans eat scrambled eggs?" she asked as an afterthought.

"Now's not the time to be asking," Janet pointed out, her eyes dancing with merriment at the thought of Robbie trying to feed her stubborn daughter.

Robbie looked down at the tablecloth, tracing patterns with a long, slender finger. "Listen, I'm kind of head of the family now. I feel I've got some responsibility to see that Rebecca here is okay."

Janet looked up from watching Robbie's hand. She had beautiful hands, with long artist's fingers. In fact, Roberta Williams was a knock out. One of those rare people who were very comfortable with and unaffected by their incredible good looks. "Were you and Billy close?"

"No." Robbie frowned.

"Robbie, Billy never saw his daughter. The Williams Family does not have any responsibility to Rebecca. I'm quite capable of raising her on my own."

"What the hell sort of relationship did my brother have with you?" Robbie asked in irritation.

Janet was saved from answering by the arrival of their food. She noticed that Robbie deliberately did not look up at the waitress. Nor had she the previous time. *She doesn't want to be recognized. I hadn't even thought about her being famous.*

"Thanks." Janet smiled, drawing the attention to herself.

"You're welcome." The waitress left them to their meals.

Janet reached over to touch Robbie's arm. "I'm sorry."

"Sorry for what?"

"For bringing attention to you last time the waitress was here. It never occurred to me she might recognize you. I'm truly sorry," she repeated sincerely.

Robbie shrugged and looked uncomfortable. "So, you tell me about your relationship with Billy, and I'll stuff these eggs into the kid, okay?"

Looking into remarkable blue eyes that seemed to glow with an inner light, Janet considered. "Okay," she said, wondering whether Robbie would understand.

Robbie determinedly picked up a fork. Janet took it away and handed her a teaspoon. "Just put a little on and blow on it first so it's cool," she cautioned. Robbie nodded and scooped up some egg and blew on it, then offered it to Rebecca. Rebecca grabbed the spoon with a laugh and tipped it over into Robbie's lap.

"Shit!" Robbie snapped. Janet raised an eyebrow. "The kid got egg all over me," Robbie protested. Janet said nothing. Robbie scooped up, blew on, and offered egg again. This time Rebecca refused to open her mouth but one egg filled hand came up and grabbed Robbie's hair.

Janet saw the look and reacted immediately. "Here," she said, hurriedly offering Robbie her napkin. "Like this." Janet took the spoon and readied a mouthful. "Here you are, sweet one, open up for mommy. That's a good girl. Do you like the eggs Aunt Robbie got you? Come on, have another spoonful," Janet coaxed, putting the spoon in her daughter's mouth then lifting it up so the egg was scraped off as the spoon was withdrawn.

Finding the exchange between mother and daughter fascinating, Robbie watched intently.

"Okay, now you try." Janet smiled, handing the spoon back to Robbie. Robbie repeated the action. Right down to Janet's expressions and voice tone. Rebecca ate her egg happily and Janet sat with her mouth open in shock. "That was me!" she gasped.

Robbie smiled and wiggled her eyebrows. Rebecca burped and spit up on Robbie's hand.

Robbie lifted her hand and watched the partly chewed egg drip off. "And just what expression do I use to describe what I am feeling now?" she asked quietly, pulling a face.

"I usually say, 'Oh dear,'" Janet offered, trying not to laugh.

"Nope. 'Oh dear' just doesn't cut it dramatically."

"Here," said Janet softly, taking Robbie's hand and wiping it clean with her napkin. "Tell you what, you eat your dinner and I'll finish feeding Rebecca. I'm used to eating with one hand."

Robbie didn't protest. She had successfully stifled, for now, any nesting instinct that might have been lying dormant within her. She looked down at her cool and partly congealed omelette. Janet's eyes followed.

"You get used to eating your food cold," she sighed. Robbie nodded and ate her dinner moodily, watching silently while Janet ate and fed Rebecca at the same time.

They left some time later, Janet carrying a now tired and grumpy child to the truck. Robbie gingerly held the crying child while Janet got in the rear seat and then, with relief, she passed Rebecca over. Janet strapped her miserable daughter into her car seat while Robbie walked around and slipped into the driver's seat once again. For a while the sound of wailing pierced the air above Janet's soothing voice. Then both child and mom went quiet as Robbie started to sing. Her songs were old Welsh lullabies and her voice was low and melodic. Soon Rebecca was fast asleep and Robbie pulled to the shoulder to let Janet get back into the front seat.

"You have a beautiful voice," Janet said as they started off again.

"Hmm," Robbie responded disinterestedly.

"Have you sung professionally? I don't remember you singing in any of your movies except in *Dark Night*, but that was just a few words and you were drunk then," pattered Janet.

An eyebrow went up. "No, I don't sing professionally. And I wasn't drunk, I was *acting* drunk; there's a big difference," the actor clarified.

"You don't drink alcohol at all?" Janet asked in surprise. She had understood that the famous director had lived a rather wild life, but the vehemence of Robbie's response made her think otherwise.

"Rarely, and never to excess," Robbie responded. "Where do I turn off the highway?"

"Just north of Bartlett," Janet replied as she studied the actor's profile.

"Nothing is north of Bartlett," Robbie observed sarcastically. "Is there something wrong with my face?"

Janet smiled. "No, you are really very beautiful, but I guess you hear that a lot. No, I was trying to understand you. You are a very complex person."

Robbie had heard she was beautiful a lot but somehow Janet thinking so made her tired spirits rise. She wasn't sure, however, if she wanted Janet to understand her. *She probably wouldn't like what she found.*

Shifting so that she leaned against her door, Janet continued to look at Robbie. She was a strange and beautiful enigma, filled with a pulsating energy that could focus in an instant in violence or in care. Janet couldn't explain why, but she really didn't dislike this woman as she had first thought she would. In fact, she found herself very much impressed with Roberta Williams.

She had found Billy's family to be a trying experience. What would they do if anything happened to her? Legally, her daughter would be handed over to Alexandria. That scared the hell out of Janet. Elizabeth seemed nice, but she lived in her own world. She wouldn't have time for an active child like Rebecca. Then there was Robbie...

"Can I ask you a question?"

"I guess." Robbie sighed, waiting for one of the standard fan questions.

"Who would you want as Rebecca's guardian?"

The truck swerved onto the gravel shoulder and then bounced back onto the tarmac. "What?"

"I thought it only fair that I allow the Williams family some input. If anything were to happen to me, I want to make sure Rebecca has someone that will take good care of her. Billy's dead and I don't have any family. I don't want Rebecca running any chance of having the childhood I did."

Robbie stole a look at the face of the serious woman beside her. "You were an orphan?"

"Yes."

"Who raised you?"

"My grandfather," Janet answered tersely.

Robbie was confused by the subject. "Are you ill?"

"No, I'm not ill. I'm responsible. I need to know that Rebecca's future is as secure as I can make it."

There was silence for a minute. "I'll be Rebecca's guardian."

That was not the response that Janet had expected. She hesitated for a minute and then spoke frankly. "Most of what I've read about you was pretty negative. You are supposed to be a creative genius, but a tyrant. Did you really cause Sally Gershman's nervous breakdown?"

"Most likely, but that is beside the point."

"It is the point. I've seen a bit of that tyrannical nature tonight, but I don't think Rebecca would be intimidated by it. I've also seen another side of you today. Elizabeth adores you, Alexandria respects you, and I've learned that you have a really soft heart."

"Crap."

"I will consider your offer," Janet said, proving herself to be just as strong willed as Robbie.

There was a long silence as various emotions washed across Robbie's face. "You do that," she finally grated out.

"I will," Janet said noncommittally, and then leaned back against the headrest.

An hour later, they turned off the Bartlett road and bounced down a rutted dirt lane pressed in by thick trees on either side. "Do you live with the bears?" Robbie asked sarcastically.

"Only in the winter," Janet yawned, as they came to a stop outside a log cabin. "This is where we live."

Robbie looked at the log cabin in disbelief. "Who with...Daniel Boone?"

Chapter 2

I like it, Robbie concluded, looking around the small log home while Janet busied herself getting an exhausted Rebecca to bed. The log walls were varnished a soft honey colour and the furniture was overstuffed, traditional and comfy. The sofa and one chair were a deep burgundy plaid and the other chair was forest green.

The focus of the room was a huge fireplace made of granite stones, which was bracketed on each side by a large window. Robbie looked out, but the night was too dark to see the view. The kitchen was to the other side, separated by a log counter with a cut stone top. The third wall was a built-in bookcase with an inset TV centre. The last wall opened onto a hallway, off of which were two bedrooms and a bathroom.

They had entered by the side door, near the kitchen. The front door was in a small entrance hall beside the living room. The front door, from what Robbie could see out the window, seemed to open on a porch that ran the length of the house.

It was small, but very well organized and tastefully decorated. Robbie put her overnight bag down on the chair and walked over to look at the large painting over the mantel. The artist was a well-known Eastern Woodland Indian painter. The image was of Corn Mother feeding her young. The subject was simple and the colours bold. *Like that, too,* Robbie thought, then wandered across the room to look at the books.

There was a smattering of popular literature, but the vast majority of the books were related to educational philosophy. *Hell! Billy married a school marm.*

"Sorry to leave you standing there, Robbie, but I had to get Rebecca to bed," Janet said as she walked back into the room.

"You're a school teacher? Over paid, under worked, summers off, don't care about basics or kids, school teacher?" growled Robbie, lifting the book in her hand to reveal the title, *Methodology in Gifted Classrooms* by J. J. Layton.

"What? Listen, you—" Janet started in annoyance, the red warming her cheeks. Then she saw the sparkle in Robbie's eyes. "I bet you were a real terror in school," she laughed, folding her arms across her chest and giving the tall woman her best teacher look.

Robbie's face became instantly innocent as she pointed an index finger at herself. "Me?"

"Hmm, it explains why you turned into a rude, overbearing, egocentric workaholic," Janet growled in her best imitation of Robbie's voice. Robbie feigned surprise and hurt. Janet walked over and took the book from her hand and placed it back on the shelf. Their bodies were very close now and again Janet sensed the warm, gentle heat and spicy scent of the famous actor. *It's no wonder she has such a wild reputation. Robbie Williams would be very hard to resist.*

She turned to find Robbie looking down at her. For a moment there was a silence that radiated tension, then Robbie stepped back and asked, "Well, are you a school marm?"

"Yes, I'm the principal at The Bartlett School for the Gifted," Janet called over her shoulder as she hurried to put the kitchen counter between her and Robbie. The way she was feeling about this woman was definitely not good. *Shit!* "Can I get you anything? I usually have a cup of tea around this time," she rambled.

Moving to stand by the dark window in contemplation, Robbie nodded. "Yeah, tea would be good," she responded after a minute. *Damn, I must be tired. I almost kissed her.*

What the hell is the matter with you, Williams? Robbie thought, trying to pull herself together. *What the hell am I doing here?*

"So just what kind of relationship did you have with my brother?" asked Robbie, going on the offensive. "You never did answer me."

Janet grimaced and put down the mug that she was holding. She looked over the counter at the tall woman who had turned to look at her. Their eyes met. Janet licked her lips. There was no point in lying. Robbie would check, she knew she would. "I needed money quickly, lots of money, so I sold my body to your brother." She was quietly pleased that her voice hadn't cracked with the emotion she was holding firmly in check. The blue eyes registered surprise followed by doubt.

Fumbling to make the tea with shaking hands, Janet struggled to get her emotions under control. The splash of the hot water and rattle of the china were painfully loud in the deafening silence that followed her statement. When she finally looked up, Robbie was still standing there looking at her, a shrewd and calculating look on her face.

"Would you like to put your bag in your room while the tea is brewing?" Janet asked to end the silence.

"Yes." Robbie met Janet's eyes, saw pain in the green eyes that looked back at her.

She followed Janet into a bedroom that was clearly hers. Here, the large logs were hung with Navaho rugs. They weren't big, but they were of good quality, Robbie noted, as she leaned on the doorjamb after placing her bag on the floor. "So you sell your body, huh?" she purred, and saw the shock and anger rise in Janet's eyes. "How much?" she enquired in a voice laced with steel.

"It was a one-time business deal, Robbie. Don't be offensive," Janet warned. Robbie stepped toward her. The tall woman looked hungry and mean, and she walked like a dark jungle cat stalking its prey. Janet instinctively took a step back, fear showing on her face.

Robbie stopped. For a long minute the two women stared at each other. "What did you think I was going to do, attack you?" Robbie snorted, one eyebrow arched in annoyance.

"No...I mean, I felt threatened by your attitude and posture." Janet blushed. "I'm not a bad person, Robbie, but circumstance put me in a difficult position. I'm tired and over stressed. I don't want to have this conversation right now."

"I need to know the truth," Robbie insisted.

"Truth?" Janet snorted and pushed past Robbie, heading for the kitchen. "After the Williams' staging I witnessed today, I'd be hard pressed to believe that truth could survive in your world." She stalked into the kitchen and found that her hands were shaking so hard, she couldn't pour the tea. Robbie stepped around the corner and Janet jumped.

Robbie rolled her eyes, poured the tea with a steady hand, and carried the mugs into the living room. She put them down on the coffee table, which was shaped like an old fashioned sled. *Janet has unusual and creative taste.* Robbie sat down in the green chair and stretched out her long legs, crossing her ankles comfortably. *But she has a secret that's too painful to discuss. That's just too bad. We need to discuss it now.* Robbie raised an eyebrow at Janet, who still stood in the kitchen, and waited.

Coming around the counter, Janet dropped into the burgundy chair at the other end of the coffee table. She fidgeted with her hands. "It's hard for me to talk about it. It was a very personal and painful time in my life, and not one I want to share." Janet's voice shook with emotion.

Robbie shrugged, unimpressed. "You will have to. If there is anything in your past the press can get their teeth into, they will. You'll have to accept my authority as head of the family. You have no idea yet what it is to be a Williams. I won't take 'no' for an answer. Everything you have ever heard about me is true, and there is a lot you haven't heard. Now, tell me what I want to know."

"I am prepared to accept your intelligence and capabilities, Robbie, but you have no authority over my life and never will. We will start to get on a lot better when you accept an equal relationship with me," the petite woman responded confidently.

Robbie lips twitched in a ghost of a smile. "I'll give you this, school marm, you can hold your own. I don't want the press digging up any dirt that I don't know about and can't counter immediately. What you tell me will not go any further, if I can help it."

Janet hesitated, then nodded reluctantly. "There isn't too much to tell. My grandfather was an inveterate gambler. As he got older, he lost some of his sharpness and all of his money. He signed my name to some debts that he was not able to pay. When he died, I found out I owed a fortune. The creditors would not consider payments and the bank would not give me a loan for that amount of money. I was facing a prison term.

"I was desperate. I met your brother at a party. He was desperate, too. He said he needed an heir but he didn't want any obligations to either the child or its mother. I said I'd bear and raise an heir for him in exchange for the money I needed." Janet stared into the fireplace, her face white with stress.

Silence.

"I'm going to bed now. Where are you sleeping?" Robbie asked abruptly, getting up.

Janet looked up, her eyes blinking at the sudden change of subject. "Here, on the couch." Robbie nodded once and was gone. Janet leaned her head back on the chair, emotionally drained by the day and by Robbie Williams. The woman was impossible, an erratic blend of fire and ice.

Robbie lay in Janet's bed, her hands folded behind her head, staring at the ceiling. She was taut with anger and she had absolutely no idea why. She had gotten what she wanted out of Janet. The woman had spirit. The bed had a lingering scent of hot summer herbs and honey that she knew was Janet's chemical makeup.

Billy had got what he wanted, too. Her heart jolted and a pain filled her chest. *Shit! That's it. I'm jealous that Billy bedded Janet. Get a grip here, lady. This woman is nothing to you. She probably isn't even gay. You're just experiencing some latent nesting syndrome because you like Rebecca. Reb is alright, really well behaved for a kid. Why did Billy suddenly feel he had to have a child?* Then an awful realization exploded in her mind. A fear gripped her heart and she rolled out of bed, grabbing her robe.

Janet was still sitting in the chair. She looked and felt completely numb. The bedroom door opened and in a few quick strides, Robbie was in front of her.

"Why did he marry you? He could have gotten an heir without marrying you. Why?" she demanded.

Janet sighed, and in a voice devoid of energy or emotion answered, "He insisted. He said his child couldn't be a bastard. We even waited a few months after we were married before... He wanted no doubt that the child was his legal heir. He said it was important."

Cold icicles of fear ran down her back as Robbie understood what her brother had done. *Billy must have found out about my illegitimate child. He wanted a child in wedlock so he could claim the inheritance. I don't give a damn about the money, but who else did he tell?* "This is important," she said seriously, fighting not to show any of her true feelings. "Did he tell you anything else?"

Janet shook her head and the towering woman seemed to relax a bit. She wore only a blue, silk bed jacket tied with a belt. The jacket ended half way between her knee and her hip. Her legs were incredibly long and shapely. *She must sleep naked*, Janet thought, and then looked away to the dead ashes in the hearth.

Robbie looked at the woman intently. *No, she doesn't know any more*, she reasoned, then turned on her heel and was gone.

Janet was so exhausted she barely noticed her leaving.

Janet woke early to the sound of Rebecca demanding attention. For a minute, she had no idea where she was, then the events of the day before filtered back into her consciousness. *I'd better get up. No doubt my damn uninvited houseguest will want a hunk of raw meat thrown in her direction for breakfast.* With a sigh, she rolled off the couch onto her feet and, blurry eyed, moved toward Rebecca's room. "Hi, sweetheart," she called to the small child who stood in her crib holding on to the bars. At the sight of her mom, Rebecca bounced with glee. "Want to shower with mommy this morning?" More giggles of delight.

After stripping off Rebecca's diaper, Janet carried her into the bathroom. The happy child played with her rubber ducky until her mom had turned on and adjusted the water for their shower. After much singing, giggling, and soap bubbles, the two emerged squeaky clean and with a warm glow. Janet slipped a Toronto Maple Leaf jersey over her head and a similar one over Rebecca's. Then mother and daughter headed off for the kitchen to see to breakfast.

Robbie's bedroom door was open and, after hesitating, Janet moved further down the hall and looked in. The bed had been stripped and the sheets left neatly folded. Robbie's overnight bag was zipped closed and lay on a chair. It was the only indication that Robbie was still around. Rebecca squirmed to be let down, and Janet came back from her thoughts and lowered her active daughter to her feet.

Rebecca looked into the room. "Mommy's 'oom," said the child pointing.

"Yes, mommy's room," agreed Janet. "Come on, Rebecca, let's get some breakfast, okay?"

Rebecca giggled and ran, wobbly on her feet, toward the kitchen.

"What will it be, partner?" Janet looked over the counter and down at her daughter, who looked back with serious blue eyes.

"Banana, peas."

"You'd like a banana on fresh bread?" clarified Janet with a smile at her daughter's good manners.

"Yes, peas," Rebecca answered, then she ran across the room and stood by the screen door. "Obbie come. Obbie come," the little child reported happily.

Janet felt her gut tighten but she smiled. "Good, Robbie can have breakfast with you, Rebecca."

Robbie kept a steady pace up the dirt road. It was nice running in the cool of the woods rather than out on the hard pavement of the city. The air smelled of pine, not diesel, and the ground was softer under foot. She picked up her pace, enjoying the high that a long run always gave her. The road bent and Robbie caught a glimpse of the lake before she dropped back into the mottled shadows that led back to Janet's log cabin.

Running up the wide wood stairs, she came to a stop on the large porch that overlooked the long, narrow lake. The view was framed by tall pines and out on the lake a pair of loons called to each other with lonely, plaintive cries.

"Obbie," came a voice from behind her and the director turned to see Rebecca standing at the screen door, looking at her.

"Hi, Rebel. How are you doing this morning?" Robbie felt herself drawn to her brother's child by a powerful inner force. She carefully opened the door and stepped in. Rebecca looked up at her aunt, and fell on her bum in the process. "Oops, you okay, kid?" Robbie asked from way above her.

Rebecca raised her small arms. "Obbie up. Obbie up," she insisted. Strong hands wrapped around her and the next minute, she shot up in the air and was looking down at Obbie's face. She laughed happily and the tall woman laughed too.

Swinging Rebecca in her arms, Robbie walked over to where Janet was working in the kitchen. "Morning," she said stiffly.

"Good morning," a cold voice returned.

Robbie smiled defiantly. "Still got our feathers ruffled, have we?" she drawled.

Janet gave her a warning look but said nothing. She sliced a banana onto a piece of fresh bread, folded the bread over and passed it to her daughter who was still wrapped contentedly in Robbie's arms. "What would you like to eat?" she asked her sister-in-law formally.

Robbie looked down at Rebecca who was busily pulling slices of banana out of her sandwich and mushing them against Robbie's shoulder. With a weary smile, Robbie watched as a partly chewed piece of sticky fruit slipped down her cleavage. "You did that deliberately, didn't you?" she asked, an eyebrow going up in annoyance.

"No." Janet smiled from behind her coffee mug as she watched her daughter be...well, her daughter. Rebecca laughed through a mouth full of banana and reached up with a sticky hand to grab Robbie's nose. Banana slime now dripped from the famous woman's face. Janet snorted into her coffee.

"Okay, Reb, you've given your mom enough entertainment at my expense," said the tall woman, going around the counter to place Rebecca in her highchair. The banana sandwich went on the floor. Robbie sighed and bent to pick it up. "I can't understand why the world is over-populated," she muttered, looking in disgust at the mushed sandwich before she dropped it into the garbage.

"Go clean up and I'll finish feeding Rebecca and get us some breakfast, too," Janet suggested, looking at the woman who now stood beside her.

Robbie looked down at Janet. The petite woman had spunk and a sense of humour. She was pretty and intelligent, too. Her little brother had picked some good genetic stock, it would seem. "So you are speaking to me now, huh?" she growled.

"It would be childish not to. However, for the record, you are not forgiven for your aggressive behaviour last night." Janet turned away. She could feel Robbie behind her, feel her warmth and the intense energy that always seemed to surround her. Then the feeling was gone as Robbie walked and passed to the other side of the counter.

"Breakfast isn't necessary," stated the retreating figure.

Janet's eyes followed the arrogant woman in amazement. *She bullies me last night for the information she needed and then gets her feelings hurt this morning because I'm still annoyed with her. That woman is the strangest piece of work that I've ever come across.*

Angry, Janet peeled the remainder of the banana and passed it to her daughter to eat. "Here you are, Reb," she said softly. *Now where did that name come from? Robbie called her that. Damn! Seems to suit my fearless daughter, too.* Perplexed, Janet turned back to the kitchen and started to prepare blackberry pancakes for the two of them.

Storming into the bedroom, Robbie stripped off her sweats. Opening her bag, she pulled out her dressing gown and slipped it on and then took out underwear, jeans, and a sweatshirt. She headed down the hall to the bathroom and was dismayed to find it smelt of the warm sweet herbs that were Janet. *Shit! Why am I angry? Who cares if she thinks I'm a bastard? I am. Damn the woman anyway,* Robbie grumbled in her head, as she slipped out of her wrap and stepped on a wet rubber ducky in the shower.

Janet had cleaned Reb up and was just placing her in her playpen when she heard the crash. She walked over to the hall and then hurried down to the bathroom door. "Are you okay?" she asked through the door.

When there was no answer, she repeated, her voice a little louder, "Robbie, are you okay?" There was still no answer, so Janet knocked on the door. Nothing. She turned the knob and looked in. Robbie lay on the bathroom floor, half in and half out of the shower. Janet's shocked mind registered three things, one right after the other: *She's naked. She's gorgeous. Oh my God, I think she's dead!*

Robbie's nausea was beginning to pass and her head was clearing from the initial pain as she enjoyed being in Janet's caring arms. Janet had covered her respectfully with a bath towel. Her knee ached terribly. She closed her eyes and played hurt to the best of her ability. Janet was holding an ice pack on the lump growing on her knee and talking to her softly. "Robbie, are you okay? This knee doesn't look good."

The actor milked the scene for all it was worth before opening her baby blues. "You left that duck there on purpose, didn't you?" she drawled with humour, her eyebrow going up in question as she looked at Janet.

Janet was shocked. "No, of course not!"

Robbie managed a weak smile. "Are we even now?" she asked seriously.

"Yes. But I didn't try to hurt you. I'm really sorry that you hurt yourself on Reb's toy."

"Why, because I might sue?" Robbie asked sharply in annoyance.

"No, because I don't like to bring harm to anyone — deliberately or by accident," Janet said with fervour.

"I might sue," Robbie grumbled with a moan as she tried to straighten her leg.

"Oh, yeah, the mighty Roberta Williams is going to sue because she was laid low by a rubber ducky," Janet mocked and the two women broke out laughing.

"Ouch, that hurts." Robbie winced and reached for her knee. As she did so, her hand covered Janet's where she held the ice pack in place. Robbie immediately pulled her hand away. "Sorry," she said awkwardly.

For a second the two women looked into each other's eyes, then Janet said, "Listen, do you want to try getting up?"

"Janet?"

"Yes?"

"My knee is twisted. I'm letting you know in case I have to lean on you," Robbie said seriously.

"You can lean on me," Janet responded, and both women knew that the friction between them had passed and that they could possibly learn to be friends. The whole weekend was turning out to have some real surprises in it.

"Janet, I am not going to your doctor!" Robbie yelled some time later from where she lay on the living room couch.

Reb, who had been sitting contentedly on top of Robbie, looked startled and then hit Robbie's hand. "Bad Obbie! Bad Obbie." She scowled.

Surprised, Robbie looked at the little girl. "Shit, you are just like your old lady," she muttered.

"Robbie, don't..." Janet walked over to continue the argument. Robbie had a package of frozen peas on her knee but the joint was continuing to swell by the moment.

"Shit, mommy. Shit, mommy," Reb repeated. Robbie roared with laughter.

"No," Janet said firmly and Rebecca looked worried. "Bad, Rebecca," Janet said and Rebecca reached up to her mommy in tears. Janet picked up her upset daughter and held her.

"Now look what you've done," growled the actor, fighting the urge to fly to Reb's defence.

"*I* did? Look, Roberta, your leg is getting worse. You need medical attention."

"I'll need more than that if I go sit in a waiting room. Have you any idea how aggressive fans can be?"

"Oh, I hadn't thought of that. Look, Bill — that's Doctor Perkins — is a friend of mine. I'm sure if I asked him, he'd come over after work and look at the knee. Okay?" Janet swung back and forth as she soothed her worried child.

"How good a friend?" Robbie demanded with a scowl, pulling herself up on her elbows.

"What?" The startled woman lowered her daughter to the floor to buy some time.

"You heard me, how good a friend?"

"That is not your business, Ms. Williams," Janet said formally, going to start the breakfast dishes in the kitchen. To her surprise, Robbie was right behind her. "Robbie. You are going to do even more damage your knee."

Robbie got that stubborn look that Janet was quickly learning meant big trouble. "I want to know."

"Don't even think about intimidating me," Janet grumbled, pushing past Robbie, who wobbled back against the counter.

"I'm family. Family has no secrets," argued the tall woman, rubbing her knee in pain.

Janet snorted as she wiped Reb's highchair tray clean. "Your family is totally dysfunctional."

"Don't try to change the subject," Robbie commanded, remaining focused on her goal.

Sighing and rolling her eyes, Janet turned to look at this stranger who had bullied her way into her life in a most irritating manner. "I'll make you a deal. I'll tell you about my relationship with Bill, if you agree to do what he says," she suggested, already planning to have Bill pack Robbie off back to a city specialist.

Robbie agreed readily; she was formulating some plans of her own. "Okay."

Janet's eyes narrowed. *What is this exasperating woman up to?* Leaning against the counter, she said, "Bill and I have an understanding."

"What the f— What does that mean?" Robbie amended as Reb came running around the corner and wrapped her arms around her mother's leg. She had Robbie's bag of frozen peas on her head. Janet reached down and took it off, placing the plastic bag on the counter.

"It means that there might be a time in the future, when Bill's practice is established, when we might consider marriage," she explained awkwardly, not looking at Robbie.

Silence. *She's a lousy liar,* thought Robbie, "Ahh, would he be a good step father?"

"Yes."

Robbie limped past Janet, picking up the frozen bag as she went, and returned to the couch to work on her laptop. Janet went back to her dishes and Reb quietly went to play in the ashes of the fire until Janet ran over and confined her adventurous daughter to her playpen.

Late in the morning, the fall day clouded over and a steady drizzle started to fall. Robbie closed up her laptop and flipped through the books on the bookshelf. There were four by J. J. Layton. Turning to the back jacket, Robbie was startled to see Janet staring back at her in black and white. *So Janet Williams is also J. J. Layton, M. Ed.*

Janet returned from putting Reb down for her afternoon nap. "These are yours," observed Robbie as Janet walked by.

"Yes, I know." The author blushed. "Bill said you were to stay off that leg until he has a chance to see it," she said, as she went to clean the ashes out of the hearth.

"I'm bored," grumbled the famous actor, putting the book back neatly on the shelf and hobbling over, stiff legged, to sit down on the couch and watch Janet work.

Janet placed the fireplace ashes in a metal pail to carry them outside. When she came back in from dumping the ashes in a sandpit, she found Robbie sitting on the floor going through the small collection of DVDs that she kept in the drawer under her TV. "Make yourself at home; feel free to go through my cupboards," she said sarcastically as she put the ash bucket in the broom closet.

"Thanks," Robbie muttered, ignoring the barb. "You don't have any of mine," she observed peevishly.

"No." Janet headed for the kitchen to put the kettle on.

Robbie looked over at the petite woman who could barely be seen over the counter from that angle. "Why?"

"They're too violent. I like things with happy endings."

Robbie schooled her face to remain still and passive. *Okay, so Janet doesn't like my movies, so what?* "You've got *Jurassic Park*. Didn't the really big dinosaurs scare you?" she asked, resorting to sarcasm.

"Nope, I always root for the animals," Janet observed. "But I was terrified for those kids."

Robbie nodded. *Putting kids or animals in danger really heightens tension in a screen play.* Much to her own surprise, she asked, "Uh, you want to watch a movie with me?" She felt heat climbing up her face.

Hesitating for a minute, Janet thought about her feelings. *I do find myself liking Robbie even though I dislike the way she tries to bully me at times. She seems to be the best of the pack in the Williams family, not that that's saying much. Reb needs to know her father's family and this woman has offered to be Rebecca's guardian if anything happens to me. Would she be an acceptable guardian? I don't know. But I think she would take the job very seriously. However inappropriately Robbie might behave, there's a sort of noble core about her. It's just a shame she's so filled with anger.*

"I was just going to make a pot of tea. I think I've got some home made oatmeal cookies. Shall we have some with the movie?" To her surprise, she saw Robbie relax, as if she had been holding her breath waiting for an answer.

"Yeah, that would be good. Those pancakes you made this morning...they were good," Robbie said awkwardly as she pretended to read the copyright information on the DVD case.

Janet smiled. *A compliment of sorts. It sounded like the first one Robbie has ever given.* She made the tea and brought it over on a tray with a plate of raisin-oatmeal cookies. Robbie slipped in the DVD and, hobbling, pulled a cushion onto the floor so that she could watch lying down with her leg flat and her knee under an ice pack. As the movie started to play, she watched intently, her blue eyes moving constantly over the screen, taking in every detail.

Meanwhile, Janet watched Robbie. *She's very beautiful and in a very real way. She isn't the product of dieting and makeup, she's just naturally good looking and healthy. She's almost larger than life in her vitality, her presence. However aggressive and commanding the woman is, she's also mesmerizing.*

"I like a good adventure show. Do you?" Janet asked the director, passing her the plate of cookies.

"Adventure show? God damn it, lady, this is Spielberg. Have you really looked at this film?"

Janet jumped in surprise and spilled cookies onto the polished wood floor. Robbie did not appear to notice; she had grabbed the remote and was rewinding the tape, a look of utter disgust on her face.

"Okay, look, the helicopter comes in low over the water. 'Copters don't do that in real life. It's dangerous, and besides aviation regulations call for five hundred feet minimum. The director chose to do that." Robbie pointed, freezing the action. "See, now look, the point of view has shifted from the 'copter to the approaching island. The viewer is forced to look up. You are approaching the Jurassic World where nature dominates and humans are made small. Spielberg is setting the stage.

"Watch," Robbie ordered, starting the film again, "Look how the 'copter has to go around the small island. Already nature is dominating. And look at the shape of the island. Tall, dinosaur-like." Robbie's mood shifted from annoyance to excitement as she warmed to her subject. "Okay, this is the valley scene. Watch. See, they go down the long valley. No 'copter pilot would do that normally. It's symbolic. You are entering the world of Jurassic Park. It is a birth image.

"Now they run into trouble. Turbulence. The missing seat belt strap. There is confusion. They can't cope. Finally, the knotted belt; it's a very human action. It draws us to the protagonist. We bond in the common experience of having to deal with the ordinary frustrations of things like seat belts. This whole section is a foreshadowing of things to come. The best-laid plans are already falling apart. And it is in that out-of-control state that we go down, down into the Jurassic World. Brilliant. See how the waterfalls in the background repeat that message?

"Right, now, here is the meal ticket," Robbie explained, freezing the action again and pointing to the screen. "The Jeep door opens and there is the Jurassic Park symbol. Blatant commercialism. I bet he sold a pile of those toy Jeeps. The guy not only has the heart of an artist but a damn good business mind, too. That one second of film promotes the show, reinforces the title, and sells a billion toys. You can almost hear him laughing all the way to the bank." One long, slender finger clicked the remote and the action started again.

"Now the Jeeps enter through the gates that close behind us. Foreshadowing, right? We become trapped in a world from which not all of us will escape. Note the pink uniforms. Female references are starting to appear. Rebirth. Subtle hints that nature's reproductive cycle cannot be controlled.

"Right, now we move out on the savannah. Note the tall trees creating that dinosaur height again. The Jeep circles around the tree. Nature dominates. The pattern the director established at the beginning of the show is now being repeated for the dim-witted. We went down the valley, now the protagonist is seen in a reverse image, rising out of the roof of the Jeep. A birth image. Human trouble again. The character, so overcome by the power of nature, falls to the ground.

"Listen to the music — stirring, building. It is female music, filled with hope and rebirth. Okay, back to the action." Robbie was now completely lost in the work. "Listen to this line, 'They're moving in herds.' Again it's foreshadowing. The dinos will work together to defeat the humans. The music crescendoes and the viewpoint shifts to the world of Jurassic Park that opens out in front of us.

"How much of the film did we look at? Maybe a few minutes, and look at how much careful planning was in it to create the perfect illusion. And you say to me," Robbie sighed and turned on Janet, "that you like a good adventure story. Shit!"

Completely taken back by the outburst, Janet blinked in surprise. The DVD played on into the silence of the room as the two women looked at each other. Robbie's expression slowly changed from frustration to confusion as if she had suddenly become aware of where she was and what she was doing.

"Well, it is what I do for a living. I guess I see it differently than most," she grumbled to hide the embarrassment she felt at having shown so much of her excitement and love of her craft.

Janet laughed, her eyes sparkling with delight. Robbie looked up sharply, her temper rising. *Is Janet laughing at me?*

"That was the most fantastic experience. I learned so much. Wow! You just opened doors for me, in terms of what I can start to pick out of film now. Please, Robbie, go on. I want to learn more," Janet begged, slipping onto the floor by Robbie in her excitement and leaning her back against the chair.

Robbie gave a nervous smile. "Yeah? You liked that? Okay, let me rewind." The director smiled and picked up the remote from where it lay in her lap.

Janet eyes followed the action, lingering on the spot where tight blue jeans covered

Robbie's sex. *Oh boy, this woman could really get my motor humming,* Janet thought, and then quickly turned her attention back to the screen before Robbie noticed where her eyes were focused.

For the next three hours, Robbie talked about her craft. She was encouraged and pleased when Janet asked intelligent, probing questions. When Reb woke from her nap, Robbie played with her on the floor while Janet prepared chili for dinner and made bread to go with it.

We'll have a fresh tossed salad with the chili, and I'll ask Bill to join us. She hadn't been really truthful about Bill. The truth was Bill wanted marriage and she didn't. Janet had had satisfactory relationships with both sexes, and she liked Bill a lot, but she'd always thought that when she met her special person, it would be a woman. Someone like Robbie.

Bill arrived at five carrying two bunches of spring flowers. As Janet opened the screen door, he gave her one and pecked her lightly on the cheek. Robbie rolled her eyes as she watched from the couch. The actor had changed into her black running shorts and a tank top of the same colour with a slash of gold down the sides. One long leg was bent up and the other out straight as she lounged back against the arm of the couch, her arms spread wide. Blue eyes, almost inhuman in their intensity, slowly stroked up the young doctor's body.

Come here, Robbie thought. *I'm going to eat you alive.*

Janet saw the look and narrowed her eyes in warning. Robbie flashed a dazzling white smile at the short, wispy-haired doctor and held out a graceful hand to accept her flowers. "How lovely," she said in the famous voice that could turn a heart of stone to lava.

"Roberta, this is Dr. Bill Perkins. Bill, this is Roberta Williams."

She knew as soon as she saw Robbie's face what the woman was going to do. She should be furious. To steal someone else's man right there in front of them was just damned disgusting. But instead, she found herself thinking it was rather funny. Janet shook her head and headed for the kitchen.

"Doctor, do you think it is just my knee? It hurts up here, too," Robbie cooed, taking the stupefied doctor's hand and placing it on her inner thigh. "Maybe I...pulled something."

It was Janet's turn to roll her eyes. She opened her mouth and put her finger inside. Robbie, watching Janet's antics over the poor doctor's shoulder, raised an eyebrow and smiled wickedly.

"Ms. Williams, I'm a big fan of yours. I've seen all your movies," the doctor babbled as he examined Roberta.

"Then we have something in common, Bill. I'm a big fan of yours because you went to all the trouble of coming out here. Imagine having a doctor that makes house calls. I'm so lucky you were nearby."

Janet buried her head in her hands and tried not to laugh.

The doctor stayed for coffee but not dinner. He wasn't invited. Janet packed him off with a personal letter of thanks from Roberta to hang in his office and a reluctant hug from Janet. Once the lovesick doctor had driven down the driveway, Janet came back inside. "That, Robbie, was a new low, even for you," she growled.

Smiling broadly, Robbie stretched like a panther in the sun. "Nope, not even close to how low I can go, kid," she gloated.

Janet walked over and stood by the couch, arms crossed. "And what if I'd really loved that guy?" she asked, tapping a foot.

"You don't and we both know it. You're a terrible liar. Besides, if he can be swayed that easily, would you want him practicing in this town with his plastic glove up—"

"Robbie!" Janet picked up a pillow and tossed it at the director.

Robbie caught the missile easily and looked up at Janet. Her blonde hair was catching the evening light from the window, bringing out the red highlights. *I am going to have you, Janet Williams. You just don't know it yet*, Robbie decided. Instead, she said, "Can we go out on the lake after dinner?"

"You have water on your knee, Robbie. Bill just told you to rest it." Janet sighed, knowing that she was going to let Robbie win the argument. A canoe trip around the lake was always special in the fall. The rain had let up and the evening was promising to be beautiful.

The three of them walked down to the lake, Robbie's arm wrapped around Janet's shoulder for support. Janet carried Reb in one arm and wrapped her other arm around Robbie's waist. Before Robbie let go, she gave Janet's shoulder a small squeeze. Janet looked up and smiled, and then eased Reb to the ground.

She turned her red canoe over and slipped it into the water. Then she brought it parallel to the shore for Robbie to step in. With a grimace of pain, the actor got in and seated herself on the bottom, leaning against the wooden crosspiece. Janet put a life jacket on Reb, checked the fit, and handed her to Robbie. Then she spun the canoe out and put one foot in, pushing off with the other. She pulled the paddle from its holder and checked to make sure there were floatation devices under both seats. Then they were off.

Robbie felt a bit awkward letting Janet do all the work, but that had been the condition for the canoe ride. "*You trying to balance on that bad knee and paddle will put all of us in the lake,*" Janet had told her firmly. "*If we go, you have to sit in the bottom with your leg out straight and hold on to Reb.*"

Sitting in the bottom of the canoe wasn't such a bad deal, Robbie decided. Facing toward the stern, she was able to observe Janet openly. It was clear that Janet knew how to handle a canoe. They quietly slid through the water at a smooth pace. Reb, tired out with an afternoon of play, snuggled deeply into Robbie's warm chest and was soon fast asleep.

"Who owns all this land?" Robbie asked, looking around. The lake was clear and deep, and the forest around it was just starting to show its fall colours. The only house on the lake seemed to be Janet's.

"My great grandfather owned it at one time, then my grandfather. He gave me one lot for my twenty-first birthday. A local saw mill holds it now. They bought it for back taxes. So far, they haven't started cutting in this area. I don't know what I'll do when that happens. It will be so sad." The petite woman sighed.

"You've got a good job, royalties on books, a house. How come you couldn't pay off your grandfather's debts?" Robbie asked moodily. *I really like Reb, but the thought of my brother and Janet together upsets me. There are pieces missing from this story, I know it.*

Janet frowned. "Hasn't anyone told you that you shouldn't ask about other people's finances?"

"I'm going to hell in a hand basket anyway," Robbie replied a little too seriously, "so I don't have to play by society's rules. Tell me and save me the trouble of having you investigated."

Janet gave Robbie a dirty look. "You would, wouldn't you?"

"Without a second thought," Robbie replied, a predatory glint in her eye.

"My home is mortgaged to the maximum, royalties on educational material are pathetically low, as are educators' salaries, and I'm carrying a student loan, too. I was only just getting on my feet and establishing my career when I found I was thousands of dollars in debt. I...it was really scary," stammered Janet, feeling all the emotion and fear of that dark time returning.

"So you made a deal with my brother." Robbie snorted, looking away so that Janet couldn't see her face.

"I love Rebecca very deeply, Robbie. I wouldn't have had a child if I wasn't prepared to be a good mother. The arrangement suited me, too. I-I...don't see myself as ever marrying and yet I wanted a child."

The blue eyes swept back. "Because you're gay?"

Janet nodded, and after that they paddled on quietly for a while until she put her finger to her lips to signal Robbie to stay quiet. They came around a point and slid silently into a small marshy bay. There stood a moose in the water, chewing leisurely on underwater plants. Robbie, a city person, had never seen a real moose before. It was the size of a horse but with coarse, crude features. It waded forward on long, knobby-kneed legs and ducked its head under the water. Some time later, the head surfaced, dripping water and with a mouthful of green plants.

"They can close off their nostrils and hold their breath for a long time," Janet explained. "That's why they can feed on the water plants. They're safe enough this time of the year, but in the spring they can be pretty aggressive. Along the roads, you'll see moose warning signs because the bulls become so territorial, they will charge a small car. They're clever, too. The hunters will tell you that moose will sometimes circle around behind them and hunt the hunter." Janet thought she was showing Robbie the beauty of nature, hoping to ease the anger that always seemed to be just under the director's surface.

Robbie nodded, enjoying listening to Janet's knowledge of the forest world. They moved on and Janet showed her the tall standing rock near the shore where red ochre rock paintings could still be seen. They were pictographs left by the Woodland Indians of the area a thousand years before. Robbie took mental notes. Had she known it, Janet was showing her scenes that she could use in her work.

When they returned, Janet made a fire and carefully locked the screen in place now that Reb had discovered fireplaces. What a mess she had been when Janet had scooped her up that morning. And there had been Robbie, her co-conspirator, watching Reb with delight as she built grey ash hills on the floor.

Later, when Reb had been tucked into bed and the fire had burned down low, Janet opened the screen again and dropped some chestnuts on the red coals. Their shells darkened as they hissed and cracked open, revealing their starchy white centres. The two women lay in comfortable silence by the fire, eating the roasted chestnuts with a bit of butter and salt.

"Dinner was really good," Robbie said, staring into the fire.

Wow! Two compliments in one day. I'm on a roll here. "Thanks."

"The 'copter will pick me up tomorrow," Robbie said suddenly. Janet looked at her in surprise. Only that morning, she would have gladly sent Roberta Williams packing at the end of her foot, but now, well, she had sort of taken it for granted that Robbie would stay until her knee was better.

"Tomorrow's Sunday. I'll still be here to help you. Monday, I have to go back to work but you are w— I mean you could stay until your knee was a little better," Janet stammered.

Robbie raised an eyebrow in annoyance. "I see. I'm not welcome, but you won't throw me out on the street if I'm injured."

"No. Robbie, it's not like that. I just didn't want to give the wrong impression," Janet tried to justify, only making things worse.

Suddenly, Robbie rolled up on her side and looked intently at Janet.

"You are welcome to stay," Janet said, playing idly with a shell from one of the chestnuts. Robbie picked up the last chestnut and peeled the white meat from the shell. She dipped it in the butter and sprinkled a bit of salt on it, then she held it to her mouth and bit off half. The remaining piece she reached over and placed next to Janet's lips. Mesmerized by Robbie's silent actions, Janet's lips parted to accept the warm meat into her mouth.

Warm, buttery lips followed and Janet found herself kissing Roberta Williams with a passion that scared her with its intensity. She pulled back in surprise, pushing Robbie away with her hands. "No!"

"Why?" asked the surprised actor. "No" was a word she used but others could not.

"No, I don't want to do this." Janet wriggled out from under Robbie's long, sexy form and stood up. "I don't want to be another conquest, Robbie. I'm not interested," she said emotionally.

Robbie got awkwardly to her feet. "You didn't kiss me like you weren't interested," she observed, moving closer.

A straight arm stopped her. "Well, I'm not interested. I'm sorry if I gave you the wrong impression. I am your brother's widow, and there is Rebecca and my standing in this community to consider."

Robbie's temper snapped. "Oh, your standing in the community. Well, we wouldn't want your standing to be undermined by the likes of me fucking you, would we? Better you sell yourself—"

Janet turned and slammed out of the house. A few minutes later, Robbie heard the car pull out of the drive. Rebecca started to cry.

An hour later, Janet was still not back and Robbie was facing some hard realities.

Okay, I can handle this, Robbie tried to convince herself. *I head a multi-million-dollar enterprise. I employ hundreds of people. What's one dirty diaper? Oh God. Gross.* "Here, Reb, just sit on the bed while I get rid of this thing," Robbie mumbled. *Can I flush these things? I don't see a hazardous waste container around.* She dropped the diaper on the floor then turned back to Reb. "Oh boy, look at the sheets. I guess I should have cleaned you up first, huh?"

Holding the now laughing Rebecca out in front of her like a time bomb, Robbie carried her into the bathroom and wedged her in the sink, then popped her out again, remembering just in time that one had to test the water or something. With one hand, she managed to get a lukewarm flow and then wedged Reb back in. The water splashed all over.

Some time later, Reb was washed and dried and training panties had been put on to replace the diaper, Robbie having forgotten to make a diagram before removing the last one. The director and the bathroom looked a little the worse for wear, but the job was done. "Okay, Rebel, bedtime. You're going to have to sleep with me 'cause I'm not making up two beds," Robbie explained as she carried the child into her mom's bedroom.

Reb fretted a bit, but Robbie sang to her until she went to sleep. For a while, Robbie lay thinking miserable thoughts about whether Janet had gone to spend the night with Dr. Respectable-Male Perkins. Eventually, though, exhaustion claimed her.

A few hours later, after driving down the back roads, Janet calmed down enough to return home. She found all the lights on, a dirty diaper on the nursery floor, and an equally disgusting mess in the crib. The bathroom was in a state of chaos and Robbie and Reb were curled up, sound asleep, like Madonna and child. For a while, Janet stood there and looked down at the beautiful pair. Then, carefully, she lifted Reb out and took her back to her freshly changed crib.

Robbie woke with a start the next morning. Reb was gone. *Christ! I fell asleep and lost the kid!* Robbie leapt from the bed. Her stiff and swollen knee gave out immediately and she crashed to the floor with a cry of pain.

Jumping up from the sofa, Janet ran down the hall to find Robbie rolling around in silent agony. "Do you do this every morning?" she asked, walking over and offering a hand to help the actor up.

"Reb's gone," Robbie moaned, trying to get to her feet without help.

"She's in her crib."

"Shit," Robbie muttered, running a shaky hand through her hair. "Where the hell did you go?" she snarled.

"Out." It was all Robbie got for an answer. "I'll get you some ice. When is the helicopter coming to pick you up?"

"Later," Robbie answered from between clenched teeth.

Robbie collapsed on the bed and, once Janet was out of the room, let the pain show on her face as she grasped her leg in agony. Janet returned silently and walked over to the bed. "It's worse today, huh?" she asked, placing the frozen bag of peas on the swollen and bruised knee.

"It's okay, just hurt a bit when I jumped out of bed," Robbie muttered, acutely aware of Janet's touch. "The 'copter will be here by ten. I'll stay in here until then."

"Want breakfast in bed?" Janet asked.

"No, thanks."

Janet nodded sadly and left the room.

The helicopter touched down on the lake at a quarter to ten. Robbie was already outside waiting, with her soft-sided overnight bag and laptop. Janet and Reb went out to say goodbye, and Robbie scooped the little child up and gave her a big hug. "You be good, Rebel," Robbie whispered. Then she passed the child to Janet, being careful not to touch the woman.

"Thank you, Robbie. I really did need someone with me to drive back after the funeral. I...ah...well, keep in touch with Reb, okay," she finished lamely.

Robbie nodded. "I will. Bye," she said abruptly, then hobbled down to get into the helicopter.

In a whirl of wind, they lifted off and Janet turned to shield Reb with her body. When she turned back, the 'copter was already disappearing over the ridge. "Bye," Janet echoed, feeling a painful loneliness settle around her. She lowered Reb to the ground and the little child looked up into the sky and pointed.

"Obbie's bird gone," she said sadly.

"Yes, she's gone." Janet sighed and took her child's hand to lead her back up to their home.

Robbie looked down at the little log home in the bush. A dull ache filled her chest and she had no idea why. She had a thousand things to do. Billy's death could not have come at a worse time with the final editing cuts of her new film under way. The dailies and their time-codes waited for her attention on CD-Rom. This procedure allowed her immediate access to any scene without the often-frustrating delay of rewinding video.

She pushed Janet and Reb out of her mind and focused instead on organizing her thoughts. Her film work was acclaimed for its artistic quality. Robbie saw herself as an "auteur", a French word that meant author. In film, it meant the director was the driving force in establishing the film's artistic elements and style. Robbie's films had a quality to them that reflected the intelligent creativity of the director in methodology, style and theme. They were not just entertainment, they were art; Robbie had the Oscars to prove just how good she was. Such success, however, was not possible without a tremendous amount of energy, talent, and focus. Robbie had all three qualities in great abundance.

Janet pressed the suit she would be wearing to work on Monday. It was vital that she meet with her staff to discuss the new guidelines set down by the Ministry of Education and establish some new curriculum writing teams. Janet believed that teaching the process of research and academic thought was just as important as factual curriculum content. That meant that all her staff had to have a common methodology woven into their classroom studies.

She sighed. She knew her staff was already doing a lot more than they were paid to do. It wasn't always easy to convince the teachers that they would have to give even more of their time to meet Janet's vision of education. But they were a really dedicated bunch that she had handpicked, and she was sure that if she approached the issue in the right way, they would be receptive.

It would make her job a lot easier, however, if each newly elected government would not change the direction of education. One of the frustrating elements of teaching was that everyone who managed to conceive a child or get elected suddenly became an expert on education. They would be a lot better off if those people with the classroom experience and training were allowed to write curriculum and policy.

Janet put away the ironing board and iron. The house tonight seemed so quiet and empty. It was silly. Robbie had only been there forty-eight hours, and yet Janet really missed the aggravating woman's presence. She hoped Robbie's knee would be all right.

She picked up her suit and carried it into the bedroom to hang up. There beside the bed was Robbie's card. Sprawled in a bold hand on the back were the words, "In case I'm needed."

I can't need you, Roberta Williams, Janet thought. *It would only lead to heartache.*

Chapter 3

The office was a glass-faced monolith, designed with a planned obsolescence of thirty years. It had fifteen years to go before it could be torn down as a really bad idea. Robbie parked her 1967 dark green Stingray between the yellow painted lines that marked off her territory in the underground parking garage. She stepped out, unfolded her long frame, and then bent to retrieve her briefcase. She wore a classically cut business suit of Scottish wool in muted heather blue, over a cut lace blouse.

Her heels clipped a slow, uneven rhythm as she painfully limped across the stained grey cement. At the elevator, she pressed up and waited impatiently. *Funny, I never noticed before how strong the stink of auto emissions is down here. It could gag a horse. I probably have lungs that look like tanned leather.*

The elevator arrived and Robbie entered, pressing the button for the twentieth floor. To her surprise, the elevator stopped on the main floor. It was unusual for staff to be there this early. Brian McGill, her assistant director, stepped in. Brian preferred traveling by train from the suburbs over facing the freeways of Toronto.

"Morning, Robbie. Gwen phoned to say you were back, so I thought I'd better get my butt in here early. It was a nice funeral. You okay? Everything go all right? "

Robbie's face was expressionless and her body strangely still. "Good decision. We can talk in my office. Thank you, I'm fine. Everything went as planned."

Brian sighed quietly. Robbie stood lost in her own thoughts, a predatory look on her face that her employees had come to know meant she had focused on something and she was going to go all out to see her concept through. "The hot set is at location A, Robbie. I'll be heading out there this morning to get things ready for the afternoon shoot. The light today should be perfect. Today will be the last of the dailies and then we can get on with the edits."

"There is going to be some major editing. I'm going to change the focus of the film to more of a love story."

"What?" Brian didn't try to hide his surprise.

"I'm changing the focus of the film."

"Does Talsman know?"

"Not yet," Robbie responded determinedly.

The elevator stopped and the doors slid open. Brian stepped aside to let Robbie go first. "He'll have your butt."

"Not in his lifetime," Robbie shot back, limping down the hall with long awkward strides while Brian made a valiant effort to keep up.

"Look, Robbie, I don't know what bee is in your bonnet, but we've got a damn good picture going to edit here — what happened to your leg?"

"Gwen, get Ernie," Robbie cut in as she hobbled across her secretary's office on the way to her own. Brian followed in her wake, rolling his eyes comically.

Gwen stood and crossed her arms in annoyance. "Not until you return my good morning and explain to the two of us why you are limping," she stated flatly.

Stopping with her hand on the knob, Robbie turned slowly to face Gwen.

Oh boy, thought Brian, wondering if the scene was going to end with him having to testify in court.

"Explain to me again, Gwen, why I haven't fired you," Robbie growled.

Gwen opened her desk drawer, and took out a steno-pad and flipped open the coiled ringed book. "I type eighty words a minute; despite my senior position, I still go out and get you lunch; I work appalling hours because I have no life; and I'm the only secretary you've ever had who hasn't given you the finger and walked out when you've thrown your first temper tantrum." Gwen snapped the pad closed.

"Gwen, you're fired," Robbie said with a stony look.

"Can't, you haven't hired me back from the last time you fired me."

"In that case, stay fired." Robbie laughed whole-heartedly. "Good morning, Gwen. How are you, your husband, the cast of thousands the two of you are raising?"

"I'm fine, he's fine, and there are only three children. You are just harbouring a grudge about the last maternity leave. Ernie is on line one." She frowned. "What happened to your leg?"

"Ah, twisted the knee in a fall, nothing serious." A blush crept up her neck. She covered her embarrassment by disappearing into her office with Brian following, a relieved look on his face. "That damn woman terrorizes me because she knows I can't afford to lose another secretary," Robbie groused, waving him to a chair.

Brian sat. As a studio man, he was rarely in the boss's office.

"Morning, Ernie," Robbie said as she sat down at her desk with a grimace and carefully straightened her sore knee before she turned to bring her computer up.

A high-pitched voice came through the phone's speaker. "Hello, Robbie. Joy and light to you. I hear the film's coming in on time and on budget. You've got a happy producer here."

"Get unhappy. I'm planning on making some modifications. There will be some major editing changes. I'll be going a little over budget and time."

"What?" came a panicky squeal.

"You heard me."

"No. Disaster knocking, I hear; you, I don't. Are you nuts? Of course you are. What am I saying? The investors will go crazy."

"It's a problem we will have to deal with."

"A problem we will have to deal with. You stupid or something? They'll pull out."

Robbie clicked uninterestedly through her e-mail. "They've got too much invested to pull out now. Remind them I know what I'm doing."

"Can you deliver?" came a suspicious voice over the machine.

An eyebrow went up and Robbie looked incredulously at the phone system. "Have I ever not?"

"Christ, Robbie, I don't know—"

"You'd better know. That's your damn job," Robbie snarled, as she reached over and clicked off the receiver button.

"'Too violent.' I'll give her a film she'll have to sit up and take notice of, damn it," she muttered under her breath. Then she looked up at Brian and smiled. "Let me outline the changes," she purred.

"Give mommy a kiss. Hmm, love you, girl." Janet smiled her thanks as she left Reb with Mrs. Chen, who took care of three other children of the staff's in a room set aside for her at the Bartlett School for the Gifted. Faced with the expensive and always problematic care of their young children, Janet and the three other staff members had pooled their resources and set up a daycare room right at the school.

Lily Chen came each day and provided a stimulating and happy environment for the four children, and the teacher/parents could pop in for a visit whenever they had a free moment. Lily was a small, Asian woman, who had emigrated with her husband from Hong Kong. Her husband was working in the town of Bartlett as an accountant for several of the local resorts. Lily had tremendous energy and an outgoing personality.

"Janet, I was so sorry when I read in the newspaper that you were at the funeral. I did not know. If there is anything I can do to help—"

"Thank you," Janet cut in, feeling the heat rising in her face. "My husband and I had been separated for a long time. I felt it important that Reb — that Rebecca attended. That will be important to her in the future."

"She comes from a very wealthy and famous family. She has good joss in having such ancestors."

"Yes," replied Janet briefly, not wanting to go down that road. "Bye, Reb. Mommy will see you at lunch," Janet called, picking up her briefcase to walk down to her office. Her secretary, Carolyn, was talking to Milka Gorski in the hall outside the office. As Janet came around the corner, the conversation stopped. Janet sighed inside. It was going to be a difficult day.

"Good morning, Milka, Carolyn."

"Hi, Janet."

"Morning, Janet. Ah, are you okay? I mean...everything go all right?"

"Everything went fine, thanks. Let people know I appreciate their concern and the flowers they sent to the house. My husband and I had been separated for some time, but it was important that Rebecca be at the funeral."

"We had no idea you were one of *those* Williams," Milka gushed enthusiastically.

"Actually, it was the first time I met Billy's family," Janet clarified. "I'd better get into my office and get caught up. Excuse me."

The two women watched Janet's back as she walked through the outer office and into her own. "Do you think it's true that Robbie Williams was staying up at her home this weekend?" Milka's eyes sparkled with excitement.

"Paul, down at the framing shop, told Stacy at the doughnut shop, who told Jason, that Dr. Perkins brought the letter in first thing this morning for framing. So, I guess it must be true."

"She's a closed one, huh? Imagine us never realizing whom she had married."

"Rebecca's only two, so it couldn't have lasted very long," observed Carolyn.

"Hmm, our Janet and Billy-the-Kid. They say opposites attract, but my God."

"I'd better get to work. See you later."

"Yeah." Milka headed off to run her science test. *Janet and Billy-the-Kid. Still waters do run deep.*

Janet sat at her desk trying to clear some of the paperwork that had accumulated while she had been in Toronto. Carolyn slipped in and closed the door behind her. "Gerald Lucier is here from the *Bartlett Gazette*. You remember he wanted to interview you about the school for an article he is writing. Be careful," Carolyn advised.

Janet's eyes snapped up. "Why?"

Carolyn shrugged. "Gerald bowls with my husband and Ted says he's made a few comments in general about education. You know, the usual myth about how kids today can't read and write, as if the adults are so literate. He thinks gifted education is elitist."

"What's new?" Janet sighed. "Another teacher basher. Sometimes I think we should all resign and let these people who know so much more about education take over."

Carolyn snorted. "Or test the adults to see how well the good old system really worked," she suggested as she slipped back out the door.

The problem with living in a small town was that everyone knew everyone else's business. Janet smiled. *I wonder if it's around town yet that Robbie stayed out at the cabin.*

"Mr. Lucier, Mrs. Williams," introduced Carolyn with a flourish.

Janet stood up. "Hello, I'm Janet. I think our paths have crossed a few times before, but this is the first time I've had a chance to talk with you."

"Gerald. Yeah, I've seen you around at functions. You're involved with the historical society, aren't you?"

"Yes. I understand you have some questions you would like to ask about our school here." Janet gestured to a seat as she sat down herself.

Lucier pulled a recorder out of his pocket, "Okay?" he asked, holding up the instrument. Janet nodded. "The taxpayer sinks a lot of money into public education. Why do we need these special programs on top of all that?"

Wow! This guy goes straight for the jugular. Janet took a second to make sure her answer was clearly stated. "The public education system was designed for mass education. It is geared, by definition, to the average child. It is very hard in a setting of twenty to thirty students, to provide specialized instruction to exceptional students. Bartlett is a privately funded institution that provides a specially designed program for the gifted."

"So, what's a gifted child? One of those absent-minded professor types that end up going around blowing up worlds?" Lucier laughed sarcastically.

Gritting her teeth, Janet managed to smile pleasantly. "No, Mr. Lucier, that concept is a Hollywood myth. In fact, gifted children tend to have it all. They are bright, athletic, and very socially aware. There are exceptions, of course, but generally speaking the gifted child has a lot going for him or her."

"So why put them in a special school and make them different? Are they that damned special that they can't mix with the common folk?"

"Well, as I explained to you already, the public school system is not designed to handle exceptional students, although it does try its best. To be gifted, you have to have a consistent I.Q. score of over 140. That puts you in the top two percent in the world intellectually. In the regular school system, three things end up happening to the gifted child." Janet ticked the points off on her fingers. "A) They are given extra work to keep them busy, so they learn pretty quickly to act out or play dumb to avoid this punishment. B) They are seated beside the troublemaker to 'be a good influence'. Good kids often are rewarded for their fine behaviour by sticking them with the kid no one else wants to be near. Or C) They skip grades and end up terribly socially isolated."

"So what do you do that is different?"

"We do not accelerate students. Instead, we provide a program that has breadth and depth. We are concerned with providing a challenging, stimulating program that will create socially responsible, well rounded, life-long learners." *If I had a dollar for every time I've said that line, I'd be rich.*

"Sounds elitist to me," Lucier argued.

"No, it's not. These are the minds that will advance and improve our world. Do we not want to encourage and support them to do so? We think nothing of singling out the best student athletes to put them on the school sports teams. Is that not elitism? We provide millions of dollars to train them. We have special ceremonies to reward their athletic achievements.

"Athletes get awards, fame, and money. What do the intelligent get for their efforts, Gerald? And what does that say about what is important in our society? Perhaps we would have a better educated population if we paid more than lip service to the importance of education." Janet could feel her emotions boiling to the surface. This might not have been a good day to have this interview. "Parents and the media are always complaining about the education system, but they rarely support it. If you are bright, Mr. Lucier, you are the brownnose, the teacher's pet, the egghead, the absent-minded professor. It is the troublemaker that society respects, not the academic."

"Hey, don't lecture me."

"You wanted answers. I am passionate about my job, Mr. Lucier. Despite the abuse that we teachers take, I am proud to call myself a teacher. Anything else?"

"No, this will do. Thanks," Lucier got to his feet stiffly.

Janet stood too, trying not to reveal with her body language just how angry she was. "Good bye."

"Bye and thanks." Lucier slipped his recorder back into his pocket and moved to the door. His hand dropped off the doorknob as he turned and asked, "Any truth to the rumour that the actress Robbie Williams is staying up at your place?"

Janet wondered if the tape was still running. "Yes, my sister-in-law provided my daughter and me with a ride home. She has now left."

"What's she like? She doesn't give interviews very often."

"She is intelligent, funny, and very dedicated to her craft," Janet responded defensively.

"She's supposed to be a tyrant," Lucier observed with a smile.

"I found her to be strong, concerned, and supportive." Janet walked over to the door and opened it. Lucier nodded and left.

Carolyn looked up and met Janet's beautiful green eyes. Janet crossed them and pulled a face, then disappeared back into her office as Carolyn laughed.

Well, that was a waste of time. She looked out the window across the soccer field to the forest on the other side. *I wonder what Robbie's doing now? It bothers me that we didn't part on the best of terms.*

"Janet?" Carolyn's voice over the intercom.

"Hmm."

"There's been another theft in the girls' dorm. I've got Angela Murphy here to tell you about it. It's her CD player that's gone."

"Okay." Janet sighed. "Just give me five minutes to make an important phone call and I'll see her."

Janet sat down at her desk and reached for the phone. For a second her hand hesitated, then she picked up the receiver.

Brian McGill emerged from Robbie's office about an hour later. Gwen looked up from her desk and smiled. Brian went over and stopped in front of her desk. "It's official," he said sadly.

"What is?" Gwen asked in surprise.

"Robbie's lost it."

Gwen laughed and shrugged. "Creative genius," she suggested.

"Maybe, but in a court of law, I think they'd label her criminally insane." The assistant director sighed as he headed out the door.

Some time later, the intercom on the director's desk clicked on, "Robbie, Mrs. Janet Williams on line two," came Carolyn's voice and Robbie almost dropped the receiver in her haste to pick it up.

"What's wrong?" she demanded by way of a greeting.

A startled voice came from the other end. "Nothing's wrong."

"Oh, then why did you phone?" Robbie asked in surprise.

There was a moment's hesitation. "I didn't like the way we said good bye."

"Yeah?"

"Yeah."

A silly grin formed on Robbie's usually stoic face. "How is your day going?"

"There is a great interest in the actress who is reported to have stayed at my home over the weekend. There is no interest in education, and someone is stealing items from the girls' dorm. How is your knee?"

"Still hurts like hell but the swelling is starting to go down," Robbie answered in her concise manner. *Shit, what do I say now?* Janet came to her rescue.

"How's your day going?"

"My secretary, Gwen, tells me that my assistant director thinks I'm criminally insane," Robbie observed happily.

"He'd be right," Janet agreed dryly. "So why did he decide this?"

"I sent him out to tell my leading lady, Tracy Travelli, that I'm going to be making some major edits to the film."

That caught Janet's interest. "Tracy Travelli, the Latin Bombshell?"

Robbie felt an unreasonable amount of professional jealousy growing in the pit of her stomach and fought it down. "So?"

"The fans voted her the one they would most like to be trapped on a desert island with. She's supposed to be hot stuff." Janet laughed delightedly.

Jealousy won. "Actually, she was a dry stick in bed."

For a second there was shocked silence. "Aha, you know her. I had heard you launched her career."

Robbie smirked. "You might say I opened her up to possibilities in more ways than one."

"That's cruel and crude."

"Sorry, but it's the truth," Robbie came back at her.

"I hope no one ever says anything like that about Reb," Janet observed, trying to make a point.

"They won't," snapped Robbie angrily.

"What if she falls in love with someone like you?"

There was silence for a moment. "I won't let that happen."

"You can't control, only teach and guide, Robbie."

"Don't preach to me."

Janet sighed. "I phoned to end the fight, not get into another one."

"So sleep with me."

"No. We would have to know each other a lot better and feel safe with one another before I would ever consider that."

"You know me."

"Which person are we talking about — the one you are or the one you pretend to be?"

"Get out of my head, school marm."

"Am I in your head? That's a start."

Robbie asked cautiously, "A start to what?"

"To being in your bed," Janet said boldly. *My God, what did I just say?*

A red-hot tidal wave swept through Robbie's body and turned her insides to the consistency of Jell-O. Her jaw hurt, her grin was so big. Mentally, she gave herself a shake. *I'm acting like a school kid.* "Verbal agreements are binding," she managed to say in an even voice.

"I'd deny it in a court of law," teased Janet. "Uh, next week is Thanksgiving. Do you spend it with your family?"

Robbie laughed. "I'd like to see the look on Alexandra's face if a dead bird was put in front of her to carve."

"In that case, would you like to come up here? The colour should be good by then. The trees are turning quickly. Uh, I usually take Reb to church and we go to the town hall dinner. Oh, maybe that's not a good idea. I mean, you're sure to be recognized," Janet sputtered. *What am I doing? Every time I open my mouth, something comes out that my mind never okayed. First, I come on to her, and then I invite her to go to church with me. She's going to think I'm insane.*

"Hey, I can handle it, if you can. Okay, I'll be there Friday night. Do I need to bring pyjamas?"

"You are so cheeky. And yes, you most certainly do. Our sleeping arrangements are not changing."

"You like me though, right?"

Janet smiled. Robbie could be so disarming. "Very much so, but I'm not going to be bullied into sleeping with you."

"I'm not a bully."

Janet rolled her eyes heavenwards. "Yes, you are, but you're a sweet one."

Robbie snorted in disgust. "Sweet."

"It's not a crime. It's a good thing." Janet laughed.

"Good thing, huh? I can do sweet."

"It won't get you anywhere," warned Janet.

"Why not?"

"Because, acting sweet wouldn't be sincere."

"You want sincere, too? You don't ask for much, do you? And they say I'm a tough director."

"I just want the best," Janet observed quietly, totally amazed at her brashness.

"Is that me?" asked the surprisingly insecure voice.

Janet considered for a moment and then responded honestly. "I don't know."

Robbie nodded at her end of the phone, a determined look on her face. "I'll fly up on Friday night. Say hi to Reb. I'll be seeing you, Janet."

"Bye, Robbie." Janet looked at the phone and then a grin broke across her face. Suddenly, the day wasn't so bad after all.

For a long time after hanging up the phone, Robbie sat trying to get her thoughts in order. She'd never met anyone quite like Janet. She was a rare blend of innocence and spunk that Robbie found extremely appealing. *I'm going to bed you next weekend, Janet Williams*, she vowed. *You just wait and see.*

She smiled confidently and got to her feet, then grimaced in pain. Picking up her car keys and briefcase, she limped out of her office. "I'm off to the hot set," she said to Gwen on her way by. A hot set was one that had been readied for the performers. Every prop was in place and had been double checked by the chief grip and the set decorator; it was now sealed off waiting for the director and the actors.

"Anything you want done?" asked Gwen.

Robbie raised an eyebrow. A smirk hovered at the corner of her mouth and her eyes danced with excitement. "Under no circumstance are you to buy me pyjamas. I won't be needing them." She grinned, then turned and left, leaving a bewildered secretary in her wake.

"Okay, Angela, let's see if I've got this straight: your new CD player was on the table beside your bed last night and it was gone this morning. Is that correct?"

"Yes, Mrs. Williams. It's awful. Someone must have been in my room last night, while I was in bed. Anything could have happened."

"Angela, let's not get carried away here. Miss Singh was on duty last night, and she has since checked the windows, doors, and surveillance cameras. No one broke in. No, I'm afraid this is an inside job."

"But that means that one of my friends is a thief!" Angela showed more distress at that revelation than at the idea of some stranger in her bedroom.

"Maybe, maybe not. The CD player might have been borrowed. Or this might be a practical joke. Try not to worry. We'll get to the bottom of this soon. That's all for now, Angela."

Angela left, not looking at all happy about not having her CD player restored to her. Janet got on the phone right away to reassure Angela's parents before a real dust up started over the issue. She had Carolyn go on the P.A. and call an assembly for the end of the day to talk to all the students about being more careful with their personal property. There was still the staff meeting to look forward to after that. It was turning into a really long day.

Robbie slowly pulled her car into the gravel parking lot so as not to kick up a stone that might damage the paint job on her pride and joy. Making sure she was as close to the set as possible and getting out carefully, she hobbled over to the area where the actors waited in canvas chairs for their calls.

Tracy Travelli caught sight of her and came running over. "What is this Brian is saying? You want to make changes to the film? Never! Are you to be making this film of yours forever?"

Robbie smiled down at the volatile actor. Her blue eyes glowed with an inner light that radiated energy and confidence. "I am going to make you immortal, Tracy. A hundred years from now, people will still talk about your role in this movie. Trust me, I am going to make you an icon."

"I do not trust you. You are a monster. But you are also the genius of film, so I will co-operate. But Robbie, you will make me great, no?"

"My word."

The day had indeed been long for Janet. At the staff meeting, she handed out the new government standardized tests that were to be administered to all eleven year olds in the province. The teachers immediately saw the flaws in the testing that would make the results totally invalid. The discussion went around in circles and got very hot.

Finally, Janet had to use her authority to call an end to the venting and remind the teachers that they had no choice but to follow the government directive, however flawed. "We are civil servants. I think we all agree that educational reform is needed to keep up with the times. We'll just have to hope that, over time, modifications will be made to deal with some of the very valid concerns that you have expressed today."

The meeting ended in sullen silence; her overly stressed staff walked out with even more paperwork to take them away from their teaching preparation time. Janet sighed in frustration as she tucked a cranky Rebecca into her car seat. The little girl had had too much change and stimulation over the weekend, and was out of sorts.

Mother and daughter rode home in grumpy silence. Usually the beauty of the northern forests and lakes relaxed Janet, but tonight she was feeling very stressed. *I guess the emotion of the weekend is starting to catch up to me, too*, she reasoned. *Time to snap out of this.* She made an effort to think of something nice.

Robbie immediately appeared in her thoughts and Janet replayed their phone conversation in her mind. The tips of her ears turned warm and her body reacted to the sexual tension that had laced their conversation. *How could I have been so bold? My God, I've actually given Robbie a green light to come on to me.*

That thought sent hot delight streaming through her. *Oh boy! I want this to happen, and at the same time, I'm scared as hell that it might.*

Once home, mother and daughter had a bath together that involved much giggling and splashing.

Both of them emerged in a better frame of mind. Janet warmed up some beef stew she had in the freezer. She carried Reb's highchair outside and the two of them had a picnic on the porch overlooking the lake.

After the dishes were done, they played in the sand on the beach. Tired and happy once again, Reb was cleaned up and put to bed. Janet ironed her raw cotton suit for the next day and then settled down on the sofa to do some paperwork. Picking up the cushion, she could still catch the faint, lingering scent of Robbie's perfume. She tucked the pillow under her chin and wrapped her arm around it. *This can't be happening! I hardly know this woman, and what I do know is bad news. Janet, for God's sakes, be careful,* she warned herself. But deep inside, she knew it was too late. She was thoroughly infatuated with Robbie Williams. *I wonder what Robbie is doing tonight.*

Robbie nipped the closest earlobe of the beautiful, naked woman who lay exhausted under her. The sex had been good. Tracy had become a more enthusiastic partner with experience. Carefully protecting her sore knee, Robbie rolled away and lay on her back, one hand under her head.

Tracy cuddled closer and nuzzled Robbie's neck. "You want I stay tonight?" she purred.

"No."

Tracy sighed and slipped out of Robbie's bed. "I do not know why I go so willingly to your bed. You are a brute."

Turning on her side, Robbie watched the Latin Bombshell searching for her scattered clothes. "Maybe you like brutes," she suggested playfully.

Tracy crawled back on the bed, an armful of rumpled clothes clutched to her breasts. She kissed Robbie passionately, pleased to feel the director respond. "You are very bad," Tracy complained.

"Hmm, *you* are very good," Robbie muttered, pulling the clothes from Tracy's hands and dropping them on the floor. She took a second to enjoy the sight of Tracy's full breasts and then leaned forward to catch one swollen nipple in her mouth. Tracy moaned and let the brute have her way again.

It was getting ready for bed after that long, demanding day that Janet's fingers brushed over a small lump under her armpit. Frantically following a row of them, she traced back to the edge of her right breast. Dread filling her, her heart fairly aching with fear, she lay down on her bed and felt with the flat of her fingers as she had been taught. There was a lump in the breast, as well, large and hard. Tears welled in her eyes. *Oh God, no!*

Chapter 4

The next afternoon, Janet was in the doctor's office. Bill Perkins palpated Janet's breast, locating the margins of the lump. He took the syringe and pushed the needle in, feeling it slide smoothly through the layers of skin and muscle and then having to push harder when the tip encountered the growth. Despite a small noise of distress at the invasion, Janet held still. Bill pulled back on the plunger. Nothing. He shifted the needle slightly, knowing that it was going to hurt, and tried again. Still nothing in the plastic syringe.

With a sigh, he withdrew the needle. "Okay, Janet, you can get dressed now and I'll meet you in my office." He discarded the needle into the red container reserved for "points" and slipped out of the room.

Her breast hadn't hurt before but now it did. Janet dressed with trembling hands, squared her shoulders, and headed down to Bill's office. Lily Chen had been kind enough to stay overtime to care for Reb while Janet visited the doctor after school. She couldn't keep her waiting too long. Whatever Bill had found, Janet was just going to have to handle it and get on with her life as best she could.

"Sit down, Janet. Well, we know some things, but not all. It's a large lump and when I tried to aspirate it, there was no fluid inside. That means that we are probably not talking about a regular fibroid cyst here.

"That doesn't automatically mean we are looking at cancer. There are other possibilities, such as a fibroid abnorma. That would mean surgery but no real danger. I am concerned, however, about the swollen lymph nodes. They indicate an infection or invasion of some sort, and we need to take that seriously. I've booked you for a mammogram and an ultrasound tomorrow in Barrie."

"Bill, I can't just keep taking time off work," she protested. "Can't I go on the weekend?"

"No. With government cuts, these services aren't as available as they were. Besides...I don't think we should wait," he finished, meeting Janet's eyes.

She saw compassion there, and worry, and dropped her objections. Swallowing hard, she nodded, her trembling hands clutched tightly in her lap.

"Look, why don't I come over to your place tonight? There is no need to worry until we know more. I could pick up a pizza—"

"That's kind of you, Bill, but I need to be alone to get this all into perspective. I...I'm going to have to make plans for Reb, too. Thanks anyway."

Bill nodded and stood. "You know I'm always here for you, Janet, as a doctor and as a friend."

Janet stood too, managing a weak smile. "I know, and I really appreciate that."

Numb, she robotically left the doctor's office and got into her car. Shock was a wall that separated her from her surroundings. She tightened her fingers around the steering wheel and drew a deep breath. *There is no hiding from this crisis. I've got to take things one step at a time, whatever comes. First, I'll pick up Reb and see if Lily can baby sit after school tomorrow as well. Then, I'll have to phone Carolyn and Milka so they can handle things at school.*

Robbie was like a bear with a sore paw. Each day now was going over budget, and the below-the-line costs would be mounting quickly. She sat in the editing bay looking at out-takes, trying to create the film she wanted with the footage she already had. With a primitive growl of disgust, she hurled a reference book against the wall. In the next room, a technician closed his eyes and grimaced at the thud.

Getting up to pace, Robbie collapsed back into her seat with a curse. The knee was greatly improved but still painful when stressed. *Okay, if I was Desiree and Napoleon had just propositioned me... No — if Janet was Desiree, how would she have reacted?* Then it came, the scene she wanted to create in the editing process, filled with passion and courage and drama.

Robbie turned back to her terminal and keyed in the footage that would give her the focus she wanted: Desiree had not been the victim, she had been a strong woman who had not been defeated by the course of history but instead had swum with the tide of events and survived.

No, more than survived...she had triumphed. Napoleon had died a prisoner and a broken man. His lover, the milkmaid Desiree, had married and become a queen. This would no longer be a movie about the exploitation of a woman, but rather the courage and intelligence of a woman of strength.

It would be a blockbuster, appealing to the romantic and the feminist alike. Painted against the background of the Napoleonic wars, it would also have enough action to keep the pace quick and powerful. Robbie grinned. *You'll watch this film, Janet.*

A few hours later, Gwen opened the editing bay door and snapped, "Damn it, Robbie, will you pick up your phone?"

"No, I'm busy," she barked. "I told you to hold all my calls."

"I think you'll want to take this one. It's Janet Williams, and by the sound of her voice...well, I think it's important."

The click of the computer keys stopped and a grim-faced director turned and picked up her receiver. "It's Robbie, Janet. What's up?" Gwen closed the door softly behind her.

"You said I could call if I ever needed your help," Janet said tentatively. "Robbie, I...I..."

"Janet? What's wrong? Look, take a deep breath, okay? I'm here. You just tell me and I'll help."

"I...Bill...I found several lumps; it might be breast cancer. I have to go to Barrie for tests tomorrow. The lady who normally takes care of Reb is busy after school and I don't know how long I'll be. I—"

"Listen, I'm on my way. I'll be there tonight and I'll drive you and Reb to Barrie tomorrow. What time is your appointment?"

"Ten, but Robbie—"

"No 'buts'. I'll be there as soon as I can. Try not to worry; everything is going to be all right." The voice was calm, confident.

"Thanks, Robbie." Janet's voice was shaky. "Robbie?"

"Hmm."

"Thanks."

"You and Reb get a fire going and make something for us for dinner." Robbie knew it was important to keep Janet busy until she got there. "I'll be there in less than two hours. Okay?"

"Okay." Janet smiled. "See you."

"Count on it." Robbie was buzzing Gwen as she hung up. "Gwen, I've got an emergency. I'll be gone for a few days. Tell Brian, I'll be in touch as soon as I can. Call for a helicopter to take me to Bartlett. I'm just slipping home to pack and then I'll head out to the island airport."

Gwen was concerned but she knew better than to pry. "Okay, Robbie."

Robbie paused as she threw clothes into a suitcase. *Why am I doing this? I can't leave my editor to handle this film cut; he won't understand my vision. And if he makes the wrong cuts, it will put us weeks behind. A delay now in editing is going to cost me millions. I should be finishing my work and then climbing into bed with Tracy for some relaxation.*

She leaned over her suitcase, balanced on her extended arms, eyes closed. *Who am I trying to kid? I gave it my all last night with her and didn't feel anything. This damn little school marm has gotten under my skin in a big way.*

A chill ran through her as she recollected, *Christ! I said I wanted to take Reb if anything happened to Janet. If I had thought I could have been a good mother, I wouldn't have... Don't go there; just deal with the here and now. Janet needs me and so does Reb, and no matter what the cost, I'm going to be there for the two of them. Like it or not, I'm head of the family and it's my duty. Besides, Janet needs me.* As if that one thought overrode any objections, she snapped the lid of the suitcase closed.

Janet stood at the screen door scanning the evening sky, while Reb made happy little baby noises from inside her playpen. A shiver went through Janet and she wrapped her arms around herself and rubbed her arms with her hands. *I shouldn't have called Robbie. I'm not her responsibility. I just wanted her here so badly. It was really weak of me. The poor woman hardly knows me.*

The *whoop, whoop* of helicopter blades echoed across the lake and the silhouette of the bug-like 'copter appeared over the horizon. Yellow eyes searched the beach and then turned, as the craft slowly settled in the shallow water. The bubble door opened and Robbie slipped out into the ankle deep water. Bent double to keep away from the blades, water sprayed around her as she reached in and grabbed her bags.

Squinting against the wind and spray, she limped up the beach and met Janet half way to the cabin. Dropping her bags, she wrapped the smaller woman in her arms protectively and let her cry. Neither one of them heard the helicopter lift off and disappear over the trees.

After a short while, Janet's sobbing stopped. She pulled away from Robbie and took out a tissue to wipe her eyes and nose. Janet smiled weakly. "Okay, sorry. My granddad always said when things get too much, find a comfy shoulder, cry your eyes out and then get on with it. Well, I've had my cry and it was a nice shoulder."

Robbie looked uncomfortable. "Ahh, well I'm here."

Stepping forward again, Janet hugged the tall woman tightly. "That means a lot to me. Come on in. There is so much going on in my mind. I'm so glad you came. Do you want tea? Reb's still up." The babbling betrayed her stress.

Robbie followed quietly into the house. She'd just sort of dropped everything and come, and now that she was there, she wasn't really sure what to do.

"Obbie's bird! Obbie's bird," called Reb from her playpen as she held on to the bars and did a little baby dance, bobbing up and down.

Robbie laughed, lifting the small child up into the air. "Hi ya, Reb." She settled the diapered backside over her shoulders and held on to Reb's long legs. The baby, laughing with delight at this new view of the world, dug her hands into the actress' hair and held on tight.

Janet laughed, the merriment almost making it to her worried eyes. She picked up Robbie's luggage from where she had left it by the playpen, and together they walked through to Janet's bedroom.

"I'll make up a bed on the couch."

Robbie carefully landed her baby pilot onto the centre of the bed and then turned to face Janet. "I'll sleep on the couch. You need to rest."

"That's thoughtful of you, Robbie, but you don't fit on the couch. The last time you were here, your feet hung over the arm rest by a foot."

"I'll manage."

"No. I need you to drive tomorrow. I...I don't think I could give it my full concentration. You need the sleep, okay?"

Robbie looked down at the remarkably brave woman. The more time she spent with this lady, the more impressed with her she was. "Okay, but I'll make the tea."

Janet chuckled. "Do you know how?"

"Funny. Come on." Robbie jerked her head toward the kitchen and flashed a famous smile that captivated audiences. Janet helped Reb off the bed and the little child ran on ahead.

Later, they sat together on the sofa, Robbie's long legs draped over the sledlike coffee table to keep pressure off her knee and Reb fast asleep between them. Janet was softly stroking her daughter's hair. "I should put her to bed."

"Hmm," Robbie agreed, feeling suddenly tired.

"I need to go to a lawyer, Robbie; you know, to make a formal will just in case..." She went on in a hurry, "Well, in case things don't work out. It's a good idea anyway. I mean, what if I was in an accident or something?"

"I'll get my lawyer to see to it. Don't worry. You just tell me what you want," Robbie muttered, looking at the glowing embers of the fire.

Janet bit her lip nervously. "Robbie?"

"Hmm?"

"You did offer at one time to be Reb's guardian."

Robbie looked up at Janet, her eyes guarded. "As I recall, you didn't seem real keen on that idea."

"I only knew your reputation then, I didn't know you. Now I think I do. Would you be Reb's guardian?"

Shifting, Robbie put an arm along the back of the couch. "Look, Janet, I'm not really the motherly type, and I'm not going to hold you to a request you are making at a time when you have some real fears about the future. If there is anyone else you'd—"

Janet's hand reached up and rubbed Robbie's where it lay on the back of the couch. "Reb loves you, Robbie. She just took to you right away. And I trust completely that you would care for and protect my daughter. It might be a rather unorthodox upbringing," she grimaced, "but it would be a good one. I've known you only a short time, but you're the one I called, not any of my friends. I just know in my heart that this is the right choice. That is, if you are willing to take on the responsibility."

Am I willing? Can I handle the responsibility of a child? "Yes, I will be Reb's guardian," Robbie heard herself say. Her fingers interlaced with Janet's. "We'll see it through together." Uncomfortable with the tension and emotional current between the two of them, she abruptly changed the subject. "Okay, I'll carry helicopter child to her crib, but you gotta do all the messy baby stuff."

"Hey, you need to practice."

"I'm counting on the kid being through college before I have to think about living up to any parental responsibilities," mused Robbie, cradling the two year old in her arms without being aware she was doing so. Janet smiled, but said nothing.

Still favouring her stiff knee, Robbie slid into the bed awkwardly and took a deep breath of the lingering fragrance that was Janet. She hadn't planned on getting between these sheets again so quickly and certainly not alone. *Damn! Everything is different now. Everything.* She lay on her back, staring up at the ceiling. The pearl moonlight coming through the window painted a kaleidoscope of leaf patterns across the ceiling. *I wish tomorrow was over.*

Janet tossed, then turned, and then gave in and got up. She looked out the window at the moon shimmering across the lake and thought about the phone conversation she'd had with Robbie only the day before. Now everything was different. It would be better once she knew what she was facing, whether it was minor surgery or a prolonged battle. *I wish tomorrow was over.* With a sigh, she walked back to her makeshift bed and picked up her pillow.

Wide-awake, Robbie counted leaf silhouettes on the ceiling. *This is stupid. I charged up here like some damn white knight and now I don't know what the hell I'm supposed to do. Damn it, this is not my responsibility. I've got an entire film production team counting on me. I should be back in Toronto.*

"Robbie?"

Robbie reached out and turned on the bedside light. Janet was standing at the bedroom door. "You need something?"

"I can't sleep."

Robbie slipped out of bed carefully.

"You're naked!" Janet's startled eyes were wide.

Looking down at her lean, muscular body with disinterest, Robbie shrugged. "Yeah, I came that way. Come on, you get into bed and I'll take the couch."

"If you put your housecoat on, we could share," Janet suggested awkwardly. "I mean, I just don't want to be alone."

Robbie smiled tenderly. "Get in. Glad you thought to bring your own pillow, I don't share."

Rolling her eyes, Janet smiled and then happily hopped into her own bed. Robbie limped around to the other side and slipped in under the sheets. "And I won't wear PJs for anyone."

The drive down to Barrie in Janet's old truck was quiet and tense. In the hospital parking lot, Janet turned to Robbie. "I can do this alone. Reb would just get antsy having to hang around a waiting room. There is a really good waterfront park. Would you take her there and play with her for an hour, and then come back to pick me up?"

"You're sure?"

"Yes."

Robbie nodded and Janet slipped out of the truck and made her way over to the hospital. When she looked back, Robbie lifted her hand in a wave and then drove off.

The park ran along the curve of Lake Simcoe. Robbie, disguised in a floppy hat and big sunglasses, hoisted Reb up onto her shoulders. Holding on to the squirmy child with care, she slowly walked down the length of the park and back again, trying to work out the stiffness that remained in her knee. Reb played with Robbie's long hair that stuck out from under the hat, and like a tour guide, pointed out the things of interest to her tall friend.

"Sea gal!" squealed the young child, pointing to the sky.

"Yes, seagulls," agreed Robbie. "You like birding, Reb?"

"Agha."

"Me, too. When I was younger, I used to bird a lot. Those are ring-billed gulls, Reb. Say ring-billed."

"Ing-billed," came the prompt response.

"That a girl." Robbie looked out at the water.

"I was going to go into science and become a zoologist. That was before...well, you don't need to know about that. No one does."

"Boat!"

"Sailboat," Robbie clarified, pointing to the sloop as it slid by on the steady wind.

"That a sailboat," repeated Reb.

"Hmm. And that's a noisy motor boat." Robbie pointed to the offending powerboat as it cut around the sailboat and sent the sloop's boom swinging in its wake.

Reb laughed with delight. "Vooom! Motta boat! Voom!"

Raising an eyebrow, Robbie looked up at her charge. "I should have known you'd go for speed and power."

She lowered her small charge to the ground and together they headed up to a playground, Reb holding on to the actress' hand as if she had known her all her short life. Robbie lifted Reb to the top of the slide and waited at the bottom to catch the gleeful bundle of delight. Then, she swung her high in the sky and deposited her at the top again. Whoosh! Down slid the happy child again.

"Why do I get the feeling I could be doing this all day?" Robbie laughed as she deposited Reb at the top once more. "I can see, Reb, why your mom has such a great body, having to chase you around all day." She looked out across the huge lake. The water on the horizon was almost the same colour as the sky, as if one could swim up into the heavens.

I lay beside Janet last night and held her hand. I haven't held anyone's hand since my first high school date, damn it. And yet it had felt nice, like a special bond you feel with someone you have known and trusted for a long time. She hadn't felt angry or frustrated at not getting any action, she had just felt...content. Robbie felt a jolt of surprise. She couldn't recall having felt content since—

"Obbie's bird! Obbie's bird," came the delighted giggle of the small child atop the slide.

Robbie looked up with a smile, which changed to a look of horror as Reb spread her arms like wings and dived off the top of the ladder.

Janet sat in the crowded waiting room, flipping through a dog-eared copy of *People* magazine from the previous year. "Mrs. Williams?" called a disembodied voice from behind a door that had been opened a crack. Janet got up and obediently entered the inner sanctum of the mammography department.

The voice turned out to belong to a springy, small woman in her thirties, wearing blue surgical scrubs. "This way, please. This is your change cubicle. We'll need everything off to the waist. Here's your gown. Open side to the front, please. Hang your clothes on the hooks, but please don't leave anything valuable in the cubicle." The woman was gone before Janet could respond.

I wonder how many times a day she has to say that. Janet stepped into her allotted space and pulled the curtain. She stripped to the waist and put on the gown that had been provided. Two of the three ties were missing. She sighed. *Once you enter the world of medicine, any sense of privacy and self-dignity becomes a thing of the past.*

"Are we ready, Mrs. Williams?"

"Yes." Janet rolled her eyes as she emerged from her area, clutching her gown with one hand and her bag with the other. Another perky hospital guide trotted by them, leading an older man clad only in a gown and black socks and shoes. The man's desperate attempt to hold the flaps at the back closed had failed, and he mooned them as he went by. *Well, at least I was spared that indignity,* Janet thought as she followed her guide to the mammography room. She was handed over to a new assistant.

"Okay...Mrs. Williams," said the nurse, checking the chart. "When was your last mammogram?"

"Ahh, about five years ago." The nurse looked up with a disapproving expression, causing Janet to add, "I've been meaning to get around to it."

"Age?"

"Thirty three."

"Any children?"

"One, she's two years old."

"Not pregnant?"

"No."

"Have you had cancer or is there any history of cancer in your immediate family?"

"No."

"Why did the doctor refer you?"

"I found a large lump in my right breast. The lymph nodes are swollen, too."

The nurse nodded and finished checking off the data on the chart. "Okay, drop the top of the gown and step up to the machine. We're going to have to squeeze you a little."

It was the heel of Reb's leather shoe hitting the bridge of Robbie's sunglasses and snapping them in two that resulted in the black eye and the cut to the bridge of the actress' nose. It was Reb's impact with the metal stud on Robbie's leather jacket that scratched her nose and gave her the shiner that matched her aunt's. Robbie's panicked dive and grab brought them both to the ground heavily. Reb, lying on top of her, was silent for a minute in stunned surprise.

Dabbing at the blood on Reb's face, Robbie tried to ascertain how bad the damage was. "Hey, you okay?" Robbie asked, her voice shaky with fear.

Recovered from her surprise landing, Reb opened her mouth and screamed with a baby wail that could have been heard in Toronto, an hour's drive south.

Robbie sat up and held the frightened child. "Hey, God damn it, Reb, don't cry. God damn it, people are going to think I'm abusing you. Shh!" As the screams got louder, Robbie looked around in a panic. She reached into her pocket and pulled out a tissue to clean the blood from Reb's face, surprised to find that it was only a small scratch producing the copious amount of blood over the two of them. Then she realized that her face was bleeding too. "God damn it," she muttered again, awkwardly getting to her feet before picking up the small child. She carried the stiff child over to a small ice-cream stand where a woman looked on with concern.

"Are the two of you all right? My, that was an amazing dive you took to grab her out of the air."

"I think she's fine," Robbie fretted over the wails. "I haven't been able to ask her any vital questions yet. Can I have an ice-cream cone in whatever flavour two year olds like? One that's big enough to fill her mouth."

The woman laughed and made up a baby vanilla cone. "That's a dollar-fifty."

Robbie rooted in the pocket of her blue jeans and pulled out a gold and silver coloured coin worth two dollars. "Keep the change," she said, taking the ice-cream cone and holding it up to Reb's open mouth. The tears turned to sobs and then to happy, baby sucking noises.

Pulling a handful of paper napkins from the dispenser, Robbie limped over to a park bench. Reb sat there happily eating her treat, while Robbie wet down some of the napkins at the water fountain and wiped herself and Reb as clean as possible. Reb's eyelid was definitely going blue. Robbie touched her own. It was almost swollen shut, and she'd had to use a piece of napkin to staunch the blood flowing from the deep cut on the bridge of her own nose. They both had blood trickled down the front of them.

"We look a sight, Reb. God damn it, your mom trusted me to take you out on loan and now I'm going to have to bring you back damaged. I'm in big trouble, Reb. Listen, can you move all your fingers and toes?"

As if to show Robbie she was all right, Reb struggled to her feet, wobbled along the park bench and deposited her ice-cream cone down Robbie's front. Robbie looked at the sticky mess that was Reb and then down at her own front. "Well, kid, at least we match."

"Alright, Mrs. Williams, we got nice clear x-rays." The nurse smiled at Janet who was waiting in the mammography room. "Now, if you will come with me, I'll take you over to the ultra-sound department."

"Okay." Janet grabbed up her shoulder bag and followed the chipper nurse down the hall. In one room they passed, through a crack in the curtain, Janet saw the old man having an abdominal ultra-sound done. *If I stay here much longer, there is nothing I'm not going to know about that old guy,* she thought grimly.

In her own ultrasound room, she dutifully lay down on the bed and let yet another technician have a go at analyzing the problem with her right breast. This time it involved covering the breast with warm oil and running a hand-held apparatus over it. The soft tissue of the area showed up in fuzzy black and white on a TV screen.

"What do you see?" she asked.

The technician smiled wearily. "I'm not allowed to read them, honey; I just photograph them. A report will be sent to your doctor and he will advise you."

Janet lay still and watched the shapes on the screen change in size and darkness. She could see the large irregular mass. Several times, the technician stopped, measured the item on the screen and recorded the shot. When it was over, she was given a towel to clean off the oil and sent back to her cubicle to dress.

Robbie had parked the truck so that she could see Janet when she came out. It had been one hour and thirty-eight minutes so far, and Robbie was starting to get worried. She looked at her watch again. An hour and thirty-nine minutes. She turned to look at Reb, who was safely strapped into her car seat, having a nap. When she looked back, Janet was coming across the parking lot. Robbie got out and went to meet her.

"Robbie! What happened? Where's Reb?"

"In the truck, what did the doc—" Robbie stopped. Janet was already on the way to the truck. *Shit! Not very good damage control there, Robbie,* she chided herself, following in Janet's wake.

Janet looked in at her filthy, but peacefully sleeping child who sported a small scratch on her nose and a bit of a black eye. Her racing heart calmed as she reached out to make sure her daughter was okay.

"She's not dead or anything," came the less than reassuring remark from behind her. "She just went to sleep because she was tired. We went for a swing ride, but she threw up. I think it was the vanilla ice cream. I should have gotten her chocolate. No one throws up chocolate," she reasoned.

Janet closed her eyes and counted to ten. She turned, folded her arms and looked at the erstwhile babysitter. Robbie was doing her best to look innocent. "Do you want to explain?"

"Nope. How are you?" she demanded.

Janet shook her head, turned and lifted Reb from her seat. Reb snuggled in comfortably and Janet started to relax. She looked at Robbie who impatiently stood waiting for an answer.

"Don't know. They aren't allowed to tell you anything; I have to wait for my doctor to contact me with the results." Janet stepped forward and ran her finger over Robbie's damaged eye. The piece of napkin stuck on the bridge of Robbie's nose was blood soaked. "Hey, are *you* okay, sweetheart?"

Almost managing to lift an eyebrow, Robbie smiled. "Sweetheart, huh?"

"It was a term of affection. It looks really sore. I think we'd better go to Emergency and get a stitch put in."

"It was a term of endearment, and I'm not going to Emergency. You can clean it up when we get home. Get in, *sweetheart*," Robbie ordered cheekily, opening the truck door.

Janet laughed. Having checked Reb over once more and satisfied herself that her daughter was okay, she fastened the child back in her safety seat and then climbed in. She waited for Robbie to go around to the other side and slide behind the wheel. "If we stop at a fast food place rather than a restaurant, there is a chance we can still get out of town without being arrested for child abuse. No murderers in your family, are there?" Janet joked.

Robbie's eyes snapped up, cold and filled with anger. Not understanding why Robbie had reacted with such intensity Janet recoiled. "It was a joke," she reassured.

Robbie laughed weakly. "Ahh, sorry. Just a little guilty, I guess, about returning the kid damaged."

"It's okay. It happens. She is a very active child." A grin spread across Janet's face. "It must have been a good fight. Just how many rounds did you go with her before she knocked you out?"

"Funny," Robbie snorted, as Janet went off in gales of laughter.

Reb was in bed and Janet now had time to think about the day. The *click, click* of the laptop keyboard could be heard coming from the living room where Robbie had commandeered the desk and connected to the Internet. Janet went into the living room and sat down in the chair near by. "You wear glasses," she observed in surprise.

Magnified blue eyes came up and made contact with green. "Only when my eye is too swollen to wear contacts," Robbie said wryly. "Don't tell my fans. It would ruin my tough girl image."

Janet watched in fascination as Robbie worked, finally asking, "How much of you is image and how much is real?"

"It gets hard to tell after a while; the image, the person, it's all one package for marketing." Robbie worked on for a few minutes, very aware of Janet's close scrutiny. Then she closed down her programs and snapped the lid shut, turning in her chair so she was close to Janet. "What?"

"You are very funny, do you know that? I almost burst a gut on the way home as you told the story about your morning with Reb. It's a side of you that people never see."

"Hmm." Robbie removed her wire-rimmed glasses and looked at Janet with steady blue eyes.

They were the colour of a calm Caribbean sea tonight, Janet observed. *Sometimes, they were dark and stormy, or flashed with an intensity that seemed to radiate from within. Other times, they were the blue of glacial ice.*

"Let's go sit on the couch where it's more comfy," suggested Robbie, getting up.

As she followed, Janet noted that Robbie still favoured her knee. They settled down again, each at opposite ends of the couch. Robbie stretched out her long legs across the sled-table and sighed contentedly.

Janet looked at the fire that was burning with a mellow glow. "It feels a little awkward...you being here, I mean."

"You called," Robbie fired defensively.

Green eyes looked up in surprise and Janet rushed to reassure. "I want you here. I guess I'm embarrassed because I needed to ask for help."

"Would you have, if it hadn't been for Reb?"

Pulling at a thread on the cushion, Janet laughed nervously. "I wouldn't have had an excuse to then."

"You don't need an excuse." Green eyes met smoldering blue. "If I was directing this scene, you would come over here, now, and whisper, 'Thank you, sweetheart', while you kissed me passionately."

Janet laughed. "If you were directing this scene, you'd have had your way with me and then my irate ex-lover would have stormed in and we'd have all been killed in the crossfire."

"Hey! For someone who never bought any of my films, you have a lot to say," Robbie growled, leaning over and giving Janet a gentle swat. They laughed, and Robbie used the opportunity to slide a little closer. She placed an elbow on the back of the couch and rested her chin on her lower arm, looking seriously at Janet. "I'm very attracted to you. Do you know that, Janet?"

Janet licked her lips nervously. "Robbie, I don't think I can handle this right now." She turned away and looked at the red-hot embers of the fire.

"I know. I'm not coming on to you, I'm just asking if you understand that I'm attracted to you." Robbie reached out and softly stroked Janet's shoulder. She felt the shiver her touch sparked in Janet.

"Yes, I understand, but I wonder why." Janet sighed. "You don't have a very good track record, Robbie." The hand stilled and Janet looked up, surprised at the hurt she saw in the blue eyes. Instinctively, Janet slid over and reached for Robbie, pulling her into a quick embrace. "Oh, Robbie, I didn't mean to upset you." She pulled back and looked into eyes filled with insecurity. "I...I like you, too. I have...right from the very beginning."

"Like?" The voice was deliberately neutral, controlled.

Janet looked down at her hands. "I'm very much attracted to you. I just have concerns about the consequences for my life, and Rebecca's, if we were to..."

"Become lovers?"

"Yes."

A silence fell between them. Janet, sensing Robbie's pain, did not pull away but instead nestled into the crook of her arm, leaning her head back against her shoulder and putting her feet up on the coffee table. *Robbie's so complex — one minute vulnerable, and the next minute iron. She's so very, very attractive and so very, very dangerous.*

Robbie forced herself to keep her arm on the back of the couch, even though she wanted to wrap it around Janet's shoulder. *Okay, you can do this, Robbie. Give the lady some space.*

It shouldn't have hurt that Janet knew and didn't approve of her wild life. It was just painfully ironic that the only person that she had ever expressed some feelings for didn't believe her. *It takes you down a peg or two, doesn't it, Williams?* To her surprise, a lump formed in her throat. She swallowed it quickly. *Get a grip,* she ordered herself.

"It's hard waiting for the results," Janet said into the silence.

"Yeah." Robbie lost the battle and her arm slipped around Janet, pulling her close.

"I'm glad you're here."

"I'm glad I'm here too, sweetheart," Robbie whispered.

They sat for a long time in each other's arms. Then, self consciously, they prepared for bed, only feeling at ease with each other after they had slipped under the covers and Robbie had turned off the light.

"Good night, Janet." Janet's hand slipped into Robbie's. Robbie sighed happily and closed her long, strong fingers protectively around the small hand.

"Good night, sweetheart," came a soft voice in response.

Robbie fell asleep with a happy grin on her face.

"Now, are you sure you don't want the truck? You could drop Reb and me out at the school and then pick us up later." Janet slipped into her business jacket, wiped Reb's mouth, and then lifted her daughter out of the highchair and down to the floor.

Rebecca giggled and waddled over to Robbie, who was standing in the living room trying to stay out of Janet's way as she got ready for work. This was a side of Janet that she hadn't seen before — efficient single mom and career woman. Janet was strong and confident in a very quiet and pleasant manner. Robbie smiled. That was about as different from her style of leadership as was humanly possible.

"Up, Obbie, peas," called a voice from below her knee. Robbie bent and lifted the small child high into the air, letting the happy baby giggles rain down on her before she tucked the baby over her shoulder.

Janet picked up her briefcase and baby bag, and took a quick look at her watch. "Okay, Reb, say good bye to Aunty Robbie. We have to go."

"Bye, bye, Anney Obbie," laughed the child, twisting in Robbie's arm to wave a chubby little arm in her face.

"Bye, bye, Rebel." Robbie smiled and gave her niece a kiss on the cheek before lowering the child down to her feet. Janet watched with soft, happy eyes. "You phone me if you hear anything, okay?"

"I'll phone you right away. I promise." Baby bag over her shoulder, briefcase in one hand and Reb's trusting hand in the other, Janet prepared to set out once again to face the workday of the single mother.

Robbie touched her shoulder and leaned forward and kissed Janet on the cheek. "Bye, love. Have a good day."

Green eyes filled with affection smiled back at Robbie. "Thanks. I'll phone."

Robbie managed a weak, worried smile as Janet led her daughter down to the truck and headed off to work.

"Robbie! For crying out loud, woman, where are you?"

Relief was clear in the voice of Brian McGill that came over the phone Robbie had tucked under her chin as she typed on her laptop. "About thirty miles north of nowhere," was her calm response.

"You do realize that Gwen and I are up against an army of Williams haters. There is talk of hiring a hit man to track you down."

Robbie laughed. "That suggestion had to come from Ernie Talsman."

"No, Ernie's comment was, and I quote, 'That's what I get for working for a God-cursed skirt. I shoulda listened to my pappy: a woman's place is in the kitchen or a man's bed.'"

"Ouch! The old 'skirt' shot, huh? I'd have thought Ernie could do better than that. Christ, if Ernie found a woman in his bed, he'd pee himself."

"Robbie, you are costing the company thousands. Travelli, the bitch on a stick, is driving me crazy. You gotta do something here, Robbie."

Robbie laughed and made an obligatory protest. "Hey, I happen to be sleeping with that bitch on a stick." She continued happily typing away as she listened to Brian's report from the front.

"Not anymore you're not. She's the one who wants the hitman to track you down."

"Hmm, did I forget to say good bye?"

"Robbie!" Brian yelled, unwrapping the tinfoil from the scruffy roll of Tums that he had found at the back of his desk drawer, and popping three into his mouth.

"Your doctor told you to lay off the digestive tablets," she reminded him, picking up the sound of the distinctive chewing at her end.

"He told me to work for someone human, too."

Robbie pressed send. "There are eight e-mails heading your way. Go do exactly what they say. Don't question; just obey. And one other thing. Tell Gwen, I need to know how to cook a basic Thanksgiving dinner. Tell her to e-mail me a recipe."

"That's it, I'm phoning the company lawyers and having you declared insane. You don't have a domestic bone in your body. You have to bring Gwen on the set when we do a kitchen scene. What the hell are you up to?"

"Do it," Robbie commanded, hanging up abruptly when she saw the call waiting light flashing. "Hello."

"Hi, Robbie." Janet's was voice strained.

"Well?"

"The nurse at Bill's office phoned. I'm going in to talk to Bill right after school. I guess I'll find out then."

"Shit! This chain of medical command is as bad as the military. I'll come and pick up Reb."

"Robbie, you don't have a car," Janet pointed out.

"I will by then. When will you be finishing there?"

"Five."

"I'll be there."

The phone went dead and Janet frowned as she looked at the receiver. *Robbie, impossible as it seems, you have even fewer social graces on the phone than you do in person. There's going to have to be a talk about the chain of command in our household pretty damn soon, too. Our household! What am I saying? I can't keep Robbie Williams as my number one babysitter and hand holder forever. And yet, that's exactly what I want to do.* Red crept up her neck. *Oh bother! I've got a crush on an actor.*

At precisely 4:30, Robbie pulled into the parking lot of the Bartlett School for the Gifted driving a new, navy blue Jeep Cherokee. She had bought it over the phone from the local car dealer and had it delivered after lunch, after the baby seat was installed. The ownership papers, license, and insurance were still being processed.

Janet's campus was beautiful. Several long, low buildings of fieldstone were nestled in manicured lawns that faded out into natural woods to the north and east. To the west, the lawns sloped to a pebbled beach and the majestic shoreline of Lake Superior.

Robbie compared it to the sterility of the building she worked in, the stinking carbon monoxide of the parking garage, and the canned, environmentally controlled air in her offices. She breathed in deeply, smelling pine and freshly cut grass. *Nice. Janet's doing all right for herself.*

The sign at the entrance read: *Report to the office upon entering the building.* Robbie looked down the hall, saw the office sign, and headed in that direction. "Roberta Williams to see Janet Williams," she said to the secretary's she found there.

Carolyn looked up from her computer screen, surprise and disbelief on her face. "Oh, my God! I mean...one minute, please," she blurted, hitting several wrong buttons on the intercom system before she connected with Janet in her inner office.

"Mrs. Williams, it's Roberta Williams. Here...in person," Carolyn said, clearly flustered.

Robbie leaned over the desk and spoke to the intercom. "Hi, school marm."

"Hi, Robbie," came the disembodied voice. "Come in, won't you?"

Carolyn flopped back into her chair in star-struck delight. Robbie grinned at the secretary, gave her a wink, and disappeared into the office.

Robbie smiled and Janet's strained face relaxed into a grin. "Hi."

"Hi."

"Busy day?" Robbie slipped into the visitor's seat with relief and smiled at the woman behind the desk. *Should be a crime to be so damn cute and smart, too.*

"Yeah, lots of things to arrange if I'm going to be off for a while with surgery, and then there is all the usual school stuff."

Robbie chose to deflect the focus from the negatives. "It's a beautiful place you have here."

"The main house burnt down years ago. What you see here used to be the servants' quarters and stables of the estate of a local lumber baron. He was the original Bartlett. He had a gifted son who committed suicide. In his will, he left the land and a trust fund to establish this school. Someday, when we have more time, I'll show you around."

"You mean someday in our future together?" Robbie wiggled her eyebrows comically.

"You never give up, do you?" Janet got up with a shake of her head and a smile. "Come on, we'd better pick up Reb."

She circled around to the front of her desk and looked up at Robbie, who had also gotten to her feet. "Uh, would you mind if I introduce you to the staff members still in the building?"

"No, it's part of the marketing I was telling you about."

Janet frowned. "I'm not comfortable using you as marketable material."

Robbie shrugged. "It's okay, really. It is, to some extent, part of the job and unavoidable." The grin flashed into place. "Believe me, you'll know when I've had enough."

Janet grimaced at the thought. Small town Canada might not survive a Williams temper tantrum if the stories about them were true. They left the office together and found Carolyn and Milka Gorski, grinning like Cheshire cats. She shot a sidelong glance at Robbie. The stage facade had fallen into place and the woman she was beginning to know had disappeared entirely.

Bill Perkins greeted Janet at his office door and got her seated. He flipped open the report on his desk. "Well, Janet, it's bad news and good news. The bad news is that the tumour is cancerous. The good news is that although the lymph nodes are infected, there is no sign of the cancer having spread to them that we can see."

Janet forced herself to remain calm by disconnecting emotionally. This was someone else they were discussing, not her. "So, what are we talking?"

"For sure, we're talking lumpectomy and radiation treatment. And it might be that a radical mastectomy will become necessary."

Janet felt the blood draining from her face. "I...I...thought they didn't do those anymore."

"Actually, we do. Granted, nowhere near as often as in the past. We are going to do whatever is necessary to stop the cancer from spreading further. This tumour appears to have grown very quickly and it has spread out through your breast tissue and into the muscle tissue. This is serious, Janet."

Janet stared at her hands as she tried to hold herself together. She felt herself reaching out to Robbie for support. In her mind, she suddenly felt those wonderful, capable hands squeezing her shoulders and the warmth of the body behind her. *We'll get through this together.* That's what Robbie had promised and Janet knew in her heart it was true. She blinked back the tears and straightened her shoulders. "What are my chances?" Bill grimaced and Janet knew he hated such a question, feeling that answering it was like playing God. Regardless, she felt she had a right to know the odds.

"It's hard to tell. I've seen patients with worse tumours survive and smaller cancers die. It depends a lot on the patient's physical makeup, strength of character, and luck. If I had to call the odds, I'd say fifty/fifty at this point in time, but I'd be willing to bet on you with supreme confidence."

Janet smiled, although the light didn't reach her eyes. "Thanks. So when is the surgery to be?"

Bill's expression reflected his relief that she wasn't going to cry or cut up rough. One of the reasons he was attracted to her was her no-nonsense attitude. "It has got to be done right away. This is Thanksgiving weekend coming up, and that means a regrettable delay. I've had them cancel some elective surgery to get you in on Tuesday. I need you to book into Princess Margaret in Toronto early Tuesday morning."

"I can't just walk out of my job. I need time. I—"

"Janet! I'm trying to save your life here. Work with me, not against me," Bill cut in with feeling, meeting Janet's gaze with worried brown eyes.

"Okay. No more arguments." Janet rose to go. She wanted to get back to Robbie as quickly as she could.

Bill stood too. He smiled awkwardly. "Since you're in town, how about dinner tonight? You're my last patient. We could talk. You need someone to talk this out with."

Janet looked at the floor, then up at Bill. "I really enjoy your company, but I think we both know that there isn't enough romantic feeling between us for a lasting commitment. It would be wrong of me to lead you on, especially now. I need you as my doctor. Can you do that for me?"

Swallowing several times before answering, Bill managed a sad smile. "Yeah, whatever you want, Janet. But I think I'll wait until you've come through this with flying colours before I give up all hope of us sharing more."

"Thanks, Bill. You're the greatest," Janet whispered, stretching up on tiptoes to kiss the bristly cheek. She thought about the smooth skin over hard muscle that was Robbie and the hot, dry, spicy scent that had become so familiar to her in such a short time. In her heart, she knew what she wanted, and it wasn't Bill.

Robbie and Reb built a castle together on the beach. It involved a massive earth works project and considerable role-playing. They stormed the castle twice, Reb's favourite part, which resulted in major renovations and rebuilding. They were now cleaning the sand out of their respective undies while Robbie explained the next order of the day.

"Okay, Reb, we are going to get dinner ready for your mom for when she comes home. I think we..." She stopped as a most extraordinary feeling of dread came over her. Somehow she knew in her heart Janet had received bad news. She didn't believe in premonition. For a second, she closed her eyes and tried to rein in her emotions. No matter what the tests had shown, she knew she would be there for Janet; no matter what the prognosis was, she wouldn't let her die.

She took Reb's hand and led her out to the kitchen. "Okay, we gotta keep this simple because I can't cook. You'll have the famous banana sandwich, and Janet and I will have frozen pizza and beer because that's what I picked up in town."

"Ugah."

Robbie stopped and looked down at Reb, who appeared to be pulling a face. "Hey, I'm new at this. Besides, I'm saving up for my big romantic evening when I cook dinner and sweep your mother off her feet with my charm."

Rebecca sat down at Robbie's feet and laughed as she undid the director's shoelace.

"Oh, you think that's funny, do you? Listen, smug baby, I'll have you know that I've never struck out until I met your mother. I might have two strikes against me in the bottom of the ninth, but she did say that she was attracted to me, you know," Robbie pointed out as she prepared their meal.

Reb listened seriously from the floor, clapping her hands together and reaching for the dangling shoelace every time it passed by.

Hearing the crunch of tires on gravel, Robbie swung Reb up and placed her in her playpen. She quickly tied her shoelace and stiffly hobbled outside. Janet was just getting out of her truck and the news she had been given was written clearly on her features. Robbie went over and wrapped Janet in her arms.

Janet clung tightly. "How did you know?"

"I just did." Robbie's voice was rough with emotion.

Her head still buried against Robbie's cotton shirt, Janet nodded. "It's cancer; it's reached an advanced stage. They'll operate on Tuesday in Toronto at Princess Margaret cancer hospital. I'll also be having extensive radiation treatment. Bill said a fifty/fifty chance of recovery. Robbie?"

"Hmm?" The emotion was muffled in Janet's hair.

"I...I might have to have a mastectomy."

The strong arms held her tighter. Robbie felt her gut twist into a knot but she spoke reassuringly. "Whatever it takes, sweetheart, just as long as we beat this thing." She pulled back and kissed Janet's forehead. "You okay?"

Janet nodded. "I think it hasn't really hit me that this is me facing this illness and not someone else. I feel a little overwhelmed." The pragmatist took charge. "There's so much to do before Tuesday. I'm not sure how long I'll be off work."

"Don't worry. Just take it one step at a time and trust others to help pick up the slack, okay? Come on; Reb's been asking about you. I told her the tooth fairy carried you off."

"Robbie! You didn't," Janet managed a shaky smile and poked Robbie, who kept her arm around Janet's shoulder as they walked up the porch. In answer, Robbie just raised an eyebrow and reluctantly removed her arm to open the door.

"Mommy! Mommy," Rebecca called, lifting her arms to be picked up. Janet reached down and kissed her daughter and then, falling to her knees, she hugged the child close and sobbed broken-heartedly.

Robbie wasn't sure how to handle this turn of events. Should she leave mother and daughter alone? Should she try comforting them? Reb was crying almost as loudly as her mother. "Okay, that's enough." Robbie roared.

Mother and daughter turned wet eyes on Robbie in startled wonder. Robbie stepped forward and picked Reb up, then offered her hand to Janet to pull her to her feet. She wrapped her arm around the woman and kissed the top of her head. "This is nothing we can't handle, sweetheart."

"I might never see Reb grow up or marry," Janet sniffed in explanation.

"That's okay, she's going to grow up to be a butch and lead a terrorist group to free the musk ox of Ellsmere Island, anyway."

Janet snorted and fervently hugged the two that she loved more than anything. Yes, she was in love with Robbie Williams. *Why did you have to come into my life now, Robbie? And how long will you stay?*

"Hey, I made dinner," Robbie said as the oven buzzer went off. She gave Janet a quick squeeze and then carried Reb over to her highchair. Janet climbed up on one of the bar stools and looked at dinner: frozen pizza and Molson Canadian. It was on the tip of her tongue to make a snide remark when she noted Robbie's pride and, with relief, the banana sandwich for Reb.

"Pizza and beer. Rob, that's just what this day calls for. Thanks." Flashing a smile that warmed Janet to the tips of her toes, Robbie served each of them a slice of pizza and circled around the counter to sit beside Janet.

Janet found, to her surprise, that the pizza and beer did go down easy. Robbie helped to further ease her anxiety by getting a pad of paper and helping her to organize a list of things that had to be done. They divided the list into things that Janet would have to handle, and things Robbie could see to. The mountain of responsibilities to discharge that Janet had been building in her mind was reduced to a long, but manageable list.

A sleepy Reb was put to bed at seven, after she had shown her mom the castle that Obbie and she had built. Janet had helped Reb fashion a flag made of a twig with a leaf, and they stuck it on top of the huge mound of sand. Now the two adults sat at opposite ends of the couch, Janet explaining how she would want the custody of Reb and her estate arranged. Robbie typed the information into her laptop to e-mail off to her lawyer. It was a difficult task to deal with, and she found that she had to force herself to keep the emotion from showing on her face. This was important, both legally, and for Janet's peace of mind. She typed on.

When they were finished, Robbie's shoulders ached with tension. Janet was wired and roamed around the room with restless energy. "You know what I need you to help me do now, Robbie?"

"No."

"Bake cupcakes." Janet stood in front of Robbie, eyes sparkling.

"What?"

"Cupcakes for the church social. Come on, Robbie, I need to keep busy."

Robbie sighed. She had thought they could be busier enjoying each other's embraces on the couch. *Damn woman.* "Okay, but if you ever tell a soul that I helped bake cupcakes for a damn church social," she grumbled, "you'll be going head first into the lake." Privately biting the bullet, she followed the tightly strung woman out to the kitchen and stoically did whatever was asked of her. They laughed a lot, and slowly the nervous energy dissipated, leaving a tired but calmer Janet.

"Almost done." Janet yawned as she iced the last few cupcakes. Robbie looked up from licking the chocolate-covered beaters.

"Good, because if I have to lick one more beater clean, I'm going to be sick."

"Don't complain. You were the one who insisted on taste testing everything."

Pleased that Janet was acting more like her old self, Robbie smiled. "Hey, it was a tough job and I didn't have Reb to help me."

Janet went over to the counter and leaned close, looking into Robbie's remarkable eyes. "You two are so much alike. I can't tell you how much it means to me that you're here. I don't know how I can ever repay you for your kindness."

Robbie ran her finger around the bowl Janet was holding and reached over the counter to paint Janet's lips with chocolate. Then she leaned over the counter, and slowly and deliberately licked off every bit of icing. The kissing became a mutual exploration. Janet put down the bowl and ran a hand around the back of Robbie's neck, pulling her closer. Play exploded into passion.

Janet finally pulled back. The two were breathless. Robbie smiled. "There, the debt's paid."

Janet's lips opened as she leaned back toward Robbie. "No, it isn't," she whispered huskily, just before their lips met again.

It was Robbie who broke this kiss to come up and over the counter in a smooth vault and wrap Janet in her arms, while her lips explored the texture and taste of Janet's face and neck. When she felt the smaller woman stiffen, she slowed and pulled back. Their eyes locked.

"I'm not being fair to you, am I? I...I mean, I...this is no time for me to get involved..."

Robbie kissed the golden hair. "We were involved from day one. I won't rush you, sweetheart. We'll go really slowly. Ready for sleep, now?" Nodding, Janet smiled. This time Robbie didn't wait for Janet to take her hand. When Janet slid into bed, demurely dressed in her nightie, Robbie turned off the light and curled her naked body around Janet's smaller form. Janet took Robbie's hand from where it lay draped over her and placed it over her breast, interlacing her own fingers with Robbie's.

Robbie smiled in the dark and nuzzled into the back of Janet's neck.

Chapter 5

Janet woke to the *Beep! Beep!* of the Roadrunner. As she blinked in the sunlight, the sleep slowly left her mind to be replaced by the jolt of memory. *I've got cancer.* The words were a shock wave crashing through her. *Why does everything sound and look so normal?* The alarm brought her eyes to the clock. *Time to get up for work.* There was so much to be done; she didn't have time to feel sorry for herself. *Okay, Janet, move your butt.*

Forcing the depressing thoughts to the back of her mind, she slid from the bed that she had shared with Robbie. To her surprise, there was a small bunch of wild daisies lying on the abandoned pillow. She reached over and slipped out the card that rested underneath. The picture on the card was of a storm over a wind-tossed sea. Janet flipped the card open, recognizing Robbie's bold handwriting.

I am not worried. There is nothing you can't handle. Robbie.

The fear that had fueled her morning depression shrunk back into proportion. As long as Robbie believed in her, was there for her, she knew they would find a way through this. A comforting warmth filled her heart. *I wish people knew Robbie as I know her.* She slipped into her housecoat and padded softly out of the bedroom and down the hall to peep around the corner.

Reb between her legs, Robbie was sitting on the floor watching the Roadrunner cartoon on TV. They were sporting matching black eyes. "See, Reb, there is good animation in the character but none in the background. That's how you save time and money. You gotta watch those below the line costs when you're a director. Good point-of-view here as the Coyote falls off the cliff again. You see him from the top and then from underneath and then below ground level, all within a twenty second time frame. You remember, I told you there are twenty-four cels to a second of animation, so that scene had about four hundred and eighty cels."

"Oadunna, Obbie! Oadunna," Rebecca squealed with delight, pointing to the screen.

"That's right, Rebel. Roadrunner."

"What's a cel?" Janet asked, leaning in the doorway and watching the two interact with delight.

Looking up in surprise, Robbie felt a blush wash up her neck. "It's a word Disney created. Short for celluloid, which is the type of plastic the cartoons are painted on."

"Do you do cartoons, too, Robbie?" Janet came over to the pair.

"Mommy," Rebecca demanded, standing up and holding her arms up to be lifted.

Robbie patted the spot beside her. Instead of picking Reb up, Janet curled up beside the director on the floor and let Reb climb into her lap.

"Morning, Reb." Janet gave her daughter a kiss on the forehead. "You, little one, are up very early."

"We went for a walk after my run this morning," Robbie explained proudly. Janet smiled her delight and Robbie found her insides melting like an over-heated candle. *My God, I want this woman!* She'd felt desire many times before, but not like this. This was a hunger that wasn't going to be denied.

"I need to get ready for work, but just share with me a little bit about what you and Reb have been talking about." Janet squeezed Robbie's arm. "And thank you for the flowers. They made my morning a lot brighter."

Snapping back from the wash of sensations, Robbie tried to remember what it had been she had been telling the kid. "Ahh, you're welcome. Reb found them. No, I've never made a cartoon. It would be fun to try but it is hard to compete with companies the size of Disney. Even Universal can't match their work."

Janet enjoyed the pride that Robbie took in her field. Robbie lost all her defensiveness when she talked about the art of film. Janet liked that side of her friend. "How are they made?"

"Well, you start with the story, the script. Then the team is brought together to make a storyboard, which is like a big comic book, only it's just rough sketches. It's a brainstorming session where ideas are developed and interrelated. Once an idea is agreed upon, it's written on the storyboard. That way, everyone working on separate parts of the production — animation, sound, background, special effects — will know how all the parts are to fit together." Janet was listening intently, so she continued.

"When you see an animated movie, you are actually seeing individual pictures moving at a rate of twenty-four frames per second. So, for every second of film, the animator draws twenty-four pictures. In reality, the animator will do only the main positions of the character. They're called the extremes. The assistant animator draws the main interconnecting stages between the extremes, called the breakdowns. The less practiced artists, called in-betweeners, fill in the remaining sequences called tweeners.

"Producing a cartoon feature takes a lot of time and money. It has to be a real team effort. A Disney or Universal production of feature length will take three to four years to produce and have around four hundred thousand drawings."

Janet looked closely at the cartoon as Roadrunner handed the coyote a stick of dynamite. "But aren't they just produced by computer now?"

"Computers are used to set colour and create reversals and things like that, but no, the only way to make a good cartoon is by hand. It is an amazing art form."

"So everything I'm seeing is done on cels?"

"The characters are. The backgrounds are painted. Each cel is set against the background, photographed, removed, and replaced by the next one in the sequence."

"I guess I'd better not make some inane remark about cartoons being cute, kid's stuff, huh?" Janet laughed, giving Robbie an affectionate nudge with her shoulder.

One eyebrow raised, Robbie smiled down at her. "Nope."

The urge to reach up and kiss Robbie was almost uncontrollable. Instead, Janet passed Reb back to her and got up. "Well, I've got a busy day. I'd better not be late."

Robbie watched Janet disappear back down the hall and then quickly picked Reb up and deposited her in her playpen. "Listen, Reb, play with Pooh Bear here for a bit and don't cry, got it? I'll be right back."

Stripping off her housecoat and nightie, Janet turned on the shower and adjusted the water temperature. She turned back to get her shampoo and hit a human wall. "Ahh! Robbie! You scared me. How can anyone so big move so silently?" Janet gasped, recovering from her shock to feel a blush flooding her cheeks as she realized she was totally naked.

An eyebrow went up and the corner of a mouth lifted in a bemused smile. "I had to follow you. You didn't give me a good morning kiss," reasoned Robbie.

"Hmm, where's Reb?"

"Penned."

"Come here," Janet ordered with a smile as she wrapped her arms around Robbie's neck.

There was no timidity this time. Open, hungry lips sought each other in a passionate dance. Tongues stroked and curled and sucked in a sensual imitation of things not yet done. Robbie let her hands slide down to cup Janet's round, firm bottom, and she felt Janet's responsive moan deep in her mouth.

Yes, now, Robbie thought and moved one hand to glide over a well-defined waist, across tight abdominal muscles and up to the soft, warm breast. Slipping her tongue deep into Janet's mouth as her thumb rubbed over a taut nipple, Robbie bathed in the heat and scent of Janet's body. *Oh God, I'm going to come right here!*

Robbie's explorations fueled a rush of heady sexual energy. Janet's whole being tingled with need and she rubbed herself along the lean hard body that encircled her. She throbbed with want, tearing Robbie's shirt free from her jeans so that she could run her hands across the silk-covered steel of the actor's chest. *Ohh, I should stop. Oh God, I can't.* Until the hand that was rhythmically caressing her breast touched the area where the tumour lay.

Janet stepped back and rested her head against Robbie's chest. "We can't."

"Why the hell not?" Robbie's frustrated response was rough and breathless with desire.

Standing on her tiptoes, Janet kissed Robbie's cheek. She unconsciously traced patterns over Robbie's bra cup with the tip of her finger. She was falling hard for this complex and moody woman. "Because I'm not going to tie you to me when in a few days time my world could turn upside down. I can't anyway. I need to get ready for work and we can't leave Reb long."

"Okay," Robbie agreed with a sigh, as she kissed Janet lightly on the brow and lowered her hands to rest on Janet's hips. Janet's hands dropped slowly, weaving patterns across Robbie's chest as she pulled her hands from under the T-shirt. Forest green eyes met winter blue. "This is not over," Robbie warned. "It's barely begun. I want you."

Janet nodded. She had crossed a line with Robbie and events were going to take her where they may in the next few days. One thing she knew was that she wanted at least one night when she could make love to Robbie. One night when she could feel whole, well, and sexy again. "Nothing I can't handle," she responded cheekily, making Robbie laugh. "Now go get my daughter fed and dressed. I'm running late and need your help."

Another quick kiss and Robbie was gone. Janet stepped into the lukewarm shower and let the water stream against her sensitized flesh. *My God, where is all this going?*

Janet gulped down the last mouthful of coffee as a too innocent Robbie and Reb stood by watching. "Okay, Wednesday, you went a round with Reb and lost; Thursday, you bought a truck; what's on the agenda for today?"

Robbie smiled. "Reb and I are going shopping."

"Well, that sounds harmless. If anyone asks for an autograph, please don't hand the baby away," Janet teased, picking up her briefcase. "You sure you want to keep Rebecca all day? She can come with me to the daycare..."

"We'll be fine. She has to get used to me in case you're laid up for a bit next week. We discussed this." There was an edge to her voice. *Doesn't she trust me?*

Uh, oh, Williams temper. "I know we did, but I'd hate for Reb to get you in any trouble." Janet giggled and placed a kiss on her daughter's cheek and then one on Robbie's.

An eyebrow went up. "Funny."

Janet turned back at the door to look at the two troublemakers standing there holding hands. "Call me at lunch?"

"I'll report in at regular intervals." Robbie smiled, rolling her eyes.

Janet chuckled as she looked back through the screen door that had closed behind her "You won't have to. Once people know you're in town, I'll get a constant report of your movements via the jungle telegraph."

Robbie snorted as Janet trotted down the porch steps and a few minutes later disappeared along the dirt road in her truck.

Robbie looked down at Reb. Reb looked up with a smile. "Kid, let's go get some things I need for me to make some headway with your mother. Come on."

Gwen cradled the phone and cursed Robbie to a lower level of Hades than she had relegated her boss the day before. She had received a number of emails questioning where Robbie was. She's fielded so many phone calls for her boss, she wished she had shares in Bell Canada; and she'd had to post a security guard at the office door to repel boarders, in order to get any work done at all. And the instructions she and Brian were carrying out under Robbie's direction strongly indicated that the woman was up to no good. To her surprise, a ring came from her purse.

Damn! The bastards have got my home number now. No, it might be one of the kids; I'd better answer it. "Hello, Gwen here."

"Gwen, Robbie. Why can't I get through on the office phone?" came the impatient voice.

"Because you are behind at least a million others in line, that's why. Come back before they break down the doors," the harassed secretary requested.

"No. Listen, I'm in the grocery store. Do you know they've got these neat carts with seats for your kid? Where do I look for the Thanksgiving food?"

Gwen was stunned into silence. Robbie was clearly in one of her moods where she was going to try to stir things up. *Patience.* "Robbie have you ever been in a grocery store before?"

"Sure I have, in grade two. Mrs. Rousseau brought the class to check out the vegetables."

"Oh, God!" came the exasperated response.

"Hey, that was the cook's job. It would have been presumptuous of me to interfere."

"How do you eat?"

"Eat out or cater in."

Gwen rolled her eyes. "How can you look the way you do and have such appalling eating patterns? Okay, listen, above all, don't lose your temper. Everyone has right of way over you because you're the new guy. Don't block the aisles, and if anything goes wrong, give your name as Gertrude Stein," Gwen ordered, doing a little stirring herself.

Robbie growled, "I do not look like Gertrude Stein, and besides, she's been dead for years."

"Hmm, first, we look for the meat counter. It's a cold section, usually towards the back of the store."

"Okay, here, Reb, say hi to Aunty Gwen while I steer this thing. I had to get the one with the rusted wheels. It probably spent the winter in a snowdrift and was only salvaged last spring," Robbie muttered.

Reb giggled gleefully. "Hi."

"Hi, Rebecca. How are you?"

"Hi."

If I wrote a book, no one would believe it, Gwen thought with a sigh. "Is Robbie there, Rebecca?"

"Hi."

"Hi, Rebecca. Where is your mom?"

"At school. Mommy teacha. Obbie di-ectta."

Robbie took the phone back. "Okay, I'm here. And people complain about violence in movies. The carnage wrapped up on Styrofoam trays back here is scary. I'd hate to meet the butcher after hours. What are you laughing at?"

"She calls you Obbie," giggled Gwen, her day improving immeasurably. "Wait until I tell Brian."

"She does not. She calls me Robbie. She just hasn't mastered r's yet. R's are particularly hard, as any actor would tell you," Robbie defended hotly.

More giggles. "Okay, you want ham, right? Two people...look for something around five or six kilograms; anything smaller and it will dry out."

"What does raw ham look like?"

"Robbie, for God's sakes, work with me here. The packages are labelled."

By the time Robbie had been talked through the grocery store by the exhausted and long suffering Gwen, word had gotten out that Robbie Williams was in town. After she paid for her groceries, she sat on the counter and signed autographs. She also gave an interview to and was photographed by the local paper. True to her word, Robbie did not hand the squirming child over to anyone else, although she did make sure not to let Rebecca's face show in any pictures.

Having charmed the locals, she headed over to the Community Centre to buy three tickets for the Thanksgiving dinner put on by the Ladies Auxiliary at the town hall. Lastly, at the gas station she asked directions to the lumber mill before heading back to the cabin for lunch.

The phone was ringing when she staggered through the door with Reb and two bags of groceries. Hurriedly dropping all three on the couch, she grabbed the receiver. "Hello."

"Hi. I could have gotten the tickets for the dinner. Should I buy extra copies of the paper so you can send the article to your family? And why did you need to go to the saw-mill?" asked an amused voice.

Robbie burst out laughing. "Wow! And I didn't even do anything newsworthy."

"We live in the Canadian back bush, in a village with a population of four hundred and ninety three, most of them related. Last week's headlines in *The Bartlett Gazette* were about the minister buying a new car. Don't evade. What's up with you and the sawmill?"

"It's a surprise."

"I can live with surprises, just not big nasty shocks. Is that Reb I hear?"

"No, that was eight cans of baked beans hitting the floor. Reb is inside the paper bag that they used to be in."

"Why do we have eight cans of baked beans?"

"They were on sale and came highly recommended by the store manager. It was a PR gesture. It was a lot cheaper than a billboard in Times Square. How are things going there?"

"Carolyn and Milka are pretty upset; the others don't know yet. I'll call a meeting after school to tell everyone about the administrative changes. Milka and I sat down and went through things with Carolyn. They are both bright women and professional. It's short notice, but if I'm not gone too long, I think they can manage."

"Good."

"Uh, I miss you." Janet could feel Robbie's smile right through the phone.

"I miss you too, school marm. Hurry home."

Robbie picked up the cans and unpacked the ham, the vegetables, and the baby. She made cornflakes and milk for their lunch. A short time later she realized that two-year-olds really needed to be asked on a fairly regular basis if they needed to go to the bathroom.

Some time later, having turned the air blue with curses, a fresh Reb and an exhausted Robbie headed out to the sawmill. It turned out to be a pretty small operation, owned by a local resident named Walter Higgins. He was fifty-six, married, and had two children that worked at the mill. Son Doug ran the circular saw and daughter Tracy was the secretary cum bookkeeper. They owned about two hundred hectares around Long Lake where Janet's cabin was situated and another thousand hectares to the east. So far, Walt had used the lake block mainly for hunting, except for the five or six hectares where the sawmill actually sat.

The sawmill was on Saw Mill Road just off Highway 11, about twenty miles north of Long Lake Road. *They certainly didn't use up any brain cells coming up with names around here,* Robbie thought as she turned off the highway.

She had gotten all her background information easily enough by simply asking for directions to the mill, as all information apparently was given out wrapped up in local history. She knew that Walt's wife May had the arthritis bad, and Tracy was seeing Lou's boy, whoever Lou was.

A big, beefy man with a friendly round face walked toward the truck as Robbie slid out and flipped back the seat to get to Reb. "Hi, I'm Walter Higgins. I heard you were heading up this way, eh. It's a great pleasure to meet you, Ms. Williams."

Robbie helped Reb down and held her hand tightly. Janet would likely never forgive her if she brought the kid home cut into two pieces. "Hi. It's nice to meet you, Walt. Is that your family over there?" May, Tracy, and Doug were standing awkwardly by the office door, grinning.

"Yup, that's them. Come over and meet the brood."

"Sure." Robbie smiled cheerfully, inwardly cursing all family gatherings to hell. Janet had laughingly told her about the languorous pace of "northern time". Robbie found nothing funny about it at all. True, no one was going to die of an ulcer, but they might grow roots. It was no wonder the north of Canada was so underdeveloped. No one had yet gotten around to starting anything.

"This here's my wife May and our kids, Tracy and Doug, eh."

"Hi. Great to meet you."

"Ohh, Ms. Williams, I saw you in *Midnight Terror*, and I was so afraid for you. It was a wonderful movie."

Robbie beamed insincerely. "Thanks. Call me Robbie. Actually, I was rather afraid myself, with all those cars whizzing past me in the dark. I kept getting drenched every time one hit a puddle." Everyone laughed and relaxed. *The actor is human*, Robbie thought sarcastically from behind her stage smile.

"Well, what can we do for you? Little Janet need some more winter wood?" Walt asked.

Business at last. "No. Actually, I have an offer I'd like to put to you. Can we use your office?" Robbie bent to pick up Reb. The child had been trying to escape since she had been released from the truck.

"Well, this comes as a surprise." Walter Higgins flopped back into his chair, looking totally shocked. "Never thought about sellin', eh. But I'll have to turn you down. I guess, someday, Doug will take over and, well, both my kids make their livin' here. Now Tracy, she has been steppin' out with Lou's boy, but..."

"Five hundred thousand."

"Good God, woman, no. My kids have got to make a livin'."

"May could go south for the winters. It would be great for her arthritis. There are more Canadians than Americans in Arizona and Florida. And I'll guarantee good jobs for the kids, once I get my business underway."

"You're going to run a sawmill?"

"Something like that." Bored by the chatty negotiation, Robbie growled, "One million, my last offer."

There was no response as the clock on the plywood wall ticked off twelve interminable seconds. "I need to talk to my family."

Robbie smiled, success all but assured. "Tell your kids that their starting salaries will be forty thousand a year. They'll be working as grips and get to be on set and meet all the stars."

"Forty thousand? Hell, that's good money for a starting salary up here. That's mighty generous," Walt blurted.

"It has nothing to do with generosity. It has to do with a union that has producers and directors by the...over a barrel," Robbie amended. "I'll let the family know that you want a board meeting."

Robbie played hide and seek with Reb around the yard, the two of them getting pretty muddy and sticky with pine gum. Some time later, Walt came out and walked over to the two. He held out a hand. "You got a deal there, Robbie."

Robbie flashed one of her famous smiles. "Let's go phone our lawyers."

Janet hung up from her conversation with the chairman of the school trustees. She rubbed her eyes and leaned back in her chair, spinning it around so that she could look down the lawns to the shoreline of Lake Superior. *Patronizing jackass.*

Carolyn burst in. "Janet, you'll never guess..."

"What have they done?" she drawled, turning back, prepared to hear the worst. She just knew deep in her heart that her daughter had found a kindred spirit in Robbie and that trouble was going to follow them like a dark cloud.

"She bought out Walt Higgins lock, stock, and barrel. Paid a million dollars."

Janet's feet hit the floor with a thud as she sat forward with a start. "She did what?"

"Okay, Reb, we gotta think in terms of dinner here. You know I'm kinda the house-mom this week. Weird, huh?" Robbie chatted happily to the baby, who was banging pans together energetically as she sat on the kitchen floor. Robbie stopped what she was doing and looked down at the percussion section. "Say, kid, maybe you'll take up jazz. I like jazz. I play a pretty good trumpet, you know...well, for an amateur. There's a clarinet in your mom's closet. I saw it when I was snooping. Maybe we could form a group and jam."

The baby giggled and slammed two pot lids together. Robbie laughed and went back to opening a can of baked beans and dumping them into a pan. *Getting all those cans of baked beans was a good idea after all*, Robbie reasoned. *Now I won't have to worry about meals.*

The door slammed open and Janet strode in, throwing her case on the couch as she went by. Robbie looked up in surprise. The sound of crashing pans had masked the arrival of Janet's truck.

"Hi," Robbie called cheerfully, licking the spoon clean of cold baked beans.

"Don't you 'hi' me, Robbie Williams, as if butter wouldn't melt in your mouth. What are you up to? You can't just come into this town and turn people's lives upside down. A million dollars for the old lumberyard? Robbie, those people make a living out there. It's one of the few industries in the town," Janet roared, standing in the centre of the living room, beet red and shaking with anger.

Robbie's body went strangely still and her facial muscles hardened into an expression totally devoid of emotion. The blue eyes that had sparkled a second before like rain drops in the sun were now the colour of glacial ice. "I wanted it. I bought it," she hissed.

"And what about Doug and Tracy?"

Robbie shrugged. "I bought them off."

"Bought them off? These are people, Robbie, not stock commodities. What the hell is a grip?" Janet demanded, white fingers gripping the edge of the stone countertop.

Leaning against the back counter, taut with anger, Robbie forced her body to relax. "It's someone who fetches and carries on site. They set up the sets under the supervision of the chief grip."

"Mommy?"

Janet ran an unsteady hand through her hair. "And just where are they going to work? Toronto? They'd hate it. Damn it, Robbie, you've ruined these people's lives on a whim."

Rebecca was upset by her mother's anger and she pulled on Janet's skirt. "Bad Mommy."

"Giving someone a million dollars is not wrecking anyone's life," came the snarled response.

"You would say that!" Janet yelled. "You stupid Williams think money and power is everything."

"Mommy!"

"Shut up, Rebecca," Janet snapped down at the annoyance that was pulling at her skirt. Reb's face crumpled into a tight knot and her mouth opened in surprise, then the tears started to fall and the wail of hurt echoed in the suddenly silent room. Janet dropped to her knees and wrapped the small child close to her. "Oh, Reb, I'm so sorry. Shh, baby, mommy didn't mean it. I'm so sorry."

Robbie looked down at the two, eyes filled with confusion and pain, then she silently left. Outside, the cool air felt good against her hot skin. Anger and hurt coursed through her in pulsating waves. She broke into a run down the path.

The miles moved past in green walls of trees as Robbie pushed herself on and on down the shoulder off the road. Finally, as the sun was dropping toward the western horizon, she came to a staggering stop and dropped down into some long, sun baked grass by the side of a beaver swamp. For a while, she lay on her back gasping for breath and trying to work the cramps out of her oxygen starved muscles.

Finally, pushing herself up, she walked down to the edge of the pond and knelt to splash cold water over her heated body, only to draw back at a whack and a splash. A beaver, angry at the intrusion, slapped its flat tail against the water and then swam out to the relative safety of its home — a dome of mud and sticks half submerged in the water. Robbie watched as the beaver slapped the water once more in warning and then dove below the surface to the entrance of its snug den. Despite her foul mood, she smiled. In the soft, honey glow of the late afternoon, the pond and its creatures were a beautiful, soothing sight.

It's been a long time, Robbie realized, *since I just stopped and enjoyed nature.* She sat down, wrapping her arms around her legs and listening to the chirp of the frogs calling to each other. Overhead, bats and swallows swooped across the darkening sky chasing insects. Robbie slapped at a mosquito. It was time to head back. She got up reluctantly, not anxious to deal with the conflict waiting back at the cabin. With a sigh, she set an easy jogging pace back. *Maybe Janet will be in bed by the time I get there and I won't have to deal with the issue.*

Thump, thump. The rhythmic tread of Robbie's sneakers echoed in the dark. She hadn't realized that she had run so fast or so far. She had been jogging back for almost two hours and she had only just reached the turn off to the cabin. It was dark now and she had actually run past the driveway, catching sight of Janet's mailbox at the last minute and doing a U-turn to drop into the blackness of the long lane.

She slowed a bit, unable to see her footing on the rutted path. *If I stay here, I'm absolutely going to have to get this driveway paved*, she thought. *That is, if I don't find my stuff on the stoop when I get back. Okay, maybe I did act a bit impulsively, but going with my gut reaction is the way I run my business.* Although she headed a multi-million-dollar company, she was an entrepreneur by nature, not a businessperson. It was the empire building she loved, not the maintenance of the corporation. *Tigers hunt and sheep stay home on the farm*, she thought. *I don't have time to worry about individuals. Everyone has to look out for themselves. So why am I feeling guilty?*

So I promised Doug and Tracy more than a salary; I promised them jobs. I've got some ideas. I'm just not ready to talk about them yet. They're not so much ideas as those gut feelings that just let me know I'm headed down the right path. How can I explain that to Janet without sounding like an idiot? In the long run, what I did today will work out all right for everyone. I just don't know how, yet.

Thump, thump. I'm not used to having to share ideas. If I'd told Janet more this morning when she asked about my plans, maybe we wouldn't have had the fight. I guess I did put her in an embarrassing position. This is a small town and all, and I'm her guest — sort of. I probably should have cut her some slack. She's gotta be strung really tight. How would I handle knowing that I had cancer and could die?

Robbie's stomach reacted violently at the thought, sending her to the side of the road to throw up. The thought of losing Janet or Reb was like a shot to her heart. *Damn. I gotta work out more. When was the last time I threw up after a run — the Boston Marathon?* Robbie wiped the cold sweat from her forehead with the back of her arm. *Shit!*

Janet sat in the corner of the couch, a small forlorn figure. She had had a very stressful day and her talk with the chairman of the Board of Trustees had been the last straw. The insufferable bastard had her dead and buried already.

"*So where do we stand here, Janet? Should we be posting your job and setting up interviews? I'm sympathetic, of course, but the school has to have consistent and strong leadership.*"

She should have told him to go to hell but instead she had been diplomatically reassuring. And then she had come home and jumped all over Robbie. It hadn't been fair. Not that Robbie hadn't acted high-handedly, but she could have at least given her a chance to explain. Robbie had dropped everything and come to provide support for an almost complete stranger, and in return she had been insulted and berated.

Janet got up and looked out into the dark night. *Where are you?* She wondered if she should wake up Reb and take the truck out to look for Robbie. She might have been hit by a car and be lying in a ditch somewhere. A wave of fear brought out a cold sweat on her forehead and goose bumps on her arms. She had to get Reb and start searching.

Then she saw the tall figure jogging tiredly into the circle of the porch light and she shot out the screen door, down the porch steps and into Robbie's arms, startling her. "I'm so sorry," she wailed into a sweaty shoulder.

"Me, too, love. Me, too," Robbie groaned, holding Janet in a tight embrace.

Robbie emerged from the shower to the reassuring smell of canned pork and beans and fresh toast. She wrapped a towel around herself and combed her hair back straight. After throwing some clothes on, she went out to the kitchen where Janet was just dishing up their late meal.

They sat side by side on high stools, eating their meal at the bar counter. Their conversation was pleasant but forced, each of them still trying to deal with the emotion of their fight. Usually a disagreement didn't bother Robbie much. If she needed to dress someone down, she did. She paid her employees well and they had an outstanding benefits package. In return, Robbie expected nothing less than excellence and a high performance level that matched her own.

But fighting with Janet had really hurt; it had left her feeling confused and vulnerable. She knew Janet was waiting for her to explain why she had bought the lumberyard. Instead, she brought up a completely different issue. "Uhh, it bothers me that you slept with my brother." *Why the hell did I say that?*

"W-what?"

"I said, it bothers me that you slept with my brother," Robbie repeated moodily, stabbing at her meal with her fork.

"I didn't."

"W-what?"

"I didn't. Do you really think I'd sleep with a stranger? It was done artificially."

Robbie tossed down her fork and turned to look at Janet. Blue moody eyes met flashing green. "You sorta implied you had. This explains a lot. I didn't think my brother... Reb was mixed up in a Petri dish?"

"Basically, yes."

"A test tube kid?"

"There is nothing wrong with that or my daughter," Janet responded, her temper rising again. Robbie broke out laughing, which irritated her even more. "What's so funny?"

"It just explains a lot. Uh...about Billy and about you. Uh...well, uh, it was just weird wanting to go to bed with a woman who had slept with my brother."

Janet slipped off the stool to remove the plates. "You make me feel like a hand-me-down shirt."

"On the contrary, you are the most beautiful and enticing woman I have ever met," Robbie said honestly.

Now it was Janet's turn to laugh as she ran hot water in the sink. "You will say or do anything to get me into bed, won't you?" She giggled, then looking over her shoulder she caught sight of Robbie's face.

"I meant it," Robbie said quietly. She turned and went to look out the window into the dark night.

Janet wiped the soapsuds off her hands and followed after Robbie. "Hey." She wrapped her arms around the actor's waist and rested her head against Robbie's muscular back. "I'm sorry. I guess it's hard for me to believe that of all the beautiful and talented people you have known, you would find me the most appealing."

Robbie knew there was a lot she should say, but somehow the words just weren't there. She never had trouble writing dialogue, but it was different when it was real emotion and you had to actually say the words. She said nothing.

"Thank you for saying it, though. It makes me feel very special. I...I care for you, Robbie." Sensing the tension in Robbie, Janet realized that the complex woman needed some emotional space. "Hey, you want to teach me some more about film? We could go through my DVDs and you could tell me about them."

Robbie turned and gave Janet a quick, hard hug. *Pull yourself together here, Robbie. You're supposed to be supporting Janet, not the other way around.* "Sure. You let me know when you've had enough. I can go on for hours."

They walked hand in hand over to the television inset and settled down once again on the rug. Robbie sorted through Janet's DVDs with disdain. "I'm going to buy you a decent collection of films for Christmas. This lot is an embarrassment."

"Hmm," Janet murmured noncommittally, allowing Robbie to find the safe ground she needed for her warring emotions.

"Okay, seeing as Reb has been buying the DVDs in this house, we'd better look at Disney cartoons." After placing a movie in the player, Robbie began her lesson. "*Beauty and the Beast* was a blockbuster. It was beautifully made. Look at this horse pulling the cart through the dark woods. The animation is great. You can feel the weight, the muscle, and the fear. It says 'draft horse' and yet the expressions are human.

"Wait until I fast forward. Okay, observe the detail in the castle. Forget about the characters, just look at the background — the depth of detail, the intense shadows, and the feel of dimension. The people who do the backgrounds are not animators, you know, they are fine artists. This work is superb. And then there is the personification of the clock, candlestick, et cetera. This is Disney at its best.

"Okay, look at this scene of the napkins spinning on the table and then parachuting off the edge. Remember that. Right here's *Fantasia*, which is the mother of classics in film animation. In my opinion, it is the best animation ever made. Okay, see this scene, where the blossoms spin down the waterfalls, where have you seen that?"

"It's the same as the napkins," Janet exclaimed, getting as involved as Robbie in what she was seeing.

"Got it in one. This is one team of animators paying homage to another. *Fantasia* was made way back before the war. Walt wanted it to be an ongoing project where the film would be morphed each season and would be reissued, but after the war there wasn't the money to do that."

"I love *Fantasia*." Janet's eyes sparkled.

Robbie gave her a quick hug. "Good girl. There's hope for you yet." Janet poked her in the ribs in response.

Leaning forward, Robbie slipped *Beauty and the Beast* back in the machine and rewound to near the beginning.

"Each character is done by one team with a manager overseeing. The woman who was in charge of the team that worked on Belle in *Beauty and the Beast* had the habit of using her hand to brush her hair back off her face when she leaned over a drawing board. The animators put the gesture in as a joke."

On the screen Janet saw Belle reach up and push her hair out of her eyes. "She did it," she laughed with delight.

"Yep, there are all sorts of hidden jokes in film. Here's another one." She popped in a new tape. "The teams that did *Beauty and the Beast* did the crowd scenes for *Hunchback* while other teams did the principal characters. But they left their mark. Look closely now, right here near the beginning of this film when they're showing the streets of Paris, see the character rounding the corner? She is only on for a half second..."

Janet laughed, clapping her hands. "It's Belle."

Robbie smiled at Janet's enthusiasm. "Right. Different coloured outfit, but it's Belle alright."

She slipped the tape out and got up to put some soft jazz on the stereo, then got out two wine glasses while Janet watched. Robbie expertly uncorked one of the bottles of Mouton Cadet that she had bought for their Thanksgiving dinner. The brick coloured wine from the private vineyards of the Rothchilds glowed in the soft light of the fire. For a while, they lay contentedly watching the flames and sipping their wine. Like so many good French wines, it had a rich, mushroomy body and peppery finish that was a delight to the senses.

"I bought the land for you," Robbie muttered, not daring to look at Janet.

Startled, Janet set down her wine and turned to face Robbie. "What?"

Robbie downed the last of her wine and set her glass next to Janet's. "You said you didn't want to see the trees around the lake cut down," she shrugged, "so I bought the land for you." Robbie stared at the rug as a blush crept up her neck.

"Oh, Robbie."

A strangled gasp and Robbie's arms were wrapping around the small woman who had just propelled herself into the taller woman's lap.

The music started slowly, a melody of rich, liquid notes that rained softly from a mellow guitar. Robbie let her mouth caress Janet's face, ears and neck, enjoying the soft, rhythmic gasps of delight from the woman under her. The guitar picked up the tempo as clothes were loosened and discarded. Now the rhythm took over, thrumming its beat in an earnest need. Hot music, hot flesh, as Janet let Robbie play her body like a finely tuned instrument. The guitar thumped out a crescendo as Janet's body moaned with each passing wave of release.

The melody was passed to the piano player who hungrily took up the age-old melody. Janet rolled Robbie onto her back and felt the ensuing groan vibrate on her lips as she nuzzled a long, muscular neck. The music rose relentlessly to a climax, allowing the pounding of the drums to take over and dominate. Then the other instruments once again took up the rhythmic refrain slowly, softly now, bringing all the elements of the music into a single sustained note that whispered off into silence.

Much later, Robbie lay on her back in bed. Janet was fast asleep, lying on Robbie with her limbs dangling, like a little golden cub asleep in the sun. Robbie was in a state of shock. *Bases loaded in the top of the ninth and who slams home the home run but the opposition team. When have I ever let go like that before? Never.* She had given herself completely, had let down all her defences, screaming in ecstasy as her body bucked with each passing aftershock. She had never before let herself be that vulnerable, never let someone control her so completely. *My God! It was wonderful.*

Tears rolled from the corners of Robbie's eyes and settled like dew drops on the floral sheets. *Good God, I'm in love*, she realized with a start. After all the years of being so careful not to make an emotional commitment to anyone, she had fallen hopelessly and completely in love without ever seeing it coming. She wrapped her arms around the sleeping form and nuzzled her face into Janet's soft hair. *What the hell am I going to do now?*

Okay, okay, take it easy here, Robbie chastised herself as her heart pounded. *I'll just end it; walk away, like I have so many times before when things were starting to get serious.* Her heart pained at the thought and the tears overflowed in a steady trickle. *I can't leave her! I can't! Somehow life without Janet and Reb would be unbearable.*

So what now? I can't just sleep with this one and walk away. I don't want her to think that this is a conquest and nothing more. I want some sort of commitment. It would drive me crazy to think of her sleeping with stupid Bill Perkins. Or anyone else, for that matter.

She was well aware that the laws in Ontario had been recently changed. She could ask Janet to marry her in a civil service. Then she could legally adopt Reb. *No.* That was impossible not after...

Well, at least I should do the honourable thing and be honest with Janet about how I feel. Not completely honest, of course, I could never burden Janet with the complete truth, but as honest as I can be at least. Tomorrow. Tomorrow, I'll tell her. It's important that before she has this surgery, she knows that I love her.

This time the stab of pain brought a groan to Robbie's lips. *Please, God, don't take Janet. Please, she's all I've got.* In the darkness of the night, Robbie held the sleeping woman close and cried.

Janet returned to the living room after putting Reb down for her afternoon nap. It had been a beautiful Thanksgiving Saturday. She had awakened in Robbie's arms, her body nestled into the curve of the taller woman's body. They had made love again. After a late breakfast on the porch, the three of them had gone for a long walk and picked wild blueberries by the sun warmed granite rocks at the western end of Long Lake. They had a picnic lunch there under the blaze of fall colour. Later, they walked back hand-in-hand along the old abandoned logging road that ran to the south of the lake.

Through the picture window, Janet could see Robbie sitting on the porch rail looking out over the lake. Her arms were hooked around one leg that was bent up on the rail. The other long leg hung down. In her cabled Scottish wool sweater, she looked every inch the star. Robbie Williams in lights. It was hard to believe that this was the same woman who had given her so much pleasure last night and again this morning. *I'm sleeping with* THE *Robbie Williams*, she told herself, but in her heart, in that special place that was filled with love for this remarkable woman, she knew that this was just her Robbie. She was a complex and supremely private person who was caring and honourable in her own vulnerable and stiff way. "I love you, Robbie," she whispered and then hid that knowledge deep before stepping out on the porch.

Robbie stood up and met her, wrapping Janet in her arms and burying her face in the soft blonde hair. "Hmm, you smell of summer heat and fresh herbs."

"And Johnson and Johnson baby shampoo. Reb and I share." To her surprise, Robbie bent and lifted her up into her arms. Eyes locked, and Janet fell into the kiss, revelling in being so free and at ease with the powerful woman. *If people could only know Robbie as I do*, she thought again and then was surprised by the sudden dart of jealousy. *No, I don't want to share. I just want Robbie to myself forever.* Tears had to be blinked back quickly. *Talk about looking for a cinematic happy ending. Grow up, Janet.* Dreams like that didn't come true. To Robbie, she was just one more conquest. Even so, she wouldn't have given up their night together for anything.

"Hmm, that's nice," Janet whispered.

"Yeah, it is." Robbie carried Janet over and placed her on the swing, then she sat down beside her and placed her elbows on her knees, looking down at the floor.

Janet felt the lump forming in her throat and steeled herself. *Here comes the famous Williams brush off.*

"Uhh, I guess you realize that...I...I...I like you."

"I hope so, Robbie. I am very fond of you."

"Fond. Uhh, good. Uhh," Robbie stopped to lean forward and pick up a red maple leaf that had drifted to the porch. She ran it nervously through her fingers. "Janet, I need you to know that there was a time in my life when I was very confused and I did things...well, that lay heavily on my shoulders now." Steeling herself, Robbie forced her eyes to look up into Janet's. "Bad things. Things that I don't think you could ever forgive me for."

This was not what Janet had expected. She sat and let Robbie say what she had to say without interruption.

"Uhh, about us..." *Go on, just say it. Tell her that you love her.*

Janet couldn't bear to hear Robbie actually say there was no future for them. "It's okay, Robbie. I was using you, too," she cut in.

Robbie hid what felt like a mortal wound behind a face devoid of expression.

"I needed to be loved. I needed you to know me as...as the woman I am now. That sounds awfully callous. It wasn't quite that scheming. I am attracted to you, Robbie. At any other time, I probably would have wanted to know you a lot better before we...but I might not have much time and..."

"Hey, it's okay." Robbie smiled. "Just as long as we both know where we're coming from, huh? Friends and occasional lovers, okay?"

Janet smiled, too, although the light had not reached either woman's eyes and the air was filled with stress. "Okay." Janet got up, her lip trembling with the pain she was holding inside.

Robbie scooped her into her arms immediately. "Shh, hey, it's okay. There is nothing you can't handle, sweet one. Shh, I'm here, I'll always be here for you...friend."

"Oh, Robbie," Janet sobbed, "Hold me. Hold me."

With Janet curled in her lap, Robbie stared bleakly out across the lake over Janet's sobbing shoulder. They sat there until Reb's howl of protest from her crib sent them inside.

It was after a dinner strained with fake happiness that Robbie's beeper went off. She got up from the couch where she had been reading to Reb and went to the window, snapping open her phone.

"Robbie, it's Gwen. I've had a call from London. There's been another incident."

Robbie stiffened and turned away from where Janet and Reb were playing. Janet saw the movement and picked Reb up and disappeared down the hall. Robbie sighed. "What happened?"

"A fight."

Robbie's stomach turned over. "Is Ryan all right?"

"Yes, but the other guy's got a broken arm."

"Shit! Contact my law firm and have them send down their detective, Polinski. He handled the last case really well. We can't afford a lawsuit or criminal charges. Tell him, whatever it costs, just make sure that this whole thing goes away, okay?"

"Sure, Robbie."

"And thanks...thanks, Gwen."

Gwen's voice softened. "I'll make sure everything is okay, Robbie, don't worry. You okay, there?"

"Yeah, fine. As well as can be expected. We'll be heading down to T.O. on Monday and after the operation on Tuesday, I'll try to get things back on schedule. How is Brian?"

"Eating Tums like breath candies. Ernie sends his love and hopes to see you in hell, and Tracy said she would quit the movie except her Robbie is such a sex machine."

"If you tell a soul that, Gwen, I'll have to kill you."

"Bring a gun when you come, Robbie; it's all over the office. See you Wednesday. And don't worry, okay?"

"Thanks, Gwen. Goodbye."

"Bye."

Robbie found her two girls playing blocks on the floor in the nursery.

"Everything okay?" Janet asked, reaching up to take Robbie's hand and tugging her down to sit beside her. It was written all over Robbie's face that something was wrong.

"Yeah, everything will be okay, just some unfinished business that needed immediate attention, that's all."

"Being here takes you away from important things. I'm so sorry."

Robbie gave Janet's hand a squeeze. "Right at the moment, there is nothing more important than you." Janet's sudden smile eased some of the pain in Robbie's soul.

Chapter 6

Once Reb was washed and changed, they were dressing to go to the Thanksgiving dinner at the Community Centre. "Robbie, are you sure you are all right with this?" Janet worried.

Robbie's head popped around the corner of the closet. "I'm fine with it. I was born famous. I don't remember a time in my life when there hasn't been a camera to smile at or someone who wanted to shake my hand. You might find it hard, though. It is a real loss of personal freedom and space. Wear your tan sweater with the navy trim, okay?"

"Oh, do you like that one?" Janet felt the warmth of the implied compliment spreading through her system.

"Yeah, it's okay. I'm just working out the costumes and staging here," Robbie muttered, pulling navy socks from a drawer.

"What? Robbie this is just a community dinner, for God's sakes."

Robbie stopped and turned serious eyes on Janet. "For a Williams, for anyone famous, it can never be just a community dinner. It is a performance. We are there, not to enjoy ourselves, but to make other people's evening more eventful. There will be record crowds tonight; you can count on it. We'll go a bit early so the first sitting sees us arrive, and we'll leave a bit late to say hello to the third sitting. If we are lucky, in between we'll have a good time."

Janet rebelled. "No! I don't want to be on display. I just want to have a community Thanksgiving dinner."

Robbie sighed. "Then I'll stay here."

"No." An eyebrow went up. It was Janet's turn to sigh. "I don't like sharing you," she grumbled.

Robbie smiled happily. "You're not. What I am is part of a very private world in which you belong. The community only sees the public face."

Janet stepped forward and kissed Robbie softly, "I...think you're something wonderful. So, what do we have to wear, oh famous director?"

"We'll all wear blue jeans for that down home look. You'll be in tan and navy. I'll wear my navy pea jacket and a tan rawhide to hold my hair back. Reb can wear that beige sweater with the navy bears on it. I'll carry Reb. We want to give the feel of family solidarity now that Billy is dead."

Janet grimaced. "Robbie, this is so calculating."

"First impressions are important. I've just become a big land owner in this community and people will want to check me out to see if I live up to my film image. Okay, you might be asked why the rest of the family is not here. Alexandria is in the south of France for her health, and Elizabeth is engaged in some very important research that could not be put off."

"Is that true? I'm not lying. These people are my friends and relatives."

"It's basically the truth. Alexandria is in the south of France catching the end of the season, and Elizabeth is always engaged in important research," Robbie muttered from inside a T-shirt. Her head popped through and she shook her hair back into place. "Just a few words of caution: never let Reb face the camera; don't indicate where you live to the press; and stay close to me."

"The first two I understand, but why do I have to stay close to you?"

"Because I think you're cute and I want to be near you." Robbie nuzzled Janet's ear and gave it a kiss, which made her laugh. "That's better." Robbie smiled. "Sorry about all this. You sure you want to be associated with me?"

The response was instaneous. "Very sure." And so the three Williamses headed out for their first official public function in Bartlett.

It was a circus. Along with the *Bartlett Gazette*, the press from several nearby communities showed up to take pictures and people leaving from the first sitting crowded around to get autographs. At first, Janet was embarrassed and awkward at the attention, but Robbie quietly drew her into the circle with light banter and silly jokes. Janet soon realized that it was a script that they repeated in a number of variations over and over again. Once comfortable with the routine, she actually competed with Robbie for who could be the most creative in saying the same noncommittal things in different ways.

Robbie's eyes caught hers and sparkled with amusement. Robbie was having fun, and to Janet's surprise, she found that she was too. Finally inside the hall, they lined up to be served their meals by the ladies of the auxiliary. Janet was careful to introduce Robbie to everyone and to her amazement, Robbie remembered every name and passing remark, and then made reference to them in her conversation.

"Hello, Mrs. Drouillard; it's a pleasure to meet you. Mrs. Butler was telling me that you make the best pumpkin pie this side of Toronto. I'll be sure to come back and get a piece. Hi, Ted. You're the brother of Dave back there on the ticket table, aren't you? I understand that you are Janet's third cousin on her mother's side." And so it went.

It was some time before they were safely ensconced at a table, surrounded by Janet's school staff. "Are you related to everyone in this damn town?" Robbie whispered into Janet's ear in frustration.

"Just about, except for the few outsiders who have moved in over the years. Most of us can trace our families back to the original logging pioneers. So over the last hundred odd years there has been considerable inter-marriage between the families."

Janet settled Reb into an old wooden highchair that had been provided. It was Robbie, however, who fed Reb the bowl of mashed potatoes, peas, and small bits of turkey that Mrs. Snoblen had made up especially for the young child.

Janet watched with pride, and thought back to when Robbie had first come into their lives. This was a performance, she realized, but she also knew that behind the show, Robbie had a real deep and loving bond with her baby daughter. *Where does the acting stop and the real person begin?* she wondered. *"The packaging and the person, are really all one," Robbie had told her.* She was starting to understand what the actor meant.

"Janet," came an overly dramatic voice. "Could I meet your sister-in-law?"

Janet looked up at a wall of a woman with a round, cheerful face and a short crop of grey hair. "Sure." She smiled. "Greta Corry, meet Robbie Williams. Robbie, this is our town librarian and president of the Bartlett dramatic society."

"Hi, nice to meet you." Robbie smiled mechanically.

"Oh, Ms. Williams, it is such a pleasure. I've been a fan of yours for years. I've followed your career intently and I want you to know I knew right from the beginning that you had star quality."

"Well, thanks, it's kind of you to say so," came the well-used response.

"I was reading on Net-Entertainment that your new movie has the Latin Bombshell, Tracy Travelli, in it. Is she everything the media makes her out to be?"

"Well, actually..." Robbie saw Janet's fork freeze half way to her mouth and a panic-stricken face turned in her direction. "She's really a lovely person. Giving. Warm. Ugh!" Robbie finished just as a shoe connected with her shin.

"Oh, I'm so glad to hear that. So often those of us involved in the Arts are seen, well, as not quite nice. It's so sad. Janet, you know, helps out with our yearly production. I do hope, however, that if you are around, you will give us the benefit of your vast experience."

An evil grin appeared on Robbie's face and she pre-emptively moved her foot before the frantic-looking Janet could connect with another blow. "Greta, I would be delighted to help out with this year's production in any way I can. My vast experience is always available to Janet...and her friends. What are we doing?"

"*The Tempest* by William Shakespeare."

"Really?" The grin got bigger. Janet covered her eyes with a hand. "Now there is a play that is perfect for Janet and me."

"Greta, isn't that your sister waving to you?" Janet interrupted in desperation.

"Is it? Oh, please excuse me, Ms. Williams. Now don't forget, we start rehearsals right after Christmas. It was wonderful meeting you in person."

"Bye, Greta."

Grabbing Robbie's arm, Janet leaned close to her ear. "What are you up to?"

Robbie played innocent. "Who, me?"

Janet bared her teeth in frustration. Robbie laughed gleefully. Reb laughed too and clapped her chubby baby hands with glee.

"Great. Gang up on me," Janet protested.

It was as they made their way slowly out of the Community Centre that Janet ran into Lucier of the *Bartlett Gazette*. Robbie had been detained several steps behind, signing autographs. "Mrs. Williams, we meet again. Let me express the paper's condolences once more on the death of your husband."

Janet stiffened. She didn't like this man. She quickly turned her daughter so that she looked back over her shoulder to where Robbie stood. Janet recited a variation of words that Robbie had used earlier. "Thank you. My husband and I were separated, as you know, but it is a sad tragedy that Rebecca will never know her father."

"Is there any truth to the rumour that you have terminal cancer and that Robbie Williams is here to take her brother's daughter?"

Janet felt like she had been hit in the gut. Before she could get any words out, Robbie was there beside her, her arm wrapped protectively around Janet's waist. "My sister-in-law will be having minor surgery next week to remove a lump. There is no cause for alarm and she plans to be back at work soon. I am here just helping out for a few weeks. We've always been a closely knit family."

Robbie propelled Janet forward and they escaped quickly to the relative safety of Robbie's truck and left as quickly as they could. "You all right?" Robbie asked, reaching over to rub Janet's hands as the smaller woman sat stiffly staring out the front window.

"The press is horrible," Janet choked.

"They can be. Most are fairly decent, but you get the Lucier types that use the freedom of the press as a means of bullying and intimidating others. You'll get used to it," she soothed philosophically.

"I don't want to," Janet snapped.

Robbie pulled to the side of the lane and switched off the engine, then turned to face Janet. "If I am going to be your...friend, it means that a certain amount of the limelight will fall on you. Also, whether you like it or not, Reb was born a Williams."

"No. I am not going to have my daughter grow up with that burden. She is going to be just another little girl growing up in an ordinary Canadian town."

Robbie sighed. "Janet, get real here. The kid's a multi-millionaire."

Janet's head snapped around in shock. "What?"

Robbie's eyes opened in surprise. "What? You didn't know? As the firstborn of her generation of the Williams clan, Rebecca inherits the remainder of my father's estate. I should think in the vicinity of five million dollars plus and, of course, the family estate near Unionville. Billy would have had charge of the money until Reb was twenty-one, but I presume that you will be taking over now." Into the shocked silence, she said, "Janet?"

"My God."

Robbie laughed bitterly as she started the truck again and pulled back onto the lane. "Nah, I don't think today's God has the power or the money that the old man had."

An over-excited Rebecca took some coaxing to get to bed that night. Finally, after the difficult child was washed, changed, and ready for bed, Robbie took over from a frazzled Janet. "You go get some work done and I'll get the rugrat to sleep."

Squeezing Robbie's arm in thanks, Janet went out to the quiet of the living room. So much had happened to turn her world upside down during the week, she was running on overload.

Robbie carried the squirming baby into Janet's bedroom and lay down with her on the bed. For a while she played peek-a-boo with her from behind a pillow, but when Reb's eyes started to blink with sleep, she curled up near the small bundle and sang softly to her until the little girl was fast asleep. Carefully, she carried the two-year-old back to the nursery and tucked her in.

Janet started when strong hands gently gasped her shoulders. She looked up into eyes as blue as a summer's sky. "Come here," she whispered and Robbie leaned down to dust Janet's soft, warm lips with gentle kisses. Desire, a rich liquid heat, flooded through them both.

Robbie slipped around the couch and lowered Janet down on the sofa cushions, her own body following.

"Oh, Robbie," came the gasp of need, husky and earnest. Robbie answered the call with all the passion that her soul could offer.

Robbie lay on her stomach with Janet's naked body sprawled across her back. *Mmm*, she thought, *this feels sooo good*. Lips brushed across her shoulder blade. "Robbie, time to get up for church," came a coaxing voice.

"We're queer and living in sin. The established church doesn't want us," Robbie protested in a voice husky with sleep.

Folding her arms across Robbie's back, Janet rested her chin on her hands so the she could see her lover's face. Sleep softened features beneath rich, dark hair tossed with lovemaking; it took Janet's breath away. The woman was simply gorgeous. "I try to separate the politics of church from the philosophy of the faith," Janet responded, leaning forward to place a kiss on Robbie's ear. "Besides, it is good for Reb to have a knowledge of the faith of her family. Then when she's older, she'll be able to make an intelligent decision about what she believes."

"This family member is a heathen who wants to spend Sunday morning ravishing Rebecca's mother's body." Robbie spun around, surprising Janet as she wrapped her in her arms.

Janet kissed Robbie long and tenderly. "It's important to me."

"They'll burn us at the stake."

"It's Thanksgiving, Robbie."

Gently brushing the hair from Janet's face, Robbie sighed. "Okay, but I'll probably be struck dead by lightning when I step in the door," she warned.

"Well, that will make a Thanksgiving service no one will ever forget." Janet laughed and Robbie retaliated by picking her up and carrying her into the bathroom to share a shower. Eventually, they only had enough time for a quick cup of coffee before they rushed off to church.

The church was small and made of round fieldstone in soft pinks and greys. The roof was cedar shingles, giving it the look of a chapel in some elfin kingdom of long ago. It was nestled in tall pines beside a fast flowing creek that tumbled over rocks to the main river below. Surrounded by the splendour of the autumn forests, the setting was beautiful.

Robbie had to admit that it was kind of nice. There was some good imagery that she could some day use in a film. Mentally, she filed away camera angles.

Other people arriving in their Sunday best said "hello" as Janet lifted Reb from the truck and they moved toward the church. Dave rang the church bell in the steeple with enthusiasm and his brother Ted handed out the bulletins and greeted each new arrival.

Inside, the church was simple and airy. Janet, holding on to Reb's hand, moved down close to the front and sat on one of the maple wood benches with Robbie beside her. The bright morning sun through the stained glass turned the dusty beams of light into a rainbow of colours that draped over the interior.

As the choir entered, the congregation stood and sang along, Robbie's beautiful, melodic voice adding a much-needed depth to the choir's. Robbie recognized Mrs. Snoblen and the librarian cum Shakespearian director, Greta Corry, in the choir loft. The minister followed in at the end of the first hymn, and everyone took their seat.

Raising his arms in a blessing, Reverend Billingsley smiled and prayed, "Dear Lord, bless us all on this fine Thanksgiving day as we come here to praise God's name..."

Reb, wearing a cute, cotton dress and sitting demurely between Janet and Robbie, suddenly beamed with joy and yelled out in a voice that could be heard all the way to hell and back, "Goddamn!" Then she giggled happily.

For a second, there was stunned silence in the church. Janet looked down at her daughter with eyes wide with shock and a face beet red with embarrassment.

Robbie slapped a hand over Reb's mouth and leaned down to whisper in the kid's ear, "Do me a favour here, Reb. Shut up."

"Well," the minister's voice broke into the silence as he smiled down from the pulpit at the offending child, "I can see with this new generation coming up, I've got good job security."

The congregation broke into gales of laughter and when it finally quieted down, the service went on without any further hitches.

Occasionally, Robbie would sneak a sideways glance at Janet on the other side of Reb, where she sat stiff and glowing with embarrassment. *Oh boy, I'm dead meat.*

After the service and much good-natured ribbing from Janet's neighbours and friends, the Williams family headed back to the cabin. There was a frosty silence in the truck cab. Reb chewed her fist with a worried expression and Robbie squirmed guiltily.

"Uhh, sorry about that."

Janet's knuckles were white around the steering wheel. "I asked you not to swear in front of Rebecca," she snapped.

"I didn't realize mini-humans absorbed words like sponges," Robbie protested. "Anyway, most people thought it was funny."

"I didn't. Reb will never live this down."

After a lengthy, uncomfortable silence, Robbie asked, "Are you still angry at Reb and me?"

"Yes."

"Forever?" came an insecure voice.

Despite herself, Janet snorted. "No, not forever, but for a damn long time."

"Don't swear in front of the kid," protested Robbie in feigned shock.

Janet laughed and swatted at Robbie, who caught the hand and wrapped her own around it, giving it an affectionate squeeze. "I am sorry it happened and I promise I'll be more careful in the future, okay?"

"Hmm, okay," Janet agreed, deciding that Robbie had squirmed enough. "You are like an olive."

"An olive? What — round, oily, and green?"

Janet sighed. "No. You take some getting used to, but you are addictive."

"I'll take that as a compliment." She turned around to look to the back where Rebecca was strapped in her baby seat. "Hey, Reb, we're out of the doghouse."

Reb squealed with delight and pounded her hands on the padded seat. The two women laughed with her, and the Sunday churchgoers headed home for a late brunch.

"Okay, Reb, here comes the helicopter. Rrrrrrrrr," Robbie narrated as she flew the last spoonful of blackberry pancake into Rebecca's mouth. Janet looked on with interest. Reb was being spoiled rotten by her aunt, who seemed to have her own private level of communication with her niece. Several times during the week, she had come on Robbie and Reb sitting quietly somewhere with Reb's little baby face focused and intent on whatever it was Robbie was telling her. This morning, while Janet had prepared brunch, it had been about birds. Robbie had taken Reb outside to see the piliated woodpecker that had been foraging in a nearby tree.

"Have I mentioned yet today that I think you are wonderful?" Janet asked as she came over and rubbed a hand across Robbie's shoulders before taking away the empty plates from their brunch.

Soft, yearning eyes followed the retreating figure. "I'm not, but I'm awful glad you think so. I know I have found something very special in your...friendship. Here let me do the dishes while you see to getting the Rebel changed."

Janet cheerily agreed and a short time later the three of them were setting out in the canoe down Long Lake. The air was crisp and clear, and the forest a blaze of deep oak red, maple orange, and beech yellow. Dark evergreens added contrast and the bright robin's-egg sky was mirrored in the still, crystal water of the lake.

Holding a sleeping Reb, Robbie breathed in deeply. "This is wonderful. One of my reasons for buying the land was to build a studio on the old lumberyard site. I'd like to get away from the pollution and noise of the city now and again, and a northern studio would allow that. I thought I'd start fairly small and see how it goes, but I was thinking of making it a kind of training centre for people who want to learn the film trade while working on some of my smaller film productions."

"Is that where Doug and Tracy will fit in?" asked Janet, gently reminding Robbie that she had some responsibilities to the Higgins family.

"Yeah, somewhere. All the pieces of the puzzle aren't there yet, but I've got this gut feeling that I've got hold of the right end of the stick."

Janet smiled and tossed her hair back as she paddled them smoothly through the water. "Do you always do business in such an unorthodox way?"

"I don't do business at all." Robbie pulled a face. "I create, and then I have an army of lackeys that deal with the fall-out."

Janet laughed. "Just how many little MBAs have sacrificed their lives to your empire building?"

"There are so many auxiliary businesses...it's hard to say." Robbie shrugged. "All totaled, maybe five thousand people work for me, directly or indirectly."

"Five thousand," Janet gasped in shock.

"Mmmhmm. You're sleeping with a rich, old bitch." Robbie smiled leisurely.

Eyes sparkling with merriment, Janet got a sassy look. "It is not your money I'm after."

Robbie suddenly straightened up and pointed, sending the canoe swaying dangerously from side to side. "What's that up there?" Janet placed her paddle broadside to the water and steadied the canoe. "It's the old lodge. It must be over a hundred years old. My great grandfather built it, but my grandfather never lived there and neither did my father. It was beautiful at one time, I'm told, but it's fallen into ruin."

Robbie could feel that visceral reaction that told her one of the last pieces of the picture was falling into place. "Pull in," she ordered.

Janet raised an eyebrow at Robbie's abrupt tone, but expertly J-stroked the canoe around to come alongside a small sandy beach. Robbie clambered out with a startled Reb tucked under her arm. She took a step forward, then remembered to turn back to hold the canoe while Janet got out and beached the craft.

Janet watched her lover with interest. It was clear that Robbie's thoughts had fixated on the old lodge to the exclusion of everything else. It was only with difficulty that Robbie waited for Janet to secure the canoe before she handed Reb over and took off with long strides toward the weather worn building. "Reb," Janet grimaced in annoyance, "I think we are seeing the side of Robbie that gives her a reputation as a focused maniac. We've been replaced by some old, moldy logs and a half baked idea she has cooking in the back of her mind."

A figure appeared on the old veranda. "Hey, Janet, hurry up. You gotta see this place, it's great."

How in hell did she get in? Janet wondered as she headed up to the lodge. The answer was obvious. The heavy lock had been pried free of the door with a scrap piece of metal. *She's broken in,* she thought, and then realized that it didn't matter since Robbie was the new owner.

The old lodge was dark, damp, and dirty. Forest animals had entered through rotting holes in the roof and dry leaves rustled in corners. The huge stone fireplace towered above them and massive logs formed the walls. Robbie was covered in dirt and cobwebs. "Hey!" she shouted with excitement, spreading her arms wide, "look what I bought."

Janet shook her head and laughed despite herself. Robbie's enthusiasm was contagious. Robbie scrambled over debris and scooped Reb from Janet's arms.

"Come and look at this, all the doors are carved. Check out the size of these logs. Mother Nature is too sick these days to grow anything this big. Haven't you ever been in here?"

"No, the land was sold to Higgins years ago. I've walked around the place on many occasions but it was locked up."

"You shoulda broken a window," Robbie muttered, looking around with interest, already making a list of things that needed to be done.

"Robbie, it was private property."

"It was deserted. It's not as if anyone was living in it."

Now that Janet had time to look around, she could see why Robbie was excited. It would take a lot of work and money to restore the place but the underlying structure seemed strong and the wood, stone, and detailing were beautiful. "What are you going to do with it, Robbie?" she asked, hoping the plan did not involve building some executive resort for burned out MBAs racing personal water craft around the lake.

I'm going to make it a home, marry you, and live happily ever after, was the fantasy that was going through Robbie's head. Instead she said, "I'm going to restore it and use it as a summer cottage. We can be neighbours as well as friends."

Janet smiled happily. "I'd really like that. No motorboats though, okay? I'll teach you to paddle a canoe."

Robbie laughed. "Okay. Come on, let's look around some more." They spent a delightful morning exploring each room and finding, in amongst the years of decay, some interesting pieces. One was an old oil lamp blackened with age and missing its flame hood. Yet the metal was sound and a delicate pattern was etched on its surface. Robbie presented the dirty antique to Janet. "To the light of my life," she said with a deep bow and then, seeing that Reb was busy chasing a chipmunk, she leaned forward and kissed Janet lightly.

Janet smiled warmly and tears filled her eyes. "Thank you, Robbie. I'm going to fix it up. I wonder if it belonged to my great, great grandmother. This room looks as if it might have been the master bedroom."

"Yeah, it does." The two women stood still, suddenly aware of the life that had once filled the house with laughter and joy. It had been a happy home. Robbie could feel that somehow, and she meant to make it a happy home again.

"You ready to head home for a late lunch, love?" asked Janet.

Robbie started out of her daydream, thinking for a minute that she *was* home. "Yeah," she responded tardily. "Let's go."

Three very dirty humans climbed back into the canoe and glided back to the east end of the lake where Janet's small cabin nestled in its grove of tall pines.

Janet sat at the large teacher's desk, the old lamp resting on a section of newspaper. With considerable elbow grease and the contents of a can of Brasso, she was slowly removing the tarnish from the metal. A delicate Celtic pattern, engraved in a broad band, was starting to reveal itself around the ball of the oil lamp. The brass was heavy and was in remarkably good condition.

Low muttered curses occasionally drifted out from the kitchen. Robbie, to Janet's surprise, had insisted on cooking dinner. *Fortunately,* Janet sighed, *Reb is down for her afternoon nap. She doesn't need to expand that particular vocabulary.*

Robbie struggled on, although the cooking thing was a lot harder than she had anticipated. It was important, though. It was the modern day equivalent of dragging home the mastodon and roasting it on the spit for one's true love. That morning, Robbie had seriously explained to her co-conspirator, Reb, that the dinner was now one of celebration rather than seduction, seeing as how Reb's mother had already had her way with Robbie the day before. She did manage to keep it in terms that a two year old would either understand in innocence or not understand at all.

"How's dinner going?" Janet asked, leaning over the stone counter and interrupting Robbie's thoughts.

"Fine, no problems," Robbie lied with a confident grin, bending over to kiss Janet. The light kiss became more earnest and both women were short of breath when it ended.

"Uhh, I'd better go get packed."

"Hmm. How is the lamp coming along?"

"It's beautiful. But it needs a lot more polishing yet. Hmm, I'd better go, you're a very bad influence," Janet gasped, reluctantly pulling away from the kisses that Robbie was tracing along her neck.

Watching Janet disappear down the hall, Robbie sighed. *Having you isn't enough, Janet. I want more. Somehow, I've got to make you love me as much as I love you.* A cold splash of reality broke through the wall of fantasy that Robbie had been building all day and filled her heart with sorrow. It had never mattered before. The things that she had done were heavy burdens that she had stoically carried alone. But if she got seriously involved with Janet, she would be exposing the woman she loved to the danger of exposure, too. Even if Janet didn't marry her, she would still be associated with the notorious Robbie Williams. That wasn't fair. That burden was hers alone, and yet she didn't think she could go on living without Janet and Reb in her life.

What if I lose Janet to the cancer? An unbearable pain sliced through her soul. *No. Don't let those thoughts even enter your head, Williams. Janet will beat the odds. She has to.*

Janet methodically packed the things that she and Reb would need for a week away from home. *Where does Robbie live?* she wondered. She had mentioned a family estate in Unionville. Maybe she lived there. But surely, that would be Alexandria's home. She couldn't imagine Robbie living with her mother, no matter how big the house.

Really, she knew very little about the powerful woman who now shared her bed. Not so long ago, she hadn't even known Robbie. Now she was going to be staying at her home, and she'd given her body, soul, and even her daughter into Robbie's capable care. *Am I being a fool? If it was someone else's life, I'd be shocked and worried about the quick turn of events. But it's Robbie, and somehow deep inside I know that no matter what she has done or will do, my soul belongs with her.*

Blinking back tears, Janet swallowed hard. *Oh, Robbie...I love you so much and I can never tell you that. I'm just another lover in your life, a passing fling with the girl next door. How am I ever going to go on when you leave me?*

The cute baby sounds of Reb waking up ended Janet's desolate thoughts. "Hey, special one, you ready to get up?"

"Up, Mommy, peas. Go potty."

"Very good, Rebecca. Okay, here we go."

Dinner was wonderful, though the ham was overcooked, the mashed potatoes runny, and the vegetables mushy. Dessert was the blueberries they had picked on top of vanilla ice cream, and not all the stems and leaves had been picked clean. But Robbie had prepared it for her, and Janet had a feeling, by the look of the kitchen, that was not something that Robbie normally did. That made the whole thing very special.

After dinner, they wrapped up warmly and went for a walk down the path. Reb rode on Robbie's shoulders and Robbie and Janet walked hand in hand. Their talk was of childhood memories and fun incidents that had happened to them as they slowly built a framework of common knowledge around their relationship.

To Janet, Robbie's early life seemed bleak. She had been born five years before her sister and brother, while her mother was still at the height of her career. Robbie had been raised by a series of nannies and then, at the age of eight, sent to boarding school. Elizabeth and Billy had been born after the famous ballerina had retired and so they had been raised at home with domestic support. Robbie's history of those years was sketchy and it was clear to Janet that she was not comfortable talking about her family, although she did tell some amusing stories about her days at boarding school.

Janet giggled. "Your science fair project was making the perfect beer?"

"Yeah. I got all the ingredients and set up secretly in the dormitory basement. I figured with a little moonshine business I could make a mint off the kids. I bottled the stuff in old pop bottles, but the fermentation continued and the gas built up until the corks shot out and beer bubbled out like mini-volcanoes. The whole dorm stank of sour beer for weeks."

"You, Robbie Williams, have always been a bad apple."

"I thought I was an olive."

"You're my olive. I'm not sharing."

Robbie stopped and looked down at Janet, searching her eyes for the truth.

The smaller woman blushed and stammered, "I'm sorry. I shouldn't have said that. We're just friends and I have no claim over you."

"Oh, yeah." Robbie resumed walking. "Well, it's all right because I don't want to share your...friendship, either."

Janet skipped a step to catch up. "You don't?"

"No."

"Oh."

After that they walked in silence, stopping to watch two young deer browsing on cedar branches near the water's edge, then heading back to the cabin in the cool twilight.

Their skin tingling from the cold of the late fall day, they sat by the fire that Janet had built and sipped Glenfiddich single malt scotch whisky from brandy snifters. Reb curled up on the couch between them and played with a stuffed purple dragon until she went to sleep. Time passed in comfortable silence as they watched the flames die down.

Robbie sighed and shifted forward, placing the empty glass on the sled table and balancing her elbows on her knees. Janet waited, recognizing the position as one Robbie took when she was trying to explain something very important to her.

Reaching down, Robbie picked up the stuffed toy that had fallen to the braided rug. "Uhh, you remember, I was telling you that I'd done things, terrible things, Janet, that I wouldn't...can't burden anyone with."

"Yes, I remember," Janet said quietly.

"I've always lived my life at a pretty casual level, uhh, avoiding commitments."

Janet felt the goose bumps rising on her skin despite the warm fire and alcohol. *Oh, Robbie, please don't leave me now*, she pleaded silently.

"There is something I need to tell you, Janet. It's important to me that you know how I feel. I can't offer you anything, I have no right, but..." Afraid to look at Janet, Robbie got up and paced nervously to the window, looking out into the dark night. "I love you."

"What?"

The voice from the other side of the room sounded startled and Robbie looked down at her feet miserably. "I love you," she repeated quietly. "I just needed you to know that it was more than friendship with me because—" Suddenly, Janet was there in her arms.

"I love you, too."

Immeasurable relief swept through Robbie, followed by a tidal wave of joy. "Ohh, God! I can't begin to tell you how much I need you in my life," Robbie groaned, raining kisses on Janet's face that was wet with tears of joy.

"Hold me, Robbie!"

Robbie lightly traced a fingertip along Janet's collarbone and then around the curve of a heavy breast.

"Mmm, I love the feel of you," she whispered, leaning over to kiss lips swollen with lovemaking. Arms wrapped around Robbie's neck and pulled her down.

"Tell me again," Janet murmured.

"I love you."

"I don't think I'll ever get tired of hearing you say that. It's something special I feel for you, Robbie. It's more than just love... I...I...only feel whole when I'm with you. I love you so much."

Robbie settled her hips between Janet's legs and kissed her lover's abdomen, smiling as she felt the muscles contract in excitement. "Of all the successes I have had in life, winning your love is the only one that leaves me in awe," Robbie whispered before she lowered her head to do things to her lover that were the eternal blend of instinct, art, and soul.

Chapter 7

The helicopter hovered over the skyline of Toronto, slowly descending to land squarely on the white H in the center of the metal pad. Robbie held Janet's hand, unconsciously rubbing a nervous thumb over her lover's wrist. They waited for the blades to stop and then Robbie opened the glass door and lifted first Reb and then Janet to the ground. The view from the penthouse roof garden was breathtaking. To the north, the entire city of Toronto spread out before them in a huge curve to the east and west. Famous landmarks such as the CN Tower, Ontario Place, and the Rogers Centre stood out amongst the clutter of big city dwellings. To the south, Lake Ontario sparkled in the sun, so vast that the United States on the opposite shore could not be seen.

Robbie led Janet and Reb to the French doors that gave access to her domicile. She was nervous, realizing that her penthouse, however luxurious, was not the warm home that Janet's simple cabin was. "Well, uh, this is our city home," Robbie said, allowing Janet and Reb to go first so that she could watch their reaction.

Walking to the centre of the morning room, Janet slowly turned around. The place was simply magnificent. It looked like it had fallen out of the pages of *Architectural Digest*. Reb was less in awe. She climbed up on the calfskin leather couch and squealed happily as she ran her hands over the cool, soft surface.

Robbie met Janet's eyes. "It needs to look more lived in," she conceded.

"I'm terrified that Reb will damage something. Reb, get your shoes off the couch," Janet called, hurrying over to remove Reb shoes.

Robbie intercepted her by grabbing her around the waist. She fell back on the couch with Janet to one side of her and Reb to the other. "Let's not worry about it. Let's just live in it as...as a family," Robbie suggested shyly.

Janet looked into the wishful, blue eyes and nodded, snuggling into the arm that wrapped around her. Reb crawled up on Robbie's lap. "Obbie, I go potty."

Janet laughed. "Kid," Robbie growled playfully, "we gotta work on your timing."

Robbie's e-mails to Gwen had included buying the necessary equipment for a two year old's nursery. Reb had been provided with the best of everything. As they unpacked and put things away, Janet shook her head at the extravagance. "Robbie, I can't let you do this. You've spent a fortune on us."

Placing her strong hands on Janet's shoulders, Robbie leaned down to nibble on an inviting ear. "You and Reb are as close as I will ever have to a family. I want my apartment to be a comfortable second home for you, just as you made me welcome at the cabin."

"That's different."

"No, it isn't," Robbie protested.

Robbie's "apartment" was the entire top floor of the Harbour Front Condominiums. Landscaped garden with a private helicopter pad led into a long morning room finished in cream Italian leather, with tables of rough and polished marble. The walls had been rag rolled to look like parchment.

The dining room held an Edwardian table that could easily seat twenty, and the walls were finished in Irish linen. The matching china cabinet contained a full set of Royal Crown Derby. The kitchen was by Smallbone, and each of the four bedrooms, one now a nursery, were interrelated in a varying theme of colour and patterns in rich, vibrant hues, each with its own en suite bathroom.

The apartment also contained a pantry, media room, gym, and library. It was the library that left Janet totally speechless. Located at the centre of the complex, it rose two stories up and was finished in oak. In beauty and content, it rivaled any of the private libraries of Europe.

And then there were the paintings. Works by Ron Bolt, Mary and Christopher Pratt, Colville, Danby, Moresseau, Mishibinjima and older works by the Group of Seven. It was an amazing collection of Canadian art. Janet thought about her only numbered print over the fireplace by Daphane Ojig and shook her head in wonder. She had found the original of her print in Robbie's bedroom.

Now, late in the evening, they sat together in the rooftop garden watching the sun set and spread its liquid gold across the deep blues of Lake Ontario. Janet got up and looked around. "Robbie, all this, I mean, this is not a world that I belong in."

Robbie's gut contracted.

"When I asked you to raise Reb, I didn't know well, about all this." Janet waved her hand about.

Robbie felt her world crumbling. *Say something*, Robbie ordered herself, but the words just wouldn't come. Finally, she managed, "Don't leave me."

Turning in surprise, Janet saw Robbie pale with shock and shaking with emotion. "Robbie, love, no, shhh, it's okay. I just didn't want you to think that Reb and I were a couple of gold diggers."

Relief swamped Robbie, sweeping away her fear. "It's hard for me to trust. I...I...I'm not the sort of person people love. You and Reb mean the world to me," Robbie got out with difficulty.

"Oh, Robbie, you mean the world to us as well. We love you. Somehow, we'll find a way to make all this work. And if...if anything happens to me, Reb will always be there for you."

"Nothing is going to happen to you," Robbie growled roughly. "I won't let it."

Janet watched the array of emotions crossing her lover's face. In many ways, facing a battle with cancer was going to be harder for Robbie than for her. "Robbie, come and sit down, okay?" Robbie let herself be led back to the garden seat and the two of them sat down, Janet cuddling deep into Robbie's side. "The odds are not good. I might die, Robbie. You have to accept that as a possible outcome."

"No."

"Shhh," Janet soothed. "We'll both fight very hard. I've got everything to live for, but Fate plays by its own rules. I need you to be able to carry on and make a happy life for Reb. I'm counting on you."

Robbie nodded, her eyes filled with tears and her throat working to swallow down the emotion as she wrapped Janet close to her. They stayed like that until the sky darkened and the city of Toronto blazed with a million lights.

The hospital administration, realizing that someone as famous as Robbie Williams could not sit in the public waiting room without causing a small riot, had allowed her to sit in one of the counselling rooms while Janet had her surgery. Looking out the grimy hospital window for what seemed like the fiftieth time, Robbie sighed and then paced around the small room again.

Janet had been so brave that morning, keeping up a cheerful front for Reb. Gwen arrived to baby sit while Robbie took Janet to the hospital. "Robbie," Janet had asked shyly as she filled in the data forms and waivers, "is it okay if I put your name down as next of kin?"

Robbie had rubbed her fingers over Janet's cold hand. "I wouldn't want it any other way."

Once through Admitting, Janet was only in her private room a short while before the orderlies came to take her down to surgery. That had been almost three hours ago. Robbie bit her lip and tried to control the growing dread and panic that was eating at her.

"Ms. Williams?"

Robbie jumped and turned to see the doctor standing at the door in his surgical scrubs. "Yes."

"Your sister-in-law has come through the surgery very well. We had to do some extensive surgery. It involved a radical mastectomy of the right breast and the removal of a number of lymph nodes, just to be on the safe side, but we are fairly confident that we were able to remove all of the tumour."

Robbie remained outwardly calm while inside her stomach churned at the news.

"She will need weeks of therapy and, of course, extensive radiation treatment, but we feel that having removed the tumour intact we can offer some hope of a successful recovery."

Crumpling to a chair, Robbie stared at the green wall.

"Ms. Williams?"

Robbie looked up. "Is she awake? Does she know?"

"Yes, she is out of recovery and I talked to her before I came down to you."

"Can I see her?"

"Yes. You'll find her a little dopey yet. Don't stay too long; she needs to sleep. If you come back this evening you'll find her more alert."

Robbie nodded dumbly and got to her feet. "Thank you, Doctor."

The doctor nodded and left with relief.

Janet looked so small and vulnerable as she slept inside the aluminum frame of the hospital bed. "Janet? Hey, love," Robbie whispered.

Sleepy eyes tried to focus on the tall figure leaning over the bed. "Hi." Even the single word was slurred.

Bending over the bar, Robbie kissed Janet's forehead tenderly. "Hey, the doctor said they got it all. That's good, huh?"

"They took my breast," Janet mumbled miserably.

Robbie reached down and took Janet's hand. "Anything, just as long as it helps you survive this, okay, Janet? I'm here for you, always."

Tears filled Janet's eyes and rolled down to the starched sheets unchecked. Robbie reached out and wiped them away with a finger. "You sleep, now. I'm going to pick up Reb and we'll be back later to visit, okay?"

Janet nodded tiredly and closed her eyes. For a while, Robbie just sat there trying to get all the emotion in check. Then she squared her shoulders and got on with it.

As her private elevator opened into the foyer, the sound of Reb bawling her eyes out reached Robbie.

Gwen came out holding the two year old who was stiff with a major tantrum. "There is no doubt that this child is a Williams," sighed the secretary, handing the angry child over to Robbie.

Robbie held the child at arm's length and just looked at her. Gradually, the cries subsided and Reb hung there looking back at Robbie with big, watery blue eyes. Robbie smiled and lifted the two year old over her head.

"Obbie's bird," laughed Reb.

Gwen leaned on the doorframe, a look of surprise on her face. "That's an unusual technique you've got there, Robbie, but it seems to work on the little hellion."

Tucking Reb into her arm, Robbie smiled. "She's cute, isn't she? Smart, too."

Gwen's eyes opened in surprise. "She's a Williams alright. How is Janet?"

Robbie's face clouded. "They think they got all of the tumour but it involved Janet having a mastectomy. I think she's worried that it will make a difference in our relationship."

Gwen's mouth opened but nothing came out for a second. "Relationship? Janet? Robbie, you're sleeping with Tracy Travelli."

A blush climbed up Robbie's neck as she stalled for time, lowering Reb to the ground. Reb stuck her thumb in her mouth and wrapped the other arm around Robbie's pant leg, holding on tight.

"I'm in love," Robbie admitted quietly. "I'm seriously involved with Janet. I...it just sort of happened."

Stepping forward, Gwen gave Robbie a quick hug, surprising her boss. "I'm happy for you, Robbie. You've needed someone in your life. You do realize, though, that when she finds out, Tracy will kill you and deep six the movie."

Robbie grimaced. "I really haven't had time to think about it. I'll have Tracy in for a talk on Tuesday."

Gwen rolled her eyes. "Actors," she snorted good-naturedly, heading for the door.

At Toronto University, Robbie turned down a long hall lined with scruffy old oak doors. Entering one, she passed through an outer office and on to the next where a woman leaned on her desk in deep concentration. Behind large glasses, grey-blue eyes blinked in surprise. "What is that?"

"It's an immature female of the *Homo sapiens* species," Robbie responded, flopping into a chair. "Her name's Reb and she'll be three next August."

"Billy's child," Robbie's sister concluded. A look of horror crossed her face. "Oh, Robbie, you didn't steal it, did you?"

"No." Robbie laughed. "She was given to me."

Elizabeth removed her glasses and chewed thoughtfully on one of the bows. "I don't understand."

Robbie sighed and leaned forward, placing her elbows on her knees. Looking up, she saw Reb reaching up toward a grouping of shiny test tubes sitting in a metal rack on a side counter. "No, Reb, don't touch," she said firmly, "You never know, one might be a relative." The child turned and looked at Robbie to see if there was any chance of a change of attitude. Robbie raised an eyebrow. Reb fell on her bum and became absorbed with her shoelace.

Robbie smiled and then frowned. "I'm in love," she told the floor. Silence greeted the admission and Robbie looked up to see Elizabeth staring at her in disbelief.

"This is not good, Robbie," she finally managed to articulate.

"Why?" snapped the actor, rising to her feet in agitation.

"I am presuming that this is a gay relationship and that could have a profound effect on your career if you choose to go public. I am also assuming it is with our late brother's wife and that, in turn, will raise some eyebrows. Lastly," Elizabeth swallowed and continued softly, "there are other issues in...the past. Does she know about—"

"Of course not."

"I don't know very much about love, but I understand that truth is one of the elements of a good relationship."

"I told her that I've done things in the past that she would find difficult to forgive. She loves me anyway."

"An abstract concept is not as offensive as a cold fact, Robbie. What about Billy?"

"He must have found out. Billy made a deal with her to have a child by artificial fertilization. I think he wanted money. I've got my lawyers auditing the estate. You know Billy and money..."

Elizabeth mulled that over with some intensity while Robbie showed Reb a stuffed baby crocodile that Elizabeth had on one of her shelves. "I do not think this relationship is wise, Robbie, but you are my sister and I owe you so much. You will, of course, have my support."

Robbie's shoulders slumped in relief and she turned and smiled at her sister. "Thank you, Beth. That means a lot. You're the only real family I've got." To her surprise, tears overflowed her eyes and she dropped into the chair and grabbed a tissue from the box on Elizabeth's desk.

Elizabeth had only ever seen her sister cry once before, so this outburst shocked her. She leapt up and came around to kneel at her sister's side. "Robbie, what's the matter?"

Robbie wiped her eyes and got herself under control. "I'm sorry. I just left Janet at the hospital. She just underwent surgery for breast cancer. It's serious, and I don't know how I'll cope if anything happens to her."

"Obbie?" came a little voice from the other side of Robbie's chair. Robbie forced a smile and picked the little girl up, swinging her over her head. "Obbie's bird," the little child giggled gleefully.

"That's right, Reb, Obbie's bird. Hey, I'm forgetting my manners. Reb, this is your Aunt Bethy."

"Hi, An Bethy," the two year old responded politely.

"Hi, Reb. Would you like a chocolate?"

The child smiled. "Peas."

"Still addicted to chocolate, huh?" Robbie laughed, trying to get things back on an even keel after her unusual loss of control.

Elizabeth tried to raise an eyebrow, with marginal success. "I need the magnesium," she justified, holding the box of chocolates out to the child.

Robbie snorted. "You need the sugar fix." Both sisters laughed and Reb used the opportunity to snitch a second chocolate.

Robbie and Reb left a short time later. Elizabeth had promised to have dinner at the apartment to get to know Janet as soon as she was up to visitors. Robbie felt good about that. She wanted to build some sort of life with Janet, even if it did have to have limitations because of her past.

Janet opened her eyes to the happy squeal of "Mommy!" There stood Reb, covered with chocolate and holding a teddy bear about the same size as herself. Behind her stood Robbie, burdened down with flowers and packages of all sorts.

"Hi, love." Robbie smiled.

"Hi, Reb, hi, Obbie." Janet giggled.

Robbie raised an eyebrow at the pet name and sauntered over to dump the contents of her arms at the foot of the bed and then, leaning over, kissed Janet softly. Reaching down, Robbie swung Reb up to Janet's good side to get a hug and kiss from mom, too.

Tears suddenly ran down Janet's face as she hugged her daughter close. "I promised myself I wasn't going to do this," Janet sniffed, trying to brush her tears away on her shoulder.

"It's okay," Robbie reassured, reaching over to touch the tear soaked material.

Janet pulled away, sobbing in anger. "No, it's not. Nothing is. Look at me."

Robbie sat on the side of the bed and scooped a confused Reb up into her arms. "Janet, there is nothing we can't handle. I believe in you."

Janet made eye contact with Robbie and a world of messages went back and forth until Robbie reached out and laced her fingers with Janet's. "The three of us, together, happy, and very much in love," Robbie whispered, and the smile that appeared on Janet's face reached her eyes and sparkled there.

Robbie watched the first real snow of the season drift down onto the black waters of Long Lake. She was tired. Bone tired. The last few months had been hell: a non-stop merry-go-round of hospital visits for radiation treatment, working on the new scenes for the film, editing, dealing with the traumatic issues of radiation sickness, and flying back and forth in that damn helicopter to catch time with Janet and Reb.

The worst was over now, but she wasn't sure her relationship with Janet had survived intact. *Yeah, what relationship?*

After the surgery, Janet would no longer let Robbie near her. They kissed and even hugged at times but they slept in separate beds. At first, it was because Janet needed time to recover from the surgery. "You understand, Robbie, I'm really tender." Then it was, "I'm too sick and weak, please don't," or else, "the radiation levels in my body liquids are too high." When Janet started to lose her hair, Robbie was banned from the bedroom altogether. "I don't want you to see me like this."

Robbie placed her forehead against the cold windowpane. She felt guilty for feeling resentful. After all, Janet had gone through hell and had never complained. If she needed space, well, that was understandable. But there was a growing worry in Robbie that the love they had shared so briefly was never going to be the same again.

She hadn't seen Janet naked since before the surgery and it was beginning to look like she was never going to. Nor had she seen Janet without the series of scarves and hats that she had bought from the store that specialized in that sort of thing. Robbie sighed. *I gotta be patient. Janet is too special a part of my life to give up on.* Yet tonight when she had arrived, she found that even Reb had been sent away. Reb had been the only bright spot in her visits recently, and now even she wasn't there.

The bleep of Robbie's phone drew her out of her moody thoughts. "Robbie."

"Robbie," Gwen's voice was quiet, "there's been a serious accident in London, an explosion in the school lab. Ryan's in a coma. There is a jet helicopter on its way for you."

Robbie sank to a chair, her knees too weak to support her as a shock wave of fear ran through her. "Robbie?"

"How bad is it?"

"I don't know, Robbie. Bad. The 'copter will take you straight to the hospital. It should be there in about half an hour."

"Thanks, Gwen."

"Keep me posted, Robbie."

"I will." Robbie snapped the phone shut, her entire world crumbling around her.

In the bedroom, Janet fussed with her short hair. It was still very short, a sandy fuzz, really. *Will Robbie hate it? Lots of women cut their hair short these days.* Janet bit her lip. *You can't put this off any longer.* She had discussed it at length with her counsellor — either Robbie was going to be able to handle the fact that Janet had only one breast, or she was going to be really turned off by it.

It wasn't fair to keep Robbie away. She'd been such a rock. She'd been patient and kind, and a second mom to Rebecca. Janet could see the hurt in Robbie's eyes each time she gently pushed her away. It was so hard. Robbie was beautiful, vibrant...and whole. She worked with people like Tracy Travelli. There were even hints in the gossip columns that Robbie and Travelli might be more than friends. Why would she want to stay with Janet now?

But tonight was going to be different. She had wonderful news to start with; the doctor had told her that there was every indication that they had gotten all the cancer. She'd made Robbie's favourite meal and she'd asked Mrs. Chen to baby sit so that they could have a special night together. She started out to the living room, then at the last minute put on the Blue Jays baseball cap that Robbie had brought her. Once they had talked a bit, when some of the tension that had developed between them had lessened, then she'd be ready.

"Hi, what are you looking at?" Janet asked, coming up beside Robbie as she stared out at the gathering night.

"I'm waiting for the helicopter. I have to leave," Robbie said tersely.

"What? You only just got here," Janet exclaimed, sounding more annoyed than she'd intended.

Robbie swung around, eyes flashing and face tense with stress. "So what! You don't give a damn whether you see me or not."

"That's not true. Look, Robbie, I don't need—"

Frustration and fear made a volatile mixture; it boiled over. "Yeah, well, I've got some needs, too."

Janet felt her own temper snap. "I thought your needs were being well taken care of by Tracy Travelli, or didn't you think I'd heard the rumours?" the smaller woman countered spitefully.

Paling, Robbie started to speak and then stopped as the bug-shaped shadow appeared over the trees, bright yellow eyes searching for a landing spot. Without a word, Robbie pushed past Janet and slammed out of the house to catch her lift to London, a city west of Toronto.

Janet stood in shock at the window and watched her go. *My God, the rumour was true. Robbie is having an affair with her leading lady.* She turned and looked around the room, hearing in her memory the happy banter of the good times they had enjoyed together there. Now there was only the *tick, tick* of the mantel clock to break the silence. On weak legs, she walked over and sank into a chair. It was over, just like that. Robbie had left her.

It had been almost three weeks. Some days, the young teenager would move or her eyelids would flutter, but Robbie knew now not to get up false hope when that happened. They were, as the doctor explained, spontaneous involuntary movements.

Ryan had been mixing some sort of rocket fuel together without the knowledge or consent of the school, and the accidental explosion had thrown the girl through a wall. The back of her skull had been cracked and there was considerable swelling of the brain. Tests indicated no brain damage, but Ryan was not coming out of the coma.

Every day, Robbie worked with her, exposing her to music, reading to her, having her smell different odours, or rubbing different textures against her finger tips; anything she could think of to stimulate Ryan's brain and unlock her consciousness. Nothing happened.

Robbie lifted the small hand. She looked at Ryan's long fingers, so like her own. They were strong, capable hands for a little girl. "I guess you've had to do it on your own, haven't you, kid? I was never there for you. You see, I'm your mother. I was just, eighteen when I had you. I was pretty confused at the time, wild, ya know. I never meant to hurt you, Ryan. I thought I was protecting you from the stigma of who I was. I love you, you see, and I..." Robbie stammered to a halt, realizing that she'd been talking out loud like she sometimes did with Reb.

She wished Reb and Janet were with her. She missed them; more than that, she needed them. She wished she hadn't yelled those things at Janet, especially when there had been no time to take them back. Robbie blinked back tears as she looked at the still form of her daughter. She placed her head down on their joined hands and tried to think of something that she had not yet tried to help her daughter.

"Water," whispered a faint, gravely voice.

Robbie scrambled to her feet and ran to get a nurse.

It was late, and the weather was nasty. Robbie drove like a maniac through the night, her mind trying to make sense of the conflicting emotions inside her. All she knew for sure was that she hurt like hell inside and needed to be with Janet. How long had it been since she had walked out? Three weeks, maybe? She'd just left Janet to cope on her own. *Damn it all to hell! What was I thinking?*

The windshield wipers struggled to clear the thick, wet snow. Icy ridges were forming on each side of the windshield of the rented car, narrowing Robbie's view with each sweep of the blades. Just another kilometre and she should see Janet's mailbox at the end of her lane. Suddenly, the lights caught the shape of something orange and huge on the road in front of her. Robbie slammed on the brakes, sending the car's light back end spinning around so that the wheels caught on the gravel shoulder. The car slid off the road and broadsided the hard packed snowbank left by the township plough, which brought it to an abrupt stop.

Janet stood at the window though there was really nothing to see. The outside lamp illuminated a near white out. It was cold, too, the wind howling through the trees. *A true Canadian snowstorm.* Janet sighed. Fortunately, it was a weekend, so classes would not be too badly disrupted by the snow. Still, she would need to get in touch with the duty teachers and make sure everything was under control. Going back to her job fulltime had helped to fill the void in her life after Robbie left. Her work allowed her to push back, for a little while, the loneliness and pain that were her constant companions.

It had only been snowing an hour and already there were several inches on the ground. Janet checked again to make sure she had matches and candles handy and a good stock of wood for the fireplace in case the power went off. Then she wandered back to the window. *Where is Robbie tonight?* The possible answers made her heart twist with pain.

Leaping out of the car, Robbie checked the snow-covered road and didn't find any blood. Whatever had loped across the road, she had managed to miss it. There was a movement to her right, and she turned and gasped. When she took a second look, she laughed. Sitting by the side of the road was the biggest, scruffiest, ugliest dog that she had ever seen in her life.

It had long rusty hair, which was knotted with burrs and clumps of mud and ice. It had long legs, like a sloth, and a face, or what could be seen of it through all the hair, like a bulldog. One ear went down and one went up, and the tail, when it stood up and wagged it, seemed to lean to one side. Robbie walked over to the beast. "You almost scared the hell out of me. You know that?" A long tongue hung from a huge, smiling mouth.

The dog was skin and bones. Robbie remembered Janet telling her that the summer tourists often lost pets in the woods and simply went back to the city without them. "Well, that car isn't going anywhere tonight." She looked back at the dog. "You'd better come with me. I've walked out on too many lives already," Robbie said bitterly as she took the belt off of her coat to form a makeshift collar and leash. Together, they trudged up the road toward Janet's, wading through the snow.

It was freezing and Robbie could barely see ahead of her. Now that she and the massive dog had turned into Janet's lane, the snow was much deeper. She had to climb over a ridge of snow left by the plough at the end of the driveway, and then push through two foot drifts that ridged the driveway where the snow blew between the pines and piled up. *Did I wander off the path? I should be able to see the lights of the cabin by now.* She was realizing that it had been a poor decision to leave the safety of the car and try to walk through the storm. All she wanted to do was lie down and go to sleep.

Running into the back end of her own truck alerted Robbie to the fact that she had found the cabin. She edged along carefully to the front of the vehicle, walking blind in the heavy, windswept snow. *Shit! No lights. Janet must be away.* She followed the log wall around to the porch and tried to look in the front window. She couldn't see anything, the curtains were closed. *Damn.* She went around to the door, the big dog close at her side seeking warmth. The door was locked. Fishing into her pocket, she hunted for the keys. Cold, numb fingers barely functioned. *Did I leave my keys in the ignition?* The dog snorted in frustration and scratched at the door, sensing the warmth inside. *Maybe I can find something to break the window.* She turned to head for the woodpile just as the sharp crack of the rifle shot shattered the air around her.

Janet was just finishing putting some hot coffee into a Thermos when the power went out. *Well, that was good timing,* she thought, tightening the lid into place. She felt her way across the room to where she had left the matches and candles, freezing when she heard a thump and muffled footsteps outside.

Oh God! Janet lived alone in an isolated area and, although she loved the solitude of her private lake, she was aware that it left her vulnerable. She tiptoed over to the phone. It was dead, too. Fear grasped at her heart. *Okay, don't panic, Janet,* she told herself as she heard someone trying to clear the ice and snow to see through the window.

She ducked below window level and crawled on her hands and knees over to where she kept her grandfather's old twenty-two. With care, she pushed a number of cartridges into place and then quietly opened the back door to circle around behind the intruder.

Through the heavy snow, she could just make out two large black figures trying to get in the door. One suddenly turned and came at her. She fired.

Robbie fell face down in the snow and the huge dog landed playfully on top of her. "Don't fire," she managed to yell above the wind. "I'm not armed!"

"Robbie?"

"Janet?"

"Oh, my God!" Janet ran over and knelt beside the prone body. "Are you all right?"

"I don't know. Did you hit me?"

"Of course not. I shot in the air to try and scare off the intruders."

"It worked," Robbie muttered, rolling over in the snow and sitting up.

Janet brushed snow from Robbie. Then she looked up into a big, shaggy face that was sitting near by. "What is that?"

"Rufus, meet Janet. Rufus is my dog. I think it's a mix of Tibetan Mastiff and tree sloth."

"Your dog? Come on, let's get you inside. I think the cold is affecting your reasoning."

Reaching out, Robbie grabbed Janet's arm. "I'm sorry. I didn't mean those things! I—"

"I had it coming." Janet reached down and gave the snowy, cold woman a quick hug. "Come on, you're freezing!"

In the firelight, Janet could get a better look at Robbie and the massive dog. She was shocked by what she saw. Robbie was soaked through. The light jacket she was wearing had been little protection against the harsh elements. She tugged the clinging coat from Robbie's shoulders and had her sit near the fire while she ran to get towels and blankets. Returning, she gently stripped the sodden clothes from the woman she loved and replaced each item with tender kisses.

Robbie moaned with pleasure and pulled Janet close, kissing her with desperate need. Her hands hesitantly moved across Janet's back and pulled her sweatshirt up so that her cold hands could stretch across warm flesh. Janet shivered at the touch and then pulled back, allowing Robbie to watch her undress.

It looked...weird, Robbie concluded, to see a woman with one breast and only an angry red scar curved around where the other should be. Then Janet was back in her arms and the feel of her warm skin sent waves of passion through Robbie.

"I'll understand, Robbie, if you don't want to," Janet whispered through impending tears.

In answer, Robbie pulled Janet down with her to the rug and made slow, passionate love to her in the rich glow of the firelight. Later, they lay in each other's arms, too exhausted to continue but still touching, nuzzling and kissing with a desperate need to be close.

"I've missed you. I tried phoning Gwen but she wouldn't tell me where you were, just that you'd been called out of town on an emergency. I was so worried, Obbie. Is everything all right now?"

The silence lengthened while Robbie tried to find some way to explain. "No. We need to talk but...not just yet, not tonight, okay?"

"Okay. Hmm, I need to go get Reb. The house is starting to cool and she'll get cold in the nursery. She'll have to sleep here by the fire with us. Is that okay?"

Robbie's eyes lit up and she smiled eagerly. "Yeah, go get the anklebiter."

Janet laughed and gave her lover a hug. "She's missed you terribly."

A sleepy bundle wrapped in a blanket was carried out by her mom. She took one look at her Obbie sitting by the fire and launched herself from her mother's arms. "Obbie, you come back."

Robbie caught the diving child out of midair, much to Janet's relief, and spun her to the ground. "Hi, Rebel. Want to see the dog I brought you?"

"What?" Janet gasped, but any objections she might have made were too late. Robbie and Reb were already playing with the big lump of wet, smelly fur that was passing itself off as a domestic pet. Janet sighed, bowed to the inevitable, and went to get a tinfoil dish of Cheerios and the left over end of a rump roast. Now that the canine mountain had rested and warmed itself by the fire, it was probably hungry. Leftovers and cereal would have to do until they could shop for some more appropriate food for the poor animal.

The household routine was in complete shambles. The power came back on in the early hours and Reb, who had played with Obbie and Rufus for hours, was put to bed at dawn, thoroughly exhausted. Janet then insisted that Robbie have a shower because she smelt very much like a wet dog. Robbie complied, insisting that she needed her back washed by her lover.

Janet ran slow, soapy fingers down Robbie's back, curving a path back and forth across rippling muscles. She scooped Robbie's cute butt in both hands and leaned forward to plant a nest of kisses between Robbie's shoulder blades. Robbie turned around and stood looking down at Janet. What Janet saw made a pool of hot lust form low in her being. Robbie was simply breathtaking. Her dark hair was smoothed back off her face and pearly beads of water trickled over muscles of steel. Eyes the colour of tropical seas traveled over Janet's exposed body.

"I like your hair like this." Robbie reached out with a graceful hand to play with a truant curl of dark gold. "You look like a pixie."

"Are you comfortable with this?" Janet gestured at her scarred, flat right chest.

Lowering her head, Robbie kissed along the red line that marked the incision, then she looked up at Janet. "You are beautiful, exciting, and everything I have ever dreamed of having. I wish you hadn't had to go through this, but it makes no difference to us. What I love is far more than the physical package; it is the woman whose soul fits so perfectly with mine."

The ball of tension that had been coiled tightly in Janet's heart began to unravel. She poured a liquid herbal soap onto her hands and lathered it gently over Robbie's body. Robbie returned the favour, each woman teasing the other to new heights. It ended with them in bed, loving each other late into the morning.

Janet lay in the crook of Robbie's arm, her free hand running down Robbie's body and her fingers gently playing in the soft pubic hairs. Robbie's arm was wrapped around Janet, stroking a flat, hard belly.

"I had a child," Robbie announced to the ceiling.

Janet froze in shock and then rolled over to look at her lover.

"A girl. I called her Ryan. She doesn't know who I am, but I've supported her all these years." Tears trickled from the corners of her eyes and she struggled to continue. "That night I...left, she was in a lab accident at school."

Janet placed a gentle hand on Robbie's chest. "Is she all right?"

"She is now, but her skull was cracked. She was in a coma for over three weeks."

"Oh, my poor love, I'm so sorry. You were not ready emotionally to take on another major crisis."

"It was hard. All the while I was sitting by her bedside, I felt guilty because I was part of Reb's life but I'd never been part of my daughter's."

"Why, Robbie? Why didn't you raise your daughter?"

"After...after a really bad time in my life, I was really mixed up. I thought I'd be going to jail and I just went wild. I dropped out of university at seventeen and just lived: wild parties, wild times, anything. When I found I was pregnant, I just hid away. I didn't want her to have to grow up with the stigma of being my daughter. I thought I was doing her a favour. It still haunts me, what I did back then. That's why I don't feel I can offer you anything permanent. I'm always waiting to be called to account for what happened."

Robbie's body was stiff with tension and the effort it had taken her to share that much. "So what do you want to do now, Robbie?" Janet coaxed softly, as her fingers painted patterns on Robbie's chest.

"I...I...don't know."

Janet sighed. *This is going to be harder than I thought. Robbie has these huge walls of defence, not to protect herself, but to protect others from her past.* "Robbie, you can't keep beating yourself up for things you did wrong as a child. How old are you?"

"Thirty-two."

"So all this happened almost fifteen years ago. Let it go, Robbie. It's time to stop hiding and start living again. Look at all you have accomplished since then. You have added so much to our world, mine and Reb's. We love you. Just like you stood by me, I would stand by you, no matter what, because I know who you are now. I am so impressed with what I see in your soul, that it's you that I would leave my daughter to if I were to die." Janet felt the spasm of fear that ran through Robbie. "Shhh, it's okay. My first check up was okay."

Robbie wrapped Janet in her arms and rolled the smaller woman over on top of her, holding her tightly and burying her face in Janet's soft hair. "I don't deserve you," she murmured.

"Yes, you do, my silly olive. So, are we going to fetch Ryan home?"

"Yeah. I just don't know how to do that."

"We'll work it out. Does she look like you?" Janet asked, trying to steer the tense woman into safer waters.

"No, well, she's got my build, but she's got your colouring."

"Mine?"

"Yeah, dark green eyes and sandy hair. My grandmother had that colouring; maybe she's a throwback." Robbie smiled with pride. "She's kinda cute, smart as a whip, and a good athlete," she concluded with a blush.

"Who was the father?"

"One of my university professors."

The teacher in Janet reacted with contempt. "Shit, Robbie, you were seventeen."

Robbie shrugged. "He was a drunk. He was killed a few years later in a car accident."

"Good riddance!" Janet snapped.

Rolling over, Robbie gave her a kiss. "Hey, you're cute when you are defending my honour, but I told you, I was wild."

"I don't care."

Robbie looked deep into Janet's eyes. "Ryan's had a lot of...problems. She doesn't get on too well with other kids and she's always trying things she shouldn't and getting into trouble. Are you sure you want to take on a kid like that?"

Janet laughed. "I've got a whole school full of kids like that."

Ryan wiggled her toes, played air piano with her fingers, touched her nose with her eyes closed, and did all the other silly exercises the doctor insisted on. She had already told the specialist that her responses and reflexes were, as always, above norms. He now knew that to be true.

"You are an unusual girl, Ryan, with a particularly hard head."

The doctor laughed; Ryan didn't. It had nothing to do with hardness, she was just fortunate that the lambdoidal suture had opened enough to release the energy of the impact rather than it crushing her skull in, which was by far the more common result. Clearly, her sutures were not knitted as closely as one would expect for a girl of fourteen. She must ask to see the x-rays.

A blonde haired woman looked around the door jamb. "Ryan? Oh, I'm sorry, I didn't know you were here, Doctor. I came to visit Ryan."

"That's okay, I'm just leaving." The doctor turned to Ryan. "I'll sign your release papers for tomorrow and arrange with the nursing station to have someone pick you up."

Ryan nodded. "Thank you, Doctor."

The specialist left to continue his evening rounds and Janet entered the room. "Hi, I'm Janet Williams."

"Billy-the-Kid's widow. You're the principal at Bartlett. I'd like to go there," Ryan said seriously. "Did my mother send you? I assumed that the lab explosion might be the last straw and I'd be asked to leave the school. This will be my third school. My mother tends to pick schools based on the strictness of their program rather than their academic excellence."

Janet blinked. She was used to precocious children, but Ryan Williams was something else. "I have been sent by your mother, yes."

"She usually sends the detective that works for her law firm. He hates me."

"Why?"

Ryan considered. "Well, I tend to treat him like a dork, and I'm not very co-operative. He tries to boss me around."

"I'm not sure your approach with him would be conducive to a good working relationship. Maybe that's why she sent me instead." Janet smiled. "Your mother was very worried about you."

Eyes cold and flashing, Ryan's response was immediate. "My mother doesn't give a damn."

So, she isn't as immune to feelings as she lets on. Janet fought fire with fire. "That is a hypothesis that I don't think would hold up to testing. You have fallen into the trap of making emotional assumptions rather than evaluating the evidence. You don't know your mother."

The chin went up in anger but Ryan checked her retort, looking at the petite woman by her bed with some interest. "Do you know my mother?"

"Yes, very well."

Ryan laughed. "Not as well as Tracy Travelli, I bet." She giggled, tossing the Saturday scandal rag in front of Janet. The picture was of Robbie leaving the studio after a promotion for her new movie; her arm was around Tracy. The headline read: *First Celebrity Gay Wedding?*

The colour drained from Janet's face. She picked up the paper and read: "'Reliable sources have told us that Tracy Travelli and Robbie Williams became more than just friends during the shooting of Williams' new film about one of Napoleon's mistresses. Was the leading lady getting personal coaching from the famous actor/director/screenwriter?' That bitch," Janet muttered, and then blushed as she realized that she had spoken out loud.

"Which one?" Ryan asked happily.

Robbie leaned over her desk in fury. "I want to know where this information came from," she growled, slamming her fist on the gossip newspaper that lay on her desk.

"I might already know," drawled Polinski, looking up at her angry face.

Calming immediately, Robbie sat down. "Tell me," she ordered in a quiet voice edged with ice.

"There's been a small town reporter by the name of Lucier asking a lot of questions about you. He's even tried, unsuccessfully, to access our files. We think he got wind of your...ahh...relationship with Travelli and sold the gossip to the tabloid. Travelli was pretty vocal about you running out on her."

Robbie sighed and rubbed her eyes. "This couldn't have come at a worse time for the film or for me. Let's see what we can do to put the wraps on this thing." Robbie spun at her desk and punched a code into her phone. "Hassan? Robbie. Listen, I need some damage control. Get Travelli on some of the talk shows to deny that she is gay. She's smart enough to know if she lets this one out of the bag, her image as the Latin Bombshell just fizzled." Robbie hung up and turned back to Polinski. "Get the lawyers to threaten a lawsuit. We'll try to put a scare into them."

Polinski nodded, then got up and left. Robbie was already on the phone to Travelli. "Have you seen the paper?" she asked angrily without bothering to introduce herself.

"We look cute together," was the sassy response.

"Latin Bombshells don't fuck gay women, Tracy," Robbie told her coldly, tapping her pen angrily on her desk. "I'm arranging to get you on some talk shows to deny the story. Be good; your chance at an Oscar is riding on this performance. I also need you to be seen around town with a male. Pick up some sucker and promise him marriage, okay?"

"But, Robbie. I meant no harm."

"Just do as I say and maybe, just maybe, we can salvage your career and my film," snapped Robbie, hanging up. Unclipping her private phone from her belt, Robbie pressed one.

At the other end, at the Victoria Hospital in London, Janet took her phone from her purse. "Hello."

"This is Robbie. A scandal rag has just published an article about Tracy and me—"

"Yes, Ryan was just sharing it with me," Janet cut in sardonically, pulling a funny face at Ryan who had her hand over her mouth trying not to laugh.

"Shit. I'm so sorry, Janet. I'm embarrassed and ashamed. At the time, I had no idea that *our* relationship would grow into something so close."

"We'll be discussing it," Janet responded coolly.

After a moment of silence, a voice laced with pathetic insecurity murmured, "I love you."

"It's got to be more than just words, Robbie." Janet hung up.

Ryan laughed merrily. "Wow! Did you toast her buns."

Janet's foul mood sent her on the offensive. "Let's change the subject. How long have you known who your mother really was, and how did you find out?"

Ryan straightened. "For a long time, I didn't care who she was. But last year, I began to wonder why my surname was Williams. Whoever was supporting me had money; that was for sure. So I started with a list of possibilities, and the most obvious were the Williams sisters. Then I accessed birth certificates and bingo, mine turned up with Robbie Williams' name on it. But that didn't mean she was supporting me, so I snuck into the school office one night and went through the files to see who was issuing my tuition cheques. It was a law firm that also represented Robbie Williams. So then I hacked into—"

"Don't tell me any more," Janet cut in dryly, holding up a hand. "There is no doubt that you are your mother's daughter."

Robbie paced around her apartment, picking up things and putting them down again. *Maybe Janet decided to go back to her cabin instead of coming here. No, she wouldn't leave Reb. Maybe she had an accident.* The traffic on the highway between London and Toronto was fast, busy and dangerous at this time of year. A new knot of anxiety formed in Robbie's stomach, then she heard the whoosh of her elevator and hurried over to wait nervously by the door. The doors opened and Janet stepped out. Robbie shifted from one foot to the other, trying to think of something to say to make it better. There weren't any words that could do that. "Ahh, hi."

Janet slipped out of her coat and dropped it on a chair, then turned and walked into Robbie's arms. Robbie wrapped her in tightly, filled with emotional relief.

"That really hurt and embarrassed me, Robbie," Janet said, her voice muffled and strained.

"Oh God, love, I'm so sorry."

"Come on, let's sit down. You want to make me a cup of tea? I'm exhausted. Then I want to know the truth, okay?"

Robbie nodded and gently kissed Janet's brow. "I'll get the tea," she whispered, and disappeared down the hall.

Janet watched her go with sad eyes. Was it too much to expect that Robbie Williams could settle down and live a family life?

"Uhh, I told you Tracy and I had a relationship years ago."

"Yes."

"Well, after the funeral, I had a one night stand with her," Robbie confessed uneasily.

"You'd made a pass at me that weekend," Janet pointed out dryly. "Were you going to service both of us?"

"No," Robbie protested, looking up from the tea mug that had held her attention. "I'd struck out with you and...and I guess my ego was bruised," she finished lamely.

Janet remained silent.

"It never happened again. I...I just sort of walked out on Tracy and came to you. She was pretty hot about it and did some talking, and that damn reporter, Lucier, got wind of it and sold the story to the tabloid. I'm really sorry."

"Me too." For a while there was an uncomfortable silence between them. When Janet thought that she had made her point, she continued with a sigh. "Your daughter, Robbie, is an olive out of the same bottle."

Robbie looked up in shock, "She's fooling around?"

Laughing, Janet shook her head, "No, at least not yet, but I've got to tell you, this child of yours is a hellion."

Janet settled back and Robbie listened intently to all she had to report.

They had been discussing the issue for several hours and were on their second pot of tea. "Okay, here is where we stand." Janet brushed her fingers through her short hair and paced back and forth across the living room. "You will call a press conference and admit to having a daughter, explaining that it was a youthful indiscretion. Having recently learned that the father is deceased, you felt it was okay to recognize the daughter that you have been secretly supporting all these years.

"In the meantime, I'll spirit Ryan away so that she doesn't get the opportunity to give a press interview herself, because God only knows what that child would say. I'll keep her under lock and key, figuratively, not literally, at Bartlett until this thing blows over."

Robbie sighed miserably from where she sat, elbows resting on her knees, staring at the carpet. "I've really fucked up, haven't I?"

"Well, one good thing about this whole mess is that it will help to bury the story about your relationship with Travelli."

Eyes flashing, Robbie jumped to her feet. "I did not have a relationship with Travelli. I love you, damn it!"

There was a moment of startled silence and then Janet started to laugh, falling into Robbie's welcoming arms. "You are such a charmer, you are," she giggled.

Robbie squirmed awkwardly. "Well, I do love you," she muttered defensively.

"Then I'm a very lucky woman." Janet stood up on tiptoes to place a soft kiss on Robbie's lips.

Robbie smiled at the woman she loved. "No, I'm the lucky one. Want to go to bed?"

"Thought you'd never ask." Janet snuggled her sleepy head against Robbie's chest as Robbie picked her up and carried her through to the master suite.

"Do you think it will be on *Entertainment*?" Ryan asked, looking up from the book she was reading as Janet drove her up to Bartlett in Robbie's truck the following Friday.

"What?" asked Janet, her own thoughts miles away with her partner.

"Do you think the press conference where Robbie announces she got knocked up as a teen will be on *Entertainment*?" Ryan repeated patiently.

Janet gripped the wheel firmly and set her jaw. "Ryan, please do not resort to crudity as a means of defence. It is in poor taste. I can understand why you harbour some resentment towards your mom; you don't yet know her like I do. You need to understand that your mom is a very private person and today will be quite an ordeal for her. Like you, she often hides her very gentle soul behind a tough facade."

"I'm not like my...like Robbie," snapped Ryan.

"You have her build and looks, despite your colouring, and you do seem to display a number of similar personality traits, although I'm sure in many ways you're very different."

"I wish Elizabeth was my mom. She is a worthwhile person, not a movie star," Ryan said with contempt.

Janet laughed. "You're mom is far more than just a beautiful face. You'll see." Ryan returned to her book. It was Stephen Hawking's *Universe*. Ryan was definitely not an ordinary fourteen-year-old. The mention of Elizabeth shifted Janet's thoughts to the dinner that she had prepared for Elizabeth at Robbie's apartment several weeks earlier.

Robbie's sister had been so nervous that she had dropped her shoulder bag twice getting into the living room. With Robbie, she had talked physics, Janet amazed at how readily her lover could keep pace with the complex maths and theories that Elizabeth was explaining. Janet had a good mind, but she only understood a general overview of what they were discussing.

Elizabeth had been stilted and formal with Janet until she learned that Janet had a master's degree in gifted education. Then the academic had asked her one question after another, absorbing information like a sponge. By the end of the evening, the conversation had become almost relaxed and normal. At least, as normal as at-home conversations with the Williams sisters would ever be.

Robbie had declared the evening a roaring success, saying that Bethy had really warmed to Janet and relaxed in her company. Janet's wide eyes had betrayed her disbelief, but Robbie had assured her that Elizabeth had been known not to speak at all at social gatherings and so the night had been a real triumph.

"Robbie, what happened to your sister? Why is she so introverted?"

Robbie had immediately become distant. "It's part of the bad times. I don't want to talk about it," she had said stiffly, and then gone out to stand alone in the roof garden while Janet was left to finish the dishes.

Now here was another generation of Williams carrying scars. Janet glanced over at the young girl. She was tall for her age, and lean. Wearing blue jeans and a green sweatshirt under a waist length parka, she looked like an average teen, even a little conservative perhaps.

"When would you like to meet your mom?"

"Never," came the response from behind the book.

"I think tomorrow would be a good time. It's Saturday, so I'll make brunch for us all and you can spend the day at the cabin getting to know each other. That will give you the rest of today to settle into Bartlett and give your mom time to recover from the press interview."

"Whatever."

Janet's voice took on an authoritative tone. "Ryan, please don't use that expression. It is not allowed at Bartlett. It carries with it a degree of bored insolence that is not an attitude that is tolerated at our school."

Ryan looked at Janet, ready to rebel, then hesitated. Janet could tell that Ryan was responding well to her no-nonsense honesty. "Sorry," Ryan said, closing up the book and looking out the window. "I guess I'm just nervous about meeting...Mom. Uhh, she's so beautiful and talented, maybe she won't like me." Ryan sighed dramatically.

Janet burst out laughing at Ryan's attempt at role-playing to win sympathy. "You are just like your mother at times, girl."

Steeling herself, Robbie strode into the room that had been set aside for the entertainment press. She moved to the front of the cluster of reporters and stood before the grouping of microphones. "I am happy and proud to finally be able to announce the birth of my daughter, Ryan." The bored group, expecting yet another promotional release, surged forward with interest. Flashbulbs went off in her face, blinding her for a second.

"She was born fourteen years ago, and I have supported her secretly until this year. Learning of the death of her father, I was relieved to be able to recognize Ryan as my heir. Recently, Ryan was involved in a serious accident that left her in a coma for three weeks. I was with her during that time and am very grateful to announce that she has made a complete recovery and is now on her way to my home."

"Ms. Williams, who was the father?"

"No comment."

"Was the child born out of wedlock?"

"Yes."

"Ms. Williams, how does Tracy Travelli feel about you bringing your daughter home?"

"I haven't discussed the issue with Ms. Travelli. The rumour that she and I were involved in a serious relationship during the making of *Desiree* is simply not true."

"Under the terms of your father's will, the first grandchild inherits a fortune. Ms. Williams, will you make a claim against Billy-the-Kid's estate now that you have acknowledged that you had the first Williams' grandchild."

"No. Thank you for your time. No more comments." Followed by a barrage of questions, Robbie turned and made for the door. *Thank God that's over!*

She took the elevator back up to the administration floor and walked down the hall to her office. Gwen had a phone propped over one ear and another in her hand. E-mail was flicking up on her screen. "Start with line two, Robbie, it's Alexandria, then line one, it's Brian. I need a raise."

"I'll build you a house in the country instead, on a lake. Your kids will love it," Robbie answered on her way through to her office. "Order the helicopter, I'm heading north."

Gwen blinked, shook her head, and turned back to her phone console.

It was late afternoon. John Bartlett, the supercilious jackass and used car salesman who chaired the Broad of Trustees, resettled himself in the chair across from Janet's desk. He had been waiting when she got back from settling Ryan into the Maplewood Dormitory.

"You understand that the Board does not want to interfere in your personal life, Ms. Williams, especially at this time when you are still recovering from surgery and grieving the loss of a fine man such as your husband."

Then why are you here? Janet thought sarcastically, maintaining a neutral expression on her face.

"But I'm sure you understand that as head of the school, it is important that you set a high moral tone. We understand that your sister-in-law, Robbie Williams, has been staying at your place and, well, she's an actress. And, well, there is talk that she is perverted. And now, on the way here, I heard on the car radio that she has an illegitimate child. Ms. Williams, do you feel this association is setting the right tone for our students?"

Janet only just stopped herself from going over the desk and ripping out the idiot's throat. She smiled. "My sister-in-law is well liked in this town, Mr. Bartlett. She is a truly talented and intelligent lady. I don't know what would make you think she is perverted. She lives a very upstanding life—"

"Ms. Williams, she is gay. That is a disgusting sin."

"Mr. Bartlett, this is the beginning of the twenty-first century. Here at Bartlett, we teach tolerance. Ten per cent of all populations — whether lions, seagulls, or humans — are homosexual. It is a natural variant. I do not object to your religious stand that such behaviour is a sin, but please, do not force your views on me, the school, or the students. And above all, do not feel that you are in a position to judge other people's life styles. I remind you that, in Ontario, discrimination against homosexuals is illegal and that this province now recognizes gay marriages, adoptions, and benefit rights."

"Well, I don't approve."

Janet shrugged. "Actually, my sister-in-law has just enrolled Ryan Williams here at Bartlett. I picked Ryan up and brought her up to the school today. I think that can only do our school good. It is, to start with, positive free advertising. And, looking at Ryan's Canadian Achievement Test scores, we are dealing with a child who is in the top one per cent in the country. She will do our school proud."

"I...ugh...well, the Board will be monitoring the situation to see if there is any negative impact on the school's image and our enrolment," Bartlett finished stiffly, getting up. "Good day, Ms. Williams."

"Good day," Janet responded, standing but letting the Chair see himself out. *Horse's ass*, she thought.

At the end of a hard day, Janet went to pick Reb up from day school and Rufus from the pen that Robbie had bought and had set up behind Janet's office window. *I've acquired more dependents lately than Rufus has fleas*, she thought, as she strapped Reb into her car seat. Rufus jumped in beside Reb, effectively filling up the back seat. When Janet got home, she almost cried with relief to see Robbie coming along the porch to meet her.

"Hi, love," Robbie murmured into Janet's ear, as she wrapped her in her arms. "You look tired. I've asked too much of you lately. You need rest; you're still weak from all you've gone through. Are you eating properly?"

Janet snorted and poked Robbie in the ribs. "You, Williams, wouldn't know a well balanced meal if one was put in front of you!"

"Hmm, I just worry about you," fretted Robbie. "You get in out of the cold and I'll bring in the rugrat and her pet rug."

It was great to be sitting with Robbie in the peace and quiet of the cabin and to feel, for a change, really healthy. Tired, she conceded, but a good sort of tired. "You nervous about meeting Ryan tomorrow?"

"Yeah."

"Be patient, okay?"

"I can do patient."

Janet smiled. "No, you can't, but try. She's got a lot of resentment that has built up over the years."

"Yeah, I guess."

"Robbie?"

"Hmm?"

"I need to talk to you professionally, principal to parent." Janet got up and went over to her desk to slide out Ryan's Canadian Achievement Test results.

"Oh boy, she couldn't have gotten into trouble that quickly. Do I have to sit at the desk?"

Janet pulled a face as she came back and curled up again next to her lover. "Ryan tests off the scale in some areas, Robbie, particularly in math and logical thought."

Robbie's stomach contracted with worry. "But she gets good marks at school," she protested.

Janet looked at her with disbelief. "I meant, Ryan is very bright. She is actually testing in the top one percent."

"Math and logic, huh? She's going to be another egg-head like Beth."

Rolling up the report, Janet swatted Robbie playfully on the knee. "Robbie! That is just the sort of bigotry I have to fight every day, please don't bring it into my home."

Robbie took the report and became serious. "So what does this mean?"

Janet watched Robbie's eyes moving as they scanned the data. When they stopped, Janet answered. "She certainly will need some enriched programs to challenge her mind. We'll want to provide her with a lot of support. This is too good a mind to waste. Ryan has had a lot to face and has not had the security of a stable family life to fall back on. We'll want to track her pretty closely."

"I don't want my kid labelled," Robbie snapped, eyes flashing with anger.

Janet's voice went cold. "We don't label kids. We educate and encourage them to be good citizens. Trust me to do my job right, Robbie."

Robbie sat forward, placing the report on the sled table and resting her elbows on her knees. She balanced her chin on her hands and stared at the fire. "It's hard not to try to over-protect her. I want to be part of her life."

Swinging her feet to the ground, Janet wrapped an arm around Robbie. "You've got to move slowly, Robbie, or she will resent you even more than she already does. Trust the school to help her adjust, okay?"

"I trust *you*," Robbie said, kissing Janet softly. "Hey, it's time for bed, love. The doctor said you've got to get lots of sleep."

Janet laughed and pulled Robbie to her feet. "We can go to bed, but we're not going to sleep. I've got a lot of nights to catch up on."

Chapter 9

Robbie pushed a piece of bacon around with her fork. "Uhh...you like your room?"

Ryan shrugged. "It's okay."

Swallowing the bacon that had finally been captured, Robbie nodded. "Uhh...you feel okay, not getting headaches or anything?"

Ryan put down her knife and fork neatly on her plate. "No, I'm fine. That was a great brunch, Aunt Janet. Thank you."

"You're welcome, Ryan," Janet responded as she scraped the last of the scrambled eggs out of the Winnie the Pooh bowl and fed it to Reb.

"I'll go clean up Reb," Robbie suggested, quickly rising to her feet at the possibility of escape.

Janet stayed her with an outstretched arm. "I have a better idea. I'd like to spend some time with Reb. While I was having treatments, I wasn't always there for her. Why don't you and Ryan get the snowmobile from the shed and go over to the lodge. You can show Ryan what you're doing over there. I think she'll find it interesting."

"Oh, okay," Robbie said, looking trapped and awkward.

Janet gave her a push toward the back door. "You two have a good time and I'll see you back here in a few hours." Janet gave Robbie a meaningful look and then turned it on Ryan.

Robbie smiled weakly; Ryan scowled. *Oh boy, this is going to be a long day.*

"Watch out for the wolves," Janet called, as the mother and daughter waded reluctantly through the snow toward the tool shed. "Ted Potts saw a pack on the other side of Blackberry Rock just the other day. If you're lucky, you might see them."

"Aunt Janet has a funny concept of good luck," Ryan observed dryly as Robbie unlocked the shed. "Can I drive?"

"Do you know how?" Robbie entered the shed and went over to fill the gas tank.

"Sure, the last school you dumped me in had winter survival classes."

"Guess it paid off," Robbie muttered, tipping the contents of a plastic gas can down the funnel she had balanced in the snowmobile tank. Snowmobiles were the winter workhorses and recreational toys of Canada. The small, motorized vehicles could carry two people, one sitting behind the other. The front of the snowmobile was mounted on short steering skis and the back on a tread for traction and power.

"If we met wolves, what would you do?" Ryan asked, looking around the shed.

"Get the hell out of there," Robbie responded, tightening the gas cap and then checking the oil level.

"Wouldn't you try to save me?"

Robbie looked up to meet intelligent green eyes, suddenly realizing that she was on trial. "I guess I'd credit you with enough sense to be right there beside me as we headed for safety. You ready?"

"Yup." Ryan mounted the snowmobile and put the key in the ignition.

Robbie climbed on behind. "Is it okay if I hold on?" Robbie asked.

There was a moment's hesitation before Ryan gave a short nod. "Sure."

Robbie held on to Ryan's waist and they headed out. She was impressed with Ryan's driving. She moved out of the shed and down the bank to the frozen lake with care and only opened the throttle on the flat, windswept lake. Even then, she kept close to the shoreline. The kid was no show off and used a good deal of common sense.

Half way down the south side of the lake, Robbie pointed up into a patch of thick pines. Ryan nodded, turning the vehicle around and slowing as they wound up between the trees to the lodge.

Ryan turned off the engine and waited for Robbie to swing off the snowmobile first. "What is this place?"

"The lodge was built by Janet's great grandfather over a hundred years ago. It's been standing empty for the past forty years anyway. I bought all this land from a lumber company in the fall and, when I saw the lodge, I decided to restore it. We didn't get too far before winter set in. Things were pretty wild, what with Janet being ill."

"She has cancer, right?"

"Yes," Robbie muttered, looking away.

"Is she dying?"

Robbie's head snapped around in anger. "No! No, she isn't going to die. Let's go see inside."

Ryan nodded and the two walked in silence through the deep snow to the door. Robbie got out the key to open the new hasp and lock that had been installed to replace the one she had demolished when she first broke in. "Are you gay?" Ryan asked, and Robbie's hand hesitated on the lock.

What the hell do I say now? Well, she's going to catch on sooner or later and Janet said it's best to be as honest as you can. "Yes."

"You're in love with Aunt Janet, aren't you?" Ryan observed, enjoying the blush that was rising on her mother's face.

"Is it that obvious?" Robbie sighed, pushing the door open and indicating that Ryan should go first.

Ryan snorted. "Oh yeah, a blind man could figure it out. You two give off vibes whenever you are close to each other."

Robbie turned to look at her very mature fourteen-year old daughter. "Does that bother you?"

Ryan met the look with hard, cold eyes and her chin rose defiantly. "I've been teased all my life for being a bastard. Now I'll be the bastard of the queer. I can deal with it. I always have."

Robbie didn't know what to say. The kid was right. She was paying for her mother's decisions. She led the way up into the living room.

"Are you going to marry her?"

Robbie stopped and turned around. "I wish I could. But I decided a long time ago that I didn't want anyone — you, a partner, anyone — to have to share the consequences of...of things I did when I was young that were very wrong. Now, well, it's been a long time and maybe I can afford to get closer to people, but I'm still hesitant to give them my name in case some day they might be humiliated to know me. I'm speaking very openly here, Ryan. I hope you understand that I don't want any of this talked about."

Surprised by her mother's candour, Ryan nodded. "You acknowledged me; you ought to marry her. She's okay. Do you think she'd have you?"

Sighing impatiently to hide her own insecurity, Robbie turned around, hands on hips, to look at her daughter. "Cut me some slack here, okay?"

Ryan pulled a face and clammed up, walking over to the impressive fireplace. Tracy and Doug had been made overseers of the reconstruction until such time as there was a real job to offer them. They had managed to open up and grade the road in, patch the holes in the roof and clear the debris from the inside before the heavy snows came.

"Look at the size of the fireplace, Mom. You could roast a cow in it."

"Maybe Janet could. You and I couldn't manage to boil water without burning the house down."

The response was a growl of annoyance. "I can cook."

"I'm glad to hear that." *Patience, Robbie.* "You want to go investigate the out building? I haven't been in there yet."

The reply was sulky. "If you want."

With difficulty, they pushed through the knee-deep snow to a small fieldstone building nestled in some tall pines. "This was an ice house. Years ago, before they got power up here, they used to cut the ice on the lake into blocks in the winter and store it in here covered with sawdust."

"It's a pretty little place. I mean, if it was cleaned up it could be a good guest house or something," Ryan mused.

"Let's see if we can get the door open." The two worked away, clearing snow from the door until they finally were able to push it open enough that they could squeeze in. After the glare of the winter sun reflecting off the snow, it took some minutes for their eyes to adjust to the gloom inside. The building was round with a conical cedar shake roof. The floor was wood, but old and rotting. A dank smell made them wrinkle their noses.

"Ugh. This place would need a lot of work before anything could live in here. It's cold and damp, too," Robbie observed with a shiver.

Moving further into the room, Ryan stopped to look at an old rusted chain and winch system that hung from the centre beam.

"I wonder what this was for." She had only just gotten the words out of her mouth when the wood below her gave way and she dropped into the cold darkness below.

"Ryan!" Robbie's scream of panic echoed against the cold stone walls.

It was a minute that seemed to last forever. Robbie saw Ryan drop out of her sight even as she dove to try and grab her daughter. Wood crumbled around her and musty dust filled her lungs. In the darkness of the void in front of her, she could hear the heavy thud as her daughter hit bottom and then the patter of wood pieces as they rained down.

"Ryan?" The silence that answered her made her heart pound. "Ryan!"

"I'm okay." The voice was shaky with shock.

"Don't move. You might have broken something." Robbie swiped tears of panic from her face and tried to calm her racing heart so she could think straight. "Did you hit your head?"

"No, I hit feet first and then landed on my bum. Stuff fell on me, but I'm okay. Just sore and stiff."

Robbie could hear her daughter moving among the debris below but couldn't see her. "I can't see down there. How far down are you?"

"I can just see you by the light from the door. I think I'm down about four metres. It's not much fun down here."

The fear was there in Ryan's voice, although muted behind her calm responses. Robbie looked around. She didn't think Ryan would want to be left alone down the pit while she went to get help. She needed to find a way to help her daughter. *What can I do? This is important. Ryan needs rescue and she needs to believe in me. Think.*

"Ryan, I'm going to see if I can get this old winch system to work so I can lower a chain down to you and pull you up. But first, I've got to check to make sure the beam is still strong. Are you okay for a few minutes?"

"Yeah, sure. I'm not going anywhere. Mom?"

"Yes?"

"Be quick, okay? It's spooky down here."

"I'll be as quick as I possibly can. Stand back in case this beam breaks. I don't want it to land on you."

Carefully crawling back from the edge and then standing by the wall, Robbie gave a jump and grabbed hold of the log beam that crossed the centre of the room. She swung her legs up and hung there from her hands and feet. The beam groaned but held. Slowly, she edged forward, working her way over the pit.

"I can see you, Mom."

"Good. The beam seems strong enough."

"Be careful. If you fall in here too, we're in big trouble."

"Have some faith, kid."

"Sure," Ryan muttered.

"Okay, I'm where the chain is looped over the pulley." Clumsily, Robbie tried to hold on with one hand and her legs while she used the other to check the pulley mechanism. She could see Ryan waiting in silence below her. "The pulley is pretty rusted but it still moves and it seems solid enough. The chains are off, so I'll need to fit them back into place. Then I'm going to hang from the chains and make sure they can hold your weight."

"Be careful, Mom."

"I will."

Robbie checked each bolt and rocked the pulley back and forth to loosen it up, then she placed the chains back into the pulley and pulled. With some protest and a lot of flaking of rust, the pulley turned and the chain lowered a bit.

"Hey, things are dropping down in here."

"Its rust. Watch your eyes," Robbie warned.

Carefully, holding on to the beam tightly with her legs, she transferred the weight of her body to the chains. They held. "I think this is going to work."

"Good."

Robbie reached up with one hand to catch the beam again and suddenly felt the chain she was holding in her other hand give. Thrown back, she grabbed for the chain wildly as her legs were pulled free from the beam. The pulley screeched wildly and the stiff chains banged loudly through the mechanism. Robbie, holding on as tight as she could, plummeted into the pit and landed in a heap of chains and wood chips.

Strong hands steadied her as Robbie freed herself from the rusty chain. "Welcome to my humble pit, Mom. Are you hurt?"

"Only my dignity."

"Are we trapped now?"

Robbie tested the chain lines. With relief, she felt them roll. "No. The chains are still in place. I can hoist you up to the beam and then you'll have to crawl along to the side where the footing is safe. Okay?"

"What about you?"

"I think I can pull myself up."

"You sure?" The edge of fear was back in Ryan's voice.

Robbie gave her daughter a quick hug. "You bet."

Robbie tied a loop in the chain for Ryan's foot and Ryan stepped on, holding tight to the chain while her mom carefully hoisted her up out of the hole to the beam above.

"Can you let go of the chain and reach for the beam?"

"I got it."

Biting her lip, Robbie watched her daughter grab the beam and hang from it until she could swing her legs up and edge along to the side like her mom had done.

"Okay, I'm down, Mom. Can you get out?"

"I'm on my way," said Robbie, sounding more confident than she actually was. She made sure her ski gloves were on tight, wrapped her leg around the chains, and slowly started to climb up hand over hand. Her arms ached painfully and her breath was coming in short pants by the time she reached the beam.

"You okay?"

Saving her breath, Robbie nodded. She reached up for the beam, and missed.

The chain spun crazily.

"Careful!" Ryan yelled.

Robbie tried again and managed this time to grab hold. Now she hung from arms far too tired to hold her weight. With the last of her strength, she swung a leg up and hooked her leg around the beam. Then she raised the other. Slowly, she edged back out of danger, dropping down to the floor as soon as she thought it was safe. She sat against the wall, gasping for breath. "That was hard work."

Ryan nodded. "Thanks."

After catching her breath, Robbie smiled. "You ready to go?"

"More than."

The two exited and, having locked up, they made their way back down through the snow to their snowmobile.

Janet was starting to get worried about how long Robbie and Ryan had been away when she heard the snowmobile returning. *I sure hope those two have managed to find some common ground.* She heard their footsteps on the porch and, lifting Reb from her chair, she went to open the door for Robbie.

"Well, that took a long—" Janet stopped mid-sentence. She was staring at two of the dirtiest humans she had ever seen. Streaks of rust ran up their snowmobile suits, chips of wood stuck from their hair, and their hands and faces were filthy. "I can't wait to see the movie they make about your afternoon."

Ryan laughed. "The floor in the ice house gave out from under me and I fell into this really deep pit and Mom rescued me. She was great."

"Hey, you did all right yourself."

"The ice house!" Janet exclaimed. "What in the world where you doing inside there?"

"Checking it out."

"That...and falling through the floor," Ryan added.

"Okay, you two, strip out of those things and head straight for the shower. You're both a mess."

"You go ahead and shower first, Ryan. I think I need to soak in a bath. Every muscle in my body aches," Robbie admitted.

"Getting old, eh? I'll be as quick as I can."

Ryan headed for the bathroom and Janet looked at Robbie. "Looks like you two made some headway today."

"Yeah."

"Do either of you need medical attention?"

"We've both had current tetanus shots so I think we'll be okay, but we've got some cuts and bruises that will need cleaning and attention."

Janet smiled. "I'll stand by with the first aid kit."

"Obbie dirty." Reb pulled a face.

Robbie sighed dramatically. "Everyone's a critic."

Later, Robbie sat in the middle of the couch. On one side, Janet was resting her head on Robbie's shoulder as she read through more education reports. On the other side, Ryan curled up close, reading a book. Reb lay on her belly across the three of them, fast asleep. Rufus lay on the floor by their feet, guarding his family.

Robbie stared at the flames in the fireplace. *How had this happened?* One minute, she was a single, lone woman, cold and aloof. The next, she had a family who depended on her and loved her. It was the most scary and wonderful thing she had ever experienced.

Today had started out badly and ended very specially. They were a family, no matter what others might say or what troubles they might have along the way. She kissed each head in turn and ruffled Rufus' fur with her foot. She pushed the soreness of her muscles to the back of her mind and drew peace from the warmth of her family around her. Being there with them...it was like a magical story. "Hey, guys, I think we need sleep."

Janet yawned. "Mmm, you're right, but it's just so peaceful here."

Robbie laughed gently and stood, holding Reb, still asleep, in her arms. "Let's go, you lot. Come on, Ryan, you can finish your chapter in bed while I tuck the Rebel in."

Ryan didn't argue. By the look of her sleepy eyes, she was more than ready for bed. Neither did Janet. "Okay," she agreed, standing up to have a stretch.

Ryan slipped into her bed just as Robbie had finished getting Reb settled. Robbie turned and sat down on the edge of her oldest daughter's bed. "You okay?"

"I guess, just sore and tired."

"Me too," sighed Robbie.

"You were pretty cool swinging along that beam today. Where did you learn to do stuff like that?"

"Over the years I've trained to do a lot of stunts for my movies. I've always tried to exercise regularly. It's part of the job."

"You're a weird mother to have," Ryan pointed out with annoying honesty.

Robbie was hurt. She had thought the events of the day had broken down some of the barriers between them. "Yeah, I guess. I've never had any practice at it."

"That's okay, you're cool," Ryan concluded as she settled down to sleep.

Smiling, Robbie leaned forward to kiss Ryan on the forehead. "You were pretty cool out there today, yourself. I was very proud of you. Good night. Pleasant dreams, Ryan."

"Good night, Mom."

The next afternoon found Robbie chopping wood and Ryan watching. Robbie's frustration with the film industry and a phone call she'd had with her assistant, Brian, was being directed at the woodpile. A large pile of kindling was quickly forming. Her muscles, already sore from their adventures the day before, were screaming in protest.

"I could stay here," Ryan suddenly said.

Robbie stopped chopping and looked at her daughter. "What?"

"I think I should stay here instead of the dorm. You're always away and Aunt Janet shouldn't be left alone. I could be helpful. You know, chopping wood and stuff."

"Good point," Robbie responded neutrally, trying her best not to break out in a goofy grin. "You think you can handle two moms bossing you around?"

"You two can't have any more rules than your average girls' dorm, believe me," Ryan grumbled.

"Well, it's not my house and it is getting crowded. I'll talk to Janet and see what she says. I don't know if she'd be allowed to do that, what with her being the principal of your school."

Ryan looked exactly like a disappointed child who was trying to pretend she wasn't. "Oh yeah, I forgot about that."

"Janet has to go into Bartlett to get groceries. I thought I'd drop her off and then head down to George Drouillard's Small Motors. He sells snowmobiles down there. Seems to me, we could do with at least one more. You want to come along?"

Ryan beamed. "Yeah, that would be cool."

"Good. We'll go as soon as you've stacked all this wood I chopped," Robbie called back over her shoulder, on her way to put the axe back in the shed.

Ryan's smile disappeared, but she climbed down off the porch and started stacking.

When Robbie walked in, Janet looked up from working at her desk. She shoved a stack of papers aside and waited for Robbie to open the conversation. There was something on her mind. It was written all over her face.

Janet looked tired and stressed. "You okay?" Robbie asked, gently, well aware of how hard Janet worked.

"Mmmhmm, fine. I'm just going over a few things." She reached out to capture Robbie's hand, needing her close.

"I was just talking to Ryan. Uh, we're getting on alright."

"She thinks you're wonderful, and she would be right."

Robbie blushed and Janet squeezed her hand. Robbie shifted from foot to foot, then said awkwardly, "She asked if she could stay here instead of at the dorm. I told her that maybe you couldn't take her because you are the principal and all."

"Ryan is welcome to stay here, Robbie. She's your daughter." Robbie smiled in relief and Janet went on. "I didn't think she would adjust so quickly to having you as a mother but yesterday's...events sort of accelerated the process. You understand, Robbie, that there are still going to be disagreements and when they occur, she is liable to bring out all the old hurts to use against you."

Robbie sat on the edge of the desk and looked at the floor. "Yeah, I guess we've got a long way to go. You sure you're okay with this? Because I'll be away a lot on the circuit promoting the film."

"Then Ryan will be good company."

"You're forgetting that she's an olive." Robbie laughed.

Janet leaned forward and kissed her. "I happen to love olives."

"Hey, I'm an impressionable kid, you know!" came a cheeky voice from behind them. "Are we going to town, or did I get conned into stacking all that wood for nothing?"

"You, Ryan Williams, are a pain in the butt," Robbie growled playfully. "Janet said you can stay if you cook dinner each night, do the house work, including windows, make all the beds in the morning, and share the dog blanket with Rufus."

Ryan's eyes got big and her mouth gaped open but nothing came out. Janet came to her rescue. "Don't listen to her, Ryan. Of course you can stay here if you feel comfortable doing so, and we'll discuss and come to some agreement on your household responsibilities. Alright?"

Ryan's face lit up. "Thanks, Aunt Janet. I'll be good. I promise."

"I'd get that in writing if I were you, Janet," Robbie cautioned, her arms crossed as she looked at her daughter with obvious affection.

It had been Robbie's plan to drop Janet at Dave Pott's grocery store, but the warning look in Janet's eyes made her change her mind. They were in this together. They all piled out. Rufus stood guard at the door, while the remaining Williams clan invaded. Ryan wheeled Reb around in her own cart, explaining to her about how neat snowmobiles were while Robbie pushed a cart for Janet.

They ended up buying twice as many groceries as they needed because Robbie kept throwing in junk food to supplement Janet's well-balanced meals. Janet, for her part, bought extra treats and a squeaky rubber ball for Rufus because he hadn't been getting as much attention of late.

Word soon got around the small town. Ryan gave a hilarious rendition of her rescue to David at the check out counter. The O.P.P. officer who boarded at Greta Corry's happened to be in the store, and he passed the story along to Greta when he dropped off her groceries. She set a new record in spreading the news of the accident and Robbie's rescue of Ryan all over town. Those fortunate enough to be in the store at the time came up to listen in and to have their own say, and there was a good deal of humour and sympathy exchanged. Janet appeared unusually uncomfortable with the friendly village chatter. Robbie kept the family close, putting a protective arm around Ryan when anyone stopped to talk.

Ryan was helping Reb decide which kids' cereal had the best toy inside and Janet and Robbie were temporarily alone. "It's silly," Janet confessed, "I see everyone now as a star-struck fan rather than a friend."

Robbie rubbed Janet's back reassuringly. "Hey, you'll get used to it. It's just being a Williams. They'll get used to having me around and a lot of the interest in us will wear off. It's just going to take some time."

"The rest of you seem okay with all this attention," Janet observed sheepishly.

"Ryan hasn't left my side all day. And...yeah, I get tired of it, but it's part of the job and I try not to let it get to me. I have been thinking about this problem, though."

Janet looked up at her lover, her curiosity clear on her face. "Thinking about what?"

Robbie shrugged. "You know, the attention that my fame causes for the rest of you."

Feeling like an old hand at grocery shopping, while Janet paid for the groceries, Robbie talked to the villagers who were in line. How quickly her life had changed over the last three months.

George Drouillard was a little taken aback when the Williams females invaded his small motor shop. Mostly, it was men that came in to discuss clogged carburetors or snapped sheer pins. Occasionally a woman would drop in with a lawnmower that just wouldn't start or to pick out an outfit from his line of sportswear, but he couldn't recall ever before having a crowd of females in his workshop.

Robbie sat on a snowmobile with Reb in her lap making vrooming noises and left Ryan to give poor Drouillard the third degree on the pros and cons of each engine. She listened closely, however, and was proud of Ryan's astute questions and comments. Ryan was showing off for mom.

Janet watched and shook her head in disbelief as her own little bottle of olives spilt out over the floor and took over the machine shed. This visit was going to keep the town in gossip for a week.

"Well, Ryan, what do you think?" Robbie asked, looking up from trying a racing helmet on Reb.

Ryan considered. "The 400 series has the power and good performance, but the 364 is the better deal because they're selling off older stock. There's nothing wrong with the 364. I guess it depends whether or not we're going to compete in the Winter Carnival."

"What?" Janet exclaimed looking out from a rack of snowmobile suits. "Oh no, you two."

"Of course, we are." Robbie grinned and Ryan's eyes lit up with pride and delight. Janet rolled her eyes and sighed. They'd have to talk.

"No!" Janet repeated again, looking back at the mean machine sitting on a flat trailer attached with a temporary hitch to Robbie's truck.

"Why not?" Robbie argued, keeping her eyes on the icy road as they headed over to Maria's Café for dinner.

"Mom's sure to win!" Ryan said loyally.

"Obbie win! Obbie win!" chanted Reb.

Janet rolled her eyes in frustration. "That's just it! You will have to win or die trying. Robbie, this is a friendly little village carnival, not the Indy 500."

"I can do little and friendly," Robbie objected.

"No, you can't! The Williams are competitors, and you, Robbie, can be bad tempered and a poor sport."

"I am not!" Robbie roared, startling everyone. "I just like to win," she finished meekly.

Janet sighed. "Okay, but there will be no famous Williams temper tantrums, and you and Ryan have to take some lessons."

"Reb too," came a little indignant voice from the child's seat.

Janet groaned. "Oh boy."

The clan piled out of the truck and took over a corner of Maria's Café. Rufus sat outside, forlornly looking in the window. Janet waved to a small, wiry woman whose dark hair was pulled back in a bun. The woman waved back and picked up some menus to take over to the table. Janet leaned over. "Maria Enrico is the mother of Lou, who runs the garage now that his father is dead."

"Lou, who is," Robbie made quotation marks with her fingers, "stepping out with Tracy?"

Janet nodded as her eyes lit up in greeting. "Hi, Maria. Let me introduce my sister-in-law, Robbie Williams and my niece Ryan."

"Nice to meet you, Maria. I hear Lou is seeing Tracy, who works for me."

"Yes. Tracy is a good girl. My Lou could do worse. I see your announcement on the TV. You were such a proud mother."

Robbie blushed scarlet.

Maria put the menus down on the table and took out a small camera. "It is okay if I take a picture? I will hang it in my café and it will be very good for business. The tourists will come, hoping to see you."

"My luck," Robbie muttered under her breath. "Yes, I'd be delighted to have my picture taken, but please, no pictures of my children. Janet, why don't you take a picture of Maria and me together?" Robbie suggested.

Janet got up beaming. Robbie had said "my" children. That sent a flood of warmth through Janet. Robbie stood by the dessert counter with her arm over the shoulder of the little woman while Janet took several pictures.

"So, afraid to get your picture taken with the bastard?" Ryan asked as her mother sat back down at their table.

Robbie looked like she had been punched. *I warned you, love*, Janet thought, but said nothing.

Robbie sat down and looked Ryan in the eye. "I'm sorry. I'm so used to the pitfalls of being famous that I take it for granted that everyone understands. I should have explained. I had to explain to Janet, too. I am a very rich, famous woman, Ryan. That means all those people close to me are in danger of being kidnapped or otherwise harmed. I don't want any of you to get your pictures in the paper or magazines because that would make you more easy to identify. If anything happened to you or the others because of me, I'd go crazy."

The anger in the teen's eyes was replaced by confusion. "Is that why you ordered the alarm system and floodlights?"

That took Janet by surprise. "What alarm system?"

"I've ordered a system for the cabin. If anyone tries to break in, an alarm will go off, floodlights will come on outside, and an emergency signal will bleep at the police station."

"It cost a bundle," Ryan added informatively. Robbie gave her a glare, which she blithely ignored.

Janet was touched by her lover's concern, but chided gently, "Robbie, that wasn't necessary. I've lived there for years with no problems."

"That was before you knew me. Besides, I have to be away promoting the film and I want to know that my family is safe."

There it was again. Janet's happy eyes met the sky blue of the actor's. She smiled softly and Robbie winked.

Ryan groaned to hide her teen embarrassment. "You two!"

They ordered pizza with the works and Ryan had them all in stitches trying to justify the list of school offences that Robbie gleefully listed one after the other.

"Hey. The kid had it coming. She'd been bullying the entire floor and when she picked on little Grace just because she had a stutter, I lost it. I was playing it cool because I knew I was down to my last chance after the 'goldfish in the drinking fountain' incident, so I just told her ever so nicely that if she took a swing at me, I'd knock her block off."

Robbie smiled and shook her head. "And?" asked Janet.

"Well, I let her get three hits in so that I had some blood for evidence, and then I decked her."

Janet laughed.

"Don't laugh!" Robbie protested. "She broke the kid's arm. I had to send Polinski up there to sort it out so she wasn't charged or sued."

"Ryan! You didn't." Janet stopped laughing, but there was still amusement in her eyes.

"I didn't mean to. She fell against the desk."

"You sure you want her at Bartlett?" Robbie asked, watching Janet wiping tomato sauce off Reb's face. Playing in pizza had been a real hit with the two-year-old.

"Mom! I *want* to go to this school."

They all laughed and Robbie paid the bill, arguing that Janet had paid for the groceries.

Later that night, with Ryan and Reb safely in bed, Janet was able to have some private time with Robbie. Janet ran a hand over Robbie's naked chest and pulled her down for a kiss. "Mmm, I'll miss you while you're away," she whispered.

"I'm going to miss you terribly. Are you sure you're alright staying here?"

"I'll be fine. I've lived here for years. But the security system that is being installed tomorrow will keep us all safe. Thank you." She kissed Robbie again.

"I'll phone each night," Robbie promised.

Janet didn't answer; she had other, more interesting ways to express her love.

A week later, Ryan and Janet sat in the wing chairs watching the TV and sharing the bowl of popcorn that sat on a small table between them. Ryan had been allowed to stay up late to see her mom on one of the late night interview shows.

"And now, ladies and gentlemen, the beautiful and multi-talented Robbie Williams!" There was much clapping and whistling, and Robbie walked on set wearing an elegant black pantsuit. The host stood and embraced Robbie and they air-kissed beside each other's head.

"Keep your paws off my...my sister-in-law," Janet muttered, and Ryan snorted and threw a piece of popcorn at her.

"Well, we are very pleased to have you on the show tonight," the host said once he had helped Robbie settle. "You don't give interviews."

"I don't? Well, I'd better leave, then." Robbie half rose from her chair.

The audience laughed and the host pulled her back. "No, I meant it is rare for you to agree to come on a talk show."

"I'm very excited about my new movie, *Desiree*. It's quite a departure in style for me and I think people are really going to enjoy it." She turned to the audience. "Don't forget to go see it!" The applause lights flashed over the stage and the audience dutifully whooped and cheered.

"It looks like Mom, it talks like Mom, but it isn't Mom," Ryan observed with interest.

"It is Robbie, but it's another side of her. This is your mom at work, Ryan. It's all a marketing game. That's what these shows are all about — infomercials for the entertainment trade."

"Pretty mercenary," Ryan said cynically.

"No, it's no different than selling any product. Your mom has over five thousand people working for her in various companies. If she makes a film that doesn't do well at the box office, then that has repercussions right down the line. That's a lot of responsibility and pressure that your mom is under."

Back on the television screen, the announcer brought up the subject the audience had been anticipating. "We had Tracy Travelli on a couple of weeks ago, Robbie, and she was furious about the tabloid story that linked you with her romantically. I've got to tell you, the men of America were very relieved to hear the two of you are still available." The laughter lights flashed and the audience giggled and clapped.

"Why, how nice. What's your number? I'll be sure to put you in my little black book."

"Ugh," Ryan said, putting her finger in her mouth.

"Little black book? You'd better stop flirting with that man, Robbie Williams, or you are going to be sleeping in the snow when you get back."

"So, tell us about this daughter of yours, Robbie. Is she gorgeous like you?" asked the television host.

Robbie smiled softly. "She is good looking, but she has many more important things going for her. She is bright, funny, caring, and adventurous. I wish I could take credit for her, but she got that way all by herself. I'm really proud of her."

Ryan sat staring at the screen, a red blush creeping up her face. Janet reached over and gave her arm a squeeze. "That was nice, huh?"

Ryan scowled. "She didn't mean it. It's like you said, just marketing."

"No!" Janet snapped, startling Ryan. "She wouldn't do that, not to people she cares about. Your mother plays hard but she plays fair." Ryan didn't respond, but Janet noticed that she wiped a tear from her eye when she thought Janet wasn't looking.

"So, Robbie, we hear that, just like Desiree, you're a real hero. What's this my research department tells me about how your daughter fell into an old mine shaft and you went down and saved her?"

Robbie went still and very serious. "It wasn't a mine shaft, fortunately, but an old pit dug as an ice house and covered up with a wood floor later. My daughter, Ryan, acted coolly and calmly and, working together, we were able to get out safely without any real injury."

"I'm glad to hear that. I understand, Robbie, that some of the profits from *Desiree* will go to women's crisis centres."

"That's right. Statistics show that at least one in every four women has been the victim of abuse. That horrifying statistic really drives home the need for women's crisis centres. It is a cause I very much believe in. Abuse and violence towards women and their children has to be brought out in the open so that this sickness in our world communities can be dealt with."

"I agree completely, Robbie. Folks, here's a number you can call for more information or to get help if you are experiencing abuse in your life. And go see this wonderful movie. It's great entertainment and a portion of the profit from each ticket sale will go to support women's crisis centres."

"That's right."

"Ladies and gentlemen, Robbie Williams! Get out there and see her new movie, *Desiree*." The canned clapping and flashing lights prompted the audience. "We'll be right back after this commercial break."

Janet got up and turned off the TV. "Okay, Ryan, bedtime."

"Do you think she really has a little black book?" Ryan teased.

"Not if she knows what's good for her," Janet growled, playing along. They hugged goodnight and went to their rooms.

Gerald Lucier had watched the show, too. He'd made a tidy little packet selling the tabloid the story about Tracy and Robbie, and although they had denied it, they hadn't sued. He'd also scooped the big papers with the story about Ryan falling into the pit and Robbie rescuing her. One of the big Toronto dailies had asked him to send in a resume.

But he wasn't interested in a regular reporter's job at his age. No way. He wanted his own by-line, and he figured that he might just have the lead that was going to put his name right up there. It was going to take some good investigative journalism, but he was good at digging for dirt. With a laugh, he took a sip from his beer and lit another cigarette. *Might as well watch the rest of the show.*

It was just after three in the morning when the alarm went off and the floodlights came on. Janet jumped from her bed, heart pounding, and ran down to the girls' room amid the wild barking of Rufus and the breaking of furniture.

Ryan barely checked the paddle she swung at Janet's head. "What are you doing with that?" hissed Janet, slamming the door closed.

"Repelling intruders," Ryan explained in a nervous whisper. "Do you have the rifle?"

"No, it's out there," she whispered back, jerking her head in the direction of the living room where the sounds indicated that a massive fight was taking place.

"We'd better lock the door," Ryan suggested, nervously gripping her paddle.

"The interior doors don't have locks. We'll have to barricade ourselves in here until the police arrive."

The two women looked around the room. One camp cot, a plastic crib and a diaper-changing table were the main articles in the room. There was certainly nothing to prevent an attacker from breaking through. Janet felt the sweat dripping down her back as goose bumps spread up her arms.

Growls and barks came from the living room. "It's an animal!" gasped Ryan.

Janet took a deep breath to calm herself. Animals, at least the four legged kind, she could handle. "Here, give me the paddle."

Ryan did so and Janet slowly opened the door. An animal lurking in the hall cast a menacing shadow on the wall. Janet gripped the paddle and looked around the corner. Rufus stood there alertly, ready to pounce. Seeing Janet instead of an intruder, he sat down happily and wagged his tail. "Woof. Woof."

"Come, Rufus." The dog obediently trotted down to the bedroom. "Okay, you stay here with Rufus, and I'll go see what's out there," Janet instructed.

"Not bloody likely. Mom would kill me if I let anything happen to you."

"Someone has to protect Reb," Janet pointed out, and Ryan nodded reluctantly, recognizing the logic in that.

"Be careful."

Janet nodded and headed down the hall. Ryan had to hold on to Rufus' collar to stop him from running down the hall after her. Janet looked around the corner into the living room. It was a complete shambles. Something jumped from the ledge above her head and she screamed. Rufus broke loose and charged down the hall; Reb woke up crying; the police arrived with sirens blaring. Ryan tore down the hall and knocked Janet flying. The intruder, a very frightened raccoon, darted out the door with Rufus in pursuit as soon as the police smashed through, guns drawn.

Early the next morning, it was a sleepy Ryan that answered the phone. "Hi, Mom. Wow, did we have a night last night. We had an intruder. Rufus fought him, and you should see the living room, wow, what a mess! The alarms worked really well. The police have just left. They smashed through the door with their guns out just like in one of your movies."

At the other end of the conversation, Robbie's heart started to pound with fear.

"No, Reb and I are fine but Aunt Janet has a broken nose and—" The phone was snatched from her hand.

"Robbie?"

"Janet. Sweetheart, are you all right? My God. I'll be home on the next plane."

"Robbie, it was a raccoon."

There was silence at the other end for a minute while Robbie's panic-stricken mind wrapped itself around this information. "What?"

"A raccoon. It fell down the chimney and Rufus chased it around the living room."

"How did you get a broken nose?"

"It's not broken; it was just a nosebleed. Your daughter flattened me in the confusion." Suddenly, Janet started to laugh. "Robbie, it was like a French farce. Wait until I tell you."

Chapter 10

Several weeks later, Robbie sat on the plane staring blankly at her video screen. A smile came to her lips as she replayed Janet's tale of the Night of the Raccoon through her mind again. She missed them. She missed them all terribly. *Where am I going to go from here? It's obvious that my relationship with Janet has gone much further than being a steady date. Hell, we're virtually living together. Janet's helping to raise my daughter and I find myself thinking of Reb as my own.*

Is Janet right? Is it time to let my ancient history go and have a real life? Or is Elizabeth right in reminding me that, for us, a commitment to anyone just exposes them to public humiliation...or worse? Damn! I don't know. I don't want to hurt Janet or the girls, but the truth is I can't live without them.

What would be the difference really? I've long since crossed over the line. If someone did dig something up on me, Janet would be drawn into it anyway.

Okay, that's it then. I love her and I'm going to ask her to marry me.

But what if she says no? Let's face it, Williams, you're not easy to get along with. We've had our fights. In fact, Janet didn't want to sleep with me in the first place because it might reflect negatively on her and Reb. So why should she marry you? Idiot!

Misery spread through Robbie's soul as she looked out at the puffy white clouds below and blinked back tears. *I love you so much, Janet.*

She had been away almost six weeks and was very anxious to get home. *Home. Funny, I never thought of the condo as home but Janet's cabin is. Home to Janet and the girls and the furry mountain that might be a dog.* Robbie smiled. *When did all this happen to me?*

Her eyes turned dark and misty. Janet and the girls would be meeting her in T.O. Janet was scheduled for a check up tomorrow. It was one of many tests she would have over the next five years to make sure they had gotten all of the cancer. *What if they hadn't?* Robbie felt sick at that thought. *Janet has to live, she just has to. Five years, the doctor said, five years before we can be relatively sure that the cancer will not return.* It was like a darkness always hovering over them.

Robbie put on her sunglasses and hat then picked up her briefcase. At the open hatch of the plane she was met by a representative from the airline who handled V.I.P.s and was taken by motorized cart through the corridors to Customs. There she was passed through quickly. A limo waited to take her to her office while the representative waited behind with her baggage claim tickets to collect and forward her bags after they were unloaded from the plane.

It took almost forty minutes to battle the Toronto traffic from the airport down to her office in the city core. Stepping out of the car, she headed for the automatic doors, then turned away and walked down the street instead, opening the heavy brass doors to DeBeers.

She looked at various displays, then, getting her nerve up, she moved over to engagement rings. The selection was amazing. Robbie sat on a stool and a sales representative showed her various gem styles and qualities. Finally, she saw the ring that she knew she had to have for Janet. It was three bands of plain gold joined as one, the centre band with a row of six perfectly matched diamonds. It was elegant and different, and a quiet expression of her love. "I'll take it."

With the small, plush box in her coat pocket, Robbie retraced her steps and took the elevator up to her administrative offices. She wasn't sure that she would ever have the nerve to ask Janet to marry her, but somehow, buying the ring was a symbol that she had at last broken with her dark past and was stepping out into the warmth of the sun.

"Hello, Gwen, I'm back. You've lost weight. I'll need Brian on line one, and then get me Ernie on two," Robbie fired as she passed through her secretary's office and disappeared into her own. The litany continued a few seconds later on the intercom. "Also, I want the balls of the fucking lawyer who is holding up merchandising in Britain."

Gwen shook her head and closed her eyes. With a sigh, she put through Brian's call. Robbie had been away for weeks but she was able to walk in and take command as if she had been out of the office for only five minutes.

Robbie leaned back in her chair. "Brian, it looks like *Desiree* is going to do well at the box office. I've got plans; I need to see you. ... Well, cancel your damn holiday. Why would you want to go to a tropical paradise like Trinidad and Tobago when it's snowing and forty below outside?" She had to watch her assistant director; sometimes he got ideas that he had a life of his own. "Here. Now. Bye." Robbie hung up and clicked to line two.

She smiled. "Hi, Ernie. So, are the backers happy?"

"Robbie, baby! We've made millions this first weekend at the box office. I hear swords and ballroom dancing are all the rage in California."

"There won't be too many balls if they're going to waltz with swords," Robbie observed pragmatically. "I need you to put together a deal for me for the spring, Ernie. I've got some ideas."

"What? Oh. Ideas. New ideas I like. So when are you going to have something for me to sell?"

"Not before spring. I'm taking the winter off to write." Robbie turned to click through her mailbox.

"Good, you write. In the spring, you give me something and I'll sell it. I hear Brian is going to Trinidad and Tobago. I passed by on a cruise ship once. It looked lovely."

"Brian has had a change of plans. I need a package put together before spring. Thirty million."

"Thirty million! You want me to sell thirty million of nothing? Am I the miracle worker?" the excited voice squeaked down the line.

"Make it happen." Robbie yawned and hung up. Gwen was standing at Robbie's desk.

"Hello, Ms. Williams, I'm Gwen Smith, your long suffering and over worked secretary, who has been holding the fort around here for weeks," Gwen opened sarcastically. "I need at least two hours of your time, and I want it now. I've made an appointment for Brian to see you at two."

Excited, Robbie swivelled back and forth on her chair. "Gwen, wait until I show you where your family is going to live..."

Janet passed the Bartlett School duffel bag up to Ryan in the back of the truck. She stowed it with the rest of the bags in the truck storage box and then jumped down. It was freezing cold and snow was falling. It was a hell of a day to have to drive to Toronto, but there was no other choice; the 'copter that Robbie told her to use couldn't fly in this weather.

"Okay, let's hit the road. We'll drop Rufus off at Amanda Singh's and then hope we can get through to Toronto. If we can get past the snow belt between Orillia and Barrie, we should be all right."

Ryan got in on the passenger side as Janet slipped into the driver's seat. She looked back to make sure Reb was firmly fastened in her child's seat and then turned on the wipers to clear the snow that had built up in the few minutes that they had taken to put the bags in the back. Brow furrowed, Janet put the truck in gear and they moved slowly down the driveway that was quickly drifting in. She would see Robbie again tonight if she had to get out and push the damn truck all the way to Toronto.

By the time Gwen finished with Robbie, three hours had gone by. Part of the time had been used up by Robbie swearing Gwen to secrecy and showing her the map of the land that she had bought. She had expected that Gwen would need to be bribed or even black-mailed, if necessary. Instead, the woman had actually hugged Robbie, told her she was a Godsend, and promised to work for nothing on Christmas Day, if need be. Robbie had had no idea that Gwen loved the north.

Brian had been more difficult. He had quit. He announced bravely that he was going to Trinidad and Tobago, no matter what, and that he was not going to live any further north than the suburbs of Toronto. Robbie was forced to resort to blackmail and bribery before the man broke. When Gwen told him that she was planning on moving north, he handed her his plane tickets.

Robbie leaned back in her leather chair and smiled happily. Tonight she was going to see Janet and the girls again and, as far as she was concerned, that made life just about perfect.

The lights of Toronto were barely visible through the snow. Robbie looked at her watch again. Janet and the kids should have been there hours ago. She had arrived at her condo to find a message on her service saying that the 'copter was grounded and that Janet and the kids would be making the trip by truck.

She had tried to get them on the cell phone but they had not answered. She'd called the police. The 400 had not yet been closed, but traffic was down to one lane in some areas. She paced around the room again, dread eating at her. *If anything has happened to my family...* The elevator started rising and Robbie was over there in an instant, nervously dancing from foot to foot. The door opened and out piled her family.

"Hi, everyone!" Robbie called happily, plucking Reb from Janet's arms and giving the child a kiss and a fly over her head. After she brought Reb in for a landing, she pulled an embarrassed Ryan close for a hug. Then she turned and let Janet, exhausted from a hellish drive, fall into her arms.

"Oh, Robbie, I am so glad to see you. What a trip. You've lost weight, love," Janet mumbled, hugging her lover close.

"I was getting really worried." Robbie gave Janet a quick kiss on the cheek. "Are you guys okay?"

"Sure, Aunt Janet can handle anything," Ryan bragged.

Janet gave Ryan an affectionate hug. "Ryan kept Reb amused for hours. If she hadn't, I'd have probably left the anklebiter upside down in a snowdrift, I was so tense."

"Well, come in. I had sandwiches and soup sent up from the restaurant. I'll heat the soup up in the microwave," said Robbie.

"Good, I'm starved. I'll just see to getting Reb settled. Ryan fed her in the truck. I'll be back soon." Janet trotted down the hall with a sleepy Reb over her shoulder, while Ryan followed Robbie to the kitchen.

Ryan looked around at the magnificent, designer living room and the expensive kitchen. Over-tired and grumpy, the trappings of wealth grated on old hurts. "So, if you have so much money, how come you couldn't take care of me?" she asked sarcastically.

Robbie, too, was feeling over-tired and stressed. She'd been on the move from city to city for six weeks trying to sell the critics and public on her new style of film. Before that, she'd had to deal with her daughter's accident and Janet's illness. "Get off my case, Ryan," she muttered crankily as she stuck a container of soup in the microwave.

"No. I want to know," the young teen whined.

Robbie sighed and turned to face Ryan. "I explained this to you before. I was in a lot of trouble at the time. I didn't want you having to live down my past while you grew up."

Ryan pulled a face and rolled her eyes. "What could be worse than getting knocked up with me? Were you turning tricks? Selling drugs? Did you murder your old man for his money?" she smart-mouthed.

"I said drop it!" Robbie yelled, heaving a bowl across the room. It smashed into pieces against the stone fireplace. Janet came running down the hall as Ryan backed out of the kitchen looking extremely afraid.

"What's going on?" she demanded, looking between Ryan and Robbie.

"Stay out of this, Janet!" Robbie snarled, her eyes flashing with anger. She'd gone through enough without having to put up with Janet defending the rudeness of this brat of a kid.

"Okay. But before you discuss this matter with Ryan, could I just talk to you for a minute? Ryan, your room is the second on the right, hon. Why don't you take your bags down there?"

Ryan nodded and escaped.

Janet had read that her partner had a violent temper. Now she had seen it, and it was pretty scary. It wasn't so much what Robbie had said or done; it was the energy that she seemed to radiate, like a reactor having a meltdown.

"Leave me alone," Robbie snapped, banging things around noisily in the kitchen.

Janet walked over and wrapped Robbie in her arms. The stiff body crumbled at the warm, gentle touch and she sobbed against Janet's shoulder. Janet held her while she got some of the tension out. Then she took a tea towel and backed up a step to wipe Robbie's face.

Taking the towel from her, Robbie sniffed back the last of the tears as she dried her face. "Damn," she croaked out, her voice raw.

Janet smiled and rubbed Robbie's back. "No, I don't think it is quite that bad, but you two sure pushed the envelope a bit. She's an over-tired teenager, Robbie. I don't know what happened in here, but I do know that teens have a Doctor Jekyll and Mr. Hyde personality. We've been pretty lucky with Ryan so far. She has been really willing to accept a lot on faith. There will be some bad times, Robbie. You have to expect that."

Robbie nodded. "Yeah. I really love the kid, you know. I...I guess I've got a lot of guilt about not being there for her. She wanted to know, if I was so damn rich, why I couldn't raise her."

Janet looked at Robbie. "You've been away a long time; she was testing. What she really wanted to know was that you still wanted and loved her. Tell you what, you clean up the mess in the living room and I'll go clean up the mess that's your daughter. Then you two can talk it out, okay?"

Looking strained and tired, Robbie nodded. Janet stood on tiptoes to kiss Robbie tenderly. "I need you, too," she whispered before she left.

Ryan had her headphones on. That was a bad sign. Ryan only put her headphones on when she was escaping. They were her sign to the world that she had an attitude and wanted to be left alone. Janet sat on the bed and waited. It took about thirty seconds to wait Ryan out.

"She's a bitch."

"Is she?" Janet asked in surprise.

Ryan took off the earphones. "Look at all this!" she exploded. "Why couldn't she take care of me? She could have hired a nurse if she didn't want to be bothered herself."

"I truly don't know, Ryan. Robbie won't discuss it with me either. All I know is that whatever happened back then impacted terribly on the whole family. Whatever happened, your mom has never come to terms with it. She is still very much afraid that her past will come back to hurt us all."

"So why has she taken me in now?" Ryan asked, fiddling nervously with the wire on her earphones.

"Because of the accident. She thought she was going to lose you. That made her realize that you were something very precious to her, and she had already lost too much time that she could have shared with you. I think, too, that she realized that children could like her because Reb did. It gave her the courage to try to be a good mother to you."

Ryan licked her lips. "I was pretty rude."

"The nice thing about being close to someone is that you can say you are sorry, and if you really mean it, that person will always give you another chance. How about if I go see to dinner and I send your mom in here so the two of you can talk?"

Ryan nodded and Janet gave her a hug and left. Blinking the sleep from her eyes, Janet forced her weary body down the hall. She found her sad looking lover puttering hopelessly around the kitchen. "Okay, your turn. Try not to throw anything valuable," Janet twigged with a soft smile. Robbie hesitated. "Go on, you big coward. You got yourself into this one, and now you are going to have to wade out."

Robbie frowned and headed down the hall as if Janet had forced her to walk the plank.

Janet watched her go with eyes filled with compassion and understanding.

"Uhh, hi," said Robbie awkwardly, from the doorway.

"Uhh, hi," Ryan responded nervously, as she sat on the edge of the bed.

"Ahh, can I come in?"

Ryan nodded and Robbie went in and sat on the bed beside her. She frowned. *What do I say? I'd best just tell it like I see it, as I usually would.* "I didn't like that. I didn't like fighting with you. I didn't like being pushed about something I just can't discuss. I didn't like making an ass of myself by losing my temper, and I didn't like having to come in here to try and talk to you because I'm not very comfortable when I feel vulnerable," Robbie said, staring at the wall.

"You're a famous screenwriter," Ryan snorted, looking at the same wall. "You should be good at this sort of thing."

"We're not acting here. This is how you and I really feel about each other and about what happened. I'm sorry. I wish I'd been a better mother. I wish...well, the only good that came out of that time in my life was you."

"I'm sorry I acted like a jerk," Ryan offered.

"It's okay. I guess we both kind of dumped on each other. You hungry?" Robbie asked, finally getting up enough courage to look at Ryan.

Ryan fell into her mother's arms. "Don't send me away," she sobbed.

Pain stabbed at Robbie's heart. "Oh, sweetheart, now that I've got you, I'm never, never going to do that."

Some time later, mother and daughter came down the hall together and Janet gave a sigh of relief. "Hey, anyone for soup?" she called from the kitchen.

After lighting the gas fireplace, Robbie, Janet, and Ryan sat around it, eating herb and salmon sandwiches and cups of lobster bisque with sherry. Robbie and Ryan soon got into a heavy discussion on modifications they could make to their snowmobile and what Ryan had learned about snowmobile racing from her instructor, George Drouillard of Drouillard's Small Motors fame. They looked up some time later to find Janet curled in a chair, fast asleep, her empty cup in her hands.

"I think Aunt Janet has had it," Ryan whispered.

"Yeah." Robbie sighed. "I guess I kind of left her to handle things," she admitted, feeling a belated sense of responsibility.

"Yeah, the drive took us almost eight hours and Aunt Janet white knuckled it most of the way. It was really scary out there with the white-outs. And then I had to go and throw a temper tantrum." Ryan was starting to feel rather like a rotten human being.

"You and me both," Robbie agreed. The two Williamses looked very guilty as they sat watching Janet sleep.

"And we didn't include her in our conversation," Ryan added to the list of their crimes. "That was bad manners."

Robbie frowned. "She looks awful pale." Tomorrow was Janet's test, and she wasn't supposed to get over-tired if she wanted to get well.

"Do you think she'll kick us out?" Ryan asked, insecurity rising. Tears welled in her eyes.

Robbie managed a weak smile and rubbed the back of her daughter's neck. "No, it's not that bad, but we'll have to think of something to try to make it up to her. We sort of acted like Williams creeps."

Ryan nodded. "You help her to bed, Mom, and I'll clean up dinner. Wait until I tell the kids at school that take-out at your place is lobster bisque with sherry and salmon with herbs. Usually we send out for pizza."

Pulling a funny face at her daughter, Robbie went to pick Janet up out of the chair. She murmured softly in her sleep but didn't wake as her lover carried her down to their room. She gently lowered Janet to the bed and then carefully stripped her down.

"I can do that!" protested a groggy voice.

Robbie leaned forward and kissed a soft, warm belly. "Mmm, let me. I've missed you," she murmured.

Janet smiled, her eyes still closed. "I missed you, too." She was fast asleep again by the time Robbie tucked the sheets up around her. She kissed Janet tenderly on the cheek, and then went to help her daughter. *I have to learn to be more thoughtful if I'm going to have a family,* she concluded as she walked back down the hall. *I've got to stop thinking like a singleton.*

There were words the next morning, too.

"I'm your partner. I should be there at your side. I want to be there," Robbie argued.

Janet gave Robbie a hug on the way to her chair at the breakfast table. "I know, Robbie, but the last time you came with me there was a near riot when your fans found out you were in the building. That's not fair to the hospital staff and I'm not very comfortable with that sort of publicity. Can you understand that?"

"Understand, yes. Like, no," grumbled Robbie.

"I could go with Aunt Janet," Ryan suggested.

"No! I want to go."

Janet shook her. "Okay, here's the plan. You can all come, but you have to wait out in the truck. Does that sound fair?"

"No, but I can live with it. If this is easier for you and the hospital staff then we'll go with this plan." Ryan nodded her agreement.

Janet took the hospital elevator down to the main floor, doing up her jacket as she went. Southern Ontario was in the grasp of a nasty cold front that had sent the temperature plummeting. She crossed the lobby and slipped through the automatic doors where she was hit by a wall of cold air and blowing snow. Janet shivered and pulled her collar up around her neck to protect her face from the elements.

"There she is," blurted Robbie. "Stay with Reb," she ordered, getting out and hurrying to Janet's side.

Janet looked up to see Robbie dodge two cars and hop a guardrail choked with snow as she bee-lined to her. *She is such a wonderful idiot,* Janet thought as Robbie scooped her under her arm. "The doctor said everything looks fine. I'll have to wait a few days for the test results to come back from the lab, but the doctor seemed fairly confident that they got all the cancer." Janet felt the relief flow through her lover.

Robbie didn't say anything. She couldn't. She just squeezed Janet close to her, protecting her from the wind as the two of them made their way back to the truck.

"Well?" asked an anxious Ryan, leaning over from the back seat.

Janet smiled, reaching up to pat Ryan's face. "I'm fine!"

"Cool," Ryan said confidently, as if it had been a given. "Let's go celebrate!"

Robbie arrived late at her office the next day, as some of the private celebrating that she and Janet had done in bed had been encored that morning. The elevator doors slid open to chaos. Personnel from several departments crowded the hall and angry voices seemed to be emanating from her office. "Okay, everyone, back in your cages," Robbie snapped from behind the gawking group.

"Williams!" someone warned, and the group hastily dispersed back to their desks.

Robbie strode down to her office. Two police officers were holding back two very angry men. Robbie recognized one of them as Brian. The other was hard to identify with the blood spurting from his nose and the swelling of his left eye, but Robbie suspected that it might be Gwen's husband. She had met him, she recalled, at the staff Christmas party one year. A security guard bent over Gwen, applying some ice wrapped in a paper towel to her jaw.

"What the hell is going on in here?" Robbie slammed her briefcase on Gwen's desk and moved to kneel by her secretary, who had a nasty bruise on her jaw. Noting the shock in Gwen's eyes, Robbie asked softly, "You okay?" Gwen nodded. Robbie stood up, radiating authority. "Okay, who sucker punched my secretary?" she growled.

"He did!" yelled Brian, as the cop held him tight. "The bastard's been cheating on her, and when she served him with divorce papers, he came in here and hit her."

"I'm going to sue you, you hear. I think you broke my nose," came a nasal voice from behind the blood.

"Brian, did you hit him?" Robbie asked calmly, looking at her assistant director with new respect.

"Twice," Brian bragged.

"Good. Remind me to give you a hefty raise." Robbie turned to the cop holding Smith. "Officer, I will be pressing charges against Mr. Joseph Smith for trespassing and assaulting one of my employees. We will also want a restraining order filed against him." Robbie stood toe-to-toe with Smith and looked him in the eye. "If you bring charges against my assistant for protecting my secretary, I will hire a battery of lawyers to see that you go to hell in a handbasket. Officer, please remove him from my office." The Toronto constable smiled and led the man from the room.

Robbie turned to the other officer. "I think it is safe to release my assistant now. He seems to have stopped frothing at the mouth."

The police officer laughed and let Brian go. He went over to Gwen immediately.

Robbie watched with a bewildered look on her face. *What the hell has been going on around here while I was away?*

It took most of the rest of the morning to fill out police reports and lay charges. Robbie called her lawyers to represent Gwen and Brian, and had the company nurse see to Gwen. Robbie now sat leaning back in her chair with her eyes closed. Brian sat across from her. She sighed, tapping a finger on the arm of her leather chair. "Okay, Brian, I'm waiting; make it good."

"I got here a little early for our meeting and found him manhandling her, so I hit him. He got up, so I hit him again," Brian explained with dignity.

Robbie nodded and lifted her hand to wave him on. Brian cleared his throat. "About five weeks ago, I found Gwen crying. She'd found out her husband had been cheating on her for some time. So, naturally, I offered her condolences." The hand waved again. "And took her to lunch."

An eyebrow arched up and Robbie looked at Brian through one blue eye. "Are you fooling around with my secretary?" she snapped.

"No. She won't let me," Brian responded with heated annoyance, which made Robbie burst out laughing.

As her private elevator rose to the top floor, so did Robbie's spirits. She was going home to her family, Janet was well, and Christmas was coming. Robbie hummed a Christmas carol as she rode up. The doors opened and Janet was there to meet her. She pulled Robbie back into the elevator and pressed down. Then she said hello properly in a long, probing kiss. On the way back up, they tried it again.

"Voom, voom," came two children's voices, one baby-like and the other starting to take on the deeper tones of adulthood. "Foot out. Lean to the curve." Robbie looked at Janet for an explanation.

"Ryan's teaching Reb how to race a snowmobile on your exercise machine," she giggled. Robbie rolled her eyes.

"Hi, Obbie. Hi, Obbie. Peas fly me," squealed a delighted two-and-a-half-year-old, running to be scooped up and spun over Robbie's head.

"Hi, Reb. Hi, Ryan." Robbie laughed, looking over her shoulder at her daughter as she came out of Robbie's gym room.

"Boy, this place is swell; it's just like a mansion on stilts. Wait until you see what I did to your computer."

Robbie paled and lowered Reb to the floor. "You were playing on my computer?" she asked weakly.

"It's okay, Mom, I saved and closed all your stuff. Boy, are you messy. So you're into special effects, huh? Wait until you see mine," Ryan bragged.

Janet put a restraining hand on Robbie to keep her from saying something she might regret. "Show us what you've been doing, Ryan," she cut in.

"Come on, Reb," Ryan called, heading down the hall to the state-of-the-art editing room that Robbie had set up.

Robbie sighed under her breath as she shed her coat and boots. Janet grimaced. "It's partly my fault. I didn't see any harm in her using your computer to do her homework."

"That is not a computer room. It is a two million dollar editing room that just happens to have a bank of computers in it." Robbie shook her head in disbelief as she stomped down to the room. *It could be worse; at least it's between films,* she consoled herself philosophically.

"Oh boy," Janet whispered, following along in Robbie's wake.

Ryan waited until they were grouped around the main computer, then in a circus announcer's voice she said, "Ladies! I present the X-rated Rebryan Production of Bear Facts! Okay, Reb, press the key."

Reb giggled and carefully pressed the key as Ryan had taught her. The screen saver flashed to DVD mode and the music to Teddy Bear's Picnic started to play. Little yellow Winnie the Pooh bears in red shorts waddled across the screen. In their midst was a cartoon character looking remarkably like Reb. The character sneezed and all the bears lost their shorts.

Reb broke into gales of laughter. "Play again, Sam. Play again, Sam," Reb squealed with delight. Janet and Robbie laughed until the tears rolled down their faces.

They laughed through dinner too, as Robbie told them the story of Brian's gallantry, and Ryan and Janet told Robbie about their trip to the nearby grocery store.

"We have a grocery store around here?" Robbie asked in amazement.

"Mom, you have to see this place. They've got the food locked up."

"What?" Robbie asked blankly. *I don't recall any food locked up at the store in Bartlett, although for what you have to pay for a good, thick steak, it ought to be.*

"They've got a locked cabinet with small rolls of truffles and pate for a hundred and fifty dollars. There was this container about the size of a bread roll of black caviar from Russian sturgeon for seven hundred dollars. They had live lobsters in tanks, too. I wanted to have lobster for dinner, but Aunt Janet couldn't bring herself to condemn one, so we bought dead lamb instead. We couldn't find toilet bowl cleaner, though, could we, Aunt Janet?"

Robbie looked at Janet. "I've got a cleaning staff."

"I wanted some to take back to the cabin with us," Janet explained as she took Reb's spoon from her and helped her clean up the last of her dinner.

Ryan giggled. "The manager was impressed that you had live-in staff."

"What?" Robbie laughed, simply because the other three were.

"The manager thought we were the maid service," Janet explained, "because I asked for toilet cleaner."

"Boy, do you live in a snobby neighbourhood, Mom," Ryan teased, holding her nose in the air.

"Don't let it go to your head, kid. I'm leaving all my money to the Canadian Tax Department."

Much later, Robbie lay in bed feeling just about as happy as a person could feel without exploding with joy. Janet lay partly draped over her body, fast asleep. She grinned. *What Janet and I have together is just...great.* She lifted her head to drop a kiss into soft hair. *Life is great.*

We'll head back up to the cabin tomorrow early because we need to drive the truck back. It's Sunday, and Janet and Ryan need to be back at school on Monday. I think I'll take a month off, practice for the winter carnival that's coming up, and then it will be Christmas.

Christmas! Robbie's eyes popped open and sleep fled. *Don't families buy presents and things? Damn it. What the hell am I going to get them?*

On Monday morning, six girls sat around Stacy Nona in the dining hall. It was their secret meeting place before classes started. "I'm telling you, Robbie Williams is gay."

"Why would she want to be gay?" Angela failed to see the logic in it. "She's really feminine and good looking. I thought only ugly girls became gay because they couldn't get a guy."

Taira blinked in disbelief. "Angela, you're talking nonsense. At one time, homosexuality was thought to be caused by over-possessive, dominating mothers. We now believe that it might be genetic. You are born gay."

"Weird."

"No, perverted and a mortal sin. We've got to do something. We don't want their kind here. Ryan must be gay too, if it's in the genes. She's even got a guy's name. I say we make her want to leave this school."

"You're just angry because she caught you taking her lab kit and made you give it back," observed Debbie.

"I needed it. I lost stuff out of mine and she wasn't using hers right then, anyway. She's a bitch. She's been kicked out of other schools, you know."

"What for?" Angela asked, loving a bit of gossip.

Stacy stirred the pot. "What do you think? Like mother, like daughter, if you ask me. And they're staying up there with our principal. Makes you wonder."

"Do you mean—"

"Shhh, here she comes."

Ryan saw the looks and steeled herself. She'd gone through enough hazings to know the signs. "Hi, guys. Some storm on Friday, huh?"

Stacy lifted her big bulk and stood in the doorway, blocking Ryan's path. "We've been talking. We know what your mother is and we don't want your kind around here."

"I'm sorry you feel that way. I don't know my mother very well yet, but she seems like a very nice person."

"She's a damn queer and so are you," Stacy snarled, pushing Ryan back into the wall while the other girls crowded around to act as cover. "You're going to leave here, got it. Leave. Leave. Leave."

The blows landed with each word. Ryan could have fought back. At other schools, she had, but she wanted to stay here. She wanted to live with Aunt Janet and her mom, so she let the blows fall.

Robbie was just coming in from doing her practice laps on the snowmobile and had to pull off her boots and run for the phone. "Robbie."

"Robbie," said Janet's professional voice, "there's been a situation. I need you to come over to the school right away. There has been a fight. Ryan's okay, but she's pretty battered."

"I'm on my way," came the grim response.

Stacy and her mother were already in the office when Robbie walked in.

"You gotta get her kind out of here!" Mrs. Nona was yelling. "She tried to beat up on my daughter. And Stacy said that Ryan's the one who has been stealing all the stuff from the girls."

Robbie saw her daughter sitting forlornly in the corner of the principal's couch, her face bruised and her lip cut. A ball of ice filled her gut as she slid in beside her daughter and let the young girl snuggle into her. "You all right?" Robbie whispered into Ryan's ear. Ryan nodded.

"It was a hazing, Mom. Stacy's got them worked up that we are all gays. She started whaling on me, but I swear, I didn't do anything."

"Lying bitch," Mrs. Nona yelled.

"That will do, Mrs. Nona," Janet snapped, interrupting before Robbie lost her temper. "We are here to piece together what happened, not to yell insults at one another."

"We know what happened, that girl attacked my daughter. There are witnesses. She's been stealing, too, and I want her out of this school. My husband pays good money to send Stacy to this school. We deserve better."

"Mrs. Nona, the thefts at the school are indeed a concern, but they have been going on for a lot longer than Ryan has been here. She is not involved in that issue. Stacy, have you any bruises, cuts, or anything that need attending?"

The girl smirked. "No. I fought the queer off and taught her a lesson."

"Neither your language nor your tone are acceptable to me. If you wish to stay in the office and participate in this discussion, then you will please talk politely or I will ask you to leave."

"Hey, stop picking on my daughter. You're just protecting your relatives. That's not fair."

A knock sounded on the door and Amanda Singh stuck her head in. "Sorry to disturb you, Mrs. Williams, but I have Debbie DeLuca out here and I think you should hear what she has to say."

Janet nodded. "Okay." Amanda entered beside a very scared looking student. "Yes, Debbie, what is it you want to say?" Janet asked gently.

"Stacy told us if we didn't support her story that she'd beat us up. But Mrs. Singh talked to us one day about what it is like to live with prejudice and I don't want to be part of that hate. Ryan didn't do anything, Mrs. Williams. Ryan always tries to be nice. Stacy said we had to get rid of her because her mom's gay." She stopped and blushed, turning to Robbie. "I'm sorry, Ms. Williams, I didn't mean to call you a name."

"That's okay, Debbie. I don't consider 'gay' to be derogatory term. Go on."

Debbie nodded. "Stacy is the one who's been stealing stuff. A lot of us knew, but we were afraid to do anything in case she might beat us up."

"You're lying! You're sticking up for Ryan because you're sleeping with her."

"Enough!" snapped Janet. "Mrs. Nona, some serious charges have been laid against your daughter. It would not be appropriate for me to investigate because I am related to the Williamses. I'm going to suspend Stacy from school and call a special meeting of the trustees. They can evaluate the evidence and make recommendations as to how to proceed. We'll notify you as soon as we have set up a time for the meeting."

"You're going to take this...this hooligan's word over my daughter's? My daughter is the victim here. Come on, Stacy. This damn school will be hearing from our lawyer." The Nonas stormed out, slamming the door behind them, leaving the room in a bubble of silence.

Robbie stood, rigid with emotion. "Thank you, Debbie, for having the courage to stand up for your beliefs," she said with feeling, offering Debbie her hand.

Debbie took it in a daze. "Thank you, Ms. Williams."

Robbie turned first to Amanda and then to Janet. "And thank you for your assistance in this matter." She reached down and helped her daughter up and left without another word.

Janet felt a migraine headache forming. Was Robbie angry at her for doing her job? This was one hell of a mess and it was going to get worse, she knew. She became aware that Amanda had said something. "I'm sorry. What was that, Amanda?" she responded absently.

"Do you want to talk to Debbie, or should I take her back to class?"

Janet gave herself a mental shake and reminded herself that she had a job to do. "No, leave Debbie here; I'll need the names of the other students involved to give to the board. Thank you, Mrs. Singh."

Robbie drove back to the cabin with Ryan quiet at her side. Ryan could see her mother was having a meltdown again, and she didn't want to remind her mom that she was part of the cause. The truck came to a halt and Robbie slammed out, coming around to help Ryan from the truck, much to Ryan's surprise.

"Do you need a doctor?" Robbie asked seriously.

"No, I'm okay, Mom. I'm sorry."

Stopping short, Robbie looked at her daughter with eyes as cold as the Arctic snow. "No, I'm sorry, for exposing you to that sort of abuse."

Ryan smiled and gave her mom a hug. "You are the greatest. Aunt Janet will work it out. We're kind of a weird family, but we are a family, aren't we, Mom?"

Robbie held her brave daughter close. "Yeah, we are. Come on. Let's get out of the cold."

Mother and daughter sat drinking tea, their socked feet side by side on the coffee table and the fire blazing. "Ryan, there could be more days like today, you know."

"Yeah, I know. I can handle it, Mom. Don't chicken out now, okay?" Ryan laughed, although there was a worried catch to her voice.

Robbie took Ryan's hand and held on to it. "I'm never going to leave you, Ryan. Doing so all those years ago was the biggest mistake of my life. I made that decision for the best of reasons, but it was still a mistake. Actually, ahh, I was wondering how you would feel if, well, ahh, maybe, if your aunt was willing, we could, I mean I could..."

Ryan laughed with glee. "You're going to ask Aunt Janet to marry you?"

Robbie blushed deeply. "Well, there isn't enough room in this place and the work at the lodge is going really well. I thought, in the summer, we all could move in over there. I don't know how Janet would feel about that. I mean, there's her job and well, she loves this house...and I'm kind of old and grumpy."

"Boy, I hope you do a better job when you ask her, Mom. That was awful. You want me to do it for you?" Ryan teased.

I know she's joking to cover up her concern. On the one hand, she wants to be a family. Of that, I'm sure. On the other, living in a gay household is sure to make Ryan a target. She must be afraid that the marriage could result in her having to put up with abuse from idiots like Stacy.

"No! You butt out of this, Ryan. I'll ask her. Sometime, maybe, when the time is right. I just thought we'd do it quietly. You know, no one needs to really know. It would just be a family thing. What do you think?" She searched her daughter's eyes. *I don't want to hurt any of you, but my love for Janet could do just that.*

Some of the tension of the day beginning to ebb, Ryan said cheekily, "So, instead of you coming out of the closet, we're all going to get in?"

Robbie laughed. "No, but I don't think we need to shock Bartlett too much. Let's let them get to know us, and in time they'll probably figure it out for themselves."

"Sounds like a plan," Ryan said with a smile, heading for the washroom.

Winking at her daughter, Robbie picked up the phone and dialed the school. "Hi, Carolyn, it's Robbie Williams. Can I speak to Janet, please?"

"Hang on, Robbie," Carolyn pleasant voice directed.

"Hi," Janet answered anxiously. She had just hung up from talking to the Chair of the Trustees, John B-for-Bastard Bartlett. Her headache was much worse and it was parent interviews tonight. She wasn't sure she could handle a showdown with Robbie, too.

"I just phoned to tell you I think you are the greatest and that I'll try to be objective when it comes to my daughter. I needed some time to calm down before I could say that."

A rush of relief flooding through Janet. "I love you. Ryan didn't do anything wrong that I can see. We'll just have to ride out this storm. The Chair of the Board is anti-gay and works with Stacy's father at the car dealership, so we'll have to see. Don't forget it's parent interviews tonight. I'll be home for dinner, but we'll need to take separate cars because I'll have to stay to the bitter end."

"Parent interviews? I don't want to go. You just tell me what I need to know," Robbie whined sulkily. The last thing she needed was to meet the Nonas in the hall tonight.

"No. You are Ryan's mother and you need to talk to her teachers," Janet stated firmly. "This has nothing to do with me."

"Why the hell am I sleeping with the principal, then?"

Janet leaned back in her seat and some of the tension of the day slipped away. "Fringe benefits."

"Mmm, I do like those." Robbie felt the warmth of desire building deep inside her. "See you for dinner."

"Okay. Let Ryan cook, would you? I can't face another meal of beans on toast." Janet fired her parting shot and hung up.

Robbie stuck out her tongue at the receiver and hung up too.

Janet never made it home. Carolyn phoned to say she was at a meeting with John Bartlett and to please bring a sandwich when Robbie came for interviews. The last hope Robbie had of faking a headache to avoid the evening faded. She was going to have to do her duty.

Robbie redirected Reb's spoon from her ear toward her mouth and looked at Ryan over her shoulder. "Hey, you're a good cook."

"Mom, it's frozen fish, carrots, and stuffed potatoes. All I did was heat things up," pointed out the ever-practical Ryan.

"More than I could do. Listen, is there anything I should know about before I go to this thing? Have you blown up any labs or anything?"

"Mom!"

"Just asking." Robbie laughed and Ryan threw her napkin at her.

Robbie looked at her watch. "I'd better get going. Don't forget to let Rufus out for a bit, then put on the exterior alarm. Make sure Reb doesn't eat anything valuable, and don't watch Aunt Janet's collection of dirty DVDs."

Ryan snorted. "You call *Simba's Pride* a dirty movie? In this house, I have to make do flipping through old copies of National Geographic."

Robbie gave her daughter a hug and slipped on her parka. The last thing she wanted to do was go to the damn school. She picked up the paper bag that contained Janet's dinner and headed off.

To Janet's surprise, John Bartlett was very conciliatory. "We don't want this to go to a board meeting, Janet. Can't have that," he said, wiping his brow. "I don't know if you realize this, but Ted Peel owns the dealership; I'm just the manager. Ted is married to Olivia Nona, that's her second marriage, so Stacy is my boss's step-child."

Janet's face showed interest; inside she was sighing. *Damn small town politics!* "If you think that puts you in a position of conflict of interest, John, you can let the rest of the board handle the situation."

"No, no. Ted, he doesn't want it going to the board. He came to me today after his wife called. He doesn't want this leaking out to the community. Seems Stacy confessed to beating on the Williams kid and doing the stealing. She's a smart enough kid to realize she'd better after Debbie blew the whistle on her. According to Ted, Stacy's a lying trouble-maker, but you know how mothers are, they just don't want to see it."

"That puts us in a difficult position, John. We need to resolve this issue. I can't pretend that things weren't stolen and that there wasn't an assault here today."

John Bartlett loosened his tie. "Look, this is what Ted wants. He said he'd shut Olivia up and move Stacy to a school in Toronto. He'll pay for all the missing stuff, and in return, we let this issue drop. I don't want any bad publicity from all this."

Janet leaned back, maintaining her poker face. Inside she was doing cartwheels of joy. She'd been worried all day that Bartlett would get his teeth into the gay issue and run them all out of town. Now, instead, she had him over a barrel.

"My sister-in-law is a very volatile woman and she needs to be concerned at all times about her public image. Very serious accusations were made and I've got to tell you, she was furious when she left here today. She has the money and power to bring a team of lawyers from Toronto and crucify all of us. All I can promise you, John, is that I will do my very best to pacify her and get her to accede to Mr. Peel's wishes. I'm sure you're worried, John. I certainly am. I'll let you know as soon as I can." *After I let you stew for a few days, you rotten bastard.* Janet stood. "Thanks for being so forthright."

John Bartlett struggled to his feet and left the office, a drained and worried man.

Robbie fumbled with the list she was given by a student at the door. *Okay, first on the list: Mrs. A. Singh, science teacher. Hey, that's Amanda. Okay, I can handle that.* As she walked down the hall, Robbie checked the numbers on the doors until she found the science lab. She walked in hesitantly, unused to dealing with Ryan's schools on friendly terms.

"Hi, I've got the seven o'clock appointment," she said stupidly, standing at the door feeling very warm in her parka.

Amanda got up. "Hello. Come on in. Have I got great things to tell you about your daughter."

"You do? Hey, that's good." Robbie beamed, moving forward as she shed her jacket. "I can do great."

In the end, Robbie was the last parent to leave, having stayed to hear what Janet had resolved with John Bartlett. Much to Janet's relief, she had been satisfied with the arrangement, and had then followed Janet home. Principal and parent walked into the cabin to find a worried daughter playing blocks with Reb.

She was on her feet in an instant. "Is it all right? Can I stay?" she asked nervously.

Janet and Robbie glanced at each other, belatedly realizing just how stressed Ryan had been about the conferences. Robbie walked over and smothered Ryan in a big bear hug. "The teachers all agree that you are human and that you can stay as long as you stop eating your peas off your knife," she joked. Into Ryan's ear she whispered, "I am sooo proud of you."

Janet smiled as she walked over to rub Ryan's back reassuringly. "Stacy has confessed to causing the problem and stealing. I've arranged for a boarding school placement for her in Toronto. That is not to be blabbed around though, okay?"

Ryan beamed, her smile the same white flash of delight as her mother's. "That's great, Aunt Janet. I knew you'd fix it."

Janet and Robbie took off their coats and Ryan went to put the kettle on for hot chocolate. When they were all seated around the fire, Ryan announced that she had a surprise. She picked Reb up off Janet's lap and stood her on the coffee table. "Okay, we've been practicing all night, haven't we, Reb?"

Reb nodded seriously, adoring eyes looking up at her cousin. Ryan cleared her throat and Reb copied her. Robbie and Janet tried not to laugh. "The letter R by Rebecca Williams," proclaimed Ryan. "Say 'room', Reb."

"Room," giggled the two and a half year old, and everyone clapped and cheered.

"Say, Rufus."

"Rufus!" yelled out Reb, her eyes sparkling with the attention she was getting. More clapping and cheering followed the successful attempt at Ryan's name.

"Okay, Reb, say 'Robbie'."

Reb giggled and hopped with joy. "Obbie, Obbie," she chanted and launched herself at her aunt. Robbie easily plucked her out of the air and twirled her overhead with much laughter.

Ryan sat down with a sigh and shook her head in dismay. Janet giggled, "I think your mom will just have to be Obbie," she concluded.

Reb, now snuggled in Robbie's arms, nodded her head and said stubbornly, "She Obbie."

The tip of Janet's tongue teased the corner of Robbie's mouth. They had settled the kids and then shared a shower, taking turns washing each other's hair. Now they lay warm and relaxed in bed, Robbie on her back and Janet curled around her.

"Did I tell you that Bill Anderson — he's the math teacher — said that Ryan is one of the strongest students that he has ever taught?"

"Yes, and you told me that Jason thought she showed talent as a cartoonist, that Amanda felt she could easily follow in her Aunt Elizabeth's footsteps, and that Milka was impressed by the maturity and depth of her writing," Janet murmured, running a finger over a hard, pink nipple.

"These parent interviews aren't so bad," Robbie concluded with a smug grin, pulling Janet in for a hug and absently kissing her on the forehead.

"You can absorb praise like a sponge, Williams." Janet laughed. "Talk about satisfied with yourself."

Robbie wore a grin so wide her jaw ached. "Hey, that's my kid."

"Shut up, Obbie, and make love to me," Janet ordered, kissing Robbie soundly.

Isabelle Selo unfolded the letter she had picked up at the post office and re-read the note from the investigative reporter who wanted to meet her. Mr. Lucier sounded like a very caring, nice man. Yet you couldn't be too careful; there were all sorts of perverts out there. She'd meet him in a public place and not tell him yet where she really lived.

She looked up at the big poster of Robbie Williams she had hanging in the hall. It was the one of Robbie dressed in a black sleeveless T-shirt, looking hot and dirty and carrying a machine-gun in her long fingered, strong hands. Although she had posters from all of Robbie's films, she liked this one best of all. She liked the way the sweat beaded on the bulge of her forearms and the way her eyes shone so blue through the dark tangle of hair.

Robbie looked around the crowded room of Carolyn's home with disinterest. It was the annual Bartlett staff and trustee Christmas party, and it was a bore. Educators were conservative and nice, and they threw really well organized and predictable parties. She thought about some of the parties she had attended in the film industry and smiled.

The man who had cornered her was John Bartlett. He managed the car dealership, and he had been going on for some time about the possibility of Robbie's companies buying from them now that she was settling in town. He was the Chair of the Trustees, and Janet disliked him. Robbie disliked him too, just on principle. Her mind suddenly clicked in to what he was saying.

"These teachers have to understand that the taxpayer wants value for their money. They're well paid to work for ten months of the year and it's a job anyone could do, just standing up there talking. Yet they're not getting the job done. Kids today can't read or write and that's a fact. Now if teachers had to work in the real world—"

Robbie lost it. "What the hell do business people know of the real world? You sit in your office all day pushing paper with your handpicked staff. If someone doesn't live up to your standards, you fire them. It's not like that in teaching, Bartlett. That *is* the real world.

"You take thirty little very imperfect kids, each one of them with a schoolbag full of individual needs. You want to talk about the real world? When have you had to deal with cases of sexual and physical abuse of children, or the trauma caused by divorce? When have you had to deal with the special needs kid, the emotionally disturbed child, the lice, the neglect, the poverty, the teen pregnancies, and all the other stresses that teachers quietly deal with day after day on top of teaching? You know dick all about the real world, Bartlett."

Bartlett turned beet red and glanced around nervously as Robbie's stage voice continued to every corner of the room. "Every damn adult who gets elected or spawns a child suddenly thinks they're an expert on education. Bull! Get a university degree, your college training, and then work in a classroom for ten years and you'll have something worthwhile to say."

Carolyn came charging around the corner into the kitchen where Janet was talking to Milka about the new language guidelines. "Janet, come quick. Robbie's telling Bartlett the truth about education."

"Oh, shit!" Janet whispered, as she put her drink on the counter and made a beeline for the living room.

"When do you think the curriculum gets researched and written? When do you think the marking gets done or the lessons planned? When do you think the sports teams practice or the field trips get planned, or the concerts are rehearsed? Do you actually think that happens in the classroom?"

"Ahh, Robbie could I see you for a moment," Janet interrupted, pulling on Robbie's arm. "Excuse us, John, won't you?" She smiled. "I have something I need to show Robbie."

"Of course, of course." Bartlett smiled weakly, backing away with relief.

Janet pulled Robbie into the now empty kitchen. "What the hell were you doing out there?"

Robbie looked annoyed and stubborn. "Telling that asshole the truth."

Shaking her head, Janet sighed as she placed her hand on Robbie's hard stomach. "Robbie, teacher bashing is part of the job. No one in politics is going to admit that they don't know what they are doing when it comes to setting up educational programs, and no parent is going to admit their child is slow or poorly raised. It is always going to be the teacher's fault."

"But a teacher with thirty students has less than five minutes of individual time with each child a day. What can they do to solve all the problems that parents dump on them?"

Janet frowned. "Robbie, where are you getting all this stuff?"

"I read your manuscript about your first five years of teaching. It's good. I think we'll make a movie out of it someday." Robbie smiled.

Janet's mouth fell open and then snapped shut. Her jaw tightened. "Robbie, my manuscript was on disc and in my desk files. I can't believe you would be so rude as to go through my personal things. Damn it, it's not finished, and I'm not sure I want it published, never mind made into a movie. It's very personal."

"Yeah, I know, that's what makes it so damn good," Robbie said agreeably.

"Robbie! What you did was very wrong. You violated my privacy," Janet snapped in angry frustration.

"Why would you want to have secrets from me?" Robbie asked, hurt in her voice.

Janet rolled her eyes and stomped a few steps away, then turned and came back. "When you were working out your plans for the land you bought, did you tell me right away?"

Robbie looked sheepish. "Well, no, I needed to work it out." She shuffled her feet and a red flush crept up her neck as she realized what Janet was saying. "I'm sorry."

"You're sorry that I'm upset; you're not a bit sorry about going through my files." Janet snorted in annoyance.

"Well, it's a start."

Janet looked at her with cold eyes. "Never again, Robbie. Promise."

Robbie looked resistant. "What if there was an emergency and I had to go through your things?"

"Promise."

Robbie surrendered. "Okay, I promise." Worry crossed her face. "Are you going to stay mad? Did I get you in a lot of trouble?" she questioned belatedly.

Janet gave her a quick hug. "Thanks for defending us teachers. Don't ever do it again, okay?"

Robbie nodded, relieved to get off as lightly as she had. *I've got to learn to see my partner's rights. This getting serious with someone takes a lot of work.*

Chapter 11

A still sleepy Janet reached a hand from under the covers and snagged the phone. "Hello?"

"They're here!" came the cheery voice of Mary Drouillard over the line. "George is just unpacking them now. Greta's T-shirt order is here, too. She's on her way over. George and I have already set two aside for us."

Janet smiled. Mary never introduced a subject; she just expected people to know what she was thinking. "*What* is here?"

"Why, the snowmobile suits in your racing colours that Robbie ordered for the whole family. Oh! George is holding one up now. It's lovely — black with a gold slash down each side. You are going to look super. Bartlett will be able to hold its head up with pride this year, I can tell you."

Janet controlled her emotions long enough to say, "Really. Well, that's great, and just in time too. We'll be down later today to pick them up."

Robbie came into the bedroom drying her hair with a towel and ran into a small but mighty barrier. "You ordered racing colours?" Janet asked.

Big eyes looked out between strands of damp, tousled hair, making Robbie look a bit like Rufus. "Yeah. Are they here? I was beginning to think that they wouldn't get here in time for the winter carnival."

"You promised me that this would just be for fun, no getting carried away. Damn it, Robbie. I was recently at a Williams funeral where the theme was racing colours, I don't want to attend another one." Janet fought to control her emotions. If anything happened to Robbie, she wasn't sure how she could go on.

To Robbie it was all fun. The show, the competition, it was just all part and parcel of being Robbie Williams. But she realized that Janet was really upset. "It's just an outfit, Janet. Team Bartlett has to look the part." She wasn't sure she understood Janet's fears. *What could go wrong?*

"Team Bartlett?" Janet fumed, hands on hips.

"Hey, it's no big deal," Robbie protested. "It seems Bartlett has never had anyone enter the regional races before, so we are sort of the town's team by default. That's all. And George said all the other teams had colours, so what was I going to do?" Robbie smiled innocently.

"Black and gold," muttered Janet, rolling her eyes. "You just remember you promised me not to get too competitive. This is just a friendly, small town race." Robbie wiggled her eyebrows and Janet threw up her hands in frustration. "I want final say. If I think it's too dangerous then I don't want you racing. It scares me," finished Janet, her lip quivering.

Robbie pulled her close, not really understanding but moved by Janet's distress. "Hey, it's just a small, friendly contest, you said so yourself. Okay, you've got final say. We Williams will be good. I promise."

Janet felt some release of the tension around her heart. It was as if Robbie was just attracted to danger. She didn't want to chain her lover's free spirit, but she did feel the need to place some checks and balances on the woman. She had a daughter and responsibilities. She wanted Robbie to learn that she couldn't just live for the moment. "Robbie Williams, you are an olive," she sighed.

"Mmmhmm. Let's have breakfast at Maria's and go pick up the outfits, okay? We can go to town on the snowmobiles." Robbie was almost dancing with excitement as she hugged Janet.

Janet smiled, lapping up Robbie's enthusiasm. "Okay. Let's get the kids up."

The four Williamses paraded into Maria's and stripped off the layers of snow wear, their faces red with the cold. Outside, the ever faithful Rufus sat looking through the window and waiting for the table scraps. The family had deliberately kept the speed of their snow-mobiles down so that the determined dog could keep up.

Maria bustled over. "Look, look, I am second to own one. Greta brought a box in for me to sell here in the store. These colours suits me, I think."

The group turned to see Maria in a black T-shirt with a four-centimetre gold stripe along the shoulders and down the sides. On the left side in gold was the logo of a racing snowmobile. Across the top it read "Team Williams" and below was written "Bartlett's own."

"Robbie..." Janet started.

"I didn't know a thing about it," Robbie cut in. Then she smiled. "We'll take four, please."

"Ahh, good. They are selling like hot cakes. Greta is using them as a fundraiser for the drama society," Maria explained, bustling off.

Janet looked around. Everyone was looking at them. She'd come to expect that, but today the other patrons were all smiling and holding up T-shirts or pointing to the ones they were already wearing.

Janet sat down, defeated. Robbie and Ryan went around signing the T-shirts. Janet looked over at Reb, who was sitting forgotten in the highchair. "We should have just driven the truck home ourselves the night of the funeral," Janet sighed. Reb blew a raspberry and laughed at Robbie across the room. "Great. My own daughter has become an olive."

The day of the carnival was beautiful — clear, calm, and crisp. There were games for the kids and rides on horse-drawn sleds. The Lions Club was playing Christmas songs over the baseball park loudspeakers and the women's auxiliary was selling hot drinks, barbe-cued hot dogs, and hamburgers.

Ryan went off with some school friends and Robbie took Reb on the small Ferris wheel with Janet, rocking the seat back and forth until Janet ordered her to stop. Then they leapt on the back of a wagon covered with straw and rode around the lake singing Christmas carols along with a handful of other townspeople.

Back at the carnival, Janet took Reb. "I have to go and do my half hour of selling at the auxiliary bake sale table. Robbie, look around but please don't get into trouble," she cautioned.

Robbie looked angelic. "I am here just to have fun, like any other Bartlett citizen," she huffed.

"Be good," Janet reinforced, and hurried off to help the ladies.

Robbie walked along checking out the various displays set up by different compa-nies. She saw a hand crafted cedar picnic table that she wanted to show Janet later. They could put it on the porch or down by the lake to use in the summer. Rounding the corner, her eyes lit up. There ahead of her was her childhood fantasy — a bright red fire engine with its yellow ladder extended. She made a beeline for it.

"What about you, Walt? The volunteer fire department needs new recruits. You get to ride on the fire truck and hack through your neighbour's roof with an axe." George Drouillard was laughing as Robbie came up.

"Sorry, George, my back's not up to it," Walt responded, moving on.

"You run the fire department, too?" Robbie said in wonder, dancing eyes staring at the big, red, fire eating machine.

"Hi, Robbie. Yup, I've been the Fire Chief of the Bartlett Volunteer Fire Department for about ten years now, because I've got the only garage big enough to keep old Betsy-Lou in."

"I want to join."

George chuckled and scratched a spot above his ear with a finger. "Well, Robbie, I don't think there is a rule against women belonging, but it's never happened before. You see that ladder there? You gotta be able to carry a full grown man down it. Not too many women can do that."

"I can." Robbie's blue eyes radiated confidence.

"Well," George laughed nervously, "I don't suppose we'll have any trouble finding a volunteer to help you with the test."

The excitement and the size of the crowd grew as word got around that Robbie Williams wanted to join the fire department. By the time they had assembled, Robbie was climbing into yellow rubber pullovers and big black boots. Standing up on a platform by the ladder was David Potts who ran the general store.

"Hey, Dave, watch where you put your hands now!" someone yelled up.

"Oh dear," flustered David.

Robbie smiled. It was well known that David, like his brother, was a shy, middle-aged bachelor. *He's going to be very embarrassed about being carried over my shoulder and no doubt will be teased unmercifully about being carried by the star who's been named one of the most beautiful and sexy women of the decade by* People *magazine.*

"Two dollars says she drops him," someone called out.

"Five dollars says she gets him down, but he dies of a heart attack with a grin on his face!" Everyone laughed and poor David, stranded at the top of the ladder, turned beet red.

"You can't do this, George! Every man in town will be setting his house on fire and rushing to the second floor." More laughs and good-natured fun followed as Robbie pulled on her work gloves and set her helmet in place.

"Hey, Mom!" hailed Ryan. Robbie looked over, saw her daughter and smiled. Ryan leaned over the rail. "You show those guys."

Robbie winked, swung up on the back of the truck and headed up. At the top, she slung David's arm over her head, crouched, and easily lifted the stocky man up on her shoulder. The crowd cheered. David closed his eyes.

This was the hard part, and the crowd fell silent. The other volunteers stood below, the fire net at the ready. For a second, Robbie was struck by the pressure that she had taken on. That was her daughter down there. She couldn't fail and she couldn't fall. Maybe that was what Janet had tried to make her see.

Robbie got a good grip on the ladder with one hand and another on David, placed her left foot securely on the rung, and swung out and around so that her other foot slipped onto the rung below. She shifted David into a more comfortable position and climbed down the ladder to cheers and whistles from the crowd. At the bottom, a few of the volunteers helped David, weak in the knees from the experience, down off the truck. Then Robbie jumped down. "You okay?" she asked David, who sat on the fender looking very pale.

"I'm fine. Dear me, nothing like that is ever happened to me before," he gasped.

Robbie laughed and leaned forward and pecked him on the cheek. Lucier, who had missed the ladder descent, had to be satisfied with a picture of Robbie's pucker and David's startled face. It appeared on the front page of the paper that Friday with the caption "Hot New Firefighter".

Janet stopped dead when she saw Robbie and Ryan advancing towards her. Robbie was dressed in the Fire Department yellow pants and jacket and Ryan was wearing a firefighter's helmet. "Guess what, Aunt Janet. Mom carried David Potts down the fire ladder, and now she's a member of the Volunteer Fire Brigade," bragged Ryan. "She's got a beeper and everything."

Robbie stood there with that silly grin she got when she was particularly happy with life and hadn't a care in the world. Janet closed her eyes and shook her head. Bartlett was never going to recover from Robbie Williams and her daughter. Somehow she had to make Robbie realize that little Bartlett was not Robbie's personal playground.

Janet had to admit that Robbie had shown considerable restraint when they walked over that afternoon to where the races were being held in the old cow pasture beyond the Lions' Hall. Big trailers with bright logos down the side provided storage for half a dozen snowmobiles and a full repair shop. The drivers had teams of helpers working on their machines. Team Williams was a pathetically small open trailer with one black and gold snowmobile perched on top. Their team consisted of the Williams clan and George Drouillard with a jerry can of gas.

What they lacked in equipment, they made up for in spirit, however. Ryan drove their team entry slowly over to the warm up area with Reb sitting in front of her. The child-sized helmet Reb wore made her look like a little alien. Black and gold homemade banners dotted the crowd, and a big cheer went up as they arrived. The Williams clan, all dressed in identical snowmobile suits, waved back. *How did I get to be part of another Williams orchestrated event?* Janet wondered. Wishing Ryan luck in the under sixteen race, Janet took Reb to find a good place to stand.

Robbie stayed behind with her daughter to review their plans for the race. "Okay, kid, remember to watch your speed into the third turn. It's icy over there, and you don't want to spin out," Robbie cautioned, checking everything over one last time before letting Ryan move up to the starting line with their snowmobile.

"Okay, Mom." Ryan smiled, a sparkle in her eye at the thought of the speed and competition to come.

Recognizing the look with a sudden spurt of fear, Robbie pulled Ryan's helmeted head close and spoke into her ear. "You be careful. I want you back in one piece. I love you." Ryan smiled and gave her mom a quick one-armed hug, then moved up to the starting line with the others.

Robbie ran around to stand with Janet at the starting line. "She'll be okay." Robbie reassured Janet and herself as she bounced from foot to foot nervously.

Janet reached out and rubbed Robbie's back, feeling the tense muscles under her racing jacket. Robbie was a great mother in her own strange and wonderful way.

Robbie needn't have worried. Ryan easily beat the other kids without really feeling the pressure to push for that extra bit of speed. A good stage mother, she hung back and let Ryan enjoy the limelight before going over to wrap her daughter in her arms and hug the daylights out of her.

The adult competition was a much larger field of competitors. Robbie moved up through the heats, coming in first each time. In the last heat, she was racing in a group of six. The most serious competitor was from Helingone, a community northeast of Bartlett. Helingone had gotten its name from the early loggers who had wintered over there, and who swore it was several miles north of Hell.

The residents of Helingone seemed to feel that they had to live down the name of their town by being fiercely competitive. They always won the snowmobile races and the summer regatta. They particularly enjoyed beating Bartlett because Bartlett's town sign read: "Welcome to Bartlett! We might be north, but at least we're south of Helingone." Helingonians did not see the humour in that.

Big Jim Ableton was their number one racer. He was a logger by trade and resembled a hardwood tree — both in size and intellect, from what Robbie could ascertain. He had gone out of his way to pass nasty remarks about the "girly" team that Bartlett was supporting. Robbie meant to wipe the course with him.

They sat in a row at the starting line, revving their engines in anticipation of the flag. They were off with a roar and a blue cloud of exhaust. Robbie let the world fall away until she was just one with the machine vibrating under her. The track tunnelled by in a blur, Robbie conscious only of what lay ahead. One by one, the other snowmobiles fell behind with each lap until it was just her and Jim jockeying for position close to the inside of the track. They came down the last stretch side by side, Robbie slowly edging forward. Fifty feet before the finish line, Jim edged his machine over, prodding Robbie's back treads with his front ski.

The tread jammed for a split second sending Robbie into a wild spin. Jim crossed the line first with Robbie spinning over a split second later. She felt the snowmobile tipping and leapt off. Her body was traveling at over a hundred kilometres an hour when it hit the snow. She spun like a top, arms and legs flinging out in all directions, then rammed, back first, into a bale of hay.

For a second, she lay there stunned, then she rose up like a mushroom cloud over Ground Zero. She was going to cut Big Jim down to size with her two bare hands. Shaking with anger, she took several steps in that direction, until she caught sight of her family standing there, horror written on their faces. *I scared them.* She smiled and waved. She'd get that bastard in the final race.

Janet fell into Robbie's arms, not caring at that moment what people thought. "Oh God, Obbie! I thought you were dead."

"That was cool," Ryan said, covering her own fear with humour. "You looked just like the blades on the helicopter. Bet you hurt."

"Obbie go booboo," Reb observed, looking up at her hero.

Robbie bent and picked up the small child. "I'm fine Ryan, really. It looked worse than it was. I was just sliding along until I hit that soft pile of hay." In actual fact, every bone in her body had been jostled and she ached, having pulled some muscles that she didn't even know she had. There was no use upsetting her family and ruining a perfectly good day.

"I'll get Ableton in the final," she promised with a smile. "I'll be ready for his tricks next time."

"No," Janet said, and all the Williamses looked at her in surprise. "Robbie, you said I could call the shots and I'm doing so. You're finished racing today. I'm not letting you get hurt in some sort of grudge match."

"Ahh, Aunt Janet..."

Robbie touched her daughter's shoulder and she fell quiet. "I promised your aunt that if she wanted me to pull out, I would. So that's what we are going to do. The family's more important than the race." Robbie smiled, burning inside with frustration. *Damn. Why did I make that silly promise?*

Just then Big Jim swaggered past. He reached out a hand and gave Janet a slap on the backside. "Hey, girly, any time you want a real man in your life, you just call. I think I can teach the school teacher a thing or two." He smirked as he walked on.

Ryan and Janet had to both step in front of Robbie to stop her from going after him. "Robbie?" Janet said, fuming at the insufferable rudeness of the man.

"What!" Robbie was about one hair's breath away from murder. No one touched Janet. No one.

"You kick his ass good in the next race," Janet ordered. For the second time in a few minutes, the other Williamses looked at Janet in surprise. Then they all started to laugh.

Ableton had the post position with Robbie to his right. When the flag dropped, they were off to a fast start. This time, however, Robbie stayed close to Ableton, just far enough back that she sat in the blind spot of his rear view mirror. Every once in a while he would take a quick look back to see where she was.

I'm getting to you, aren't I, tree stump?

Just after the last curve, Robbie made her move, dropping suddenly to the inside and burning past Ableton. He tried to move to the outside. Robbie moved with him, keeping him right behind, in her ruts and exhaust. She kept one eye ahead of her and one on Ableton, watching out for his tricks.

Sure enough, he tried to ram her back end. She kept just that couple of feet ahead of him right across the finish line. The crowd of black and gold shirts clapped and hooted their approval. Robbie was pushed on a tide of well-wishers over to the platform to get her trophy. "Thanks to George Drouillard and my daughter Ryan and the rest of the Williams team, and a big thanks to the people of Bartlett for their support!" she yelled out above more applause and cheers.

The Williams clan, Drouillards, Greta Corry, and several of Ryan's friends all sat at one table in the Lions' Hall and feasted on burgers. It was a tired family that hitched up their snowmobile trailer and headed back to the cabin in the late afternoon. Dinner was a plate of sandwiches by the fire, Janet holding the sleeping Reb at one end of the couch, Robbie at the other, and Ryan nodding off in one of the chairs.

"Don't you ever again not tell me when you are hurt!" Janet commanded later that night as she straddled Robbie's naked backside and massaged her aching muscles. Robbie moaned with pleasure and wiggled her backside between Janet's naked thighs. Janet leaned forward and kissed the back of Robbie's broad, muscular back. "I think you have misinterpreted my nurturing activities," she whispered into Robbie's ear.

Robbie growled. An arm shot up and around Janet, and the next thing Janet knew she was under Robbie, being kissed long and deep and hungrily. Robbie lowered her hips between Janet's legs and moved rhythmically. It was Janet's turn to moan as Robbie slipped down and did things to Janet's body that made her go crazy with desire. She was getting close, panting with need, when Robbie's beeper went off.

"Nooo!" Janet gasped, burying her head in the pillow as Robbie leapt up and ran to the closet to slip into her clothes and firefighter outfit.

"Sorry, love, I'll be back. Save my place," Robbie said as she hopped about getting her rubberized pants on.

Janet threw a pillow at her, then called out as Robbie headed out the door, "Don't do a thing, just watch. You haven't had any training yet."

Several hours passed while Ryan, who had been awakened by the commotion, and Janet, who was too stimulated to sleep, waited for Robbie to return. They filled in the time baking cookies for Christmas. Finally, the fire truck, flashing red lights, pulled up at the side door. Janet was there just as Ted Potts raised his hand to knock.

"Evening, Janet, we brought Robbie back, on account of she was in no good condition to drive."

Janet paled. "Where is she?"

"The boys are bringing her along now." Ted stepped aside so that George Drouillard and Moe Singh could help Robbie in.

Robbie was soaking wet and an awful shade of blue. She walked along on stiff legs with an arm around each man's shoulder for support. Looking up and seeing Janet, she said sleepily, "I'm hurt."

"Oh, Robbie. Ryan, put the kettle on, please," Janet instructed. "We need to get something warm into her right away."

"Why, thanks, Janet, we could do with a cup of tea," George said. "I'll get the rest of the boys."

The sun was showing on the horizon by the time Janet and Ryan had stripped Robbie of her clothes, gotten her into a hot bath and then into a sleeping bag on the sofa. She had refused to be put to bed while everyone else was drinking mugs of tea and eating fresh-out-of-the-oven chocolate chip cookies in the living room.

"So, Larry Butler did a little too much celebrating after the race today and made the poor decision to take a shortcut with his snowmobile over Turn Back Bay. Course, the ice there is no good, every fool knows that, what with the winds. Sure enough, the ice breaks up and he's left adriftin'. He calls his wife, Flo, on the cell phone and she calls us out. By the time we get there, his vehicle has slid off the ice and into the lake, and so has he," George explained between sips of tea.

"He managed to pull himself up on a small ice floe, but it's clear he isn't long for this world if we don't get to him. We try a few times, but the ice keeps a-crackin' up under us. Finally, Robbie here, bein' the lightest, slips into a harness and crawls out to the open water, but by that time old Larry is too far gone to care. He isn't even tryin' for the rope she's tossin', so damn if the lady doesn't keep right on a-goin'. Swims about ten feet to him, hooks him on to her harness, and we pull both of them back in." George stopped to chew a cookie philosophically.

"Larry will be okay. I figure he had too much alcohol in his blood to freeze. It was quite a night. Just like one of them Williams movies."

Ryan, who was sitting on the floor by her mom, looked up with pride; Janet shook her head. They finally got to bed about six. Reb had them up by seven.

The following week, Robbie had to fly down to her office.

"Why don't you invite your sister Elizabeth for Christmas while you are in Toronto?" Janet suggested during one of their many phone calls.

Robbie snorted. "My sister? She only leaves her secluded world to go to physics conferences, and then only once in a blue moon. I'm not sure she realizes Canada spreads further than the suburbs of Toronto."

"Please," Janet wheedled. "Family is important and Ryan really wants to meet her famous aunt."

Robbie's voice took on a pouty tone. "What's wrong with her famous mother?"

Janet laughed. "Ryan adores you, but you are not the scientist."

"Where would we put her? The cabin is overcrowded as it is. You practically have to book ahead to have a bath."

"I've got it all worked out. I asked Bill Perkins and he said we can borrow his trailer. It has a good electrical furnace and a reasonable-sized bathroom. We can run a power cord from the house. That way, if Elizabeth needs some private time, she can escape to her trailer. How does that sound?" Only silence greeted what she thought was a good idea. "Robbie, how does that sound?"

"It sounds like you had dinner with Bill Perkins."

"No, coffee at Maria's after the drama society meeting," Janet confessed. "Jealous?"

"Yes."

Janet knew that you could only pull the tail of a Williams once before you were likely to get a reaction that would be less than amusing. "Good. You'll get back here to me faster. I miss you."

"When, between coffee dates?" Robbie sniped, partly in jest and partly out of a real need for reassurance.

"I miss you all the time, especially at night when I reach out for you," she whispered gently, knowing her lover would be thinking the same thing she was.

"Mmm. I like that. I'll talk to Elizabeth, but I make no promises. I'll phone you tomorrow. Bye, my love."

"Bye, darling." She really did miss Robbie terribly.

Elizabeth wrote a complex equation on a piece of paper and looked at it with a half smile. *Physics is so beautifully pure; loyal to the laws of nature and yet so complex in its structure. It's like dropping a stone into the pool of the universe and watching the ripples of energy create eternity. I wish people could understand enough math to be able to see that beauty. It seems a shame that only a handful of people in the world can read God's blueprint—*

"Hi."

Elizabeth looked up with a start.

"Sorry, Elizabeth, I didn't mean to scare you."

Elizabeth wiped the sweat from her upper lip with a shaky hand. "It's okay. I usually keep my door locked when my secretary has left, that's all."

Robbie nodded. "So, is this a good time to talk?"

Elizabeth's eyes focused on Robbie sharply. What was going on with her sister? She had read with some surprise that Robbie had at last acknowledged her daughter. She had also seen an article about Robbie saving Ryan from a well or a pit or something. She was glad she lived in the relative safety of the academic world. There were no surprises. She hated surprises. "Of course. What is it you wish to discuss?"

Before she lost her nerve Robbie poured out: "You know how I feel about Janet, Bethy. I wanted you to know that I've decided to ask her to marry me. Would you like to join our family for Christmas?"

Elizabeth blinked, then blinked again. These were not surprises; they were two whopping big shocks, blows to her state of well-being. It took the better part of half a minute for Elizabeth to recover. "Love, I understand, is irrational, which explains the lack of logic in the rest of your statements," she observed.

Robbie nodded. "My daughter, Ryan, would really like to meet you. She thinks science is wonderful. She's already blown up a lab and she's only fourteen. Janet can borrow a trailer. It's like a home on wheels, so you can have all the privacy you want. The cabin is kind of small. It would mean a lot to me, Bethy."

It had taken a lot for Robbie to get that all out, Elizabeth realized. Robbie was not good at sharing personal information. She noticed a sheen of sweat had even formed on Robbie's upper lip. Elizabeth did not want to go. She didn't think she liked kids and she hated strange places, but Robbie had asked her, and if Robbie wanted it, then there was no choice. "If you want me to, Robbie, I'll come."

Robbie smiled. "That's great. I'll take care of you, Bethy; you know I will."

Elizabeth smiled. Robbie always took care of things. Robbie was wonderful. She knew she could trust her.

"Listen, I haven't actually asked Janet to marry me yet, so don't say anything, okay?"

Elizabeth frowned. "You do know I don't approve of this relationship, Robbie," she said nervously doodling numbers on her paper. "We agreed that because of our past, involving others in our lives was not fair."

Robbie face clouded and she sighed. "There are days when I don't approve either, Bethy. I must be crazy to risk recognizing Ryan and bringing Janet and Reb into my life, but I can't go back. I don't want to go back. For the first time in a very long time, I've been happy."

Elizabeth looked down at the numbers that gave her such beauty and pleasure. Robbie should have happiness, too. "Then I will support you, Robbie," she promised. "I want you to be happy."

Frowning, Robbie drove through the wintry streets of Toronto. She hadn't noticed before how truly dreary winter in the city was. The yellow-grey sky hung low and wet, and the snow, piled to the sides of the streets, was pitted with dirt. *My lungs probably look like that,* she reasoned, pulling a face. She thought about the piles of white, fluffy snow in the north and the clear blue skies. *I can't wait to get out of here.*

It had been a busy week and Robbie was tired. The "Brian, Gwen, Joe" triangle seemed to have resolved itself for the time being, thanks to the company's bank of lawyers. The film was making millions, was even being hailed as the best love story ever. Ernie was making headway in selling nothing to the backers, and she had managed to get her Christmas shopping done.

That had been by far the most exhausting part of the week. It was dangerous out there. She had no idea how frantic and ruthless Christmas shoppers could be. No wonder they threw Christians to the lions. By the end of the week, she had been quite willing to participate in that age-old Roman tradition.

Now she was driving her BMW — her Stingray never saw winter — over to the island airport to take the company helicopter up to Janet's. She could hardly wait. Damn, she missed her family. The last six months of her life had been like a rebirth. Her whole world had changed from icicles to fire. The cell phone rang, cutting into her thoughts. She picked it up off the seat. "Robbie."

"Hi, Mom."

Robbie felt her particular cup of joy spill over. *I've got one great kid,* she thought proudly. "Hi. What's up?"

"I phoned to warn you: don't come home; dye your hair, change your name, and move to Argentina. She might not be able to track you down there."

As she turned into the parking lot of the commuter airport, Robbie's eyes widened in surprise. "Who and why?" she asked calmly, as she punched the button to get her parking ticket. Robbie was used to having people gunning for her.

"Aunt Janet has spent all week watching your movies. First, she watched the ones you directed and wrote, and then she started on the earlier ones you acted in. She said they are works of art and clearly show that you should be locked up as a deranged and sick human being."

Robbie beamed. "Works of art, huh? Why am I sick and deranged?" she asked conversationally as she found her spot and pulled in, shoving the car into park while she leaned back to talk to her daughter.

"You killed the dog in *Cold Night Walking*; she and Rufus took it personally. We all sat around and cried."

"That's what you were supposed to do," Robbie protested. "Is that why I'm in the doghouse?"

"Nope, you're in trouble because of *Female Marines*. I quote, 'Robbie and *that* woman have something going. That Julie Devon is all over her like a rash.' You're in trouble."

"That was ten years ago!"

"She has big boobs...*two* of them," Ryan explained, less than subtly.

"Uh oh."

"I'm to take Reb to the library this afternoon for Read Along. She wants me out of the house so there are no witnesses. So, were you sleeping with Julie Devon?"

Robbie looked at the phone in shock. "What are you, the teen from hell? You don't ask questions like that."

Ryan giggled. "Thought so, you could see the chemistry."

"What would you know about chemistry? No! Wait, don't tell me, I don't want to know. I wouldn't be able to sleep nights."

"Bye, Mom. Good luck!"

"Thanks, kid," Robbie said softly, and hung up. *Oh boy, I'm in trouble. Maybe a gift... Is there a store at the island airport?*

Grinning with happiness, Robbie ran up the steps. "I'm home," she yelled. Janet met her at the door and Robbie scooped her up in her arms to kiss her. "God, I've missed you!"

"Mmm. I missed you too." They kissed again, long and slow, desire building like a tidal wave.

"Anyone around?" Robbie asked between kisses.

"No." Robbie carried Janet to the bedroom.

Later, they sat by the fire, waiting for the kids to come home, Janet snuggled against Robbie's side and Robbie wrapping a possessive arm around her. "Umm, I've been watching your movies. They really are good."

Uh, oh, here it comes.

"When you made *Female Marines*, were you and Julie Devon...well...you know?"

Janet was too smart a lady not to pick out a lie, otherwise Robbie might have considered it. "Yes," she stated flatly. She'd decided that the only way to make their relationship stronger was to be honest with Janet.

"Oh." The tone was disappointed, pained. "She's very beautiful. Is she nice?"

"Yes, she is very beautiful and she was a real pleasure to work with. She's up-beat, funny, and a hard worker," responded Robbie honestly.

"*ET* said there are rumours that she will star in your next movie." Janet rubbed Robbie's hand with the tip of a tense finger.

"I don't have a screenplay yet. I'm going to take some time off this winter and write. I have talked to Julie about the story line, though, and she is leaving herself available for the role next year." The body she was holding went still. Janet's hand stopped moving and she held tightly to Robbie's hand.

Robbie gently wrapped her hand around Janet's. "Does that bother you?"

"Yes." Janet started to shake with tears.

Robbie's heart spasmed with pain. She lifted Janet into her lap and held her close. "Shh, love, it's okay. There is only one person I will ever need in my heart and my bed from now on, and that's you."

"I'm grotesque," Janet sobbed, holding Robbie tightly and dripping tears down her neck.

"No, you are not. Don't ever think that or say it again," Robbie said sharply. She pulled Janet away and forced her to make eye contact by lifting up her head with a gentle hand. "You turn me on. You satisfy me. You have given me more joy and happiness than I thought possible. Do you really think I'm such a low life that I'd cheat on you?"

With tear filled eyes Janet mumbled miserably, "You dumped Tracy Travelli."

"Tracy was a convenience. She knew it. I knew it. We were just using each other. Things are a lot different for me now. I've fallen in love, deeply in love. I've got this...family. I don't need or want anything else." The words fell well short of what she felt inside.

"Oh, Robbie," Janet moaned, wrapping herself around her lover again. "I love you so much. Every time you do something dangerous or go away, I feel so vulnerable. I don't mean to be so jealous and possessive."

"It's okay, I kinda like being wanted." Robbie smiled, holding Janet close. "I work with a lot of beautiful and famous people, Janet. If I act, I'm likely to do a love scene. It's just business, nothing more. Sure people come on to me at times, males and females. You have to know, though, that you are something special and I'm never going to risk that."

Janet held on as tight as she could. "I love you, Robbie."

This was not how she had planned to stage it; there was going to be soft music, a shining Christmas tree, and a quiet drink. Instead, her proposal wasn't going to be a performance, it was going to be real, here and now, with a lover whose nose was red from crying.

She slipped Janet off of her lap and on to the couch, then left her for a moment to get the ring box out of her briefcase. On her return, she sat beside her lover and kissed her softly. "You are my soulmate. I have always loved you, and I always will. Would you do me the honour of marrying me this Christmas?" Robbie's stomach fluttered nervously as she waited for the answer.

"Oh, Robbie, we can't...the kids...my job... Oh, yes! Yes, Robbie! I love you so much!"

Robbie took out the blue velvet box and slipped out the ring she had bought. With great reverence, she removed Billy's band of gold and in its place slipped her own pledge of loyalty and love. For a long time the two of them said nothing, too overwhelmed with the step they had just taken to find the words to express what they had found together.

"It's beautiful Robbie. Everything is so beautiful now that I've found you," Janet whispered softly, feeling warm and cherished in the circle of Robbie's arms.

Chapter 12

The next day, Robbie found David Potts sweeping out his small general store right at closing time. He smiled. "You just made it, Robbie, I was just going to put the lock on the door."

"We've gotta talk," Robbie said seriously, closing the door behind her and switching the cardboard sign around so it read "Closed".

"Oh dear!" He looked truly frightened.

Robbie didn't look much better, but she'd proposed and there was no backing out. "I...uhh...need a favour. I understand you are the Justice of the Peace in town."

David smiled in relief. "That's right. I bet you want your passport signed. I can take your picture, too. I've got the camera back there by the meat counter."

Robbie licked her lips. *This is nothing to be ashamed of, Williams. Just ask the man. Even if he refuses, Janet said he could be trusted to keep quiet.* "This is a confidential matter."

"Well, I don't think I do things like that." David frowned. "My job is for the public record. Maybe, you should see a lawyer, Robbie."

"I want to buy a marriage certificate and I want you to marry Janet and me," Robbie got out in one deep breath.

David looked stunned. "Oh, my."

"We don't want it to become a circus. We just want to quietly exchange vows and adopt each other's children. Can you do that?"

"Well, I don't know." David was flustered. "I mean, I can, but I never have. Most people go to a minister."

Robbie just stood and looked at him, one eyebrow up in annoyance and her arms crossed.

"Oh! Oh dear! I guess that wouldn't do, would it?" David bit his lip and then smiled. "You know, I always wanted to be a minister. I've got the licenses right over here. Oh, this is so exciting!"

Frowning, Robbie followed him. "We don't want a lot of people to know. We don't want it getting out to the media."

David stopped and looked at her in shock. "Ms. Williams, I would never tell a secret," he said indignantly.

It was Friday afternoon, and Janet had asked Carolyn, Milka, and Amanda to pop into her office before they left. They now sat in a row in front of her desk looking vaguely worried. "Umm, this is a personal and confidential matter," Janet began, feeling embarrassed. "You are not only part of my staff, but friends. I want you to know that I'm gay and that I've been seeing Robbie Williams."

She waited. There was no reaction. The three women just sat there with smiles, waiting.

Janet cleared her throat and went on. "We've decided to get married and wondered if you would feel comfortable being at the ceremony." This time there were whoops and her friends got up to hug and congratulate her.

Carolyn said knowingly, "We spotted the ring days ago."

"We thought you'd never tell us. It was all I could do to not say something," groaned Milka.

"When is it going to be?" Amanda asked. "Can Bert and Mohammed come?"

Janet blushed brightly. "Yes, of course, they can come if they feel comfortable at a gay wedding. It will be on Boxing Day, at the cabin. Robbie would like it outside, so we hope the weather will be nice. Uh, you understand, you can't say anything. If the media got hold of this, it would be a mess, and very hard on the kids."

"Hey, we can keep a secret. We're your friends. This is just so neat," babbled Carolyn. "Who's doing the ceremony?"

"Umm, Robbie is arranging something today," Janet stalled, not wanting to mention David's name until she knew he had agreed.

Gwen got the announcement in an e-mail. "This is for Brian and your eyes only, Gwen. Janet and I are getting married on Boxing Day. You two are invited. The 'copter will bring you up. R."

Gwen shook her head. *Typical Williams. Didn't have the nerve to tell me face-to-face. And where am I going to get a babysitter for three kids on Boxing Day? They'd just have to go stay with their father and his new live-in, because not for the world would I miss seeing Robbie Williams get her wings clipped.* She hadn't been sure about Janet at first, but she had come to realize that the quiet principal was the perfect match for Robbie.

Christmas was wonderful. To everyone's surprise, including her own, Elizabeth felt very safe and comfortable at the cabin. She liked the small coziness of the trailer, too. After the rather startling noise and confusion of her sister's family, she could lie in her bunk at night in the northern stillness and look out the window at the clear stars. She knew many of them by name and number and spectrogram.

She liked Janet. She was like a mother ought to be — friendly, caring, and she could cook, too. She liked that. Elizabeth tended to warm some canned soup in a beaker over a Bunsen burner or stick a frozen dinner in the microwave. She could well afford to have a cook or maid, but she needed her privacy more than such services. At Robbie's they had real Christmas cake and sugar cookies cut and decorated with icing. There were stockings hanging on the fireplace, even one for her, and all sorts of parcels under the tree. She was glad that she had ordered a gift for each of them. It was like the Christmases she had read about but never had.

And her sister was so different — relaxed and funny, and just great with the kids. Robbie was happy at last. That made Elizabeth happy. Ryan and Reb, she found, were fun. Reb liked to sit in her lap and play with her glasses. She called her "Annie Beth" and her sister "Obbie". Ryan was full of mischief and could be quite startling in what she would say and do. She was so very much like her mother. Yet, when Elizabeth talked about physics with Robbie, Ryan was right there and asked intelligent questions.

Elizabeth nodded in the dark of her trailer. Yes, she liked having nieces. She must find out when their birthdays were and send them a little something each year. Why, that monkey Ryan had even taken her for a ride on her snowmobile into town to buy extra milk and butter and introduced her to the nice looking man who owned the store. Ryan had told her that he was also the Justice of the Peace and would be the one that would marry Robbie and Janet. There was a man who could turn his hand to anything.

At dawn Christmas Day, Ryan was banging at her trailer door with a coffee. Elizabeth slipped over to the cabin in her wool housecoat and boots and joined the family around the tree. Janet handed out the presents and wouldn't let anyone open any until they had all been distributed. Then it was pandemonium.

Once all the gifts had been exchanged with many hugs and kisses, much to Elizabeth's surprise, they had a breakfast of homemade braided loaves and jam made from the blackberries they had picked that fall. Then they all went to church. It was...magical.

Janet and Reb had gone for a much-deserved nap and Elizabeth sat in the window by the fire, watching Ryan and Robbie down on the lake, industriously rolling snowballs. *What in the world are they up to now?* Large snowballs gradually formed a semicircle on the lake near the beach. Then, at ninety degrees to the arch, a second row of three large snowballs was hoisted into place. Two more were placed on the top of these and then one. The semi circle now had a central tower.

Elizabeth pushed her glasses up the bridge of her nose and watched with interest. Two wooden benches from the cedar picnic table were carried down and placed inside, with an aisle left between them. *Why, they are building a snow chapel,* Elizabeth realized. *How lovely.* Carried by the moment, Elizabeth went and got her coat, and then helped her sister and niece wet and polish the snow walls until they shone ice blue.

Smiling with delight, Elizabeth inspected the winter fairy castle under the dome of a robin blue sky. Later, when Janet joined them, Elizabeth, in a rare moment of insight, took Reb from Janet's arms and indicated to Ryan to follow her up to the cabin.

Janet stood with Robbie and watched the setting sun turn their chapel to soft pink then royal blue. "I love you, Robbie. Thank you."

"I love you, too." Robbie sketched a bow. "And you are welcome." Hand in hand, they walked back up to the house.

"Robbie?" came a soft voice in the dark.

"Mmmhmm?"

"Why are you still awake?" The sheets rustled as she moved closer.

"Why are you?" Robbie evaded, kissing a bare shoulder affectionately.

"Because I'm scared skinny about tomorrow," Janet admitted, kissing a soft breast.

Robbie laughed. "Me, too. I do film, not stage."

"Terrific. All we've gone through to get to this point, and now we both have cold feet. It's a very big step we are taking into the unknown. There could be some real tough moments ahead for us and the kids," Janet fretted.

"Yeah. There are sure to be. But gays have fought long and hard for the right to enjoy the responsibilities and privileges that legally married couples have always had. We would be foolish to let our fears of what society might say and do stop us from taking this step."

"I know, we've never talked about money or anything. I have a mortgage and—"

"*We* have a mortgage and we will pay it off."

"That's not fair. Why should you pay my debts?"

"Because we are not going to be a 'you and me' after tomorrow. We'll be a we. Janet, have you any idea how rich I am?" Robbie's tone was amused.

"Rich enough to have a spare million anyway," Janet sighed.

Robbie snorted. "Last year, my personnel income, not that of my companies, just mine, was over fifteen million. I think we can afford to pay off the mortgage." Robbie felt and heard Janet giggle. "What's so funny?"

"Damn, you're a good catch."

Robbie was obliged to show her just how good.

The ice chapel shone under the clear blue, northern sky. Evergreen trees, bowed with white pillows of snow, framed the scene as the guests arrived and took their places. On Robbie's side sat Gwen, Brian, and Elizabeth. On Janet's side were Mika, Carolyn and Bert, and Amanda and Moe. Bill Perkins was there, too. He fancied himself an amateur photographer, and it was his bittersweet duty to photograph the event from the sidelines.

David Potts stood proudly in front of the snow wall. Robbie had wanted to buy him a blue parka to wear for the ceremony, but he had refused. This was his first wedding and he planned to do it right, he told her. He had braved the cold in his Sunday-best, navy blue suit.

Robbie and Ryan waited nervously beside him. They both wore black pants and boots and buckskin jackets in soft cream. Indian bead work in bright blues and reds formed small panels from each shoulder.

Soft Celtic harp music played as Janet and Reb, hand in hand, came down the small aisle. They wore black pants and boots, too, with matching white Eskimo parkas. Simple native patterns decorated the hemline in the same bold colours as was on the buckskin jackets. The four made a beautiful grouping as they stood in front of David.

David smiled shyly and then gathered himself together. "Who gives away this lady?" he asked.

Janet squeezed Reb's shoulder and the little girl giggled. "I do."

Everyone smiled and Janet winked at her tiny daughter.

"Ladies and gentlemen, we are here today, under God's immense sky, to witness the marriage of these two fine ladies. Marriage is a sacred bond. It does not deal with gender, age or religion, but with the love, loyalty and trust between two individuals, such as Janet and Robbie. They have chosen to join their lives together as one. If anyone knows of any reason why these two should not be wed, please speak of it now." David paused. When no one dissented, he continued with the vows.

"Janet Jean Williams, do you take Robbie to be your lawful partner, trusting in her love and loyalty to guide you through your life together?"

"I do."

"Roberta Nichola Williams, do you take Janet to be your lawful partner, trusting in her love and loyalty to guide you through your life together?"

"I do."

"If you would place the rings on this Bible," David instructed.

Ryan took the two simple bands of gold from her pocket and placed them on the white leather Bible that David held out. "Robbie, if you would take one and make your pledge to Janet."

Robbie took the ring and placed it on Janet's finger. "My love, my loyalty, my trust, always."

Janet took the remaining ring and slipped it on Robbie's finger. "My love, my loyalty, my trust, forever."

"In this special place made by our Lord God, and before these witnesses and friends today, I declare you legal life partners. Please seal these vows with a kiss."

Robbie leaned down and brushed a shy kiss across Janet's lips while their family and friends applauded. Robbie and Janet hugged Ryan and Reb and then accepted congratulations from David and the others.

Janet and Robbie, now one, led the party back to the cabin to sign the certificate and to cut the wedding cake that David had surprised them with that morning. He had baked and decorated the cake himself.

David and Elizabeth took the marriage certificate and carefully folded it and put it inside the Bible. They walked over to where Robbie and Janet stood hand in hand and took them aside. "The Bible I used today was bought for you by your sister, Elizabeth. In it is your marriage certificate. Best wishes to you both," he said, giving them the white leather Bible.

Tears filled Robbie's eyes. Unable to put into words how she felt, she gave her sister a big hug. For the first time in a very long time, Elizabeth didn't flinch at the touch but instead hugged back gently.

That night Ryan and Reb had a sleep over in Aunt Beth's trailer. Janet and Robbie sat for a long time by the fire. They held hands and watched the brightly burning flames, content to be together as partners. It was a new world and a new beginning.

The night was icy cold and Janet shivered as she waited for the truck's heater to pump some warmth into the frozen cab. There was no moon, and driving through the dark back roads of northern Canada with only the stars visible, brilliant over head, was like flying through space. Janet smiled softly, enjoying the sensation of commanding a lone vehicle through the cold darkness.

Beside her, Ryan sat quietly. Her breath made little clouds, tinged pink by the dashboard lights. The clouds drifted across the inner space of the cab and froze to the windscreen beside Janet. She turned up the defroster to clear the ice away.

"Aunt Janet?"

"Yes, love."

"Do you think Mom will help us?" Ryan asked anxiously.

Janet felt her heart contract. Ryan was so outgoing and confident that one sometimes forgot that she was, in many ways, a very insecure and fretful teenager. Her years of isolation away from her mother and family had left some deep wounds.

"I think she will give me an awfully rough time, Ryan. I'll have to eat crow, that's for sure, but your mom will help us if she can. Obbie would do anything for you; don't you know that by now? She loves you very much."

There was no answer, but the tense body beside her seemed to relax a bit.

Robbie looked up from the computer screen, her blue eyes framed by her reading glasses. The eyes were not focused on the room. Instead, they saw, as though through a camera lens, a scene set a thousand years ago.

Harold Godwinesson, King of England, stood in the darkness and looked at the night sky over Westminster. It was the eve of Letania Magna, April 24th 1066; the night the longhaired star had appeared. Some called it a comet. For the next seven nights, it would shine over England. Just as Harold, the only king of true English blood, would reign for a brief time over the island kingdom. Like Haley's Comet, Harold would appear out of the Dark Ages, shine for a brief second in time, and disappear. Yes, the film would start in black and white and explode into colour on the flare of the comet's tail.

Headlights flashed across tree trunks outside the cabin and Robbie realized with a start that her wife and daughter were home. *The rehearsal must have ended early*, Robbie thought, glancing at her watch and frowning. The Bartlett drama society was staging William Shakespeare's *Twelfth Night* and Ryan had been given the role of Viola, one of the twins who had been cast ashore in a storm. Janet was directing this year, not feeling well enough yet to act. Greta Corry had agreed to take the role of Sebastian, Viola's twin brother. She hoped the rehearsal had gone well.

Her family entered on a blast of frigid air. Robbie got up and went over to help Janet out of her coat. The muscles on the side where Janet had her surgery were still weak, and little things like slipping out of a coat could be awkward for her.

"Hi, loves, you two are home early." Robbie saw the worried look that Ryan shot at Janet. Robbie's gut tightened and she instinctively wrapped an arm around her daughter. "What's wrong?"

"Uh, Ryan, why don't you get ready for bed while I talk to your mom, okay?" Ryan nodded, slipped out from under Robbie's arm and disappeared down the hall to the bedroom she shared with her sister Reb.

Cold blue eyes targeted Janet's. "What happened?" Robbie demanded, her voice sharp.

Janet put her hands on Robbie's chest. "Hey, easy. Nothing has happened to hurt Ryan, I promise. I just need to talk to you, and it's going to be embarrassing enough without Ryan looking on." Janet felt the tension in Robbie subsiding. She took her partner's hand and led her over to the chair by the fire. Robbie sat. Janet paced.

"Ahh...Greta Corry has to have her gall bladder out. She's had to drop out of the play. There's only a few weeks before opening night and we don't have an understudy. Ryan's really disappointed."

Robbie's lip curled into a smug smile. An eyebrow went up as she crossed her long legs and looked patiently at the squirming Janet. Janet saw the jig was up. She sighed in defeat and the red tide of embarrassment washed over her features. "I need your help," she muttered, looking at the rug. At the continued silence, she looked up into eyes sparkling with devilment. "You're going to make this hard, aren't you?"

"Very," Robbie whispered, trying to control the laughter that was building inside. *Oh God, I'm going to enjoy this! This is sooo sweet.*

"You are the only one who could take over that part so the play can go on."

"I know." Robbie arrogantly flashed a delighted smile.

Janet started to lose her patience. "Oh, come on, Robbie, this is for Ryan. You've got to do it."

Robbie got up and circled behind Janet. She whispered into a soft, warm ear, "Who me? Who was told, by you, that under no circumstances was I to show my face at the Drama Society meeting, even though I'd been personally invited by Greta Corry at the Thanksgiving Dinner?"

Janet turned to look at her and Robbie stepped away. "Let me see. What was it you said: 'I am not going to let you continue to use Bartlett as your personal playground, Robbie Williams.' Wasn't that it?" she asked innocently, enjoying watching Janet squirm.

Janet laughed and shook her head. "You are loving every minute of this, aren't you?"

Robbie grinned from ear to ear. "Yes." She wrapped Janet in her arms. "So what are you going to do for me for helping you out with this little problem?"

Janet took a deep breath, drawing in her wife's spicy smell. "I guess I am yours to command," she whispered, nuzzling Robbie's strong neck.

A dark head bent and hungry lips caught Janet's in a long, deep kiss. "I'm going to be a very demanding taskmaster," Robbie warned, dropping a kiss on Janet's nose.

"You'll play the part?"

"Sure, anything for the kid." Robbie smiled as Janet gave her a tight hug.

"Go tell Ryan, okay. She's really worried and disappointed at the moment."

Robbie dropped another kiss on Janet's head. "Okay."

Watching from the bedroom doorway, Robbie saw Ryan sitting on her bed with her earphones on. Janet always said the earphones were a sure sign that Ryan was upset. They were her "I've got a problem" indicator.

Ryan's green eyes looked up and searched deeply into her mom's. She turned off her radio and hung her earphones around her neck.

"Hi," Robbie whispered, so as not to wake Reb. "Can I come in?"

Ryan nodded nervously. Robbie walked in and sat down on the edge of Ryan's bed.

"I don't do stage; I do film," Robbie began. Ryan's face crumpled with disappointment before she was able to school the muscles into an expressionless mask. "So I'm going to have to rely on you to train me for the role."

Ryan was in her arms in an instant. "Thanks, Mom! You're the greatest!"

"Hey, what could be better than being on stage with my own daughter? Mind you, I'm not sure about the director. What's her name...Williams?"

Ryan giggled, then covered her mouth so as not to disturb her little sister's sleep. "You'd better not let Aunt Janet hear you say that. She's tough. You'll have to learn the lines, Mom."

Robbie rolled her eyes. "Have I not been helping you to practice your lines every night for almost two months? Believe me, I know the lines. Come on, let's see if we can get the director to make us some hot chocolate."

The next day, Janet stepped into David Potts' General Store with a sigh of relief. She had left her truck at the dealership up the road and walked into town in the bitter cold of the afternoon. David waved and called "Hi" from the back of the store as she wandered over to the card section.

Ryan's birthday was coming and she wanted the perfect card to give her. She sorted through the various options and finally settled on a card with a photo of a sunset over a northern lake. Inside was printed Happy Birthday. It was ideally suited for Ryan: beautiful but not mushy.

Smiling, she took her choice over to the counter. David rang it up for her. "So, who is having the birthday?"

"Ryan. She's going to be fifteen in a few weeks. We're planning a birthday party for her. It's a surprise."

"Well, that's great, just great. She's a nice kid. I hear Robbie is going to take Greta's place in the play. It'll be nice, them getting to be a mother and daughter act. Ticket sales are really up. I'm sold out and people have been asking if the show will run for an extra weekend. What do you think?"

Janet laughed. "Well, I'll have to ask the cast. It sure would help the drama society's finances. Do you think enough people would buy tickets to run another two nights?"

"To see THE Robbie Williams on stage? You bet. You know, she doesn't look the same in fire pants."

Janet snorted. "I'll let her know you said so."

"Oh dear! She won't be mad will she?" he worried.

"That ego-maniac? Not likely."

David grinned, and then frowned and scratched his head. "Listen, Janet, while you are here...you wouldn't know anything about computers, would you? I just got one and I'm not sure how to use it."

"Well, I don't know a great deal, but I do know most of the basics. Let's have a look."

He led Janet into the small office he had at the back of the store and stepped aside for her to enter first. She looked into the room and then at David, repressing her laughter. "I think it will work a lot better, David, if you take it out of the cardboard boxes." She giggled.

David blushed a bright red. "I didn't want to lose any parts foolin' around with it," he admitted sheepishly.

Janet poked him good-naturedly and took off her coat to tackle the assembly of David's computer system.

"There are some excellent software packages you could use for inventory and ordering, David," Janet observed some time later, as she fitted the various cables into place in the back of the hard drive tower. "Is that why you got a computer?"

His face turned a luminous red again. "Oh, dear, well actually, no. I've hooked up to the Internet."

"Really?" Janet plugged the line into the phone jack. "Do you know how to access your mail? I could show you."

He looked very relieved. "I don't want to keep you, Janet, but that would be a great help to me."

"No problem." She gave him a wink and slipped into the chair in front of the keyboard. "My truck is in for a tune up so I'm waiting for Robbie and the girls to pick me up. They're over at Drouillard's Small Motors, so you know how long they are going to be."

David nodded. Robbie and Ryan's fascination with all things mechanical was common knowledge in the town, thanks to the members of the Bartlett Fire Department who saw Robbie as one of the boys and Ryan as the crew's radio assistant and mascot. Ryan had taken to going to the meetings with her mom and, although she was too young to train, she had made herself useful cleaning and repairing equipment and operating their old, fussy radio system when they were out on a call. Robbie teased that Ryan was a bit smarter but less obedient than a station Dalmatian. Robbie had bought the station a Jaws-of-Life apparatus for helping to get trapped people out of the mangled remains of car accidents. Today some of the volunteers were over at Droullard's learning how to use it on a wreck they had dragged out of the dump. Ryan and Reb were playing the victims.

Janet showed David how to connect to the Internet and watched with surprise as eight messages immediately appeared in his in-box. The address on all of them was EWilliams <mailto:EWilliams@flymail.com>.

Janet turned to look at David in surprise. He fairly glowed with embarrassment. "Tell me all," she demanded with a grin.

"Oh, dear." David cleared his throat and shuffled his feet. "Well, you know, she is a wonderful woman and her research is terribly important. But I couldn't help but notice," impossibly, David got even redder, "that she was underweight. You could tell she hadn't been taking proper care of herself. You know how much I enjoy cooking, and there is only my brother Ted and me, so I thought it wouldn't hurt to courier her the occasional pie or box of muffins. Bethy and I have found we have a lot in common and have kept in touch since the wedding."

Janet grinned mischievously. "David Potts, do you mean to tell me that you have been secretly courting Robbie's sister?"

"Oh, dear, no! I mean, yes...well...no," he stammered.

Janet waited for David to compose himself. *This is just too cute.*

"I mean, we are just friends, but I had been considering asking her out to hear Yo Yo Ma perform at Roy Thomson Hall in Toronto next month. I confess that I am a little nervous about approaching Robbie on the subject."

Janet's eyes widened in surprise. "You're going to ask Robbie to ask her?"

"Dear me, no. But since Robbie is sort of the head of the family, I felt it proper to ask her if it would be all right if I stepped out with Elizabeth," David explained with awkward dignity.

Janet bit her lip to keep from laughing. She just had to be a witness to this moment in Williams history. "David, I think that's very honourable of you," she managed.

"Hi, Aunt Janet. Hi, Mr. Potts," Ryan called from the doorway. "Mom's out in the truck with Reb. Reb's crying because she wasn't allowed to bring the Jaws of Life home with her. She thinks it's really fun to hide behind a seat and be rescued."

Janet stood and cast a critical eye over Ryan's body. The teenager was covered in dirt, rust, and cobwebs. "Is Reb wearing the other half of the town dump?"

Ryan grinned. "Pretty much."

Janet laughed and shook her head as she retrieved her coat. Ryan quietly stepped forward to help her settle the one arm into the sleeve. Janet smiled and gave the teen an affectionate bump. Saying their goodbyes to David, they went out to the waiting truck.

It was only when Robbie had turned off the lights that night and slipped into bed beside Janet that the teacher finally had the opportunity to tell Robbie about the computer and

David's intentions. To her surprise, the light was snapped on again and Robbie was standing by the bed, bristling with anger.

Janet pulled the bedclothes around her chest and sat up. "Robbie! What's wrong?"

"If he goes anywhere near Elizabeth, I'll...I'll...stop him," Robbie growled.

Concern flooded Janet's face. She wrapped the sheet around her and stood up to hug the naked woman who towered angrily over her. "Hey, easy, love. Come on. I need to talk to you, and it's too cold to be standing here by the bed naked."

Robbie didn't want to lie down again. She wanted to get dressed and go down to David Potts' and beat the daylights out of him. But she didn't want to upset Janet, so she sat on the edge of the bed and let her wife curl up beside her.

"Robbie, the e-mails, all eight of them, came from Elizabeth. They like each other. What's wrong with that? It would be good for Elizabeth."

Robbie's head snapped around so that cold blue eyes challenged soft green. "No, it wouldn't. You don't understand."

Those green eyes searched Robbie's quietly for a very long time. "This has to do with the dark time, doesn't it? Something happened to Elizabeth and you are trying to protect her."

Robbie stiffened and tried to pull away, but Janet wouldn't let go. "No, Robbie, I'm not going to push for information. It's okay. I know you can't talk about it. I just want you to realize that your reaction stems from whatever happened then. This is now. Elizabeth is reaching out, first to your new family and now to David. That's wonderful, Robbie. Don't let your fears put an end to that."

Robbie swallowed hard and Janet could feel her partner shaking with the effort to control her emotions. "I don't want her to be hurt again," Robbie managed to force out of a tight throat. "She carries such deep scars already. We all do."

"Hey," Janet smiled and gave Robbie an affectionate shake, "we're talking David Potts here. He is the nicest man I have ever met. He's polite, caring, and ever so sweet. You know that, Robbie."

Robbie wiped sweat from her upper lip. "People aren't always what they seem," she muttered bitterly.

"No, they're not, but David is. He told me that before he asks Elizabeth out on a date, he is going to ask your permission to 'step out' with your sister. Isn't that cute?"

Robbie swallowed but said nothing. She stared vacantly at the Navaho rug on the floor.

"Robbie? I need you to be brave. I need you to trust David to take Elizabeth out, okay?" The seconds ticked by and then Robbie nodded. "If David talks to you, you're not to terrorize him," she warned, knowing all too well how a Williams mind worked.

Robbie frowned. "I've got a right to know what his intentions are," she grumbled.

Janet giggled and bumped against Robbie, surprised to feel the sheen of nervous sweat that covered her partner's body. "His intentions are a Yo Yo Ma concert at Roy Thomson Hall."

Robbie rubbed her face and stood up, turning to look deeply into Janet's eyes. "Okay," she finally said. "I gotta go for a run."

Janet nodded and watched as her partner dressed in sweats and left to run through the cold wintry night. *I think I'm one step closer to getting Robbie to show me whatever is festering deep in her soul. But what will it cost her?*

Sighing, Janet got out of the now cold bed and remade it. She wouldn't be able to sleep until Robbie returned anyway. *Time for a hot bath, and then I'll work at my desk until Robbie gets back.*

She went down the hall to the bathroom and turned on the water, then slipped off her nightie. As always, an emotional shockwave knotted her stomach when she caught sight of the red scar where her breast once had been. She blinked back the tears. It was hard to deal with the issue of a new self-image, a new way of dressing, a new way of feeling, the awkwardness that sometimes came over her when they made love. All those things were hard enough, without having to see every day that constant reminder that she'd had cancer.

She'd talked to her counsellor about it and to her doctor and she knew what she wanted to do. How Robbie would feel about it, she wasn't sure. One of these nights, when they were tucked into bed and it was their quiet time together, she was going to have to broach the subject with her lover.

It was two hours later when Robbie returned, wheezing with the effort of taking warm air into cold, oxygen deprived lungs. Robbie had run full out until her muscles screamed and her head was too dizzy to think anymore. Then she had forced herself to keep up a steady jog back to the cabin.

Janet met her there, wrapping her in a quick hug and then getting the shower ready while the runner stripped off her sweatsuit. They showered together, Janet washing Robbie's hair gently and soothing her as she would a child. Robbie went along numbly, needing the love and security that Janet was providing but too upset and exhausted to articulate her thoughts.

In bed, they made love, Robbie needing to be as close as she could to her wife. Janet responded with open trust, trying to reassure Robbie that love was good, safe and beautiful. Much later, Janet fell asleep, sprawled on her belly with her lover already fast asleep on top of her.

The letter from the lawyer arrived on Friday morning but it was Saturday before Robbie opened it. Janet could see by the change in Robbie's expression that the contents of the letter upset her. She finished wiping down the counter and then went over to whisper in Ryan's ear as the teen helped clean up Reb from her morning breakfast of Pablum. "I need to talk to your mom. Could you keep Reb busy in the bedroom for half an hour?"

Ryan looked over to where her mother sat at Aunt Janet's desk. She was wearing the emotionless look that Ryan had come to realize meant that the feelings inside were running high. "Sure, Aunt Janet. Reb and I will go make your bed. She likes to play hide and seek with the covers."

Janet smiled and gave Ryan a squeeze. "I'll tell you about it later," she promised, as her adopted daughter swung Reb from her highchair and led the small child out of the room.

Janet went over and placed her hands on Robbie's shoulders, leaning over to kiss the top of her lover's head. "Anything I can do?"

Robbie sighed. "We need to talk. You'd better come sit on the couch."

Janet could feel the tension as she followed Robbie. *What could have gone wrong?* A frown formed on her face.

Robbie sat on the edge of the settee looking really uncomfortable. A deep blush slowly seeped up her neck. "This letter is from the family lawyer. It is about the settlement of my brother's estate. You know that each of my father's children got five million on his death. Alexandria got thirty million. The remaining five million and the family estate were held in trust to go to the first grandchild born."

Janet nodded.

"When Reb was born, that trust was handed over to my brother to manage, as dictated by the terms of the will," Robbie explained nervously, making eye contact with Janet.

"Robbie, Reb doesn't need the money. It should be Ryan's anyway. I don't care about it," Janet said by way of reassurance.

Robbie shook her head in irritation. "No, Reb's the legitimate heir. I have no problem with that. Ryan will inherit half of my estate and you the other half. That will leave you both very wealthy women. It's Reb I'm worried about." Robbie took a deep breath and mumbled with embarrassment, "Billy spent a good deal of the money."

"He spent Reb's trust fund?"

"Three million of it," Robbie revealed sadly.

Janet's voice rose in disbelief. "On what?"

Robbie squirmed. "Billy had some problems...because...because of before. He couldn't...I mean, he never...well, he just couldn't do *it*. That's why we were all kind of suspicious of you having Billy's child, because we knew that he'd never been capable before. It looks like he had gone through his own money for establishing himself in racing and in getting treatments for...his problem at a Swiss clinic. He needed more money, so he had an heir. He took Reb's inheritance to pay for the artificial fertilization and also for treatments for himself."

Janet shrugged. "Oh well."

Robbie looked up in surprise. "It wasn't right. He stole from his own kid. He had a child to get money because he had gone through his own," she snapped.

Janet shrugged again. "Okay, I agree it was wrong. But he's dead. Trying, no doubt, to prove he was a man. I've got Reb and that delights me. Were my motivations any more nobler than his?"

Robbie blushed and looked away.

Janet answered for her. "No, they weren't. I wanted money and I wanted a child. So I'm partly responsible for Reb's inheritance being misused. But I don't care. I'm happy, Reb's happy, and we are doing just fine. Don't worry about it, Robbie."

"I'll make it up to the kid," Robbie promised, taking Janet's hand.

"You already have. You, Ryan, and that thing you dragged home and insist on calling a dog. Rebecca loves you all dearly. You've brought so much into Reb's life, that's all that matters. You write your silly law firm and tell them just to finish off the paperwork and not to worry about the mismanagement of the trust. Reb was worth it." Janet smiled, then she giggled.

Robbie put an arm around her. "What's so funny?"

"I just know that when Reb is much older and can understand all this, she is going to really enjoy being the product of an illegal act."

"Hey! That's our daughter you are taking about and she is perfect," Robbie protested.

Janet bumped her forehead lightly against Robbie's. "No, she is a Williams, and that spells trouble."

Trouble arrived the following week with the annual old timers' hockey tournament. Several years before, Greta Corry had organized an all-women's team to compete. LIPs — Lady Ice Players — had never won a game against a male team, whose players had all played in amateur hockey leagues at one time or another. Everyone had a good time, however, and the all-girl team always drew the crowds when they were playing.

This year, Greta could not take her place in goal because of her gall bladder surgery, and Janet couldn't take the left wing position because of her mastectomy. They had to settle with managing and coaching the team.

Amanda Singh was recruited for goal, and Robbie and Ryan were picked up as forwards. Suddenly, the women found they had a team that could actually win games. One Friday night, they surprised the Creaky Joints from Harriston with a three to two win, and then on Saturday they went on to defeat the Bartlett Golden Jets by a score of four to one. Sunday they were to face the Helingone Rusty Blades in a grudge match final.

Janet reviewed her game plan options. Amanda skated poorly, but she had played goal for her school's soccer team as a child back in India. She was flexible and fast in net despite the large pads and protective gear she had to wear. Carolyn Carr could hold her own on defence, having grown up playing backyard hockey with her brother. Gladys Billingsley, the minister's wife, was a little weak on left defence, but she made up for it by providing hot chocolate and cookies for the team. Robbie had taken figure skating as a child and was quick and confident on her skates. She had a powerful shot, although not an always accurate one. Ryan was a good skater, too. She had played hockey on school teams, and she played smart. Unlike her mother, her shots were always on the net. They would play the forward wings. At centre, Greta and Janet had decided on Stacy Barlow from the doughnut shop. She was a tough, wiry woman who never gave up.

The rules for old-timer hockey were pretty flexible. The games were just for fun and body contact was not allowed. You were supposed to be an amateur and be over thirty to play. But in the small northern towns, where the populations were small, anyone who wanted to continue to play hockey after they had outgrown the leagues could pretty well join as an old timer.

Corry had convinced the organizers to waive the age restriction for the women so that they could get enough players to make up a team. The women's team was mostly women in their thirties and forties, but Ryan was a teenager and Amanda and Janet were still in their late twenties.

Janet stood by the boards and used Robbie's camera to take pictures of Ryan and Robbie warming up on the ice. Mother and daughter skated around the rink at a leisurely pace, holding Reb by the hands. Reb was wearing a pair of double-bladed skates and was dressed up in a hockey sweater and helmet just like her big sister and second mom. Robbie had paid Flo Butler to cut a team jersey down to Reb's size and had bought her a kid-sized helmet. A miniature hockey stick completed the outfit. Janet had to admit that Reb looked cute as a button.

Reb idolized her big sister and aunt. Most of the time Janet thought that was just great. Her daughter couldn't have a better pair of role models, at least ninety percent of the time. Then there was that ten percent of the time when that "no limits, no fear" attitude of the Williams family came out, and that scared the hell out of Janet. She understood that it was the quality that allowed them to take their natural talents and push them to greatness, but it was very worrying and stressful to deal with at times. She had come to realize that one of the things she could do in her marriage with Robbie was to help her partner use her tremendous focus for positive rather than negative things.

Janet smiled and brought her focus back to the game. Helingone had a good team. The game was being billed as a grudge match because Jim Adleton was the Rusty Blades' star player. Everyone knew that there were bad feelings between Robbie and Jim because of the Winter Carnival snowmobile race. Janet frowned. She needed to remind Robbie again that this was a friendly game and not to lose her temper.

There had already been some underhanded play. A very embarrassed official had come to Janet and Greta and told them that according to the Hockey Association regulations, all players had to wear athletic cups. It appeared that someone on the Heligone team had pointed out to the officials that if there was an injury, they could be liable if the women were not wearing the proper protective gear.

"An injury to what?" Janet had exploded, but the red-faced official had just shrugged.

It had been Amanda Singh who had saved the day by phoning her husband, Mohammed, who owned the local clothing store. He arrived with a large grin and enough athletic cups for the team. There had been joking and giggling in the dressing room as the team fitted the useless gear into place. Stacy had the team nearly in hysterics when she announced that she thought she'd start wearing one full time because it was a handy spot to tuck her tips.

Greta's voice cut into Janet's thoughts. "Okay, ladies, come over here!" The team headed over to the bench for their final instructions.

Robbie bent down and lifted a beaming Reb over the boards to her other mother. "There you go, Reb. Don't forget to cheer for us, now."

Reb looked at Robbie with big, baby blue eyes. "I won't forget, Obbie. I cheer," she promised seriously. Robbie leaned over and patted Reb's helmeted head.

"Okay, it is the Williams/Barlow line out there first." Janet balanced Reb on the boards. "Stacy, you take the face-off and try to get the puck to Obbie. She'll take it down the ice with Ryan at her heels. Once over the blue line, Ryan, you cut ahead and go behind the net. When you come around the other side, Obbie will have passed the puck and you tap it in the corner. That's our entire game plan. Any questions?" The team shook their heads and prepared to head out to centre ice. "Obbie," Janet called.

She came back to the boards. "Hmm?"

"Remember this is a fun game. Be good," Janet warned.

Robbie scowled good-naturedly and skated off to her position, shadowing Jim Ableton. As the referee got ready to drop the puck, Ableton smiled at Robbie and in a voice just loud enough for the players to hear, said, "So, Williams, you wearing an athletic cup?" Several of the male players snorted.

Robbie winked at her daughter on the other side of the face-off circle. "Sure am, Jimmy. I keep trophies in it. But you're safe, 'cause I only keep the big ones." The referee dropped the puck. Stacy snapped it over to Robbie and the Williamses were on their way down the ice while the men were still laughing at Ableton. Ryan rocketed behind the net, Robbie passed and Ryan was there to jam the puck into the corner of the net before the Helingone goalie could react. Less than a minute into the game and the ladies were leading one to nothing.

"It worked! It worked!" Greta screamed from the bench.

"Kill 'em!" Reb yelled at the top of her baby lungs. Janet looked down at her daughter in shock. The Williams genes had struck again.

The less-than-friendly game was tied at two-two in the third period when Ryan was fed a pass from Stacy and found herself on a breakaway. She picked up speed and careened down the ice with Jim Ableton in hot pursuit behind her. Seeing he couldn't catch Ryan, he dove with his stick out, stretched, and tripped her up. Ryan skidded across the cold ice on her face and went into the corner boards. Her helmet flew off and she lay motionless on the ice.

For a second, everyone froze in horror, the only sound the grating of Ryan's helmet spinning like a top on the ice. "Ryan!" Robbie screamed into the silence. Dropping her stick and gloves, she charged over to her daughter.

Janet passed Reb to Greta and went over the boards. She ran down the ice and slid in beside Robbie, who knelt by the still figure of her daughter, afraid to move her.

Robbie's voice was shaky. "Ryan, honey. Ryan, are you all right?"

Ryan heard her mother scream her name but she was so winded from landing on her stick that she couldn't get a word out. She struggled to get air into her lungs so she could reassure her mom that she was okay. The lungs wouldn't work. She tried rolling over.

"Don't move, Ryan," a panicky voice commanded.

Ryan felt her mother's hands trembling as they tried to support her neck and head. "I'm okay, Mom," Ryan finally got out with a gasp as she laboured to get her breathing regulated. "Honest. I just fell on my stick and winded myself." She smiled and coughed several times.

"The kid shouldn't be playing anyway," Ableton justified from behind Robbie.

Robbie gave a growl of anger that echoed through the arena like a war cry. She rose like a mushroom cloud above her teammates, who were clustered around Ryan. Ryan saw

Ableton swing his stick up in reflex when he saw the fire in Robbie's eyes. Her mom pulled the stick out of Ableton's hands in a lightning quick move.

Another Heligone player skated over to try and grab Robbie from behind. Amanda casually stuck out her goalie stick and tripped him up, sending him sprawling into Stacy, who went down.

Gloves came off, sticks dropped, and a bench-clearing free-for-all exploded around Robbie. The crowd cheered them on. Janet pulled Ryan clear of the action and secretly hoped that Robbie would knock Ableton's block off.

A frustrated, overworked referee ended the game, sending the players to their dressing rooms and calling the game a tie.

Janet drove her truckload of Williams olives home in stony silence. Two guilty Williams sat wedged in the back seat with Reb. Ryan rested her head on her mother's shoulder. Robbie held a tissue to the bloody nose she had gotten in the brawl. Ryan poked her mom and nodded toward the front seat.

"Ahh. Are you mad at us?" Robbie asked nasally.

Her back to her family, Janet smiled into the silence. *Let them sweat.*

Robbie felt Ryan's hand slip into her own and she gave her a squeeze. "I mean, I know you must be upset, but you're not going to stay mad, are you?"

"Well, let's see...in three years, LIPS has never had a penalty and in just one game, the Williamses managed to cause a bench-clearing brawl. Then there is the not-so-little matter of one of you having trained Rebecca to chant, 'Kill 'em.' I could probably be philosophical about all of this had it not been for the lecture I just got from the referee on teaching my team some sportsmanship. Like it is my responsibility to keep you motley crew of Williamses in line," Janet growled in feigned anger.

"We're sorry," Ryan said, worried. Robbie gave her a hug to reassure her that everything would be okay.

Janet snorted. "I don't believe that for a moment. You three were in your element, up to your collective backsides in trouble."

"Obbie killed 'em," Reb offered helpfully.

Ryan whispered, "Shhh, kid."

"Uh, Reb, don't say that, okay?" Robbie reached past Ryan to pat Reb's shoulder. "It's not nice."

"Ryan say it," Reb protested incredulously, refusing to believe that anything her big sister did could be wrong.

"Ryan isn't going to say it anymore, either," Robbie stated firmly, giving her daughter a pointed look. Ryan smiled sheepishly.

Janet decided that she had made her troublesome family squirm long enough. "The only reason the three of you are not sleeping in the snow tonight is the shiner Obbie gave that big bully Ableton."

Ryan's worried face broke into a big smile. "Mom rocked, didn't she, Aunt Janet?"

"You bet she did," Janet agreed, and chuckled at the collective sigh of relief from the back seat.

"Does this mean we can still order pizza?" Robbie asked tentatively.

Janet laughed and shook her head as she pulled up in front of their cabin. "We might as well, since I imagine we are all too hyper to sleep."

Much later that night, Janet rolled over to kiss her lover's sore nose. "How are you doing, champ?"

"Okay," came the nasal response and Janet smiled.

"Robbie, how would you feel about reconstructive surgery?"

"My nose isn't that bad," she muttered.

"I meant for me."

Robbie sat up and turned the light on, watching her partner blink in its glow. "What?"

Janet pulled herself up beside her lover. "How do you feel about me having reconstructive surgery to replace my missing breast? I...I've been reading up on it."

Robbie blinked, started to say something, stopped and tried again. "Well, I don't know. I mean...I never thought about it. It doesn't bother me that you've had a mastectomy, but the thought of you having more surgery does bother me. Why would you want to? Did I say or do something that made you think I don't find you appealing?"

Janet looked at her hands that lay folded on the bedclothes in front of her. "No, you've been great."

Those days when Janet had been ill had been like a nightmare. Robbie just wanted to forget and move on. The last thing she wanted to do was walk through a set of hospital doors with Janet again. If anything happened to Janet... No. She didn't want to deal with even the slightest possibility. "Well, then, forget it!" she said irritably.

"Robbie, unlike other surgeries, a mastectomy is a day-to-day reminder of your battle with cancer. The reminder is there in the morning when I wake up and it's there when I take a shower. It's there when I go to bed or when I'm trying on clothes, and it is definitely there when we make love.

"You've been a wonderful partner through it all, but I can't help but wonder if you are affected more than you would ever admit. These little insecurities pop into my head now and again. I think I handled the whole episode pretty well emotionally and intellectually, but I have to tell you honestly — there are days when I don't want that reminder. Can you understand that?"

Robbie licked her lips and tried to absorb what Janet had told her. She nodded reluctantly. "I understand. What would they do?"

Janet got more comfy. "Well, there are different procedures depending on the type of mastectomy. For me, it would be quite a long process. First, they would insert a saline implant that can be inflated and then muscle from either the stomach or back would be placed over top. Over a number of weeks, the implant would gradually be inflated to stretch the muscle and skin. When the muscle has been stretched sufficiently, the inflatable saline implant would be replaced with a permanent silicone one."

Robbie's eyes were wide with fright. "No! Those implant thingies are dangerous."

Janet smiled and gave her partner a reassuring hug. "Actually, the hullabaloo over silicone is greatly exaggerated. Most problems occurred in the early years of testing or because of inexperienced doctors. Normally, everything goes just fine."

Silence enveloped them then Robbie presented what struck her as a logical argument. "Don't you need that muscle in your stomach or back?"

"The use of stomach muscle is not recommended for active women because if you lift heavy things, you risk getting a hernia. The loss of the muscle in the back does weaken it, but with proper exercise the remaining back muscles can compensate and you can regain that strength."

"Oh." Robbie felt a tension headache coming on. She knew she had to work through this with Janet, but it was hard to set aside her fears.

"Once the permanent implant is in, then they'll reshape my unaffected breast so the two match and have a more youthful shape," Janet finished.

"Shit! More surgery?" Robbie exploded. She definitely didn't want this to be happening. Okay, so it was a bit weird having a wife with one breast...but, hell, it didn't matter. It wasn't affecting their sex life...was it?

Robbie turned and looked deeply into Janet's eyes, searching for the truth. "Aren't you having good orgasms? I mean, is it bothering you to the point where I'm not satisfying you? I thought it was good. I mean it's great with you. Am I doing something wrong, 'cause—"

Janet's lips ended the flood of insecurity. "You, Robbie Williams, are as sexy as hell in bed and there is nothing wrong with our sex life. I just...I just want to feel whole."

Robbie saw the pain in Janet's eyes and pulled her close. "Okay, lover. If you want this, then I want it too. When?"

"Not for a few years, I think. I want to make sure...well, that they got it all. I need time to get over the treatments, too." She hugged Robbie close, feeling the tension in Robbie's body. "You okay with that?"

"Yeah, I'm okay with that. Thanks for talking to me about it. It will give me time to...you know, get used to the idea."

Janet smiled. Her big, brave hockey star was a wuss when it came to anything that was going to affect her wife. *Love you for that!* She leaned over for another kiss. "We could just run a test to make sure my evaluation of you as a super lover is accurate," she teased.

Robbie happily obliged.

Robbie and Rufus dropped Janet, Ryan, and Reb off at The Bartlett School for the Gifted and drove into town to run some errands. The last stop was David Potts' General Store to pick up a large bag of dog food of the type that Rufus preferred. Rufus sat by the window, watching. Inside the store, Robbie hefted the heavy bag onto the counter and waited for David to ring it up.

"Robbie, before you go...," the colour rose in his face, "I wonder if I might have a word with you."

The colour drained from Robbie's face as quickly as it had risen in David's. *Oh shit!* "I'm kind of busy," she evaded.

"Please, Robbie. It will only take a minute."

Robbie nodded and followed David through the store and back into his office. A new Pentium IV sat on the desktop. Robbie sneered at it.

"Won't you be seated, please?"

Robbie sat, trying to look relaxed although she was anything but. *Remember, you promised Janet*, she kept repeating to herself as she watched David carefully take off his apron, straighten his tie, and slip into his jacket.

"As the head of the Williams family, I thought it proper that I make my intentions known to you and ask your approval to step out with your sister," David managed to get out, determination winning out over his natural shyness.

"Just what are you intentions?" Robbie asked, a little more sharply than she had intended.

David swallowed nervously. "Well, I have told Elizabeth — we communicate daily by e-mail — that you and Ryan are going to star in *Twelfth Night*. I offered to buy her ticket if she was free and if you were willing to set up Bill's trailer again for her to stay in. Also, Elizabeth has a season concert ticket to the Roy Thomson and I was going to ask if I could buy a ticket and join her to hear Yo Yo Ma next month."

Eyes as cold as ice, Robbie looked at David. He stood quietly with embarrassed dignity. Robbie stood and looked directly in his eye. "Yes, if Elizabeth wishes, she may come to see *Twelfth Night* with you. Yes, I will arrange for the trailer. Then I'll talk to Elizabeth and decide about the Toronto concert. I don't want my sister hurt, David."

David looked truly upset. "Robbie! I wouldn't do anything to hurt Elizabeth or anyone else."

Robbie smiled, letting go of some of the tension. Janet was right, David was just plain sweet. "Yeah, I know, but Bethy, well, she's not outgoing like me..." Robbie fumbled for words. *This is not David's business, damn it!*

David nodded. "I know. She has been badly hurt in the past. She told me so," David revealed softly. "I haven't had much experience with dating, but I feel very comfortable with Elizabeth and she needs me. You know that condo she owns is such a burden to her. She can't seem to find a decent manager and—"

"Elizabeth owns a condo?" she exclaimed, eyes wide.

"Yes, the one she lives in. She is doing very important research and she doesn't need to be bothered with number 32A's leaky showerhead, now does she?" he asked, coming to Elizabeth's defence.

Robbie smirked. "No, leaky heads are a bitch," she acknowledged, knowing David would not pick up on the double meaning.

David nodded in agreement. "And you know she doesn't take care of herself. She gets so involved in her work that she forgets to eat properly. I've been sending her some treats. She is very fond of my sticky buns."

Robbie tried not to laugh. She had never thought she would end up enjoying this conversation with David.

Unaware of Robbie's merriment, David went on. "I thought I'd take my tool box down to Toronto, that's if it is alright, and see what I can do to help out around there. I'm not as active as my brother Bill, but I think I can handle a tool as well as any man," David finished with feeling.

Gathering all her stage presence, Robbie managed to say, "I'm sure you can, David. Please tell Bethy we'll look forward to seeing her. The kids will be delighted that they will be seeing their aunt again." Then she escaped to the truck. Rufus sat on the front seat beside her and watched her with a puzzled expression. As she steered the truck back to the cabin, Robbie kept bursting out laughing and wiping her eyes to see the road.

Some nights later, Janet sat at her desk working on her computer, listening with one ear to the family noises. Squeals and laughter floated out from the bathroom where Robbie was dying Ryan's hair to the same colour as her own and helping her with her make up for the play's opening night. In the living room, Reb had recently discovered that Rufus followed voice commands and she was making the shaggy dog's life a living hell.

"Sit!" commanded the small figure, looking up at the huge dog that stood in front of her. Rufus extended his massive muzzle and licked the top of Reb's head affectionately before sitting as he had been told. "Good dog!" Reb praised, petting the wide, shaggy chest.

"Reb, play with your toys and leave poor Rufus alone. He needs to sleep."

Rebecca looked at her mother with big, serious eyes and then back at the dog. "Sleep, Rufus," she ordered, and then sat down on the rug to play with the blocks that Ryan had bought for her.

Some time later, Janet looked over to see her daughter fast asleep, curled up against Rufus' side. Quietly, she got out Robbie's camera and took a picture. Sometimes she loved her daughter so much it almost hurt.

She carefully lifted her daughter with difficulty and got her ready for bed. Carolyn and Amanda were going to take turns babysitting on the play nights. She went into the bedroom to change. A few minutes later the other half of her family barged in, all smiles. Janet started in surprise. With the expert make up job and change in colouring, Ryan was the spitting image of her mother. "My God! You two could be twins," Janet gasped. Both Williamses smiled.

"Mom's a bit taller, but I'm gaining on her."

"Kid, you are never going to be as tall as me," Robbie teased, giving her daughter a poke. "I'm just going to check on Elizabeth, and then as soon as Carolyn arrives we can be off."

Janet looked at Ryan. *The resemblance between Robbie and Ryan is amazing.* "Are you nervous?" she asked.

Ryan frowned and thought about the question in the same serious, intense way that her Aunt Elizabeth had. "I would have been if I'd been playing opposite Greta, but not with Mom. Mom will make sure everything goes all right. If I forget a line or something, she'll ad-lib. She's cool," Ryan observed proudly.

Janet nodded. "Yes, she is. That sounds like Carolyn's car, so we'd better get our coats on. You'll need lots of time to change into your costumes and review before the performance."

At the trailer, Robbie tried to stall until David arrived. "I don't really think I should leave Elizabeth alone."

Pointing out the obvious, Janet said, "Carolyn and Reb are in the cabin only a few feet away if there's a problem."

Robbie chewed on her lip and tried to think of another excuse to delay her leaving.

Janet gave her a warning frown and herded her into the truck, noting Elizabeth's look of relief as she did so.

Ryan blossomed on stage, with a sense of timing that had the audience in stitches as she played Viola, the shipwrecked twin who had disguised herself as a man, taken service with Duke Orsino, and been sent by him to court the Lady Olivia, only to have the Lady fall in love with her. Robbie played Sebastian the male twin, and the audience howled as she was courted by Olivia, who thought she was still the male Viola.

The play was a roaring success. Elizabeth had a wonderful evening with David, and the entire family, including David, ended the night with a late dinner at Maria's. The next day, Elizabeth took the helicopter back to Toronto. David showed up in time for the good-byes and was so bold as to kiss Elizabeth on the cheek. Janet tightly held on to Robbie, just in case.

The following weekend, Janet had time to note how Robbie carefully let her daughter have the limelight. She only took over the stage when Ryan was not on with her. Janet realized that Robbie was good down to the centre of her being, but she hid it behind that protective wall of aggression. From the wings on the last night, Janet used up the rest of the film in Robbie's camera. The cast took their final bow and walked off stage to a standing ovation.

The cast party was a cheery affair and the Williams clan slept in a bit the next morning. Robbie and Janet were up in time to get a special breakfast ready. It was Ryan's birthday, and Robbie was trying to make up for all the birthdays she hadn't been there for her daughter.

Finally Robbie could stand it no longer and she went in to wake up the birthday girl. "Happy Birthday, Ryan." She hugged her daughter close to her as she sleepily sat up in bed. She felt Ryan stiffen and knew the old hurts were returning. Robbie was getting better at dealing with them, though. "Ryan, I wish I could make up for all those birthdays when I should have been there for you. Please, just indulge your mother today and let me try to show you how much your birth meant to me in my heart. I love you, Ryan."

Ryan's body relaxed and she hugged her mom back. "I love you too, Mom."

"Come on. We've got a birthday planned for you that will be the talk of the town." Laughing, Robbie pulled her daughter out of bed.

The morning was a happy, riotous affair. They breakfasted on French crepes filled with ham and scrambled eggs, followed by more crepes filled with fruit and whipped cream. Then they sat around the fire and Ryan opened her presents. Reb's present was opened first. It was a crayon picture of Ryan in a sailboat on Long Lake. It had been carefully framed down at Paul Digby's art and framing shop.

Ryan gave her little sister a teary hug. "I'm going to hang this on our bedroom wall, I promise."

Janet had bought Ryan her own life-vest and had a cherry wood paddle made specifically for her with her initials etched into an oak leaf pattern on the blade. Ryan ran her hand over the polished wood and looked up with tears rolling down her face. "Thanks, Aunt Janet," she said hoarsely.

Then Robbie's gifts were brought out: a table saw, jig saw, tool kit, and a set of plans for the building of an Australian sailing dory. "I thought we could build it together this spring," Robbie explained nervously. Ryan didn't say anything, she just wrapped herself in her mother's arms and stayed there sobbing. Janet took Reb to clean up and left the two alone.

"You okay, Ryan?"

Ryan nodded and pulled her mother closer. "We're going to stay together, right, Mom?"

Pain shot through Robbie's heart and she stroked her daughter's hair. "We are a family, Ryan. That's forever, I promise."

"That was some birthday," Ryan sniffed, pulling away to wipe her eyes.

"Kid, this is only the beginning. We're going to have a great day. Come on, let's get dressed, and go and have some fun."

The Williams clan was just slipping into their coats when there was a knock at the door. Janet opened it and found Constable Jarvis, who boarded down at Greta's. "Hi, Jerry, come in. We were just celebrating Ryan's birthday."

A pained look crossed the young constable's face. "Robbie, this isn't correct procedure, but I asked the sergeant if I could come in and leave the others outside. We all know you, what with all of us volunteering on the fire brigade, and well, this isn't easy." He drew a deep breath. "Roberta Williams, I'm arresting you for the murder of your father—"

"What?" Janet moved to stand by her partner.

Robbie's hand touched her shoulder lightly before falling away. "Shhh, Janet. Let him read me my rights."

Jerry Jarvis bit his lip. "I gotta put these cuffs on you, Robbie. It's the rules." Robbie nodded and turned around, putting her hands behind her. The constable stepped forward and nervously snapped the metal cuffs around her wrists. She turned back again and Jarvis took out the card to read Robbie her rights.

"You've got to come now, Robbie," he explained regretfully when he was finished. The room was deathly quiet and he felt very uncomfortable.

Robbie looked around the cabin that she had come to love. Her eyes met Ryan's and saw the pain of betrayal. Ryan turned and walked out of the room. Reb's eyes were wide with fear and she was on the verge of tears. At last her eyes met Janet's and she saw that Janet knew the truth and loved her anyway.

Janet reached up and kissed Robbie. "I'll come as soon as I get in touch with your lawyer, love." Robbie nodded.

Jarvis looked at his boots. He'd heard rumours that Robbie and Janet were gay, but he hadn't believed it. This was turning into a hell of a day.

"Is the press out there too?" Robbie asked quietly.

"Just Lucier so far."

Robbie grinned cynically. "An exclusive, eh? Lucky him. Let's go."

Janet watched Robbie leave with the Constable. She never looked back.

Chapter 14

The library of the hundred and ninety-five year old house was warm and cozy. One wall was bookshelves rising to the ten-foot ceiling. On the second wall, a fire in the old hearth crackled softly against the morning chill. The third contained an archway of French doors, and the last held a carved Victorian china cabinet. The walls not covered by books were rag-rolled to look like soft suede. Displayed on them was an eclectic mixture of rare art: a fragment of an ancient Egyptian painting on papyrus, an illustration from a 16th century Persian manuscript, and two 18th century wood block prints from a Japanese pillow book. On the mantel was a section of rock containing fossilized fish from the Green River prehistoric fossil beds, and sitting on the oak library table, where the woman worked, were three Nigerian clay inkpots tied together with bark. An Edwardian chandelier bathed the room in mellow light and Antonio Vivaldi's *Larghetto Concerto Op. 3* played softly in the background.

It was a scholar's room, the remaining furniture consisting of two overstuffed wingback chairs and the library table's sturdy armchair. The woman sitting there was a jarring contrast to the surroundings. She was tall and lean with the wiry muscles of an athlete. She wore running shoes, sweatpants, and a T-shirt that read "FORENSICS: The Dead Do Talk!"

The dark head leaned forward, holding the magnifying glass close to the small object that she held in her other hand. She was examining the left anterior view of a fragment of a jawbone. The frontal, zygomatic, and alveolar process were present, as was the anterior nasal spine.

Deciduous teeth — only DI2, DC1, and DP3 remaining. Considerable charring. Doctor Aliki Pateas placed the fragment back in the cardboard box that held the rest of the bones. *Male, approximately three years old. A First Nations' pot burial*, she concluded, closing her eyes and letting her senses drift with the flow of the music. The child in the box had been forgotten.

The oak-cased pendulum clock on the wall had just softly chimed the hour when a vibration in Aliki's pocket indicated a phone call. She sighed, slipping a long, slim hand into her pocket to pull out a small cell phone and flip it open. "Pateas."

"Al, it's Tom Bates. There's a squad on the way. I need you to exhume a possible murder victim before the press gets word of it. This one looks like it's going to be high profile. The body was buried in a shallow grave about fifteen years ago."

"Terrain?"

"Woods."

"Shit! I hate acting like a pig hunting truffles," Pateas growled.

The man snorted. "As if. Al, it's the Williams' case. The body's possibly the old man, Philip Williams."

Aliki Pateas sat up straight, suddenly very interested. "Philip Williams, the father of Robbie, Elizabeth, and Billy Williams?"

"The same. A witness, who was a kid back then, got an attack of conscience and came to tell us. She saw the grave being dug and led police to it."

Pateas sneered. "So how much did the tabloids pay her to discover her conscience?"

"Enough, I guess. She had a reporter in tow; he was claiming to be doing his civic duty. I need you out there quick before the place is crawling with them. Once this guy publishes his exclusive, all hell will break loose. Go get the bones and I'll do the examination as soon as they arrive."

Aliki looked out the window. It was a grey, cold, blustery spring day. Yesterday, it had rained heavily. Rank had its privileges. Still, this was a case she most definitely wanted to be involved in for far more than professional reasons. "I'm on my way, sir."

Bill Gorski had been on the force for less than a year, but he knew of Doctor Aliki Pateas. She worked out at the same fitness centre as he did. She was gorgeous. Nice enough, too...as long as you didn't try to get too close. Word had it in the police rumour mill that she had about as much emotion as the dead she worked with. A pretty strange profession really, examining bones for a living. Why would anyone want to do that? Still, if his grisly remains were ever found in a shallow grave, he sure hoped it was Pateas' beautiful hands fondling his bones. He smiled at his own joke as he turned off the car engine and opened the door.

A cold, wet wind blew around him. *This is going to be a hell of a day to play in the mud.* He sighed as he walked up the pathway. He rang the doorbell, reading the blue metal historical plaque on the wall as he waited. *The Sinclair House, 1805.*

The door opened. "Come in. I'll be right with you. You might as well enjoy some warmth while you can."

The tall figure of the beautiful woman moved away from him down the hall as he watched. "Ahh, thanks."

"What's your name?" she asked from inside a closet.

"Gorski, ma'am. Bill."

Pateas reappeared carrying a big gym bag and wearing a warm rain jacket. "I'm Aliki. Let's go, Bill."

Entering the grounds of the estate near Unionville, Bill drove the squad car down the long paved drive and around the back of the house. Off in the distance, across the perfectly manicured lawns, yellow police tape could be seen tied to trees at the edge of the bush. It fluttered wildly in the wind. Aliki sighed and opened her door, letting the blast of the blustery spring day into the confines of the warm car.

While Bill radioed in their position, he watched Aliki get her bag out of the back seat and hoist the strap up on her shoulder. As they headed out over the cold, soggy grass, he suspected that Aliki was glad she had changed to waterproof rain shoes before leaving her house. He could feel the dampness already seeping into his own leather boots as he followed her. He wondered if he should offer to carry the heavy looking bag, then decided that he had better not. The lady seemed capable of taking care of herself, and word was that you didn't want to offend the doctor.

Several miserable looking officers stood around a partly excavated grave. The outline of a skeleton could be seen in the wet, black earth.

"Morning, men. Hell of a day," Pateas greeted, dropping her gym bag and squatting by the hole. "Did you guys do the digging?"

"Yes, ma'am," said a burly looking cop standing on the opposite side of the grave.

"I'll need the dirt collected and boxed for sifting. There might be evidence in it we can use. Did someone take photos?"

"Yes, ma'am."

Pateas stood and then bent over the gym bag. She pulled out a pair of hip waders and stepped into them. Taking off her jacket, she passed it to Gorski to hold while she slipped her suspenders into place. She gratefully took the jacket back. Next, she pulled a cement trowel out of the bag. Without a word, she stepped down into the grave and started to scrape away the debris.

Bill realized that, like the others, he had been standing there staring at the mesmerizing woman who now straddled the dead man and casually worked dirt out from around his ribs.

"Come on, you two, let's find something we can put this dirt in," he growled. They left Pateas to her quiet, methodical work.

After Robbie was taken away, Janet contacted Robbie's law firm and Amanda, then she sought out Ryan. She found the teenager curled in a ball in the corner of her bed, her ear-phones in place and her eyes closed.

"Can we talk?" Janet asked, standing at the bedroom door with Reb in her arms. Ryan stared at her coldly but nodded. Janet walked in and sat on the bed. Reb immediately squirmed out of her arms and into Ryan's, curling up quietly into her big sister's lap and sucking her thumb.

"Reb never sucks her thumb." Ryan's voice was dull, lifeless.

"No," Janet agreed. "She's scared. We all are."

Fighting back tears, Ryan asked, "Did she do it?"

"I don't know what really happened that night. Robbie never wanted to talk about that time in her life. I do know that your mom is not capable of murder."

"Robbie's not my mother. I might as well not have had one." Ryan looked up and met Janet's eyes. She saw only trust and confidence there, but her pain was too great for her to believe again.

Ryan being so controlled, so emotionless, was disturbing. *Why doesn't she cry or yell? Anything to get her pain and disappointment out.* "Mrs. Singh is going to come to baby sit Reb. I'm going down to the police station to make sure your...Robbie's okay. Do you want to come with me?"

"No."

Janet tried not to let her worry and anger show. She got up and looked down at Ryan. "Whatever happens, Ryan, you remember this: with your permission, I adopted you as my daughter, just as Robbie adopted Reb. I am very proud to have you as my daughter. I love you, and so does Robbie. We will always be together as a family."

Ryan snorted. "Yeah, my...Robbie said the same thing only a few hours ago."

Janet cringed inside but outwardly remained calm and smiled. "Good, because she's right. We are a family and we will stay together. Don't give up on us, Ryan. This damn branch of the Williams family is worth fighting for."

For a second, their eyes held in silent communication, then Ryan slipped her ear-phones back in place and, hugging Reb tight, closed her eyes. Janet leaned down and kissed each of her daughters on the head and then went out to wait for Amanda.

Robbie sat on the bunk in the Bartlett jail staring at the stained cement floor. She had been sitting like that since they had booked her and apologetically locked her in the only cell that Bartlett had. *What the hell have I done to the people I love and swore to protect? Wrecked their lives, that's what. I wasn't supposed to get involved. I knew that. What the hell have I done?*

"Robbie?"

Dull blue-grey eyes looked up to meet soft, worried green. The eyes widened and Robbie was at the bars in an instant. "What are you doing here?" she growled.

Terry quietly opened the gate and let Janet in. Quickly locking the door shut behind her, he walked away. "Where else would I be?" Janet stepped closer so Robbie could wrap her in her arms.

Instead, Robbie backed off. "You shouldn't have come. Where are the girls?"

Janet was taken aback. Fear and pain crossed her face and then were replaced with tender understanding. "Amanda's at the cabin with them. Don't do this, Robbie. I'm your legal partner." Janet moved close again and grabbed onto Robbie before she could elude her. Robbie's body was rigid and unresponsive; Janet stroked her lover's back, pretending not to notice. "I love you. I married you knowing that you kept a dark secret you feared would some day come back to haunt you. You were honest with me, Robbie. You tried to warn me off, but I didn't care. I still don't. I love you and that's forever."

Strong arms came up to pull the smaller woman in close. "I'm so sorry!"

"Don't be." She reached up to plant a kiss on Robbie's chin.

Robbie looked at the far corner of the room, her jaw working nervously. "Does Ryan hate me?" she mumbled.

Janet hesitated and then told the truth. "She thinks she does." Seeing the pain on her lover's face, she reached up and cupped her chin, forcing Robbie to make eye contact. "Don't you dare give up on us," she demanded angrily. "Because we are not going to give up on you."

Robbie swallowed, fought for emotional control and then spoke, placing her hands on Janet's shoulders and looking intently at her partner. "You listen, that joint bank account I established... I put a lot of money in it. You take a leave of absence, get our kids out of here. Change your name, just disappear."

"No."

Robbie pulled away in exasperation, walked to the corner of the cell and turned back to look at her determined wife. "You have no idea what it will be like. The press is going to have a field day with this. How long do you think its going to be before the marriage certificate comes to light? Jesus, Janet! Just go away. I should never have gotten involved with you in the first place, or thought that it was safe to contact my daughter. Christ! What have I done?" She sank down onto the cot in despair.

Janet sat stiffly beside her. "Don't you love me anymore, Robbie?" she asked quietly.

Robbie's head snapped around, eyes blazing. "Of course, I love you. That's what makes this whole thing so wrong. You don't hurt the people you love."

Janet shrugged. "It sometimes happens," she responded philosophically, taking Robbie's cold hand. "If it was the other way around and I was in here, would you leave?"

A moment's silence was broken by a humourless laugh. "No," Robbie admitted. "I'd be ripping the walls off to get to you."

Janet giggled and lifted the strong hand to kiss it. "Well, I didn't have to go quite that far, but I did have to get pretty firm with Terry and the desk sergeant. I got permission to leave my cell phone here with you, too."

Robbie pulled Janet against her in a hard hug. "I don't deserve you."

"I like that attitude," Janet said, kissing her lover's ear. "It gives me the upper hand. I'm going to get you out of this, Robbie. I don't know how, but I—" Cold fingers pressed against her lips, stopping her.

"Janet," Robbie whispered, "I did it; I killed him."

Green eyes hardened. "I am going to get you out of this," she repeated with determination. "Now that you've started, tell me the rest." She knew that her lover was going to lie.

Robbie squirmed, swallowed, and made her confession.

An hour later, Janet drove home with a lump in her throat that was threatening to choke her. This was no time for tears. Later tonight, maybe, in the privacy of their bedroom, but not now. She had the girls to think of, particularly Ryan. As she pulled into her driveway, she tried not to think about the pressure headache that was threatening to take the top of her skull off. *Just keep it together for a few more hours,* she commanded as she slid out of the cab into the cool afternoon air. Amanda was waiting at the door, worried sympathy on her face.

"How's Robbie?" she asked as Janet stepped up on the porch.

"Upset."

Amanda nodded, knowing not to push. "Nothing on the news. I checked," she reported.

Janet smiled weakly, too tired to be glad of the brief stay. Amanda helped her out of her coat and gave her a hug. Janet allowed herself to be held for a second, relishing the emotional warmth and support. *How did I become so dependent on Robbie so quickly?* She felt like part of herself had been torn out. Before she completely lost control, she pulled back and smiled at Amanda. "Thanks for helping out. Where are the kids?"

"I put Reb to bed. She fell asleep in Ryan's arms. Ryan paced about a bit and then said she was going to chop wood. I wasn't sure I should let her, given her present state of mind, but I didn't know how to stop her. She's so...so controlled. I've been watching her from the window until I heard your truck."

Janet nodded again, aware now of the sound of an axe splitting wood. The rhythm was similar to the pounding in her head. For a second, she closed her eyes.

Amanda took her arm. "You okay? Do you want me to stay?"

"No. I'm fine, just a headache. I need to talk to Ryan. Listen, could you just quietly let the rest of the staff know? I don't want them to be surprised if they wake up tomorrow to find the news media on their doorsteps wanting interviews."

Amanda smiled at Janet's attempt at humour. "Sure thing." She slipped into her coat and, before heading out to her Honda Civic, turned to look at Janet. "Call if you need anything. You know you have friends. Don't be afraid to lean on us."

Janet smiled through misty eyes. "Thanks." Amanda nodded and was gone.

Taking up her coat, Janet crossed the living room and went out the front door to find Ryan placing a log on the old stump. With a powerful swing of the axe, the wood was split in two. The teen put the axe down and bent to throw the pieces onto a nearby pile.

"The first thing Robbie asked was whether you hated her," Janet said. "I told her you thought you did."

A cry of pain rose from deep inside Ryan. She took the length of wood she was holding and smashed it against the tree stump, over and over again. Janet waited, letting Ryan work the anger out on the tree. When she saw the blows start to weaken, she went over and wrapped Ryan in her arms.

"Why?" sobbed the heartbroken child. "Why did they take Mom away from me?"

"Shhh, love, shhhh, don't you worry. We'll find a way to bring her back to us," Janet soothed, gently rocking the teen as she would Reb. She held her tight for a very long time. When the painful sobs subsided, she pulled back a little and smiled. "I left my cell phone with your mom. You want to phone and say hi? It would mean a lot to her. She's really down on herself."

Ryan nodded. And the two walked back into the house together.

Robbie lay on the cell bunk, staring at the cement ceiling. She wasn't sure that she could spend years locked up like this. She closed her eyes and tried to fight down the fear and desperation. Silently, Janet's phone went off in her pocket. Like a drowning woman reaching for a life preserver, she pulled out the phone and flipped it open. "Hello."

"Mom?" a quiet voice said tentatively.

Robbie's heart contracted and the blood roared in her head. "Ryan. Ryan, I'm so sorry," she choked through her tears.

"I was angry." Then she added, "For an actor, you sure have bad timing."

Robbie sniffed out a laugh. "Yeah, I sure do. I love you, Ryan."

"I know, Mom. You okay?"

"I am now. How about you?"

"Okay, I guess," she said evasively. "Aunt Janet wants to say goodnight." She handed the phone over to Janet.

"Is she okay?" Robbie asked after Janet said hello.

Janet thought about that for a minute as she watched Ryan disappear into the bathroom. "No. But she will be in time. She had herself a good Williams scene when I got back and that let out some of the pain. She is a remarkable child, Robbie. Strong, like you. She'll work through this; it's just going to take time."

"No kid should have to work through something like this. I love you all so much. I never—"

"Robbie," Janet cut in, "we're past that. Now we are moving forward as a family to see this through to a happy conclusion that can bring you back to us."

"Janet..."

"I love you, sweetheart. Feel my arms around you tonight. I am still with you and always will be." Tears silently rolled down her face. She knew Robbie was crying too.

"I love you too, Janet. I am so lucky to have you. Goodnight, love."

"Good night."

The next morning, Janet woke to the sounds of the doorbell ringing and Rufus barking. She was just slipping into her housecoat when Ryan appeared at her door in a run. "Reporters. They're all over the place. I pulled all the drapes."

Janet sighed. They would have to run the gauntlet on the way to work. The phone rang and she went over to her bedside table and picked it up. "Hello, Janet speaking."

"Hi, it's Carolyn. *The Herald* out of Toronto has broken the story of the arrest this morning. Wouldn't you know it's Lucier's story. I'm going to kick him where it hurts next time I see him. Listen, Janet, I phoned to warn you: the front page has a picture of Robbie in handcuffs being put into the police car. You're in the background. There is also a copy of your marriage certificate on page two."

"Oh shit."

Ryan's eyes widened in surprise. Aunt Janet rarely swore.

"As soon as I saw the paper, I headed over for coffee at the doughnut shop. I figured you'd want to know what was going down. The town is crawling with reporters. Stacy took me aside and told me that there is a meeting of the school trustees this morning. They sent Larry Butler over to get them all doughnuts and coffee. They're meeting in the boardroom at the car dealership and then going out to see you at the school."

Janet sank down on the bed. "That doesn't sound good," she murmured. Ryan came to sit beside her and Janet wrapped an arm around her, needing Ryan's warmth as much as Ryan needed Janet's reassurance.

"Yeah. Gladys Billingsley stopped in. You know how she and Reverend Billingsley powerwalk with God in the mornings?"

"Yes."

"Well, they've got a mess of righteous indignation up their back ends and it looks like they're going to take steps to ask you to leave the church. You're living in sin."

"No, I'm not," Janet argued dryly, "but I want to be."

Carolyn laughed. "Opinion is going to be split in town, Janet. You know that. Just remember you and Robbie have a lot of friends, no matter what."

Janet smiled. "Thanks. That means a lot to me, Carolyn. I appreciate you calling to let me know the lay of the land. I'd hate to be facing today blindfolded. It's going to be ugly. Our cabin is surrounded by reporters. They keep ringing the doorbell. I'll get us to school as soon as I can. Try to keep everyone on the regular schedule and warn them not to talk to the press. Phone the police and see if they can spare an officer to be up at the school. I don't want the students getting harassed."

"Okay. Bye for now."

"Bye, Carolyn. Thanks." Janet looked at Ryan.

Their eyes communicated their feelings. Suddenly, devilment danced into the worried principal's eyes. "Let's phone your Mom and give her a rough time for being the biggest damn olive in the Williams jar."

Robbie paced one way, then the other, trying to fight the urge to smash at the bars. The constable on morning duty had brought her *The Herald* with breakfast, a big, grin on his stupid face. *Damn! This is going to be a nightmare for my family!* She checked her watch again. Still a little too early to phone and warn Janet. The vibration of the cell phone interrupted her thoughts. "Hello."

"Morning, love. How are you doing?" Janet's tense voice was raised over the sound of the doorbell ringing. The ring stopped abruptly. "Thanks, Ryan," Janet called out.

"Lucier broke the story in *The Herald* this morning," Robbie said. "Is that the press at the door?"

"Since six this morning. We are under siege here. Carolyn phoned to warn us." Janet smiled up at Ryan who, having disconnected the doorbell, had just walked in with Reb and Rufus.

"Phone! Phone!" squealed Rebecca, running over to her mother. She had just recently discovered the magic of phones.

Janet laughed and held the phone to her daughter's ear. Reb's eyes sparkled and she grinned broadly with delight. "It's Obbie," Janet explained to the child.

"Obbie?"

"Hi, Reb."

"Are you on a plane?"

"No, Reb. I...I had to go away for a bit," Robbie evaded, feeling her heart filling with loneliness.

"You come home," commanded Reb with a pout.

Shit! What do I say now?

"Obbie will come home when she can," Robbie heard Janet say to her daughter. Then there was the sound of the phone changing hands again.

"Hi," Ryan said. "You okay?"

Robbie snorted. "Probably better off than you are. I've got police protection. You okay there?"

"Yeah. Here's Aunt Janet."

"Hi. Well, my favourite olive, you have really spiced the pot this time," came Janet's happy voice again.

Robbie could hear the tension hidden behind the brave front. "Janet, I never meant—"

"Robbie! Don't, okay?" Janet snapped, running a nervous hand through her hair. "We are going to get through this. The news of your arrest has just been broken, so there was bound to be a bit of a sensation."

"They published the marriage certificate. How is that going to impact on you?"

Janet was silent for a minute. "Our friends are being very supportive. There are going to be some repercussions, obviously. You are well liked in this town, Robbie. Once the nine-day wonder is over, we'll be fine. Your law firm will have someone there today for you. I'll be around as soon as I can. Don't worry."

"I am worried. You keep the kids close and stay away from strangers. I don't want some right winged, neo-asshole hurting any of you because of me," Robbie snarled, the impact of the situation mounting within her by the minute.

"I promise," Janet said calmly, trying to relieve some of the stress that her partner was under. "We have to go now. I'll phone you as soon as we are safe at the school. Don't worry."

"Be careful. Don't let the press stop you. Don't talk to them," Robbie advised in a nervous rush.

"Okay. Love you, bye"

For a long time, Robbie stood there looking at the phone in her hand. *Dear God! This is awful!*

An hour later, Janet helped Rebecca into her spring coat while Ryan stuffed her books into her school bag. "Okay, this is it. Ryan, you carry Reb. Keep your faces away from the cameras if you can. I'll go first with our stuff and open the truck doors. We'll take Robbie's truck. Stay right behind me, and no matter what happens, don't react or speak."

Ryan nodded nervously and Janet moved forward to give her a big hug. "You don't know how much your support means to me. I know this is a terrible thing for you to have to go through. Just remember, it won't last forever, and there will be better times ahead."

Ryan nodded, hugging her aunt stiffly, then bent to pick up Rebecca. Janet looked at the big hairy dog that brushed protectively against her knee. "Rufus, don't bite anyone. Well, at least not too badly," she amended, smiling up at Ryan and giving her a wink. "Keep Rufus by you."

The nervous teen nodded. "Heel, Rufus," she commanded quietly, and the lumbering orange dog came to sit beside Ryan's knee.

"Good dog," Reb encouraged, looking down from Ryan's arms. Rufus wagged an affectionate tail.

"Ready?" Janet asked. When Ryan nodded, Janet opened the door to the soundwave of clicking, whirring cameras. As they stepped off the porch in a tight formation, reporters swarmed in from all sides.

"Did she do it?"

"How is Robbie handling her arrest?"

"Have you spoken to her?"

"What's it like to be in a gay marriage with Robbie Williams?"

"Is she pleading guilty?"

"Did your mother tell you she'd killed her father, Ryan?"

They were jostled about, unable to make much headway until Rufus let out a threatening growl and started barking. The shaggy monster came off the porch in a rush and scattered reporters in all directions.

Janet nudged Ryan, and they used the opening to get to the truck. Rufus stood behind them growling menacingly at the stunned crowd as the Williams unlocked the doors of the truck, stowed their bags, and strapped Reb into place.

Janet started the engine. "Come, Rufus," she called, and the big dog leapt into his regular place beside Reb. Janet reached back and closed the truck door and they were off.

Things were a little better at the school. Carolyn had arranged to have an Ontario Provincial Police cruiser at the gate for the start of the school day and had hired more security guards to help patrol the grounds. Once Janet had slowly edged the truck through the swarm of reporters at the gate, they were safe.

Parking the truck in the spot reserved for the principal, Janet felt a cold dread spreading through her. She turned to look at the silent teen beside her. "I might lose my job today. If that happens, I'll come and get you and Reb, and we'll get out of here. Robbie set up an account just in case something like this occurred. Also, her law firm is doing everything it can for us. Robbie tried her very best to protect us. Try not to worry. We are going to get through this, no matter how rough it gets in the short haul."

Ryan nodded, her jaw white and clenched with stress. "I'll take Rufus to his pen."

Janet squeezed Ryan's hand before she opened her door and then turned to open the back door to get Reb out of her car seat. Holding her daughter's hand, she watched Ryan and the big, ugly dog disappearing around the corner. Ryan was like her mom; she internalized too much. How much could one child handle emotionally? With a worried frown, she left Reb in their small daycare centre and went to her office.

Carolyn Carr came out from behind her desk to give Janet a big hug. "They're down in the staff room waiting for you."

Janet nodded, knowing that "they" had to be the members of Board of Trustees. "I need to speak to Amanda and Milka first. Have Jason, Alex, and Wanda cover for them and get them down here as quickly as you can."

"Sure thing, Janet."

"Ask Jason to keep an eye on Ryan, just in case there are problems. She seems to be fitting in nicely now, but...well, ask him," Janet fretted.

"Done."

Janet nodded her thanks and went into her office. She wanted to get her paperwork caught up just in case. Ten minutes later, Amanda Singh and Milka Gorski came into the outer office and Carolyn waved the two worried women on into Janet's office.

Janet was all business, needing to maintain a barrier between her work and her emotions until she had everything organized. "Have a seat, ladies."

"Janet, we're all so sorry. You know you have the support of the staff, don't you?" Milka said.

"Thanks. That means a lot to me. I'm surprised I have Wanda's support. She is very religious."

Milka laughed. "She said that she couldn't approve of your lifestyle but she didn't think it was any of her business. She thinks God will get you, so she doesn't need to bother."

"Oh brother." Amanda sneered and rolled her eyes.

Janet shook her head in disbelief. "Well, I appreciate her tolerance, if not her mindset." Janet sighed. "Okay, down to business. There is a good chance I will be asked to resign. I won't, so that means they will have to place me on leave with pay or buy out my contract. Either way, I think it's fairly safe to say that after today, my career is done like dinner."

"It's just not fair. You're so good at what you do," Amanda protested, and Milka nodded her agreement.

"Thanks, but the Board of Trustees is undoubtedly going to have trouble with the image of their school principal being in a gay marriage with a suspected murderer," Janet responded cynically.

"Bored trusses," Milka muttered, using the teachers' favourite expression for the Board of Trustees.

"I need to review with you how to handle things when I'm gone. I'll recommend both of you as possible replacements. You both have the education, knowledge, and experience to take over."

"Please," Amanda interrupted, "I would like to help any way I can, but I have a young family at home. They come first in my life at the moment. I don't want the job, not yet anyway."

"I want it but not like this," Milka protested.

"It won't be your fault if I lose my job, Milka, and I'll feel better leaving knowing the person taking over will do a good job. Okay, let's go through this stuff quickly; the Board's waiting."

Ryan walked down the hall to her locker, aware of the wake of silence around her.

Jenny Kingsley, who had the locker beside hers, leaned around the beige metal door. "Hi, Ryan. We're really sorry to hear about your mom. Look, if there is anything we can do to—"

"Thanks," came the sharp response. Then more softly, Ryan added, "Thanks, that's good of you. I don't know what's going to happen. The press are like vultures out there."

Debbie DeLuca stepped over and patted Ryan on the back. "Yeah, that's the trouble with having a famous parent. Look, when you first got here...we didn't treat you very well because we were all afraid of Stacy. We'd like to make it up to you this time around."

"No need. Look, I know a lot of you are not comfortable with the gay issue. You don't have to pretend you are. If you want to help, just stay out of it. Okay?" Ryan slammed her locker shut and hurried down the hall to homeroom.

"Well, she wasn't very nice," Nona grumbled.

"Cut Ryan some slack," snapped Debbie. "Shit! Her mother's a queer married to her principal and probably killed her grandfather. How would you feel?"

"Talk about your bad hair day," Angie interjected, trying to ease the tension.

Debbie agreed with a nervous giggle. "Yeah. Come on, let's get to class."

An hour later, Janet sat on an orange plastic chair looking at the elected citizens who were in a position to judge her despite the fact that not one of them knew anything about education. The old tradition of a community body overseeing the local one-room school somehow seemed ludicrous in modern society.

Bartlett got straight to the point. "Mrs. Williams, ah, the Board met this morning and we don't feel that the situation you are presently in is good for the school's image. We know you have two years left on your contract, but we feel we have no choice but to ask for your resignation."

I should have let Robbie finish tearing him apart at the party. "My marriage is quite legal, and in this country, people are still innocent until proven guilty. I do realize that this is embarrassing for the school, but I will not resign. I have done nothing wrong."

"Yes, well, of course, you are right, but Bartlett relies on its paying clientele, and image is everything in this business. We would ask that you reconsider, for the sake of the school," he said, adopting a more-in-sorrow-than-in-pain tone.

"No."

The Trustees squirmed uncomfortably in their seats and looked from one to another. Bartlett sighed. "Then I'm sorry, we have voted to put you on leave of absence with pay until your contract runs out. Your contract will not be renewed."

Janet showed no reaction. "Fine. You would do very well to promote either Milka Gorski or Amanda Singh to my position. They are both well qualified."

The Trustees looked surprised. "We have been very pleased with your work, Mrs. Williams. It is just an impossible situation for the school. We hope there are no hard feelings," one member said.

Janet smiled. "Yes, there are hard feelings. If I decide to take this to the Equal Rights Commission, they'll make mincemeat of you. It might, however, be quicker just to sue for damages, since you have no cause for my dismissal. You have made a very poor decision today. Good day." *Let the assholes chew on that.* Janet got up and walked out of the room.

Janet signalled to Ryan through the small window in the classroom door. Ryan got up quietly, took her books, and left.

"Hi," her aunt greeted awkwardly.

"You fired?" Ryan asked bluntly.

Janet smiled cynically. "No, I'm on permanent leave."

Ryan rolled her eyes and looked sadly around the school hall. Janet knew that Ryan had been happy at Bartlett. It was a school she really wanted to go to at last, and one where she could have gotten a good education. *Today is just as hard for Ryan as it is for me.*

"So, I could home school you, if you like," Janet said, watching her niece and adopted daughter closely for a sign of what was going on inside. *Both Ryan and Robbie are always charged with emotion, but it only shows in subtle movements of a muscle under the skin or a slight twitch of a nerve. Their faces never show their emotions openly. They're always on guard, always afraid that if they show their feelings they'll be hurt. I have to deal with my partner and my daughter so gently.*

Ryan's muscles tightened, causing her jaw line to whiten. A small vein throbbed at her temple. "Sounds like a plan to me," she grunted toughly.

Janet nodded. "Let's clean out your locker and get Reb. You want me to call a few of your friends out to say good bye?"

Ryan looked back through the glass. New friends sent furtive, worried glances toward the door. "I was kind of abrupt with them earlier. I think I owe it to all of them to say good-bye properly."

Janet smiled and hugged her. "You are one of a kind. I hope Reb grows up to be like you. Go say good-bye. I'll be back to get you."

Chapter 15

Aliki read about the arrest of Roberta Williams in the morning newspaper as she sat in the white wicker chair on her sun porch. She lifted her coffee and took a thoughtful sip as she looked at the picture of the handcuffed director being put in the squad car. Memories of snippets of whispered conversations that she had overheard as a child came back to her. *Could Roberta Williams be related to me?*

In the background of the photo, a small blonde stood in a doorway looking on worriedly. *Cute,* Aliki observed idly, and then let her eyes drift back to the figure of the director. The bones she had dug up appeared in her mind. Something...yes, something about those bones didn't fit with the substance of the police report. She made a mental note to have another look at them now that they had been cleaned up and Bates had finished his work.

Later that day, she sat on a tall stool in the lab, her face only inches away from the skull of Philip Williams as her magnifying glass edged along a deep indentation in the left temporal. The blow had shattered the articular eminence and filled the squama of the temporal with a web of hairline cracks that formed a concave dish. It had been a hell of a blow. So had the one that had cracked his jaw.

"Are you double checking my work?" came an amused voice from behind her.

Aliki straightened and twisted to look seriously at Doctor Thomas Bates, the chief pathologist in the Toronto Forensic lab. "No. Your report is quite accurate. There is just something here that I'm not comfortable with and I don't know what it is."

Bates picked up the left ulna, playing with it absentmindedly. "It's our job to just report the medical facts, Aliki, not to draw conclusions. That's for the lawyers."

"But the lawyers will want to know what we can deduce," the forensic anthropologist protested, her eyes blue and clear as she looked at Bates.

Aliki knew what Bates would be thinking before he said it. He, too, had been idealistic at one time, as eager to find the truth. Bates still did his job well, but he'd told Aliki many times that he had come to realize over the years that truth was a very slippery eel. In the end, no matter how clear the facts, it was court procedure and jury perception that would prevail, not necessarily truth. Truth lurked, her boss had told her, in the muddy depths of people's consciences and was rarely caught, no matter how highly prized.

Aliki was relatively new to forensic work and she had a lot to learn, she knew. Her early research had been on prehistoric Inuit sites. With some luck and Bates' steady guidance, she'd quickly made a name for herself. She knew she had that special combination of intelligence, observational skills, and instinct that was needed for the job, and she was cool under cross-examination in court. But she was also aware that sometimes she thought like a cop, not a scientist.

"Doctor Pateas, I could tell you to just do your job and not try to be a hero or play God, but you wouldn't listen. You never do," Bates drawled, tossing the arm bone back on the gurney and taking out his pipe. He slowly and lovingly filled his old briar with the strong St. Bruno tobacco he favoured, then continued. "So tell me what you have observed and perhaps whatever is bothering you will reveal itself in the process."

Aliki smiled. She liked Doctor Bates. She had learned a lot from him in a short time. She especially appreciated his tolerance now, and as a result was willing to forgive him his noxious smoking habit. He never actually lit the pipe inside the building, but the smell of stale tobacco tended to follow in his wake. Most people in this line of work smoked. In the

Forensic Department, as in the morgue, a good sense of smell was not necessarily an asset.

"The subject was struck with a blow to the left side of the mandible, close to the mental foramen, resulting in this green fracture. It was not the cause of death, although most likely it resulted in unconsciousness."

"An assumption, Doctor," Bates murmured, sucking happily on the stem of his pipe. He did not seem to notice that the damn pipe was not lit.

"Yes, an assumption," Aliki acknowledged. "But it is on fairly safe ground. It was a blow hard enough to cause a broken jaw and he was an older man."

Bates nodded but said nothing, so Aliki went on. "That was not the blow that killed him. The one that did was to the right temple area after the subject was on the ground."

"Explain."

"The first blow was an upper cut by a right handed person. The second blow was a down stroke..." Aliki stopped and stared at the skull. "The murderer was left handed!" she exclaimed.

Bates smiled, his eyes sparkling. "There were two different people there the night the murder took place."

Aliki looked at him in surprise. "You knew that?"

"It's a possibility."

"But you didn't state it in your report."

"No. It is an assumption, although highly likely. The defence will have their own medical experts to analyse this data. Based on the evidence and on my report, they will draw the same conclusions and it will most likely come out in court under cross examination."

"What if it doesn't?"

"We report scientific facts. We also work *for* the police, not against them. That's why they have two sides to the courtroom, Aliki." Bates wiggled his eyebrows mischievously. "All the information is there. Each side can do with it what they will." Bates patted her arm affectionately, and walked back toward his office as Aliki looked down at the bones and brooded.

At his office door, he turned and remarked, "Of course, Doctor, it could have been a gentle blow to the jaw that caused the damage if the victim had osteoporosis. He was, after all, getting on in years. Also, had the attacker been facing the opposite direction, the blow to the temporal squama could have been made by a right-handed killer. Please verify your facts, Doctor. Lawyers are very exacting." Having played devil's advocate, Bates disappeared into his inner sanctum.

Aliki stood there looking over her shoulder at the closed office door. "Shit!" she mouthed silently and then sat back down on the stool to cover the bases she had missed until Bates had pointed them out to her.

The ride to Toronto in the back of the paddy wagon was boring. Robbie sat in the tin box with a female police officer whose job it was to prevent her from doing anything drastic. She looked at her handcuffed hands, which were linked to a chain around her waist, as were the ankle cuffs they had put on her. *You'd have to be pretty imaginative to do anything drastic,* she thought wryly.

Robbie spent the rest of the time coming up with variations on that theme. She'd come up with twenty-seven possible scenarios by the time they had reached Toronto. Six of them, she felt, were quite feasible.

The booking process was humiliating. Once again, she was fingerprinted and photographed. Then she was ordered to strip and shower with a matron watching on. *Lady, if I was going to do anything drastic, I'd have done it in one of twenty-seven creative ways before*

I got here, Robbie thought as she stood in the grotty stall and made herself presentable for her prison debut. She was drying her hair on the thin, small towel when she saw the matron walking toward her wearing plastic gloves. *Oh shit!*

The search for illegal substances was embarrassing and disgusting. Afterwards, Robbie was given an orange coverall to put on. It was a little short in the arms and legs and a bit baggy in the hips and ass.

Once again she was fitted with her stainless steel jewelry and led to another room where she stood at a counter with the matron. The ferret-faced woman handed Robbie's personnel effects to the clerk, who slowly and laboriously listed each item on a form.

"You gotta take the ring off, too," he growled, shoving a manila envelope over for her to put her watch, gold chain, and wedding band in.

"It's my wedding ring," Robbie protested as she slipped off her watch.

"Yeah, so I hear," the clerk sneered. "Put it in the envelope, lady. Gold is valuable. She ain't worth getting mugged over."

Robbie took the ring off. It was just a ring, she knew, but removing it filled her heart with dread. It was as if she had broken some precious link that joined the two of them together. *Janet, I'm sorry.* The ring dropped into the brown envelope and was quickly sealed in.

"Look this list over and sign that's all you got," ordered the clerk.

Robbie read and signed. The matron took her arm and led her to the first of the barred doors that led to her cell and her new life.

"What? ... When? ... Well, Jesus, why didn't somebody notify me? Okay, okay. Where was she taken? ... Yeah, I'll pick up my phone when I get the chance. Good bye."

Ryan sat in the chair across from the principal's desk and looked at Janet, who was obviously upset. *What's gone wrong now?* She felt a tightening in her stomach; was her mom safe?

Janet hung up the phone angrily. "Your mom was transferred to Toronto today. She'll be held there until she is remanded for trial, then she'll be sent down to Kingston." She ran a nervous hand ran through her hair.

Ryan could see she was fighting for emotional control before she spoke again.

"Obbie's not going to be able to handle being locked up very well. She wanted to phone me but they wouldn't let her take the time. They took the cell phone away from her before she was transferred." Tears spilled from Janet's eyes and she covered her face with her hands.

Ryan silently pulled some tissues from the box on the desk and passed them to her aunt. Janet gave a weak smile in thanks, wiped her eyes, blew her nose and squared her shoulders.

Ryan smiled reassuringly. "So, what should we do now?"

They left the school grounds by a little used service road and, once at the cabin, the remaining Williams family packed hurriedly while the press was still unaware of their location. By three, they were on the 401 heading south to Toronto.

"Are we going to stay at Robbie's?" asked Ryan.

Janet, preoccupied with her own thoughts, responded briefly, "Yes."

Ryan would have liked to ask more, but was afraid. It looked like she'd lost her home as well as her school. They hit rush hour traffic, moving along like a vertebra in a slow moving metal snake. Ryan could see her aunt gripping the steering wheel in angry frustration and she stayed quiet. *Everyone's nerves and patience were ragged after today. It was not a good time to talk.*

It was nearly seven o'clock when they finally turned into the condominium complex by Lake Ontario where Robbie made her home. With a sigh of relief, Janet activated the garage doors to enter the underground parking lot. Swinging around a pillar, she was surprised to find a Ferrari in one of Robbie's parking spots. Did Robbie own that too? Janet had no idea. She knew Robbie had the Stingray and the BMW and, of course, the truck she was now driving, but she wasn't sure if Robbie owned any other vehicles. Really, she knew very little about Robbie.

Dread crept into her heart with that thought. Robbie had so willingly moved into her small-town world. Except for the funeral, Janet had had very little contact with Robbie's world. How much did she really know about the history of the woman she had married? How much of the legend of the Williams family was true, and how much lies?

Fatigue overtaking her, she unloaded some of the basic luggage they would need and herded her family into the private elevator that would take them to the penthouse. Janet leaned back into the corner of the lift and allowed her eyes to close for a minute while she listened to Ryan explain to Reb that they were going to stay in Obbie's house for a while. Reb was being fretful and difficult. She didn't blame the poor kid. Her routine had been turned up side down in the last twenty-four hours.

Janet opened her eyes and leaned forward to rub Ryan's shoulder affectionately. "Here, let me take her. It's just been too much for her and she's overtired. We all are," Janet said with quiet reassurance.

Ryan also had just about had all she could handle. She nodded and handed over the whining child.

The door to Robbie's home slid open and a sharp voice stunned them out of their exhaustion. "Just who are you and what are you doing in my daughter's home?"

"Ryan, meet Alexandria," Janet provided with a roll of her eyes as she stepped out of the elevator, followed by her children and shaggy dog. "I'm sure you haven't forgotten me, Mrs. Williams. I am your son's widow and your oldest daughter's wife," she pointed out with a forced smile.

"It's preposterous! I simply will not accept it! What was Robbie thinking of?"

"Sex," Janet shot back unfairly, for the shock effect. "She is a very basic individual."

"Couldn't she have just slept with you?"

"Not and lived," Janet observed, helping Ryan carry in bags.

Ryan kept quiet, but her eyes sparkled with amusement as she listened to her aunt spar with Alexandria.

Reb, released from Janet's arms, made a beeline to the stranger and looked up. "Where is Obbie?" she asked earnestly.

Alexandria looked down in surprise. "What...is...an...Obbie?" she demanded.

Janet took Ryan's hand and went over to capture Rebecca's sticky little hands just before the child made a grab for Alexandria's furs. "That's what Rebecca calls Robbie. Alexandria, you remember my daughter, Rebecca, and this is Robbie's daughter, Ryan," Janet introduced politely.

Eyes the same colour as Robbie's snapped up to look at Ryan curiously. "Oh yes, I have heard rumours over the years of Robbie's bastard."

Janet felt Ryan stiffen and she gently ran her thumb over Ryan's hand, hoping the gesture would calm Ryan as it always did for Robbie.

"Alexandria, Robbie and I are very proud of our children. Don't you ever speak to them that way again. I think I must ask you to leave now. The children and I have had a very taxing day and we are not up to entertaining."

Vicious anger flashed across Alexandria's face, and for a second Janet thought the older woman was going to strike her. Instead, sudden amusement sparkled in the cruel eyes. "Well, I don't think you'll be getting any sleep for a while. The police have gone through the place looking for evidence," said the tall woman as she swept past and stepped into the elevator. "I just had to co-operate with them." She smiled as the doors closed.

"Hope the cables snap," Ryan muttered.

Janet shot her a warning look and Ryan fell silent.

The condo was a mess. Drawers had been opened and furniture cushions and mattresses tossed aside. Janet wasn't completely sure that it had been totally the work of the police. It didn't make sense that Alexandria would come here or that she would co-operate with the police. Suddenly, anger boiled over inside Janet and she heaved a pillow across the room. It was that damn "dark time" again. There was a vow of silence around it that the remaining Williamses cherished. She loved Robbie deeply, trusted her completely, and yet the trust had not been returned a hundred percent. Janet had always been left on the outside, finding out things that everyone else in the family knew only after it was necessary for her to be informed. *Damn all Williams to hell.*

The anger passed as quickly as it had come. Janet just didn't have the energy to stay mad after their exhausting day. She looked around for her family. Reb, the resourceful toddler that she was, had crawled into an armchair and was fast asleep, with Rufus guarding the little body with his big, shaggy bulk. Ryan had wandered out onto the barren garden terrace.

Janet quickly set up Reb's portable playpen and carefully laid the sleeping baby into it, then went out to Ryan, who was sitting on a garden bench looking out over Lake Ontario. Ryan didn't react as Janet slipped in beside her. "Penny for your thoughts," Janet said softly.

"I thought I had a home and mother at last, and I wasn't going to be a bastard anymore," Ryan muttered, the tears spilling over with the effort of expressing her emotions.

Janet felt her own tears well up and stream down her face. "Oh, Ryan! Honey!" She pulled her niece and adopted daughter into a deep, tight hug. Ryan held on tightly and sobbed. Janet let her and then, after a few minutes, she offered Ryan her tissue, wiping her own tears away with the back of her hand.

"Ryan, a home isn't a building. It's the family that lives there," Janet said earnestly, taking the teen's hand. "We are a family. Robbie didn't leave you, honey, she was taken away. Her first thoughts were of you."

Ryan broke eye contact and moodily looked out over the water.

Janet went on quietly. "I know you've lost faith in Robbie again. That's okay. The two of you will have time in the future to work that out. But I won't allow you not to believe in us. You are my legal daughter and I love you just as much as I do Reb and Robbie. We are a family, and you are a very important part of it. That's not going to change, not where it counts, here in our hearts."

Ryan swallowed, blinking back tears. She turned to look deeply into Janet's eyes that were, surprisingly, so very much like her own. "Can I call you Mom instead of her?" she asked bluntly.

Janet didn't hesitate, although she would have liked time to consider the consequences that such a decision might have on Robbie's tender soul. Ryan had to come first, and Ryan needed this. "Ryan, I'd be very proud and honoured if you called me Mom, too." Janet smiled through eyes brimming over with emotion.

Ryan nodded seriously and looked back out across the huge lake. "Okay."

Janet laughed in relief and gave Ryan's hair a muss. "Come on, you. I need some help in there or we are going to have to sleep in kitchen drawers tonight."

After an hour of tidying and making beds, Janet made up a box of macaroni and cheese for the three of them. Once Ryan had showered and Reb had been bathed, she tucked them into bed and told them stories.

Janet sat in the girls' room until she was sure her daughters were both asleep. Then, with relief, she walked back to the master bedroom, showered, and crawled between the cold sheets. She was so tired, and yet now that she was there, alone in Robbie's bed, the sleep wouldn't come. Instead, the tears fell, and she sobbed her heart out until exhaustion finally claimed her.

Elizabeth sat curled up in the corner of her couch. She had been at home all day, having phoned in sick when she had heard of Robbie's arrest. She knew what Robbie had told her to do and say, but the emotions and fears that rocketed around inside her made it hard for her to think. It was wise to stay in here, away from everyone.

All these years she had guarded the secret, and now it had come out. Only part of it, that was true, but enough that she now felt very vulnerable. How could she cope without Robbie's towering strength? Her big sister had always been there for her. Her thumb tip slipped between her teeth and she absently rocked back and forth. Robbie promised her that no one would ever know the whole truth. Robbie always kept her promises.

She wanted to phone the jail and talk to her, make sure she was all right, but that would mean talking to others, strangers, and she didn't think she could at the moment. Besides, Robbie's instructions had been quite clear. She was not to contact her. Robbie had gone over it with her so many times. She knew what Robbie expected of her. She always did what Robbie said. Yet inside, she felt awful.

Her eyes shifted to the computer as the screensaver flashed off to be replaced by incoming e-mail. It would be David. He and Robbie alone knew her home addy. She couldn't communicate with David anymore. It wasn't right. He was nice and had high moral standards and she...

Elizabeth stood suddenly, pushing the rest of that thought from her head. She never thought of those things! Never! She wouldn't allow herself to now, either. With the look of grim determination that all Williamses seemed to share, she walked over to her desk and lost herself in the beauty of numbers and the poetic structure of physics equations. Quantum Mechanics was like a balm for her tortured soul.

Oblivious to the panoramic view of evergreens and lake to his right, Ted Potts drove the heavy dump truck down Lakefront Road. He'd been out at Larry and Flo Butler's place picking up his pay cheque, and now he was on his way over to the Bartlett Car Dealership to get the truck's safety certificate for another contracting season.

He liked working for Larry Butler well enough. The pay was okay and Larry was good to his employees, even if he was kinda short tempered at times. In the summer, Ted drove the dump truck, running loads from Larry's gravel pit down south of Indian Gorge to whatever site the company was working on. In the winter, he drove a snowplow. But he was getting on a bit in years, and the lifestyle was getting harder, especially in the winter when he'd have to get up in the middle of the night. It was no fun. When the snow started to fall, he'd be called out into the freezing cold and be on the plow for eighteen hour stretches, trying to keep the roads open.

Ted sighed. When he was younger, he'd thought his brother David was really stupid for tying himself to that grocery store and a big mortgage. But now David had paid off his bank loan and he seemed to be doing real well. He was his own boss, made his own hours, and didn't have to go out in the cold if he didn't want to. David always was the smart one.

A split second later, a deer ran out in front of Ted's truck. He slammed on the brakes and swerved around the fleeting creature. The wheels locked and the back end of the vehicle spun out on the wet spring pavement. Over went the truck, rolling into the ditch and slamming the roof of the cab against a large granite boulder. Moisture shaken from the stark branches above rained softly on the twisted and silent cab.

David came out of his office feeling depressed and annoyed. There was still no response from Elizabeth. He hoped she was all right. He thought they had been getting on very well together. Each day they e-mailed each other, and when she had come to the Drama Society play, she'd had a very good time. She'd agreed to go with him to Roy Thomson Hall, but now, when she should want a friend, she had completely cut him off from her life.

Okay, David, don't let your hurt feelings cloud the issue, he scolded himself. *Christian charity begins at home. You know that Bethy is very insecure and easily hurt. Naturally, she has hidden away from the press. It must be awful for her.* He'd seen Alexandria on TV the night before, and she was very upset. She had cried and said that she just couldn't talk about it, that the thought of her poor Philly lying in a cold, wet hole all those years was just too much for her to bear. David had been quite moved. He was sure that his Bethy would be even more upset than her mother, especially with Robbie under arrest for the murder.

He walked over to the door and flipped over the open sign, then undid the latch. David had just turned around when his beeper went off. He looked at the code screen: Vehicle Accident: Lakefront Road. Quickly, he switched the sign to "closed" and locked the door. Removing his apron, he tossed it on the counter and headed out the back way to his car. He could see other members of the volunteer fire department already taking off down the road.

As soon as David saw the truck, he knew it was his brother. Ted always drove the same truck for Butler. He pulled to the side and leapt out; he was met by a worried Larry Butler. "David, it's Ted. He's alive, but he's pinned in there good and tight. It's hard to know how bad it is. He's in a lot of pain. Said it was his back and right leg," Larry explained as he walked with David down to where the huge truck lay on its side.

George Drouillard, the fire chief, was lying on the cab door with his head through the smashed passenger window talking to Ted, while Paul Digby and Moe Singh readied the Jaws of Life. David climbed up the fire ladder that had been leaned against the undercarriage. George moved aside and let David take a look.

"Hi, Ted. How are you doing?" David's voice was tight with worry. Below him he could see his brother's head and shoulders sticking out from underneath a twisted lump of metal that had once been the roof of the cab. Beside him, halfway through the front window, was a muddy Doctor Perkins.

"Sure...hurts, David. But...that...might be a good...sign, eh?" Ted replied through gasps of pain.

"Yeah. Look, we're going to use Robbie's Jaws of Life to get you out. You just hang on." Ted nodded, his eyes now closed and his face ashen. David looked at Perkins.

"His vital signs are good, David," Bill Perkins said with reassurance.

George patted David's arm reassuringly. "Okay, Moe, it will have to be you going in there, on account of you bein' the skinniest. Paul, you and Walt get more four by fours to shore up this truck. I want a good cribbing in place before we start using the Jaws."

Then he looked around and yelled over to the fire engine, "John! You get on that fancy car phone of yours and see what the ETA is gonna be for the hospital helicopter. Remind them to land it in the skating rink parking lot. Then phone over to White's Funeral Home and tell them to get the hearse up here. We're gonna have to put a backboard under Ted and we'll need their stretcher."

George looked over at David and smiled. "Sure wish we had that little Ryan here. She could always get the damn engine radio to work, eh. Could do with Robbie squeezin' down into the cab, too. Damned if I ever thought we'd need women on the fire department, but those two are all right. I guess in the city you get a lot of females on the fire department now days."

"I guess," David responded absently, watching Larry Butler wedging timber against the truck to make sure it would not roll or shift while they were working on it.

George cleared his voice awkwardly. "Ahh, you heard anything? You know, about Robbie and the family? Folks have been askin'. They're well-liked, although some are a bit turned off by their, ahh...peculiarity."

David looked up sharply, but saw no disapproval in George's face. "No, no, I haven't heard a thing. Janet left with the girls, not because of the town, but because the press wouldn't leave them alone. And of course, stupid Bartlett over there had Janet fired!"

George looked over at the man on the car phone. "Well, John's always been a jackass, right from a boy. Accordin' to my mama, he comes from a long line of them."

Moe climbed up the ladder and then reached down to grab the heavy apparatus that would be used to get to Ted through the twisted metal. "You be careful, son," George warned, patting Mohammed on the back. "David, I gotta ask you to get down now, so as we have more room to work."

David climbed down the ladder and stood at a safe distance with Paul. He watched as Moe carefully lowered himself as far as he could into the mangled cab and then waited as George handed down the Jaws of Life. Moe looked around thoughtfully, decided where the best place would be to start pulling the metal away from Ted's body, and slipped in the metal prongs. Holding on to the handles, he held down the start button and the scissor-like prongs slowly spread, edging the wreckage away from Ted's pinned body.

On the edge of the action, David tried his best to stay calm. He knew George was watching carefully to make sure the operation went smoothly and safely, and Doctor Perkins was monitoring Ted's vitals from his position in the muddy ditch. An hour later, they were able to carefully strap Ted to the backboard and slide him out the front window of the cab. David joined the other men in gently carrying Ted up the slippery bank and sliding him into the back of the hearse, which in Bartlett doubled as their ambulance. Ted was soon on his way to the helicopter that would fly him to the Barrie hospital, miles to the south.

Robbie spent some time with her lawyers, who had arranged for her transfer to Toronto and for the court hearing for formal charges to be held the next day. They told her not to plead guilty to the charge of first-degree murder. They wanted to enter a plea of accidental homicide. Robbie didn't really care; her worst nightmare had become a reality.

The matron led her by the arm down into the cellblocks and placed her in a cell with another woman, whom she introduced as Tracy. Robbie looked around. The cell was small, with a bunk on each side and a metal toilet and sink at the end. The walls were brick, spray-painted cream. The whole place smelt of cheap disinfectant and sewage.

She looked at her cellmate. She was a wiry, tough looking woman with bulging muscles covered in poorly done tattoos. Her hair was cut real short. She ignored Robbie as she sat reading a *Hard Metal* comic book.

"I'm Robbie." She stepped further into the cell. "Is this my bunk?" she inquired politely.

"If I say so."

Robbie gritted her teeth and tried to stay calm. *Just my luck to get a stupid bitch with an attitude.* "Well, you were here first so I guess you get first choice. So, which one is yours?" she asked, letting her impatience show.

"Both," the woman responded, uncoiling slowly, like a snake, and standing up. "You can sleep on the floor until I decide about you. Right, girls?" she said, speaking a little louder so those in other cells could hear. A chorus of cheers came back.

Robbie smiled. *So this is the sort of hazing crap that Ryan has had to put up with over the years. I think I'm getting really, really pissed.* "That's not acceptable to me. I think you'd better choose...now."

The con brought her fist up and slammed it into Robbie's temple. Robbie let it happen. She didn't want to have started the fight. Satisfied that the hit had left a mark, she went for Tracy, letting out all her pent up anger. Three blows and the con was on her knees, dazed.

Robbie stuck two fingers up the woman's nostrils and lifted her off the ground by her nose. The woman screamed in pain as the cartilage in her nose tore and blood poured out. Robbie slammed the half conscious woman against the bars, holding her high so that she had to stand on her toes to ease the pain. She looked out at the silent women who were watching. "No one messes with me, got it?" she snarled, letting Tracy sink to the floor. Disgusted, she went over to the sink beside the toilet and scrubbed her hands as well as she could under the circumstances.

Aliki sipped at a liquor glass of Benedictine. She watched the reflection of the flames from the living room fireplace dance across the polished oak floor that edged the Persian rug. The case had more than a professional interest for her. She was drawn by curiosity like a moth to a flame. She had followed Robbie Williams' career with interest, and this case might give her a chance to get to meet the woman. Aliki recalled the talk about her father having had an affair with a ballerina with the Winnipeg ballet before he married her own mother. There'd been whispers between the adults that would end abruptly if any of the children walked in. *I've heard enough, though, to put two and two together; it makes me wonder. More than once people have said that I looked remarkably like Robbie Williams in some lights. Could we be related?*

Leaning back into her armchair, she closed her eyes and thought about her findings. Philip Williams had not had osteoporosis. She had dug out the photographs of the murder scene. The body had fallen with the top of the head near the base of a love seat. The second blow could have only come from one side. The first blow had been right handed, the second, left. There were either two people involved in the murder or, Aliki smiled, foreseeing her boss' next point, the killer was a switch hitter.

She opened her eyes, took a second sip of her nightcap, and took up the statement that Robbie had made to the police in the presence of her lawyers.

"I argued with my father that night over my sexual preferences. He took a swing at me and I blocked it and hit him back. He fell to the floor. I thought he was unconscious.

"My mother was out of town that weekend. I went to find my kid sister and brother who were upstairs in their beds, to make sure they were okay. I found them asleep. I went back downstairs, planning on leaving, but I found that my father was dead rather than unconscious. I panicked and buried him in the woods. Then I drove to the Port Credit harbour, took his sailboat out a couple of miles, and made it look like he'd fallen overboard and drowned. I swam back to the shore. I told my brother and sister that my father had called me at my university residence and asked me to baby sit so that he could take his boat out for the weekend. He sometimes did that. The next afternoon, I reported my father missing."

Aliki smiled softly as she put the paper down on the sherry table beside her chair. *Robbie Williams, you are lying and I'm going to prove it. And maybe in the process I'll get an opportunity to answer some questions that I've had for a long, long time.*

Janet had been notified early in the morning about the hearing. It was to be at eleven o'clock. She was anxious to get there and see Robbie, although the lawyer had reassured her that her partner was alright. Ryan was content to stay at the condo and baby sit Reb while Janet went alone to the courthouse.

Kissing her two daughters good-bye, Janet took the elevator down to the parking garage and got into her truck. She was preoccupied, upset, and overtired, and she didn't sense any danger until she stopped at the end of the driveway and her door was yanked open.

"Fucking pervert!" the teen screamed, as he grabbed Janet and tried to pull her from the truck. Another teen leapt into the passenger side and started hitting Janet to get her out of the driver's seat. Fear clutched at her as she tried to fight off her attackers. A blow to her right temple sent her reeling out onto the sidewalk. The first teen leapt out of the slowly moving truck and joined the other as they started to kick at her.

That morning, Aliki had tried unsuccessfully to contact Robbie's sister, Elizabeth. At ten o'clock, she had decided that she might have better luck if she tried to contact Janet Williams, Robbie's wife. Besides, she was curious about Janet. She made a few phone calls and found out through the police that Robbie's family was staying at her condo not many blocks away. On impulse, she decided to take her morning jog past Robbie's condo and check it out. As she rounded the corner, she could see two skinheads kicking at someone on the ground. A truck left in gear had rolled across the road and was buried in the hedge. Aliki accelerated from her jog and hit the two punks at full speed. A few carefully placed kicks and the thugs took off.

Breathing heavily, she took a second to get her breath and then squatted down beside the figure that was curled in a ball on the ground. "You okay?" The figure shrank away at her light touch. "Hey, it's okay. They've gone now. I'm Doctor Aliki Pateas. I'm going to call 9-1-1 and get you some help."

The figure stirred and a bloody face looked up. "No! Please. I'm okay. I have to go... I mean...I've got an appointment. I'm late." Only with grim determination and with the support of the tall woman beside her was Janet able to get to her feet. Her head was throbbing and, to her embarrassment, she threw up on the sidewalk. The stranger stood behind her and, with strong hands, held her by the shoulders.

"First, I have to take you to Emergency. Then, if they say it's okay, I'll take you to your appointment," Aliki said firmly.

"No! I'd be hours at Emergency. Please! I'm okay. I'll clean up in the Ladies when I get to the courthouse." Janet held her side in pain.

Blue eyes snapped up to meet green. "Are you Janet Williams?"

The green eyes looked cautious and worried. "Yes."

Aliki smiled. "I was on my way over to see if I could talk to you. I'm one of the forensic team members working on the case. Look, let me get you into the truck and get it out of the hedge. I'll drive you over to my house, which is just a few blocks down the road. You can clean up there while we talk, and then I'll take you to the courthouse."

Janet opened her mouth to protest but Aliki held up a long, graceful hand to stop her. "Janet, no security guard is going to let you into the courthouse looking like that. Better you're late than not there at all. Come on, we'll be as quick as we can."

She nodded and let the confident woman take her by the arm and lead her to the truck. Aliki was worried. Janet looked pretty badly beaten, and it was clear that she was dazed and disoriented.

Aliki backed the truck off the curb and onto the street. She was concerned when she heard the soft gasp of pain from the small woman. Janet was pale and her eyes didn't look too focused. Aliki considered taking her to Emergency anyway, then decided against it. She'd get faster care if Aliki just took her home.

The next real clear impression that Janet had was sitting on a toilet lid gazing at the T-shirt covered breasts in front of her face; they belonged to the woman who had rescued her. *Nice breasts, nice abs. This woman is in great shape,* Janet observed, as confident fingers worked to clean and bandage the cut over her eye.

"There, I think that's going to be okay. Your shirt is blood-soaked. I've got a sweat-shirt here that you can put on."

Janet looked down in surprise.

"I couldn't get your nose to stop bleeding."

Janet nodded. "What's your name again?" she asked in embarrassment, struggling to her feet as her rescuer stepped back. She was beautiful, with dark, curly hair cut short and neon blue eyes like Robbie's.

"I'm Doctor Aliki Pateas. I'm a forensic anthropologist working for the Metro Toronto Police. I was the one who recovered Philip Williams' remains."

Janet's eyes widened in surprise. "Oh." Janet turned, steadying herself by holding onto the sink. Her side hurt terribly and she was finding it hard to breathe. Looking into the mirror, she was shocked to see what a mess she was. The right side of her face was swollen and bruised, and a large plaster covered the cut on her eyebrow. Her nose was red and swollen and her chin scraped.

"Look, you need a real doctor," Pateas observed.

Janet's pleading eyes looked at the woman behind her in the mirror. "I have to be there for Robbie."

The woman grimaced. "Janet, it's already too late. The hearing will be over before I could get you there."

"Oh shit," she groaned, closing her eyes and feeling both emotional and physical pain sweeping through her.

Firm, warm hands took her shoulders. "This is what we are going to do. I'm going to take you to the clinic down the street and get you looked at, then I'm going to bring you back here. You can't stay where you are in your present state if you are going to be a target."

Janet couldn't think. It was just too hard, and blackness was invading her vision. "I need to go to the clinic," she admitted, and felt strong arms wrap around her and lift her off the ground. She should protest, she knew, but instead she found herself resting her head on a broad, comfortable shoulder. "I'm worried about my children," she managed to say before passing out.

The next few hours were kind of fuzzy. She saw a doctor and had x-rays and was then taken home. She was stripped and put to bed. She thought she had held Rebecca for a while and that Ryan had talked to her, but she wasn't sure that she hadn't just dreamed it. Through all the misty images was the figure of the quiet, dark woman who had rescued her.

Robbie sat on her bunk and stared at the wall. Yesterday, she and her cellmate had come to an understanding. Once she had cleaned the blood off herself, she had dampened a towel and taken it over to the woman who huddled in the corner.

Squatting down, she had held out the cloth. "I really lose it when I get mad," she said quietly. "Don't make me mad again."

The bloodied woman nodded, fear in her eyes as she cautiously took the towel.

"We are stuck in here for a little while, so let's make it as pleasant as this hell hole can be. I don't get in your way; you don't get in mine. Agreed?"

The woman nodded again, grimacing as she tried to clean away the blood from her broken nose.

Robbie looked at it critically. "It should heal pretty straight if you tape it." She held out her hand and after a moment's hesitation the battered inmate wrapped her hand around Robbie's wrist. Robbie got a grip on the woman and hauled her to her feet. After that things had gone better.

Until the hearing.

Janet hadn't been at the hearing. The lawyers had told her that Janet had e-mailed to say she was at Robbie's apartment and they had phoned her to let her know about the hearing, but she hadn't come. None of Robbie's family had. Not that she could blame them. This must be horrible for them. And Janet was still pretty run down from her cancer treatments. As for Ryan, well she'd pretty well betrayed that kid's trust and love. Robbie buried her head in her hands. She hurt so bad inside.

"Hey, the hearing not go so well?" asked a nasal voice.

Robbie looked up at the woman across from her. *What had happened at the hearing?* She was so upset at not seeing Janet, she hadn't really taken much in. She'd pleaded not guilty as her lawyers had instructed her. The Crown had argued for more time to prepare their case because other charges might result, pending further investigation. *What charges?* Her lawyers had tried to get her out on bail. The request had been denied. They were appealing. *Where were Janet and the kids?*

"The hearing was okay. I don't know where my partner and kids are," Robbie answered, surprising herself as much as her cellmate.

"Didn't they show today?" Tracy shifted a bit, grimacing in pain.

"No."

"She got somebody else?"

"No!"

"Okay. Easy," Tracy soothed, holding up her hands. "I was just askin'. It happens a lot, ya know. They get sick of waitin'."

"Not Janet. We've got something special going." Robbie knew she was trying to reassure herself as much as Tracy. Tracy nodded and let the conversation drop, returning to her ever present comic book.

Several hours ticked by with Tracy reading and Robbie staring at nothing, then two guards appeared outside their cell. "Williams, you've got a visitor. Marlow, step to the back, Williams, place your hands on the back of your neck and step up to the gate."

Tracy gave the guard the finger from behind her back and slowly walked to the rear wall and leaned on the sink.

Robbie smiled slightly. *If they think that having me put my hands on the back of my neck is going to protect them, then they're fools.* Still, she stood obediently and waited while one guard put chains on her and the other stood by watching.

Robbie's stomach fluttered; maybe it would be Janet. She really needed to see Janet. They led her through the corridors and up an elevator, and finally down a hall to a small room. It was divided in half by a counter and a thick glass partition. To Robbie's surprise and disappointment, the woman standing on the other side was a stranger. She was tall and well built, with dark curly hair cut short. Robbie was aware of intelligent blue eyes appraising her as she moved over to the partition.

"Hello, I'm Doctor Aliki Pateas. I'm with the forensic department. Janet sent me."

Robbie's eyes flashed with concern. "Where's my family?"

"They're okay. They're at my place. Sit down. We need to talk."

They stood looking at each other for a few seconds, sizing each other up. The woman had an unfair advantage — information about her family. Robbie would have to play along. She let Aliki win by looking away, then she sat.

"Janet got worked over pretty good by a couple of skinheads that live in your building." Aliki watched the colour drain from Robbie's face to be replaced by white anger. The prisoner leapt to her feet and smashed herself against the wall, howling in anger. Aliki stood and watched helplessly from the other side of the glass as Robbie cried.

When the guard came running in, she ordered, "Leave her! She's okay. She just got some really bad news, that's all. Give her a chance, for God's sake." The guard hesitated.

He looked again at Robbie, who seemed to have calmed some, then shrugged and went to stand outside the door again, watching closely through the window.

"How bad is it?" Robbie asked, her face against the wall.

"She'll be okay. A concussion, three cracked ribs, and a cut over the eye that took three stitches. I'm going to see the boys are charged. They're the teenage sons of some wealthy right wing business executive. They're spoiled rotten and looking for a cause."

"The girls?"

"They weren't there. The incident happened at the end of your driveway when Janet was on the way to the courthouse." She saw the flicker of emotion cross Williams' face. "I had the police go and pick up your children. I wasn't sure how secure your place was, given that the boys live in the same building. The children are safe now at my place, sort of under semi-police protection."

Robbie was silent for a few seconds as she tried to control her raging emotions, then she walked over and sat down, looking up to met the other woman's eyes. "Thank you."

"No problem. They're a nice family. Ryan was really upset. I had to let her stay with her mom. She just wouldn't let go of Janet."

Ice blue eyes looked up. "Ryan's my daughter," she said quietly.

"Oh." Aliki frowned. "She calls Janet 'mom' so I thought Reb must be yours."

Robbie looked down at her manacled wrists. "Maybe that's for the best."

"Janet sent you a note. Here it is." Aliki pushed the letter through the slot. Robbie took it and held it tightly. "She sent some books for you, too. The guards will bring them down once they've been checked over," she finished awkwardly.

Aliki swallowed and tried to regroup her thoughts. *I'm not used to dealing with emotion. My work is objective, scientific, and when the dead speak it's in sign language, the screams long gone with their lives. This is harder than I thought. Having followed her career all these years, I feel like I know her. Could we be related?* "Look, I need to talk to you. I know you lied in your statement to the police. I want you to tell me the truth."

Robbie looked up slowly from the letter, her emotions now masked behind still, hard muscle. "I made my statement. I've nothing else to say," she spat.

"At least answer this. Are you left or right handed? Or can you use both equally well?"

"I'm right handed."

Aliki looked at her steadily and decided that now was not the time to push. She got up and signalled to the guard who was watching through the window. "You need to change your mind about talking."

"I won't," Robbie responded. Aliki frowned and turned to leave. "Aliki?" The doctor looked back. "Thanks," Robbie said again.

"I'll see that nothing happens to them, Robbie."

Robbie nodded as the guard took her elbow and led her back to her cell.

"Jesus fucking Christ, Bates! The Crown's got a watertight case here! Damn it, she admits to hitting him and covering up his death. We have a witness who saw her bury the body. What do you want, a trail of blood to her doorstep?" The police officer paced as best he could inside Tom Bates' small, overcrowded office.

The scientist sucked happily on the cold pipe. "I told you at the time not to be too quick to pick her up. Now you've got a charge that you might not be able to make stick," he mused.

The homicide officer stopped his pacing and leaned over the desk. "Oh, I'll make it stick all right! With or without your help!" he snarled. "We found an old letter at Robbie's that she had sent to her mother just after the murder. In it, she said she hated her father and wouldn't be at the memorial service because she hoped he rotted in hell! Now what do you think about that, Doctor?" The officer didn't wait for an answer. He stormed out of the office, almost sideswiping Aliki as she walked toward the door.

Bates saw Aliki Pateas looking into his office with a worried frown. "Come in, Aliki," the old man invited cheerfully. "And close the door."

"Are we in trouble, Doctor?" she asked, moving aside a dried, weathered bone that had been left on the only other seat. She placed the human bone carefully on an already overcrowded shelf and sat down on the now empty chair.

Bates smiled; he knew that Aliki didn't understand how he could work in such clutter. Her domain was fanatically ordered and neat. He was almost afraid to touch anything in her office. He didn't answer for a bit. He put down his pipe and was toying absently with a jar that contained the remains of a severed hand in formaldehyde. It had been partly dissected.

"This hand is from one of the victims in the restaurant shooting last week. I'd like you to render it down to the bone and have a look at it. I'd like your opinion, Doctor."

"Yes, sir," responded Aliki, taking the jar. "What am I looking for?"

A quick smile flashed across the worn face and devilment danced in pale eyes as Doctor Tom Bates picked up his cold pipe again. Leaning back in his chair, he gave a dry chuckle. "Now, telling would spoil the surprise." For a second, Bates contented himself with sucking on the stem of his pipe, a thoughtful look on his face. "Yes, the police are not happy with us. We've rather thrown a monkey wrench into the Williams case."

Aliki leaned back and stretched out her legs crossing her ankles. "Don't they want to catch the right person?"

Bates wiggled his eyebrows. "They think they have. The examination of human bones is not an exact science. For all our little charts and graphs, in the end you rely on the gut feelings of the forensic examiner. Lawyers throw fits when you answer that you've looked at a thousand bones and this one just wasn't quite right." The old man laughed, enjoying his little joke. "You know that. You get used to the bones of the general population that you work with. If you have to deal with the different bone structure of another culture, you are at a disadvantage because you sometimes miss the subtle differences."

"I've talked to Robbie Williams," Aliki blurted.

Her boss was amused rather than irritated. "And?"

"Her statement is a lie, I'm sure of it, but she wouldn't tell me the truth. I tried to talk to her spouse, but I arrived just in time to see two skinheads pounding the stuffing out of her."

The pipe popped out of Bate's mouth and he leaned forward. "Is she all right?"

Aliki nodded. "I put the boots to them. Janet's got a concussion, and is pretty sore and shook up yet. She's at my place. So are their kids."

He closed his eyes and shook his head. "Why is it, Al, you can't just practice the science of forensics? Why must you always get personally involved?" Bates sighed. "If you must solve cases single-handedly, join the police force and train as a detective!"

"It just happens," she said defensively.

Bates looked at her, and then decided to let the matter drop. Aliki was young, brilliant, idealistic, and driven by some inner demon. Over the years, he'd learned that it was best not to go looking for demons in others.

"Whatcha readin?" Tracy asked, coming back from making use of their loo.

"A book on Greek architecture that my wife sent," responded Robbie moodily.

The con snorted. "Ain't you high-bred? Give me a good old super-hero comic book any day."

"Same thing," Robbie muttered.

"What?"

She just wanted to be left alone to try to deal with the news that Aliki had brought, but it would be stupid not to take an opportunity to get Tracy on her side. Tracy could be bad news and not above sticking a knife in her ribs while she slept. "Same thing," she repeated, sighing as she rolled off her bunk.

"Oh yeah," Tracy scoffed.

"No. Look." Taking some books, Robbie shifted over to sit beside Tracy on her bunk. "See, here's a picture of a male Greek sculpture."

"Oh, nice cut," Tracy moaned.

"Exactly. The ancient Greeks set the standard by which we judge the male body. Because of the nature of marble, their figures tended to have a foreshortening of the limbs that emphasized the chest muscles even more. Now look down here." Robbie pointed to the spot where the abdomen met the hipbone. "See how the abdominal muscle extends over the hip bone? That's called a Greek Fold. The ancient Greeks thought it was a sign of a well developed body and it was greatly admired."

"I'm admiring! Them Greeks were really hung, huh?"

Robbie rolled her eyes. "The fold, Tracy," she reminded her cellmate.

"Oh yeah, the fold."

"It's actually a genetic trait and only twenty percent of males have it. No females do. Okay, now look at the picture of Adam here in Michelangelo's painting in the Sistine Chapel." Robbie flipped through another art book. "See the bunchy muscles, the foreshortened limbs, the Greek Fold...same style."

"You mean, Michelangelo copied some ancient Greek?" Tracy took the book and looked at the picture closely. "He didn't copy the dick. That thing's puny."

"The artists of the Renaissance, really all artists, learned their anatomy by copying the works of the ancients because nude modeling was considered a sinful act. So, they picked up the style."

"So?" Tracy tossed the book back, having lost interest.

"So, artists still do that. Look at your Batman comic here — bunchy muscles, foreshortened limbs, Greek Fold. Three thousand years later and our concept of how to draw the human form has stayed the same."

"Hey, cool, Batman's Greek! Hey, look, so is Superman!"

"Modern day cartooning has very close parallels with classical work. Look at the dramatic, heroic movements in your comic. They look just like the figure in this Greek frieze of a battle." Feeling that she had made a point, Robbie took her books and went back to her bunk.

Tracy looked for a long time at her comic books, flipping from page to page and book to book. "Tell me something else," she demanded at last.

"About what?"

"About my comic books," Tracy snapped impatiently.

Robbie took off her glasses and rubbed her eyes. If she stayed locked in there much longer, they might have to convict her of Tracy's murder. "The Greeks established theatre as an art form. Our concept of the hero is very much that of the ancient Greek hero," Robbie explained patiently.

"Yeah?"

"Uhuh. Take the original Herakles. Not the TV show or the cartoon. Herc has all four elements of a Greek hero," she pointed out. *I'm lying on a damn metal cot in a cement cell lecturing some Joe killer about dramatic form. I think I've lost it.*

"So are you going to tell me what the four things are?" Tracy growled, interrupting Robbie's thought.

"Oh, sure, sorry. An unusual birth or childhood, super-human abilities, a tortured soul, and a need to help others. Look at Herakles. He has the unusual birth, all right. His mother is a mortal and his father is Zeus. And he has unnatural strength that makes him super-human. His soul is tortured because he killed a man. That's why he had to do the twelve labours, as a punishment. And he was always going around doing good deeds to get noticed by his father. He is a classic Greek hero."

"Oh, so?"

"Well, take a modern day hero...ah..."

"Xena," Tracy suggested with an evil grin.

Robbie rolled her eyes. "Okay, Xena. Unusual birth? Maybe, if she is the daughter of Ares. Certainly she had an unusual childhood, because her father tried to kill her. She has super-human strength and reflexes, so the second criterion works. Tortured soul? You bet. She kills half the Greek nation at least once a week and always regrets it. And she has this need to help others."

"Hey! That's cool!" Tracy exclaimed. "Do it for one of the comic book guys!"

"Okay. Superman, unusual birth because he comes from another planet. He's an alien. He definitely has super powers. He has the tortured soul thing because he has lost his family and world and is living on an alien planet. And of course, he has an almost pathological need to help others. He's a regular Boy Scout."

There was silence for a minute. "Do Batman."

"No! Let me read!" Robbie snapped. Tracy went back to her comics and when Robbie thought she was asleep, she again pulled out the letter that Janet had sent.

> *I'm so sorry I wasn't there in court for you, Robbie. You warned me to be careful and I wasn't. I will be from now on. Don't worry, the girls and I are alright. We are staying for the time being with Aliki until I feel better. She's really nice and the girls like her. She stopped the guys who were beating up on me and then just took over and saw to things. She's great. We'll be all right now, I promise. I'm going to get you out, Robbie. I won't stop until I do. I love you. I love you. I love you. Don't forget that.*

She read it a few more times and then folded it carefully and tucked it back into her bra. Tears rolled down her face. She felt like she had lost everything she had ever wanted out of life.

Brian McGill placed his hand on the small of Gwen Smith's back to reassure her as they waited for the guard to let them through the barred gate.

"This place is awful!" Gwen murmured, just loud enough for Brian to hear.

"Yeah." His voice was strained from worry and fatigue. It had been a hell of a spring. First there was the stress of Gwen's marital break-up, and then the confusion and frustration he was experiencing in his feelings towards Gwen, and now the extra burden of Robbie's arrest. All hell was breaking loose at the office.

They were led by the guard into a room divided by a glass partition. They sat down on the metal folding chairs and waited. After a while, a door on the other side opened and Robbie was escorted in. She wore an orange coverall, and her hands and feet were chained and linked to her waist. Her face was lean and her eyes haggard. Brian heard the stifled gasp of shock that escaped Gwen's lips at seeing Robbie.

Robbie shuffled over and sat down. Her smile was thin and brittle. "Hi, guys. Thanks for coming." The blue eyes moved to Brian. "How is it going?"

"Shares are down in the DVD, special effects, and production companies. Your other interests are holding their own because no link has been made to you yet. The investors are complaining, but so far have not taken any legal action. The film's making too much money for them to worry about any splash effect from the bad publicity."

Robbie smiled cynically. The bleak eyes turned on Gwen. "Well?"

"Lots of calls, Robbie. Three companies want permission to do made-for-TV films of your story. I declined on your behalf. Most of the CEOs of your companies have touched base. They're pretty nervous."

"Afraid the greenback well might dry up?" she jabbed bitterly.

Brian gave Gwen a nudge to let Robbie's question pass. After all, Robbie had a right to feel bitter. A lot of feeder companies made their money off her drive, talent, and success.

"I've got those forms for you to sign." Gwen folded them so that they would fit through the slot at the base of the glass. The guard came forward and took them away.

For a second, the old spark flashed across her eyes, then the blue dulled again in defeat. "My censor board will have to approve my reading material first," she joked sarcastically. "I'll get them back to you as soon as I can."

Gwen nodded. "We've been to see Janet and the kids."

The blue eyes flashed up. "Is Janet okay?"

Brian grimaced. "She's pretty banged up, Robbie. They kicked her about the face and chest. She's still really swollen and sore, but she and Aliki both said that the doctor felt she would be fine. She hopes to visit in the next day or two, as soon as the ribs will let her. She's in a lot of discomfort."

Robbie nodded, her jaw moving under her pale skin. She said nothing.

Gwen laughed. "Ryan has decided she is going to be a detective now."

Blue eyes flashed. "No, she is not. She's going to get her doctorate in physics like her aunt."

Brian and Gwen exchanged looks. "Oh," the secretary responded noncommittally. "I've been searching through the files. The name of the Crown's witness rang a bell with me and I thought I'd just check it out. Isabella Selo is the daughter of a gardener that worked on the Williams estate. That's why she was around and saw...well, what she says," Gwen stumbled. She went on quickly, "Last year, she wrote asking to be president of your official fan club. We turned her down nicely, explaining that you already had an official fan club."

Robbie sneered. "A disgruntled fan."

"It appears so. I told Janet, and she is going to pass the information on to your lawyers. They might be able to use it to discredit the witness."

Robbie shrugged and said nothing. They talked about business after that, avoiding anything that touched on the case.

Two days later, Robbie was again taken upstairs to see a visitor. To her surprise, she was searched, then she was taken to a different room. The room held only two wood chairs placed side by side and facing in opposite directions. The chairs were bolted to the floor. Janet was sitting in one.

She rose gingerly, a look of shock and worry on her face as Robbie shuffled over and stood looking down at her. The guard waited by the door, watching. Robbie's face was cold and masked all feeling; her lovely eyes were dull and lifeless. Janet stepped closer and wrapped her arms around the stiff figure, holding her tight, feeling the chained hands separating their bodies. After a second's delay, Robbie lowered her head and rubbed against Janet's. Janet looked up to see eyes filled with pain. "I love you, Robbie," she whispered before hard, demanding lips met hers.

Janet pulled away from the kiss. It had not been tender or loving, just demanding and crude. This was not the Robbie she had fallen in love with. This was the old Robbie — cold, ruthless, commanding. "Ahh, ribs hurt. Sorry. Can we sit down?" she murmured, not wanting to get into an argument with her lover when their time together was so limited.

"You okay?" Robbie asked with concern, showing emotion for the first time.

Janet nodded, tears welling in her eyes. "Robbie, Aliki knows you are not telling the truth. Please, hon, you have to."

Cold blue eyes looked up. "You've never called me *hon* before."

She was startled by Robbie's reaction. "What?"

"So who is your *hon*, Janet?"

Janet's face reddened in anger. "That was not called for, Robbie," she said quietly. She tried to keep her temper in check. "Reb asks about you. She can't understand why she can't phone you whenever she wants."

"And Ryan? I hear she calls you 'Mom' now," Robbie commented, looking at a corner in the room.

"Ryan is really having trouble with this, Robbie. She is feeling very insecure. She's afraid she has lost you and that I'll abandon her. She is trying to strengthen the bond with me in the hopes that won't happen. She is a very scared child, with a lot of baggage," Janet explained softly.

Eyes burned bright blue. "You think I don't know that?" Robbie snapped.

Janet swallowed and wiped away the tears that had overflowed. "I tried to contact Elizabeth, but so far I haven't been able to get through."

"Leave Bethy out of this," Robbie commanded.

Janet looked into the ice blue eyes that had once shone with love. "I will do anything for you, Robbie, except let you rot away in here for something you didn't do."

"Read my statement, Janet. I did it."

"Aliki said you didn't and Gwen has proof that the witness could be no more than a disgruntled fan."

"Fuck Aliki," Robbie snarled, getting up. "Or do you already?"

Janet got to her feet awkwardly and slapped Robbie across the face, then she walked to the door and slammed out. Robbie let a smirking guard lead her back to her cell.

Chapter 16

When Robbie returned to her cell, she picked up the newspaper that she had been reading before she left. She stared at the black and white photo of Janet leaving the police station the previous day after making her statement. She was tucked under Aliki's protective arm. Aliki carried a smiling Reb, and Ryan followed along behind. The picture sliced through her and trashed her emotions. She wanted to stop looking at it but the photo held her with a morbid fascination. The caption read: "The Williamses and a close family friend."

The heat of Janet's slap burned against her cheek. She reached up and touched it. Janet had hit her. She ran the tip of her tongue over her lips recalling the sweet taste of her wife. *I was a bit rough,* she conceded. No, she'd been more than rough; she had been a first class bitch. *What the hell did I do?* she thought as realization hit. *Damn, I acted like a jealous jackass.* Robbie leapt to her feet and flung herself against the bars. "Hey, guard, hey! I've got to use the phone. Hey, it's an emergency. Come on," she screamed, banging at the bars. Tracy watched with interest from her position on her cot.

After a while a guard came down the hall. "Quiet down, Williams."

"Look, I've got to use the phone."

"Sorry, block time is over. It will have to wait until tomorrow."

"I can't," Robbie screamed, shaking the bars in angry frustration.

The nightstick slammed against the bars in front of Robbie's face. "You can and you will. Now settle down, Williams. You're disturbing the whole block. Keep it up and you'll get isolation."

Suddenly, Tracy was there between Robbie and the bars. "Fuck you, turnkey. We just wanted to send out for pizza."

The guard sneered. "Cute, Lanker," he said, his attention drawn away from Robbie.

Tracy gave him the finger as he walked away, then she turned to look at Robbie. "You crazy or somethin'?"

Robbie put her head against the bars. "Yeah, I just might be," she muttered.

"So what is it worth?" asked her cellmate with a smirk.

"Huh?"

"So what is it worth to you to make that phone call?"

Blue eyes turned and made contact with brown. "What do you want?"

"Thousand bucks."

"No, you'll spend it on drugs and I'm stuck in here with you. I'll get you a decent paying job when you get out of here and cover the lawyer fees for your appeal."

Tracy chewed her lip and considered. "That would be more than a thousand dollars."

"A lot more," Robbie agreed.

"Okay. Come here, ye're gonna have to help."

Robbie carefully drained the water out of the toilet bowl with her toothbrush cup as Tracy had instructed, pouring it back into the sealed tank until it was full to the brim. Tracy sat on the bed and kept a look out while she explained. "See, the pipes are all connected. So once the water's out, you can stick your head in there and pass a message from block to block. We got a guy upstairs who'll place the call and pass on the message. It'll cost you twenty bucks and he only allows ten words."

"You're kidding," Robbie growled.

"Listen, you wanta get the message out or not?"

Robbie sighed. "Okay. Do it."

Tracy came over and started rapping on the toilet bowl. A short time later, a muffled rap came in response. Tracy nodded to Robbie. "Gimme the phone number."

Robbie looked at her blankly. "The phone number," Tracy snapped.

"I don't know it," Robbie admitted.

"Shit, woman. Whatcha thinkin' of? Well, give me someone's fuckin' number."

Thinking desperately, Robbie gave Gwen's number, hoping Gwen would be able to pass the message on. Tracy tapped out the code, then gave Robbie her final instructions. "State your first name and your message. Don't yell, but speak loud."

Robbie stuck her head into the bowl. "Robbie. Janet, I'm sorry. I love you." She turned to look at Tracy.

The woman smirked. "Ahh, ain't that sweet."

"Screw off," Robbie muttered, getting up and brushing the dust from her knees.

Tracy laughed. "See ya put the water back in or the damn water rats come crawlin' up the crapper."

Aliki could tell that Janet was upset as she walked across the prison parking lot to where the scientist sat waiting in the van. Janet got in out of the cold wind and sat white and stiff beside her.

"You okay, hon?" asked Aliki.

Janet's head snapped around. "What did you call me?"

A slow red washed up Aliki's neck. "Hon. I asked if you were okay. I was concerned."

It was Janet's turn to look embarrassed. She nodded. "Yeah, I'm okay. Robbie picked a fight. She's...she's different."

Aliki nodded and said no more. She started her Honda van and slipped into the busy Toronto traffic, leaving Janet with her thoughts.

It was much later that night, after Janet had kissed both girls goodnight, that Aliki called upstairs to say that Janet had a phone call from Gwen. Janet picked up the phone, a feeling of apprehension taking hold. *Why would Gwen be phoning at this hour? Unless something has happened to Robbie!*

"Uhh, Janet. I just got a really weird phone call from some guy who wouldn't identify himself. The call came from a pay phone; I checked. He said, 'This is a message from Robbie in prison: Janet, I'm sorry. I love you.'"

Janet's knees gave out and she sank onto the end of her bed.

"You there?" asked Gwen.

"Yes, thanks, Gwen." Janet laughed weakly. "Thanks."

"Well, goodnight."

"Goodnight. Thanks," Janet responded in a daze. *How did Robbie manage that?* She smiled; that was more like her Robbie.

Ted Potts had been transferred to Toronto. He had suffered a broken back and hip in the rollover. David drove to Toronto to be with his brother. Now, forty-eight hours later, he was standing in the hospital parking lot wondering what to do next. His hand rubbed against a two day old stubble. He needed food and a place to sleep.

Getting into his car, he considered what street would be the most likely to have a decent hotel where he could stay at a reasonable price. That was going to be no small order in an expensive city like Toronto. He started his Ford and headed off. Much to his surprise, he found himself driving toward Elizabeth's condominium. He needed to see

Elizabeth, he admitted to himself. Her calm, practical reasoning would put Ted's accident in the proper perspective.

Walking into the lavish entrance hall, he pressed the unmarked intercom button that he knew would connect him to Elizabeth's apartment. There was a long wait, followed by static but no greeting. David took the chance. "Elizabeth, is that you? It's David Potts."

A distressed voice came from the speaker. "David? Oh, David. It is so good to hear your voice. I don't know what to do."

"Open the door, Elizabeth, and I'll be right up," David instructed, and was pleased to hear the latch on the security door release almost immediately. David pulled the door open and entered.

Aliki paced down the large living room. Antique walnut furniture shone richly in the fire-light and the soft glow of the Chinese lamp. The lamp had been a gift to herself when she had gotten her present job. The fine china bowl was hand glazed in 24-carat gold and the shade was pure silk. It had been very expensive. Aliki usually shopped for bargains and meticulously refinished each piece herself. But this piece had been so beautiful and, to Aliki, it represented the changes that she had fought so hard for in her life. The lamp was more than decorative; it was a symbol of victory.

She sighed, placing her hands on her hips and looking moodily at the floor. She wasn't feeling victorious tonight. She was feeling foolish. This evening had been...disturbing. It wasn't the dog hair that was forming dust bunnies the size of a walrus in her hall, or the copper pots and pans she found Rebecca pounding together in the kitchen. It wasn't Ryan's ten million questions about her life as a child on a western cattle ranch, or the way the kid followed her around. It wasn't Janet's panties she found left inside her dryer. It was the whole thing, and the sitting down at a table with a family and hearing happy voices around her. She hadn't felt that sort of closeness in a long time. It...it felt good.

She liked the girls. They were very different and yet both really neat. And Janet, hell, she more than liked her. She found herself very attracted to the woman and it was hard to keep reminding herself that her beautiful, vivacious guest was married to somebody else.

She looked around. Her meticulously ordered domain was in a state of chaos. Ryan's runners were by the couch where she had kicked them off while reading. The forensic book Ryan had taken from the library shelf was on the end table. Reb's doll, which Rufus had carried in, was lying near the hearth with the big shaggy dog sleeping beside it. Janet's notes on Robbie's case were scattered over the campaign trestle table in the corner of the room. What surprised her was that she didn't care. She liked it. It was sort of a ready-made family. A nice one.

"I got a message from Robbie," Janet announced, bouncing into the room.

Aliki forced a smile. "That's good. I take it from your smile that the fight is over."

Janet nodded, her eyes sparkling. "Yeah, she sent a message to say she was sorry and she loves me."

Aliki smiled but said nothing. She saw Janet smile back shyly before she turned to look at the paintings on the wall.

"These are beautiful!" she exclaimed.

"Thank you," Aliki responded. "I painted them for...a friend many years ago."

"You painted them?"

Aliki felt the heat climbing up her neck. "Yes."

"I love them. You really **are** very talented. Did you paint this big one, too?" Janet went to stand in front of the **large** picture of summer flowers that hung over the couch. The flowers were in full bloom, soft and sensual in their rendition.

"Yes."

Janet turned to look at Aliki. "You are amazing, you know. Did you do all the art in the house?"

Their eyes met and locked. Aliki was the first to look away. "No," she said, "only in this room. The rest are pieces I've collected over the years." Aliki needed time alone to cool the heat that was spreading through her, desires focusing on the small woman who stood happily in front of her. *Remember she looks happy because her partner just sent a message to say she loves her, damn it, Aliki.* "I'll make tea, if you like, while you get on with your research." At Janet's appreciative nod, she stomped down the hall to the Victorian kitchen. *Don't make a fool of yourself.*

Aliki sat reading by the fire, her tea cooling at her elbow. Janet was back at the desk researching the news clippings from the time of Philip Williams' death. "Aliki, could a child have killed Philip?" Janet asked, chewing on a pencil.

Aliki hated chewed pencils but Janet looked so cute doing it. She considered. "How old?"

"Twelve."

The scientist thought about it. "Yes, if the weapon was something that could pick up force from being swung, such as a golf club or bat," she concluded. "By the shape and size of the depression, I'd put my money on a golf wood or perhaps a fireplace tool. There was a fireplace in the room."

"If it wasn't Robbie, it had to be either Elizabeth or Billy," Janet observed.

"The police don't like dealing with child killers," Aliki said dryly, taking a sip of tea and then frowning at it. It had gone cold while she had been caught up in her reading.

"They are not children now," argued Janet. "And Robbie is covering for someone."

Aliki looked at Janet. "She is covering for Elizabeth, Janet. We both know that, but why?"

Janet sighed. "I wish Elizabeth would talk to me."

"She can hardly talk to you if she's hiding the fact she is the murderer, Janet," Aliki pointed out practically.

Janet stood up and paced around the beautiful room. "It's a Catch-22. If I find evidence to free Robbie and that evidence points to Elizabeth, Robbie would never forgive me." Janet groaned at her dilemma.

Aliki didn't say anything. She had an emotional bias and now was not the time for her to be offering advice. She didn't wish any harm to Robbie, but then again, having Robbie out of the picture would suit Aliki just fine. It was paradoxical: all these years she had been fascinated about her possible relationship to Robbie, and now she just wanted the woman's influence out of her life.

Suddenly, Janet stopped and snapped her fingers. "If Elizabeth won't talk I know who will — Billy!"

Aliki's eyes got big. "Janet, the man's dead. Even I couldn't get that information out of his remains."

"Al, for years he took therapy at a Swiss clinic. What if he told his doctor about the killing?"

Aliki's eyebrow quirked up. "That's a possibility. You'd have to get your lawyers on it to make it legal. I've got some friends with Interpol that could probably put some muscle behind a legal request for disclosure."

"Let's do it," Janet decided.

Aliki stood to go to the phone. Much to her surprise, she found herself being hugged by Janet who reached up and kissed her cheek. "Thanks."

Aliki smiled weakly and tried hard not to be so petty as to wish that they would find out that Billy had identified Robbie as the killer.

Robbie walked the yard, trying to soak in as much of the weak spring sunlight as she could. She wasn't sure how she was going to survive years in prison. The walls closed in on her and she was exhausted from trying to force down the panic and anger that built up inside. She looked across the yard to where Tracy was busy making a drug deal. *Shit. Another night of Tracy in la-la land.* Voices were getting louder, Tracy apparently felt that the price was too high. A push. Retaliation. In a second, a brawl had started.

Robbie watched as Tracy was surrounded by three inmates. She was giving as good as she got until one of the women grabbed her from behind and pinned her arms. The other two set in on Tracy and Robbie charged across the yard and started swinging.

The next day, Janet arrived right at visiting time, lining up with other loved ones and families. She was anxious to see Robbie again and sort out the emotions that were driving a wedge between them. She signed in and went through the metal detector, and then requested to see Roberta Williams. The guard clicked down the list on the computer screen.

"Sorry, Roberta Williams is confined to her cell. She is not allowed visitors for a week."

"What? Why?"

The guard rolled his eyes. "Bunch of them went at it in the yard yesterday. A real free-for-all, from what I heard."

Janet paled. "Is she hurt?"

The guard looked back at the screen and brought up Robbie's individual data file. Janet watched his eyes scanning down the screen. "She wasn't sent to infirmary so she must be okay."

"Can I get a message to her?"

The guard looked up and grinned. "Sure. Here's some paper and an envelope."

Janet smiled her thanks and wrote a note to Robbie, folded it and sealed it in the envelope, then handed it back to the guard. "Thanks."

"No problem," the guard replied, not looking up from his computer screen. Janet walked away, disappointment and frustration bringing tears to her eyes.

The letter reached Robbie in the late afternoon. She was alone in the cell. Tracy was with the lawyers that Robbie had arranged to help her with her pending appeal. She took the letter from the guard and went over to sit on her bunk, looking at Janet's neat teacher handwriting on the envelope. Then, carefully, she opened the flap and pulled out the letter.

Fear held her heart in a tight vice. *What if Janet's not going to forgive me? What if she's had enough of the problems I'm always bringing into her life?* She unfolded the notepaper.

Good morning, my love. I got your message. Thank you! You are so wonderful, darling. Well, my beautiful olive, you've done it again, haven't you? I hope you are all right. It must be awful for you to be in there. I'm going to get you out, Robbie. I know you don't want me to involve Elizabeth and I won't if I can avoid it. But nothing is going to stop me from getting you back with us. Robbie, I love you. That is the only thing at the moment that is a constant in our lives. Trust me, Robbie. I know that trusting is hard for you, but trust me. I am your soulmate, your wife, and your lover, now and forever. I miss you so very much. Be careful.

Robbie read the letter over and over, her hands nervously straightening the paper on her lap.

Janet, I love you. Oh God, Janet, I don't deserve you, but don't ever leave me. I miss you and the kids so much. Tears rolled down her face unchecked.

When Janet returned from the jail with her disappointing report, Aliki did her best to cheer up the Williams family. She took them to the Toronto Zoo. Sitting in the Don Valley, the zoo covered hectares of parkland. For the most part, the animals were confined by natural barriers, such as water or deep ravines, rather than by fences. Each wildlife area had been specially designed to reflect the natural environment from which the animals had come. There were also huge pavilions, each representing the flora and fauna of a specific hemisphere.

They walked about for hours, Ryan looking at everything with a scientific eye and asking Aliki and Janet a thousand questions, and Reb laughing joyously at every new animal she was shown. They returned to a warm fire, hot chocolate, and Aliki's homemade apple pie.

Reb was put down for her nap and Ryan went off to do the studies that Janet had assigned for her. Janet curled up on the couch in the living room and read through the home study curriculum that she was using for Ryan. *It had been a much-needed day of relaxation,* Janet mused, looking over at the red embers that still glowed in the hearth. They certainly owed Aliki a lot. Off in the distance, Janet could hear soft classical music playing and smiled. Aliki had beautiful taste in everything. On impulse, she went in search of her new friend.

She found her in an empty room toward the back of the house. One wall was all windows looking out on a small oriental rock garden. Aliki was in a black exercise outfit that emphasized every muscle in her body. In each hand, she held a long thin knife with a horn-like hilt of metal. Highlighted in the evening sun, she became a living sculpture — beautiful, powerful, and fascinating. The music started again — Johann Pachelbel's *Canon in D major*. It floated softly through the air and pulled Janet into the room. She sank slowly to the floor by the door and watched as Aliki swayed in gentle, sensual motion.

The music was soft and flowing and Aliki moved in a slow dance, the knives an extension of her form, flashing in the sun and forming silver arches of light around her. It was as much a dance as it was martial arts, each movement balanced, graceful and liquid. Every position became a single note in a harmonious worship of peace and power. Yin and Yang. Love and hate. Life and death.

A shimmer of moisture coated the dancer's body, glistening off soft tanned skin that rippled with controlled strength. This was more than training, more than art, it was a powerful dance of love: sexual, forceful, and beautiful. Aliki's breathing deepened as the music rose to a climax. Her body spun, arched and heaved, following the lines of the twin blades.

Janet's lips parted, sucking in air as she was carried away on a tidal wave of feeling. The music reached a climax and, for a second, blue eyes turned to caress green. Janet's emotions reached a pinnacle and then tumbled out of control down the other side as the glance was broken and Aliki's body slowed to the music that flowed in an aftermath of sound.

The French call a climax the "little death". That was what Janet had felt and she knew that Aliki had experienced it too. The air was heavy with the musky scent of desire and still the dancer swayed to the music, the sharp knives now thrusting slowly to the rhythm. Janet stood fascinated by the dance of the little death. As the music ended, Aliki moved toward Janet like a lover — dark, mysterious, and deadly.

For a moment, the dancer looked down at her. Janet followed a single bead of moisture that curled down the planes of Aliki's face and dropped like a pearl to her breast. As she looked up, soft, warm lips met her own and hands carrying deadly weapons drew her gently into safe arms. Janet's hands slid up hot muscled arms and the kiss deepened, igniting their desire.

"You need to trust me, Elizabeth," David said. "There is nothing that you can say to me that will make me think less of you. I am not going to judge; I am going to accept you as you are."

Elizabeth sat stiffly at one end of the couch, her hands folding and unfolding in her lap. David sat at the other end, earnestly searching Elizabeth's eyes for a clue to the secret she kept hidden.

The physicist nodded, swallowed, and tried to collect herself to relate a story she had only ever revealed once in her life, and not for fifteen years. "My father, he...he sexually abused Billy and me," she whispered.

David said nothing. He slipped slowly across the empty space between them and took Elizabeth's cold hand in his own, waiting.

"He did horrible things to us," Elizabeth went on, the tears now following freely. "That night, Robbie came home for the weekend and found him...on me. I was trying to fight him off. Billy...he'd hidden upstairs. Robbie pulled my father off and called him a name. He swung at her and she ducked and then hit him really hard in the face and he fell down. Then she wrapped me in her arms and picked me up and carried me upstairs.

"She helped me shower and washed my hair, then gave me a pill and I went to sleep in her arms. When I woke up it was much later. Alexandria was home and Robbie was gone. I could hear Alexandria singing in the room down the hall. I just lay there, terrified, until Robbie returned in the morning. She took Billy and me for a walk and told us that our father had gone sailing and she had come over to baby sit. But I knew that wasn't what had happened. Later, when he was reported missing, I asked her and she told me that she had killed him when she had hit him that night and that I must never tell the truth." Elizabeth sobbed convulsively against David's shoulder.

He held her and whispered softly to her, "Everything will be all right now."

Aliki felt the body that had molded to her own stiffen and pull away.

"Aliki, I..." Janet backed out of the dancer's arms. "That was wrong. I shouldn't have done that."

"I know. I'm sorry. I won't do it again. I just couldn't help myself." Aliki gave a sad, lopsided smile. "I think I've fallen in love with you, Janet."

Green eyes, soft with passion, looked up. "I want..." Her tongue flicked over her lips and she sighed. "I can't love you as any more than a friend, Al; you're not Robbie. Robbie is more than my lover, she's my soulmate. I'm sorry; I could have loved you but not now, now that I've found the one who was meant for me."

The bitter smile hovered again at the corner of Aliki's mouth. "What if you are *my* soulmate?" she asked softly.

Janet shook her head. "It doesn't work like that. Everyone has that special somebody. You can love many, but there is only one who can bond to your soul. I'm not her, Aliki." Janet searched the dancer's eyes. "I belong to another. You have yet to find your soulmate."

"Will I?" Aliki asked sadly.

Janet reached up and brushed a soft kiss across lips swollen with their kiss. "I hope so. The lucky ones do. You will find someone who loves you very, very deeply, Aliki. You are a very special person, and I love you as a dear friend, for who you are." Janet turned and left, leaving Aliki to return to her dance alone.

Robbie woke with a start, knowing that something was wrong. She rubbed shaking fingertips over her mouth, removing the sheen of sweat that had formed on her upper lip. Suddenly a feeling of utter peace and security flowed through her and she smiled. *I love you, Janet,* she thought and lay down again to stare at the cement ceiling and listen to Tracy's soft snoring.

Ryan had taken Reb out to play in Aliki's backyard. The two adults sat over their morning coffee, a little embarrassed in each other's company after the kiss they had shared the night before. Aliki was quieter than normal and sat looking moodily into her coffee mug. Janet, uncomfortable with the silence, tried to think of something to start a conversation, realizing that they had to move on.

"You were so beautiful to watch yesterday. Tell me about the knives."

Aliki looked up and smiled sadly. "They are called sais. They are a branch of the original seven disciplines of the martial arts. Their history is associated with the ninja class, but their doctrine has deep spiritual ties with Shinto."

"Are you very good? You seemed to be." Janet buttered another piece of toast.

Aliki leaned back. "I have a ninth dan." Janet looked at her blankly and Aliki smiled. "That is the ninth level of black belt."

"Oh! That's very good, isn't it?" Aliki shrugged. "Can I see your sais?"

"Sure." She got up and left the room. In a few minutes, she returned and placed a black leather case on the table. She opened it to reveal the two knives fixed in place on a red silk bed.

"Oh, they're beautiful!"

The blades were octagonal and the prongs were intricately etched with detailed designs. The handles, too, were works of art. Coloured string had been woven into interlacing patterns creating depth and beauty.

Aliki smiled with pride. "They were hand forged in Che Chao-po. The blades were tempered using the traditional clay process that has been used there since 700 AD. The hilts are covered in stingray skin and then finished in Japanese cotton cord wrapping."

"Have you studied for long?" Janet looked directly into Aliki's eyes for the first time that morning.

"Since I was a child living on the ranch in Alberta. There was a Japanese master living nearby. During the war, he had been taken from his home in Vancouver and put in an internment camp and later just stayed on in the area. I learned a lot from him."

Janet nodded. "You know, you told me the first day we were here that the only thing you took from the West was your name, but that wasn't really true." Aliki's eyebrows went up in surprise. "I hear you telling Ryan stories about your childhood in the foothills of the Rockies and your voice is filled with love."

Aliki closed the case. "You read me wrong, Janet." She went and sat down again. "I worked my tail off so that I could escape being a cattle rancher's wife."

Janet laughed. "Maybe. But you still love the land and you have lots of happy memories. Do you still have family out there?"

"Two of my three brothers and my father are still alive. We still keep in touch. My mother died when I was twelve." Aliki warmed her coffee up from the carafe that sat on the table.

Janet was amazed that the private woman was being so open. "Do you go back often?"

"Only a few times since I left the ranch for university fourteen years ago."

There was silence from across the table. Aliki looked up into concerned eyes. "You need to go home," Janet said.

Aliki snorted and passed Janet the last of the toast to distract her.

It was later that Saturday morning when Janet received a phone call from Elizabeth. "Janet," her voice was raw with emotion, "I'm sorry I haven't answered your calls. David is here now. Can we meet you a-and talk?"

Janet smiled tenderly. She realized that this was a very hard thing for the reclusive scientist to be doing. She must love Robbie very much. "I need you to know, Elizabeth, that Robbie doesn't want me to talk to you. I told her I would not involve you in the case unless there was no other way."

There was a moment's silence. Then in a clear, firm voice Elizabeth said, "Robbie's wrong. I need to end the secrets and come to some sort of closure on what happened."

"I think so, too. I'm proud of you, Bethy. I'll ask Aliki to pick you up in her van. The press might know your car and follow you, otherwise."

"No, that's okay, Janet. David has his car here and no one will recognize it. I feel safe with David."

Janet smiled. She gave Bethy the address and hung up.

It was a quiet, obviously shaken pair that arrived some time later. They stepped into the house and looked around nervously. Aliki made them feel welcome, settled them in the living room and brought tea. Then she herded the girls out and left Janet to talk to Elizabeth and David.

Ryan watched Reb as she played with Rufus on the kitchen floor. She would hold on to one end of a short rope and the massive dog would pull on the other end, dragging the small child across the floor on her backside as he backed up. Then Reb would let go and Rufus would trot back across the room with the rope in his mouth, to wait patiently for Reb to get up and run over to do the whole performance over again.

"Reb, come here and get your hands washed before you have your snack." Aliki placed a plate of cookies on the table and poured three glasses of milk. "Just what kind of dog is Rufus?"

"We have no idea. We're not even sure that he's a dog. Obbie thinks there might be tree sloth in him," Ryan explained.

Aliki laughed at the family joke as she lifted Reb up on the counter and took a cloth to wash the child's hands. "It sure is one big, ugly thing."

"Nah, he's one big, ugly, orange thing," said Ryan. "Whatever he is, we've been treating him like a family pet and he's responded very well. Rufus is very loyal."

Aliki shook her head as she lifted Reb into her arms, carried her over and placed her on Ryan's lap since they did not have a high chair. Ryan gave Reb a cookie and she chewed on it happily.

"Is it bad in prisons?" Ryan asked after a few seconds. "You know, you see movies and stuff and..."

The cookie on the way to Aliki's mouth halted and returned to the plate. *Shit. What do I say now?* "Prison is not a nice place to be, Ryan. You spend hours locked up in a small room with another person. You are surrounded by dysfunctional individuals, many of them capable of considerable violence. There is no privacy and no time when you can completely relax. Robbie can hold her own, however. I don't think you need to worry," she finished.

"I wasn't worried," Ryan protested. "You just hear things about prisons, you know. Mom said Obbie got into a fight."

Aliki finished chewing the cookie that she had finally gotten to her mouth. "Yeah. I phoned some of the people I know just to make sure everything was okay. Her cellmate, Tracy, got into an argument in the yard. That's the area where the prisoners are allowed to walk outside twice a week. She got jumped and your mom waded in to help her out. The three who started it got solitary and the others, including Robbie, just got confinement to their cells for the week."

"She'd hate that," Ryan muttered, pushing crumbs around her plate with a finger. "She's pretty active. Always moving about restlessly."

Poor kid, she sure is going through a lot.

Reb looked up at her big sister. "Obbie come home soon, Ryan?"

Ryan kissed the child's dark head. "I don't know, Reb," she answered honestly.

That night, Janet had time to share with Aliki what Elizabeth had revealed. "So, we are not much further ahead. If Bethy is telling the truth, and I think she is, then her story is the same as Robbie's. In a way, I'm glad. It would kill Robbie if Bethy was put in prison for the murder. So it looks like we can get Robbie off on the charge of second degree murder, but we are still looking at manslaughter." Janet sighed. "What would she get for that, Aliki?"

"Two to seven, most likely," the scientist responded. "But I don't think manslaughter is going to hold up. There were two blows, most likely from two different people. We now know that, initially, Robbie only hit her father once, just like she said. Either someone else came into that room and finished him off while Robbie was upstairs, or Robbie came back down and deliberately killed him."

"Robbie wouldn't do that," Janet protested, looking up sharply from where she sat on the couch. "She can be hot tempered but deliberate murder, no; Robbie would never do anything like that."

Aliki rested her head on her hand. It was really hard trying to go on with business as usual when she was hurting like hell inside. Worse still, she found herself in the position of having to help the one woman she would rather see in hell. Aliki spoke to the fire. "If it wasn't Robbie or Elizabeth, then it had to be Billy. He was the only other person in the house that night."

Janet sighed. "God, I hope our inquiry turns up something."

"They might not be willing to release the information. Patient/doctor confidentiality and all that," Aliki suggested wishfully.

"Well, I was his wife, and Robbie's lawyers are asking, too. They should be willing to release that information to us. After all, he's dead," Janet responded hotly.

Aliki's eyebrow went up. Janet's marriage to Robbie's brother seemed very strange to her. The Williamses' relationship tangle made the Gordion Knot look simple. Maybe Janet married the guy and then realized she was gay. It was pretty obvious that she had never loved him.

It was near the end of a very long week when Robbie's lawyers contacted Janet with the information sent back from Switzerland. The response was brief and to the point. Billy had talked about the weekend his father had disappeared. He had said that his father had died in a boating accident. Janet curled up in Aliki's arms and had a good cry.

Aliki kept her face passive. Her heart ached for Janet and she felt sorry for Robbie, but most of all she felt damn sorry for herself. It was only with great effort that she was able to remain supportive in a drama that she wanted no part in. *Love is a bitch!*

Later, Janet paced the floor restlessly. Back and forth. Back and forth. She could hear the classical music coming from the back of the house, but images of the beautiful and deadly dance were buried beneath her fretting for Robbie. Back and forth she walked, and in the back of the house, the music went on and on.

Aliki trained until she almost dropped from exhaustion, then she leaned against the wall and watched the red spots dance across her eyes. If she could make it upstairs to her bedroom, maybe she could sleep tonight.

With a groan, she pushed herself off the wall and dragged herself upstairs. She stripped down and took a shower, only to find that sleep was still elusive, no matter how tired her body was. The bedroom was large, with hard maple floors. At one end was a writing desk of oak with a matching set of drawers. At the other was a sitting area. The central area was dominated by a large oak sleigh bed, and on the opposite wall was the third of the three fireplaces in the house.

Aliki slipped into navy blue silk pyjamas and sat down in the comfy wingback chair by the fire. Leaning down, she put a light to the kindling and pulled the screen into place. It promised to be a long night. She must have dozed, because Janet rushing into her room woke her with a start.

"I know who did it! I know!"

Aliki caught her in her arms and spun her around, laughing with her. "So, are you going to share the answer, Mrs. Holmes?" Aliki asked playfully, acutely aware of the feel of Janet's body through the thin layer of fine silk. Did Janet know what she was doing to her? *No.* Aliki sighed inwardly. Janet was focused on one thing and one thing only — getting her soulmate back. Aliki pulled away and went to get her housecoat from the closet. Putting it on, she turned to see a worried face.

"Oh, Aliki, I'm sorry. That was pretty callous of me," Janet apologized. "It's not me you love so much, Aliki, as it is having a family. You're happy with a house full of kids, a pet, and a partner. When this is over, go home, find yourself. Then you'll be able to really find love."

Aliki shrugged and gave a weak smile. "I sure hope someday someone will love me as much as you love Robbie. Here, come and sit by the fire and tell me what you have worked out."

Janet gave Aliki a quick hug and kissed her cheek then she went to sit in the other armchair on the opposite side of the hearth. "It was something Elizabeth said. She said that she heard Alexandria come in and she was singing. Doesn't that strike you as a strange thing to do if you have two children in bed? Unless you wanted to be heard because you needed to set the time for when you got home so it was after the murder," explained Janet, her eyes sparkling.

Aliki rubbed her chin and considered. "You think she came home early, maybe witnessed what had gone on, and while Philip was out cold decided to take the opportunity to be rid of him?"

Janet nodded. "It explains why Alexandria was so willing to help the police. She planted that letter in Robbie's apartment in the hopes of making the case against Robbie stronger. Why would Robbie have a letter she had sent to her mother years ago? She wanted to prove Robbie had attacked Philip and harboured really angry feelings toward him."

"It makes sense," Aliki concluded, "but how are you going to prove it?"

"I can't. But you can help me flush her out." Aliki's eyebrow went up and Janet smiled at her wickedly.

Janet lined up with the other visitors queued up to see an inmate. This time she was given clearance to see Robbie. Once more she was led to a small room with two wooden chairs bolted to the floor. The woman who entered barely looked like the woman she loved. Her face was pale and her eyes deep set and dark. Someone had raggedly cut her hair short. She looked haggard, hard, and depressed.

Robbie walked over and stood quietly looking down at her. Hesitantly, Janet wrapped her arms around the woman who was her soulmate. The stiff body convulsed at the touch and Robbie lowered her head and rubbed her cheek against Janet's head like a kitten seeking affection. They stayed that way for a long time, each afraid to speak in case they hurt the other.

Finally, Janet looked up into sad blue eyes. "Kiss me?" she requested, and Robbie lowered her head and gently caressed her lips. "Here, sit down, love," Janet instructed, frightened now that Robbie had not spoken. "You don't look so good," she commented, using her fingers to comb Robbie's short hair into some sort of order.

"I don't feel so good," came a whisper, from a voice that sounded rusty from lack of use. "I...I don't like being locked up."

Janet nodded, tears welling in her eyes. "It will be a little better now that you can get out of your cell again sometimes," she soothed, pulling the unresponsive body into a hug. She hated the sound of the chains when Robbie moved and the smell of stale cigarettes and sewers that clung to her clothes. Keeping Robbie locked up was like hamstringing a racehorse.

Robbie didn't answer. She just nodded and rubbed her head against Janet's again. Janet smelt of the outside; of summer days and wild herbs under a hot sun. How could she tell Janet that she was slowly going crazy in there?

"I can't tell you anything, Robbie, but Aliki and I are onto a lead that we think will get you out of here," Janet whispered.

Robbie forced herself not to react. She didn't want to fight with Janet, but she was getting sick of hearing Aliki's name. Now they had secrets they were keeping from her. *Could you blame her, Robbie, if she found someone else? How honest were you with her?* "I love you," Robbie croaked out in desperation.

"I love you, too," Janet whispered. They didn't talk after that. They just sat together, Janet's arms around the handcuffed woman, two very lonely lovers, close but apart.

Aliki paced around the parking lot waiting for Janet. She'd been in there a long time. The thought of someone else touching Janet ate at her. Anger hardened the muscles in her face and she forced them to relax into a deadpan expression when she saw the petite figure heading through the parking lot in her direction.

Janet smiled. "The first really warm day. Maybe our April showers are over."

Looking around, anywhere but at Janet's lips, Aliki nodded. "Yeah, summer's close now," she responded, pleased by how normal her voice sounded. "Ready to go and get this over with?"

Janet nodded. "This has got to work. If we can't flush her out, I don't know where to go from here."

Aliki gave her hand a pat. "We'll make it work," she promised.

They drove north out of Toronto then headed west to Unionville. Once again, Aliki pulled into the driveway of the Williams estate, not to pick up the bones of Robbie's father this time, but to pick at the soul of Alexandria Williams. If Janet was right, this woman had let her daughter carry the guilt of the death of Philip Williams for years, and then had callously tried to set Robbie up to be wrongfully convicted of that murder. It was hard to believe that anyone could be that coldly self-serving.

They were led by the maid into a morning room were Alexandria lay lounging with a *Vogue* magazine. "Oh, it is Robbie's little friend," Alexandria drawled. "I am surprised to see you here."

"You shouldn't be," Janet retorted. "I own this house."

"Really! You are common, aren't you? The estate has been used by the family for years."

Aliki smiled when Alexandria tossed the magazine aside with her left hand.

"Not by you anymore. I will be selling the place. I want you out as soon as possible," Janet snapped. "You're likely to put off prospective buyers."

Aliki listened to the catty exchange, eyes wide with surprise. This fiery bobcat was a part of Janet's personality that she had not seen before.

"Alexandria, this is Doctor Aliki Pateas. She works for the Toronto Police Forensic Department; she has made some interesting discoveries. Doctor?"

"Mrs. Williams, it might be of interest to you to know that the forensic lab can prove that Philip Williams was struck twice that night — once by a right handed swing to the jaw by Robbie, and once by a club of some sort swung by a left handed person. It was the second blow, to the temple, that killed him. You are left handed aren't you, Mrs. Williams?"

Alexandria's eyes had narrowed at the introduction, but now her covert interest in the doctor was replaced by self-interest. "What are you saying? How dare you!" Alexandria sputtered, shaking with anger.

"We can also prove that you planted that old letter in Robbie's condominium. Why would you need to do that, Alexandria, except to divert the blame to Robbie?"

"I never did. This is character assassination. Haven't I gone through enough? My husband murdered by my perverted daughter... The things I have suffered. And now this!" Alexandria carried on dramatically.

Much to Aliki's amusement, Janet ignored the melodramatic acting.

"You should be warned that we can prove what time you got home the night of the murder. The same woman who witnessed Robbie burying the body also witnessed...other things," Janet bluffed.

Aliki noted that Alexandria turned pale, and her long, bony hands twisted nervously around each other.

"You bitch," Alexandria whispered.

Janet's eyes narrowed. "Whatever it takes to clear my wife's name. You are, unfortunately, Robbie's mother. For that reason, and only that reason, I am here. The truth is going to come out within the next few days, Alexandria. I don't want Robbie and Bethy to have to waste time with you. Leave. Get out of the country as quickly as you can. Disappear or face the consequences." The veiled threat having been delivered, Aliki took Janet's arm and they walked out without another word.

Back in the van, Janet wore a grin from ear to ear. "Yes!" she exclaimed excitedly. "We've got the bitch on the run."

Aliki laughed and put the van into gear. "Lady, I'm sure glad you're playing on my team." Then her face went serious. "I hope Robbie appreciates just how special you are."

A gentle hand touched her arm reassuringly. "Robbie is a very complex and moody person. She doesn't always react the way you would want her to, but she loves me, Aliki, above all else. I don't doubt that, and I love her above all others."

Aliki sighed. "Yeah, I know," she said dejectedly. The hand squeezed her arm in sympathy before withdrawing.

Robbie was surprised when she was taken from her cell again and told she had visitors. It wasn't visiting hours and usually they were pretty strict about that. Maybe it was her lawyers. They had been milling about in a near panic ever since she had been arrested. To her surprise, she was led to the family room. Inside, she found herself facing her two daughters across the room. Their reactions were different. Ryan's face showed shock and fear. Reb's lit up with recognition and she came running across the room to Robbie.

"Obbie! Obbie!" She laughed, reaching her arms up. Robbie bent down and scooped the child up as high as the chains would allow her. She hugged the small child close, blinking back the tears that threatened to spill. She carefully lowered Reb to the ground and walked over to Ryan. Ryan backed up a step.

"Reb wanted to see you," she said defensively. "She was worried, even though Aliki said you could handle yourself in here. You don't look so good."

Robbie let Ryan get away with the face-saving lie. "Does Janet know you are here?"

Ryan shook her head. "We took a taxi."

"I'm okay," she assured her daughter as she stroked Reb's head. The little child had wrapped herself around Robbie's leg and was holding on tightly.

"Obbie, Mom said she and Aliki are going to get you out. Don't worry, okay, 'cause Mom can do anything," Ryan reassured awkwardly.

Robbie swallowed her pain with difficulty. *Okay, so I'm Obbie now, not Mom. What did I expect! The only birthday I was ever at and they drag me away in handcuffs. At least she cared enough to come and see for herself that I'm all right.* "Listen, Ryan, Janet loves you very much. She's a good mom. You...you be good for her. You take care of her, okay?"

The guard came forward. Ryan licked her lips and started to say something, then stopped. Tears welling in her eyes, she reached down and pulled a scared looking Reb away. "Come on, Rebecca, we have to go now. Say good-bye to Obbie," she instructed through a tight throat.

"Bye, Obbie." Reb waved as Robbie walked backwards across the room.

"Goodbye, girls. Ryan..." Robbie tried to formulate the words she needed to say to her daughter, then gave up. "Just be careful on the way back."

Ryan nodded.

The phone call came the day after Janet had talked to Alexandria. Gwen was so excited that she could barely make herself understood. "Janet? It's Gwen. Listen, I got to thinking about what you told me and I thought to myself — if Isabelle Selo saw Robbie bury her father, maybe she saw other things, too. So I hunted up her address from our files and Brian and I went over there.

"Boy, what a weird place. She's got pictures of Robbie all over, and candles and things. Robbie would have a fit. Anyway, she did see something. She saw Alexandria's car go up the road toward the house hours before she supposedly got there. You were right, Janet. Alexandria was there when the murder took place."

Janet closed her eyes and sank to the chair.

"Janet? Are you there?"

"Yes. Yes, I am. Gwen, I can't thank you enough. We are no longer bluffing now. We've got Alexandria on the run. I can't thank you enough. You and Brian are such good friends."

"Hey, anything for you and Robbie, you know that," Gwen responded happily. "I'll let you go. Give Robbie our love the next time you see her."

"I'll do that. Thanks, Gwen." Janet hung up and then danced a little jig.

Alexandria looked around the room with disdain. She walked over to the chair that sat by the partition and made sure the guard noticed as she cleaned the seat with a tissue, dropping the soiled item on the floor when she was finished. The guard's face remained frozen in an expression of disinterested boredom.

With a flourish, Alexandria arranged herself on the chair and watched through ice-cold eyes as her daughter was led into the room. Her lip curled in a cruel smirk as she observed Robbie shuffling over to the seat on the other side of the division and sliding awkwardly into the chair. The chains made a tinkling sound, like ice crystals rushing through black, cold water.

She looks like hell. How delightful! Alexandria observed. *She's skin and bones. And what a hollow, mean look.* "Your bitch and her new mate have been to see me," Alexandria remarked, and was rewarded by the flash of pain across Robbie's face. Robbie remained silent.

"They were all over each other. Really, it was so infantile," dramatized Alexandria. *Still no reaction.* "The bitch actually had the nerve to threaten me." Alexandria laughed. "I don't take that sort of thing well."

Dark eyes stared back at her, now cautious and interested. Alexandria leaned back and smiled. "I've decided to go overseas to live. Your little escapades have made it impossible for me to live here, what with the press and all. But before I go, I have a little secret to share with you." Alexandria leaned forward. "I hate you," she whispered cruelly.

Shock registered on Robbie's face, then disappeared behind a well-trained facade. "More than anyone else?" Robbie asked sarcastically, going on the defence.

"Yes. You are not a Williams, you know." Alexandria was rewarded by the expression of utter shock on Robbie's face.

"What?"

Alexandria laughed. *Oh, that one hurt, huh? More than knowing your sweetheart is cheating on you.* "That's right, you are not one of the remarkable Williamses. Your father was someone else, a loser, like you turned out to be." She smirked. "I told Philly you were his and the fool believed me. Philly had money, your father didn't."

Alexandria got up and looked down at Robbie. Her daughter looked utterly defeated. "I just thought that now that you are all grown up," she oozed sarcastically, "you should know. Good riddance, Roberta."

Robbie watched as Alexandria's sharp heels clipped across the floor. "Wait!" She blurted out, leaping to her feet. "Who was he?"

Alexandria shrugged. "I don't care to reveal that information. He was a loser, like you," she finished in satisfaction, and walked out on her daughter.

Tracy watched Robbie out of the corner of her eye. She had been getting increasingly worried about her cellmate. Robbie was one of those who was going to snap someday. Tracy had been in and out of prison enough to know the signs. You could see that she was one of those people that couldn't be locked up and survive.

She kind of liked Robbie, as much as she liked anyone. Besides, Robbie had kept her word and gotten her a law team that was going to help her beat this rap. Being nice to Robbie was important, at least until Tracy got paroled. You had to watch Robbie, though. She'd learned that the first day. The glamour queen had a side that was vicious when she lost her temper, and she had the muscle and skill to back up her threats. It was best to tread easy around her.

Something had happened upstairs, that was for sure. Robbie was white and silent when she came back from the visitors' section. She had been sitting on the very edge of her cot ever since, staring at the wall like a zombie. Tracy watched Robbie over the top of her comic book, feeling the actor's anger radiating off of her like sound waves. She had just glanced down at her comic when it happened, taking her completely by surprise even though she had been expecting it. A scream, and then Robbie went berserk.

Tracy just managed to take cover under her bunk before Robbie's plastic water bottle smashed against the wall. Water splattered over everything. Mattress stuffing went flying about and, absorbing the water, sank to the bottom of the melee in soggy lumps. Robbie was hurling herself at the bars now, and the women in the other cells around moved forward to watch. It was a scene that most had seen many times before, but it drew them with morbid curiosity. There was satisfaction in seeing it happen to someone else. It was a visual reinforcement of the fact that the horror and panic each felt inside was shared by all.

The guards arrived. Tracy covered her face and held her breath. Robbie took the pepper spray to the face, but that didn't stop her. It took three shots of the irritant to finally bring Robbie to her knees.

The pain was intense. Her eyes burned like hot coals, and tears and mucus ran down her face. The gate clanged open and heavy footsteps surrounded her. She heard Tracy curse as she was dragged out from under the bed and dumped down beside her cellmate. Robbie blindly lashed out at those who were manhandling them. Once again, the spray burned her face and she sucked it into her lungs, setting them on fire. Their arms were cuffed behind them and searching hands probed their bodies for weapons.

Robbie was lifted up and half led, half dragged away. At one point, she vomited, the burning now spreading from her lungs to her throat. Her breath came in raspy, watery gasps. Blackness closed in around her.

They took the ferry over to Toronto Island that day. Reb wandered into the children's maze and had to be rescued by her big sister, who could see over the hedges. They fed the ducks and geese pieces of bread by the water's edge while Reb explained again how Ryan had shown her the way out of the maze. "Ryan, knew the way out, Mommy. She tall, so she could see the path. Ryan showed me where to turn and then I got out. It was a trick place, Mommy, but Ryan knowed the trick."

"Knew, sweetheart. Ryan knew the trick and you are right, your sister is very smart. A real hero." Janet poked Ryan with affection as she talked to her younger daughter.

Reb nodded her head in the same serious way that Robbie and Ryan had. "Ryan a hero," she agreed, wrapping herself around her adopted sister.

Ryan hugged the child close, letting the warmth of the innocent child warm her cold soul. Even the heat of the warm spring day could not remove that icy spot. Visiting Robbie had upset her far more than she was prepared to admit. To do so would be to concede that she still loved her mom, and that would leave her open to being hurt again. She was not going to allow that. Robbie was never going to get the chance to abandon her again because she was not going to let her back into her heart.

Ryan listened to the gentle teasing and banter of the others, letting it seep into her soul and locking it up safely there. The family they had formed had filled a large hole in Ryan's life, but now the security that she had felt so briefly had pretty much been snatched away. Today was okay, though. They were pretending that everything was all right. And Aliki was there, filling a big void in their lives. Ryan wanted to cherish every second of the day. It was like a salve on the wound of her teenage soul.

She stood as close as she dared to Janet, watching Aliki and Reb playing on the playground equipment, soaking in the strength and gentle warmth that was her aunt. A lump formed in her throat and she swallowed it down. She had to be brave, too. It was important. She took a step away, trying to show a courage and resolve that she didn't feel.

Later, they ate at the restaurant in the Skydome and watched the Blue Jays baseball team play Detroit. It was a happy day in the midst of a very dark time, one that they would all remember with affection.

Late that night, Janet and Aliki got word from Robbie's law firm that Alexandria had left the country and that they would be calling for a new hearing based on the evidence that Janet and Aliki had provided. Janet had gone to sleep that night relaxed and happy, and feeling that at last there was a light at the end of the tunnel.

Some hours later, Janet woke with a start. *Something's happened!* The dread she had felt earlier that day was back and flooding her soul. She wiped the sweat from her face and started as the phone rang. It was a nurse calling from Toronto General Hospital.

Robbie woke with panic gripping her heart. She was restrained in a bed and her eyes were sore and her vision blurred. She suspected that she'd been given some kind of drug, too, because her thoughts came slowly, and even the action of opening her swollen eyes took tremendous effort. A warm hand slipped around her own.

"Shhhh, love, I'm here," came Janet's voice. "Lie still." Robbie tried to say something but all that came out was a dry croak. "Would you like some water?"

Robbie nodded. She felt her bed being raised up and then a cool arm wrapped around her shoulder as a straw touched her lips. Robbie sucked the water up noisily, feeling the cool liquid ease some of the burning inside.

"There. You inhaled a lot of pepper spray and it's in your eyes, too. It's going to take some time until you feel better," the voice of her lover explained gently.

Robbie nodded, the action causing tears to roll down her cheeks again. "Where am I?" she managed to croak out.

"The hospital," came the quiet answer. "What happened, Robbie? What did Alexandria say to you?"

Janet saw Robbie's body physically jerk then still. *Please, Robbie, no more evasions and secrets. Just trust me.* Janet waited. Robbie didn't answer. Janet smiled sadly as she looked down at their inter-linked fingers. *Maybe she's not my soulmate after all. Maybe she doesn't feel the same way I do. Something is missing from our relationship.* Gently, she started to slip her fingers from the grasp.

Robbie listened intently, trying to figure out what was going on as her thoughts ran wild within her. She wished that she could see Janet, watch the emotions cross her face. This was hard. *All my life I've built a wall between me and others. Compartmentalized my life so I was never completely exposed to anyone, never vulnerable. Kept my secrets deep inside where no one could use them against me. I learned survival so young, now it's a natural part of me. I wear my defences like a second skin. Should I, can I let them down and trust Janet has...will remain loyal to me? Especially now, when I can't even see?*

In the end, it wasn't trust that made the words come out, but the very real fear of losing what was most precious to her as Robbie felt Janet slowly slipping her hand away. "No!" she got out in a rough exclamation, tightening her fingers around Janet's hand. "Don't leave me!"

"I didn't leave you, Robbie; you're shutting me out. You can't talk to me about what is wrong with you and that puts a wall between us," said a quiet, sad voice.

Finally, the words came in a desperate torrent of emotion. "She said Aliki was your new mate, that you were all over her. She said you threatened her. B-be careful, she hates you," Robbie managed to get out, choking on the tears. The bed moved and suddenly she could feel Janet's body next to hers. She wanted to reach out and pull her lover in close, but the restraining straps prevented that.

"Robbie, I love Aliki, but as a friend nothing more," Janet began gently, feeling the pain lance through her lover. "I made a mistake. I kissed her." Robbie was shaking now, the tears running freely in choking sobs. "Then I apologized to her because I knew my heart could never belong to her because it belongs to you. Robbie, I used Aliki. I was lonely and scared and missing you so very much, and she was kind and strong. It was wrong, because there could only ever be you, in my heart, in my soul and in my bed. I love you, Robbie." The body beneath her slowly calmed. Janet wiped away tears with her hand.

"Did you tell her that?" Robbie asked insecurely.

"Yes. Immediately."

"Hold me." Robbie was surprised to hear herself say it. She rubbed her head along the side of Janet's, wanting, needing the warmth that her partner's love gave her. For a long time they lay there.

Finally, from deep inside, Robbie released the pain. "She said she hated me, a-and that Philip wasn't my father. She said my father was a loser with no money. She told Philip that he was the father so she could marry him for his money. I-I didn't mean to kill him," she cried, the sobs once again convulsing her body.

"Robbie! Shhh, lover, it's okay. You didn't kill your...you didn't kill Philip Williams. All you did was knock him out. Aliki can prove that. The blow that killed your father came later and was most likely delivered by someone who was left-handed. Someone who came home early that night and saw an opportunity to get rid of her husband and put the blame on the daughter she resented."

The body beside Janet went still for a very long time. "Alexandria killed him?"

"We think so."

"She killed him and let me live with the guilt," Robbie repeated, anger now dissipating the pain of the secret that she had held all those years.

"It looks that way, Robbie," Janet soothed gently. She wasn't sure she was handling this right. They had sent for her in the middle of the night when they were unable to settle Robbie down. Even when they had given Robbie a sedative at the hospital, she had fought against it, screaming in her sleep. It had been Janet's quiet, soothing voice that had finally allowed her to fall into a deep slumber.

According to the guard on the door, Robbie had come back from the interview with her mother and had simply gone berserk. Now Janet understood why. Robbie was always so strong, but how much could one human being take? She'd taken on a ready-made family, then almost lost her own daughter in an explosion, rebuilt a relationship with Ryan only to have it stolen away the day of her arrest. She'd stood by Janet through all the surgery and cancer treatments, and then had thought that on top of everything, Janet had found someone else.

Then there was the guilt and shame that she had carried all those years because she thought she had killed a perverted father in the heat of anger. Robbie thought she was going to spend a good part of the rest of her life behind bars and, if that wasn't enough, her mother revealed her hatred for her and told her that the man she killed wasn't even her father! *My God! It's no wonder Robbie lost it!*

"Aliki and I have written up a report for the lawyers and we hope to get a hearing in the next few days. They haven't got enough to make the charge of murder stand, Robbie. I'm going to be taking you home soon."

"I don't want Elizabeth involved."

"Elizabeth went with David to your lawyers and made a complete statement about what happened that night." Robbie's body stiffened. "That was Elizabeth's idea, not mine. She needed to bury a few ghosts too, Robbie."

"Is she okay?" Robbie fretted.

"Yes."

"Where's Alexandria?"

"She's disappeared. She left Canada for Argentina, but we think that she got off somewhere on the way. It is likely that there will be a warrant for her arrest issued once your name is cleared, but I don't think they will find her. Alexandria is a survivor," Janet finished bitterly. She stroked Robbie, trying to keep her calm as she coped with all the information and emotions that had been dumped on her.

"You didn't threaten her. You warned her so she'd have time to get away, didn't you?"

Janet gave a soft, weak laugh. "Well, a little bit of both. She is your mother. I didn't think you needed to go through her trial for murder."

"I...I love you, Janet," Robbie whispered, her voice brittle and rough with emotion.

"I love you too, my sweet olive. I always will," Janet responded with feeling, capturing Robbie's lips with her own. They tasted acidic and peppery, and her own lips came away burning. "You sleep. I'll be here when you wake again."

Robbie was released from the hospital two days later and taken by squad car directly to the hearing. Walking in with her guard, she saw her family sitting with Aliki in the front row. The whole proceeding took less than a minute. The Crown, having read the brief submitted by Robbie's lawyers, dropped the charges and requested that a warrant be issued for the arrest of Alexandria Williams.

Robbie held her hands out while the cuffs were removed, then Janet was in her arms. Reb had her by the leg and Elizabeth had tears running down her face and David patted her affectionately on the back. Ryan stood nearby, her lip trembling but her face expressionless. Aliki stood behind her, the scientist's face a still, quiet mask.

Robbie eventually pulled out of the embraces and walked over toward Aliki until they faced each other. Blue eyes locked with blue and a silent message of understanding passed between the two women. Robbie offered her hand and Aliki took it, then Robbie turned away and smiled softly at Janet. She walked over and gently took Ryan's hand, leading her over to where Elizabeth stood, then wrapped her daughter and sister in a big embrace, deliberately keeping her back to Aliki and Janet. She trusted Janet. There were no more secrets. She owed it to both of them to let them say good-bye in private.

Janet looked up at Aliki through watery eyes. Aliki smiled. "I'm happy for you. You're taking a piece of my heart, you know," she confessed through her own tears.

"And you'll always have a piece of mine. Thank you for giving me back my soulmate," whispered Janet, into Aliki's ear as she wrapped her arms around the woman who had been her anchor through this horrible time. Aliki held her tight and then gave her up. Janet reached up and softly kissed her cheek, then turned and walked over to Robbie. Together the Williams family walked out of the courthouse to meet the press.

Robbie stood in the roof garden of her condominium, Janet tucked safely under her arm. A full moon had risen and was sending shimmering diamonds of light across Lake Ontario. The night was warm. Summer was on its way. It was time for them to step out of the shadows and take their place in the sun. It was time to grow again after a stormy spring.

Not too far away, Aliki swung a bag into her van and then slid into the driver's seat. It was time to go home. She'd been away too long.

Summer Heat

Chapter 17

Janet looked out the window to where her lover sat on the porch. Robbie had been restless since they returned to the cabin four days earlier. She had always been filled with a surplus of energy and ideas, but now it was different. Her actions, once so focused, seemed random and lacking purpose.

We share the same bed but we haven't made love since she was released from prison. Life goes ahead on the surface but the family teasing and banter doesn't reach her. She's so moody.

Janet sighed and walked across the living room and up the hall to their daughters' bedroom. She paused at the door. Reb was making the soft baby noises of sleep, but Ryan's figure was still and quiet in the darkness. "Ryan, love, are you still awake?"

"Yeah."

Janet walked in and sat on the edge of Ryan's bed.

"Has she come back yet?" Ryan asked casually, although worry made her voice rough.

"About half an hour ago. She's sitting out on the porch," Janet knew Ryan wouldn't sleep until her mother had returned from the run she had suddenly decided to take.

Ryan nodded and relaxed a bit. For a minute there was silence. "I didn't support her like you did," she said regretfully. "I was kind of mean to her."

"Yes, you were," Janet agreed honestly, then went on to lessen the sting. "But I think your mom understands. Your relationship with your mom is still pretty vulnerable."

"I shouldn't have stopped calling her mom," sighed Ryan, the tears evident in her voice.

"Well, that is easy to fix. Just start calling her mom again."

The anxious reply revealed one more hidden root of Ryan's distress. "She might get angry. Maybe she doesn't want me as her daughter anymore."

Janet took Ryan's hand and gave it a squeeze. "Maybe, and maybe pigs can fly! Come on, Ryan, if you know anything by now it is that your mom worships the ground you walk on. Get out of bed." Janet pulled on Ryan's hand as she stood. "That's right. Now march out there and tell your mom that you'd like to build that boat she gave you for your birthday."

"What if she says no?" fretted the edgy teen.

"Then I'll be running outside to see the flock of pigs fly over the lake," Janet snorted, giving Ryan a push in the right direction. "Go on, Ryan, here is your chance to help your mother. She needs you, sweetheart."

A moody Robbie looked out across the lake. *When I first came here, the horizon seemed endless. Now the trees seemed to have grown in close around.*

"Hi, Mom," said a voice from behind her.

Robbie's heart skipped a beat as she leapt to her feet and spun around. Ryan was in her arms almost immediately. Robbie held her close and rubbed her cheek against Ryan's soft hair. "Hi, Ryan," she managed to get out, her voice cracking with emotion. Robbie drew back but kept her arm around her daughter's shoulder. "It's a nice night."

Ryan nodded. "You enjoy your run?"

Be open, be honest. Don't make the same mistakes a second time, Robbie warned herself. "It helps control my panic. I can't seem to get over the fear of being confined," she confessed.

Ryan turned and looked at her, searching for something in her mother's eyes. "If we build that boat you gave me for my birthday, we could take it out on the lake and then you could really feel free," she said nervously.

Robbie's emotions almost crumbled under the surprise offer. She smiled through tears that rolled down her face. "You know, Ryan, that would be just about perfect." She pulled her daughter close and thanked whatever powers there might be for giving her yet another chance to bridge the gap between herself and her daughter.

Ryan pulled back awkwardly. "Well, I'd better get back to bed. Aunt Janet is re-enrolling me at Bartlett tomorrow."

"Sure." Robbie smiled and leaned forward to kiss her daughter's cheek. Ryan gave her mom one more hug, and then hurried off to bed. Robbie sat down on the stoop again and watched the stars reflected in the still, deep waters of the lake as she wiped away the remaining tears with a shaky hand.

Janet came out with two cups of tea in hand. "Hi, can I join you?"

The tension returned to Robbie's frame, but she gestured to the stoop beside her. "Sure."

"Nice night," Janet remarked, sitting down next to Robbie but leaving space between them. That's the way things were now, close but not quite one. They sat for a long time watching the changes in the early summer night.

With a sigh, Robbie put down her cup and, still looking out at the lake, she said, "I need to ask you something. I need to know."

"Okay." Janet mentally braced herself for what might be coming. *Don't leave me, Robbie.*

"Would you have slept with Alika if you hadn't had the surgery? Is that what stopped you?"

Janet absorbed the blow to her senses for a few seconds. "I think if it had gone that far, the mastectomy would have been a factor, Robbie. So much of what we are as women is tied to our concept of our bodies. But it didn't get that far, not even close. That evening, I was very vulnerable and the moment was very sexually charged. I never planned to kiss her, and I never would have slept with her. When I did kiss her, I told her right away that I'd made a mistake, that you were my soulmate."

Robbie was stiff and quiet for a long moment. "Ryan wants to build that boat."

"That's a good idea," Janet replied neutrally, fighting for emotional control. *Oh God, Robbie, don't do this.*

"Yeah...I'm having trouble with all this, Janet. I thought I'd found everything that I could possibly want in life and then suddenly it all just turned to sand and ran through my fingers. Hell, I don't even know who my father is, who I am anymore!"

Janet turned to kneel in front of Robbie. "Do you know that I love you? Can you believe that?"

Robbie looked down at her feet. "I know what you went through to get me out of there. I don't know if that was loyalty or love. Aliki and you..."

Janet leapt to her feet and jumped down the stairs to pace angrily back and forth. She stopped directly in front of Robbie. "There is no Aliki and me. There never was. Can't you get that through your thick head?" she stormed. "I kissed her. I shouldn't have. It wasn't fair to you or to her. I'm sorry, but damn it all, Robbie, I'd had it. I don't often feel sorry for myself, but I'd gone through cancer and struggled with the insecurity of losing a breast. Out of the blue, I find my wife being arrested for a murder that she didn't trust me enough to tell me the truth about. Then I had to cope with the press and your refusal to talk. I was kicked out of my church and my job. I was beaten up by a bunch of skinheads just for loving you, and had you yelling at me and accusing me of sleeping with another woman. I'm sorry I kissed Aliki. It was a lousy thing to do to her and you but damn it, I am not super woman and I've heard enough about it, Robbie. Enough!"

Turning on her heel, she stomped up the stairs and into the cabin, leaving a stunned silence behind her on the steps. For a long while, the emotions swirled inside Robbie's head and nothing made sense. Then the litany of things that Janet had given her registered one after the other. *Christ! They fired her. Teaching was Janet's life; that must have been devastating for her. I never questioned why she had time off; I just presumed she'd taken a leave. God, I'm arrogant. Okay, Robbie, here is the bottom line. You can either walk away because she kissed Aliki and told you, or put it behind you and try to make a life with Janet and the kids. What's it going to be?*

There wasn't any question.

Janet had a blistering headache, one of the worst she had ever had. *Nice play, Janet. Of all the times to feel sorry for yourself, this had to be the worst. If Robbie wasn't planning on leaving you, she is sure to be now.* She rooted around in the medicine chest but could not find any painkillers. Then she came across a bottle the doctor had given Robbie after she hurt her knee the year before. It was almost empty, but there were a few pills left in the bottom. Relieved, she swallowed two and got ready for bed.

Her head started to swim and she felt dizzy and disoriented. *Oh no,* she thought and went to get the bottle. *Now you read the label.* Sure enough, the pills had codeine in them. She knew from past experiences that codeine caused her to have a drug reaction and pass out. *I'd better get to bed and sleep this stuff off.* It was the last thought she had for a while.

Robbie got up and stretched her back that had stiffened in the damp, cool air. *Okay, Robbie, it's time to stop wading knee deep in self-pity and get on with life.* She entered the cabin, locked the door and turned off the lights, using the brilliant moonlight to find her way to the bedroom. Lying on the floor was the ghostly figure of her wife. In her hand was an empty pill bottle with two white pills spilled out on the floor. Robbie's heart lunged and stopped.

"Damn it, woman, if you aren't the worst patient I've ever had to treat I don't know who was," grumbled George Drouillard as Robbie fought to get free from the paper bag he was holding over her mouth and nose.

"W-what?" Confused, Robbie became aware of a room full of people. George Droullard leaned over her with a paper bag on one side and Ryan stood on the other, a bloody tissue held to her mouth. "Ryan! What happened?" Robbie exclaimed, bolting upright and almost sending George on his backside.

"You happened. I was trying to help Mr. Droullard hold the bag on your face and you socked me," she complained good-naturedly. "You hyperventilated and passed out. Boy, did you lose it when you thought Aunt Janet had killed herself."

"Janet!" Robbie screamed, as she bounded over the back of the couch and ran into the bedroom.

George Droullard looked at Ryan and shook his head. "Now that's where your artist's temperament comes in, Ryan," he observed, nodding his head wisely.

"Aunt Janet says the Williams are like olives; we're nice, but we take a lot of getting used to." Ryan smiled.

George chuckled in agreement. "You know, she was just as wild the night Jim Ableton put you into the boards at the skating rink. If Lou Enrico and Bill Perkins hadn't pulled her off, I was a-thinkin' we'd have been taking Ableton out of the rink feet first."

Ryan smiled, pleased that her mom had come to her defence with the same intensity that she had fought for Janet's life. By the time Ryan had leapt out of bed, her mom had already called Doctor Perkins and the Bartlett Volunteer Fire Department.

"Mary," George called over to his wife, who had come along when she had heard that Janet had tried to commit suicide, "you'd better be making some sandwiches to go with that tea. I know the guys aren't going to want to leave Robbie in the state she's in, her bein' one of the boys and all."

Mary waved and laughed, and cheerfully took a few loaves out of the cupboard. She couldn't be happier than to find herself in a kitchen with an entire room of hungry people to feed. Several O.P.P. officers emerged from the bedroom with Doctor Perkins. Through the window, by the glow of red and yellow emergency lights that flashed on several vehicles, Mary could make out the arrival of several more cars. That would be the Ladies' Auxiliary come to lend a hand with the emergency and find out what was happening.

"Janet!" Robbie bounded into the bedroom and almost knocked down the two police officers who were trying to find out what had happened.

"Easy, Robbie, or you'll be hyperventilating again," warned the local doctor. "She's fine."

Robbie sank to her knees by the bed and took Janet's limp, cold hand in her own. "Janet, sweetheart..."

Green eyes opened a crack with effort. "What has my favourite olive done now?" she asked sleepily.

Robbie looked up at the doctor.

"It took me a while to wake her up enough get some sense out of her, but it seems she had a headache and was out of painkillers so she took two of some I had prescribed for you. They had codeine in them and Janet is allergic to codeine. It knocks her for a loop. Give her twelve hours for the stuff to work through her system and she'll be fine," Perkins explained with a grin.

Robbie slumped with relief and placed her head on the bed. "Oh, God. I thought she'd done something drastic because we had a fight."

Perkins patted Robbie on the shoulder. "She'll be fine, Robbie. It was just an accident." He signalled to the police officers and the three of them left the room. Perkins closed the door to give the women some privacy.

"I didn't mean to scare you," Janet said, her voice slurred with sleep.

"I've never been so afraid. I think I panicked." Robbie kissed the small hand that was intertwined with her own.

Janet laughed softly. "So I hear. I love you, Robbie Williams."

Robbie looked up so their eyes met. "I love you too, Janet Williams." She smiled and leaned in for a kiss. Janet was asleep again before the kiss had ended.

The Bartlett Fire Department, two O.P.P. officers, one doctor, and two children — one with a fat lip — were served tea and sandwiches in the living room while Doctor Perkins explained to everyone's relief that it had just been a misunderstanding.

Some time later, Mary stuck her head into the bedroom to find Robbie lying curled up beside Janet, both women fast asleep. She saw to Reb and Ryan getting back to bed and then shooed the men home in the pre-dawn sky.

The women did the washing up and left a plate of sandwiches and squares for the family before they left for home, too. "You know, Mary," George observed as he drove, "them two are very much in love."

"Really, George?" Mary commented dryly.

The sarcasm was lost on George. "Yup, almost as much as I love you, pretty thing," he chuckled, taking Mary's hand in his own.

Mary leaned her head on her husband's shoulder. She was a very lucky woman.

Janet woke to the happy sounds of her family.

"Up, Obbie. I want up, peas."

"Up it is, Reb. Voom, voom. Reb Air coming in for a landing in Highchair Airport!" came Robbie's voice over Reb's giggles.

"Hey, Mom, should I wake Aunt Janet? She's supposed to take me into Bartlett and get me back into school."

"No, let her sleep, Ryan, I'll take you and Reb in. Do you want cereal or toast for breakfast, because that's all I can cook."

Janet smiled sleepily, feeling a hummy sort of warmth spread through her. She had her Robbie back. Her eyes closed and she slept peacefully for the first time in a very long while.

Robbie and Ryan dropped Reb off at the Bartlett Day Care Centre and reassured Lily Chen that Janet was fine. All of Bartlett knew, of course, about the incident the night before. Some had heard it on their police scanners, some from husbands in the Bartlett Volunteer Fire Brigade, and the rest heard it at the doughnut shop that morning. Now daughter and mother walked side by side down the still empty halls of the school.

Ryan bit her lip nervously. "Uh, Mom, you're not going to make a scene, are you?"

"Scene? What do you mean?" Robbie asked tightly.

"About Aunt Janet getting fired. I can tell you're angry 'cause you're clenching your jaw."

"Stupid, damn Bored Trusses. I ought to—"

"Mom."

Robbie stopped and glared down at her daughter, who glared right back at her. "My other mom is pretty cool, and she can fight her own battles," Ryan said quietly.

Anger flashed across Robbie's face to be replaced almost immediately by a slow smile. "Okay, kid, I'll be good," she promised. Ryan looked relieved as they continued up the hall to the school office.

Carolyn Carr came out from behind her desk and hugged Ryan and then Robbie. "It's wonderful to see you two back. Welcome home. How's Janet?"

"She's fine. We left her to sleep in. Things got a little hectic last night." A blush crept up Robbie's neck.

Ryan giggled. "Mom went postal."

"So Burt told me." Carolyn laughed. "That is so sweet, Robbie," she said, giving the embarrassed woman a poke.

"Robbie, Ryan, hey. How's Janet?" called Milka, as she came out of the principal's office and hugged each Williams in turn.

Ryan snorted. "She's fine. She always was. It was Mom here who had the problem."

Robbie gave her daughter a dirty look as the three laughed at her expense. There was a time when that would have set her temper off, but now, well it just made her feel like she belonged.

"I'm here to enroll Ryan. We can't stand having her around the house all day," Robbie growled playfully. "We're willing to pay you to take her off our hands."

"Nice, Mom," Ryan exclaimed, snuggling against Robbie's side as her mother wrapped a protective arm around her daughter to reassure her that her words were just in fun.

"Well, come on in, then, and we'll see to the paperwork. Looks like we might get some rain today. We sure need it. It was a really dry spring."

When she got back to the cabin, Robbie let Rufus outside to run, then she stole quietly into the bedroom to check on Janet.

"Hi," came a sleepy voice from the tangle of sheets.

Robbie dropped to her knees by the bed and leaned over to place a soft kiss on Janet's cheek. "How are you feeling?" she asked softly.

"Take your clothes off, get in here, and I'll show you," Janet whispered, reaching up to draw Robbie down into long, sensual kiss.

They spent the morning in bed, talking out their feelings and reclaiming each other's bodies with slow burning passion. Eventually, hunger drove them out for a leisurely lunch by the fire. Then they lay on the couch, Janet tucked between Robbie's long powerful legs, her head pillowed on the actor's chest.

"Looks like there could be a storm brewing," Janet observed. "I'd better fill the oil lamps in case we lose power tonight."

"Mmmhmm. I'll bring in some extra wood for the fire before I leave to pick up Ryan and Reb. Janet, about your job, I don't think they had a legal right to—"

Fingers came up to caress Robbie's lips. "I know. I did think about taking them to court, but I just don't want to bother with any more lawyers and reporters. It would be such a hassle and I'm not sure I would want the job back under those circumstances. It's hard, but I've got a little saved and I can get into the supply pool at the local public high school. It might give me some time to finish writing that novel."

Robbie wrapped her close, knowing that the loss of her career would have cut Janet very deeply. "You don't have to worry about money, damn it. What's mine is yours, you know that. You are far too qualified to be supply teaching at the local high school," she grumbled.

"I know you're rich, Robbie, but I don't want to be kept. I want to have an independent income. It is a matter of pride. Nor am I so arrogant that I think I'm too good to work in the classroom. That is, after all, where the real educating is done," Janet protested, giving Robbie a kiss for being so protective and loyal.

"Hmm, that tasted nice," purred Robbie, stretching her frame like a cat. "Come here."

"Janet, do you know how to teach the talented as well as the gifted?" Robbie's voice was husky with lovemaking. They were now on the rug by the fire, having found the couch way too restrictive for their activities.

"Well, my degree is in gifted education and that includes both the academically gifted and the creatively gifted. It really shouldn't, because educating talent takes a totally different thinking process than working with the gifted. The academically gifted are very logical and methodical in the thought processes that eventually lead them to understanding. The talented, on the other hand, tend to work backwards. They start with this spark of an idea and then make it happen. We really need to do a lot more research into what makes people talented."

There was silence for a minute, then Robbie slid over Janet and scooped a handful of ash from the fireplace, spreading it evenly over an area of the hearth. Janet smiled, *If ever there was a definition of a truly creative thinker, it's my Robbie. She gets that intense look and then just does whatever she needs to achieve the concept that's materialized in her imagination.* Janet realized that genius made Robbie a tyrant to work for, but it also had made her and her companies the amazing successes that they were.

Robbie, totally absorbed in her ideas, was unaware of the mess she was creating. With a dirty finger she put a dot on her ash canvas. "Okay, here we are and here is Long Lake," explained the director, adding a line with her finger. "Down here is Saw Mill Road. My plan, as you know, is to tear down the mill and build a state of the art studio complex there, real high tech stuff. Down here, east of Saw Mill Road, is Kettle Lake. I'm going to run a road around it and subdivide it. A lot of people will be moving into town and Williams Construction is going to put in a pretty nice subdivision here. There will be parkland around the lake to protect it from overuse, and a public dock. We'll have a rule that people can't use motorboats on the lake, too. Gwen is going to love it. She's from the north, you know."

Janet leaned over and kissed her ash-covered lover. She loved this woman so very, very much.

Robbie paused to return the kiss, then went on. "I shared a cell with a woman who had killed her boyfriend 'cause he had been cheating on her. We got to talking about comic books and Greek art and things, and I got this idea...don't laugh now. What if we built a school for the talented that would be affiliated with my studio?"

Janet blinked, then blinked again.

Robbie waited.

"Are you serious?"

"Well, yeah. Would it be really hard to do? I figured you ought to be able to handle it," Robbie stated cavalierly.

"Me?"

"Who else? It will be a lot easier for you now that it will be your only job," Robbie pointed out. Janet lay back and laughed and Robbie smiled, liking the feel of the warm body vibrating with mirth beside her.

"You are such an olive!"

"Well, will you help me start The Kettle Lake School for the Talented?" Robbie leaned absently on an ashy hand.

Janet looked up with sparkling eyes. "Only if you have a bath before you make love to me again, Robbie Williams. You are an absolute sight."

"Hmm, so does my new principal give back rubs?" Robbie purred, leaning in to kiss Janet and unintentionally spreading the ash to her partner.

"Mmm, sounds good."

Robbie was a little late arriving at the school to pick up Ryan and Reb. She blamed it on the thunderstorm that was now in progress. Picking up Reb, she ran with Ryan to the car where a very worried Rufus sat with his large orange muzzle pushed through the window that Robbie had left down a bit for him. A soggy group of Williams family members piled into the car and Rufus licked each of his humans in greeting.

"No, Rufus! No, lick," Reb ordered sternly.

Rufus' ears dropped. He looked so pathetic that Ryan reached back and petted his massive, shaggy chest. "It's okay, Rufus. You're a good dog."

Reb smiled up at her massive canine buddy. "Ryan said you are a good dog, Rufus," she bragged.

At the sound of "good dog" Rufus barked happily into Robbie's ear. Her startled reaction almost put their truck in the ditch. "So when does the good part come in?" she grumbled. "I should have left him in a snowbank."

"No, Obbie. Rufus is a good dog," Reb declared, defending her pal from criticism.

Robbie and Ryan laughed. "You're right, Reb. Rufus is a perfect dog," Robbie agreed as she pulled out of the long school driveway and put them on the road for home.

A pair of pale male eyes watched from an old pick-up truck hidden in the brush. On a scrap of paper, a strong hand wrote the time of the Williams' departure in big, clumsy numbers. On the sagging seat beside him was a messy pile of pictures of the Williams family torn from various newspapers. The hand reached up and put the vehicle in gear. It bumped out onto the road and followed at a safe distance. When the Williamses turned off down their lane, the rusted grey truck kept on going.

The storm produced a sudden downpour that lasted only a few minutes and was instantly absorbed into the dry soil, but the sky lit up with lightning. Neon forks crackled across the sky or arced to the ground and sheet lightning lit up the heavens, silhouetting the black rolling clouds.

When the power went off, Robbie lit a fire while Janet got a few oil lamps going. Out of boredom, the kids were teasing Rufus. "Eh! Leave poor Rufus alone," Robbie warned as she poked at the logs irritably, feeling trapped by the storm.

Janet came to the rescue. She had a plate of hotdogs, several long handled forks, a basket of buns, and a bag of marshmallows. The mood in the Williams household immediately improved as they settled to their cook out on the living room floor. When they had all eaten, Janet began to tell them a story.

"The False Faces are spirits of the woods. There are many of them but the most powerful are Broken Nose, Spoon Mouth, and Blower. When you walk in the forest, they will often play tricks on you — tripping you up with a fallen branch hidden under the leaves, placing a muddy puddle under your moccasin, or warning the animals that you have come to hunt.

"Once Manitou and Broken Nose argued about who was the greatest god of the First Nations. Broken Nose took a stick and carved his image into the land. Then he bounced about, bragging about how powerful he was and the greatest of all the False Face spirits. Manitou smiled quietly and raised his hand. Slowly, the earth responded to his command and lifted up high into the sky, forming the great Rocky Mountains.

"Broken Nose was so full of himself that he didn't notice until he turned around and slammed face first into the mountains. That is how he got his broken nose and that is why our masks of him always have a crooked nose. Broken Nose cried a river of tears filling up the holes he had dug and forming the Great Lakes."

Reb's eyes were big with wonder. "That true story, Mommy?"

"It is one variation of an ancient myth," responded Janet, letting her daughter crawl into her arms sleepily.

"I like miffs," Reb concluded.

When Janet came out from tucking Reb into her bed, she found Robbie and Ryan playing poker for pennies by the fire. "Aunt Janet, come and play with us," Ryan called.

Janet smiled but shook her head. "No thanks, Ryan, I never play cards."

"Aw, come on, schoolteacher, live a little," Robbie teased.

"No."

"Afraid of being beaten?" Robbie grinned and poked Ryan, who giggled. "We'll go easy on you, won't we, Ryan?"

Janet stood arms folded tapping her foot. *A lesson is going to have to be taught here.* "Okay." She walked over and joined them on the floor around the sled coffee table. She took the cards from Ryan's hands and shuffled them as quickly as the flash of lightning outside. With a sweep of her hand, she spread the cards out in an even row on the table and pulled out the ace of hearts. With a flip of the last card, the row turned over and Janet swept them up again.

While Robbie and Ryan watched in open-mouthed fascination, Janet reinserted the ace, shuffled, and dropped the deck to the table. The top card flipped up: it was the ace of hearts. She shuffled again and dropped the cards to the table. Remaining in her hand was the ace of spades. Then she reached over and removed the ace of clubs from Ryan's hair.

Lastly, she laid down nine cards in three rows of three cards each. Janet turned over the centre card: it was the ace of diamonds. Picking up the cards to shuffle again, she noted with an evil smile, "You might recall that my grandfather was a professional gambler. Shall we play for who does the chores next month, ladies?"

Robbie looked at her daughter across the table. "Ryan, I think we just got ourselves into a whole lot of trouble."

The game went on for a few hours. Janet would let them win for a while and then quickly win everything back. Throughout, she would perform different card tricks, much to Robbie and Ryan's delight. By the time Ryan said goodnight, she owed her aunt and second mom a life of servitude. When Ryan had gone off to bed, Janet picked up the cards and shuffled them professionally. "Okay, Robbie Williams," she grinned evilly, looking across at her mate, "now we play strip poker."

Janet played to win. The room, warmed by the fire and bathed in soft light, was charged with sexual tension as her lover, with each loss, slowly stripped off an article of clothing as Janet watched with hungry eyes. When she had her lover naked before her, Janet placed the deck on the table and cocked a finger. "Come here, now!" she ordered in a husky whisper. Robbie, her lean muscular body highlighted in red firelight, slipped around the table and into Janet's arms.

Eventually making their way to bed, they made love well into the night, finally falling into a deep, relaxed sleep in the early hours. At five thirty, Robbie's beeper went off.

Janet sighed as she felt her lover slip from the bed and fumble in the darkness, getting into her fire-fighting gear. "Well, at least their timing is getting better. You be careful."

Robbie leaned over to place a kiss on Janet's forehead. "No fire could be as hot as you, my love," she teased, and was gone.

Robbie drank deeply from the water bottle. She was on her second, trying to replenish the water that the work and heat of the fire had sucked out of her. She stood leaning on Larry Butler's bulldozer at the edge of a tired group of Bartlett Volunteer Firefighters.

Bush fires are a bitch, she allowed, wiping at the sweat that had etched black trails of soot down her face. Her skin felt scorched and tight. *I must look like hell. I'd better clean up a bit before heading back to Janet and the kids.*

Blue eyes scanned the firebreak that she and the others had created over the last ninety-six hours. With Pulaski shovels, Council fire rakes, chainsaws and the bulldozer, they had cleared a strip of land through which the fire could not burn. Then they had used Drip Torches. The goosenecked canisters contained wicks that drew up a gasoline/kerosene mixture. They had used those to set back burns to consume the material that the approaching fire would need to feed on. The firebreak had done its job. The fire had been stopped on this front and that meant that the town of Bartlett was now relatively safe. Beyond the brown strip of barren earth, charred trees still smoked and cracked with heat. The ash blanketed the ground like newly fallen snow.

I think most people would find a burnt out area like this an eyesore. I don't. Now that the danger has passed, I like the stark landscape, the soft ash and warm land. I find patterns in the charred wood and the red of glowing embers. I guess I see it with an artist's eye and appreciate this surreal beauty. I like the way it fades in and out in swirls of blue smoke.

Still. It makes me feel good, having done my part to protect lives and property while the fire burned its course.

Robbie finished the second bottle of water and pitched the empty plastic container into the garbage bag tied to the back of the bulldozer. Her stiff, sooty Bunker fire jacket and pants squeaked as she settled into a more comfortable position against the side of the bulldozer. She smiled at the others. The Bartlett crew had become family. Hell, they'd lived in each other's pockets for two weeks as they rotated through shifts with other crews. They had practiced together as a team and had now proven themselves out in the field, trusting each other with their lives.

Do I trust Janet that deeply? Once I did; now I'm not so sure. That bothers me. I know I should trust Janet. Janet risked everything to get me out of jail. Janet loves me and I know that I love that little blonde nearly to distraction. I've made the decision to move on, to leave all the crap of those days behind. Yet there's a little worm of doubt that still burrows through my subconscious.

The rumble of a truck engine drew Robbie's attention from her musings. Like the other tired firefighters around her, she straightened. Fire-tanned and dirty, they reflected the tired pride of all heroic fighters. She smiled as Ryan swung out of the truck and looked around at the sooty faces. Ryan picked her out from all the other smoke eaters and trotted over.

"Hi! Did you have fun?" she asked. "I sure wish I could have fought the fire."

"I don't think fun is quite the word, but I feel pretty smug about being able to help out. That is, when I can summon enough energy to think at all," Robbie confessed.

"I did get to help co-ordinate all the crews. The District Chief would give me the work sheets and I'd get on the radio and dispatch crews to different areas," Ryan bragged excitedly.

Robbie squeezed her daughter's shoulder. "Yeah, I know. I recognized your voice," she acknowledged as they waited their turn to swing up into the back of the truck. "You did a great job!"

Ryan blushed with pride. Pleasing her famous mother meant a lot to her. "Aunt Janet is working at the field centre in the Lions' Hall. They've set up a hospital and field kitchen. The food that we shipped out to the crews was prepared there."

Robbie was instantly concerned. "Hospital? Were there that many hurt?"

"Aunt Janet told me yesterday that they had already treated over fifty."

"Fifty!"

"Well, only nine were humans," Ryan admitted. "The rest are animals that Greta Corry and the Girl Guides keep rescuing. That's their job. We have a deer in a pen in the baseball diamond. Can we keep her, Mom? She's got smoke inhalation."

"Sure. We can have smoked venison next Christmas," Robbie joked.

"Mom!"

As the tired parade of firefighters entered the hall, Janet looked up like she always did, searching for Robbie. She knew her lover had been working on the other side of Indian Gorge and would take her breaks at the Town Hall in Harriston, but she always looked anyway. She missed her partner and worried about her. A major forest fire was a danger-ous situation even for well-trained, experienced firefighters, never mind amateurs like Robbie. Ryan came back each afternoon and told her where Robbie was and what she was doing, but still Janet worried.

Then, there she was, tall and quiet behind Ryan. Wearing her fire gear and covered in dirt and sweat, Janet thought she had never seen anyone look so damn sexy. The other members of the Bartlett crew hugged wives and greeted friends. Ryan went off in search of food and Robbie stood looking uncertain and perplexed.

Janet smiled. They'd been outed by Lucier and the media, so what had she to lose? Putting down the tray she was carrying, she walked over to Robbie and gave her a big hug and a kiss. The wall of silence around them was almost deafening as everyone froze in surprise and stared.

"Hi, love," Janet's voice echoed in the big, quiet room. "I'm so happy to have you back."

Robbie's face lit up with a big goofy grin and the worm that had been digging tun-nels of doubt in her mind shriveled up and died.

The four of them sat at a wooden table in the hall eating Sloppy Joes and drinking choco-late milk while they told their stories. "I got to feed the deer and the cats, and Miss Corry got needles in her hand from the pork-pine and she called it a—"

"Rebecca!" Janet warned with a stern look.

Reb gave her mom a broad grin, then stood on her chair and whispered in Robbie's ear.

Janet frowned.

"Oh, a no good porcupine, eh? Well, that is bad." Robbie laughed, hugging her little daughter. The other Williamses laughed too.

"Hi, ladies," smirked a voice from behind them and a flash went off in their faces as they turned. "Guess who the city papers sent up here to cover the fire? This will make a nice little follow-up to your release, Robbie." Lucier smiled.

Janet grabbed Robbie, but would not have been able to hold her back if it hadn't been for a big meaty hand suddenly wrapping around Lucier's camera and yanking it from his hands.

"Hey!" he protested as his film was ripped out. Lucier's objection was cut short when he was picked up by his collar and the seat of his pants, and carried out the back door to a round of applause from everyone in the room.

There were several decisive thumps and a wail of pain, and then the wall of a man sauntered back into the Lions' Hall. Jim Ableton walked over to the Williams' table. "Don't for the life of me know what this town sees in a queer like you, Williams, but I owed you one for bouncing that kid of yours off the boards at the rink," he growled. "No hard feelings," he said, offering his hand.

Robbie took it, surprised to find her own large hand buried inside Ableton's. "No hard feelings," she agreed, then amended, "until I kick the shit out of your boat in the Bartlett Regatta this September."

"Ain't gonna happen." Ableton laughed, pounded Robbie on the back, and walked away.

Janet gave Robbie a pointed look.

"What?" the director asked innocently.

"You just couldn't let it lie could you?"

"No," the Williamses all answered together, and the table of four broke into gales of laughter.

From across the room, pale eyes looked up, watched for a few seconds, and then dropped once more to an empty plate. *Soon now. This damn fire has delayed my plans but soon now everything will be back to normal. Then I can put my plan into action.* The man smiled.

The Williams crew headed home. Ryan amused Reb while Janet took Robbie for a shower and then tucked her into bed. Robbie, warmed by the water and relaxed by Janet's touch, was asleep almost before her head hit the pillow. Janet watched TV with the kids, sending each off to bed at her respective bedtime. Then she gladly locked the door, turned off the lights, and crawled into the bed that she planned on sharing with Robbie for the rest of her life.

The next day, Robbie slept in and Janet took the kids to school. "I should be working," Ryan sulked. "They need me on the radios."

"You need to be in class," Janet answered firmly. "We only just got you enrolled again and then you were away for another two weeks. Honestly, what sort of mother are they going to think I am?"

"I had to fight the fire," Ryan argued. "I'm part of the crew."

Janet smiled and patted the teen's knee. "I know, love. But the fire is almost out and most of the crews have been sent home. It's only burning along the shoreline near the gorge now. I think they can manage without you."

Janet dropped Ryan and Reb off outside of the school, courage failing her when it came to walking into the building that she had once thought of as her domain. Ryan seemed to understand and made no comment as she took her little sister's hand and, waving good-bye, disappeared into the building. Janet watched them go, then shifted the truck into gear and headed back to the house. She was glad now that Robbie had insisted that Reb stay at daycare while they worked on putting their life back together. Fortunately, Milka, the new principal, had no problem with allowing Reb to stay in the school's program, even though Janet no longer worked there.

Another lazy day with Robbie sounds just about perfect. Maybe this being unemployed isn't so bad after all.

"Hey, about time you got back," Robbie called from the kitchen as she chewed on a piece of burned toast.

Janet waved her hand in front of her face and squinted her eyes as she looked through the smoke. "Did you bring some of the brush fire home with you or have you been cooking again?" she asked dryly.

"I burned the toast." Robbie smiled, happily crunching on the burnt offering.

"Well, don't eat it," Janet scolded as she opened a window to air the place out. "There is enough smoke in your lungs already. Here, sit down and I'll make a proper breakfast for both of us."

"I love you." Robbie smiled, kissing Janet on the forehead as she changed places with her in the kitchen. Robbie sat on a bar stool and watched while Janet made scrambled eggs and toast. "You know what?"

"What?" Janet dished the eggs over the golden toast she had made.

"The lodge is ready. You want to go over and have a look?"

Janet looked up into eyes glistening with excitement and smiled. Robbie was just a big kid at heart. She kissed the end of her lover's nose. "I'd like that."

They ate quickly and left the dishes in the sink while they went to get the canoe out of the shed where it had been stored for the winter. They lowered it into the lake and clambered in. "You remember the first time we did this?" Robbie asked.

"Uh huh. You'd twisted your knee slipping on Reb's rubber ducky and I was stuck with you. As I recall, oh wanton woman, you made a shameless play for my ex-boyfriend."

"Did you a favour." Robbie grinned without remorse. "You'd have ditched him anyway."

They canoed on in silence, listening to the steady swish of the paddle through the water and the cry of a raven in the trees. "I think I loved you from the moment I saw you," Robbie confessed suddenly.

"You had a funny way of showing it." Janet laughed, then relented. "I know I was very attracted to you."

Robbie suddenly stood up in the bow, turned around and walked back in the canoe, causing it to rock wildly in the water. Janet hurriedly used the flat of her paddle to try and maintain their balance. "Robbie! What are you doing?"

Robbie knelt down and leaned across the thwart to take Janet's hands. "You are the single most important thing in my life. When you came into my world, my black and white existence exploded into Technicolor. I love you, Janet Williams, with every ounce of my being."

Janet settled her paddle into the canoe. Then, carefully, she slid over on top of Robbie as they dropped into the bottom of the canoe. They lay there together, drifting slowly in the wind as the blue sky and warm sun blanketed them in peace.

A little later, Janet turned around and around in the living room at the newly refurbished lodge. "Oh, Robbie! It's...it's beautiful!" The massive room was dominated by a fieldstone fireplace that now — after being sandblasted — reflected the multiple colours of the earth. The huge log beams that stretched above the room shone like honey with several coats of fresh varnish. The log walls were the soft cream of natural wood and the floor was so highly polished they could see themselves in it.

"Probably could do with some furniture," Robbie observed philosophically.

Janet reached up to capture yet another kiss. "You are wonderful. Show me our bedroom," she whispered.

Their room was at the corner of the house. One large window looked out over tall pines to the lake itself, while the other framed trees and a small stream tumbling down the hillside over mossy rocks to feed the lake. Janet peeked into the walk-in closet and the master bathroom that had a sauna, and a sunken tub built for two beside a window of one-way glass that looked over a shaded hillside of white and purple trilliums. Tears slid slowly down her face as Robbie wrapped her close.

"It's like a dream. It is all true, isn't it, Robbie?" Janet sniffed into her favourite shoulder.

"You bet it is, lover. I'm going to move my family here and live the picture-perfect life with you at my side."

Janet looked up. "What about my house? I don't want to sell it to strangers and I don't want it to stand empty, either."

"I was thinking about that. You know it would make a good summer place for Elizabeth. She likes how clearly she can see the stars up here and—"

"Robbie! You are a genius. It would make a perfect wedding present for David and Elizabeth!"

The exuberance faded as Robbie went cold and still. "What wedding?" asked a deep, deadly quiet voice.

Janet looked up into storm-dark eyes and reached up on her tiptoes to kiss stiff lips. "I think that David and Elizabeth's friendship, if left alone, will blossom into a very special kind of love, and you know that David would want to do the honourable thing."

"You are just saying this to scare the shit out of me," rumbled Robbie.

"No, I'm saying this so you have lots of time to get used to the idea," Janet countered.

Robbie sulked. "I won't."

Janet gave her overprotective wife a hug. "Yes, you will, once you realize that David makes Elizabeth happy. The dark times are over, Robbie. You can move on and Bethy needs to, as well. Come on, worry wart. We need to get back and clean up that kitchen."

Chapter 18

"Ryan, over here," called Debbie, as Ryan moved the soccer ball down field. With a swift sidekick, Ryan shot the ball across to her friend, who drilled it into the net.

"Way to go, Deb," Ryan said, running up to pat her school chum on the back.

"Thanks!"

"Okay, girls, time to head for the locker room," called Jean Bissell, who had been hired to fill Milka Gorski's teaching position.

The two teams walked off the field, replaying the game and teasing each other. Ryan waved over at Reb and the other young children, who were going for their morning walk down the driveway with Mrs. Chen. An old grey truck pulled out from the school parking lot and drove slowly down the lane. It went past the children, and then stopped.

Ryan watched curiously as the man got out and walked over to talk to Mrs. Chen. The next instant, he hit her, knocking her to the ground, grabbed Reb into his arms, and was running for the open truck door.

Ryan started to run. She angled across the field at top speed. As the truck slowed to make the turn out onto the main road, she came alongside, grabbed hold of the truck's side and did a pony-express mount into the flatbed.

Lily Chen sat up and dazedly watched the grey truck disappear down the road as the other students and Jean Bissell ran over to help her and to gather up the remaining children.

The police and a distraught Milka Gorski were waiting on the beach as Janet and Robbie paddled across the lake. Janet could feel the panic and anger rolling off her mate when she saw the police.

"It's okay, Robbie, don't be upset. You have been declared innocent; they are not here to arrest you," she reassured her partner. Paddling in the bow, Robbie nodded stiffly but did not answer.

Despite the reassurance she **had** given Robbie, she could feel her own insides turning over with worry. For Milka **to be** there, something serious must have happened at school and that meant that one of **their** daughters was in trouble.

Robbie leapt out of the canoe **and** pulled the craft high up on the beach before helping Janet out. "What's going on?" she demanded, holding Janet's hand as she faced the police.

It was Milka who answered. "Janet, Robbie — I'm so sorry. Reb's been kidnapped. It happened when Lily was walking the children down the lane. A truck pulled up and the driver got out and hit Lily, grabbed Rebecca, and drove off."

"Is Lily all right?" Janet asked, her voice shaky in response to the gut-wrenching blow to her emotions that Milka's news had dealt.

"Yes, but—"

"Where's Ryan?" Robbie demanded.

Milka looked sick. "She was out on the field playing soccer and witnessed the kidnapping. She ran after the truck and swung into the flatbed as the truck slowed to turn out on the road. He's got both of them."

"Shit!" Robbie groaned, pulling her shocked wife close to her. "Don't worry, Janet, we'll get them back. He'll demand money and we'll give it to him, whatever he wants."

The adults walked up to the cabin and Robbie let them in. Rufus greeted them with an uncertain wag of his crooked tail and a low growl as the faithful animal sensed their stress. "Shhh, Rufus," Janet whispered, reaching out a shaky hand to reassure the huge animal.

"I'll use the cell phone to contact our lawyers. We'll want to leave the cabin line free in case he phones."

Janet sat on the edge of the couch and looked up at her partner. "W-what if his motivation was not kidnapping. W-what if he's..."

"Don't even think it. Let's plan for what we can deal with and pray that it's nothing worse." Robbie rubbed her lover's back. "It's going to be okay, Janet," she said reassuringly. "It's got to be." But inside, she felt like a bomb had exploded.

Milka returned to the school and ran pictures of Reb and Ryan on the photocopier. The teachers handed them out to anyone they could find working in the vicinity. Friends quietly came and went from the cabin during the day, bringing casseroles, sympathy, and their love. Meals were warmed and served, lawns cut, dishes done, and innumerable cups of tea consumed. Janet and Robbie ate little, talked less, and were unaware of much of the quiet support that was going on around them. They were grateful not to be alone, yet too overcome with horror to interact with those around them. Mostly, they sat together on the couch, holding hands and waiting for the phone to ring, but it never did. The hours ticked on endlessly.

The province-wide evening television news broadcasted the children's pictures and requested the public's help. The national and international news services were pouring into Bartlett seeking stories about the famous Williams family and the kidnapping. And that evening, *The National Tabloid* even ran a front-page story about "The Curse of the Williams Family".

Disgusted, Moe Singh removed the tabloids from his store and from David Potts' grocery store that he and his staff were manning while David was in Toronto with his brother. The town rallied around Janet and Robbie, protecting them from the media. They had learned a lot since the spring about dealing with the press. By common agreement, no one talked. Other than that, there was little anyone could do at this stage but wait.

To the south, the fire barrier that Robbie and the Bartlett Fire Department had cleared had checked the leading edge of the fire. But to the west, along the shoreline of Lake Superior, a flank fire still stubbornly edged forward, feeding on the high temperatures and dry air. It was hoped that the natural firebreak of Indian Gorge would stop the fire. Still, the Bartlett Volunteer Fire Department had been called out again that afternoon, and as a precaution, they assisted in the evacuation of The Bartlett School for the Gifted. They were stationed there now, to protect the school building should the flank fire not be checked.

Janet and Robbie were aware of all that, and it added to their worry. Somewhere out there, the children were being held prisoner. They could only pray that they were at least safe from the fire. The police force was stretched to its limits in dealing with the extra responsibilities of the fire emergency. And that meant virtually no one was officially assigned to look for the two missing children.

Late in the night the last of their friends left, and Janet and Robbie were alone. Janet sat staring into the fire, her mind numb with shock. She tried not to think about what might have been done to her daughters. Robbie was right; they had to look on this as a kidnapping and not let the panic of uglier possibilities take over in their hearts and minds. It was hard, though. It was terribly hard. The house was so empty and quiet without the girls. Half the fabric of their existence had been ripped from their world, stolen away in the blink of an eye. Tears rolled silently down Janet's face. It was not knowing that was the worst. *Why the hell doesn't the bastard phone?*

Robbie had slept some, sitting by Janet on the couch and holding her tight. She woke before dawn, however, and paced back and forth. She refused to let her mind dwell on what might have been done to her daughters. If she had, she would have gone mad. Instead, she used her reasoning, trying to design a course of action. There had to be a way to help her girls. There just had to be.

Janet woke from a fretful sleep, aware that Robbie had stopped pacing. The tall woman turned as Janet sat up and blue eyes met green. "He turned left onto Highway 11. Ryan wouldn't panic, she'd use her head, and that means there is a good chance that she left a trail for us to follow."

"What?" Janet got to her feet.

"I'm sure of it. There will be a trail. Ryan is no fool." Robbie got out the cell phones and checked the batteries. "I'm going out to look. You stay here and wait for that bastard to phone. I'll report back every half hour."

"Robbie, be careful!"

Robbie nodded, pulled Janet into her arms for a hug, and kissed her head. "We'll find them, I promise," she whispered, and was gone.

Janet stood at the screen door and watched her soulmate back the truck around and head down the driveway. If anyone could find their girls, she had no doubt it would be Robbie. Pulling herself together, she got out paper and pen and made a list of questions to ask if the kidnapper did phone. She planned for different scenarios and worked out how she would handle each one. Robbie and the girls were counting on her and she meant to handle the situation to the best of her ability in the event that the kidnapper phoned. With the positive action, her spirits rose. Robbie was right; they were going to get their girls back.

Robbie parked the truck on the shoulder of Highway 11. Taking her flashlight and phone, she started walking. Half a mile down the road, she found a small square of blue and gold cotton tied around an old rusty bolt. Blue and gold were the Bartlett school colours. *What had Milka said? Ryan had been out in the field playing soccer. Could this be part of a sports bib that Ryan had been wearing to identify which team she was on?*

She flipped her phone open. Janet answered on the first ring. "I might have found something. I won't be able to tell until I go further down the road. I found a small piece of striped cotton in the Bartlett school colours—"

"Part of a sports bib?" Janet interrupted excitedly.

"Maybe. Ryan might be dropping them out of the truck. I'll go on down the road and see if I can find more. You phone Jean Bissell and see if Ryan was wearing one during the soccer game."

"Okay. The kidnapper hasn't phoned. The fire has jumped the gorge and is spreading toward the school. You be careful," Janet reported quickly, not wanting to hold Robbie on the phone.

"I've got my fire gear in the truck. I'll be careful. I love you." Robbie snapped the phone shut, marked the place where she had found the material with a small pile of stones, then broke into a run back to the truck.

Moving slowly along the side of the road, Robbie used her high beams to search the shoulder ahead of her in the predawn light. Had she missed it? It would be easy to do so in the poor light or if the bolt had bounced or rolled into the bush. Should she turn back or go on? Then she saw it.

She pulled the truck to a stop and got out. Another torn piece of material tied to an old bolt about a kilometre down from where she had found the first one. She smiled and bent to make another pile of stones. *Way to go, Ryan.*

Janet reached for the phone and had the receiver to her ear before the first ring had died away. "Hi. I found another one. Ryan is leaving a trail, alright," came Robbie's voice, sounding confident and proud.

Robbie's voice spread like a cooling lotion over Janet's stress. "Jean said she was wearing a blue and gold striped bib," Janet confirmed. "The fire is out of control, Robbie. They managed to save the buildings at Bartlett by pumping water directly out of the lake and onto the structures, but the woods around it are gone. It's spreading in a long finger along the shore heading north. I can smell the smoke here."

Robbie's worry split in two. "Are you safe?"

"Yes, as long as the wind doesn't shift. If it does, I'll head into Bartlett, I'll leave a message on our house phone with our cell number in case the kidnapper phones. George Drouillard is organizing the Lions' Club in case they have to evacuate Bartlett."

"Go if you need to get out. Don't stay there too long," ordered Robbie.

She knew it was useless to ask the same of Robbie as long as their girls were missing. The best she could do was to not become another distraction for her love. "I won't."

The trail led Robbie back to Long Lake Road. *The son of a bitch had the nerve to take the road right past our house.* Robbie cursed and followed along the lane, her eyes beating back and forth, looking for scraps of material. At the fork, Robbie found one of Ryan's socks. The truck had turned left away from the long driveway leading to their cabin and headed down past the lodge toward the end of Long Lake. The lane, Robbie knew, would join the Lakefront Road where Larry and Flo Butler lived, which was right in the path of the advancing fire.

"Janet, I'm near you, love. It looks like the bastard took them down Long Lake Road and then cut west. I think he must have headed up towards Lakefront Road. I just found one of Ryan's socks. She must have run out of bib."

"Robbie, that area is on fire."

"Yeah, well, our kids are up there. I'll keep reporting back to you." Robbie snapped the phone shut. She was not going to let Ryan down again, not even if she had to go to hell and back.

Robbie could see the orange glow of the fire to her left as she turned right onto the Lakefront Road. She came to a stop and got out into air made heavy with blue smoke. In the middle of the road was the other sock. Robbie set her jaw and got back in the truck and headed off again. *Close now*, she thought; she could feel it.

Ryan had hit the truck bed with a thud that knocked the wind out of her. Curling into a ball, she'd huddled under the back window so that she would not make an easy target and tried to get air back into her lungs. *Funny, it seems so easy when I see people in Mom's movies do that,* she mused, rubbing her bruised knees. She licked her dry lips and fought back the fear that flooded through her body along with a rush of adrenaline.

What would Mom do? She'd leave signals. Ryan ducked her head out of her sports bib and with shaking hands, tore it into bits. *I sure hope the school is going to be reasonable about this,* she thought. Wrecking or losing sports equipment was almost a capital offence at Bartlett. She could almost hear Bissell going on about the three R's of the equipment room: Respect, Responsibility, and Return. With a shrug of resignation, the fourth R in Ryan's opinion, she tied the first piece of cloth to a rusty old bolt that she had picked from a soggy cardboard box in the flatbed. Hoping that the driver would not notice, she tossed the first marker over the side of the truck. She looked up and through the back window of the cab, big blue worried eyes looked down at her. Ryan managed a smile and waved at Reb. She could see her sister mouth her name but the roar of the old truck drowned out any sound.

The driver turned and swore, grabbing Reb by the arm and pulling her out of sight, but not before Ryan saw the pain in her little sister's face and the tears that sprang to Reb's eyes. Anger boiled inside Ryan's guts. *No! Stay calm. Reason,* she ordered herself. *That's what Mom would do.* She prepared another marker and threw it over the side. *Whatever you are up to, you are not going to win, you bastard.*

Ryan had gone through her pieces of bib and had thrown out both socks as they bumped along. She could smell the fire as she threw her last sock over the side. She thought she could see heavier smoke snaking through the trees to the south. *Oh shit. This is not good!*

Instead of tossing the last sock over the side as she had done the other markers, she balled the fabric up and tossed it off the back so that it lay on the road and not the shoulder. If the fire did come this way, maybe the fire wouldn't burn the marker if it was on the road. For the first time, Ryan's fear grew as she realized that she and Reb were in very deep trouble with no one to help them out.

Ryan swallowed hard and took a deep breath. *Stay calm. Stay focused. What should I throw next? Not my shoes, I might need them if we get a chance to run. Not my clothes if I can avoid it; that would be asking for trouble with a jerk like this. Okay, first the watch, then I'll rip the pocket and collar off my shirt.*

She grabbed onto the side of the truck with one hand as they bounced off Lakefront Road and onto a rutted track through the bush. Quickly, Ryan threw her watch over the back of the truck, hoping that someone would see the entrance to the trail. *Okay, Ryan, you must be getting close to the place where this guy is taking you. No one is here to help you and Reb, so think of what to do next.* Her green eyes serious, she surveyed the dirty truck bed and its contents. In a partly-broken quart basket, she saw a number of rusty tools.

Ryan crawled over and searched through awkwardly as the truck bounced over the rutted trail. Her hand closed around a long, heavy iron wrench. She knew she could not overpower the man once he was out of the truck. The only time he was going to be vulnerable was when he opened the truck door and led with his head as he got out. She had to be ready to hit him then. *No hesitating, no checking the swing, just hit him,* she coached herself. Her hand ached from the tension in her muscles as she held the wrench tightly. She could smell the rancid stench of her own fear as the sweat trickled down her back.

The truck slowed and backfired. It turned slightly and came to a jerky stop in front of an old rundown trailer. For a second, there was silence. Ryan braced herself. The door of the truck creaked open and Ryan saw an unkempt mat of greying hair. She hesitated, then struck the man's head a glancing blow with the iron wrench.

The kidnapper cried out in pain and he lashed out at her. The blow caught Ryan on the bridge of the nose and filled her eyes with tears. "You fucking bitch!" the man yelled, grabbing Ryan by the hair and pulling her over the side of the truck. She landed with a thud on the ground and the wind was knocked from her lungs.

"You get out of the truck," the man ordered, and Reb was crying as she was dragged from the floor of the cab.

Ryan forced herself to her knees and Reb squirmed from the man's grasp and fell crying into her big sister's arms. "Shhh, it will be okay, Reb. You'll see. Our moms will find us. I know they will." Even as she tried to reassure the small terrified child, Ryan was sure that she had never been so scared. Her hand shook as she stroked Reb's dark locks. She looked up to see the angry man towering over them, rubbing his ear.

"You're going to get yours before this is over, you bitch," the man vowed, as he grabbed Ryan roughly by the arm and pulled her to her feet. He half dragged, half carried them to the trailer and pushed them inside.

Ryan's heart was now pounding in her chest. She realized that by leaping on the truck, she could very well have put herself in a situation were she could be raped and murdered. Her eyes searched the small shabby interior for a weapon and she tried to think past her fear to what she should do next.

"Mommy! I want my mommy!" Reb sobbed.

"You take that brat and get in the washroom. You make her stop crying, you hear, or I'm going to make her stop. You got me?" the kidnapper snarled.

Ryan nodded and wrapped Reb closer as she backed toward the closet sized washroom. She stepped in and closed the door, not sure if she should be relieved to have a door between them and the kidnapper, or more concerned because she was now trapped with no escape. She could hear the man wedging something against the door. For the time being, anyway, they were safe.

She sat down on the cracked toilet seat and tried to think of what to do next. "Hush, Reb, you've got to be quiet so we don't make the bad man mad. Hush," she whispered. Reb stifled her tears slowly and clung to Ryan as tightly as she could.

When Reb was calmer, Ryan took stock of her surroundings. The small space barely had room for a toilet and a small sink with a storage area below it. There was a yellowed window, but it was too small for Ryan to squeeze through. She might be able to push Reb through, but then what would the small child do? She could smash through the aluminum wall, but the man would hear her and, no doubt, would stop her in a way that she would regret. She bent around Reb's small body and looked under the sink. A piece of dried, cracked soap, a balled up stiff piece of rag, and a rusted can of insect spray were all that were there.

Reb whimpered a protest as Ryan reached to grab the can. "Shhh, it's okay, Reb. I think we've got a way out of here." She shook the can and sprayed into the sink. Her heart pounded with relief as she realized that the can still had lots of pressure and repellent in it. It wasn't exactly pepper spray, but it would buy them some time.

They sat there the whole night — cramped, hungry, and miserable. The reek of the toilet was nauseating and there wasn't even water in the tap. The smell of frying bacon and eggs that evening added to their misery. Dressed only in her light gym outfit, Ryan was shivering with cold and fear by the time the sun started to rise. Several times the evening before, she had heard the man's angry voice. She couldn't make out the words, but it sounded like he was arguing with someone on a phone. That meant he might not be working alone. Ryan knew, now that it was light again, that she was going to have to act quickly before any other kidnappers arrived.

"Hey! My sister is sick. Hey! Come on! You've got to do something," Ryan yelled. She held the can of insect spray in her hand and winked at Reb, who sat wide-eyed with fear on top of the sink cabinet where Ryan had put her.

Ryan heard the barrier being moved and the man, looking angry and rumpled with sleep, opened the door. Ryan reached out and sprayed the insect repellent directly into the man's eyes, then she kicked him aside with her foot and wiggled past him. She looked around wildly, saw the dirty cast iron frying pan still sitting on the cold propane burner, and grabbed it. No hesitation this time, she slammed the kneeling man over the head as hard as she could. He didn't even moan; he just dropped to the floor.

Stepping over him, she scooped Reb from her perch in the cramped bathroom and made for the door. She ran to the truck and slipped a startled Reb along the seat. "Don't worry, Reb. We're out of here." Ryan smiled and reached for the ignition. *No keys! Oh shit.*

"Hang on, Reb. I just have to see to something." Ryan smiled at her sister and forced herself to step back out of the safety of the truck. Her nerves were at a breaking point as she silently stepped up into the trailer. She expected that at any minute the angry man would pounce on her. She stood in the doorway and surveyed the space. No keys. She couldn't see him putting them away in a drawer, and since it was clear he had slept in his clothes, it was likely that he had the keys in his pocket. Ryan edged forward and looked over the small counter.

The man lay on his belly on the floor of the trailer, his head to one side and his mouth partly open. Drool dribbled down the prickly facial hair on his chin. *What if he grabs me?* Ryan thought, as she slowly knelt beside the man. Her heart was pounding in her chest. *If he moves, I'm going to have a heart attack and die right here.*

She felt his pocket. The keys were a hard lump beneath the material. *I wonder if I killed him. Oh my God, I'm a murderer and now I'm robbing a corpse.* Swallowing her disgust, she wiggled her hand into the pocket and pulled out the keys. Then, quick as a jackrabbit, she hopped out of the trailer and ran for the truck again. Shaking with fear, she slammed the door shut and put the keys in the ignition, turning the key with trembling fingers. The engine turned over and died.

Oh God! I'm going to wet myself. Ryan moaned silently, as the sweat ran down her neck. *Calm. Don't panic or you'll flood the engine,* she commanded herself. She pressed down on the gas and turned the key. This time the engine caught. Crying with relief, Ryan turned the truck around and headed back down the trail, leaving the still body of their kidnapper on the floor of the old trailer.

Robbie turned back, fighting the panic that was growing in her heart. Somehow she had lost Ryan's trail. By now, she should have found another marker. Either she had missed it or Ryan was no longer able to leave a trail. That thought made her heart convulse. With the back of her hand, she wiped the sweat from her upper lip. *Christ! This is a thousand times worse than being in prison.*

Now in front of her, she could see the head of the fire. Blue-black smoke billowed into the sky and fire blazed behind. While she stared, a tree caught and a ribbon of flame raced up the trunk and set the branches into a blaze of fire. *How far away? Maybe a few miles. Time is running out.* Then she saw it — a narrow, overgrown trail to her left. She stopped her truck in the middle of the road and got out. A vehicle had gone down there recently. The weeds and grass were flattened into two tracks from the tires. A flash caught her eyes and bending, she picked Ryan's watch from a clump of tall grass.

Setting her jaw, Robbie turned and ran back to the truck. She slammed the vehicle into gear and turned into the brush path, bouncing along as fast as she dared. Rounding a corner, she came bumper to bumper with a beat up old Chevy. She was out of her truck in a split second and was pulling the driver from the truck in near blind anger when realized that she had hold of her daughter. "Ryan! Love! Are you all right? Did he hurt you? Where's Reb?"

"No, I'm okay. Reb's in there. She's okay too, but scared," Ryan sighed from the safety of her mother's arms.

Robbie pushed Ryan gently away. "We're in trouble. Get Reb out and into our truck. Where does this road go?"

"It's a dead end. It goes to an old trailer," Ryan said as she fished Reb out from the floor of the truck. Reb slid from Ryan's arms into Robbie's.

"Obbie! I want to go home. I want my mommy!" the little girl wailed.

"It's okay, Reb. We're all going home," Robbie soothed, as she listened to the phone in her hand connect. It was answered right away.

"Robbie?"

"Yeah."

"Where are you? What have you been doing? I've been so worried. You've got to get out of there."

"I've got them, Janet. Both of them," she cut in, half crying with relief. She held up the phone to Reb's ear.

"Mommy! Mommy! You come get me, Mommy. I want to go home!" Reb cried.

Robbie pulled the phone away from the frightened child. She could hear Janet crying and trying to soothe her daughter at the other end. "Listen, Janet, we're in a real fix here. The fire is only about two miles behind us. There is no going back. I'm on a track off to the east of Lakefront Road. Ryan said it comes to a dead end and there is an old trailer down there. Do you know the spot?"

Janet fought the rising panic, and when she spoke, her voice was surprisingly calm and controlled. "Yes, I know it. Lakefront dead-ends about ten kilometres farther on and the fire is likely to catch up to you. It seems to be fingering along the shoreline, pushed by a wind out of the south. So far it has only spread about a kilometre inland. They are evacuating Bartlett, though. Listen, Robbie, go back to the trailer and head due east. Follow the ravine. It will lead you to Beaver Creek. I'll meet you there with the canoe and we'll paddle back down to Long Lake. Hurry, Robbie. There's very little time," Janet finished, the fear cracking through into her voice.

"We're on our way. Don't worry, Janet; we'll meet you at the creek." Robbie snapped the phone shut and swung into action. "You two get in our truck," Robbie commanded as she got into the old grey vehicle and reversed it into the brush. She threw the keys into the undergrowth as she ran to their truck and jumped into the driver's seat. She rammed the truck into drive and bolted forward.

"He's down there. I...I hit him on the head with an iron frying pan. I...I think I killed him, Mom." Ryan's voice was shaky, and she buried her face into Reb's neck and hugged her little sister close.

Robbie couldn't risk looking away from the rough path, but she nodded, reached out and squeezed Ryan's knee. "You did what you had to do to save Reb and yourself. I'm proud of you. Don't worry," she reassured.

They broke clear of the trail and came out into the overgrown clearing that had hidden the dilapidated trailer. "He's in there," Ryan exclaimed. "He was lying on the floor."

Robbie nodded an acknowledgement, but was intent on following Janet's directions. She saw the ravine sloping down behind a canted outhouse and drove directly toward it. The truck smashed through the flimsy structure and sailed down the steep embankment into an empty flood gorge. Robbie wheeled the truck around on the opposite bank and dropped it down onto the dry riverbed. Popping the transmission into low gear, she moved steadily forward, smashing through fallen branches and thumping over rocks.

Ryan held on tight to Reb and tried to protect her head as they were thrown about violently inside the cab. "Shit, Mom, the owner of this truck is going to be pissed," Ryan observed dryly, as branches scraped the paint off the sides and they left their muffler behind on a rock.

"Don't swear. And the owner is good and pissed, believe me," Robbie responded with a playful growl.

They traveled on for several kilometres until the truck stuck fast in mud. "Out!" ordered Robbie.

Ryan did as she was told as quickly as possible with Reb clinging to her in silent fear.

Robbie ran to the back of the truck and slipped into her fire gear. She dumped the supplies from her knapsack onto the ground and used her jackknife to cut the corners out of the bottom of the canvas bag. "Here, turn around," she said to Ryan and slipped the knapsack onto her daughter's back. Then she lifted the now screaming toddler from Ryan's arms and stuffed the stiff child none too gently into the makeshift baby carrier.

Robbie rubbed Reb's head and looked into her little daughter's eyes. "Reb, I know this is scary, but it is okay. We're going to find your mommy now. You be good for Obbie, okay?"

Reb's big eyes were fearful and brimming with tears, but she nodded silently. Robbie smiled and dropped another kiss on the child's head. "Ryan, I'll carry the gear; you follow with Reb. The wind is coming around to the east. We are in big trouble. Let's move!"

Ryan did not need any more encouragement. She followed her mom at a quick pace down the dry, rugged ravine.

Janet phoned Milka to let her know what was going on, then she got the first aid kit and some other needed equipment and ran for the canoe. Using powerful strokes, she drove the canoe swiftly through the water along the east side of Long Lake, turned in to Moose Swamp, and steered through the lily pads until she got to where Beaver Creek drained into the bog.

Thank God the creek is fairly deep and slow moving, she thought as she pushed on. Even with the dry weather, the creek still was about four metres wide and one deep. *Hang on, Robbie, I'm coming.* Gritting her teeth, she gave it everything she had to move the canoe upstream.

The sweat dripped steadily down Janet's face and the muscles in her arms burned with effort. *How far have I come? Maybe four or five kilometres.* The smoke had turned the world around her into a blur and the air felt thick in her lungs. Stopping, she took out one of the towels she had brought, wet it in the creek, and wrapped it around her nose and mouth. A sudden draft of wind stirred around her and the woods ahead crackled and snapped like a bonfire.

Janet looked up in horror as the tops of the trees, visible beneath the rising smoke, flashed into flame one after the other. *My God, the trees are crowning. It's a firestorm.* The wind was blowing furiously now, and the air she sucked in was oven hot. A few kilometres ahead of her, where she knew her family waited, the fire had become a solid wall. She watched, mesmerized by the sheer power of the force Nature was unleashing ahead of her. *Oh God, what have I led them into?*

The fire roared and swirled in licking tongues of orange and red, devouring trees and sucking the air from the defenceless forest. Animals charged in panic, their natural foes forgotten as they fled from one of Nature's greatest enemies. Flaming trees and branches crashed down, spreading a carpet of fiery death that rolled out across the brush. It was hypnotic and terrifying, powerful and mad. Only a few kilometres in front of Janet, the world had become a scene from Dante's inferno. And somewhere within it was her family.

Ten minutes later, the worst was over. Ahead of her, where less than half an hour before there had been a green forest, the blackened remnants of hundreds of years of growth now burned slowly. Janet felt numb. Her mind refused to deal with the enormity of what she had just witnessed and the consequences to her family if they had been caught in the conflagration.

Like a robot, she picked up her paddle and moved the canoe forward toward the devastated wasteland. Her arms stung as she stroked. Looking at her hands with disinterested eyes, she noticed that her skin was red and scorched. The realization did not cause any reaction, but was simply a disconnected observation. Her shock at what had just happened was too great. With stubborn determination, she did the only thing that she could think to do. She went on.

Sometime later, she was in the burnt-out path of the fire's passing. Around her, through the veil of smoke, fires still burned in patches and trees smouldered, cracked and twisted in the heat. Her world had been reduced to black and white, like a fussy old TV. Painfully, she tore another towel into strips and wet them in the blackened water, using them to awkwardly wrap her blistered hands. Then she picked up her paddle and moved on. *Not far now. The ravine is less than a kilometre ahead.*

It was slow going. Burned and burning branches and tree trunks had fallen across the creek. Some she slid under, but she was forced to pull the canoe over to negotiate others. More burns, more delay; tears now stained her sooty face. Still, she moved on.

It was after one such portage that she looked up and her heart simply ceased to beat. A low, agonizing groan escaped her. There, lying on the bank of the river, one arm outstretched over the water, were the blackened, fire eaten remains of a person. Janet stared in horror at the charred bones, the raw meat and black cavities. *Someone tall. Robbie.* With staggering steps, she forced herself forward, leaving the canoe wedged against the ashy shore.

Her whole body shook with cold shock. She made herself look. A belt buckle, remains of shoes. *Men's shoes. It isn't Robbie.* Janet's lungs sucked in air through the damp, dirty towel. *I'm sorry, whoever you are, but thank you, God. Thank you. It isn't Robbie.* She stumbled back to the canoe through the knee high water. Grabbing the gunnels, she half pulled, half floated the craft past the burnt remains and continued on her way.

She had seen evidence of what she was likely to find, but still she went on. They were her family.

Robbie and Ryan hurried on. They had only stopped long enough for Robbie to tear her shirt to bits and wrap the strips around their noses and mouths. Reb had gone quiet and didn't look well. Robbie was very worried. When she looked back, she could see the orange glow of flames, though still off in the distance. Then ahead, she saw the trees thinning. They must be close to Beaver Creek.

The attack came from her right, sending her crashing into the embankment. She looked up just in time to see a man swinging a heavy stick at her head. She ducked and took the blow on her shoulder. Her heavy Bunker jacket had just enough padding to prevent a broken collarbone, but the pain still drove Robbie to her knees.

Ryan managed to slip off the knapsack in which she was carrying Reb and place her sister on the ground, then she made a flying tackle at the man's knees. He went down with a curse. Robbie was up in a second and helped Ryan pin the kidnapper to the ground.

It was the wind suddenly switching direction that warned Robbie. The fire behind them was sucking in the air, building towards a firestorm. The air was heating rapidly. "Run! Run for the creek!" she screamed, pulling Ryan up and pushing her forward. She grabbed Reb in her arms and ran after her older daughter.

They broke into the open on the bank of the creek. *Maybe three metres wide and half a metre deep. Not much, but our only chance,* Robbie evaluated. She pulled a package from her pocket and ripped it open and pulled out a fire tent. It was only large enough for the girls. She didn't need to say anything to Ryan and Reb. They had practiced with her many times, both at the station and in their own living room.

Ryan took the tent and splashed into the water, where she tucked her feet under the elastic edging of the fire shield. She dropped into the water and pulled the thin protection over her, holding the elastic edging down with her hands. It created a small pocket of air for breathing until they would have to duck under the water completely. Robbie knelt down and tucked Reb underneath, trusting Ryan to do what was needed to try and protect her little sister. She herself would rely on her firefighter's gear to afford her as much protection as possible.

The smoke thickened quickly, nearly blinding Robbie. The air became superheated and before she took a deep breath and ducked under the water, she was startled as the empty blanket bag that she still held in her hand burst into flame from the pure heat in the air.

It was hard to stay under the shallow water. Even with her eyes closed, Robbie was aware that the swampy water around her glowed orange, reflecting the savage fire rolling over them. Her back and legs stung as they caught the impact of the blast-furnace heat.

She struggled to get deeper in the soot-filled water. Her lungs ached. She held her nose and breathed in, as she had been trained to do, forcing the oxygen that remained in her mouth and throat down into her lungs, then released her nose and exhaled just a little bit to get some of the building carbon dioxide out of her system. She was in unimaginable pain and could feel herself close to blacking out. *Please God, let Ryan and Reb live.*

Ryan pulled Reb under her as she had been taught and Reb dutifully clung to her big sister's neck. "When I tell you, Reb, take a deep breath and don't ever let it go, no matter how much you want to," Ryan instructed earnestly. "This is for real, Reb. You do just as I say. It's important." She gauged the heat and knew that the moment had come.

"Now. Big breath." The air that Ryan sucked in, not a second later, felt like fire in her lungs. She crouched in the water with Reb clinging under her and the fire tent stretched over her back. When she couldn't tolerate the heat any longer, she sank lower, pulling the struggling Reb with her. She jammed her elbow over the edge of the fire tent to keep the corner from blowing up with the fire-wind and used her freed hand to clamp her hand over Reb's nose and mouth as she held the two of them close to the bottom of the bog.

The water warmed until it felt like a hot bath. Reb's little body stopped struggling and went limp.

Ryan counted off the seconds. *Two minutes.* She broke the surface with a gasp but made sure the fire tent still formed a protective dome around them. Pulling Reb up, she shook her gently in the darkness. There was no reaction. Ryan's heart lurched. *Oh God. I've drowned Reb!* She took a breath of the sweltering, oxygen-depleted air and breathed it into Reb's mouth. Once, twice, three times... The small body started to struggle. "No, Reb, you got to hold still. The fire has burnt over us but it's still really hot. We have to wait a bit yet. You know, like we practiced."

"I scared, Ryan," Reb whimpered.

"Me, too," Ryan choked, her lungs stinging from the smoke that now seeped under the wet fire tent. "Hang on."

After waiting another two minutes, Ryan cautiously lifted the lightweight fire resistant blanket. The area around them was completely burnt out. The heavy smoke had dissipated and now a low hazy blue surrounded them. Ryan pulled her wet cloth more firmly around her nose and mouth and sucked in air that, after what they had just gone through, tasted surprisingly fresh. Reb clung to her like a barnacle, looking around in fear with big reddened eyes.

Ryan gave her a hug. "You were so brave, Reb. I am really proud of you. Wait until I tell the guys down at the fire hall. Now listen, I have to find Mom. You sit here under the tent and wait for me, okay?"

"No. Ryan, no go!" Reb bellowed, tightening her grasp on her big sister.

Ryan didn't have time to argue; she had to find her mom. She hoped that what she was going to find would not be something that would live in her nightmares forever. She pushed off the fire tent and stood knee deep in water, Reb still wrapped around her chest.

Looking around, she couldn't see any movement. Panic rose like bile in her throat. She sloshed through the water, pushing hot debris out of her way and squinting in the smoke. Then she saw the blackened body washed up on the opposite bank. "Mom?" she called, afraid of going over to see what she might find. "Mom?" she called again, louder this time, the fear edging her voice.

"Ryan?" came a harsh croak.

"Mom!" Ryan cried, splashing over to the black form.

Robbie's Bunker outfit was almost completely burnt through but it had held, with the help of the creek water, and protected her from the worst of the fire. Her hair, that had just started to grow out, was singed. A face black and distorted with pain looked up from the ash. "You and Reb, okay?" Robbie whispered with effort.

"Yeah. Some small burns, that's all. Reb is scared shitless." Ryan eased down beside her mom, wondering what she could do to help.

"It's okay now, Reb," Robbie said reassuringly. "Your mommy will be here soon." She refused to listen to her fear that perhaps Janet had been caught in the firestorm too. "Ryan, you watch...Reb. Wait here...until your...mom gets here. She... should be...here soon." For a few seconds she rested, the air wheezing as it left her lungs, then she continued. "Ryan, I love you. I'm...really proud of..you. Tell Aunt Janet...I hurt. I promised...always to...tell her." Robbie's voice faded out.

Ryan sat beside her mom, afraid to touch her and cause any more pain. She held Reb close to her and adjusted the rag over her nose and mouth. Then she quietly told Reb about how they were going to build a sailboat and win the Bartlett Regatta in the summer. All the while her eyes swung back and forth, checking her mother's breathing and looking downstream for her Aunt Janet.

Around their huddled forms, the roasted earth cooled, cracking and popping with released heat. The light smoke twisted into ribbons that threaded through the burned out trunks of trees, and the ash settled in a snowy carpet. It started to rain. The smoke and debris from the fire had salted the water-laden air from off the Great Lake and created its own weather.

Ryan shifted closer to her mother, protecting her body and Reb's from the big, heavy drops of dirty rain that formed craters in the ash around them until the world was pocked, and streams of ash drained into the creek and swirled away in silver ribbons. Ryan had never felt more exhausted...or more alone.

Then the phone rang. Ryan leaned forward eagerly and undid the flap on Robbie's torn pocket. The phone came out damp and dirty but still, miraculously, working.

Chapter 19

Janet had gotten the canoe as far as it was going to go. The creek ahead of her was an obstacle course of burned and smouldering trees that had fallen across the water. The rain that had started a few minutes earlier was steady now. Heavy splatters stained everything in grey streaks of wet ash and smoke. She sloshed back through the water and shouldered her knapsack onto red-hot, stinging shoulders. She pulled out her phone. She hadn't dared to use it before in case it slowed Robbie's flight from the fire. The phone rang and rang.

Janet could feel the cold ball of despair building in her dissipate when she finally heard a click and a "Hello?"

"Ryan? Is that you? Are the others with you? Are you all right?" Janet demanded, trying to keep the panic from her voice and straining to hear over the static on the phone.

"Aunt Janet, where are you?" Ryan cried in relief. "I need you! Reb is asleep and Mom is unconscious. We are at the base of the ravine."

Tears rolled down Janet's face. "I am about thirty metres down river from you. I'll be there soon. Hang on, baby, everything is going to be okay now," Janet sobbed, closing the phone with shaking hands. The thought of reclaiming her family pushed back her exhaustion and she scrambled forward through the debris.

"Mom, I can hear you," came a voice from up ahead.

Then Janet was there, wrapping her children in her arms and looking down with fearful anxiety at Robbie where she lay wheezing in the mud. Her children still under one arm, Janet twisted to reach out and touch her lover.

"She said to tell you she hurts," Ryan reported with concern.

Janet nodded, biting her lip. She leaned down and kissed her lover's dirty brow. "Hey, you in there?"

Eyelids opened with effort. "Janet? Knew you'd come. Missed you."

"I missed you too, my silly olive," she whispered.

Robbie managed a hoarse laugh. "I feel more like Olive Oyl."

Janet smiled tenderly. "Hang on, I'm going to see if I can reach anyone on the phone. There is so much junk in the air, reception isn't very good." Janet tried Bartlett numbers first, without luck. Then she tried the province's emergency number. Someone answered but the static was so bad, conversation was virtually impossible. Janet leaned over Robbie. "Sweetheart, do you think you could walk to the canoe?"

Robbie nodded, saving what breath and energy she had for the grueling task that she knew she would have to face to get her family out of there.

"Okay, I'm going to help you up. Ryan, could you help Reb?" Ryan nodded, worry for her mom etched on her face.

"Obbie sick," Reb said. "You make her better, Mommy," the little girl ordered fretfully.

"I'm going to, hon," Janet reassured both her daughters as she helped Robbie to her feet. "You go ahead, Ryan, and I'll bring Obbie along shortly."

Ryan nodded and lifted Reb up on her shoulders. She headed off in the direction Janet indicated, leaving deep footprints in the ash.

Janet turned and looked at Robbie. "How bad is it? I can't tell what is coat and what is you."

"I hurt. But I don't think I have any serious burns." Robbie stopped to catch her breath. "Mostly my lungs are aching. Help me out of my Bunkers. I'll be lighter...and it will be easier to move."

Janet nodded and with a grimace helped Robbie peel out off her burned firefighter outfit. *Thank God she had it on! It saved her skin from really serious burns.* She discarded the charred material, and saw that Robbie's back and legs were red but not extensively burned as she had feared. There seemed to be mostly light burns with a few more serious places, as her lover had said. Robbie seemed to be suffering from smoke inhalation, and was in terrible pain. Infection was also going to be a major risk. She pulled her own T-shirt off and insisted that Robbie slip it on to keep the dirty rain from infecting her damaged skin.

They traveled slowly, Janet being very careful that Robbie did not scrape herself or get any more dirt on her sores. Robbie concentrated on just trying to get enough oxygen into her inflamed lungs to keep going. They moved on, Janet talking softly, offering encouragement and love, and Robbie stifling the groans and gasps of pain that ripped from her throat when she stretched her scorched skin too far. It took a long time to reach the canoe.

With Ryan's help, Janet laid Robbie on her stomach in the bottom of the canoe and placed a ground sheet over her to keep as much of the rain off her as possible. They tucked Reb in the bow and then waded through the water together, pulling the canoe along through the fallen debris. Reb was fretful and Robbie cried out in pain each time they had to scrape the canoe over a fallen trunk that blocked the creek. Both Ryan and Janet kept stumbling in fatigue, but neither complained; they just pushed on. At last, they came out of the worst of the burned tangle and could get into the canoe themselves.

Janet took Ryan's arm and whispered, "Down around this bend is the burnt body of a man on the right bank of the creek. I...it's not very pretty. I don't want Reb to see him. When we get to the corner, I need you to distract Reb until we are past."

Ryan nodded. "It's probably the kidnapper. He jumped Mom in the ravine and they fought. But when Mom realized that the fire was coming, we all made a run for it."

Janet squeezed her oldest daughter's arm. *Ryan is quite the kid.* "You get in the bow with Reb. I'll take the stern," she instructed. Janet waded along the gunnels and reached in to touch her lover's hot face. "How are you doing?"

"I hurt," Robbie mumbled, barely conscious.

"Not long now," Janet promised. She stabilized the craft as Ryan settled into the canoe, kneeling in the bow with Reb in front of her. Then Janet leapt in lightly, pushing off with her foot as she stepped in. Janet and Ryan picked up their paddles and started the next leg of the journey home in the pouring rain.

Robbie woke to the sound of hospital machinery and her sister's quiet voice. "Robbie, hi, how are you feeling?"

Slowly, Robbie managed to get her eyes open. "Janet? The girls?" she whispered.

"They're okay. David has taken Ryan and Reb to Burger King. Janet is sleeping over at the motel. I insisted that she try to get some rest. She's been sitting at your side for the last forty-eight hours. She wouldn't move until the doctor told her you were out of danger."

"I don't feel out of danger," Robbie muttered. "Tell Janet I love her and not to worry." She coughed harshly and then drifted off into sleep again.

The next morning, Robbie opened her eyes to find Janet there, watching over her.

"Hi, lover, how are you doing?" she asked, leaning over to peck Robbie's lips.

"You call that a kiss?" Robbie protested sleepily.

"Hmm, I can see you are better." Janet smiled, leaning forward to do a better job of the hello kiss.

"Yeah, I feel a little better. Help me escape before the night nurse comes back on duty," Robbie demanded earnestly "She's gunning for me."

Janet's eyebrows went up. "What have you done?"

"It wasn't my fault. If that chocolate bar hadn't been sticking out of her pocket and if she hadn't just told me gleefully that the kitchen was not going to be open for another ten hours, I wouldn't have stolen her chocolate bar and eaten it while she was getting me another pitcher of ice water."

"Robbie!"

"I was hungry and it was the middle of the night."

Janet laughed. "You are impossible! I'll buy you some chocolate bars so you can pay her back tonight. The doctor said another few days, just to make sure the infection in your lungs has settled down."

"I want to go home," Robbie pouted.

"Me too," Janet agreed. "Just a couple of days, love. We can't get into our place yet anyway, not until the fire department feels the area up there is safe. There are still spot fires burning to the northeast of us.

"You wouldn't believe the cards and flowers that have come for you. I told the hospital staff to share some of them with patients who don't get flowers. There are a few messages from fans that we need to discuss, by the way. Who is Sweetchops and why will she proudly wear a tattoo of your name over her heart forever?"

"Really? Did you get her return address?" Robbie teased.

"Over my dead body. You belong to me lock, stock and barrel, Robbie Williams, and don't you forget it!" Janet warned with a laugh.

"Hmm, I won't," Robbie promised, reaching up to pull Janet down for another kiss.

Some days later, Robbie lay on the couch propped up on pillows, covered with a fresh sheet, feeling dazed. *When did all this happen?* Janet was in the kitchen with David, sharing recipes and making peanut butter cookies. Elizabeth was at Janet's desk, loading a physics program that she wanted to work on. Ryan was sprawled on the floor reading the plans for the boat they were going to start building next week, and Reb was motoring a toy racecar around Rufus who lay contentedly by the couch.

She supposed there must have been hints that she was developing an extended family life, but somewhere along the way, she had missed it. Janet's small cabin looked absolutely packed. They really needed to move over to the lodge as soon as possible. *Damn. I'm happy*, she thought, a grin spreading across her face. She looked up and met Janet's eyes. *She knows what I'm thinking.*

Janet blew her a kiss and the smile on Robbie's face spread even wider.

What a year it's been. But it bound us all together in an invincible family bond, Robbie thought contentedly. *What can go wrong now?*

There was a brief knock at the door and Janet wiped her hands on a tea towel and went to answer it. "Aliki!" she squealed with delight, wrapping her arms around the new arrival in a quick hug.

Robbie was up off the couch and standing behind Janet in one swift movement.

"Hello, Janet, it's good to see you again." Aliki stiffly offered her hand. "Robbie."

There was a slight hesitation before Robbie took the hand in a firm, brief handshake.

"Hi, Aliki," Ryan beamed, coming up to the tall, quiet woman's side.

Aliki reached an arm around the teen and gave her a hug. "Hi, kid."

"Aliki! Aliki!" laughed Reb, and Aliki bent down to stroke the head of the little child who was wrapped around her leg.

"Hi, Reb. Would that be Rufus I see over there? Are you two still best friends?"

Big, serious eyes looked up at Aliki. "Rufus and Ryan are my best friends," she corrected. "Ryan is going to build a boat and take me on it."

"Really? That's great, Reb."

Janet bumped the sullen Robbie aside. "Come on in, Aliki. You know David and Elizabeth. I'll put the kettle on while Robbie gets you settled." She turned to give Robbie a meaningful look.

Robbie smiled weakly and gestured to Aliki to follow her over to the conversation area around the fireplace. She indicated a single chair for Aliki to sit in, well away from the one Janet usually used. "So, what brings you here?" Robbie asked bluntly, with a tone that barely passed for friendly.

"I saw the request for a body identification and retrieval, and when I saw where it was and who reported it, I asked to come. We'd have been here a lot sooner but we had to wait for the fire department to lock down the spot fires and give the okay for personnel to go into the area. I thought it would save us a lot of aggravation if I just stopped in here and asked for directions."

"We've only been back a few days ourselves," Janet answered from the kitchen. "Robbie was in hospital with smoke inhalation and, like you, we had to wait for an all clear in this area."

Robbie nodded in agreement, feeling somewhat more relaxed but still suspicious of Aliki. *Damn the woman anyway. Why doesn't she just leave us alone?*

Aliki looked at Robbie with concern. "Are you okay?"

"Yeah. The kids and I just got a little cooked."

Janet came over with a tray. "Here we go, tea for everyone. And you're in luck; we have freshly baked peanut butter cookies. David and I have been comparing recipes. This one's David's and it's great."

Aliki took the tea that Janet offered and a cookie from the plate that Elizabeth brought around. "Hmm. These are super. I wouldn't mind the recipe too, David."

David beamed from where he sat on the arm of Elizabeth's chair. "I'll write it out for you right now before I forget," he said, getting up and bustling off to the kitchen.

I'm going to throw up, Robbie thought in disgust.

"David can turn his hand to anything," Elizabeth said proudly, her eyes sparkling as they followed David into the kitchen.

"Aliki, you must stay for dinner. Robbie is going to fire up the barbecue and we're going to have burgers," Janet said, finishing giving the girls their milk and coming to sit next to Robbie and leaning her back against her lover's chest. *Come on, Robbie, relax. I love you.*

Robbie's arm dropped protectively around her, but she didn't say anything. Janet filled in the silence. "So, how are you?"

"I took your advice and went home, and it was the best thing I ever did. Thanks for forcing me into it," Aliki said in her straightforward way. "I met a woman, Dawn, and her daughter Mackenzie, and we really hit it off. It was great to see how well my family is doing. I guess I mended some fences while I was out there and put some ghosts to rest."

"I'm so glad." Janet's eyes sparkled with mischief. "So, who is this Dawn? She's someone special, isn't she?"

Aliki blushed and swallowed. "Yeah, she's special," she admitted softly, looking into her teacup. "We really got on well together. I think I'll be seeing her again."

"Is she married?" Robbie asked dryly, and got an annoyed poke in the ribs from Janet.

Aliki looked up and blue eyes met blue in open hostility. "No, she's not."

"Robbie, love, why don't you see about the barbecue and I'll show David how to make my home-made burger sauce. Ryan, could you take the canoe and show Aliki where to find the mouth of Beaver Creek?"

"Sure thing, Mom." Ryan swallowed the last of her milk and got up from the floor. "Come on, Aliki, it's a great day for a canoe ride."

After Aliki and Ryan were safely out on the lake, Janet turned to Robbie, who was moodily cleaning off the grill with a steel brush. "Robbie..."

"Don't start. I am very grateful that she helped get my miserable hide out of prison and took care of my family when I couldn't, but sweet Jesus, she made a play for my wife," Robbie snapped, using more force than was necessary to clean the grill.

"That jealous, huh?" Janet asked, leaning on the porch rail, arms crossed.

The steel brush stopped dead. "What?"

"You know — jealous, insecure because you don't think you can measure up," Janet said nonchalantly.

The brush dropped with a clang and Robbie towered in front of her. "I can measure up just fine," she growled.

Janet snuggled into Robbie's arms. "Well, I thought so. That's why I married you, because I knew that I'd never meet anyone else who could measure up to the love that I found with you, but maybe you don't feel the same way. Maybe there is an insecurity about your...abilities that makes you so jealous of even harmless competition."

"I'm not jealous!" Robbie insisted.

"Good, because I think you and Aliki could be friends if the two of you would just relax in each other's company." Janet stood on her tiptoes to kiss Robbie's throat.

There was silence for a moment while Robbie responded. "Janet?"

"Hmm?"

"You just baited me, set the hook and reeled me in, didn't you?"

"Yes."

Blue eyes sparkled down into green. "Okay, I'll be good. But I don't have to like her."

Janet grinned. "You won't be able to help yourself. She's nice, but she is not you, Robbie. I love you. You remember that. Aliki isn't even in the running and she knows it."

Robbie beamed arrogantly. "Yeah, I'm pretty good, aren't I?" she joked, wiggling her eyebrows.

Janet wet a fingertip on her tongue and ran it down Robbie's nose and onto her lips. "We'll see just how creative you can be tonight," Janet responded, as Robbie's lips lowered to claim her.

Dinner turned into a merry affair and ended with everyone going for a walk beside the lakeshore along Robbie's jogging trail to see the newly renovated lodge. On the trip back, Aliki and Robbie found themselves some distance ahead of the others.

"I'm sorry about the girls being kidnapped, Robbie. That must have been hell for you and Janet, especially after what you had just been through," Aliki said awkwardly, attempting a friendly conversation.

She'd try. She had promised Janet she would try to talk with Aliki. "It was awful. We felt so helpless and...and hell, it was our kids."

"Yeah. I imagine it was the publicity over your arrest that gave the guy the idea to try a kidnapping. There were enough pictures in the paper to ID the kids, and in a small town like this, it wouldn't be hard to work out your schedule in order to pick a good time for a grab."

Robbie nodded. "I've got some plans. I want to drop out of the public eye, work behind the scenes more. It's not good for my family to have to hide from the media all the time."

"That's good. Janet and your kids, well, they're pretty special. She sure loves you deeply. You're very lucky."

"Yeah, I am."

They walked a while in silence. Aliki surprised herself by saying, "You remember I told you I'd met someone out west? She has a daughter too."

"You two hit it off?"

Aliki nodded. "Ever since I was a little girl, I fought to be someone. To get away from the ranch and have a life where I could use my mind and expand my horizons. I felt guilty because I didn't want to be a mother to my brothers, or a housemaid for my father, or a good wife to some rancher. I felt I'd shame my family if they knew I was gay. Then, well, something happened that led to some pretty bad blood between my older brother and me, and I just left and never went back. Janet made me realize that I had to face those ghosts in order to really move on." *Why am I telling her this? It's strange, but despite the antagonism between us, I kind of like Robbie. Could it be that a bond of family does exist between us? Someday, I'm going to have to talk to my father and find out the truth. Someday.*

"Yeah, she's good at that empathy stuff." Robbie stooped to pick a handful of wild blueberries from a low bush growing in a crevasse in a flat rock outcropping. She shared the tasty treat with Aliki.

"Thanks. Yeah, she is. Then I met Dawn and Mackenzie. You know, I mean, I think I might be in love but...well...there were other issues to deal with and...and I just wasn't ready for a serious relationship."

Robbie stopped and looked at Aliki. "You panicked and ran, didn't you?"

Aliki sighed and looked over the lake. "Pretty much," she admitted miserably.

"You gotta go back," Robbie said bluntly, as a way of showing her support.

"Going to. My brother's getting married in the fall. I told her I'd see her then."

"Good. You can work it out then."

Aliki nodded and they walked on, the two women figuring that they had pretty well exhausted the subject and straightened out the problem. Robbie decided that Aliki wasn't so bad...now that she had a girlfriend of her own.

Chapter 20

Ryan sat on the snowmobile seat and watched as her mom took her turn hand-sanding the decking of the two-person sailboat. It had been fun working with her mom, and she thought that she understood her a lot better now. "Mom?"

"Hmm?" answered Robbie as she worked the wood with capable, strong hands.

Since the fire, they had moved over to the lodge, and Ryan knew her mom had finally found time to write. She knew her mom was happy and content at the moment because things were going well with the business, and the foundations were in for the new studio and school.

"How old were you when you lost your virginity?" Ryan asked conversationally.

The sandpaper in Robbie's hand slipped off the end of the wood and caused her to lurch forward. She came back up tense with concern. "What?"

"Your virginity... It can't be so long ago that you can't remember," teased her daughter.

"I remember just fine. I was forty-five."

"Mom!" sighed Ryan with a chuckle. "You are only in your thirties, and I'm fifteen."

"You were an act of God."

Ryan snorted. "Come on, Mom, how young were you?"

"Too young," Robbie said honestly.

Ryan looked down at her hands. "Do you regret doing it, having me?"

Robbie put down the sandpaper that had somehow gotten all scrunched in her hand and walked over to where Ryan sat. She slid in beside Ryan on the snowmobile bench and wrapped an arm around her daughter. "No, never. But I do greatly regret not being mature enough to care for you and provide you with a decent childhood. I will regret that until the day I die." Robbie leaned over and kissed Ryan's head.

Ryan smiled and hugged her back. "Did you love my father?" Ryan asked.

Robbie looked sad. "No. No, Ryan I didn't. He was a university lecturer. I had a schoolgirl crush on my teacher. I was very confused and upset at the time. I thought I'd killed my father. All I wanted to do was live while I could, because I thought I was going to spend the rest of my life in prison."

"Have you slept with lots of people?"

"Uhh, this is getting kind of personal," Robbie stalled.

Ryan saw the blush that replaced the chalky white her mom's face had taken on when this conversation had started. "Over the years, I've read about you in the tabloids, and about all the wild parties and lovers you've had. I just wanted to know how much was true."

Robbie looked at the cement floor and toyed nervously with her wedding band. "You can't believe what you read in the tabloids, Ryan. I was never that wild. I couldn't have been and gotten to where I am now. But I have had a few affairs with both men and women," she answered honestly.

Ryan sat quietly at her side, thinking things over. "Does Aunt Janet know that? 'Cause I don't think she slept with a lot of people before you."

"No, she hadn't, and yes, she knows. I think she is as uncomfortable with my past as I am."

Ryan turned so that she could lean her back against the handlebars of the snowmobile. "How many times have you been in love, Mom?"

"Once. When I met Janet. Before that, I'd had infatuations but never anyone I wanted to spend my life with." *Christ, kid! I can't handle this. Couldn't we have started with the birds and the bees? I want to be honest with you but this is really hard.* "When I met your other mom, I just couldn't get her out of my system. I...it was different."

"How did you know you were in love?"

Robbie's eyes targeted her daughter's. "Why?" she asked suspiciously.

"Well, you know, a person gets...frustrated and..."

"Oh boy."

"Well, I do," Ryan admitted defensively, looking at her mother, who had gone rather pale again.

"Ry...you...Ryan, you aren't...involved with someone, are you?"

"Sleeping around, you mean?" Ryan supplied with a grin.

"I hope not. No, I meant — is there someone in your life?"

"No, Mom."

"So, why all the questions?" Robbie slid off the seat and onto the floor of the garage. She leaned against the snowmobile, her eyes closed.

"I guess I'm just ready to understand things I have wondered about for a while."

"That makes sense. I'll try to be as honest and as open as I can with you, Ryan, but, well, there are just parts of my life that are private. They will be in your life, too."

Ryan nodded. "You know I went out with Paul, and then it got pretty heavy with Jason in the back seat of his dad's car—"

Robbie looked up at her daughter with a startled expression. "What?"

"Easy, Mom, nothing much happened," Ryan clarified. "I was just explaining that I've had some experience with guys, but I've never had any experience with girls."

"Oh." Robbie got up to sit on the upturned boat. "Ah, well, I mean — do you like boys or girls or both?"

"I don't know. That's why I thought I'd ask you," Ryan said with a worried frown. She watched as her mother wiped her mouth with the back of her hand nervously and tried to get more comfortable on the boat.

Robbie cleared her throat several times. "Ryan, you don't want to make the mistakes I did. Be choosy and cautious. If you are not sure which sex you are attracted to, then take your time and date casually. See how you feel with different partners. It should become clear to you who really excites you on all levels of your senses and who just gives you a physical response. I think you need to go slow. I...it's an important decision. Just because your parents are gay doesn't mean you are going to be."

Ryan nodded. "Do you think a person could meet their soulmate and know it when they are very young?"

Robbie considered carefully before answering. "Yeah, I do. But I think it would be a mistake to get too serious too quickly. You need time to experience life as a 'one' in order to establish who you are before you are ready to join in a partnership with someone. I think a lot of marriages of high school sweethearts fail years later because people grow and mature along different paths."

Ryan stood up. "Thanks, Mom," she said with a smile. She picked up a piece of sandpaper and started working on the boat again. Her mom's hand came down to rest on top of hers.

"Ryan, ahh, the world has changed from when I was young. There's AIDS and Hepatitis B and C and—"

"Mom, I know all about safe sex. We learn that stuff in school now," Ryan cut in reassuringly.

"Yeah, well, I'd rather you—"

"I know; you don't want me to sleep around. I don't think I will, Mom. Like you said, I'm young yet so it's hard to know, but I think I'd like to wait for that someone special. I see you with Aunt Janet and, well, the two of you are so cute together."

"Cute!" Robbie scoffed, pulling a face. Ryan laughed. Robbie went on more seriously. "Yeah, well, if things ever get, you know, serious with a partner, if you need anything or if—"

Ryan leaned over and kissed her mom's forehead. "I'll always come to you and Aunt Janet, don't worry."

Robbie gave her daughter a proud smile and a friendly punch, and then the two of them returned to their boat-making.

Some time later, Robbie walked back into the lodge, pale and somewhat shaken.

Janet looked up from where she was playing with Reb on the living room floor. "Robbie, what's wrong?" Robbie had pretty well recovered from her smoke inhalation, but there was still cause to be concerned about infections. Janet got up and went over to check her mate's forehead for a fever.

"I just had The Talk with our daughter. It was much tougher than I thought it would be. I've got to go lie down," Robbie muttered, heading for their bedroom.

Janet smiled at the retreating figure. Motherhood looked so good on Robbie.

A short time later, Ryan came in. "Hi, Mom, hi, Reb."

"Ryan," Reb squealed, getting up and running over to the big sister she adored. "You said we can go to see the pecker."

Ryan cringed. "That's woodpecker, kid. You are going to get me in trouble with Aunt Janet about the words I'm teaching you."

"As if it would be the first time," Janet snorted.

"Can we have some cookies to take with us, Mom?"

"Sure, Ryan, but only two each. Dinner will be in an hour or so." Janet went into the kitchen and got a plastic bag big enough to carry four cookies.

Ryan followed her into the kitchen. "So where is my other mother?"

"Robbie's lying down." Janet handed over the cookies. "She has a headache."

"Thanks. Yeah, that's because we were comparing our sex lives," Ryan casually tossed over her shoulder as she left to collect Reb.

Janet's eyes widened in shock. Suddenly she felt the same symptoms as Robbie.

"How are you doing?" Janet gently placed a cool cloth on Robbie's head. Her partner sighed dramatically.

"My daughter is a teenager," she moaned pathetically.

Smiling, Janet soothed Robbie's brow. "There, there, love. It happens in the best of families."

"I'm not ready," Robbie groused, wrapping Janet close.

Janet snuggled into the side of her lover. "I don't think any parent is."

"Robbie, are we running a film business here or a construction company?" Brian protested, stepping around a ladder and over several planks that lay on the floor of the new building that would house the Williams' Studio by next year.

"A bit of both at the moment," Robbie observed disinterestedly.

"Look, we have a cast, and a movie to produce by next year. I don't want to seem unreasonable here but a script would be nice." Brian bumped into Robbie, who had turned to face him, radiating anger. He took a step back. *Oh boy! Pushed her too far.*

The explosion never came. Robbie turned away and continued walking. "I've had a few things to handle this year," she answered quietly.

Brian sighed in relief. Robbie had been through hell and back this last six months, that was for sure. Still, it hadn't been too pleasant at his end of the swamp either. He'd been left with a multi-million dollar company to run and no artistic genius at the top to lead the way.

Robbie stopped to watch as a construction worker lowered a load of drywall to the ground with a forklift. "I have a script. *Harold, King of England* will be ready for filming in England by September. We'll bring the cast together for a read-through next week. I want to film on location as much as possible. This is a very special love story—"

"Love story? Robbie, you don't do love stories. *Harold, King of England* is supposed to be a great war epic. Guts and gore and heroism. Are you s—"

Robbie laughed. "Don't worry, Brian, there will be enough mindless violence to appeal to my most rabid fan. But I think I've grown. I think my work is taking on a new depth of understanding. *Harold, King of England* is not about a tragic hero who loses the battle that changes history forever. It is about a love story between a man and his nation. He was the last of the true English kings. That quality, that timeless love for one's nation is something I want to capture on film."

Brian stood speechless, looking at the famous director whom he both loved and feared. *Don't panic here, Brian. Aliens from Venus have clearly kidnapped your boss and taken over her body.* He became aware that Robbie was still speaking.

"I'm not going to direct *Harold*, Brian; you **are**. I've decided to become a full time producer. I want to be a backroom boy."

Shit! It's the change of life. She's chemically imbalanced and not responsible for her actions. "No."

Robbie turned around and looked at her assistant, one eyebrow arched up in annoyance. "What?"

"No, I won't let you leave film. Hell, Robbie, your work has set a new standard. You're multi-talented. You write, direct, and act in your own movies. You've never had a film that hasn't claimed awards. You can't just stop being the best."

Robbie folded her arms over her chest and looked at him. "I don't want to be away for months on location. I want to be here with my family," she said with quiet determination.

Brian knew the look. Robbie had dug her heels in. But this issue was too important for him to just walk away from. "Okay, I can see that. But there has to be a compromise. How about we co-direct? I'll do the fieldwork and you can sit back here and be the inspiration. That way you'll only have to do some short trips over to check on things. I can send you the rushes daily. Well?"

"You can make your own films, Brian. You're a good director."

"I am and I do, but I'm no fool, Robbie. I can make good movies, entertaining movies, but I'm never going to be in your league and I know it. I stick with your company and put up with your tyrannical ways because I want to have a piece of the action that surrounds you," Brian answered bluntly.

Robbie blushed and turned away. "Get real, McGill."

"You'll think about it?"

"Yeah, okay. I'll think about it."

Brian smiled. Now all he had to do was convince Janet before Robbie had the chance to discuss it with her. *Geniuses. Shit!*

Gwen looked up from her desk at one end of the trailer and watched Janet as she worked at her desk at the other end. In just the short time since she'd arrived, Gwen had come to realize that Janet was truly Robbie's equal partner. The tyrannical director had walked in and said, "I want a college level school for film making," and Janet was quietly making it happen. *When Robbie realizes the talent that Janet's putting together, she is going to flip.*

Really talented and experienced behind-the-camera people were going to be working in partnership with academic teachers to provide a balanced curriculum of theoretical studies and practical experience. Students would not just study film, they were going to make films.

Janet would phone people to ask them to get involved, and they would say "No", but before the soft spoken schoolteacher had finished, the person at the other end would not only be saying "Yes", but would be really excited. *This lady should be bottled and sold as a secret weapon. Robbie has really lucked out on this one,* thought Gwen.

Of course, I haven't done so badly the second time around. Brian is just as good a director as Robbie and he's great with my kids. When my divorce comes through, Brian and I will plan a simple wedding in our new home by the lake. The house is going to be beautiful.

Brian and Gwen had picked out the plans together and Robbie was having it built as a wedding present to the two of them. *How many bosses give you a four-bedroom house as a wedding gift? Robbie might be difficult, but inside she's a real sweetheart.*

The sound of the door opening drew Gwen's attention. It was Brian. He winked at her and then trotted down to the other end of the trailer and slumped into the visitor's chair by Janet's desk.

Janet looked up from the paper she was reading and smiled. "You're out of luck. Gwen and I shared the last bagel with cream cheese an hour ago."

"Well, at least get your secretary to bring me a coffee and some of the home-made shortbreads you have hidden in the tin over there. I need fortifying. I have to talk to you about Tyrannosaurus Rob."

"Oh, you are a man in need." Janet chuckled. "Quick, Gwen, a first aid mug of java, please; the man has done battle with my wife today."

Gwen laughed, poured two mugs of coffee and brought them over to Janet's desk. There was an evergreen stamped on the side of the mugs and arched across the top it read, *Maria's Café, Bartlett.* Gwen knew using the mugs was a political gesture as well as a convenience. The company had a whole set that had been ceremoniously presented to the Williamses one night when they had stopped in as a family for dinner. Robbie, however, still preferred her Bartlett Volunteer Fire Brigade mug with the Dalmatian pup looking with some relief at a red fire hydrant.

"My hero," Gwen smirked, kissing Brian's head before turning to lift down the tin of cookies.

Janet leaned back and got comfy. Gwen smiled. Janet had quickly gotten used to running damage control for her lover. Robbie thought she was just getting better at dealing with people. *"They just don't seem as stupid as they once were, or as disagreeable,"* Robbie had explained one afternoon, to Gwen's amusement.

"So, what has Olive Oyl done this time?" Janet asked.

"She's decided to give up directing," Brian stated.

"What?" the two women exclaimed together.

Janet sat bolt upright in her chair. "Why?"

"So she can spend her time with her family." Brian sighed theatrically.

Janet smiled and leaned on her desk. "Aww, that's so sweet."

"No, it's not. It's a disaster for film and the Arts in general. Janet, you have to talk to her."

"I think I have a conflict of interest. I don't want Robbie away for months at a time and I don't want her making up to any leading lady," Janet admitted honestly.

Brian laughed bitterly. "We all have a conflict of interest. I don't want to lose the money or the perks that come from working on a Williams film. I've suggested to Robbie that we co-direct. I'll do the on-locations and Robbie can be her usual creative genius back home. Come on, Janet, you know she is not going to be able to survive without a project. She'll drive everyone bonkers, and Bartlett will probably tar and feather her and run her out of town on a rail. She'll be starting fires just so she can put them out. Convincing Robbie to stay in film is an act of mercy. The government will probably give you the Order of Canada. You are the only one who can control Tyrannosaurus Rob."

Janet laughed and shook her head. "Hey, that's my partner you're talking about."

Brian feigned shock. "Janet, we all love T-Rob. She provides our livelihood and takes years off purgatory for us, but let's not let her run loose in the world."

As Janet covered her mouth with her hand, trying not to laugh, Gwen looked up, turned white, and tried to signal to Brian to be quiet. Brian looked up at her in question, then his blood ran cold at the icy whisper in his ear.

"Take Gwen for a walk, Brian, before I wrap your balls around your ears."

Brian was on his feet immediately and backing toward the door with Gwen in tow. "Right...walk... I'm gone, boss."

After the door had closed, Janet burst out laughing. "T-Rob! I love it!" she giggled. "Is that what they call you?"

Robbie stood still and quiet. "That and 'the fucking bitch'," she answered coldly.

Janet looked up in surprise. Robbie was really upset. She got up and moved around the desk and wrapped the stiff body in her arms. "Hey, no, don't let it hurt you. They love you. You are their hero. They take pride in the fact that they can work successfully for someone as artistically demanding as you."

The body remained still and unbending. *Uh, oh. This has cut deep.* "Robbie, why do you think Brian is in a panic? And believe me, he is. You are important to him." She put her fingertips over Robbie's mouth before she could argue. "No, not as a meal ticket or an easy route to fame, but because he really cares about you. It's just his silly way of expressing what is in his heart. Robbie, trust me on this. I know. I dealt with all these people when you were arrested, and when you were recovering from your smoke inhalation. They are very loyal to you." The body relaxed a bit in her arms.

"He shouldn't be using you to get at me. I won't have it," she grumbled moodily.

"He wasn't using me. This is your decision, love. I am not going to influence you one way or the other."

"A co-directorship might work," Robbie admitted grudgingly. "If I could find a director I can work with."

"Robbie..."

The taller woman arched an eyebrow and looked down at her beautiful partner. "You said you wouldn't try to influence me."

"And I won't...as long as you make the right decisions," she responded impishly.

Robbie snorted and lifted her wife up into her arms and kissed her softly. "How did I ever live without you?"

"You ate out and had affairs with your leading ladies," Janet responded playfully, punching Robbie's arm.

Robbie held Janet close. "You and the girls mean the world to me. I don't ever want to go back to existing like that." After a hesitation, she went on in a small voice. "I don't want you hearing those things about me. It might make you leave me."

Janet's heart twisted in pain. Robbie was so easily hurt; inside there was a very vulnerable individual. Janet snuggled deep into the arms that held her against her partner. "I am never going to leave you, sweetheart. I love all of you. It's a pretty great package, believe me." She kissed her insecure lover with gentle passion.

Robbie smiled down into the face she adored. "Let's bribe Ryan to baby sit Reb and I'll take you out for a romantic dinner at Maria's Café."

Janet gave Robbie another kiss. "Damn, if you don't know how to show a girl a good time."

Doctor Aliki Pateas and the local Ontario Provincial Police constable had paddled up Beaver Creek and brought the burnt corpse out in a plastic body bag. The constable had thrown up three times. To be truthful, Aliki had felt pretty sick herself. The greasy, sweet smell of burned flesh permeated clothes, hair, even lungs. It was a smell that her brain refused to ever let go. Due to a business trip overseas, there was a delay of several weeks before she had the time to examine the deceased who had been burnt alive. That hadn't improved the odour any.

Working at the Toronto lab, she used a trick that Doctor Bates had taught her. She wore a surgical mask and slipped a bruised leaf of mint inside it. Tom Bates kept a large pot of mint growing on the windowsill for just such jobs. The smell was still overpowering but she just forced herself to focus on the scent of the mint instead. Doctor Bates had explained that his father had been a house painter and he had always gone to work with a sprig over his ear.

Poking around with a dental tool inside the blackened mouth of the unidentified victim, Aliki cleaned some more char away from the corpse's teeth. Dental records would help identify the victim, especially if he had ever been in prison. As she went along, she carefully noted every abnormality, filling, and missing tooth on a chart. She doubted the guy had seen a dentist in a while. The fillings were old and worn, and the layer of plaque was almost as thick as the soot.

She straightened up and stretched to get the kink out of her back. She was not enjoying the examination. To start with, the guy had scared the shit out of the Williams family and that really upset Aliki. On top of that, even before the firestorm he must have been nothing to write home about in terms of personal hygiene.

She put the used tools in the pressure washer to clean them, tidied up the work area, and then turned to the corpse's hand that she had sealed in a plastic bag containing form-aldehyde. He must have been trying to crawl to the water as the firestorm consumed him. One blackened arm had hung over the bank, the hand just a knob, the fingers having been burned off. The other hand, however, had been under water and although swollen and distended, it was in fair condition.

There were at least three fingertips that were unburned — or at least sufficiently intact that Aliki felt that she would be able to get fingerprints. Not in their present state, however. The skin was soft and waterlogged. Aliki took a scalpel and carefully cut around the finger just below the first phalange. Then she gently peeled back the little cup of skin that had been the end of the man's index finger. She cleaned away the soot and then slipped it over her own finger. Now the man's print was firm and clean. Aliki had literally gotten inside the man's skin and taken on his identity, at least as far as the fingerprint evidence went.

She rolled the tip of his finger on the inkpad and then rolled it again from one side to the other on a fingerprint ID card. A near perfect print of the dead man's finger appeared on the card. Aliki smiled. *If this guy has a record, I have the bugger.*

Robbie sat in Janet's seat in the trailer and worked on the financing and equipment for the new school. She had been stunned by the amount of talent that Janet had drawn to the program. *If we get this school up and running, it's going to be* the place *for learning the art of cinematography. I can hardly wait!*

With a sigh, she forced her mind back to the computer screen. The creativity was the easy part. The hard part was making enough profit to pay salaries and leave enough over to grubstake the next picture. Nothing could be left to chance. She prided herself on being just as good at the production end of the business as she was as a filmmaker.

The phone rang and she silently mouthed a curse. "Robbie Williams."

"Robbie, it's Aliki," came the soft, quiet voice over the line.

It made Robbie's heart stutter. She had come to like Aliki well enough, but there was still that uncomfortable fear that stemmed from her possessiveness and love for Janet and the girls. *Now what?*

"I just got a positive ID on the kidnapper. His name is Jose Pennon. He's got a record as long as your arm."

Robbie's stomach tightened. *This hadn't been some yoyo trying to make a quick buck; this guy was a hardened criminal. He could have really hurt the kids.* "Christ!"

"Robbie, I'm concerned. Pennon hasn't ever been involved in kidnapping for ransom. He's a cheap hired gun. Mostly, he has worked as an enforcer for drug dealers when they have a transaction go sour. But he's not above making a few extra bucks popping off an unwanted spouse or the like."

"So what's going on here?" Robbie asked.

"Maybe nothing, but we do know that until recently, Pennon had been doing business in South America for the last few years. Things got pretty hot for him Stateside. Robbie, you need to be really careful."

"What do you mean?" Robbie twisted a pen in her long, strong fingers.

"I mean, maybe Pennon was not planning to ask for a ransom. Maybe he was hired to cause you and Janet a lot of pain."

Robbie opened her mouth, but all that came out was a distorted gasp. She tried again. "You think someone hired him to kill our kids?"

There was a moment's silence at the other end of the phone. "Your mother disappeared and she presumably was making her way to Argentina, wasn't she?" the voice asked softly.

Robbie slumped back into her chair and pushed her glasses up on her forehead to rub her eyes with her free hand. "Come on, Aliki, that's pretty far fetched," she argued.

"Yes. Yes, it is. But so is Pennon kidnapping kids in northern Canada. The guy has a record sheet that goes back twenty-odd years. Kidnapping for ransom is just not the guy's style. He's a murderer. Believe me, Robbie, there is more to this case. Maybe I'm wrong, but I'd hate myself if anything happened and I hadn't warned you. I just have this gut feeling."

Robbie looked at the ceiling and blinked back tears. She just didn't want this to be happening. She'd had enough.

"Robbie? Are you still there?" Aliki asked anxiously.

"Yeah. Yeah, I am. Thanks, Aliki. I'll take what you said seriously. I...I appreciate you phoning."

"I'll let you know if I learn anything else. Just...just be careful, okay?" came the worried voice.

"Yeah. We will. Thanks."

"So which film would you pick as the best cinematography ever?" Ryan asked. She was sitting on the floor, carefully cutting pieces of sail cloth along a pattern.

"Mmm." Robbie removed the pins from her mouth as she sat back against the desk, pinning the pieces of sail together for sewing. "Hard one. Technology has changed so much it is hard to compare. But if you are looking at major breakthroughs in film, first on my list would be *Gone with the Wind*. Hell, the thing was made in 1939. It's amazing even today."

Ryan mulled over this bit of information. She had recently started to learn about film and was inclined to give her mother the third degree whenever she could. "Why did you pick that one?"

"It raised film to a new height. The silhouette scenes, the aerial shots of the troops waiting at the Atlanta train station, the size and scope of the setting...it was inspired.

When it was filmed, there were only four motion picture cameras of that quality in the world and three were used in the filming of *Gone with the Wind*. Then there is the fact that it made twenty-five percent profit. That record held for thirty-five years. The film was a watershed in cinematography."

"Because it was popular and made lots of money?" Ryan challenged.

"No. Because it was great art." Robbie reached up and handed the pieced sail to Janet.

Janet sat at her sewing machine, running the seams of the sail together in strong rows of stitches. She winked and blew a kiss at Robbie. Robbie wiggled her eyebrows back. A silent request and promise had been exchanged between the two lovers.

"So what would you pick as number two?" Ryan persisted.

"Well, there were some incredible films that advanced cinematography: *Fantasia, The Philadelphia Story, A Streetcar Named Desire, 20,000 Leagues Under the Sea, The Bridge Over the River Kwai, Ben-Hur, Psycho, Lawrence of Arabia—*"

"Mom!" Ryan protested, looking up with big green eyes that seemed to look right into her soul.

Robbie smiled at her daughter proudly. "Mmm, *Psycho* for major leaps forward in scriptwriting and directing. But for the actual through the lens stuff, the next film to turn the business upside down was *2001: A Space Odyssey*."

"You're kidding. I thought that was boring."

Robbie gave her a stern look. "You have a lot to learn, oh child of the Nineties. Kubrick led the way. He fathered special effects and the high-tech movies. *Star Wars, Close Encounters, Alien* — they are all built on his foundation. I've watched that film a hundred times, and every time I do, I learn something new or see another layer of symbolism. It was filmed way back in 1968. Amazing." Robbie shook her head.

Janet, who had been listening to the exchange with interest, now asked a question. "I've noticed that there tends to be a group of really super movies and then a time of very average stuff. Why is that, Robbie?"

"Most years there are good films, but you are right, certain times have bred a series of great films. Part of it is breakthroughs in film making, or a great director, like me, comes along." Here the remaining Williamses rolled their eyes and Ryan threw a sofa pillow at her mom, which Robbie caught and threw back without really looking. "But times of social stress tend to promote creativity. Probably the greatest decade for film was from 1965 to 1975, when the Cold War was at its height.

"Think about it: *Doctor Zhivago, A Man For All Seasons, The Graduate, 2001, Butch Cassidy and the Sundance Kid, Midnight Cowboy, Easy Rider, M*A*S*H, Patton, Summer of '49, The Godfather, The Poseidon Adventure, Deliverance, The Sting, American Graffiti, Jaws, One Flew Over The Cuckoo's Nest* and lots more. That's a pretty impressive list. The '90's had some outstanding films, but that is because of a very few truly creative people. Overall it was pretty dull," Robbie concluded. "I think you'll find this decade a far more creative time with the rise in terrorism and problems related to global warming."

Janet looked over at Ryan and winked. Ryan smiled and shook her head in disbelief. "How do you remember all this stuff?"

Robbie laughed. "It's my job. Film is what I do. You can't create in a vacuum. You have to know where you've been so you can move into uncharted waters."

They worked quietly for a while until Ryan made an announcement. "I don't think I'll go to university. I think I'll study film and become a producer."

Robbie went very still and her eyes turned an icy blue. "You are not going to waste your life. You are going to university. You are going to study science like your Aunt Elizabeth," she said firmly.

Stormy green eyes met her mother's in challenge. "It's my life; I'll choose. I'm not sure I want to be a physicist. What's wrong with producing film anyway? You do."

Robbie got up and dusted herself off. "Your aunt put her studies first. I would have liked to study biology. There is nothing wrong with film, but there are some pretty self-interested individuals in the industry who are not above taking advantage of young women trying to break into the business. I don't want you involved in that crap. I...I don't want you hurt."

Ryan stood up as well. "I can take care of myself. I always have," she shot back and saw her arrow hit home as her mother's face paled. "Damn it, Mom, don't be so controlling. Besides, at the moment Aunt Elizabeth is more interested in sleeping with David than in physics."

Robbie's eyes snapped around to Janet. The answer to the unspoken question was written all over Janet's face. The blue eyes turned back to Ryan. For a moment, everyone held their breath. Then Robbie was in motion. In three strides, she was across the room, had pulled her truck keys from the hook on the wall, and was out the screen door. Janet was only a few steps behind her.

"Robbie. Robbie! Stop!" Janet called, finally catching up to grab her lover's arm as she stopped to open the truck door.

"Why? So you can lie to me again?" the taller woman growled, rounding to loom over Janet.

Janet held her ground as she looked up into the angry face. "I didn't lie."

"An omission is as good as a lie. I think you would have thought to mention that David is sleeping with my sister," she said sharply, turning to get into the truck.

Janet slipped in between. "David is a decent man and this is your sister's life, for God's sake, Robbie! This is just the reason I haven't shared the information with you. When it comes to Elizabeth, you just don't react rationally. I wanted them to have some time together to establish a strong partnership before they had to deal with you."

"This is my family!" Robbie barked.

"No," Janet remained calm, quiet. "This is *our* family. We are all equal partners in the Williams clan. Or have you forgotten that?"

"Of course I haven't. Don't try to change the subject. You told me this guy was honourable. Bethy was raped, damn it, by her own father. She's got some deep emotional scars."

Janet sighed and sat down on the edge of the driver's seat. "Robbie, he is honourable. Elizabeth had a hell of a time seducing him," she revealed.

"I don't—" Robbie was shocked. "What?"

"Elizabeth seduced David. I know this because she phoned me several times for advice."

Robbie looked dumbfounded. Then she turned, paced about a bit and came back to stand in front of Janet. "Errr, is Bethy okay with this? I mean, are they all right together?"

"By all reports, they are having a marvellous time. David e-mailed me that Elizabeth has gained five pounds. They are taking dancing lessons together and David has taken up painting spacescapes. Bethy said he is very good."

"Yeah, yeah, I know — David can turn his hand to anything," she quoted impatiently. "Why didn't Bethy discuss it with me?" she demanded in a tone that made it clear she was hurt.

Janet got up from the car seat and wrapped Robbie in her arms. "Because you are a wonderful sister, who sacrificed everything for Bethy, but you are just a wee bit overprotective."

"I just want the best for her. I don't want her hurt again."

"I know, love, and Bethy knows that too." Janet reached up to steal a kiss. The kiss lengthened.

"Thanks," Robbie whispered against Janet's soft, warm lips.

"For what?"

"For not letting me drive to Toronto to pull David's tongue out and nail it to the floor," Robbie murmured.

"I think Elizabeth would have been upset." Janet grinned, leaning back to kiss the end of Robbie's nose.

"What about David's store?"

"David is staying in Toronto and becoming the manager of Bethy's condo. David's brother, Ted, is going to run the store as soon as he has healed enough to manage. His back is never going to be strong enough to do construction work again. It is an ideal solution for everyone."

Robbie's face turned grumpy. "Am I the last person to know?"

"No. In fact, I was stunned at what Ryan said. I don't know how she knew."

Robbie smiled wryly. "She probably stopped by the doughnut shop. They know everything there before it happens."

Janet laughed then went serious. "Robbie, you can't control Ryan's life either. You can advise, support and protect, but you can't direct, bully or refuse. You need to talk to her," Janet said, holding her lover close so that she felt secure.

"I want her to be a scientist," Robbie protested.

"Not your call, Robbie," Janet responded firmly. "She has to make her own decisions and accept her victories and her lumps like all of us."

"I'm her mother. And I'm paying the bills," Robbie argued, pacing.

"Robbie that argument is guaranteed to drive a wedge between you and Ryan. Think about it, how would you react to a statement like that?"

Robbie stopped pacing and looked up at the northern stars. The stars were so much bigger and brighter up here than in the city and there were so many more of them. Bethy liked to look at the sky up here. She was going to have to let David take care of Bethy now, and she was going to have to give her teenage daughter some room to grow as well. *Damn, this is hard.*

Janet walked over and hugged Robbie close to her. "Please?"

Robbie sighed. "Okay, I'll talk to her. But I'm going to remind you of this conversation when Reb runs away with Jim Ableton's son to open a bait store in Helingone."

"God forbid!"

Chapter 21

Robbie found Ryan in her room. "Uh, can I come in?" she asked the teen who sat on her bed doing homework with her earphones on. Ryan nodded, turning off her music and pulling her earphones off. To Robbie's surprise, the teen got up and came to hug her.

"I'm sorry. I got angry and said things that were hurtful," Ryan admitted.

"Yeah, well, I acted like a jerk," Robbie responded. She led her daughter over and they sat together on the bed.

Ryan now had her own room, furnished in French country oak. On the wall was a row of movie stars, both men and women. They were framed black and white promotional pictures. Robbie had gotten each one signed by the actor. On the chest of drawers were a set of family pictures. There was one of the four of them standing around their snowmobile at the Winter Carnival. The one Robbie liked best, though, was a picture Janet had taken of Robbie and Ryan's faces as they talked quietly together. She thought Ryan liked it, too.

"Listen, I really would like you to go to university, but I realize that you have to do what's best for you. I just worry. I didn't make very good decisions as a teen and I hurt a lot of people because of it, including myself. I love film, Ryan, and I'm good at it. But by dropping out of school, I closed a lot of doors of opportunity. I would have liked to be a scientist like your Aunty Bethy."

Ryan smiled and leaned against her mom. "Well, I hadn't planned on quitting school any time soon."

Robbie wrapped an arm around her daughter and laughed at herself. "I guess I did kind of over react. Let's make a deal. Once our school is up and running next year, you can sit in on some of the night classes as long as it doesn't affect your marks at Bartlett. Then you can see how dull cinematography is compared to memorizing the periodic table."

Ryan laughed. "Mom! You are impossible."

Robbie gave her kid a hug and snorted. "And you're not?"

"Uh, I hope I didn't get Aunt Bethy in trouble. It didn't occur to me that you didn't know that she was having a relationship with David."

Robbie got up and paced about the room. "I guess I'm still dealing with some emotional baggage. I'm a little overprotective when it comes to Bethy, too. She was for a long time...very introverted and scared. I guess I just got used to riding shotgun for her."

"She thinks you're wonderful."

Robbie smiled impishly and wiggled an eyebrow. "Yeah, well, I am."

Ryan laughed.

"But if I have a fault, it's that I'm overly protective of my family."

"That, and you can't cook," Ryan teased, leaning on one elbow on the bed.

"Nope, I fixed that problem. I married your mother," Robbie countered with a proud smile.

"You'd better not let Aunt Janet hear you say that or you'll be eating your own cooking for a month."

"Good point." Robbie pulled a face. "So, how did you know about Bethy and David?"

"Ted sort of implied it. He's wearing a brace but he's back in town and working a few hours each day in the store, learning the inventory and books. Moe's clerks are still doing most of the work, though. Sally and Beatrice don't mind the longer hours, because they can use the extra money."

Robbie raised an eyebrow. "I gotta get out more. I'm not hearing the hot news in town." She smiled. "You finish off your homework while Janet and I complete the sail. Then we'll raid the cupboard because I think your other mom has some of those cranberry muffins hidden away somewhere."

"Cupboard on the right, top shelf, blue tin box," Ryan stated.

Robbie threw her a look over her shoulder as she headed out the door. "You better not have eaten them all, you little sneak," she warned.

"Takes one to know one," Ryan responded, her nose already back in her book.

Bending over Janet, who was still working at the sewing machine, Robbie gently nuzzled, her ear. "I love you," she whispered.

Janet turned and looked up into those amazing eyes that at the moment seemed grey with worry. "Are you still fretting about Bethy?" Janet asked, before accepting a lingering kiss that sent shivers down her back. A moan escaped her lips as they parted.

"No. Well, a little. But I need to talk to you about something else. Aliki phoned me at work today." Robbie frowned as she shifted back and forth on the balls of her feet.

Uh, oh, insecurity alert. Janet stood to snuggle deeply into Robbie's arms, and slowly rubbed against her lover. "Can this wait until after we have made passionate love to each other for most of the night?"

"Ooooh, nice. But no. We need to talk," Robbie stated firmly, stepping back.

Janet frowned in concern and led Robbie over to the couch. They got comfy in their favourite spot: Robbie propped in the corner with her long legs running the length of the couch, and Janet sitting in between them with her back resting against Robbie's chest. "What is it, Robbie?"

"They've identified the kidnapper as a guy named Jose Pennon. Seems that he was an enforcer for drug dealers. He's been in South America for a while, staying one step ahead of the law. Aliki's worried because he has no history of having worked in Canada or being involved in kidnapping for ransom. She thinks someone might have hired him to hurt our kids."

"Robbie, that's insane!" Janet gasped, turning to look at her lover. "Who would do such a horrible thing?"

Robbie said nothing. She just stared back at Janet with sad, bitter eyes.

"Oh, no, Robbie, she wouldn't?" Janet groaned. "Surely not."

Robbie sighed and buried her head in Janet's soft hair for a minute, taking comfort before she spoke. "We ruined her life by exposing her as my father's murderer. She has killed once in revenge. Maybe it's possible that she's prepared to do it again. I don't know, Janet. I just don't know."

"What should we do?" Janet asked, curling deeply into Robbie's arms, seeking her warmth.

"I don't know," Robbie sighed. "Go on and hope that Pennon was working alone, I guess. But I think we need to take precautions for a while, Janet. I'm going to hire a bodyguard for the girls."

Janet sat quietly for a minute, one finger absently drawing figure eights on her lover's hand. "I hate the thought of that," she finally admitted.

"I know, but the alternative... I don't know about you, but I can't go through that again." The tightness in her chest made Robbie's voice rough and strained.

"No. No, neither can I. It was awful. How much are you going to tell Ryan?"

Robbie sighed and hugged Janet close. "I'm afraid it is going to have to be everything. A bodyguard is not someone who can discreetly follow along behind."

"No, I guess not."

"You know what we need?" Robbie asked into her wife's ear.

A shiver of desire ran through Janet. "Hmm, what?"

"Cranberry muffins, toasted, with blackberry jam on them."

Janet laughed and rolled to her feet. "You and Ryan were scheming in there, weren't you?" she said, offering a hand to her partner and hauling the taller woman to her feet.

"Well, the subject of cranberry muffins might have come up briefly in our conversation," Robbie admitted with a wiggle of her eyebrows.

"Yeah, I can just imagine." Janet laughed. "I'll put the kettle on. You get the muffins down. They're—"

"Top shelf, right side, blue tin," Robbie recited.

"How did you know?" Janet exclaimed in mock annoyance.

Robbie grinned shamelessly. "I sent my spy in to gather data before I started my campaign."

One Williams was a handful; a house full of them was impossible. Janet shook her head and headed for the kitchen.

The day after she spoke to Janet, Robbie phoned the managing partner of Polinski Legal and Investigative Services. Polinski sent her Roger Sullivan, a man who had been a cop in Bramford but had quit after five years and gone solo. Most of his work now came from law firms, investigating damage suits or divorce cases. Sullivan would have declined the job, but Polinski didn't leave him much choice.

Polinski said the kid is a spoilt brat and nothing but trouble. I would have turned this case down if times were better, but summer is a slow season. Having been warned by Polinski that Williams was not easy to please, Roger Sullivan dressed for the part. He knew he was relatively fit, if rather average looking. He'd dressed conservatively and had a quiet, calm manner about him. The overall effect, he hoped, was one of quiet competence as he faced Roberta Williams.

"I'm sure you have heard that our children were kidnapped," Robbie began.

Outwardly, Sullivan didn't react, other than to nod his head in acknowledgment. Inwardly, he sighed heavily. *Baby-sitting two gay women's kids. What a job. I should have stayed with the police force.*

"There is some concern that the kidnapper might have been working for someone else. The police are looking into that. In the meantime, I don't want my girls left alone. If Janet and I are not there, you will be. The daycare will be locked from now on and you'll only be able to enter if you are on an approved list. Bartlett is too big a school to make completely secure, so you will need to stay with my eldest daughter during the day."

Sullivan nodded.

"Once the girls return to the house you are free for the rest of the day, and of course weekends. Do you have any questions?"

"Your oldest is a teenager, ma'am. Is she going to be comfortable with this? I really need her co-operation in order to do the job properly," Sullivan stated firmly. He saw Robbie smile down at the desk, enjoying a private joke. *She probably knows that whoever Polinski picked for this job would have been warned that the kid is trouble.*

Robbie looked over at Sullivan. "She is not happy about it, but the kidnapping was a very scary experience for our two girls. Ryan understands that a bodyguard is necessary until we can find out for sure who was responsible. She won't cause you any trouble."

Sullivan felt some of the tension draining. *Williams doesn't seem to be the holy terror she is supposed to be, and it sounds as if the kid is going to be reasonable. I'll give it a shot.* "Okay, I'm satisfied. When do you want me to start?"

"This Monday. Greta Corry rents rooms at her place, mostly to the Ontario Provincial Police officers stationed up here. She provides breakfast, too. She's a hard lady to track down. If you go into the doughnut shop, Stacy should be able to tell you where you can find her. When you find her, she'll set you up, and tell her to send the bill to me." She extended a hand.

Sullivan took it. "Thanks. I'll be in touch."

He smiled as he walked among the trailers that currently made up the nerve centre of Robbie's new studio complex. *Williams is just as beautiful in real life as she is in the movies. Wait until I tell the guys down at the gym that I've been away working for Robbie Williams! Their jaws'll be trailing the ground. No need to tell them I was really protecting the kids.*

Saturday morning found the Williamses all in the lake. "No, Ryan!" Rebecca shouted, "I don't want to swim with you."

Ryan had been looking forward to teaching her baby sister how to swim. "Why not?" she asked in surprise.

"You drowned me."

"Reb, I had to hold you under the water so you wouldn't get burned," Ryan wheedled, feeling embarrassed and hurt by her sister's attitude. In the past, she had silently enjoyed Reb's complete adoration. "If it hadn't been for me, you'd be a crispy critter."

"No swim with Ryan!" came the stubborn response from the small child as her lip curled into a pout.

Realizing that Ryan was starting to get upset, Janet slipped off the dock and came over. This situation needed to be defused quickly. Ryan was easily hurt still. It didn't take much for the emotionally insecure child to feel she was not wanted. "Ryan, could you help me try to find the old anchor we used to tie a raft to? Robbie wants to build a new one so we can swim out to it. I've got some idea where it was. If we can find it, we'll tie a rope and plastic jug to it until the raft is ready."

"Sure, Mom. What about Reb?"

Janet smiled wickedly at Ryan and winked, then she looked up to the beach where Robbie lay on her stomach on a lounge chair reading over her script. She wore a black bikini and her skin was lightly tanned. She looked great. *Especially from this angle*, Janet concluded. Her wife had a nice ass.

"Robbie, could you give Reb a swimming lesson? Ryan and I are busy."

Robbie looked back at her family over a muscular shoulder glistening with suntan lotion. She flashed a smile. "Okay."

"Suckered," Janet whispered to Ryan, and the teen giggled. "Come on, race you out there!" Janet yelled and pushed Ryan playfully as she ran and dived into the deeper water. Ryan was right behind her, the competitive Williams nature surfacing immediately at the challenge.

Robbie smiled as she got off the chaise lounge and walked down to the water's edge where Reb sat on the sand. She watched the two bodies as they sliced through the water, arriving at the dive spot at the same time. Two wet heads bobbed up and down, giggling and chatting. Robbie was filled with pride, and the warm, fuzzy feeling she got whenever she realized how lucky she was.

"Obbie, I go too," Reb demanded.

Robbie said, sitting down next to her little daughter. "You can't, Reb."

"Why?"

"Because you can't swim," explained Robbie.

"Why?" "Why" had become Reb's mainstay of conversation.

"Because you wouldn't let Ryan teach you." Robbie bent down to come nose to nose with the child.

Enormous liquid eyes turned stormy blue. "Ryan drowned me."

"Did she mean to?" Robbie asked in surprise.

Looking confused, Reb shook her head. "No."

"Oh. Was it an accident?" the child's adopted mom persisted.

Reb frowned. "No."

"Hmm, I don't get it, Reb. Why did Ryan drown you?"

"Because of the fire," Reb explained impatiently.

Robbie looked all around. "There isn't any fire now, Reb. It's all gone."

"All gone?"

"Yes, all gone." Robbie smiled, slipping an arm around her daughter.

"Why?"

"Because the rain put it out."

"Why?"

"Because water drowns fire," Robbie explained patiently. "You want me to show you how to swim while Ryan is busy?" she continued, before another "why" came her way.

For a minute, Reb sat watching her mom and big sister laughing out in the water and diving for the elusive anchor. "You no drown me, Obbie," she stated.

"Okay," Robbie agreed cheerfully. "I'll be careful."

Janet dove down into the cool, clear water and skimmed along the sandy bottom looking for the barrel of rocks that they'd used to anchor a raft when they were children. When her lungs started to burn, she arched her body and with strong strokes of her arms rocketed to the surface again. She hadn't played like this in years. It was so super to be a family. Ryan was a wonderful child, a much more stable blend of personality traits than her mother. She had an interesting blend of her Aunt Elizabeth's quiet logic and Robbie's creative spark and daring.

Janet wondered if Robbie had any idea just how bright Ryan really was. She wondered if she should talk to Robbie again about Ryan's test results and then rejected the idea. Ryan needed space to decide for herself what she wanted to do with her life. If she talked to Robbie, Janet wasn't sure that her focused partner would not force Ryan into a lifestyle she didn't really want.

She looked over at her gorgeous lover as she patiently fitted water wings onto Reb. Robbie was such an amazing mixture of fire and ice; it was sometimes hard to know which way she would go. She had been wonderful about the swimsuit. Robbie had walked in and found her sitting on the bed crying as she looked at the swimsuit that was specially designed with a pocket for a breast mold to be added.

Robbie had sat down beside her and held her close. Then she had stripped the housecoat off her and they had made love tenderly. Later, Robbie had taken the swimsuit from the floor where it had fallen and gently slipped it on her lover with a good number of kisses and caresses.

"*You are beautiful. You excite me. And I am so proud to be seen at your side,*" Robbie had said in such a sincere manner that Janet never again felt awkward slipping into her swimsuit. Robbie could be so wonderful.

"I think I saw it!" Ryan yelled, breaking the surface to the right of where Janet was treading water.

Robbie smiled and brought her focus back on the job at hand. "Okay, Reb, this swimming is easy. Even Rufus can do it."

The dog looked at the two humans with mild disinterest. Rufus had no intention of going in the water. Lying in the sun was so much more fun.

"First, you have to lie on your stomach in the shallow water, like this." Robbie demonstrated. "Then you kick your feet and move your arms. Okay, you try."

Reb, who watched with big intent eyes, rolled over on her belly and dutifully kicked and stroked with her arms as she had seen Obbie do.

"Great, kid. Now you have to remember to keep your fingers together to scoop the water. That's right." Reb giggled as she splashed water all over Obbie as she dog paddled, anchored to the shore by her belly.

"Now, this is what happens next." Obbie walked out deeper in the water and did the dog paddle for Reb to see, then she returned to shore where Reb sat looking apprehensive.

"I'm going to support you with my hand, just like the sand did. We'll move out into deeper water slowly. You know I won't let go of you, Reb, so you just relax and splash me all you want. You are really safe. Swimming feels good, Reb. It's just like when I used to lift you up and let you fly."

This idea appealed to Reb. Robbie kept the child in the shallow water for a bit so Reb could still feel the bottom, then gradually she drifted her small charge out into deeper water. Reb kicked and splashed in glee as Robbie spun her around in circles like she used to do over her head, when Reb was smaller.

"Obbie! I fly, Obbie!" Reb laughed.

"No, you are swimming! Way to go, Rebel!"

"I swim by myself," Reb demanded.

Robbie caught her daredevil daughter up into her arms before the small child could wiggle free. "No, Rebecca, you have to practice a lot first. It takes more than one lesson to learn to swim."

Big, liquid blues looked seriously back at Robbie. "I can swim. I go swim with Ryan and Mommy," the child stated firmly.

"Okay, Rugrat. But you have to hold on to me, okay?" Robbie negotiated. Reb nodded, a smile flashing across her face.

Janet was just tying the line to the empty bleach bottle that Ryan held when she was hit in the face with a splash of water. "I swim, Mommy! I swim! Look, Ryan, I swim. Now I can't drown."

The small child wore a full life jacket and clung to Robbie by the back straps of her bathing suit.

Janet laughed. "That's great, Reb. Good for you," praised her mother.

"Ryan, I swim with you now," begged the now fearless child.

Ryan looked a bit sulky. "Thought you didn't trust me," she muttered.

"I trust, Ryan. I swim like Ryan, too," Reb protested.

Her big sister was won over by Reb's enthusiasm. With a few strong strokes, she was beside her mom and the small child. Robbie slipped Reb carefully from her own shoulders to Ryan's. Reb wrapped her arms around Ryan's neck and her legs around her big sister's waist. "Go, Ryan, go. We fly!" Reb giggled as Ryan did a breast stroke through the water around her parents.

Rufus woke with a start and ran to the end of the dock, barking and growling, suddenly realizing that his cub was out in the deep water.

"Hi, Rufus!" called a cheery voice from out in the lake.

Rufus howled in frustration, took a few steps back and then, with a short run launched his big hairy body out into the water. The splash was like a small tidal wave. With huge orange paws, the fretting Rufus quickly covered the distance between the dock and Reb.

"Easy, Rufus. You're scratching me." Ryan laughed as she tried to push the big, worried dog away while keeping Reb above water.

Suddenly, Robbie and Janet were on either side of their daughters and acting as guards against the upset Rufus, as they were all herded toward the shore by the annoyed dog.

Once on shore, Ryan looked down at the soggy mound of orange fur. "I bet you are pleased with yourself, you stupid dog. You almost drowned us."

"No, Ryan." Reb came to her canine friend's defence. "Reb can swim now."

Janet shook her head. *Olives. I have a family of olives.* "Reb, you are doing very well but you can't swim by yourself yet. You are not to go near the water unless one of us is with you. Promise."

Reb looked rebellious. Robbie tapped her little daughter on the shoulder and when Reb looked way up, Obbie raised an eyebrow significantly. Big eyes got wider. Reb looked over to her mother. "Okay, Mommy, Reb no go near the water," she promised.

Janet looked at Robbie with relief and then at Rufus with annoyance. "It is going to take a week to dry this monster out and the whole house is going to smell like wet dog."

"Rufus can dog paddle, too," Reb pointed out proudly, reaching up to scratch the massive dog's ear. Rufus turned and started to lick Reb dry. The little girl giggled.

"No, Rufus," Janet said as Robbie picked up the small child and put her on her shoulders.

"Time for burgers on the barbeque. Let's head up to the lodge," Robbie directed, and the family happily gathered up their belongings and took the trail through the trees back up to their new home.

The woman looked around the rented one-room cabin with contempt. It was living like a savage. *Why would people think coming here is a holiday?* Still, the cabins were close to the lake where the Bartlett Regatta would take place. That was important. Now it was just a matter of waiting for the right moment. The bitch had betrayed her and for that, she was going to die.

She realized that she should have killed Robbie long ago; she had been far too patient. Now that her mind was made up, she could see that it was the right course of action and had been for some time. It was foolish of her to have hired Pennon. She had wasted money that she could have put to far better use. Still, it was only a minor setback. The stupid fool had been killed in the fire and so had not been able to betray her to the police. The police must not know she was here. That was very important.

She laughed softly as she sorted through her bag to find her swimsuit. It wouldn't hurt to get a better tan. That way she would not stand out among the summer people at the regatta. She knew boats. She had spent every summer by the lake. *Boating accidents happen. Tourists can be so careless, especially if they have been drinking.*

As she left the cabin, she slipped her sunglasses on and turned to carefully lock the door. Then, pulling her straw hat low over her face, she sauntered down to the small beach that was part of the Pioneer Cabins property. This late in the season, the beach was deserted. The vast blue waters of Lake Superior spread out in front of her, sparkling in the late summer sun. *Life is good*, she thought, as she arranged herself on the chaise lounge and took out a book to read. *Life is very good.*

Robbie was feeling happy and mellow. She flipped a hamburger onto a bun and then joined the rest of her family at the picnic table.

Janet watched with amusement as Robbie piled on the hot peppers, lettuce, pickles, mayonnaise... "Don't even think about going for those onions," Janet whispered into Robbie's ear.

Blue eyes slowly came around to look down into green. An eyebrow arched in challenge. A warm hand squeezed Robbie's thigh in reply. Robbie took a big bite of her burger and chewed slowly. *Life is sooo good!* She ate her burger with a happy grin pasted on her face as she watched Ryan wipe ketchup off Reb's nose.

Ryan seemed to hesitate for a second and then said, "Uh, there's going to be a dance at the Lions' Hall on the Friday night before the regatta. John asked if I would go with him."

Robbie swallowed her mouthful of burger without chewing and nearly choked. Janet patted her on the back and passed her a glass of iced tea. Robbie took a long drink, put down the glass, and looked at her daughter. "No. You are only fifteen. Who is this guy anyway?"

"He's Paul and Mary Digby's son. You know them, Mom, they run the art and framing shop in town. It's not really a date, Mom. He's just picking me up and we're meeting the rest of the gang there."

"He drives? How old is this guy?" Robbie squeaked through a throat tightening with stress. She rubbed her moist palms on her shorts and started when Janet's hand wrapped around one of her own and held on tight.

"Almost seventeen," Ryan responded moodily.

Janet could see that Robbie was dropping into her hyper-protective mode. If she didn't step in, Ryan was going to be getting her old age pension before her mom was willing to let her date. "Hmm, attracted to older men, huh?" Janet joked, holding Robbie's hand even tighter. "Well, if it's the whole gang meeting together, and if I'm allowed to come and pick you up, I think your mother and I would agree it was okay for John to take you to the dance. Right, Robbie?" She nudged her lover firmly in the ribs.

Robbie wiped the sweat from her lip. *Shit, this is awful! What if the guy makes a pass at Ryan?* She felt sick. She opened her mouth; nothing came out. She tried again, "We'll pick you up at eleven. You phone us when you get there and you are not to leave the building. Sullivan will be there, of course." Suddenly, having a bodyguard for her daughter seemed like a really positive thing.

"Sullivan! Awww, Mom!"

"Ryan," Janet interjected calmly, "this is really hard for your mom. You know that. She has said you can go. Let's just take this dating thing one little step at a time, okay?"

Ryan's eyes flashed with anger, but she nodded. "Okay," she agreed, picking up her burger.

Janet smiled in relief. Robbie had agreed to let Ryan go, but if Ryan had pushed it, she knew that her partner's legendary temper would have erupted and then Ryan would have never gotten a chance to date.

Robbie looked down at her burger with disgust. *If I eat that, I'll throw up.* Janet nudged her and looked at the burger significantly. Robbie smiled weakly, picked up the burger and managed to force it down.

"She's only fifteen," came a voice out of the darkness of the room.

"And it's only a town dance, not a real date," responded a voice with a yawn.

"Everything is changing," the first voice complained. "My sister is dating and now my daughter is going to dances. I don't think I'm ready for all this."

The light switched on and Robbie blinked like an owl into the face of her annoyed wife. "Hold it right there, Williams. A: your sister is very much in love with a very sweet man who adores her. B: your daughter is old enough to have a young man take her to a community dance. We know the family and I know John. He is a very nice boy and—"

"That's what you said about David and now he's sleeping with my sister," Robbie grumbled. "What the hell is going on with my family?"

Janet rolled her eyes and prayed for patience. For a creative genius, Robbie could be as dense as a hardwood plank at times. "I'll tell you what is going on, Robbie. Your family is healing. Elizabeth doesn't have to hide in fear anymore, and Ryan doesn't have to wear a chip on her shoulder because she doesn't have a mother. They are reaching out for human companionship in a very normal way. Let them, Robbie. You're healing too, my love. You don't have to keep looking over your shoulder. You can plan for a future and not have to keep people at bay with your temper and sharp wit. You can be loving, and caring, and part of this family and community." She paused for a moment, watching for a response. "Robbie, you've got to let go of all the old baggage," she pleaded.

Robbie sat silently, her back against the headboard. Tears welled in her eyes. "I'm afraid for them," she finally admitted.

Janet pulled her lover down so that Robbie's head rested in her lap. She gently rubbed her lover's temple with the tips of her fingers. "I know. It's not easy letting go. But Elizabeth and Ryan and someday, our Reb, need to make their own way in life. We'll offer all the support, advice and love we can, but in the end we have to let them decide. No one makes good decisions all the time. Our family will get a few scars along the way, Robbie. Just like we did. Are you happy, Robbie?"

"I am now, with you and the girls," she answered honestly.

Janet could feel her lover starting to relax. She smiled and bent to kiss her temple. "See, even with the scars you acquired in life, you are still happy. Elizabeth and our girls also deserve to be happy, even with their scars."

"How do you know?" Robbie challenged. "There are a lot of really unhappy people out there."

Janet laughed. "Because we taught them that happiness is not given to you, it's made inside. We taught them to stand on their own two feet and live life for all it is worth. And we taught them never to dwell on the scars you collect as you go along the way."

"Did we?" Robbie looked up at Janet with big blue eyes that were so much like Reb's.

"Well, we'll have made a good start if we leave Elizabeth and David alone and let Ryan go to the dance." Janet playfully wiggled Robbie's nose.

Robbie caught Janet's hand and kissed it before it could escape. "I'll try," she sighed.

"That's my Olive Oyl." Janet smiled. "I have an idea, seeing you can't sleep."

"What?"

"I'll get the rest of the chocolate icing out of the fridge, you put on some soft music, and I'll show you just how kinky our sex life can be."

Robbie smiled. It sounded like a perfect scenario for a creative genius.

Aliki went through her routine with total focus, reaching deep for the controlled strength and balance of mind and soul that was necessary to reach a height of perfection in a martial art. Her sai blades whistled through the graceful flowing movements, not reaching *for* an imaginary opponent but *through* one. She made it look effortless: a deadly dance on the brink of violence — beautiful, entrancing, powerful. Aliki had never lost a tournament.

When she was finished, she smiled. The missing piece of the puzzle had just fallen into place. Aliki knew who was after Robbie Williams. She looked out the window and watched as the setting sun kissed the twisted boughs of her Japanese Maple. She'd shower and change first. It was Friday night and no doubt the Williams family was unwinding after a busy week. She knew Robbie had hired a bodyguard, so there was no imminent danger.

The feeling of contentment and peace that she always enjoyed after a serious workout did not last long. An uneasiness that she had come to recognize as a warning to her conscious mind kept growing within her. She cut short her shower and dressed quickly in faded blue jeans and a white T-shirt, then bounded down the stairs to look in her phone index for the number for Robbie and Janet's cabin. She paced the room impatiently as the phone rang and the answering service came on. The tone indicated she should leave her message.

"It's Aliki Pateas. Be careful. I've got a bad feeling. Call me on my cell phone. I need to talk to you," the doctor stated calmly.

She hung up, feeling anything but calm. That niggling feeling inside was working its way into a full-blown alert. Aliki loped upstairs, threw a few things in a bag, and headed out. She should be able to get to Bartlett by two in the morning if the weather was good.

Robbie paced while Janet did her best to ignore her. To be fair, Robbie had been wonderful. She had been polite and relaxed with John Digby when he had come to pick Ryan up, and except for telling him three times that Ryan was not to leave the hall until she was picked up at eleven, she had been a role model for understanding parenthood. Once the car had disappeared down the driveway, however, Robbie had let her internal monsters out.

Other than a few grunts, the only two words Robbie had uttered in the last four hours would not have been found in the Oxford dictionary. As Janet worked at her laptop on organizing course requirements, she watched Robbie pace past her desk yet again. The teacher wondered whether the courts would be lenient if she got her squirrel gun and shot the legs out from under her lover.

The pacing stopped in front of her desk. "It's ten o'clock. You should be going now," Robbie prodded.

"It's a fifteen minute trip," Janet pointed out.

Robbie looked about ready to burst. "So, you could be a little early!"

"No!" Janet said emphatically. "And don't ask again!"

Robbie looked like she was going to argue but stopped herself when she saw the look Janet gave her. Instead, she went over and looked out the window into the night, swaying back and forth on the balls of her feet.

Janet considered dropping something to see if Robbie would jump out of her skin then decided against it. In the mood her lover was in, she was liable to go through the roof and turn around twice before she hit the ground. When she did land, she would not be in a good humour.

At ten thirty, Janet took mercy on her partner. "Okay," she said, snapping her laptop closed, "I'm going. You are to stay here. Your job is to baby sit Reb. I will phone you if there is any problem. Robbie, do try to relax and remember what I said — no third degree. A girl has a right to her privacy. She will tell you what she wants to tell you."

Robbie sank into a chair, weak with emotional exhaustion. It had been a hell of an evening. Janet came over and kissed her tenderly.

"You've done wonderfully, Obbie. Not long now, okay?"

Robbie nodded dumbly, feeling anything but okay.

Ryan waved goodbye to several teens at the doorway of the Lion's Hall and slid into Janet's new truck, a gift from Robbie. Janet had stopped for gas in order to arrive at just the appointed time, but she was pleased to see Ryan waiting for her.

"How's Mom?" the teen asked as she did up her safety belt.

"A wreck," Janet answered honestly. "How was the dance?"

"It was great! John's nice but he can't dance worth a damn. I think Sullivan is putting the moves on Stacy Barlow. She brought a bag of day olds from the doughnut shop and he got to choose first. Debbie's got the hots for Larry Butler. Can you imagine! The guy's a dork. Angela danced with Ted Peel Junior. I think they make a nice couple. Both their dads own car dealerships, so they bonded. But if they married, Angela's sister-in-law would be Stacy Nona. I think she'd rather live in sin," Ryan babbled happily.

Janet laughed as she rooted in her purse for her phone. Winking at Ryan, she punched in the lodge number. Robbie answered it on the first ring. "Hi, love. I've got Ryan beside me and she seems to have had a good time. We are on our way home now. Put the kettle on, okay?"

"Was she really that upset?" Ryan asked.

"I could have wiped her off the floor with a mop. This evening was really hard on her, Ryan. Be gentle, and for God's sake, don't tease her. It will be easier after this, I'm sure. Ryan, your mom, well, she has a lot of emotional issues still to deal with from her youth. Sometimes you'll just have to be a little patient with her."

"Yeah, I know. She's a great mom, you know, but I'm glad I have you, too. You sort of balance each other."

Janet smiled. "We were meant to be together. You'll find your special person some day, Ryan."

"Hope so," Ryan mused as they turned down the lane toward home.

Aliki tried the cabin number and Robbie's business number every time she stopped, but no one was answering. Construction had really slowed her down and she realized that she was going to have to stop for a few hours sleep before she fell asleep at the wheel. Reluctantly, at one in the morning, she pulled into a small motel roughly three hundred kilometres south of Bartlett.

She booked in and went to her sparse, cold room feeling grim. Setting her alarm for six, she crawled into a saggy bed between sheets that were stiff with starch and damp with lack of good air circulation. She forced herself to relax. She would be in Bartlett by eight in the morning and then she should be able to find out what was going on.

Robbie towelled down after her shower and then slipped into worn blue jeans and a white T-shirt. Her hair had grown long enough that she had been able to have it styled into a cut that looked almost decent. Another six months or so and it would be back to a good length. Janet liked her hair long.

She followed the smell of homemade French toast to the kitchen. Reb saw her coming and ran over for a hug.

"Hey, about time you woke up," Ryan called as she set up the table. "I wanted to sic Reb on you, but Aunt Janet wouldn't let me."

"I need all the beauty sleep I can get at my age," Robbie mumbled with a yawn. By the time they had shared a pot of tea the night before, and chatted about everything that had happened at the dance, Robbie had been near dropping with exhaustion. Her daughter's first date had taken a real toll on her.

Janet winked at Ryan and Ryan laughed.

Robbie grabbed her teen daughter from behind and tickled her ribs. "Laugh it up, kid. Wait until it's your daughter, then I'll get the last laugh."

"Hey, you two, no rough housing in my kitchen. Sit down and be good before the food gets cold," Janet ordered.

"I got a date like Ryan," announced Reb, who felt a need to be just like her big sister.

"Please tell me it is with Ableton's son." Robbie smiled evilly, looking across the table at Janet.

"I got a date with Rufus," Reb revealed proudly. "Mommy said I could walk Rufus tonight."

"Rufus, huh?" Robbie mused. "I hear he's a better dancer than John," she teased.

Reb nodded. "He is," she agreed loyally and everyone laughed.

The family cleaned up quickly and then piled into the truck for the ride to a beach back near Harriston where the Bartlett Regatta would take place. The scheduled location at the beach by the Bartlett School was not being used in order to allow the fire-scorched vegetation time to recover.

Arriving at the site of the competition, the Williamses spent the morning preparing *Tubby*, their sailboat, for the races in the afternoon, and in exploring the various booths at the fall fair. At noon, they sat under the boughs of an old maple and ate corn on the cob, freshly cooked by the Lions' Club and dipped in butter. Then, for the first time that day, they separated — Robbie and Ryan going to do some practice laps before the big race, and Janet and Reb reporting to the starter's launch to act as judges.

Aliki looked at her watch; it was almost noon. She had wasted a good deal of time driving out to the cabin to find it empty, then going on to the lodge to find that the Williams family was not there. A quick enquiry at the gas station resulted in the frustrating discovery that she must have driven right past the Williamses, who would be at the Bartlett Regatta back near Harriston.

Now she pushed through the crowds along the waterfront, looking for any member of the Williams family. The gut feeling was growing; it was a perfect place to seek revenge.

"Aliki! Aliki!" called a voice.

The scientist looked up to see Ryan standing by a boat ramp, waving her arms over her head. The tall woman smiled and headed over to the young teen. "Hi, kid. Where's the rest of the clan?" Aliki tried to sound casual.

"Aunt Janet and Reb are out in that boat over there." Ryan pointed. "Mom went to get the entry form for the race and told me to wait here, but I gotta get the boat in the water. Others are waiting to use the ramp. Can you help me?"

Aliki could see that Ryan was stressed. Several boaters were waiting with their boat trailers ready to back down the ramp as soon as the Williams outfit moved out. "Okay."

Ryan took the lines, while Aliki got into the cab and backed the boat trailer out into the water. She then hopped out of the truck and walked back to release the cable so that the boat could slide into the lake.

For a small boat, it sure is sitting low in the stern, Aliki thought as she released the lock and the handle of the winch spun wildly. Instead of the boat sliding easily into the water, the stern dropped and the bow snapped up and caught Aliki firmly under the jaw. Aliki let her body relax and went with the blow. Even so, the impact sent her flying back into the water and knocked her senseless.

From a cluster of trees, some distance off, a tall woman smiled cruelly as she looked through a set of binoculars while people ran to fish the body out of the water. This time Isabelle had done her job right! The smile turned to a scowl and the binoculars lifted again to focus on a figure madly trying to get through the crowds to where the accident had taken place.

Robbie pushed through the crowd to see Ryan kneeling beside a body that looked remarkably like herself. "Ryan! Ryan! Excuse me. Sorry. Ryan. Are you all right?"

"Mom, it's Aliki. She's really hurt," Ryan called in distress.

Robbie splashed into the water and knelt beside Aliki. "Don't move," she said. "Someone find the ambulance service. We need a neck brace here."

The victim lay still, letting the faraway sounds pass over her until her scrambled mind could start to make sense of what was going on around her.

"No, I'm okay," Aliki mumbled through a jaw she thought might be broken. *Damn!* "Robbie?" She felt the figure beside her lean forward. "That was meant for you. Pennon is Selo's cousin. You remember Isabella Selo? She's the disenchanted fan who ratted on you to the police. She might have testified that she saw your mom that night but it wasn't to help you, it was to cover her own butt. She's still got it in for you, I'm afraid. You be careful."

"Shit," Robbie growled. "I've had it with all this crap. Hang on, Aliki; we'll get you to the hospital."

Aliki, now feeling more alert, shook her head weakly. She moved her jaw cautiously, and was relieved to realize that all the bones and muscles were still in place, if severely bruised from the impact. Next, she moved her arms and legs and, lastly, her neck. "No, I'm okay. Just got my bell rung. Help me up, Robbie."

"You sure?" Robbie asked anxiously.

"Yeah, bones I know," Aliki managed to get out despite a badly swollen and bruised face. Robbie and Ryan carefully helped steady Aliki as she got to her feet. The crowd clapped and Aliki flushed with embarrassment. She looked at the boat. The stern was submerged in a few feet of water and the bow was sticking in the air. "Go check that boat," she said into Robbie's ear.

Nodding, she ordered, "Ryan, don't let go of her." Robbie waded out to look under the canvas covering of the small sailboat. The stern was stacked with bricks. Her eyes looked up to meet Aliki's. "Bricks. The stern is filled with them."

"That's a pretty lousy practical joke," someone snorted in disgust.

"Coulda killed someone," observed another.

"Come on, let's give the ladies a hand," offered a third, and people pitched in unloading the wet bricks to the dock and bailing the small craft so that it floated properly.

Robbie, Ryan, and Aliki stood by and watched. The ambulance driver wanted Aliki to go to the hospital, but she chose instead to sign the waiver of responsibility and stay. Robbie offered to take her to the hospital, but Aliki insisted she was fine.

When the boat was tied safely alongside the dock, and the mast had been stepped and the sail attached, the three walked over to where they had parked the boat trailer. Robbie squatted down and examined the winch. "It's been tampered with. The teeth have been filed so that they wouldn't catch."

"Where the hell is your bodyguard?" growled Aliki, who was fighting a blazing headache that had started in her right temple.

"He doesn't work weekends," Robbie sighed. "Besides, his job is to protect the girls."

Aliki rolled her eyes. "Great."

"I need to contact Janet and let her know what's going on." Robbie frowned. "She has the cell phone. We'll need to find a pubic phone."

Aliki could see the logic in that. "Okay, you first, Robbie, then Ryan, I'll bring up the rear. We are heading up to my van by the school over there."

Hands on her hips, Robbie looked rebellious. The crowds flowed past them. "Why?"

"To get my cell phone so you can contact Janet. You just got put under police protection," Aliki stated.

"You're a cop?" Ryan asked in surprise.

"An RCMP officer, actually. Come on," she said, nudging Ryan on, knowing Robbie would fall in immediately. Sure enough, Robbie was right at her side.

"You don't have an ounce of authority, do you?"

"No. But I'm all you've got," Aliki pointed out with a wry grin.

Keeping in step with Aliki as they hurried along, Robbie asked sarcastically, "So what are you, my big sister?"

Aliki stopped and looked at Robbie in surprise, then she seemed to think better of expressing her thoughts. "Come on, let's go. We need to warn Janet to be careful, although I suspect you are the principal target now."

Isabella Selo waited by the beverage tent, as she had been instructed. Everything would go well this time; she knew it. Her part had already been done. It had proven to be much simpler than she had anticipated. Now all she had to do was wait for her friend to tell her when to act. She looked around once more. Still no sign of the person for whom she was watching. She shifted from one foot to the other. Her heeled sandals were not a good choice for a northern Canadian town. Isabella loved the city. She couldn't see why anyone would want to live surrounded by woods and wild animals. Then she saw her friend and hurried over. "I did well, no?" she asked with smug pride.

There was a moment's hesitation, and then her friend said, "Yes, very. Robbie will be looking over her shoulder now. We will play with her like a cat with a mouse. Now, I suggest a lovely meal and a few cold drinks while we make our final plans. Come."

Isabella smiled and followed obediently. She was not a smart woman. Had she been, she might have lived.

"Janet?" Robbie was calling from Aliki's van, playing nervously with a small dried bone that had been sitting on the table between the two front seats.

"Robbie, I'm so glad you called. Something happened and—"

Robbie straightened. "Are you and Rebecca okay?"

"Yes, but I'm sure I was deliberately pushed from behind. I almost fell between the dock and the boat, but someone grabbed me. Fortunately, I'd already lifted Reb up onto the launch or she could have easily fallen in. Robbie, I think we have a problem."

"I know we do." Robbie went on to tell her about the bricks in the sailboat and the doctored winch.

"What are we going to do?" Janet asked, feeling frustrated at being out of reach of her lover and other daughter.

"Nothing right now. We'll just have to be really careful. You and Reb are probably safe out there, but still, be on your guard. Aliki is here. Did she ever mention to you that she's a cop?"

"Aliki? N-no, I thought she was in forensics," Janet spluttered in surprise, as she unconsciously pulled Reb closer to her and stroked her daughter's hair.

"It seems she is a lady of many talents," Robbie observed dryly, making eye contact with the woman that sat beside her. Aliki felt the heat rising in her face. "She has offered herself as police protection."

"Take it. Robbie," Janet ordered. "You and Ryan be careful."

"We will," Robbie reassured her. "The race is starting soon. We'll be safe enough out on the water. In the meantime, Aliki is going to watch our backs."

"Okay, just be careful," Janet repeated, and the two hung up.

"What's this?" Robbie held up the small bone.

"A scaphoid."

"What?"

"A small human hand bone near the base of the thumb. It fell out of a box. I keep meaning to put it back," Aliki observed.

"Jesus Christ!" Robbie dropped the bone on the dash. "And they say my films are bloody."

Aliki raised an eyebrow and gave Robbie a look. Ryan, sitting in the back seat, laughed.

Janet stood at the rail, looking across the water at the beach crowded with merrymakers. It was such a happy scene and yet somewhere in it there was one speck of real anger that was poisoning their lives.

Isabella didn't feel well. Perhaps it was the heat, or the beers they'd had with lunch. She didn't want to say anything to Mrs. Alexandria. She had been a most generous friend, and it would be insulting to say that the lunch had made her sick. She wiped a large hand, calloused by work, over her wet face. She had done well today, and Mrs. Alexandria was no longer upset that her cousin Pennon had failed. In fact, she was so pleased with her that she had now entrusted her with a very important mission.

Mrs. Alexandria promised that once they had finished here, she would take her back with her to South America and she could be in charge of Mrs. Alexandria's household. Isabella was very pleased. She would write her relatives in the old country and brag.

But first, they had to punish Robbie. She was an evil woman. Robbie had killed her father and then somehow framed Mrs. Alexandria for the murder. She had been rude to Isabella, too, not letting her run her fan club, and embarrassing her by twisting the truth when she, Isabella, had taken her story about the grave to the police. Isabella felt Mrs. Alexandria's plan to give Robbie a very bad scare was a good one. It was a light punishment for all she had done, but if the police would not help, then it was about all they could do. She felt she was helping Mrs. Alexandria get some justice when the police had failed. Also, she would get revenge for Robbie Williams embarrassing her.

When they had finished here today, Robbie would always be looking over her shoulder, waiting for the next attack, just as poor Mrs. Alexandria must now live watching always for the police. It was fair justice. Already, Mrs. Alexandria had said, Robbie had hired a bodyguard. So perhaps her cousin Pennon had not died in vain.

"Are you sure you can drive one of these things?" Alexandria said, cutting into Isabella's thoughts.

Isabella looked at the controls of the powerboat in which she was sitting. "Yes, Mrs. Alexandria. My uncle owned a small fishing company on Lake Erie. In the summer, I would often stay with my uncle's family to earn pocket money."

"Yes, yes," the tall woman cut in impatiently. "Now remember what I told you — you must go very fast and go very close to the boat called *Tubby* to swamp it. This is a very good boat. You can get very close and then yank the wheel around at the last minute to swerve away."

Isabella's head was starting to ache and her stomach was roiling. She was not looking forward to going out in the boat, but she would not disappoint her new employer. Her mother, God rest her soul, would be so proud of her when Isabella was head of Alexandria's household. Her mother was never more than cook's helper. "I will not disappoint you, Mrs. Alexandria." She was unaware that her speech was slurred.

Alexandria smiled. "I know you won't."

"Are you sure you're all right, Aliki?" Robbie sat on the edge of the dock, her legs holding *Tubby*'s gunnels to the side of the dock. Ryan was already aboard, sitting on the deck with her back against the bulkhead as she coiled the sheets.

"I'm fine," the scientist mumbled through stiff jaws. "You go have a good race and don't worry. I'll be walking up and down the shoreline to see if I can spot her."

"Well, don't take her on. You already look like you lost a fight with a kangaroo," Robbie grumbled, trying to express her concern for the woman who, however unwanted at first, had somehow become part of her life.

"Better me than you," Aliki countered teasingly. "At least I know how to fight and not just act like I can."

"Mom can handle herself. She had to in prison," Ryan said defensively.

Aliki's eyes darted to Robbie's. A message of pain and understanding traveled between them. Robbie reached over and patted Aliki's hand. "Be careful," she said, slipping into the sailboat.

"You, too." Aliki gave the dory a push out with her foot.

Alexandria put her sunglasses on and lowered the brim of her hat further over her eyes as she watched Isabella awkwardly manoeuvre the speedboat out into the lake. Alexandria knew her reflexes would be as slow as her thought processes by now. And just to ensure success, Alexandria had filed through the steering cable so that only a few strands held it. When Isabella yanked the wheel to avoid a collision with Robbie's sailboat, the cable would snap and the boat would continue on its deadly course. When they fished Isabella's body out, they would find that she had been drinking and taking drugs, no doubt to get enough courage to kill Robbie Williams. It was just so beautiful.

Alexandria turned her back and walked away casually. It wouldn't do to be too close to the accident.

Everything was working out nicely. She had thought at first that Isabella was going to be annoyingly stupid. When she recommended her cousin for the taking of the youngest Williams, Isabella had not known that Alexandria meant to hurt the child. Alexandria assured Isabella that she planned all along to give the child back. She convinced Isabella that it was just a game of cat and mouse to scare Robbie. Alexandria carefully explained to the disenchanted fan how they would come here and plan a series of mishaps. It would be their harmless but effective revenge. The slow witted and vengeful Isabella had fallen right in with Alexandria's plans.

Alexandria smiled. She had never been fond of her children. Robbie had been an accident and the others were simply to keep Philly happy. She had particularly hated Robbie. Every time she looked at her oldest daughter, she was reminded that she could have done better than the clumsy and boring Phillip Williams. A giant in business he might have been, but his dick and his talents as a lover had been pathetically small.

Aliki almost missed her. She was looking for Isabella Selo among the crowds on the beach. It was only in a passing glance that she noted the lone figure walking down the dock by the boat rentals. It was the movement that registered in her mind first. The figure moved like a cat, like Robbie. Then the hair and the shape of the long, strong body registered. If it wasn't Robbie, then it was Alexandria. Aliki cursed as she pushed through the throng, trying to get closer to the figure that had left the dock and was now mingling with the festival crowds.

Robbie and Ryan tacked around and came up to the starting buoy just as the gun went off. Robbie pulled the sheet tighter, bringing the sail in closer to the wind. The craft heeled over and Ryan shifted to sit on the gunwale and hike over the side to keep the boat from leaning over so far that it took on water.

They shot forward, the water rushing past the hull of their little craft and the wind cracking off the edge of the mainsail. Ryan looked over at her mother with a big grin pasted on her face. Robbie smiled back, her eyes sparkling with excitement. She looked over her shoulder. Ableton had dropped back to third as another boat owned by a summer resident had passed him to the windward side and stolen the air from his sails. She grinned and looked back at Ryan. Her daughter gave her the thumbs up.

They came up to the first buoy and cut in close, letting the boom fly across at the last moment. *Tubby* shuddered, then lifted and took off as the wind filled the sail. Ryan held on to a safety line and now actually stood on the side of the hull, using her body weight as a counterbalance to the strong winds they were picking up further from the shore. She laughed with glee and Robbie, at the rudder, watched the streamers on the mast stays to judge the direction of the wind in an effort to get the maximum hull speed from their little vessel.

As they crossed the finish line an hour later, they were a good fifty metres ahead of Ableton, who had made a valiant effort on the last stretch to make up the distance between them. Robbie waved to Janet and Reb as they shot past the judges' launch. Looking back at her family, it was Ryan's warning cry that snapped Robbie's head around to see the lifted bow of a fibreglass speedboat bearing down on them. Robbie tried her best in the last few seconds to tack clear. She launched herself forward at Ryan as the hull of the speedboat smashed down on *Tubby's* stern section.

Janet watched in horror as the speedboat came across the bow of the judges' launch and smashed into the small sailboat with a crack that shook the windows of the cabin behind her.

The settling water revealed a debris field of bits of white fibreglass and jagged bits of red plywood. There were no bodies visible. She stood dumbly, holding on to Reb, vaguely aware of the pilot giving orders to lower the life raft.

Aliki moved closer as she followed Alexandria out across a green towards a car park on the other side. "Alexandria?"

The woman ahead stopped and pivoted around gracefully. She smiled, but the truer emotion in her eyes was hidden behind dark sunglasses. "Now, let's see if I can get this straight. You are my daughter's slut's lover, aren't you?"

Aliki's lip curled in contempt. "I'm Doctor Pateas. I'm also an RCMP Inspector. And you, Mrs. Williams, are under arrest."

The ex-dancer laughed. "Really! Dear me, it is just like the movies. Did my bastard daughter write the script?"

Aliki's eyes turned thoughtful. "Tell me, Mrs. Williams, did you ever know my father, Georgeos Pateas?"

The thin lips parted briefly in surprise. For a minute, a pocket of silence isolated them from the far-off noise of the beach crowd and the traffic passing by on the other side of the park. "It is such a small, ugly little world, isn't it? I knew your father. Robbie is his. I'm sure you have realized that." Alexandria took off her sunglasses and slipped them into the summer bag she had over her shoulder. When the hand withdrew, it held a small, snub-nosed revolver.

"Why don't we take a ride and you can tell me all about your father," Alexandria suggested in a cold, quiet voice.

Aliki tried not to show her surprise. *Stupid, Aliki. How did you manage to get yourself in this situation?* "I don't think so, Mrs. Williams. I think instead you should come with me. You are under arrest, you know."

The older woman laughed thinly. "You have your father's panache, I'll give you that. It is a shame that I'm going to have to hurt you in order to be sure that you don't tell the police that I am in the country."

Aliki watched Alexandra's gun hand closely. "I don't—"

A loud crash and screams made Aliki look toward the beach. From the corner of her eye, she saw Alexandria raise the gun, and reacted before she even thought. She dove to the right and kicked up and out with her left leg. A searing pain gave evidence to the bullet that screwed its way through the epidermis layers of her left thigh.

Aliki's kick knocked the shot off target but Alexandria still held the weapon. The scientist landed heavily on her side and struggled to get back up to her feet. Alexandria held the gun on her, now looking desperate and angry.

"You stupid bitch," the woman hissed, pointing the gun once more. Aliki's hand moved in a flash and Alexandria gave a surprised little gasp. The gun slipped from her fingers as she crumpled to the ground, the handle of a knife sticking out of her chest.

Aliki felt dizzy, partly due to the shock of losing blood, but mostly at the realization that she had just taken a life. She looked around. No one was paying any attention to them. The crowds were some distance away, milling around and looking out at the lake. Aliki knew something had happened; she just hoped it didn't involve Robbie.

A man walked across the grass heading for the parking lot. "Excuse me, sir," Aliki called as she sank to the ground. "Could you get the police and tell them there is an officer down."

Chapter 22

Robbie broke the surface and found herself in a large air bubble beneath the white folds of the sail. She grabbed hold of a piece of the mast and pulled Ryan up close to her. "Are you all right?" she asked, treading water and gasping for breath.

"Yeah," coughed Ryan, reaching out to take hold of the mast as well. "You know, a kid could end up with some deep feelings of social rejection living in this family. I don't like to complain, but this is the third time this year that someone has tried to kill me."

Robbie was silent for a second. "You don't regret being with us, do you, Ryan?" she asked quietly, the pain evident in her voice.

Ryan laughed and reached a hand over to touch her mother's arm where it lay wrapped around the shattered mast. "Mom, I was joking."

Robbie smiled weakly. She hadn't been very successful at this mother thing, she knew. She only wanted to provide the best for her daughter, but somehow things always ended up like this. "Next year will be better," she promised.

Ryan laughed. "It couldn't be better, Mom. This has been the best year of my life. Aren't you having fun?"

Robbie smiled. "Yeah, I've never been happier," she admitted. "Come on, let's try to get out from under here."

They edged their way along the mast and then dove under the folded layers of sail-cloth to pop up amongst the debris. Someone gave a yell behind them, and they turned to see a small rowboat making its way toward them.

"You two okay?" asked one of the officials, his face worried.

"Yeah, just cuts and bruises. We haven't seen anyone else. Did you pick up the passengers of the powerboat?" Robbie asked, as she and Ryan swam to grab hold of the rescue craft. The water was cold and Robbie was starting to feel the effects. She looked at her daughter and saw that her lips were blue and her teeth chattering.

"No other survivors that we've seen yet. You ladies hold on and we'll pull you over to the launch." The man sitting in the stern reached over to take hold of each of them. "Pretty cold in there, eh?"

"Yeah," agreed Ryan, through chattering teeth. The shock and cold were starting to affect her.

Robbie moved closer, cocooning Ryan between her arms and the stern of the rescue boat. Ryan lowered her head to Robbie's arm and they were silent the rest of the short trip back to the launch. There, helpful hands reached to pull the two wet sailors up the stern ladder and onto the deck.

"Obbie!" screamed a worried voice, and Robbie curled an arm around her little daughter, who clung to her tightly. Janet knelt beside her, with Ryan supported in her lap.

"Hi." Robbie smiled up at Janet through the wet hair that plastered her face. "I hurt."

Janet's eyes filled with tears. She gently brushed the hair from Robbie's face with a shaky hand. "You two have more lives than a cat," she joked weakly. Then blankets arrived and Ryan and Robbie were wrapped up and given cups of hot tea, while the lifeboat and launch searched for any sign of the occupant of the speedboat.

The Williamses trooped off the launch, Ryan and Robbie feeling warmer and better after an hour's recuperation. They both had suffered a bit of bruising and some serious scrapes, but were in unexpectedly good shape considering the circumstances. Robbie's last-second dive at Ryan had pushed the two of them over the side and deep into the water, protecting them from most of the shattering debris.

To Robbie's surprise, it was Ableton who was there to help them down from the launch. "Most people just dock their damn boat after a race," he grumbled. "So, are you gonna have another craft for next year?"

Robbie rose to the challenge. "Like I'm going to let you win anything again."

"You ain't got a chance next year, queer. I'm ordering the new 822 snowmobile racer and building a new boat. You and Bartlett are going down."

"When hell freezes over, Ableton," Robbie teased, as Janet rolled her eyes and shepherded her family along the dock.

A police officer slipped through the crowd and came up to them. "Robbie Williams?"

"Yes," she responded through stiff lips, her stomach tightening into a knot.

Janet moved closer and wrapped an arm around her lover. Robbie, she knew, still had difficulty dealing with the police after her arrest and imprisonment.

"Could you come this way, ma'am? Inspector Pateas of the RCMP needs to see you about a matter."

Robbie gave Janet a quick, worried look and then stooped to pick Reb up in her arms so that they could move quickly through the crowds. Janet made sure Ryan was close, and they followed the police officer toward an ambulance sitting near the Community Centre, lights flashing.

Stepping into the building, they found Aliki lying on a stretcher. One bloody pant leg had been cut away and a white bandage covered a wound.

"Shit! What happened?" Robbie asked.

"I need to talk to you, Robbie," Aliki said quietly.

Aliki looked pleadingly at Janet. Janet nodded slightly and took Reb from Robbie's arms and gave a jerk of her head to indicate to Ryan that she should follow. She led the girls over to sit on a couch by a window and wait. She wasn't sure what the news was, but she knew that whatever it was, Aliki needed to deal with it one-on-one with Robbie.

From where she sat, she could watch Robbie's face. She saw shock and sorrow register there, and then caring as her partner reached out and took Aliki's hand. She watched closely as they talked for a few minutes, and then the ambulance attendants came and took Aliki away. Robbie followed behind the stretcher, but returned a short time later and walked over to where they sat.

"Alexandria is dead," Robbie stated flatly. "So is Isabella Selo. Her body was picked up by the police boat."

Janet reached up and took her partner's hand, pulling her down to sit with the rest of the family. It had been a hard time for them, but now the hate and secrets that had festered for all those years were out in the open. They couldn't hurt Robbie any more. She squeezed her partner's hand and waited for Robbie to tell her story in her own way.

The story came out in fits and starts and was tempered by a need to protect the girls from a lot of things that they did not need to know until they were older. Ryan listened intently, while Reb sat on her mom's lap and was soon asleep.

"There are a lot of things that I don't know yet. I'll be going to the hospital to be with Aliki, and when she is feeling better, I'm sure she'll tell me more. There is something though, something she is not sure of but she felt I needed to know. She knew I was worried about who my father is. She wanted me to know that there had been rumours in her family that her father had an affair with Alexandria before he moved west and met her mother. She thinks we might be related," Robbie finished, her voice quavering with emotion.

"Aliki is your half sister?" Janet asked in shock.

"She doesn't know for certain. She just wanted me to be aware that there might be a connection. She said she has known of the possibility for years, and that's why she took such a personal interest in my case."

The others looked at her in shock. Finally, Ryan spoke. "You look kinda alike," she observed.

"It would be weird," Robbie mumbled. "This whole day has been weird. I mean, I've been one of the Famous Williams all my life. Now maybe I'm not. Up until now, I kind of just didn't accept what Alexandria had told me. Now I guess I have to. It's just all so weird."

"It doesn't change who you really are, Robbie. This information might just help you find new roots. Better roots, maybe," Janet said in reassurance.

Looking up in bewilderment, Robbie asked, "What will I tell Elizabeth?"

"The truth," Janet answered immediately. "Elizabeth is your sister, Robbie. It has little to do with blood and a lot to do with how you feel about each other. I know it will be a shock for her, but in the long run I doubt very much if it will make any difference in your relationship. She loves you as a sister and that will not change."

Robbie frowned. "I'm not sure how I feel about Aliki being my half sister."

Biting her lip, Janet considered how awkward it could be if Aliki was to become a part of their life. *It's not that I wanted Aliki. That was just a moment of weakness brought on by my neediness and fear. But the kiss I shared with her could be an open wound that'll prevent the two from ever really getting to know and love each other.*

"Robbie, I love you. You have a very special chance here to start a new chapter in your life. A very special one that will give you more family you can love."

Nodding, Robbie smiled at her family, but her eyes still showed insecurity and worry.

Janet leaned close. She knew that later, after the girls were safely in bed, she would need to hold Robbie and help her come to terms with Alexandria's betrayal and the fact that she just might have a whole new family that she knew nothing about. She knew she would need to reassure Robbie that their love was true. They had all gone through so much this year, but Robbie carried the heaviest burden, added to which was a mother who was truly evil and a father she didn't know. Janet realized that only in her arms would Robbie be able to find the comfort she needed after today.

When Aliki opened her eyes, it was Robbie who sat quietly by her bed. "Hi."

"Hi. I was just talking to your doctor. I...I told him I was your sister." Robbie blushed.

Aliki smiled. "So, how am I?"

"He said you're going to be fine, but you'll need some physical therapy."

"That's good." Aliki tried to sound less relieved than she actually was.

Robbie chewed on her lip. "What you said, you know, about your dad, do you think it's true?"

Their eyes met. "Yes. I have always been curious, but once I met you I had no doubt. We have the same bones."

Robbie laughed. "Like that would hold up in a court of law."

"It might, but I'm agreeable to a blood test to support my professional opinion."

"There's Janet." The words were out, cold as ice, before Robbie could stop them.

A blush traveled up Aliki's neck. "I owe you an apology. I was way out of line that night. It was wrong and it won't happen again. It was no more than a moment of weakness on both our parts. Janet knew that immediately. It took me a while to discover she was right. I regret my actions because I took advantage of Janet's trust. I don't want to compound that error by making it an issue that will keep me from knowing a sister who I admire." Aliki reached out with a weak hand.

Robbie grasped it, feeling the warmth of her sister's hand. "I can't say that it doesn't bother me, but I trust Janet. I've learned that I can trust you, too. Let's see about that blood test soon and make it official. How do you think your family will handle it, finding out that there's another member?"

Aliki laughed. "You gotta be kidding, right? A house full of men suddenly discovering their sister is the famous and beautiful actor, Robbie Williams! They won't even notice I'm in the room. They'll be tripping over themselves to make you welcome."

"I want them to like me for me, not because of who I am." Robbie frowned.

Squeezing Robbie's hand reassuringly, Aliki smiled. "They will."

Janet looked out the window as Robbie's car pulled into their driveway. She met her partner at the door. "You okay?"

"Yeah."

"Aliki?"

"The doctor said she should make a complete recovery." Robbie looked awkward. "Uh, her being my sister and all, maybe she should stay here for a few weeks, you know, until she's feeling better and we have some results from the blood test to verify that we are related."

"Whatever you want, Robbie," Janet responded, giving her partner a hug and enjoying Robbie's warm response. *The worst is over. Our family has pushed away the dark times and grown closer and stronger this year. Autumn will be here soon. We have our lives ahead of us, and many dreams yet to fulfill.*

The hot summer robed itself in the colours of fall, but lingered on into the warm, lazy days of Indian summer. Predictably, the seasons rotated one after the other, and it had been over a dozen years since the lodge on Long Lake had been restored and occupied. Janet and Robbie Williams had settled into operating their studio and the College of Film and Animation, and to raising their family. There were three homes on Long Lake now: the lodge, the small cabin that Janet had owned and that was now occupied by David and Elizabeth Potts, and a cottage that Aliki Pateas had built some summers ago after her marriage to Dawn Freeman, the woman she had met out West during her trip home.

Janet was thinking about Aliki's cottage when the phone rang. She picked up the phone on the second ring. "Hello."

"Hi, Janet, it's Brian-the-long-suffering. I need to speak to T-Rob."

Janet smiled. Brian had become a notable film director and producer in his own right, but even after nineteen years of working for the company, he lived in awe of Robbie's legendary temper and creative genius.

Janet looked out the window to the view of her wife's tush as she leaned under the hood of the 1956 Buick that she was rebuilding. "She's sort of up to her hips in work at the moment, Brian. Can I give her a message and have her phone you back later?"

A moan came from the other end of the phone. "It's rubbing off! You are aiding and abetting an AWOL creative genius. I know what she's doing; she's working on that damn car. That is all she can think about these days."

Janet laughed. "It's Sunday, Brian. Even creative geniuses get a day off now and again."

"It's not the weekend here in Australia, it's Monday, and I have big Monday problems on the film set."

Janet could hear the crackle of wrapping as Brian unrolled his stomach tablets. When Brian started eating digestive pills like candy, it meant he really did need to speak to T-Rob. She sighed. It seemed as if she and Robbie never had any time together anymore. There was always something, and at the moment Robbie was pretty annoyed with her. "Hold on, Brian. I'll get her."

Janet put the phone down and headed out of the huge log home that had once belonged to her great grandfather, and that Robbie had bought and restored for them. She hoped Brian's call did not mean that Robbie was going to have to fly to Australia. There was such a lot going on at the moment. There were some issues that she and Robbie really needed to work through, and the family was all coming up for Thanksgiving. Plans had to be worked out for the wedding, too. Aliki and Dawn's adopted daughter MacKenzie was marrying a lawyer from Toronto in the spring, and she wanted to have the wedding at Long Lake.

Robbie was deep in thought as she worked on the old car's engine. The thoughts had nothing to do with the carburetor that she was trying to remove; they were about her interpersonal relations. This time of year was always bad. This was when she and Ryan had fought and Ryan had walked out, but it was particularly bad this year because Janet didn't trust her anymore.

"Robbie?"

Robbie started and her head smashed against the raised hood of the car. "Shit!" she muttered, and emerged rubbing the sore spot at the back of her head.

Janet smiled and shook her head, then stood on her tiptoes and kissed Robbie's cheek. "You okay?"

Robbie smiled. "Yeah. I was thinking and didn't realize you were there."

Janet gave her partner a quick hug and immediately felt Robbie stiffen. She tried not to let it bother her. *Okay, I was wrong to arrange the surgery while Robbie was away filming, but I was hurt and jealous and handled things badly. Robbie just has to understand that this procedure is so very important to me, to my emotional healing.* "Brian's on the phone. It sounds like he has a serious production problem."

Robbie nodded, dropped a quick kiss on Janet's forehead, and headed over to the house with long strides, wiping the grease from her hands on a rag. When Janet came in, she found Robbie sitting at her desk in her office, glasses on the end of her nose and reading the fax material that was coming through from Australia. Janet left her alone. When Robbie focused on a problem, it was with the same intensity that she did everything in her life. She would not wish to be disturbed.

This is a bad time of year for Robbie, Janet mused It was on a Thanksgiving weekend, some years ago now, that Ryan had announced that she was not going on to do her masters in science, but had instead enlisted in the Canadian Armed Forces. There had been a hell of a row and the end result had been that Ryan had packed up a few things and left. Janet had tried to mend the fences between Robbie and their elder daughter, but her success had been marginal. Old hurts ran deep between the two of them and, although the love they had for each other went just as deep, pride kept them apart. Ryan had kept in touch, but the fact that she had never returned home, even though she had often been invited, hurt Robbie deeply.

Janet decided that while Robbie was on the phone was a good time to head over the College of Film and Animation, of which she was the director, and see to a bit of paperwork herself. First, however, she went down to the lake to let Rebecca know where she was going.

Reb was in the process of trying to train Dufus how to follow a scent. A few years before their old dog Rufus had passed away, he had managed to corner Walt and Mary Higgins' prize Golden Retriever and do the deed. The Higginses were still trying to get over the shock of that violation of their purebred animal. The infusion of prize-winning genes seemed to have no effect whatsoever on the issue of the union. The three puppies looked exactly like Rufus — big, orange, ugly, and crooked tailed. David and Elizabeth had taken one pup, Aliki and Dawn another, and Dufus had stayed to eventually replace his dad, Rufus.

"Reb, honey, I'm just popping over to the school to do some paperwork. Obbie is on the phone to Brian. Could you let her know where I am?"

The beautiful sixteen-year-old looked up and flashed a smile that melted hearts. "Sure, Mom. Look, I think Dufus has the idea now."

Janet looked down. Reb was holding a sweater that looked a lot like Robbie's, or at least it had before it was covered in mud and dog slobber. "Is that—"

Reb quickly cut her mother off before she could get going. "Obbie said I could use it. I thought I'd better practice with Obbie's stuff first because she is the one who always goes missing."

It was a joke, but Janet could see the worry in her daughter's eyes. Being part of a family of wealth and fame had not been easy. They had gone through some dark times together. She pulled her daughter in for a hug and kissed her head. "You are quite right and I love you for thinking of it. Does Dufus have as good a nose as Rufus did?"

Reb looked at the big hairy animal sitting obediently at her side. "I think so. He picks up a scent and gets on a trail easily enough, but if a squirrel crosses his path, we've had it. Dufus hates squirrels."

Janet smiled and gave her daughter another hug before heading up the path that led behind the house to the large garage that housed their vehicles. Starting her car, she drove down the road with a smile on her face. They might have their problems, but generally, life was pretty good.

Major Ryan Williams pulled her Jeep into the driveway about half an hour later and sat looking past the corner of the house to the lake. The teen with the dog was Reb, she realized with a jolt. Ten years, and everything had changed. She swung out of the old vehicle in one smooth movement and strode down to where her sister stood working with Dufus. She'd kept in touch, of course, through letters and email, but she hadn't actually seen her sister in years. The school pictures she got periodically could have been of some stranger. In Ryan's mind, Reb was frozen as a strong willed, rebellious six-year-old.

The dog growled dangerously and took two quick steps toward Ryan, and Ryan stopped.

"Stay," Reb commanded and looked up at the tall, stern soldier on the path above her. "Can I help y— Ryan? Ryan!" The teen ran up the hill and jumped into her sister's arms as she had when she was six.

Ryan held her close, hiding the emotions swirling inside. "Hi, kid. I've missed you."

Reb was crying. "Ryan, I can't believe it's you. I have missed you so much! I knew you'd come home some day. I just knew it."

Ryan stiffened with tension and stepped back a little from her sister. Gently, she wiped a few tears from the teen's face with her finger. "I don't know how long I can stay," she cautioned. "Ah, I don't know if I'm even going to be welcomed."

Reb put her hands on her slim hips. "Of course you are welcomed, Ryan. You're part of our family. Obbie frets all the time about you not being here. She loves you, Ryan."

Ryan's tentative smile reflected insecurity. Her eyes were dark and filled with pain. She tried to sound nonchalant. "So, who is here? Uh, are the Pateases here yet?"

Reb looked up with sharp, penetrating eyes. "Oh shit. You've come back because Mac is getting married, haven't you?"

Ryan didn't say anything. Her jaw locked in a determined line.

"Ryan, you can't!"

Eyes the colour of ice met Reb's. "Watch me."

"Oh boy, this is going to be another one of those Williams things that the tabloids love to write about." Reb sighed in frustration, waving her arms in the air dramatically.

Ryan couldn't help herself; she smiled. "So, who is here?"

"Just Obbie at the moment." She saw Ryan stiffen and hurriedly went on. "Mom is at the college. She'll be back in an hour or so. Obbie's on the phone with Brian, so that's good for a couple of hours of yelling. Come on, I'll sneak you into the house and we'll figure out some way of letting them know you're here."

At the college, Janet cleared her desk of a few items of paperwork that had been on her mind, and then headed back to the house. She was anxious to know whether the problem that Brian was having with production on location in Australia would become a problem for them all. Deep in thought, she almost bumped into her daughter, who was standing in the doorway and positively squirming with excitement.

"Shhh! Mom, you are never going to guess who's here," Reb said in a stage whisper.

"Who?" Janet asked, already visualizing an evening with Robbie in a temper and some poor houseguest cringing in the corner. Her daughter pulled her into the kitchen.

An army officer stood up as she entered. "Hello, Aunt Janet."

Janet stopped dead. Her mouth opened, closed, opened again, and still nothing came out. Then she simply gave up, ran to her adopted daughter, and held on tight, crying.

Ryan was embarrassed, feeling emotional and flustered. She tried to cover up with a joke. "Some welcome. Hell, so far everyone who has seen me has cried."

Reb pulled some tissues from a box on the counter and handed them to her mom, and then stood close to her big sister's side. "Ryan is a major, and she just got her doctorate in physics like Aunt Elizabeth."

Janet stepped back and dabbed at her eyes as she gave Ryan a once over. "You could have told us. All those letters from all over the world. We had no idea what you were up to in the military."

Ryan smiled but said nothing. Her work over the years had been classified.

"Does your mom know you are here?"

Ryan shook her head and smiled at her kid sister. "From what we can make out, she's having a conference call with Brian and some others. Things must be working out because she hasn't sworn or yelled now in several minutes."

Janet rolled her eyes. "You wait here."

Janet walked into Robbie's office and found her partner pacing back and forth, barking instructions at poor Brian and his assistants. Much to Robbie's surprise, Janet reached up and placed two fingers over her lover's mouth. "Brian? This is Janet. Listen, love, we have a guest and I need Robbie right away. Do you think you can manage without my wife?"

"Sure, sure, no problem, Janet," Brian babbled, relief in his voice. T-Rob had spent five minutes solving the problem and an hour and a half yelling about it.

Janet hung up and looked at Robbie. Robbie crossed her arms and raised an eyebrow in question. Janet touched her partner's arm reassuringly. "Ryan's in the kitchen," she said softly. Robbie swayed, blinked, gasped, and made a beeline for the door. Janet followed at a more reasonable pace.

Robbie rounded the corner into the kitchen so quickly that Ryan instinctively felt under attack and stepped in front of her little sister. The two Williamses stood looking at each other. They had different colouring but the same bone structure and build. There was no doubt they were mother and daughter. Reb gave her stubborn sister a gentle push from behind.

Ryan stepped over to Robbie. "I'm home, Mom."

Robbie wrapped her daughter in her arms and held her silently. So many emotions were running through her that she felt light headed. Quietly, Janet signalled to Reb from the doorway and they left Robbie and Ryan alone; holding each other.

"I'm sorry, Mom." Ryan's voice was rough with emotion. "I felt I had to prove something to you. I was wrong. Can you forgive me?"

Robbie held on even tighter. "Yeah, you were wrong, but you were a kid and I was the adult. I acted like a horse's ass. I'm sorry, too."

"You going to let me go?" Ryan asked, laughing nervously.

"No. You might be a dream and I don't want to lose you."

Ryan hadn't come home for this; she hadn't thought it possible that they could mend any bridges. When she saw her mom again, it just happened. Now that it had, Ryan felt an incredible need to protect her mom and make sure she was never hurt again. "You are never going to lose me, Mom. I...I'm your daughter."

Robbie forced herself to step back and give Ryan some room. "Yes, you are and I'm proud of you."

Devilment sparkled in Ryan's eyes for a second, like it used to when she was a teen. "You don't know much about me."

Despite herself, Robbie reached out and touched Ryan's cheek. "I don't need to. You are my daughter. I love you and I know what sort of person you are. Whatever you have done with your life, it would be what is right and honourable."

The tears slowly ran down Ryan's face, despite her fight for control. She smiled and swallowed hard. "Thanks, Mom."

Robbie wiped away her own tears and tried to pull herself together. "Sit down. Have you eaten? No? I'll make you something."

"No way!" Ryan laughed. "I want to live to see tomorrow. No one in this family willingly eats your cooking. How about I make something and you see to brewing some coffee?"

Robbie looked stubborn. "I can cook."

Ryan pulled her in for a hug. "No, you can open a can and burn toast."

Robbie laughed. "Okay, you get something, then. Look at you. You're all grown up. Captain?"

"Major, brand new."

"That's good, Ryan. Are you going to be a career soldier, then?"

"Five more years. I just got my doctorate, Mom, in astrophysics."

Robbie sank onto a kitchen chair. "You're a physicist?"

"Yes, and I think a reasonably good one." Ryan smiled, pleased that her mother was clearly overwhelmed with her achievement. Her mom looked like she was in shock.

"A scientist. I always wanted to be a scientist," Robbie mumbled.

Ryan came up behind her and bent to wrap her arms around her mother. She whispered softly, "I know, Mom. You'd have been a good one too, but you had me instead."

Robbie kissed the strong hand resting on her shoulder. "No regrets there. You were the best thing to come out of my youth."

When Reb stuck her head in a half hour later, she found the two of them munching subs and drinking bottled beer.

"Can I have some?" she asked, bouncing in and taking a seat beside her sister.

"Sub yes, beer no." Ryan laughed and handed her sister half her sandwich.

Reb pulled a face at her, but took the sandwich eagerly. "I'll probably choke to death with nothing to wash this down with," she warned.

Robbie got up. "I'll pour you some milk. Ryan, could you make a few more of these? I'll go get Janet."

"Sure, Mom." Ryan turned and tipped Reb from her chair. "Come on, teen-slug, give me a hand."

Reb gave her a playful punch. "Hey, who are you calling a teen-slug, starched shorts!"

Robbie left them pushing and shoving their way to the fridge and went to find Janet. She needed to see Janet. Ryan was home. She found her in their bedroom, folding laundry, and tackled her to their bed, giving her a big hug and kiss, in her happiness forgetting for a moment that things had been a bit awkward between them recently.

"She's wonderful," Robbie stated, less than modestly.

"Yes, she is," Janet agreed, smiling about as broadly as was humanly possible.

"Come and have lunch with us."

"I didn't want to disturb you. I thought you and Ryan would have things to talk about."

Robbie bounced up and pulled Janet to her feet. "Hey, we are both her mother. We want you there. We're a family. Reb already snuck back in. I think she has glued herself to her sister."

Janet laughed and wrapped an arm around her lover as they headed out of their bedroom. "That little monkey. I told her to give you two some time alone."

Dr. Aliki Pateas sat biting her lip with worry as she looked across the room at her grown daughter. The years had gone by so quickly. It seemed like only yesterday that she had thrown her bags into her van after the Williams murder investigation and headed west as Janet Williams had suggested. There, at her father's house, she had met the petite, blonde Dawn Freeman.

Dawn was a remarkable woman who had grown up with her family in an isolated little log cabin in the foothills of the Canadian West. Dawn had started writing children's books and had then gone on to write several adult best sellers. She was not only an accomplished writer, but also a wonderful public speaker. Aliki was very proud of her partner, but she missed Dawn fiercely when she had to be away on speaking engagements or book promotions.

When Aliki met Dawn, she was already the mother of an adopted First Nations child, MacKenzie. The natural mother had been a Salish Indian friend and the child's father had been Aliki's older brother. Poor little MacKenzie had witnessed both her mother's death from cancer and her father's grief-induced suicide. The trauma had left her mute for most of her early childhood.

Love had come easily among the three of them, but it had taken them a long time to finally meld together as a family. That was many years ago. MacKenzie was now a beautiful young woman — tall and slim, with the bronze colouring of her Salish mother and the blue eyes of her father. Having taken an active interest in both her mothers' careers, Mac had been talking recently of becoming a mystery writer after she finished her schooling. Aliki and Dawn had raised Mac together, and she was just as much Aliki's daughter as she was Dawn's. So Aliki felt she had to talk to Mac about her engagement.

Aliki sat now on the edge of her chair in the living room of their Toronto home, trying with some difficulty to have a sensitive talk with MacKenzie. She had been really proud to be asked to stand in as Mac's father, in the place of her brother who had killed himself. But yesterday, she had accidentally overheard Mac arguing about it on the phone with her fiancé Stewart. After a night of tossing and turning, she had decided to broach the topic with Mac. She wished she could ask her partner what to do, but Dawn was away on a speaking tour and wouldn't be back until tomorrow.

She swallowed hard. "Umm, I know...Stewart's parents are not very comfortable about your parents being two gay women. I...I don't have to give you away, Mac. I mean, I could just sit with your mom and we could ask your Uncle David to give you away."

Mac looked up in surprise, and then blushed deeply as she realized that Aliki knew that Stewart's family was ashamed and embarrassed by her family. "Aliki, I'm going to tell you what I told Stewart. I am neither ashamed nor uncomfortable about the fact that my aunt and my parents are lesbians. I am sorry it causes his homophobic family problems, but nothing would make me deny my family who loves me...not even him."

Aliki squirmed as she felt the red creeping up her neck to her face. "Ahh, he is going to be your husband. You know, he has to come first in your life. I...I mean, we'll understand that."

Dark blue eyes flashed. "I wouldn't. As well as being proud of my gay parents, I am also mixed race. You and Mom have raised me to be proud of my Salish heritage. Where do I draw the line with Stewart's family? Do I say: you don't have to accept my parents for what they are, but you do have to accept what *I* am? I don't think so. What I am bringing to Stewart's family is a little social tolerance and a wider view of this world's variations. They can accept that or stick it up their asses."

Aliki laughed. "Damn, I'm glad we raised you to be a lady."

Mac flushed. "Well, it's true." Flustered, she resorted to the language of her youth when the trauma of seeing her father's death had left her unable to speak. She signed *I love you.*

Aliki signed back, *I love you, too.* For a while they sat quietly, enjoying the comfort of the bond of love they had, then Aliki pulled her courage together and broached the other issue that was on her mind. She started hesitantly. "Uhh, Stewart seems nice. He's got some good goals and will be a responsible partner."

Mac nodded. "Yes."

"Sensible, level-headed guy."

"Yes."

Aliki looked at her in worry. "Are you sure he is the one?"

Mac suddenly went somber, looking at her hands for a minute while she organized her thoughts. "Some years ago, I met someone I fell very much in love with. There is no doubt in my mind about that, but it didn't work out between us. Sometimes it just doesn't." The young woman shrugged her shoulders. "I've learned since then that love isn't enough. A partner needs to be a friend, too, and someone you can count on. That's Stewart. He's a good friend, he'll treat me well, and I love him. Stewart is responsible, caring, and he loves me, too. He'll provide me with companionship and children, and we'll be happy together. He knows that there was someone else, but he also knows that is past history and that it's him I love and want to marry."

The scientist's eyes showed shock and worry. She wished desperately that Dawn were there to handle this one; she was way out of her depth. "I don't want you settling for second best. Are you sure Stewart is the one and not this other guy?"

"Yes, I am." Mac laughed, coming over to sit on the arm of the chair and give her aunt and adopted mother a hug. "You can't make someone into the person you want to love. Besides, it wasn't a guy, it was a woman."

Aliki swirled around and looked at her daughter, her blue eyes wide with shock. "You have never even dated a girl; it's always been guys. How could this have gone on without me knowing?"

Mac shrugged. "I guess I was experimenting."

By now, Aliki was near the free-babble stage. "You and this woman, you've..." She made some gestures of frustration when words failed her, and then jumped instead into another train of thought. "I mean — have you...with men? No, wait, I don't want to know. That's none of my business." Aliki leaned back and tried to gather her thoughts. This conversation was not going as she had expected.

Mac chuckled at Aliki's distress. She was a wonderful person, and Mac adored her, but for a lesbian, Aliki was awfully straight. "No, I didn't sleep with her and no, I haven't with any guys, either. Well, you know, we've—"

"Don't tell me." Aliki got up and retreated to the other side of the room. "There are some things that should remain private."

Mac slid from the arm of the big, overstuffed chair into the seat that Aliki had vacated. It was still warm and there was a lingering scent of spice that was very much Aliki. It felt like a secure hug. She smiled at her mom but said nothing. Her parents were intelligent and wise, and she had been expecting this question. It was easier with Aliki, who always had trouble addressing personal issues. Her other mom would have asked disturbing and thought-provoking questions and that would have been much harder.

Aliki pulled herself together and tried again. "Warning bells are going off in my head here, Mac. It seems to me that staying single would be better than marrying someone you know is not your first choice."

Mac saw the pain in the older woman's eyes and got up immediately and went over to hug her gently. "But I do love Stewart. He is a fine man. There are many types of love. Love is not enough; some relationships are good for you and some are not. I will have a good life with Stewart. I know that."

At the lodge, the Williams clan stayed up late talking, freely at times, as family do, and awkwardly at other times because they were strangers after ten years. Finally, Reb went to sleep with her head against Ryan's shoulder and they all decided to call it a night. Sleep did not come easily to the three adults. Ryan lay in her old room that still reflected the interests of her teenaged mind and she pondered the bridge that had been crossed by coming home. It was one she had doubted could ever exist again. It was strangely comforting on the one hand, and rather unnerving on the other.

Robbie tried sleeping but tossed and turned until Janet turned on the light and handed her partner a script. "Read, and don't think about Ryan. That's an order."

Robbie smiled sheepishly and took the script, settling down and letting Janet use her for a pillow while she focused without understanding on the pages. The sun was rising when she finally went to sleep, her head resting next to her lover's.

Ryan woke to find Reb snuggled in beside her. She scrunched up her eyes and mumbled cheekily, "Go away, you're not my type."

Reb laughed and gave her big sister a playful nudge. "Actually, I'm into males, Ian Fraser to be exact. I'm a black sheep bouncing along the family rainbow."

Ryan pulled herself up to lean against her headboard, and gave her eyes a rub, then she pulled a face. "Be sure, kid. I dated guys all through high school, but it never felt right. In university, I gradually moved into lesbian relationships. It didn't take me long to realize that was my true orientation. Now, when I think about kissing a guy, I think, yuck!"

The two of them laughed. Then Reb sobered. "I shouldn't laugh. With Ian, it's serious, Ryan."

Ryan went still and worry clouded her eyes. "How serious?"

Reb rolled her eyes. "We are not sleeping together, Ryan. I'm talking about the family. Having a family that glows rainbow colours in the dark is hard enough to explain. Try explaining that one of my moms has been arrested for murder, that my other mom is a Williams because she married both my father and my aunt, that my other aunt has won the Nobel Prize in Physics but can't drive a car, and that my sister wears army boots. How am I going to explain all that to Ian?"

"We are a bit eccentric." Ryan smiled.

"Eccentric?" Reb spluttered. "We are the only people I know who have their own page each month in the tabloids. The spring edition had Obbie running away with her co-star and Mom threatening to reveal all in a feature movie if she didn't come home."

"Knowing what I do about Obbie's early life, that would be some blockbuster."

"My point exactly!" Reb flopped dramatically back onto a pillow. "I love you all dearly, but *Ripley's Believe It Or Not* has nothing, I repeat, nothing, on you lot."

"So, do Obbie and Aunt Janet know you are seeing this guy?"

"Sort of. They know I've met him a few times at the riding stables. He wants to take me to the fall dance, and that means bringing him home. The last guy I brought here went home crying because Obbie was standing on the porch railing, rehearsing a scene from *Galaxy Wars* using a tree branch as a laser sword, and Mom was trying to wash Rufus in tomato juice in a tub because he'd said hello to a skunk. Billy thought it was alien blood and ran most of the way home. He still avoids me — and that was in the third grade."

Ryan smiled at her sister who lay sprawled at the end of the bed. "Tough one, kid. Maybe you could tell him that the insanity is not genetic, but a curse placed on us by aliens after the *Galactic Wars*."

Reb pulled a face. "Big help you are. And now I suppose you are really going to mess up my life by causing a scene about Mac's engagement to Stewart Farton."

Ryan looked shocked. "No scene. Mac is just not going to marry him."

Reb wrapped an arm over her eyes and moaned pathetically. "I'll have to resign myself to being an old maid, or join a convent and dedicate my life to God."

"God wouldn't have you." Ryan laughed unsympathetically. "You are a little rotter."

She slid from the bed wearing only her undies and a T-shirt, and stepped into a pair of sweatpants. "Come on, I need coffee before I can solve the problems of the world."

"Holy shit! It's a Willy Jeep!"

The words penetrated Janet's sleep just enough for her to register that her olive was up and active. There was no doubt about it; the Williams family was just like olives. She heard the pounding of feet as her lover ran down the hall and the slam of the screen door as she headed outside. Janet smiled and slipped deeper into sleep.

Reb stood at the kitchen counter pouring Ryan and herself a second cup of coffee and looking at Obbie sitting in Ryan's Jeep, pretending she was driving through a minefield. Various vooms and kabooms drifted through the window. "Mom has found your Jeep. She's behind the wheel and seems to be having a fantasy that might lead to an orgasm."

Ryan got up from the breakfast nook and went over to have a look. "You know, you are far too worldly for a sixteen-year-old." She looked out the window. "Okay, so you might be right. I'd better get out there before she ruins my seat covers."

Reb smiled. Ryan just wanted to be with her mom. "Whatever you do, don't give Obbie the keys to the Jeep. Mom will never forgive you." The warning came too late. Ryan was already gone.

Back in the bedroom, Janet sighed and let the dream of a sleep-in fade as she opened her eyes to see her indignant younger daughter standing at the end of the bed. "The creeps drove off and left me here."

"Forgive them, Reb. It was the Jeep. Obbie and Ryan are beyond human reason once they see a collector car."

Reb sighed. "Well, it will give us a chance to have a mother and daughter talk about the older man in my life while they are gone. Here, I brought you a mug of coffee to help you wake up."

Janet was already awake. The phrase "older man in my life" had brought her to a sitting position and full alert. "Older man?" she inquired, in a tone she hoped sounded calm and reasonable.

Reb gave her mom a look, and then climbed on the end of the bed to sit cross-legged. "Mother, I am very mature for my age. How many sixteen-year-olds do you know who have visited their mom in prison, been kidnapped, and survived a firestorm? And those are only the highlights of my life."

Janet was not to be sidetracked. "Who is this older man?" she asked, annoyed to see her hand shaking as she took a sip of her coffee.

"Ian Fraser. He is eighteen. He's working up here for the year with the forestry services. At the moment, he's planting trees. You remember, I met him at the stables. His parents emigrated from Scotland five years ago. Ian just finished his first year of university at Guelph. He wants to be a vet, but he has to earn some money to finish his undergraduate degree."

"Eighteen."

"That's only two years difference," Reb pointed out.

"There is a significant gap between being sixteen and eighteen." Janet sighed; her stomach tied in a knot.

Reb frowned. "I know, I know. I've just heard the lecture from my sister." Her voice changed to sound just like Ryan's as she mimicked her sister's words. "Reb, the difference between sixteen and eighteen is the difference between virginity and carnal knowledge."

Janet held up her hand. "Stop. I don't even want to go there. The difference between sixteen and eighteen is jail time. Keep that firmly in your mind. Well, that, and the fact that Obbie will skin him alive if he does anything he shouldn't. Now, tell me all about this fellow."

Reb smiled and relaxed. Her mom was going to be cool about Ian.

The Jeep motored along the highway with Ryan and Robbie sitting side by side, grins on their faces as the wind whipped their hair about.

"She's a 1943 Willy MB with a four cylinder L-head, side valves, and a three speed synchromesh transmission. She's built like a little tank — heavy steel channel sides with five cross members and one K member. Her grille is made from welded flat iron bar," Ryan explained, yelling over the wind. "You can tell she is a 1943 Willy MB by the small head-lamps inside the grille, the two pane windshield, and because the spare wheel and jerry can are located on the back panel." As her mother drove, Ryan looked around happily at the familiar territory of her childhood. "Slow down and turn off here to the right."

Robbie slowed and pulled onto an overgrown logging trail that cut a slash through a secondary-growth forest. They bumped along slowly, enjoying testing the old vehicle's ability. Some twenty minutes later, they came into a clearing filled with tall grasses and milkweed. Robbie killed the engine and Ryan swung out, looking around with pleasure.

"This was Lovers' Lane when I was a kid, but I used to come here and look around for artifacts. It was a lumber camp at the turn of the century, but over there," Ryan pointed towards a rocky outcrop, "there's an old mineshaft or something. They must have been looking for nickel or gold, I should think."

Robbie nodded absently, feeling strangely shy and at a loss for words around her grown daughter. There were so many things that she needed to ask, to resolve between the two of them. "I never meant to force you to leave."

Ryan turned to look at her mom. "You didn't. Oh yeah, I was pissed about you get-ting all upset about me joining the armed forces, but that was just window dressing." She pulled a length of grass free and stuck it in her mouth, enjoying the bitter-grain taste.

Robbie looked at her hands on the wheel. "So, why then? Why did you leave?"

Ryan got back into the Jeep and nervously played with the edge of the window frame. "I had to prove that I could do it on my own...that I didn't need you."

Robbie felt as though she had been struck. She swallowed hard and blinked back tears.

Unaware of how much her statement had hurt, Ryan continued. "I loved being with you, Aunt Janet, and Reb, but there was still a part of me that felt like a loser. I guess I felt that if I allowed you to pay my way, I would never know for sure if I would have been a failure if you hadn't always been there to bail me out whenever I ran into a problem."

Ryan felt a tightening in her chest. Spilling her guts was harder than she'd antici-pated. "Even before I knew who my mom was, you were always sending your people down to take care of me and get me out of trouble. I was a royal fuck-up, but you and Aunt Janet brought me home anyway. I was so afraid that I would fail and you would send me away."

Tears rolled slowly down Ryan's face. Robbie reached out and took her daughter's hand, kissing it softly. "You meant the world to me. I would never have sent you away. I was very proud of you."

Ryan nodded. "I knew that on an intellectual level, but emotionally there was this little, hurt kid trying to prove she wasn't a failure and deserved your love."

Robbie turned, tears in her eye. "Ryan—"

"Mom, it's okay. It wasn't anything you did or didn't do for me; it was something I needed to do for myself. I made a mess of my childhood by being bitter and angry and lashing out at authority in any way I could. You and Aunt Janet gave me unconditional love, and I realized that the problem restricting my opportunities and future wasn't the system putting me down but my own attitude."

Ryan's mouth settled into a confident, determined line, so like her mom's. "So I needed to try again, all by myself, to be the success I should have been all along. That's why I joined the armed forces — to prove myself. I wasn't running away from home, Mom, I just wanted to walk through your door again, this time as a success."

Robbie nodded but no words came out. She buried her face in her hands for a few seconds and tried to get her emotions sorted out. She needed to do it right this time, needed to understand things from Ryan's point of view as well as her own. "I...I think I understand. I...I have missed you very much. I love you, Ryan, and I'm very proud of what you have achieved — on your own."

Ryan smiled broadly. "Thanks, Mom. I love you, too."

That seemed like about all the emotion and sensitivity that the two of them could handle, so Robbie wisely tried to lighten the conversation. "So, Mac and her family will be here tomorrow. I imagine you two will have a lot of catching up to do. Are you going to be able to come back for her wedding in the spring?"

Ryan's hands tightened into fists. "That's the other reason I'm here. There isn't going to *be* any damn wedding in the spring."

Aliki picked up Dawn at the airport the next day and they enjoyed a pleasant evening as a family. Mac cooked a special meal, and the three of them talked and laughed as Dawn related some of the experiences she'd had while promoting her latest book. Now she and Aliki were alone in their room and, instead of the passion they usually shared when they had been separated for a time, Aliki paced and fidgeted about.

Dawn looked up from the book she was reading. "You want to tell me what's on your mind, lover?"

Aliki sat down on the bed's edge. "I think you should ask Mac to delay her wedding."

"What?"

"I just want her to be sure she should marry Stewart. Or maybe *I* need to be sure. She told me that she had been in love with someone else."

Dawn smiled sadly and took her partner's hand. "Yes, I know."

"You do? Did you know it was a woman?"

"Yes."

"How come everyone knows this but me? Who?"

Dawn leaned forward and gave her partner a hug. "She has always been in love with Ryan Williams."

"What! I'm going to have that Ryan's head on a platter. What the hell was she doing corrupting Mac? What did she do with our daughter?"

Dawn reached up and put her hand gently over Aliki's mouth. "She did nothing and that was the whole problem. Ryan was never anything more than a good friend, and then she went away."

"This is Robbie's fault. If that damn half-sister of mine hadn't argued with Ryan..."

Dawn flopped back against the pillows in frustration. She'd had enough. "Aliki, shut up. You are ranting and making no sense at all."

Aliki's mouth snapped shut, but she looked at Dawn with cold, blue eyes that sparked with annoyance.

"Now listen to me, you can't make Ryan love Mac. Nor can you ask me to try to have Mac delay the wedding. This is Mac's decision and we need to give her support and understanding. She's all grown up, Aliki, and we have to trust that she knows her own heart. She seems to love Stewart very much, and quite frankly he will make a far more stable and sociably acceptable partner than Ryan ever would."

Aliki looked rebellious and when she spoke, she sounded sulky. "I only want her to have the depth of love that we have."

Dawn smiled and sat up to hug the woman she loved. "I know, Aliki, and I'm sure she will."

David leaned across the car seat and made sure his wife's safety belt was done up.

"Now don't fuss, David. I have done up my belt carefully." Elizabeth smiled at him.

David blushed. "I just know you are inclined to have your thoughts on other things and forget all about putting your belt on."

Elizabeth smiled softly. "Is Quasar fastened into his car harness okay?"

David looked back at the big orange dog that took up most of the back seat. "Yes, he's fine."

"I am looking forwarded to spending a few days with Robbie and the family. Imagine little Mac getting married this spring. Doesn't it make you feel old?"

"It does. There will be a new generation coming along soon, Bethy. You know, not that I am a judge of these things," David said, as he started the engine and pulled out of their underground parking spot, "but I always thought that Mac and Ryan would have made a rather nice couple. They became such good friends after the Pateas family and the Williams family discovered their connection."

"I have to admit that I, too, suspected that their pairing would have been the case, but I suppose it was totally illogical of us to assume Mac would be a lesbian just because Ryan is," Elizabeth reasoned.

David frowned. He knew that Robbie had not been happy about Ryan leaving. "Does Robbie hear much from Ryan?"

Elizabeth sighed. "Just some brief emails once a week, and a letter or card a few times a year. She seems to have travelled quite a bit with the military. She never tells Robbie much, and of course, you know Robbie, she just gives Ryan the basics in return. Janet gets so frustrated with those two. Janet writes long newsy letters to Ryan, I understand, and Reb writes to her sister as well. I know Robbie has invited Ryan home on many occasions, but Ryan always has some reason why she can't come."

"It's a damn shame."

Elizabeth tried to look relaxed as David merged onto the freeway that would take them north. "Yes, it is. Ryan, you know, has a brilliant mind. She would have made an excellent mathematician. I was extremely disappointed when she enlisted. I had high hopes for her in a field related to my own."

David nodded and reached out to pat his wife's leg. The world of academics, dealing with string theory and the possible origins of the universe itself, was a small, prestigious group. There were few who could understand the mathematics or grasp, even on a lower level, the complexities of a possible all-encompassing energy theory. It would have been nice for his Nobel Prize-winning wife to have someone in the family who could really understand the mathematical complexities of her theories.

"I wonder if Ryan keeps up her violin. She could have made a career in music, too. She's a Williams all right — multi-talented."

"Janet says she does," he returned, but a glance showed him that Elizabeth had started to jot down neat rows of equations on a pad of yellow paper in her lap. David let their conversation lapse, knowing that it was Elizabeth's practice to work on her research in the quiet of the afternoons. Instead, he gave his full attention to his driving. He, too, was looking forward to being back in the small northern town of Bartlett that had been his home for many years. He hadn't seen his brother, who now ran the local grocery store, since Christmas. Their family had grown and they all had disparate interests that kept them apart. He was glad that it had become a family tradition to gather each spring and fall for a few days together.

Miles to the north, Ian and Reb sat hand in hand on the bench in the back room of Potts' Grocery Store and listened to David's brother, Ted, spin his tale. He'd had to go and serve a customer and had only just returned, wiping his hands on his white apron as he came in. "Now, you were asking about the old mine up where the lumber camp used to be. I don't know how much stock you can put in it, but the old folks used to say that a meteorite struck there years ago and melted the ground around about. My great Grandpapa and your mom's granddaddy, Rebecca, used to brag how they saw a river of gold. Course, no one took them seriously. They were both good storytellers, if you know what I mean, especially if they'd had a few Johnny Walkers by way of limbering up their throats."

Reb snuggled closer to Ian, who was trying his best to look manly. "Do you think there really is a gold mine, Ted?"

Ted considered for a second. The emerging whiskers on his chin made a rasping noise as he brushed his finger over them. "I don't figure as there could be. I'm thinking any number of people must have checked it out while they were lumbering up there at the turn of the century. And I'm sure others with the gold itch have had a look since. No, I figure it's just an old tale. Not many people know about it now. How did you to come to hear of it?"

"Ryan told me."

Ted looked both surprised and delighted. This was a good piece of gossip by the sound of it. "Ryan? Have you heard from Ryan, then?"

Reb nodded. "She's here. She arrived yesterday. She's out with Obbie in her Jeep at the moment, so Mom sent me in to pick up the groceries."

Ted beamed. This was good gossip that would have people popping into his store all weekend once the word got out. "Well, I'll be tarred and feathered; Ryan Williams back home again. That girl used to play a mean fiddle at the Firefighters' Ball, and George Drouillard said she would have made a fine firefighter, like her mom. Not much you Williamses are afraid of, by all accounts."

Ian beamed down at his girlfriend. "We'd better be getting the groceries into the truck, Rebel. Then we'll have time to catch lunch at Maria's before you have to head back home."

They thanked Ted for his hospitality and walked down the street to the local café. Ian held the door for Reb and they took seats in a quiet corner. Maria waved from behind the counter and Reb smiled and waved back. The Williams family had frequented Maria's since they had first come to town.

Once they had placed their order, Ian broached the topic that had been on his mind. "When can I meet your family?"

Reb nervously played with her napkin. "Er, well, soon. Actually, they will all be here this long weekend. It's sort of a tradition for the clan to gather."

Ian smiled. "It might be a good time to meet them, then."

"Well, I don't know..."

The young man's frustration showed on his face. "Rebel, you said you couldn't come to the Thanksgiving dance at the hall unless your mom met me and said it was okay. How is that ever going to happen if I am not allowed to see your family?"

Reb pulled a face. She was going to have to tell him. "It's just, well, they're a bit...unorthodox."

Having been in town for a while, Ian had heard some stories about the Williamses, but he felt he owed it to Reb to let her give him whatever firsthand information she wanted to share. Clear, intelligent, grey eyes met hers. "How so?"

This is it. Reb sighed. "My mother is married to the actor/director Robbie Williams. Yes, they are a lesbian couple. My big sister is a genius. I am not exaggerating, she really is. She is a major in the armed forces. She has just come home after ten years. Oh, and she also has a doctorate in physics and plays the violin beautifully. My aunt is Dr. Elizabeth Williams, the woman who won the Nobel Prize for her work on naked singularities. My uncle owns the grocery store and Ted is his brother. My father was the racing driver Billy-the-Kid Williams. He was killed on the track when I was two. And my grandfather was the local gambler. Other than that, we are perfectly normal family. Oh, I forgot my other aunts. They are a gay couple as well. One is Dawn Freeman, the writer, and her partner is a forensic anthropologist and RCMP officer."

Ian blinked, and blinked again, then asked cautiously, "You're joking, right?"

Reb's hackles rose. "Wrong."

Ian looked stunned and a little wary, as if he suspected that she was pulling his leg. Her brief summary far exceeded the scope of the stories he had heard. "Naturally, I've heard of the actor Robbie Williams and I know her brother was the race car driver, Billy-the-Kid. I also know that one of the Remarkable Williams won the Nobel Prize for Physics. I think it's pretty common knowledge that Robbie Williams is a lesbian. What I'm having trouble with here is that you never thought to mention that this was your family. Are you telling me the truth?"

Reb gritted her teeth. "Yes."

The young man considered this. "I heard that Robbie Williams had a place up this way near the Film College. So, you're rich?"

Reb felt her anger mounting as each of the standard responses came out of Ian's mouth. Why couldn't anyone accept her and her family as just people like everyone else? "I'm not. Certainly, my family is."

Ian read the tension and emotion in Reb's eyes. *Okay, meeting them is going to be really, really freaky but it's Reb's family.* "Uh, my dad won a bowling championship once," he joked.

Reb laughed and he joined in. The tension was broken.

"So you think you can handle this?" Reb asked, some of the stress leaving her.

Ian frowned and took a bite of his clubhouse sandwich, chewing it slowly while he tried to come to terms with what she'd told him. To his credit, he did not give her platitudes. "I don't know, Reb. They sound awfully...different, and rather intimidating. But I think I should be given the chance to try."

Reb nodded, her face set in cautious lines. "I'm very proud of my crazy family, Ian. I don't want them hurt and I won't have them judged. I have no time for gay and lesbian bashers."

Again Ian took his time in deciding how to respond. "To be truthful, Reb, I've always felt I was pretty liberal about such things. I have always maintained a live-and-let-live attitude. I can't say I understand why anyone would be interested in the same sex, but I figure it's none of my business. I have to tell you, though, I have never mixed socially with anyone who is a gay or lesbian, or at least if I have, I wasn't aware of it. So I have no idea how I'll react. I can promise you one thing, though — I won't make a scene or anything."

Reb looked out the window for a second and regained her composure. This was not easy. She wondered if she would stay with Ian or if she would have to go through this conversation over and over again throughout her life. She shook her head. "Believe me, if you don't make a scene, you will be one of the few people there who doesn't."

Robbie turned off the light and gave Janet a kiss on the cheek before rolling onto her side away from her partner. Janet frowned; enough was enough. "Robbie, turn the light on. We need to talk."

"I'm tired," came a pathetic moan from deep under the covers.

Janet snorted. "No, you're not. You are a coward. Come out, you big suck."

There was thrashing and mumbling in the dark and the light snapped on. Robbie sat with her back against the headboard, arms crossed and looking grumpy.

"We need to talk about my breast surgery."

"I don't want to talk about it." Panic written all over her face, Robbie slipped down under the covers.

Janet sighed, looked at the mound of bed sheets and shook her head. This was the woman who had won Academy Awards and ran a film empire. She gave the mound a poke. "I regret to inform you that the problem with my breasts is not going away, so you will just have to face it." The mound didn't move. Janet's face hardened into troubled lines. She was just about to make a cutting remark when she heard a sob. "Robbie...love, what's the matter?" Janet slid down and wrapped her partner closely in her arms. "Robbie, talk to me."

"It never bothered me that you'd had a mastectomy. I didn't want you to have that elective surgery. I didn't want to go to the hospital again and see you in pain. It was awful. Why did you do that? When I got the call, I just freaked. I love you, damn it!"

For a while, Janet held her complex partner tight and tried to sort out what was going on inside Robbie's head. When she spoke, it was quietly, tenderly, trying to make her partner understand her reasons. "I know you never wanted me to have the reconstructive surgery, sweetheart. I know that you really had a hard time with me going through the cancer treatment. Sometimes it is just as hard on the caregivers as it is on the victim. I understand that. But is it possible that my being seriously ill so early in our relationship made you a little overprotective?"

Robbie considered that. She didn't want to be having this discussion, but Janet was helping to make it easier. Still, her answer came out between sobs. "Yes. You are the best thing that has happened in my life. I can't bear the thought of losing you. Sometimes I have nightmares. I...I don't mean to be overprotective."

"I know, lover. It is understandable that you would feel that way because you went through a really traumatic time with me when our love was just developing. I have some emotional issues from that time, too, Robbie. Do you want me to tell you about them?"

There was a moment's hesitation while Robbie fought her demons, then she rolled over and pulled herself up into a sitting position. She took a tissue from the box beside the bed and wiped away her tears, then she pulled Janet into a hug. "Okay, I want to hear what you have to say."

Janet got comfortably nestled inside the circle of her lover's arms. "It's not about appearances, Robbie. You have been wonderful about that. I still get a little insecure, but you have been nothing but a pillar of strength. Robbie, cancer is like a violation of self. You don't want it inside you, taking over and growing in your organs. Even though I won that battle and it's been more than ten years since then, there is still a fear deep inside me that it's still there and I might have to go through that horror again."

Robbie pulled Janet closer into her arms, as if to shield her from her memories, and dropped a kiss on her wife's head.

Janet snuggled in. "Sure, having a mastectomy was hard on the ego, and having to wear a prosthesis is uncomfortable and awkward, but it is so much more than that, Robbie. Every time I change, or have a shower, or have to stop to fit the damn prosthesis into place, I am reminded that I had cancer and that it could come back again. It was more than a loss of a breast; it was a continual reminder of what the cancer did to me...what it still could do to me. I needed to have the reconstruction surgery so I could be whole again, not on the outside but on the inside. I had to show the cancer that I could recover completely, that it was not even going to leave its mark on me. Do you remember talking about this years ago, love?"

"Yeah, I remember, but I thought you'd forgotten about the idea. I thought we had a good relationship and you trusted me. I hated the thought of you being in the hospital, but you explained how important it was to you. I would have understood that you'd decided to go ahead with the surgery. You didn't have to schedule it while I was away filming," Robbie muttered, her voice laced with hurt.

Janet kissed the strong, capable hand that rested on her shoulder. "I was wrong. It was a really immature thing to do. I...I was jealous."

Robbie's head shot up in surprise and she looked down at Janet with wide eyes. "What?"

"You were acting again, and with Colette Cummings. The two of you have such chemistry, such passion. And she has nice breasts."

Robbie was flabbergasted. "I only took the part because my other leading lady was too banged up from a car accident to play the role. Time is money and I couldn't find anyone else suitable for the part on such short notice. You know I don't want to act."

"I know, Robbie." Janet blushed.

Another thought suddenly hit Robbie like a sucker punch. "You don't think I had an affair with Cummings, do you?"

Janet wiggled with embarrassment. "No, not on an intellectual level, but I guess emotionally... I mean, I am married to one of the Williams family, and it happens to be the one who has been voted most sexy woman of the decade. Not to mention your list of conquests before you met me. I can't explain it. I know you wouldn't cheat on me. I just felt so insecure — seeing you with another woman on screen."

Robbie couldn't believe what she was hearing. It was bad enough that Janet didn't trust her to be at her side while she was having her reconstruction surgery, but she didn't even trust her to be faithful "You don't trust me!"

Janet pulled away and rolled from their bed in frustration. She paced around the room in irritation, on the edge of tears. "Damn it, Robbie, listen to what I am telling you. I am insecure. You would be too if you had a disease that could kill you before you could see your kids grow up or have the life you want to have with your partner. Yes, I acted childishly in accepting a surgery date while you were away. It was stupid and unfair and I regret it. I owe you an apology, but damn it, I needed this breast reconstruction. I needed to remove the scars of what the disease did to me. I needed my confidence back so that I could be a healthy, whole woman. I needed to be able to look in a mirror and see me, not the effects of cancer. And I guess I needed it to give me the confidence that you would always want me. Please, Robbie, I need you to understand."

Robbie started to retort, then took a long, intent look at her partner's face. She slipped from the bed and took Janet in her arms. "I'm sorry. I was so caught up in my own issues that I didn't listen. You've been trying to tell me all along, but I was afraid of you being in the hospital again and I just wouldn't look past that." Shaking with emotion, Robbie kissed Janet's head. "By avoiding the issue all these years, I let you down, and that allowed the mistrust to grow."

Janet kissed her lover's neck softly. "I never believed that you would cheat on me, Robbie. I was just...jealous. I'm sorry."

Robbie nodded. When the call had come from Janet telling her that she would be having surgery in the morning, Robbie had dropped everything and chartered a jet to get her back to Canada immediately. She had arrived shortly after Janet had been taken back to her room from Recovery. Janet had been in pain those first few days and Robbie had been nearly sick with worry. She knew intellectually that there was very little danger inherent in the procedure, but emotionally she just couldn't deal with Janet being back in the hospital and having to go to doctor appointments. It brought back those terrible days when they were fighting the cancer. Everything that was good in Robbie's life had come because of Janet. She couldn't imagine life without her partner.

For a few minutes they just held each other, glad that they had cleared the air of some of their issues.

Janet waited until she felt Robbie relax in her arms and then said quietly, "I want to show you what they have done."

Robbie nodded — the look on her face so tragic and pale that Janet almost laughed. She bit her lip and busied herself slipping out of her sleep shirt. It was necessary to tread softly with Robbie when she was revealing her emotional side. For all her bluster, joking, and tempers, Robbie was an unbelievably fragile person emotionally. Robbie trusted Janet with her soul, and Janet did her best to protect it at all costs.

To Robbie's relief, there wasn't much to see. The old scar of Janet's mastectomy ran around the base of where her breast had been to up under her arm. She had been fortunate in that her skin had remained healthy and there had not been too much scar tissue to remove before placing the expander. The expander, as Janet had explained it, was positioned under the pectoral muscle after the scar tissue had been removed. The expander had a small tube and a fill ball with a metal backing placed under the skin below the implant. Each week or so, Janet had to go into the hospital and have sixty cc's of saline injected into the implant through this small ball. The implant already had two hundred and fifty cc's of solution in it when it had been put in place and Janet thought she would need about twice that to be a B cup.

Robbie swallowed and ignored the cold sweat down her back that made her shiver. This was what Janet needed and wanted, and that was all that really mattered. If Robbie had not made such a fuss about it every time the subject had come up over the last ten years, Janet probably wouldn't have felt she had to accept a date for the surgery while Robbie was out of town. Gently and nervously, Robbie reached out to caress the swelling that would be Janet's new breast. Her hand barely touched Janet's skin before she withdrew it. "What if it pops or something?"

Janet laughed. "It won't. It is quite durable."

Robbie nodded. "Okay, okay. Ahh, is there anything else?"

Janet knew there were all sorts of things yet to discuss, including the surgery that would be coming up in a few months to remove the expander and replace it with a saline implant. Her other breast would then be reshaped to match her implant. But Robbie had handled about as much as she could for the time being. Although she was trying to put on a brave front, she was pale and shaky and cold to the touch. "There is one more thing."

"What?" Robbie asked, eyes big with fear.

Janet leaned over and kissed her partner softly, wrapping her arms around her lover's neck. "Make love to me," she whispered, as she nibbled at the soft, warm underside of Robbie's throat.

Robbie whimpered with need. "Are you sure it's safe with the expander in there?"

"Trust me."

"I do," Robbie whispered, pulling her lover down on to their bed and moving over her. Her mouth sought Janet's breast as one hand slipped the sleeping shorts down off the petite figure. "You are so beautiful, and I never get enough of being this close, this intimate with you. You are my passion, my desire and my home," Robbie whispered as she slipped into the warm, wet folds of Janet's being.

Across the lake from the lodge, the Pateases arrived at their cottage around noon the next day and, once settled, they piled back into their van and headed around to the Williams home. It was Aliki who noted the Jeep parked by the garage and walked over to look at it.

"Must be one of Robbie's new toys," Dawn said as she and Mac busied themselves pulling Thanksgiving baking out of the back of their van.

Aliki went over to help. "I don't think so," she said thoughtfully, and cast a sideways look at her daughter. She changed the subject, grumbling, "How much did you guys bring?"

"Don't you give me any of that, Doctor Aliki Pateas. Most of this is your baking. We've got enough pies here to feed all of Bartlett."

Aliki blushed. She liked cooking, and when she was occupied with a problem she tended to cook more. At the moment, she was worried about Mac and she had cooked up a storm during the last few days.

"I'm sure Uncle David will show up with boxes of treats, too. We'll be so fat after this holiday they'll be able to roll us down the 400 Highway back to Toronto." Mac laughed, but it stopped suddenly, and Aliki and Dawn turned to see Ryan standing behind them.

It was Dawn who recovered first. "Ryan! Oh Ryan, it is so good to see you, sweetheart." Dawn stepped forward and wrapped her arms around the tall, lanky figure.

Ryan hugged her back. She had always felt close to the Pateas clan.

When Dawn released Ryan, Aliki extended her hand, a cautious smile on her face and then, forgetting her concerns, she drew Ryan in for a hug, too. "I'm glad you're here."

Mac stood totally still, shock and uncertainty written on her face. Ryan had gone from a cute, devil-may-care teen to a beautiful, confident woman. Even in her old blue jeans and military sweatshirt, Ryan reeked of raw strength and sexuality. This was not going to be easy.

It was Ryan who walked over to her, taking the bags from her hands and placing them back in the van. She looked down at Mac with that crooked, sexy smile that had always sent arrows of need deep into Mac's being. "Hi."

"Hi," Mac returned with a nervous smile.

Dawn grabbed Aliki's arm and tugged her reluctant partner toward the house. "Leave them alone," she whispered.

Ryan and Mac stood there looking at each other, eyes sending messages that neither one of them could find the words to express. Finally, Ryan took the last step closer and wrapped Mac in her arms. Her head bent and she captured the smaller women's lips with her own. It was not a kiss of welcome; it was a kiss of passion, need, and ownership. Mac gasped and Ryan's tongue entered her mouth, curling, caressing with her own. When the kiss finally ended, they were both shaken, clinging to each other for support.

"This can't be happening," Mac groaned, clinging to Ryan's shirt. "Not now. Not after all these years."

Ryan lifted her head from Mac's hair and kissed a soft, warm ear. "I love you."

Mac pulled away instantly. "Don't talk like that! A...and don't kiss me like that again. I...I'm in love with Stewart. You know that. We're going to be married this spring."

Ryan stood legs apart and arms folded. "No, you are not."

Mac's eyes flashed and her jaw clenched in anger. She reached for the bags that Ryan had taken from her and placed in the van. "Oh yes, I am!" With a toss of her hair, she tried to pass the tall, arrogant woman.

Ryan reached out and grabbed her arm in a strong grip. She leaned close. "You didn't kiss me like you were in love with Stewy Fart-on."

Mac pulled her arm free and glared at Ryan with contempt. "His name is Stewart FarTON. I am marrying him and you can just go fuck yourself, Ryan Williams!"

She stormed off and Ryan watched with eyes filled with hurt and worry.

After the initial family greetings, Aliki pulled her half sister into the back hall for a talk. "Robbie, what's Ryan doing here?"

Robbie's face hardened. "She doesn't have to give any reason for being here. I'm her mother and this is her home."

Aliki was not to be sidetracked. "Is she here because Mac is planning to get married? Because if she is, I don't want your daughter fucking with my kid's head and messing things up for her."

Robbie couldn't quite make eye contact with her sister, no matter how good an actor she was. She tried evasion. "I think we should let them sort it out for themselves."

Suspicions confirmed, Aliki shook her head. "She is, isn't she? She's here to cause trouble. Mac is engaged and Ryan needs to back off. If she really cared for Mac she wouldn't have gone away."

They were two mothers, each protecting her own. The famous Williams temper rose to boiling point in Robbie as Aliki dared to lecture her on good, moral behaviour. "Don't you go down that road, you damn hypocrite. Who was kissing my wife while I was in prison, damn you."

Aliki snorted in frustration and met Robbie's stare with equally cold eyes. "I didn't know you then and I barely knew Janet. It was a kiss, a mistake, and past history and you know it. Don't you fling that crap at me; it is not fair to Janet."

Stiffening in anger, Robbie's hands balled into fists. "Don't you tell me—"

"What's going on here?"

Both women started and turned to see Janet looking at them with an annoyed expression. Aliki recovered first. "Nothing. We were just discussing Ryan being home. I'd better go see what my family is up to."

Janet watched Aliki stalk off, her body language tense and hostile. Janet's intelligent green eyes swung back to Robbie. Robbie squirmed. Janet's eyes narrowed. "Well?"

"She wanted to know why Ryan is here. She thinks Ryan is going to mess things up for Mac and Stewart."

Janet folded her arms and looked at her partner. "And is she?"

Robbie felt the heat of embarrassment and frustration creeping up her neck. "Yes. She doesn't want Mac to marry him."

"And you told Aliki what?"

Robbie blushed a deep red. She didn't want Janet to know that she had brought up the night when Aliki had made a play for Janet. "We argued. I told her to let the kids sort it out for themselves."

Janet looked at Robbie thoughtfully for a few seconds. She had heard her name mentioned and she was worried as to why. *Better not push,* she concluded and moved forward to hug her partner close. There was no hesitation this time. Robbie returned the hug with need. Janet snuggled close. "I know we haven't seen eye to eye these last few months but you do know I love you, don't you, Robbie?"

"Of course I know you do, love."

"Good. And you and Aliki stay out of the kids' problems."

"I didn't start it," Robbie protested, leaning back in Janet's arms to see her face better.

Janet reached up and kissed her partner's lips. "Good, and now it is finished."

While Dawn and Mac were sorting things out in the kitchen, Reb gathered her courage and tackled Janet. "Mom?"

"Hmm?" Janet replied, her head inside the freezer as she looked for some ice cream.

"Looks like there's going to be a good-sized gathering of the clan tonight. Er...Ian has asked me to the Community Centre dance and I didn't want to say yes until you had a chance to meet him. So I was wondering if I could phone him and invite him for dinner tonight."

Ice cream in hand, Janet crawled out of the freezer and smiled at her daughter. She hoped her nervousness did not show in her voice. Reb dating both pleased and scared the hell out of her. "Yes, of course you can, sweetie. Ahh, better warn him about your Obbie."

Reb smiled with relief. Her mom was one cool lady. "I already have. And Mom, don't call me sweetie while he's here, okay?"

Janet tried to look serious. "Okay, Rebecca."

Reb nodded and then went in search of her big sister. She found her outside, throwing a stick for Dufus. "Mom said I can bring Ian to dinner."

"Great, kid," her sister replied without much interest. Her mind was on deeper, darker thoughts.

"Ryan, don't pick a fight and don't wear army boots, okay?"

Ryan looked at her little sister in surprise. "I know how to behave! And I don't clump around in army boots."

Reb smiled, gave her sister a hug, and went to find Obbie. This was the one that was going to be tricky. Obbie was in her study, looking stormy and preoccupied. Most people would be reluctant to disturb T-Rob when she had that look on her face, but not Reb. She went in and flopped into a chair.

Robbie looked up over her glasses. "You can't have an advance on your allowance or the keys to the car."

"We are not in negotiations here. I have already won." Reb smiled. "Mom said I could invite Ian to dinner."

Robbie went still and her expressive eyes flashed. "I think that's a good idea. I think I should meet this guy and talk to him. His name has come up once too often around here."

Reb rolled her eyes. "Ian Fraser has asked me to the Thanksgiving dance and I'm bringing him to dinner so you guys can meet him."

Robbie frowned. Reb had a date. "Uh, Reb, uh..."

Reb held up her hand. "Don't say it! Promise me you will be good and not give him the third degree or insist on a blood test before he kisses me again?"

"Again?"

"Obbie!"

Robbie crossed her arms and looked at her younger daughter, who had stubborn defiance written all over her face.

Reb quickly went on. "Obbie, he is a real gentleman. He has taken a year off from his studies and is up here working with Forestry to earn money for university. At the moment, he's planting trees in the burnt-out areas. He wants to be a vet. Please give him a chance. No rehearsing science fiction scripts on the railing and brandishing a stick, threatening to slice him through, and no kissing Mom in front of him."

"You do hold a grudge. That unfortunate incident was years ago. And why can't I kiss your mom? He does know that we're gay, doesn't he?"

Reb ran her long, graceful fingers through her hair in frustration. "Obbie, the *world* knows about my famous family. I'd just rather he get used to you all...slowly. Just behave, please."

Obbie rubbed her temple. "If your mom has okayed it, then I will be all charm and grace," she promised with a weak smile.

Reb got up and went around the desk to give her other mom a kiss on the cheek. "Just don't scare him off. Meeting this family is hard enough without any of you acting more weird than you usually are."

Robbie waited until Reb had disappeared and then made a beeline to find Janet. She was with Dawn in the kitchen, Mac having been sent to cut some fall leaves for the table centrepiece. "Who is this guy Reb is inviting?"

Janet looked up at her partner in the doorway. "He's an older man."

"What?"

Janet shrugged unhappily. "He's eighteen and just finished his first year at Guelph University."

"And you said she could go to the dance with this guy? She's just a kid."

Janet turned from preparing the roast and looked at Robbie with annoyance. "Reb will be seventeen in a few months, Robbie. And I don't think forbidding her to go to the dance is a good idea. We'll set some guidelines and curfews and trust Reb to be responsible. As she often points out to us, my olive, she is the only sane one in the family."

"No teen is sane. They are not genetically programmed to act normal." Robbie flopped down on a kitchen chair and watched Dawn shell peas. Quick as lightning, her hand shot out and scooped a few from the bowl to eat.

Dawn raised an eyebrow but said nothing. She didn't want to get caught up in this discussion. She remembered vividly when Mac had started to date. She had practically had to hold Aliki down to keep her from tailing Mac and her dates, and she had a sneaking suspicion that Aliki had run police checks on some of them. The two sisters were very much alike in many ways.

"I don't like it," Robbie grumbled.

Janet went over and kissed Robbie's head. "Olive, don't judge all suitors by your wild behaviour at that age. If you had your way, neither of our girls would have had a chance to date until they were thirty."

Robbie eyed the bowl of peas gloomily and Dawn, feeling sorry for her, pushed the bowl closer.

"Thirty is a good age to start dating." She smiled, picking out a few more of the tender, sweet peas to eat.

Ryan watched Mac from a distance. She had been attracted to Mac since she was a kid. It had taken her time to explore and understand her sexuality, and later she just hadn't been ready to make any sort of commitment. She had needed time and space to prove herself and she still needed time to accomplish her final goal before she was prepared to think about raising a family with someone.

The trouble was — she wanted that someone to be Mac, and it didn't look like Mac was prepared to wait. Then there was this Stewy Fart-on. *Is Mac really in love with him? Is she straight?* Ryan's jaw set in a determined line. There was one thing that she was sure of — she meant to find out, one way or another.

By seven, everything was in place for a nice family meal. The table was set for ten, and silver and glass sparkled in the light from the fireplace and the candles. Most of the family was on the porch with a before-dinner drink, watching the last rays of light settle on the lake. Reb had gone to pick up Ian for what Robbie was calling the family inquisition. Mac, not feeling very sociable, had disappeared into the kitchen with the excuse of checking on things.

After a few minutes, Ryan quietly slipped out and followed Mac to the kitchen. She stood in the doorway, watching Mac feed Dufus a piece of turkey. "Just as spoilt as Rufus was, eh?"

Mac looked up in surprise then forced herself to relax. "Dufus isn't too bad. Reb has a way with animals. Our Moppy, Dufus' sister, was well trained by Aliki, but she's a terribly dumb animal, much to Aliki's disgust. She's so sweet, though. The spoiled one of the litter is Aunt Elizabeth and Uncle David's Quasar. That animal has no idea it is a dog. They've raised it as a spoiled child."

Glad that Mac was not going to hold a grudge about the confrontation they'd had earlier, Ryan smiled. "I'd like a dog but it is just not possible at the moment."

"So, now that you have your doctorate, what's the next step?"

Ryan looked over her shoulder to make sure no one had followed them. She had to pick her time carefully in telling her moms what she planned next. It was one of the reasons she had come home. There would be no keeping this quiet. "I'm in the Canadian Space Program. I'm training now for a shuttle flight in two years' time, and a stay at the space station to do some research."

Mac looked startled, making eye contact with Ryan for the first time. Ryan could see the pride there, but also the fear.

"How long will you be gone? I mean, up there?"

"Probably three months."

Mac smiled and ran a shaking hand through her hair. "I guess a dog isn't a good idea, then. Another Williams about to make a name for herself, huh?" The laugh showed her nervousness as she turned to busy herself pouring the creamed peas into a china dish. Elizabeth and David had arrived from their cottage about half an hour ago, and Reb should be back any minute with Ian. Then they would eat.

"Mac, I'm on leave for a month. I want to spend some time with you. You can't deny that there was once something there between us. I think we need to be sure. I won't push you—"

"Won't push me!" Mac snorted, turning around with the bowl in her hand. "I have a month to fall in love with you and then you are going to take off for parts unknown to prepare for a trip into space! But no pressure there. Just fall in love with you, and then step aside so you can get on with your life."

"That is not what I meant," Ryan hissed.

"It was just what you meant. Face it, Ryan, you are not capable of a meaningful relationship. It's all about proving yourself."

Ryan felt her temper rising. She couldn't think rationally when the woman was around. Somehow Mac always seemed to get under her skin. "Who made you the fucking wise woman on the mountain? You don't know what I am capable of in terms of a relationship. I can tell you one thing for sure — I'll give you a life of more passion and fun than Stewy Fart-on will ever be able to provide." Ryan saw blue eyes spark with ice-fire as Mac ground her teeth in anger.

"I told you not to call him that."

It was not wise to bait a Williams. They could never let a challenge lie, and Ryan was no exception. "What? Stewy Fart-on? That's his name, isn't it?" The creamed peas came at Ryan as fast as the words had left her mouth and she stood there in shock, dripping in the hot white sauce and peas.

There was a moment of shocked silence and then Ryan reached for Mac with lightning reflexes. She had meant simply to wash Mac's face with the sauce that dripped down her, but Mac danced away and slipped on the pea-and-sauce that splattered the floor, fell, and crashed into the kitchen table that held two large warming trays laden with food. Things shifted and rattled, and a plate of turkey went sliding, along with a bowl of roasted potatoes. Ryan moved to help Mac; Mac swatted Ryan's helping hands away.

From the corner of her eye, Ryan saw Janet walk in with Dufus at her heel to see what had happened. "Okay, that's enough. You two are not tracking right."

Dufus, who was on overload from the wonderful smells coming from the kitchen, was nearly bouncing with excitement. The word "tracking" was all the excuse the dog needed. It was the command word that Reb used with him. With a bark of glee, the big dog leapt forward into the kitchen mess, sending the already wobbly table flying. Dishes crashed in all directions. The family came running in from the veranda.

Ryan stumbled against Mac as Robbie entered and pushed past her to grab the flaming tea towel that Mac had carelessly dropped close to the burner. She stamped it out while Ryan was still blinking in surprise at the cloud of smoke spreading out and hanging at shoulder level in the room. Holding on tightly to a struggling Mac, Ryan turned to see Janet trying to pull Dufus away from the spilt food until she slipped on the mess and fell. Aliki, arrived next, helped her up and held her as she tried to clean some of the mess off her jeans.

Then Ryan saw Robbie look up from the tea towel to see Aliki holding Janet. Before Ryan could untangle herself from the struggling Mac, Robbie had crossed the room in three steps. She pulled Janet away and sucker-punched Aliki with what Ryan imagined was ten years of smouldering anger. Aliki, caught off guard, went sprawling, landing on Dufus, who, in his surprise, snapped at Ryan. Ryan gave a howl of pain, grabbed her wrist, and went down in a tangle of limbs with Mac. From her viewpoint on the floor, she saw Elizabeth stop in the doorway with David behind her.

"Oh dear. David, stop the family fighting while I let Dufus outside," Elizabeth ordered, clearly totally confident that her David would sort things out when no one else had been able to. She carefully navigated around the debris to Dufus and grabbed the beast by the collar. David waded through the smoke, trying his best to separate the various warring factions and to calm everyone down.

Ryan tried to pull her hand away from Mac, who was attempting to stop the bleeding where Dufus nipped the wrist. In the background, Ryan was aware of Janet yelling at Robbie and trying to stop her from taking another swing at her sister. Dawn was helping Aliki up and trying to stop her from going after Robbie, and Dufus, having gotten over the shock of being landed on, was wolfing down slices of turkey before he had to give in to Elizabeth's insistent pulling on his collar.

The door opened, and Reb and Ian entered. Everyone froze and looked in their direction. There was a moment's awkward silence, then Reb said quietly, "Ian, this is my family — not necessarily on one of their better days. We don't usually eat this informally." At that point, the smoke detector activated the kitchen sprinkler system, soaking everyone.

David took charge. The sprinkler system was turned off, the window opened to air the place, and Dawn, Janet and Elizabeth were sent to get dry clothes for the family members from the other houses. Ryan and Robbie, who could clean up and change at the house, were sent to do so and, once Ryan's wrist had been bandaged to cover the minor bite injury, they were ordered outside to chop enough wood for the next two years. Reb and Ian were dispatched to get enough pizza for ten, and Aliki and Mac were left to help David clean up the mess.

"I didn't mean to wreck everything," Mac muttered. "I'm sorry."

Aliki shovelled food onto a dustpan with a spatula. "I still don't know what the hell happened. I think we really messed things up for Reb."

David was busy picking up broken crockery and dropping it into a box. "I'm not certain, of course, but I suspect that Reb rather enjoys complaining about the crazy nature of her family." He looked with dismay into the box. "It is a shame; this was the good set of serving dishes. I hate to see waste."

Mac sniffled as she mopped the counters dry with a rag. "It's just that Ryan won't leave me alone. I am so confused."

Aliki left what she was doing, and went and took her daughter in her arms. "Hey, don't try to solve any issues before you have time to sort out your feelings."

"What would you do, Aliki?" Mac asked, holding on to her adopted mom.

Thinking back to the discussions she'd had with Dawn, Aliki paraphrased as best she could. "I guess I'd have to decide what was more important: an unconventional and sometimes difficult life with someone I felt was my soulmate, or a comfortable, secure life with someone I respected and loved because he loved me."

Mac moaned in frustration. "I thought I had everything worked out."

"Did you?" Aliki looked surprised. "It has been my experience that love is almost impossible to work out, even after years of marriage. It is a totally irrational element that coexists in what is generally a very rational and conservative society."

Mac giggled. "You sound like an anthropologist."

Aliki laughed. "No, just a woman who has made all the mistakes in the book on her way to finding a wonderful partner and love. Look, Mac, Ryan is here. Don't repress your feelings because you think you have made a commitment to someone else. Leave the door open and know for sure what you want; then you will have no regrets no matter what your decision is."

"I feel I would be betraying Stewart if I did that."

"In a way, I guess, but better that than marry him and then discover that your unhappiness is going to grow and destroy both of you. You don't want to go through your life with a 'what if' hanging over your head. You want to take your vows having no doubts that you are doing the right thing. Now come on, we have to get this mess cleaned up before the pizza arrives."

Ryan stacked the wood as her mom chopped the cords into kindling. "We're in big trouble," she sighed.

"No, *you* are in trouble. I'm as good as dead."

"Is Aunt Janet that mad at you for suckering Aliki?"

The axe shattered the wood with twice as much force as was necessary. "She did mention something about me completely humiliating her, before she stormed from the room."

Ryan smiled unsympathetically. "You're right, you're dead. You won't get any until you are too old to care."

Robbie shot her daughter a dirty look. "Thanks. I knew I could count on you to understand. So, what's going on with you and Mac?"

Ryan sat down on the woodpile with a groan. "I'm getting nowhere. The truth of the matter is Stewy...Stewart holds all the cards. He's got a good job, he's responsible and reliable, and he can provide her with children." For a minute neither of them spoke. The issue of children was always touchy in a lesbian relationship. "All I can offer her is my love and a promise that some day I'll settle down in some sort of research job."

Robbie tossed the split wood to Ryan, who caught it easily and placed it on the stack beside her. "You're an officer, don't you qualify for housing?"

"Yeah, but it isn't as easy as that." It was time to be completely honest with her mom. "I'm in the Canadian Space Program. I'm training for a mission that will be flown in two years' time. I'll be traveling back and forth between here and the United States for training, and then my mission will require me staying at the space station for about three months."

Robbie put down the axe and looked at her daughter. The silence was filled by the hammering of a woodpecker on a far-off tree and the gentle lapping of the lake at the shore. "You had this planned right from when you went away to university, didn't you?"

Ryan squirmed with guilt. "Pretty much."

"I'm proud of you." She nodded, then went back to chopping the wood. She *was* proud of Ryan. Proud, but also scared stiff about what the kid had planned. But there was no way she was going to discourage her daughter. She'd made a lot of mistakes while being overly protective, particularly with Janet, and she wasn't going to make that mistake again this weekend.

Ryan beamed. "Thanks."

"Does Mac know?"

The gloom returned to Ryan's eyes. "I told her in the kitchen."

Robbie tossed pieces of kindling one by one and Ryan caught them, placing them on the growing pile. "Is that why you got anointed with the creamed peas?"

"That started the argument. She feels I'm just taking a brief holiday from my life to fuck up hers and then I'll be off again."

Robbie frowned. "I can see why she would think that way. So why did she throw the peas at you?"

Ryan slipped from the woodpile and dusted off her blue jeans. "For calling her fiancé Stewy Fart-on."

"Dumb move, kid." Robbie chuckled.

"So I discovered."

As they drove, Janet vented to Dawn and Elizabeth about Robbie's temper, her fear of Janet's breast reconstruction surgery, and her ridiculous jealousy and overprotective nature. She finally wound down as they arrived at her former home, now Elizabeth and David's cottage. "I'm really sorry about going on. And I feel terrible about Robbie hitting Aliki, Dawn."

Dawn smiled and patted Janet's knee. "It looked good on Aliki. The only thing hurt was her ego. Those two are so damn competitive. Don't worry about it, Janet. There's no harm done. They love each other very much; they're just too pig-headed to admit it."

Elizabeth blinked several times, still feeling rather dazed by the turn of events. "I don't think I have ever witnessed a brawl before. Isn't it amazing how quickly they can erupt? Thank heaven David was there. He is so good; he can turn his hand to anything."

Janet and Dawn looked at each other and tried not to smile. Dawn turned off the engine and opened her door. "I don't know if that could really be classified as a brawl, Beth. More like a food fight."

Elizabeth nodded her understanding and got out. Janet slid out after her. "It was another olive event," she sighed, "and my olive is going to be paying big time for it."

Reb drove and Ian sat beside her in silence. "What do you suppose happened back there?" he finally asked.

Reb shrugged. "Hard to say. No doubt we'll hear the whole story over pizza. That is, unless you don't want to have dinner with us," she said casually, though truthfully she was pretty worried about how Ian was going to react.

He laughed. "And miss the next exciting installment? Not on your life!"

Reb frowned. "Ian, ahh, the family does not like publicity, at least not that kind. We are private people, although you wouldn't know that by the press coverage. I'd appreciate it if you didn't tell anyone about today."

Ian looked at his girlfriend in surprise. "I wouldn't gossip about your family, Reb. I haven't even told my parents who you are. I have to admit it was a bit of a shock to discover that you are one of *the* Williamses. To be truthful, it makes me wonder what you see in me."

Reb took her eyes off the road for a second to flash him a smile. "Well, for one thing, I've known you over two months now and you haven't started a food fight yet." They laughed and some of the tension dissipated.

"So, who were all those people?"

"Hmm, let's see. The one wearing the creamed peas was my sister, Doctor and Major Ryan Williams. The one bandaging her wrist and calling her names was my cousin, MacKenzie. Her mom, the author Dawn Freeman, was the one holding onto the woman with the black eye. That's her partner, Doctor and Inspector Aliki Pateas of the RCMP. The tall, angry one, I am afraid to admit, is my mother, the actor-director Robbie Williams, and the woman wearing the mashed potatoes on her backside and trying to talk some sense into her is my other mom, Janet Williams. She's the president of the Bartlett School of Film and Animation. The woman battling with the dog over the remains of the turkey was my aunt, Doctor Elizabeth Williams, the physicist, and the man trying his best to bring order to the chaos is my Uncle David. He's married to my Aunt Elizabeth."

"Ugly dog."

"Yeah, but a great tracker if there are no squirrels around."

"An amazing family."

"They're all nuts."

"That, too."

By ten o'clock, the kitchen had been cleaned, everyone had showered and changed into clean clothes, and Thanksgiving pizza had been eaten. Ian had survived Robbie's third degree and seemed to have gotten a temporary Good Housekeeping Seal of Approval. He had formally asked Janet if he could take Reb to the dance, and she had agreed, on the understanding that he have her home by eleven. Most of them were now lounging in various places in the living room in front of the huge stone fireplace, catching up on family news.

Robbie followed Aliki into the kitchen on the pretext of getting more beer. "Umm, I shouldn't have hit you. Is your eye okay?"

Aliki pulled some cold beer from the wine and beer cooler that Robbie had in the pantry. "Yeah, it's okay. So, what the hell is the matter with you?"

Robbie blushed. "Janet and I...well, we haven't seen eye to eye on this breast reconstruction thing. She doesn't trust me. She doesn't think I understand."

Aliki twisted the top off a bottle and handed it to her sister, then opened one for herself. "Do you understand?"

"I understand why she feels she needs to go through this process — I guess. I'm just not handling it very well. If anything happened to Janet..." Robbie swallowed and couldn't go on.

Aliki frowned. "Dawn and I have been in a similar situation. My police work can be dangerous."

That was an understatement. There had been a number of close calls for all of them. Robbie nodded. "Yeah, I know."

Aliki sighed. "Dawn and Mac came to terms with the danger much more quickly than me. I felt I had to go it alone and protect my family at all costs. I was wrong. You want to protect the ones you love, but you also have to give them room to take chances and do what they feel is right. This partnership thing, I've discovered, is all about love and commitment without boundaries or ownership."

Robbie ran her hand through her hair. "Janet and I haven't talked about it yet, but I know there is more surgery to come. I don't know how I'm going to get through it."

"Is there any real danger?"

"No, not really. It's just that I can't stand the hospital, knowing Janet is vulnerable again..." Tears welled up in Robbie's eyes and she wiped them away with annoyance.

Aliki wrapped an arm around her sister. The spectre of cancer had always been there for Robbie and Janet, right from the start of their relationship, and that must have been hard. "Janet is going to be fine. You gotta believe that, just like I have to believe that my family will be able to handle any danger that my job might bring their way. There are enough real problems that we all have to face without looking for more."

Robbie swallowed hard and then revealed a big part of her soul. "Janet made my life work. Before her, I was so unhappy. I can't go it alone again."

Aliki pulled her in for a quick hug. "First, that is not going to happen. Janet is well and strong and will outlive you for sure, considering the way you abused your body in your wild days," she teased. "Second, you are not alone anymore. You have family, and we're all here to get you through the rough times. Now come on, people are waiting for their drinks. And Robbie?"

"Yeah?"

"Hit me again and I'll knock your block off."

In the living room, Ryan stayed on the edge of the group talking quietly with Elizabeth about her research until David came to get his wife and show her how much Dufus had grown compared to their beloved Quasar. Then she just sat quietly in the shadows, enjoying being near her family again but feeling embarrassed about ruining the Thanksgiving dinner. After a while, Mac came over and sat near her.

"Hi."

"Hi."

Mac wasn't sure how to broach the subject, so she just attacked it head on. "Did you really come back because I got engaged?"

Ryan looked away but nodded. "The time was right. I'd achieved what I felt I had to achieve to prove myself, and I knew I had to tell my family about the mission before they heard it on the news. I knew you'd all be here...the time was just right. I'd put it off because I didn't know what sort of a reaction I would get coming home after all this time. But hearing you were engaged...I just had to know."

Mac couldn't look at Ryan. She stared over at her family. "I have always loved you, Ryan. I think of you as my soulmate, but you went away and you were gone for so long."

Ryan's voice was hurt and bitter. "I wrote and emailed you all the time!"

Mac snorted. "About work, not love. And I could read between the lines; you had some relationships."

Ryan blushed. "Nothing serious." She swallowed hard. It was none of her business but it was eating at her and she needed to know. "Are you sleeping with him?"

"No. I haven't slept with anyone."

After that, they sat in silence until Mac reached out and took Ryan's hand. Their fingers intertwined but neither of them said anything or went any further.

Reb was sitting on the couch with Ian, a jealous Dufus wedged between them on the rug. "Uncle David, we were talking to Ted about the old mineshaft down on Lovers' Lane. Do you know anything about it?" Robbie shot Ian a murderous look and Reb quickly went on. "I haven't been there, but Ryan told me about it."

It was Janet who answered. "Oh God, not the old mineshaft again."

David chuckled. "Go on, Janet, you are in a better position to tell them."

Janet rolled her eyes. "Reb, as you know, your great grandfather was a gambler. He and Ted, that was David's grandfather, were good buddies and the town con men. Whenever they were down on their luck, they would spread the rumour about a meteorite hitting up there and the river running gold after. Then they would sell shares in the mine. There must be hundreds of people with shares in that worthless mine."

"So what sort of a mine is it?" Reb persisted.

Janet shrugged. "I don't think it ever was a real mine. Granddad always said it was an Algonquian First Nations site."

Mac looked up with sudden interest. "We have to go."

"I'm in," Dawn said, sharing her adopted daughter's interest in First Nations folklore, particularly that of the Salish because of MacKenzie's Salish blood.

"Caves, cool, I'm game." Robbie beamed, always ready for an adventure.

Mac looked at Ryan who smiled and nodded. "We're in on the expedition."

"I have tomorrow off. If you are going, then I'd sure like to go along," Ian said a little nervously.

"Of course you're welcome, Ian." Robbie smiled, and saw Reb beam with delight.

David made things easy for Elizabeth. "Well, you lot enjoy. Bethy has a paper she needs to be working on and I plan on doing some repairs around the cottage. Pop by on your way out tomorrow and I'll have a picnic lunch for you to take and we'll see that there is a dinner for you when you get back."

"Thanks, David. Could you take Dufus and Moppy for the day, as well?" Aliki asked.

"Certainly. Quasar will enjoy the company."

The only one who looked worried was Janet. She didn't say anything, but she wasn't sure about the mine at all. Her granddaddy had always said it was haunted. Not that she believed in any of that stuff, but implanted childhood beliefs can often persist in disturbing even the adult.

Chapter 24

It was late at night and the family members had drifted back to their various homes. Ian had left right on the dot of eleven to show he could be a responsible and trustworthy date for Reb. Mac stayed on after her parents left, and she and Ryan went for a walk down to the lake. The night was clear and the stars hung close, brightly reflected in the still water. The air was fresh and crisp, and Ryan hesitantly put her arm around Mac to share body heat as they sat on the wooden bench by the dock.

"Wouldn't being gay ruin your chances at getting a place on a shuttle flight? I mean, I would think NASA is very careful of its public image," Mac said.

Ryan squirmed with embarrassment. "I have to stay pretty much in the closet publicly, but there has been speculation in the tabloids over the years about my orientation. I just don't deny or confirm the rumours. It's hard to have a private life when you're a Williams. People are watching to see if I can live up to the name."

"Does that bother you?"

"I don't know if 'bother' is the right word. I'm driven by a need to prove myself for many reasons, you know that." Ryan wanted to be honest, but she also needed some breathing space. She wasn't used to heart-to-heart talks. She changed the subject. "How is the master's degree going?"

"I've just about finished my thesis on how Greek mythology has shaped our modern concept of the superhero. I hope to have my degree by the spring."

"Then what?"

"Marriage was the next thing on the list." Ryan stiffened. "Then I think I want to write like my mom. I've already had a few short stories published in magazines."

Ryan got up and walked to the end of the dock to stare at the heavens. Some day soon, she would be up there, free-floating on the edge of the universe. It was something she had wanted since she was a child. She turned to look at Mac. "If it would make a difference, I will drop out of the space program and ask Mom to lend me the money to buy out my commission."

Mac looked up in shock. "I would never ask that of you, Ryan. I know how much it means to you to reach your goals your own way."

Steady green eyes looked into blue. "I know you wouldn't ask. I am offering to do so because there is nothing in this world more important to me than winning your love."

Mac stood and walked over to Ryan, hugging her close. "You have always had my love, Ryan. Always. I'm just not sure that is enough. I'm not sure if this is just another Williams who has to win at all costs and will lose interest once she does. I'm not sure if you really do love me."

Ryan swallowed hard. "Then how do I prove it to you?"

"I don't know. I'm pretty confused at the moment, Ryan. Your coming back has really turned my world upside down."

They stood in each other's arms under the stars, gathering strength from gentle caresses and warmth. Ryan waited. It had to be Mac's decision.

"Ryan?"

"Mmmhmm?"

"Make a fire in the boathouse fireplace and then make love to me, please."

The room above the boathouse was large and beautifully decorated, with a small bar and comfy, overstuffed furniture. Sliding doors led onto a small balcony, and beyond it, the lake and stars blended into one.

Ryan wanted it to be perfect. Mac was giving her a wonderful gift and Ryan meant to show her just how much she was loved. Ryan got a good fire going and while they waited for the chill and dampness to leave the room, she lit some candles, turned on some soft music, and shot the bolt on the door so they wouldn't be disturbed. She was as nervous as if this was her first time.

She knew Mac was nervous, too. She could feel Mac's eyes on her as she moved about the room. When she risked a glance, Ryan saw both the hunger and the embarrassment in Mac's eyes. She had often dreamed of this moment but now it was here, it was so real, so intense, that it was scary as hell.

Ryan poured two glasses of wine and they sat close, looking out at the night in silence as they drank. Then Ryan put down her glass and stood, offering MacKenzie her hand. Mac rose and Ryan took her into her arms and swayed against her to the sound of the music. Mac's hands ran up the front of Ryan's shirt and wrapped around her neck, her fingers gently playing with the hair at the nape of Ryan's neck.

Shivering with desire, Ryan decided that she liked very much that Mac could cause that reaction in her. She could feel herself becoming wet with need.

They moved well together, bodies close and movements intimate. Finally, Ryan stopped and stepped back. She did not speak but instead used American Sign, Mac's first language. She signed confidently and was pleased to see Mac blink back the tears of happiness that Ryan had learned to sign for her.

I have loved you from the moment you came into my life. I have waited for the day when we were each old enough and ready to share this very special moment. You are beautiful down to the centre of your soul. I know in my heart that you are the one that I am meant to be with. Ryan dropped to one knee and signed again. *I do not want you to answer yet, because I know you need time, but I need you to know before we go any further. I love you. Will you marry me?*

Before Mac could respond, Ryan stood and gently pulled her close again, dancing slowly to the smouldering music. Mac cried a little, and then nestled into Ryan's arms. Ryan wanted to show her the gentle, loving side that she rarely showed to others. She rained kisses on Mac's neck, then slowly lowered her lips to brush Mac's. The kiss was fire — spreading passion to her wet, warm folds. She was swollen and ready, to the point where the need was a hurt. Ryan forced herself to go slow.

With trembling hands, she undressed Mac. Her trim, golden form, limned by the firelight, made Ryan squirm with desire. She stepped back, reluctantly breaking contact, and slowly removed her own clothes. Ryan heard the gasp as Mac's hungry eyes drank in her well-toned, lean form.

Ryan stepped close again and the touch of their naked bodies made them both moan with want. Dancing now as they explored each other with touches and kisses, Ryan was very aware of Mac's excitement, wet on her thigh. Unable to withstand it any longer, she stooped and lifted Mac into her arms, carrying her to the daybed. Her body lowered between the spread legs of the woman she loved and she felt the warm moisture of wet hair against her belly. "I love you. I want to make love to you. Is that still okay?" she whispered.

In answer, Mac wrapped her legs around Ryan and reached up to capture her mouth with her own. Ryan gave a soft growl of need as their tongues explored, entering into warm wetness, foreshadowing what was to come.

Ryan's voice came softly as she slowly let Mac get used to the touch, the feel, and the scent of her. She nuzzled at Mac's ear and the soft underside of her throat. "There's always a faint scent of mountain herbs to your hair. I remember your body when we were young, and how it used to turn me on, but those memories didn't prepare me for the beauty of the woman you have become." Ryan kissed small breasts, teasing the hard nipples with her tongue and letting her hands stroke and fondle soft, supple flesh.

"Oh, Ryan," Mac moaned, bucking with need under the hard, lean body.

Ryan's hands stayed on Mac's breasts but her head lowered, dropping kisses on a tight stomach and using her tongue to tease Mac's navel. "I am going to make you mine, lover. I'm going to enter you slowly and gently, and do everything I can to make you feel all the love that I have for you. You excite me. Your soul lies gently with mine. This is right." As she whispered soft words of love and comfort, Ryan slid down Mac's body and, for the first time, enjoyed the feel and taste of Mac.

Her tongue caressed a swollen bud of desire and slipped between moist, hot lips to taste Mac's essence. She felt the petite woman shudder with want. Slowly, Ryan slipped two fingers into warm velvet. When she felt resistance, she stopped and pleasured Mac with the rhythmic movement of her hand. "Mac?" she asked.

"Take me. Please take me," came the soft answering moan.

Ryan pushed through and held Mac close until her pain had passed. Then she moved within her again. Slowly, gently, in the rhythm of love, she built the tension between them, whispering words of passion and need into the most intimate places of Mac's body. With a cry, Mac grabbed Ryan tight and went over the top in a long shudder of release. Ryan remained inside her, feeling the contraction of her muscles around her fingers as the aftershocks continued to pulse through her lover.

"I love you. I have always loved you and I always will." Ryan kissed the wet, warm sex of the only lover she had ever really wanted.

They lay like that for some time and then slowly, reluctantly, Ryan withdrew from the warm centre. "You okay?" she asked softly.

Mac looked at Ryan, now her lover. "I am a whole new person and I feel wonderful." She leaned up and kissed Ryan's lips, tasting herself there. The thought of where those lips had been just a short time ago rocketed sensations low in her centre. "You are amazing."

Gently, Mac slipped down underneath Ryan's form, kissing and sucking on hard nipples and feeling her lover's taut muscles contract as she kissed along her abdomen. Then she was where she wanted to be. She wrapped her arms around her lover's thighs and buried her face between Ryan's legs. Ryan on hands and knees bucked with want as Mac ate at her. Then fingers were pushed into her and Ryan rode them as her lover enjoyed her sex. With a cry of release, Ryan sat up, contracting around fingers deep inside her. She was kneeling over Mac's breasts, her passion wetting Mac's hard nipples. With one last shudder she collapsed beside Mac, totally spent.

Much to Aliki's surprise, she woke to the smell of freshly brewed coffee. It was rare that she wasn't the first one up in the morning. Blurry eyed, she slipped into sweats and ran a comb through her hair before going into the kitchen. Mac met her in the doorway and gave her a big hug and then poured her a mug of coffee. "You were so right, Aliki. Thank you."

Aliki smiled, not sure what she was right about but glad that Mac was happier this morning. "Good. 'Bout what?" she mumbled sleepily, taking a sip of the morning brew.

"Sleeping with Ryan."

Aliki choked and Mac rushed to pat her on her back. "What?" Aliki managed to squeak out between gasps.

"I just got home. I stayed with Ryan last night."

Aliki held up a hand and bounced about the kitchen in a near panic. "I never told you to do that."

Mac laughed. "Mom said you wouldn't be able to handle it."

"Your mother knows? You didn't tell her I told you to sleep with Ryan, did you?" Horror was written on Aliki's face at the thought of having to explain this one to her partner. "Because I didn't."

Her eyes filled with mischief, Mac took her time in answering. "Well, not in so many words," she conceded. "But you did tell me to be sure."

Aliki sank to a chair, feeling weak and shaky. "Are you okay?"

Mac smiled gently and went over and wrapped her arms around Aliki. She'd teased enough. "It was the most wonderful night of my life. I love her very much and if it hadn't been for you, I would have been too stubborn and hurt to see that."

Aliki's hands came up to pat Mac's. "That's the way it should be. So, where do you go from here?"

Mac sat down and took her mug of coffee. "That's a tough one. Ryan has asked me to marry her. I haven't answered yet. I think I owe it to Stewart to end that relationship before I make any decisions with Ryan. I'm not sure whether Ryan and I are ready for a permanent commitment."

"Umm, how did your mom take all this?" Aliki asked weakly, still in a state of shock.

Dawn came in with Moppy on a leash and their old cat Sally-slurp following along behind. "I told MacKenzie that I was very relieved to have her following her heart instead of settling for conformity."

Moppy ran forward and stuck her big orange head under Aliki's arm, demanding attention and almost knocking over Aliki's mug of coffee. "Dumb dog," Aliki muttered affectionately, scratching the dog's floppy ear. Sally-slurp jumped up and curled contentedly in Mac's lap.

Dawn kissed Aliki's head and then joined them at the table. "You need to go wash up, Aliki. Ryan is coming over at eight to talk to us."

The look on Aliki's face was priceless but both Mac and Dawn managed not to laugh until after Aliki had hurried off to shower.

Mac's eyes looked thoughtful. "I wouldn't hesitate for a moment if I thought I could have the relationship you have with Aliki."

Dawn tried to be diplomatic. "Ryan has a brilliant mind, she's talented, and a hard worker, and I am sure she loves you."

Mac's sighed. "Oh, she is all that alright, but she is also quick-tempered, moody, driven, and totally confident that what she wants is right."

Dawn chuckled. "She's a Williams. But Janet seems to be able to handle Robbie with no problem."

Mac played with her empty cup. "That's because Aunt Obbie believes that without Janet she would totally fuck-up. I don't have that leverage over Ryan. I'm going to have to live in the background while Ryan trains and flies off into space."

Dawn's eyes widened in feigned shock. "Then more the fool you. If Ryan is getting on with her aspirations, then so should you. A commitment to someone doesn't mean that you can't have a life of your own. Ryan has five years to serve; you use those five years to make something of yourself. If you think you can make something work with Ryan, it had better be an equal partnership or you will soon grow to hate her."

Exactly at eight Ryan drove into the yard. Mac went out to meet her and they kissed, holding each other close. Dawn watched from the window. It seemed so right and natural, and yet she knew the decision to live an alternative lifestyle was not an easy one. Still, in Ryan's arm's Mac looked relaxed and happy. In Stewart's arms, she had always looked like an unhappy little girl clinging to her big brother.

Aliki came up beside Dawn. "I never told her to sleep with Ryan," she insisted.

"I know, sweetheart." Dawn smiled. "You just gave her the push she needed to take a chance on love."

Aliki frowned. "What if it doesn't work out?"

"Then it doesn't. No 'what ifs', isn't that what you told her?"

Aliki nodded.

They sat down in the morning room and waited for their daughter and Ryan. Dawn's heart went out to the two of them when they walked in looking so happy and holding hands. Ryan clearly had raided her mom's wardrobe for the occasion. She was wearing pressed black dress pants and a grey, brushed cotton dress shirt.

"Good morning," Ryan said formally, not able to hide her smile behind her formal manner. "I asked Mac if I could come here this morning because I wanted to tell you that I love your daughter and that I have asked her to consider marrying me. I hope you would feel comfortable in giving us your blessing."

"Of course we would, Ryan," Dawn said before Aliki could say anything. "We want Mac to be happy. Come and sit down." When they had complied, she continued. "We like you very much, Ryan. I think what we are going to ask is that you give Mac time to work things out. She is engaged to someone else, as you know."

Ryan looked stormy and her hand tightened around Mac's.

"Mac needs time to be sure and to settle things in a way that will be kind and fair."

The look of defiance faded and Ryan nodded. "I understand."

Dawn looked at Ryan with new respect. Ryan had grown up, and the woman had control and a better understanding of others. She had lost her chippy attitude.

"You have to accept whatever decision Mac makes, Ryan," Aliki warned.

Ryan looked up with calm, sincere eyes. "I could never accept that I am not the one for Mac. I have always known in my soul that we were meant to be together, but I give you my word that I will respect Mac's decision."

Aliki smiled and reached out and squeezed Ryan's shoulder.

Dawn smiled. She liked Ryan. She liked the old fashioned way Ryan had come and asked for their approval. Stewart had not done that. He had merely announced that he had given Mac a ring and that they were engaged, as if she and Aliki should be thrilled.

Mac's smile assured Dawn that the approval of her parents was important. Dawn thought of the discussion that Aliki had overheard between Mac and Stewart about the awkwardness of her parents being lesbians. There wasn't really any need for awkwardness; that was just the outer trappings of bigotry. Today felt so much better.

Dawn decided it was time to let Ryan off the hot seat. "Well, if we are all meeting at ten to go explore the cave, then we'd better get a move on."

Ryan went home to change, and the Pateas family quickly got ready.

When Ryan walked into the morning room in her parents' house, three pairs of Williams eyes looked up at her with curiosity. "You're wearing my clothes," Robbie observed, raising an eyebrow.

Ryan nodded and licked her lips. This was harder than talking to the Pateas clan and that had been hard enough. "I went to ask for Mac's hand in marriage," she admitted.

Everyone looked at her in stunned silence. "Mac has stopped throwing dinner at you and has agreed to marry you?" Reb asked in exaggerated disbelief.

Ryan blushed. "Not exactly. I have asked Mac to marry me and we've...expressed our love to each other. Mac still has things to work out. I...I'm trying not to push her."

Janet smiled. "Don't you think asking for her parents' approval is pushing just a bit?"

Ryan shifted from one foot to the other. She knew she was glowing red with embarrassment. Her family was not making it easy. "I...I just wanted to do things right."

Reb giggled. "Did you get down on your knees or did you just wear creamed peas?"

"Funny, kid. Your turn will come."

Janet looked at the clock. "You'd better go change. Ian will be here soon and then we'll need to head over to the Potts'."

With relief, Ryan made her escape and went to change. A few minutes later, a soft tap came at her door. It was Robbie. The two women looked at each other and then her mom took her in her arms.

"You are quite the woman. I'm so happy for you. I couldn't think of a better daughter-in-law."

"Thanks, Mom. She hasn't said yes, though."

"She will. She couldn't find anyone who'd love or care for her better than you would."

"I gotta tell you, that was the scariest thing I have ever done."

Robbie chuckled and released her daughter. "Understood. Been there, done that." Her face went serious. "This is your home. You remember that. You and Mac are always welcome here. We will support you in any way we can. Now hurry up. Ian is here and we're about ready to go."

With the three dogs running around the Potts' backyard, and David's picnic lunch stored in two knapsacks, the family piled into the Pateas van and Ryan's Jeep to explore the mine that was located on the tract of land that Robbie had bought years earlier. They bumped slowly down Lovers' Lane and came out in the clearing. Everyone piled out, and there was a good deal of joking about Ian being the only male in the group. With smirks and knowing looks, the women all passed him their knapsacks, canteens, ropes, and other equipment until he was nearly buried in the stuff.

Ian took it all in stride. Spreading his legs and folding his arms across his chest, he insisted, "Hey, you can't all be femmes! There have to be at least a few dykes among you. Besides, I am more into swinging from vines and pounding on my chest than lifting and carrying." He wouldn't have believed a few days ago that he could have said something like that to Reb's parents, but the family had quickly put him at ease and were so open and natural about their relationships that in a very short time he had simply accepted a different worldview.

"Wouldn't you know, ladies, we gotta help the guy." Robbie laughed, and everyone picked up their stuff for the expedition.

The mineshaft went straight down about twenty feet and then seemed to tunnel out north. One by one, they rappelled down the rocky sides until they were crowded in at the bottom of the shaft. Robbie and Janet led the way down the tunnel of rock. It was about two meters wide and four high, and seemed to be more of a natural fissure in the rock than a man-made tunnel, although here and there they could see that it had been widened. The roof above their heads was sometimes rock and sometimes just a mass of roots and dirt. In places, pencil-thin beams of sunlight penetrated the gloom.

Behind Robbie and Janet came Reb and Ian, then Aliki and Dawn, and at the back were Ryan and Mac. Slowly, they followed the fault along for fifty metres or so.

"This must have been open to the sky a hundred years ago," Aliki commented.

Janet moved her light over the rock walls on either side of them. "It's certainly no mine."

"Maybe it's a sinkhole that washes out through this fissure," Ian suggested.

Reb laughed. "Or that's where great-granddad's meteorite hit."

Dawn shone her flashlight across the pebble and rock floor. "Look!" To their amazement, the uneven path shone with bits of gold.

"Wow!" Reb whispered.

Janet laughed. "Fool's gold. Pyrite. So this was the river of gold. I wonder how many people got suckered in by those two old coots' tale of riches."

Ian looked around carefully. "You can see a water line here on the rock. I'm thinking maybe a stream runs through here in the spring with the winter run off. That's probably what washes out the mineral deposits."

Janet sighed. "One thing is for sure, too many people got suckered with dreams of gold. I see light up ahead." Several of them picked up some of the pyrite as a souvenir before they moved on.

Dawn looked at Aliki and winked. Years ago her uncle had found gold in the Swan Hills of Alberta. The nuggets he had panned had made Dawn rich. It was not common knowledge and they didn't talk about it. First, because they did not want the beauty of the area destroyed by miners, and second, because Aliki was a little sensitive about the fact that she drew a very middle class salary for her work as a forensic anthropologist, while many of the other members of her family, including her partner, were very rich. Dawn gave her partner a hug. There wasn't enough gold in the world to replace the one she loved.

They had to take off their packs and wedge sideways to get through the long thin crack in the rock that sloped on about a forty-five degree angle. Squeezing out one by one, they found themselves on a small grassy ridge. In front of them, the cliff dropped off sharply to join hills of tall pines that undulated to the shores of Lake Superior far below. The view was breathtakingly beautiful. A hundred metres behind them, the cliff rose another ten or fifteen metres to a ridge of pines reaching to the sky.

"Awesome place!" Reb commented, and they all murmured agreement.

The cliff that rose behind them was not made of the granite rock that they had found in the fault line, but appeared to be made of layers of sandstone and shale. "An old shoreline or lake bottom that got lifted up at some time," Ryan suggested. "It is certainly lift and fold geological action. See how the stratification isn't horizontal but is on almost a forty-five degree angle, and...look. Are those mineshafts?"

The others looked where Ryan was pointing. They could see the normally horizontal layers of rock were on a sharp angle and that ten or fifteen dark spots on the cliff face indicated the entrance to caves or tunnels.

"Yes!" Robbie laughed, nearly bouncing with glee. "Ladies, and token male, pick your cave and let the fun begin!"

They spent several hours checking out the low caves and tunnels. Some of them proved to be natural, while others had been mined. When they stopped for lunch, the conversation was the usual banter of Williams wit. Mac, however, was quieter than usual. Ryan kept glancing at her, wondering what she was thinking and hoping against hope that Mac was not going to turn her down. As soon as the picnic was over and couples started to break up to tackle the higher caves, Ryan whispered into Mac's ear. "I love you. Please don't leave me."

Mac looked up, startled to see the worry in Ryan's eyes. "Ryan...I'm sorry...I wasn't thinking about us."

Ryan's face crumpled in misery. "Oh."

"No, silly. I was thinking about the Shaman cave."

"What Shaman cave?"

"Ryan! The First Nations cave Aunt Janet's granddad talked about was most likely a Shaman cave."

Ryan snorted. "By all accounts, my great granddad wouldn't have known the truth if it was squeaking under his foot!"

Mac laughed and took Ryan's arm. "I know he could tell a good story, but it seems to me there is always a grain of truth in what the old guy said. There was a hole in the ground. It's just that it was a sinkhole, not a meteor crater. There was a river of gold, but it's pyrite. So I figure there is a First Nation site, too — of some sort."

Ryan rolled her eyes. "Let me guess, you have to find it."

"Of course. If it is a place of the ancestors, a sacred place, then I want to see it"

Ryan opened her mouth to say something, then saw the intensity of the conviction in Mac's face and thought better of it. Learning about and respecting Mac's mixed heritage was something she was going to have to undertake. "Okay. Where are we going to look?"

Mac looked out over the panoramic view of Lake Superior far below. "I'm going over the cliff."

"No you're not!" When Mac gave her a questioning look, Ryan squirmed as warring emotions argued it out in her head. When she spoke, it sounded peevish. "I suppose you're going to tell me the Salish are natural climbers from living on the edge of the Rockies for thousands of years."

"No. I'm going to remind you that I have my advanced certificate in rock climbing," Mac said pointedly. "I am qualified to instruct, and I have paramedic training."

Ryan felt the embarrassment climbing up her face. "Sorry." She hesitated and then went on. "I might need some instruction."

Devilment flashed in Mac's eyes. "In rock climbing or tact?"

Ryan laughed. "Can we start this conversation again? You think the Shaman cave is over the cliff; why?"

"Because it would show courage to get there and that is important." Mac moved over to the edge carefully and dropped down on her stomach to look over the side. Ryan felt Mac stiffen as the vertigo hit with force. She reached out and held on to Mac's legs so she wouldn't feel as though she was sliding off the edge.

"Thanks, Ryan." Mac scanned the cliff face while Ryan held on. "I can see the entrance. There are faint traces of red ochre pictographs. We're going to need a rope."

Reb and Ian followed Dawn and Aliki up a rock chimney. Backs against the one rock face and feet braced against the other, they wriggled crab style up about twenty feet to a large, relatively flat ledge. The old wooden supports not far inside the mouth showed that this cave had been mined and fairly extensively. Carefully, checking for cracks every few metres, they moved deeper into the cave. It went in nearly twenty metres in a fairly straight line. Here and there they could see chippings along the side or cold drill bores where the miners had taken samples or had planned to branch off in other directions.

Reb found an iron hammer and chisel, and further on, Dawn found a rusty old oil lantern. When they reached the end without any additional discoveries, they made their way back down.

Janet and Robbie chose a cave farther along than the others, but it turned out to be only a short passage. On the way down, however, Robbie pointed out a dark, low recess almost completely covered by bushes some distance away from the other caves. They traversed the rock face carefully, making their way over to the spot. The opening was several metres wide but less than a metre high, so they crawled in on their bellies, side by side.

"Watch your plastic balloon thingy," Robbie cautioned.

Janet rolled her eyes, although in the sudden darkness Robbie wouldn't see. When Robbie decided to worry about something, she gave it the same intensity that she did everything else. "What is the point, Robbie Williams, of getting breast reconstruction if you are going to keep reminding me I have an implant?"

"Sorry...but be careful."

Janet gave her lover a poke and moved her flashlight beam around in a slow arc. The cave was large inside, about the size of a standard living room. The two women crawled forward and stood up. The blackness seemed to swallow the light from their torches. Cutting the darkness in slices, they could see that the cave had been used as a shelter. Smoke blackened rock and bits of charred wood marked several old fire pits. On the far side, the rock rose sharply. Here someone had used charcoal on the rocky wall to express discouragement. "No gold. No money. No luck. Haunted. Moran 1898."

They circled the cave carefully but there was nothing else to see until Robbie discovered a narrow crevice high on the far side. She crawled up and stuck her arm and head through so she could look around. "It's another chamber, Janet. Come see."

Janet crawled up and Robbie moved aside so her partner could have a look. "It looks about the same size as this one. Lower, though. It looks like quite a drop."

"About five feet and then a steep bank down to the cave floor. I think we can do it. Do you want to try?"

"Sure."

Robbie slipped through feet first and got herself balanced on the steep embankment. "You'll have to be careful, Janet. It's slippery and muddy."

"Okay." Janet wiggled through, being careful of her implant although she certainly was not about to admit that to Robbie. She felt Robbie guiding her legs down to the ground. The mud oozed around her boots. "Yuck!"

"It looks like sediment must wash from the upper cave down into here. Careful going down." Robbie had barely gotten the words out of her mouth when the ground beneath them started to crumble and slide. Their feet slipped out from under them and they went skidding down the hill in an avalanche of mud and stone.

Janet landed on her back and had the time and instinct to tuck her arms over her chest and cover her face. Still, she took an awful pounding on the way down, and from her shoulders down, she was trapped in deep debris. Robbie was not so lucky. She tumbled and bounced to the bottom in a wall of mud and rock and was buried.

Mac and Ryan rappelled down the cliff face and then edged along a narrow shelf to the mouth of the cave. It was not deep, only four or five metres, but Ryan could stand upright inside. On the walls were pictographs and pictoglyphs made by the First Nations hundreds of years before. The simple cave had a presence about it, an air of sacredness. Ryan felt very much an intruder.

"Do you know what they say?" Ryan asked, her voice almost a whisper.

"No, not really. This culture is very different from my own. I could guess at some of the uses and meanings. This is a very sacred place. These female figure pictoglyphs and the carvings on the floor with the hole dug in the pelvic area are fertility cult symbols."

Ryan looked shocked.

"No, it's not what you think. The hole might have been used for semen, but it was more likely used for an offering of corn, tobacco, or sweetgrass. It helped ensure the health and wealth of the tribe."

Ryan nodded but didn't comment. This wasn't her world and she had much to learn.

"See here. The old fire pit has a ring of granite rock, but there are also more porous sandstone rocks inside the ring. I suspect that this is a dream house. The cave front would be covered with a hide and these porous stones would be soaked and placed on hot embers to create a steam bath. The people would fast and cleanse their bodies and souls to enter into a dream-like state that would put them in tune with the spirit world."

Squatting on her heels at the entrance of the cave, Ryan looked out at the magnificent view far below. A canopy of trees in golds and reds dotted with the deep green of evergreens ran in a wide arc, framing the great lake that sparkled in the autumn sunlight until it mixed with the blue of the sky. Inland, a high cliff formed a necklace that separated the trees below from the craggy hills behind. It was a pristine and beautiful wilderness.

"I don't know how you couldn't feel close to the spirit of the land here," Ryan said with a smile, anxious to let Mac know that she respected her heritage.

Mac smiled back. "Over here, the red and black ochre paintings, or pictographs, are easier to read. The dots represent days and the wiggly line is water. So it was a four-day trip over water to come here. The circle means fire and this triangle shape is an island. So they camped on an island somewhere nearby. Probably that one out there." Mac pointed.

Ryan looked at the symbols on the walls with new interest. "That is fascinating. So the First Nations really did have a written language."

"Not so much a language as universal symbols for communication. Before the Europeans arrived, the First Nations had trading links from coast to coast and right down into Mexico. A lot of the lighter colours have faded away. They used white, yellow, red and black to represent the four directions." Mac looked suddenly sad. "I think the place has been violated by people who should never have been here. I'd like to do a purification rite from my own people. Would that upset you, Ryan?"

Ryan looked out over the panorama. She had no god and yet, up here, with the breeze gently caressing her face, she could believe, if only for a little while. "You do whatever you have to do to put things in balance again. Any little effort toward peace and harmony has to be good."

She sat at the mouth of the cave, her back to Mac, allowing her soulmate the privacy to perform the rituals that would give peace to her and to this place. She could hear Mac's voice chanting softly in her Salish tongue and after a while, she could smell sweetgrass burning. Mac always carried sweetgrass, usually braided into a thin bracelet or woven into a hair band. She always wore her spirit bag, too, but this she never opened or revealed what was inside. Ryan knew it would carry the symbols of her totem — her spirit.

After a while, the chanting stopped and Mac came and sat beside Ryan. "I'm glad you came, Ryan."

Glad. Ryan's gut writhed. *"Glad" is not a word you use about someone you love.*

If Mac noticed the tightening of Ryan's jaw, she didn't react, but continued with what she had to say. "You made me realize that I would be endangering who I am by marrying Stewart. It would have been an awful mistake."

"I wouldn't stop you from being who you want to be."

Mac looked out over the spectacular view with eyes dark with worry. "I don't know, Ryan. You are a Williams, and whether or not you are willing to admit it, that means you will steam ahead through life using your intelligence and talent to achieve whatever you want. I don't see how I fit into that picture."

"I am not asking you to fit into my picture. I want us to form a composite."

Mac laughed and leaned over to kiss Ryan's cheek. "You are impossible. Come on, we'd better be heading back. The others will be wondering what happened to us."

Reb and Ian continued to explore caves, looking for Robbie and Janet while Aliki and Dawn called it a day and climbed back down to the small meadow. They packed things up and made sure the site showed no trace of them having been there, and then lay down in the grass to cloud-gaze.

"Ian seems nice," Aliki stated after a while.

"Were you looking forward to having a son-in-law, Aliki?"

The scientist considered the question in her logical, analytical manner. "Not Stewart. He's a stuffed shirt. Having a son-in-law would have been all right. I'm used to males, having grown up in a house with a dad and three brothers." She went silent for a bit and then continued. "It would have been easier for Mac if she had not been a lesbian. You know what I mean."

"Yes, I know."

"What do you think?"

Dawn turned around so her head rested on Aliki's strong, lean chest. "To be truthful, I'm not sure what I think. Ryan and Mac are meant to be together, but I'm not sure that Mac is strong enough to stand up to Ryan. I don't want to see her losing who she is. I mean, she was prepared to live a lie with Stewart. I don't think you can ever really be happy if your partner forces you to be someone you're not. I'm glad she's going to end her engagement to Stewart. I am worried about her not being strong enough to handle Ryan. You bunch are all...well, olives."

Aliki tugged gently on a piece of Dawn's hair that she had been curling around her finger. "Hey! I'm not a Williams."

Dawn snorted. "You all share the same blood and, believe me, you are an olive."

"Is there anything we can do to help Mac?"

"No. And that's the hardest thing about being a parent. You do your best to train them to be strong, compassionate and intelligent people, and then you have to stand on the sidelines and watch your kids play their own game of life."

Aliki thought about that for some time as she sky-watched. "I wish I had those years back so I could tell Mac what was ahead and prepare her better."

Dawn laughed. "You and every parent on the globe."

It was a few minutes later when Reb and Ian dashed up, looking worried. "I can't find Obbie and Mom. Ian and I have looked everywhere."

Dawn, who had gotten up at the sound of running feet, put her hand on Reb's shoulder. "Don't worry. Ryan and Mac are not back either. I imagine they're all together." But a short time later, when only Ryan and Mac arrived from their climb on the main cliff face, the others started to get worried too.

"Isn't that typical of my sister to get herself lost?" Aliki muttered, scanning the cliff. "What cave were they going to explore?"

The group spent the next hour retracing their steps and calling for Janet and Robbie. As the sun shifted off the face of the cliff, the shadows moved and changed, making it harder to find the caves. They gathered at the base of the cliff again.

Aliki looked at her watch with concern. It was nearing four o'clock. They didn't have more than three hours of sunlight left.

"Reb, you and Ian go up to the truck and telephone George Drouillard to call out the fire department. We're going to need more people for the search. Meanwhile, we'll start over and check the caves again."

Reb nodded grimly and headed off with Ian at her heels. The others watched them go, fear now eating at them.

It was Dawn who shook them from their shock. "Come on. They would be back by now for sure. Something has happened. We need to find them before it gets dark."

Once again the four climbed up to the caves, calling Robbie and Janet's names and checking each cave carefully. Mac could feel Ryan's fear like a cold mist that made them both shudder. Ryan was devoted to Janet, and had easily accepted her as her other mother. Her relationship with her biological mother was far more difficult. But for all the problems Robbie and Ryan had with their relationship, there was no doubt that Ryan adored her mother. Part of the problem had always been Ryan's near pathological need to prove to her mother that she was worthy of being Robbie's daughter.

Mac reached out and rubbed Ryan's back. "It's going to be okay, Ryan."

The response was choked with emotion. "It's always okay, but one of these times it isn't going to be. They've gotta understand they're getting older. They can't keep taking chances."

Mac smiled. "They are risk takers, just like you are, but they are not irresponsible. You can be sure they would take every precaution and that they know what they are doing."

Too emotional to answer, Ryan nodded.

Dawn and Aliki stood at the mouth of a cave that they had just checked, trying to decide where to go next. Aliki's eyes darkened. This was so like her sister to get herself lost. It never occurred to Aliki for a minute that this might be Janet's fault. Janet was the reliable, sensible one of the pair, just as Dawn kept *her* on an even keel. Aliki looked down and pulled Dawn to her, dropping a kiss on her partner's head. "I'm lucky to have you. Let's try that cave over there."

"I'm with you," Dawn replied.

Reb and Ian hurried along the rocky fissure back to the vehicles where telephone communication could be established. She flipped up her phone and pressed George Drouillard's number. For many years, George had been the fire chief but a few years ago he had stepped down and her mother had been voted in as chief. George was still second in command. "Mr. Drouillard, it's Rebecca. My moms are missing at the old mine down Lovers' Lane. We came out to explore the caves and they didn't come back. It's getting late and we don't have much sunlight left to look for them. ... Thanks. Okay. Could you stop at my Aunt Elizabeth's and Uncle David's and pick up Dufus? He knows how to track Obbie."

Reb flipped the cell phone off and bit her lip in worry. "We are to stay here and wait for the guys so we can lead them to where the others are," she explained.

Not knowing what to do or say, Ian nodded.

Reb sighed. She knew things like this didn't happen in his family. In hers, these sorts of crises were almost expected, if dreaded.

"Is there anything I can do?" he asked. He put his arm around Reb's shoulder, but Reb, filled with restless energy and nervousness, shook her head. Fortunately, Ian gave her only a brief reassuring squeeze and released her.

"No. We'll just have to wait. Dufus will find them. I hope." She put her cell phone away and, wrapping her arms around herself, she paced back and forth. Ian leaned against Ryan's Jeep and waited.

George called a 9-1-1 immediately and cursed his way into his rescue gear. Janet was one of them. Her family went back to the first pioneers who had settled in the Bartlett area. The arrival of Robbie Williams in Bartlett had been a shock, but also a blessing. Her companies and support had taken the small, northern community that was struggling to get by and made it into a viable concern. Many of the citizens' lives had been improved because of the Williams Corporation.

Not that it had been an easy transition. Having an openly lesbian couple in town was, to say the least, awkward. George had come to accept the relationship, as had the others who worked with Robbie on the volunteer fire department. She had become one of the guys, and Janet and Robbie's daughters, Ryan and Reb, had both been accepted as members of the team. It took some getting used to, though, having women doing men's work. But he figured that you had to move with the times or be left behind.

There were those in town who *were* being left behind. You were either for the Williamses or against them, and that had certainly split the community. Still, most people had warmed to Robbie, especially as she had sorta married in, what with living with Janet Williams and her sister marrying David Potts.

When he headed out of his small motors shop, firefighters were starting to arrive, pulling their cars and trucks into any available space. One of the arrivals was David Potts, leading Dufus on a leash. Those firefighter volunteers who lived close would ride in the truck or follow behind, while those farther away would meet them at the site. George pulled open the doors on the new shed to reveal the emergency rescue vehicle that Robbie and Janet had given to the town a number of years back to help with the medical emergencies that were on the rise. More and more city folks had bought in the area and built homes or cottages, swelling the population of the small town. He knew that the Williamses were also part owners of the new medical clinic that had been built in town. That was the good side of them. The down side was that a lot of time and energy seemed to be spent in rescuing that family from one thing or another.

"Come on, boys, we gotta rescue Robbie and Janet again. They got themselves lost up at the old caves, looking for the river of gold, I suspect. You know how damn curious that family is."

The others laughed though they were taking the situation seriously. Within minutes, they were on their way.

Janet had somehow spun around as she had skidded down with the debris. So when her forward movement had finally stopped, she was facing head down, buried from her feet up to her shoulders in mud and rock with her legs higher than her head. She tried to move her feet and discovered that, other than being able to wiggle her toes inside her boots, she was pinned tightly by the debris. The blood running to her head and the total darkness around her made her feel disoriented and kind of sick.

"Robbie?" There was no answer. "Robbie?"

With effort, Janet managed to free one of her arms and then worked to get the other one out. It was slow and difficult. Each small movement caused loose rocks and stones to rain down on her face and she was afraid of being buried alive. Still, she knew she had to take the chance and hurry because if Robbie were buried, she would not have long to live.

The cold and pain seeped into Janet's body, along with the fear. She could hear herself whimpering as she worked to free her other arm. She knew the flashlight was on a cord around her wrist. She was hoping it had survived intact, had stayed on her wrist, and that she could use it to locate Robbie.

Suddenly, as she scooped dirt away from the flashlight, there was a glare of light in her face that was blinding. She closed her eyes against the pain and watched red and orange swirl across her vision as she wiggled the rest of her arm free and grasped the torch. Stones and dirt bounced around her, but she was beyond fear now, working mindlessly to free herself.

Finally her arm and flashlight broke free of the dirt. With a cry of relief, Janet fumbled to get a good grip on the torch. "Robbie?" She tried to control her panic as she forced herself to move the beam in a slow arc around the chamber. The beam quivered, reflecting her shock and nervous tension. Nothing. "Robbie!"

There! She saw something out of the corner of her eye. She moved the beam back. Only a few feet ahead of her, she could see the dirty tangle of a few strands of hair sticking out of the mud. Robbie was buried.

Janet reached out as far as she could but could not quite reach the dark locks. She sobbed in frustration and fought against her imprisonment. Over and over she reached, but she was just that little bit too far away. She wiggled and strained and suddenly something gave. Rock and mud slid forward and she fought in a panic to stay on top. When it settled once more, she again focused her flashlight where Robbie lay buried. By some miracle or blessing of the gods, she had slipped further down, but on an angle that brought her within a few centimetres of her partner. There was no time to be either careful or gentle. She wrapped her hand in the hair and pulled for all she was worth. Mud and stones shifted and ran farther down the hill and Robbie's head and shoulders, grey with mud, came clear of the muck.

"Robbie?"

Janet cleared the mud as best she could from Robbie's nose and mouth. Her partner was not breathing. Fear gripped Janet and, twisting her head and shoulders at a painful angle, she started mouth to mouth.

He was standing there with his back to her, his hands rhythmically washing his near-naked body with the smoke from a bundle of sweetgrass. Robbie could hear his low chant. The deep rumble of his voice, although soft, seemed to fill the chamber. She forced air through a narrow opening, getting only enough to keep her going. Perhaps it was the smoke that made it so hard to breathe.

The sweetgrass was pushed into the hole that was part of the carved female figure on the rock floor. Not a rape, but a coupling of the man and nature. At first, she had thought him a monster. He wore a carved wooden mask over his face, the nose twisted and the eyes large circles of luminescence like the inside of a clamshell. The mask was red, and from it hung long black hair that mixed with the man's own.

She tried to let the poisonous gases in her lungs leak out the way she had managed to pull the air in. It was so hard. Every cell in her body was screaming for her to suck in more air. She could hear the gurgle of her own choked breathing — a death rattle.

The man now had a rattle, too. He had picked it up after he had placed the burning sweetgrass in the hole. The rattle was made from a turtle shell and was tied with leather to a wooden handle worn smooth and shiny from use. The sound it made was a sharp, pulsating beat, like the laborious beating of her heart.

Would her own heart stop when the beat of the rattle ceased? Her eyes were blurry. Perhaps this was because of a lack of oxygen or maybe it was the blue, sweet smoke that hung in a cloud around the figure. The smoke swirled around the man as he danced, the slow hopping step in soft moccasins making a *shhh, shhh* sound. *Shhh, don't talk. Shhh, don't breathe. Shhh, sleep.*

Robbie's eyes closed, but the ache in her throat wouldn't let her sleep. She gasped again, drawing in a painful, thin stream of life. *Not yet.* She wasn't ready yet. She needed to see what the man would do.

He danced on and on, the rattle and his chant a cold wind through dried branches. *Shhh, shhh.* His tawny skin shone with sweat, and Robbie could now see that he had painted patterns on his body in red, black, yellow and white. He disappeared into the smoke, reappeared in parts and broke up again, as if drifting in all directions on the wind.

He wasn't really there, Robbie knew. He was dead. She could only see him because she was half dead, too. Most of her was now cold but a small, warm hand still clung to her arm, just one spot of colour and warmth holding her back. She forced the carbon dioxide out and then gasped and gurgled down more oxygen, giving herself another minute of life.

The man stopped suddenly and threw his hands into the air with a cry of anger. Then he turned suddenly, and for the first time, Robbie stared directly into the face of Broken Nose, one of the many False Face spirits of the woods. She choked with fear.

The rattle was now the blunt end of a stone club. The man walked toward her. She had disturbed a sacred place, ruined the magic. She could no longer get her breath. Far away, she could her someone sobbing, "Breathe, Robbie! P-please. Breathe!"

Back near the road, George Drouillard and the volunteers of the Bartlett Fire Department had arrived in a convoy of trucks and cars bouncing down the rutted trail. They pulled up in a fan-shaped pattern in the long grass. Car doors slammed as the firefighters got out and unloaded equipment. George hurried over to where Reb and Ian stood.

Reb fidgeted impatiently as David opened the back door of the truck and Dufus bounded out, a large, orange mass of excitement. Some of the men pulled on backpacks of equipment, while others unlashed a ladder to place in the pit. David brought a rope and harness over to her and she worked to get the massive Dufus into the contraption. A few of the men had already headed down into the sinkhole with rescue equipment by the time Reb and Ian walked the dog over to the pit.

Reb took hold of her pet's massive head. "Dufus, you are not going to like this part but we have to find Obbie, so don't be a big suck about it. Come." That said, she stepped on the ladder and she and Ian lifted the whimpering but docile dog over the side. Careful hands lowered the beast down beside Reb as the girl talked reassuringly to the animal as he was lowered.

While Reb calmed Dufus, Ian followed her down the ladder. Reb tried her best to control her nervous energy. Around her, everyone seemed so calm and matter of fact about the rescue. She wondered if Ian was starting to suspect that, as startling as it might seem, days like this occurred quite regularly in her life.

Reb was just getting the shaking Dufus out of his harness as Ian stepped off the ladder. "Dufus, track Obbie," she commanded and the dog gave a bark and wagged his crooked tail with delight as he sniffed the ground with mighty snorts and slobbering jowls. Dufus picked up the trail quickly and happily bounded down the tunnel with Reb and Ian in hot pursuit.

They emerged at the other end a few minutes later to see Dufus running around the grassy meadow following Robbie's trail, ears flapping with each bound. They ran over to where Aliki, Dawn, Ryan and Mac stood, looking worried and talking to the firefighters who had arrived ahead of them.

"Where are they?" Reb asked.

Dawn looked uncomfortable. "We have checked all the caves and can't find them. We were just discussing widening the search in case they got lost in the woods."

Reb's face hardened into determined lines. For a second, she looked very much like a Williams. "Dufus, track Obbie."

The dog looked up from sniffing the knapsacks that contained the remainder of lunch and took off toward the cliffs. The others followed behind. Narrow, crumbling footpaths ran in zigzags across the cliff face. In some spots, Ryan and Mac, following right behind Dufus, had to help the whimpering dog from one level to the other while Reb spoke soft encouragement to her pet.

Twice the dog backtracked and then, picking up the scent in a new direction, the animal headed cautiously down an embankment and onto a thin trail that led away from the caves to the other side of the cliff. In a minute, Dufus had disappeared behind some bushes. The others followed as best they could. Ryan and Mac moved ahead, both having had practice in traversing rough terrain, while the others moved more cautiously with crab-like movements through the loose, sliding gravel.

Pushing the bushes aside, Ryan and Mac could now see the low entrance to the cave. Side by side, the two of them slid in. Dufus was barking excitedly at the far end of the cave, but for a second the two women, blinded by the sudden dark, stood still, fumbling for their flashlights.

"Help! Hurry. Please hurry!"

Janet's voice came to them from somewhere far off, muffled by the rock but edged with the strength of fear. They hurried over and slid up the rock slope to look inside.

Janet blinked like an owl in the beams of their searching lights. Blinded, she scrunched her eyes closed and yelled out her concern. "Robbie can't breathe right. Something is blocking her throat and I can't get it out. We're trapped under debris. Hurry!"

"I'm coming!" Ryan started to move forward, then she forced herself to stop. "Hang on. Mac has climbing and EMT training; she'll be down in a second." Ryan turned and moved aside. "Save my mom," she pleaded. Mac nodded and headed in. Ryan's hand grabbed her. "Be careful."

"I will. I have a lot to live for."

Mac slipped over the side and Ryan lowered her down the rock face until her boots sunk into the loose debris. Slowly and carefully, so as not to trigger another slide, Mac edged her way down the slope to where Janet and Robbie were buried.

"She wasn't breathing when I pulled her free of the mud. I did mouth to mouth as best I could and she is breathing now, but not well. Her lips are blue." Janet tried not to let her panic show in her voice as she kept to the basic information that Mac needed. "She can't speak, and she is only semi-conscious."

Mac did one quick sweep of her flashlight around to make sure the bank was holding and then turned her light on her Aunt Robbie. The woman was grey. When she took a weak breath, it was more of a gurgle. Mac forced Robbie's mouth open wide and shone a light in. She could see the grey sides of a rock down her throat. There was no time to be polite or even careful. She pulled off her leather climbing gloves and stuck her fingers down Robbie's throat. Robbie gagged and struggled. Mac got one finger to the side of the stone and flipped up. The stone dislodged but did not come out. Mac pulled her hand back to use the flashlight to have another look. Robbie was hacking with dry heaves and Mac did her best to keep her head turned to the side. Suddenly, Robbie gagged loudly and stone, mud, and vomit spewed out of her mouth in all directions.

Janet lay back into a more comfortable position and closed her eyes against the harsh light. Her fingers tightened on Robbie's arm.

"What's happening?" Ryan called, her voice tight but controlled.

Mac could hear that there were others there now, too. "Obbie was sick," she minimized, as she cleared the vomit from her aunt's mouth with her fingers. Was she breathing? Yes, a gasp, more vomit, another breath, deeper this time. "She had a stone caught in the back of her throat. She is breathing now but with some discomfort and difficulty. Oxygen would be good."

"I'm on it." Ryan turned to the others and instructed, "We need oxygen. Mac can handle this. It's pretty unstable in there and we don't want to take any chances of burying them."

At the entrance to the cave, the rescuers stood around in anxious groups, waiting for Ryan to pass word back to them from where Mac worked deeper in the cave. A worried crew of firefighters, who were very fond and proud of their actor-chief and her partner, passed the oxygen up to Ryan. Gritting her teeth against her natural instinct and training to take action, the soldier let her lover handle the situation. There was no doubt Mac knew what she was doing. Ryan tied the tank to the line and lowered it down to Mac, who had carefully climbed back up the bank a bit to get it. Ryan watched from above, keeping a light on the three of them so that Mac would have her hands free to render assistance.

Once the tank was safely in Mac's hands and she had carefully returned to where Robbie lay buried, Ryan turned to look around at the worried faces of her family and friends.

Reb knelt beside her, her face buried in Dufus' furry neck. "You're the man, Dufus," Reb kept repeating softly, tears of relief in her voice.

Ryan reached over and gave her little sister's shoulder a squeeze. "Thanks to your training. I'm really proud to be your sister, Reb. Don't you worry; Mac will handle things."

Broken Nose moved toward her, not like in a movie but in freeze-frame, disappearing in the smoke and reappearing closer. His club was raised. Robbie would have cried out but a cold hand covered her mouth. She couldn't breathe. She was choking and fought with all the strength she had left. The icy fingers dug down deep in her soul, and death spread roots through her being. The club dropped. Through the blackness, there was a soft female chant. A different language, Robbie thought, but couldn't be sure. Cold rills of terror retreated from her being and warmth bubbled up like a spring. She threw up, vomiting out the evil, the death. She gasped, and air heavy with the taste of damp earth entered her burning lungs. She was alive.

"Janet?" she croaked.

"I'm here. Hang on, Obbie. We're going to be okay." Tears of relief stained Janet's face. That had been as scary as hell.

In the end, it was Ryan and Mac who slowly and carefully dug Robbie and then Janet out. Each was strapped to a backboard and carefully lifted up to the chamber above. Then Ryan and Mac climbed out, more relieved than they would admit to escape the unstable lower chamber.

Janet insisted that she was all right, other than some bruising, but George and the boys said they needed the practice anyhow and insisted on taking her out on the backboard and on to the clinic. Robbie had not yet regained consciousness, but she was moving and reacting, and breathing with the help of the oxygen.

Back at the sinkhole, David and the other firefighters carefully raised each of the two women up in a metal cradle, while Aliki and Dawn stood on the ladder to keep the cradles steady and stop them from hitting against the side of the sinkhole. Reb and Ian saw to Dufus, who was not as willing to be hauled through the air on a rope the second time.

Once everyone was up, and Janet and Robbie had been carefully loaded in the back of the truck, Ryan and Reb, by unspoken consent, piled into the emergency vehicle with the other firefighters. With lights flashing, they set off to the clinic. The others stayed behind to pack up the equipment and go back to the lodge to wait for news.

A few hours later, having phoned the lodge to let them know that Janet and Robbie were going to be all right, Ryan sat with her arm around her kid sister on a black couch in the waiting room of the clinic. "You okay, kid?"

Rebecca shrugged. "I'm used to it. I was raised on adrenaline rushes evoked by family moments of terror and near panic. I hear other families associate their moms with commonplace things like cookies and milk. Hard to believe, if you ask me."

Ryan chuckled. "We did get cookies and milk."

"Yeah, after the crisis was over. Do you remember the time you nearly drowned me in the firestorm?" Reb rolled her eyes.

Ryan tugged a piece of her sister's hair. "You're not still holding a grudge, are you?"

"Of course I am," she joked. "I wonder if Ian will still be taking me to the dance at the hall."

Ryan lifted her arm from the back of the seat, stood up, and stretched. "Not much to him if a little thing like a couple of Williamses nearly being buried alive bothers him."

Reb smiled. "Good point." She picked up a magazine to read and Ryan paced around the small room. For a few minutes there was silence except for the soldier's soft tread.

The door opened and Mac stuck her head in. "Hi, any other news?"

"The doctor said they both look to be in good shape, but he won't release them until he is sure Mom's breathing is okay. He said you did a great job. The stone lodged in her throat probably saved her because it stopped her from getting muck in her lungs."

"That's great. Ryan, I need to talk to you. Can you step out here for a minute?"

Ryan suddenly became aware of the serious frown and Mac's worried eyes. Her heart contracted. "Sure. Back in a minute, Reb."

Out in the hall, Mac gave Ryan a tender hug. "We put the news on when we got back to the house, love. The *Columbia*...it broke up on re-entry. There are no survivors." Mac felt Ryan's body jerk with the shock, then go still.

"No, there wouldn't be." She pulled Mac to her and held on to the small woman, needing her quiet strength and warmth.

"You go on home so you can follow the reports as they come in. I'll stay here and bring Reb and your moms home when they're released."

Ryan nodded into soft, fragrant hair. "Thanks. I love you."

Mac held her close for a second before stepping back. "I love you, too. Now go. I'll handle things here."

Reb looked up in surprise as Mac came in the door and her thoughtful, intelligent eyes followed her cousin as she crossed the room and sat down beside her. "What's up?"

"The space shuttle broke up on re-entry. Everyone's dead. I sent Ryan home so she could watch the bulletins on TV."

"Oh, no. Did Ryan know any of the crew?"

"I don't know, Reb. I imagine, though, that she identifies pretty strongly with those who have gone before."

Reb nodded, then sighed and rolled her eyes. "Another family member I have to worry about."

Mac smiled. "I'll be around to help. Would you feel more comfortable if Ryan wasn't in the Space Program?"

"Yes, but I'm proud of her. This is something she has always wanted. I want it for her."

"Think you could train Dufus to wear a space suit and track along orbits?"

Reb laughed at the ridiculous thought of a big, shaggy dogface looking out through a space helmet. "Well, they have had dogs in space before, but not quite as big as Dufus. He'd need a booster rocket for sure."

Janet, tired and sore, sat beside Robbie's bed holding her hand. Robbie, worn out and still a bit dirty around the edges, looked up at her. "I've been thinking."

"That's always dangerous. Please tell me it does not involve having to get out of this chair. Every muscle and bone in my body is on strike."

Robbie's beautiful, expressive eyes clouded with distress. "I'm sorry for dragging you in there."

A reassuring hand squeezed hers. "Hey, we were having fun together. Good adventures, even Saturday afternoon ones, always have an element of risk."

"That's what I need to talk to you about."

Janet looked at her partner and saw the determined, serious set of her jaw. "Okay. I'm listening."

"It's this breast thing."

Janet rolled her eyes.

"No, wait, give me a chance. The other day you made me realize that this is important to you, important enough that you were willing to go it alone if I wasn't going to support you." Janet opened her mouth to object, but Robbie raised a hand and gently placed two fingers against her lips. "Shh, I'm only warming up. I went along because you wanted it, but I wasn't overjoyed about the whole idea. I know it is a small risk, but I didn't want you back in hospital. I really hate you being in hospital."

"I know, love," Janet said sympathetically.

Robbie squirmed. "Anyway, today it was brought home to me that you can't protect the ones you love from life, that life happens and there are no guarantees. I wasn't protecting you, I was letting my insecurities limit you. I'm sorry. We both could have died today."

"Yeah, but we didn't."

Robbie smiled. Janet was about as special a partner as anyone could have. She took Janet's hand in her own. "So, how about you tell me what else they have to do to you?"

Janet looked up in surprise. "Sure you're up to it?"

"Yup, I am. I want to know so I can help out any way I can."

Janet got comfortable, laying her head down on Robbie's bed, pleased to see Robbie's colouring was back to normal and she was breathing without a rasp. "Once the extender has stretched the muscle to the right size, it will be removed and a permanent implant will be put in."

"Is that process painful?"

"Not really. When the solution is first put in, it's a bit uncomfortable and the muscle feels tight, but it loosens in a few days," Janet said. "The worst part is it sometimes itches in there. I have to move it around a bit to get some relief."

"Ahh, too much information!" Robbie joked.

"Once they put the permanent implant in place, then they build a new nipple. They usually use part of the ear lobe to do that, although there are other methods. I think I can afford to lose a bit of my ear lobe."

Robbie looked at Janet's ears with clinical interest. "How much will they take?"

"Just a little. You won't even notice much. The last bit of surgery will be to lift and tuck my real breast so that they match and look perky and young again."

"Perky is good." Robbie wiggled her eyebrows.

"I'll have a scar around the base of the breast and also vertically up to the nipple but it will soon fade," Janet finished.

Robbie nodded and grinned wolfishly. "I guess I can handle this."

Janet laughed. " Robbie! You are so bad!"

Ryan sat alone on the couch. She'd been there for several hours watching the DVD of *Columbia* over and over, focussed on every update. From time to time, the others joined her and then wandered off again to see to other responsibilities.

"You need to talk to her, Elizabeth," David stated quietly as he rinsed a plate and put it in the drainer.

Dr. Elizabeth Williams picked it up and dried it while she considered. "I really have no experience with children. I am not sure what I could say, David."

David wiped his hands on his apron and turned to look at his wife. When he spoke his voice was gentle but firm. "Bethy, she is not a child. She is a young astrophysicist and by all accounts, a good one. She is also your niece and has looked up to you all her life. Her mothers are not here. No one is more qualified to talk to her now than you are."

Elizabeth looked worried but she nodded. "I suppose you are right. I can always count on you, David, to see things clearly. I'll leave you with the rest of the dishes, then, and go and have a talk with Ryan."

David smiled and his wife gave him an affectionate kiss as she went by. Elizabeth squared her shoulders and walked down the hall, slowly trying to work out what to say. She quietly entered the media room and took a seat on the couch beside Ryan. "Has there been any more news?"

"No, not really. Nothing concrete."

"I'm sorry, Ryan."

The younger woman nodded and swallowed hard. "It's hard. They were good people, some of the best. Their loss, and that of the craft, will set back the program immeasurably. You know it can happen, but when you are training and surrounded by such brilliant and talented people, you start to feel invincible. Then something like this happens, and you realize that, for all our technological knowledge, we are still flying by the seat of our pants."

"Ryan, I can't say that I have ever had the desire to be an explorer or adventurer, but I understand why they risk their lives to push our frontiers a little further. I like to think that, in my own way, I have expanded the world's understanding and experience, if only with pencil and paper. Most people are content with being surrounded by the familiar and the known. There are a few of us who are blessed with the ability to see a small part of the beauty that is, for want of a better description, God's hand in the universe. There is no greater honour or responsibility than to be one of those rare few that will take us closer to understanding.

"Don't give up your dream, Ryan. Don't grieve for those who have been lost doing what they loved best. Instead, honour them in a special place in your soul and step up to take their place. Of all the billions of living things on this planet, we are the only ones that look up and wish on the stars. Use your talents and your intelligence, Ryan, to make all our dreams come true."

Ryan blinked back tears as she looked at her aunt. Bethy could see the love and admiration that showed on her face. "What if Mac doesn't understand?"

Elizabeth frowned. "Of course she will. She loves what you are. Loving someone is wanting to support your partner in reaching for the stars. There are no boundaries with true love. That is why love always has been and always will be the most beautiful and most daring of adventures."

Ryan smiled and leaned over to drop a kiss on her aunt's cheek. She might have said something, but the noisy arrival of the others from the clinic interrupted the moment. They got up and hurried out to the family room, both glad of a reason to end the delicate talk.

Aliki and Dawn had volunteered to drive Ian back to the makeshift park of Forestry trailers that served as mess and barracks for the summer workers. Ian sat in the back, trying to come to terms with the experiences he'd had in the last twenty-four hours. "Do you think Reb's moms will be okay?"

Dawn smiled. "Yes, they'll be fine. They are a lucky pair, though. It could've been much worse."

Ian nodded. "I'll say."

Aliki frowned and glanced in the rear view mirror at Ian. "The family would appreciate it if you didn't talk too much about the incident or give interviews to reporters. Publicity is a necessary evil for my sister, but we do like to pick and choose what we throw to the ravenous dogs at the door." Aliki's words were off hand enough, but her tone made it clear it was not a request.

Ian took the hint. "Yes, Inspector." He saw Dawn wiggle her eyebrows at Aliki at the title, and was surprised to see the red of embarrassment climbing up Aliki's neck. New thoughts drifted into his mind. "Reb is amazing with animals, isn't she? I mean, Dufus doesn't just follow commands, he seems to know what Reb wants."

Aliki nodded. "She's got a way with animals. She'll make a good vet."

"Nothing like this happens in my family. I mean, I was never involved in a food fight, even at school. It would never happen at home. And the only time we had a family emergency was when Dad broke his wrist skiing down the bunny hill at the conservation area."

Dawn laughed and turned to look at Ian. "Amazing as it seems after the last twenty-four hours, the family can manage to go for months on end without creating a sensation or scandal. You have definitely not seen us at our best."

Ian nodded. "Yes, ma'am." He saw Aliki give Dawn a poke in response to his formal address. He could see that they had found the titles of "inspector" and "ma'am" amusing, but then Aliki and Dawn seemed rather informal. Even so, he'd only just met them and was trying his best to make a good impression. "Do you think it would be all right to tell my parents I met you all? We don't know any rich or famous people, and I've met a whole bushel of them this weekend."

Aliki snorted. As a scientist and police officer, she was neither rich nor famous. Dawn laughed. "The rich and famous are no different from anyone else. They are just fortunate to have more opportunities. Sure, I think it would be okay to tell your parents you met Reb's family. Just be careful what you say and make sure they understand we value our privacy."

Aliki pulled up in front of the Forestry complex, but kept the engine running. Although she wouldn't admit it, she was anxious to get back and make sure Robbie and Janet were okay.

Ian opened the door and started to get out, then he hesitated. "Would you let Reb know that I'll phone tomorrow and see if it's still okay for her to go to the dance?"

"We'll do that. Thanks for your help today, Ian," Dawn smiled. "Goodnight."

They waited until Ian had unlocked the door of the barracks trailer and then headed back to the lodge.

Aliki and Dawn arrived back at the lodge just a little after the others had returned from the clinic. David was already bustling around getting Janet and Robbie comfortable on opposite ends of the couch and promising sandwiches, tea, and homemade pie as soon as possible. Dufus, the hero of the day, was given loads of attention and extra dog biscuits, and Reb beamed with pride. Everyone did their part, and once enough food and tea had been consumed to satisfy even the most ravenous of appetites, they all settled down to sort through the events.

Dawn sat on the floor by her partner, their backs against the couch that Robbie and Janet shared. "Reb, Ian wanted us to tell you he'll phone tomorrow to make arrangements about going to the dance."

Reb's expressive eyes sparkled with excitement as she carried refills of tea in for her moms. "Yeah? You mean I still have a boyfriend after a weekend exposed to you lot? Wow! This guy's a keeper. He's got nerves of steel and no common sense at all. He should be running for the hills."

Janet took her mug with thanks and gave her daughter a playful swat. "To hear you talk, you'd think we were the worst parents in the world. It is amazing that any of your friends have the nerve to come here at all."

Reb handed the second cup to her Obbie and smiled. "I make them draw lots to see who has to come and be exposed to you. In town, it's called Williams Roulette. I try to be caring, though. The ones that are still under intense therapy from their last visit, I don't make draw."

Robbie snorted. "Funny! See if this household throws any more parties for your motley crew of friends." The parties at the lodge for Reb's teen friends had become something of a tradition enjoyed by all.

Reb dropped a kiss on Obbie's head. "I take it all back then, because I'd really like a graduation party before we all head off to university."

"Mercenary!" grumbled Obbie.

"Takes one to know one," Janet laughed, before taking a sip of tea.

Obbie frowned. "I gotta tell you guys about this weird dream I had while I was out of it in the cave."

Mac smiled and interrupted. "Broken Nose came to you wearing the red mask. The sacred place had been violated. He was caught with one foot still among his people and the other on the path that leads to the spirit world. This made him angry."

Robbie's mouth dropped open and everyone turned to look at Mac. Although none of them yet knew Robbie's story, by the startled look on the actor's face, they could tell that Mac knew what Robbie was going to say.

Robbie swallowed and her eyes locked with Mac's. "He was going to hit me with a club, but then he reached his hand down my throat and tried to rip out my insides."

"He wanted your soul. He needed a way to the other side."

Robbie looked thoroughly uncomfortable. "Shit! I don't believe in stuff like that."

Mac smiled from where she sat beside Ryan. "That's okay. There was a stone stuck in your air pipe and I put my fingers down your throat to dislodge it. That made you throw up."

Janet looked at Mac with curious eyes. "I saw you do that. Is that what really happened?"

"Yes, that is one of the things that happened. While the rest of you were up on the ridge, Ryan and I went over the cliff and found a spirit cave. It has some amazing pictographs and pictoglyphs. It is an excellent site, but I think it had been entered by people who did not respect the ways of the people."

"Did you make things right?" Dawn asked, as she gently rubbed Aliki's leg.

"Yes. I did a purification ceremony. I think everything should be all right now."

Reb gave herself a shake. "Oh boy! Freak me out. I'm sure glad Ian wasn't here to hear this. He'd go screaming into the night."

Everyone laughed and the tension was broken. Yet, somehow, each felt in their own way that something out of balance had been made right again.

The party broke up some time later. David and Elizabeth headed back to their cabin, Aliki and Dawn took the boat over to theirs, and Ryan and Mac discreetly disappeared to walk hand in hand down to the boathouse.

Satisfied that Ian would be taking her to the Community Centre dance, Reb headed off to bed with her faithful hero at her side. "Don't you worry, Dufus, Ian said he doesn't mind that you sleep at the end of the bed."

Robbie's eyes got big. "She's joking, right?"

Janet rolled her eyes. "I hope so."

Robbie gave the leg that was wedged down beside her thigh a squeeze and looked into the gentle green eyes of her lover at the other end of the couch. "You saved my life...again."

"You're worth keeping around for a bit yet," Janet teased.

"I would make passionate love to you, but every muscle in my body has seized up and I think I am going to need help just getting off this couch to go to bed."

Janet laughed. "You are such a romantic."

"No regrets?"

"None. You?"

Robbie slowly and stiffly got off the couch and offered her hand to her partner and lover. "None. My life began with you, and each passing season makes me fall deeper in love with you."

Janet stood and kissed Robbie's fingers that were wrapped around her own hand. "They have been seasons of love, seasons of joy. Come to bed, my olive. It's late."

There was no awkwardness this night. Mac went willingly to Ryan's arms as soon as she had locked the door. The kiss was long, demanding and needy. It was only after several minutes that they parted long enough to get a fire going and pour two glasses of wine. They lay together by the fire, snuggled into a pile of pillows.

Mac reached out and stroked Ryan's tense jaw. "Are you okay, love?"

Ryan put down her drink and blue eyes the colour of ice-fire turned to look at her. "No, I'm not. My moms could have died today, some of the best people in my program *have* died today, and all I can think of is how will those two events influence my chances with you."

Mac lay back on the pillows and stared at the ceiling. She needed to organize her own feelings before she spoke and she couldn't do that with Ryan's intense, intelligent eyes watching the play of emotions in her own. "I've spent time doing some thinking myself over the last twenty-four hours. When that news flash came across the screen, the castle of dreams I was building came tumbling down. I empathized so strongly with the partners and family who were waiting for the shuttle to land and in a split second, lost everything. The cold hand of death touching so near made me physically shiver. I thought that could be me in a few years, that could be your flight."

Ryan said nothing. She rolled over in one smooth movement and was on her feet pacing. Mac understood Ryan's sudden withdrawal. Ryan needed to move, to do something. She was a person of actions, not words.

"I told you. If it is too hard, I'll leave the Space Program."

Mac slipped forward and poked at the fire, watching the patterns change and the colours intensify with the heat. "A number of years ago, I went to the hospital with my mom to see Aliki when she had been seriously hurt in the line of duty. I hadn't been allowed to go for the first week because she had been in Intensive Care. She had been beaten so badly, I wouldn't have recognized her. I knew Mom and Aliki had argued bitterly about Aliki's decision to do an undercover investigation during a very dangerous case. That decision almost cost her life. She was a very long time recovering. It almost destroyed our family and my mom. I never heard my mom say a thing about it ever again. She just put her heart and soul into making Aliki well."

With misery in her eyes, Ryan looked at the small figure curled close to the fire for warmth. "I know it was a bad time."

Mac nodded. "Yes, it was. Today, I saw the fear in Aunt Janet's eyes as I worked to help Aunt Robbie. But I saw something else there — the same look I saw in my mom's eyes as she sat by Aliki's bed. It was courage. Not the courage to be brave, but the courage to let go and let their partners be the very special people they are."

Mac tossed her stick on the fire and turned to look at Ryan, standing tall and proud just at the edge of the ring of light. That's who Ryan was — a person who would always be stepping from the safety of the known into the unknown. "I want you in the Space Program if that is what you want. And if I lose you, it will be to a great cause that you believe in."

Ryan felt dizzy and realized it was because she had been holding her breath. She breathed in raggedly and moved to sit beside Mac. "I learned something today, as well. I learned that in you I have someone who is my equal in every way. Who I can trust with the things and people who are the most dear to me. You saved Mom's life. I'm not sure I could have. Thank you."

Mac blushed and turned to look at the fire. In profile, Ryan could see her Salish heritage and her quiet strength.

"I need to finish my degree, Ryan. That is important to me. I think I might want to go on and do my doctorate, as well. I want to be a writer like my mom, but I don't want to write as she does about the tension between humans and the environment. That's not me. I want to write about the bond that is never far away between us and the spirit of the universe. I want to write about how we have only lost our way."

"Like the spirit in the cave."

"Yes, like the spirit in the cave. That reality is very different from your hard-nosed science."

"Is it? I was talking to Aunt Bethy tonight. You know what she told me? She said that most people are content with being surrounded by the familiar and the known, but there are a few who are blessed with the ability to see a little part of the beauty that is God's hand in the universe. She said there is no greater honour or responsibility than to be one of those few who will take us closer to understanding. I think we are after the same thing; we are just searching in very different ways."

Mac looked up into eyes filled with life and passion. "I love you, Ryan. Will you marry me?"

Ryan felt herself smiling like an idiot. "Yes."

Mac smiled impishly as she moved closer to kiss the woman she knew was her soulmate. "I'll ask your parents for your hand in marriage first thing in the morning."

Ryan pulled Mac into her arms as she lay back on the cushions. "You are likely to find them still in their pjs."

"That's okay. We're all family."

Back at the lodge, Robbie snuggled closer to Janet. There was a winter chill in the air, blown in on an autumn wind. Indian summer was over and winter not far away. She smiled. Life was good. The seasons passed, but the love they shared only grew stronger.

Anne Azel lives in Northern Ontario. Now retired, she loves travelling whenever she can. She enjoys canoeing, kayaking and walks with her dog when she isn't writing.

You can contact Anne at a_azelca@yahoo.ca.

Other works by Anne Azel:

Gold Mountain

(Winner of a 2007 Golden Crown Literary Society's Award for Lesbian Dramatic General Fiction)

Gold Mountain has a unique and distinctive Canadian flavour which embraces the cultural diversity found in Canada today. It is a story of two women, not only on opposite ends of our cultural scale but also on opposite ends of our justice scale. It is the story of Kelly, the daughter of the concubine of a Chinese immigrant to Canada, and her struggle to find her place in both the Caucasian and Chinese world, both of which prefer their women heterosexual. It is the story of Jane, a woman who appears to have found her place in the world, but in fact her place is waiting to be discovered. Discovering for Jane and a place for Kelly come as a result of the night that Kelly's half-brother, her father's only son, an indulged young man, is murdered.

ISBN: 978 - 1 - 933720 - 04 - 3
(1-933720-04-2)

Available at your favorite bookstore.

Coming Soon from Anne

Murder in Triplicate: The Aliki Pateas Mystery Series, Book 1

Dead Fall — Aliki Pateas goes home after many years to make peace with her family but finds that her bedroom is now occupied by another woman, Dawn Freeman. Resentment turns to love when Aliki and Dawn find themself caught up in the investigation of a mysterious plane crash and a murder.

Dead Funny — There is nothing funny about the serial killer the press was calling the Fire Clown. Aliki tries to balance family and a murder investigation, but the Fire Clown tips the scale when he goes after the one that Aliki loves the most.

Dead Aim — When Robbie finds human bones at the site of her new office she recruits her half sister, Aliki, to help her hide the evidence. A comedy of errors follows that leads the family into grave danger but help comes from a very unexpected source.

Coming Soon from Anne

Three Doses of Murder: The Aliki Pateas Mystery Series, Book 2

Dead Dude — All Aliki Pateas wanted was some time alone to propose to the woman she loved, but a family gathering becomes a fight for survival when ritual sacrifices brings Aliki into a complex murder investigation.

Dead Right — Investigating a downed airliner was hard enough but when a serial killer lets Aliki know she was the cause, Aliki goes undercover to catch the murderer. The price though might just be Aliki's relationship, her sanity, and even her life.

Dead Ringer — Mummified bodies and a mysterious dissappearence takes Aliki and her family on a wild adventure in the desert of nothern Chile.

Printed in the United States
93747LV00012B/59/A